Mortality is beautiful.
Art is beautiful.
Art is immortal.

INSTANT VANITIES
Or: At the Intersection of Pleasure and Suffering

Jesse David

ROT IRON LLC

4030 Wake Forest Rd. STE 349 Raleigh, North Carolina 27609

rot-iron.com

Originally published in paperback by ROT IRON, June 2025.

The publisher is not responsible for websites (or their content) that are not owned by the publisher.

Library of Congress Cataloging-in-Publication Data

Name: David, Jesse, author.

Instant Vanities : At the Intersection of Pleasure and Suffering / Jesse David.—First Edition.

Identifiers: LCCN 2025904077 (print) LC record available at http://lccn.loc.gov/2025904077

ISBN 979-8-218-60664-0 (paperback) 1. Literary—Fiction.

Proofreading by Zeynep Şen.

Book Design by Jesse David. Drawing by Jesse David.

Printed in the United States of America

For Logan

TABLE OF CONTENTS

A BRIEF INTRODUCTION FROM THE EDITOR

[August 22, 2033]

Dear Reader,

My time spent in the company of our dearest, Joseph Henley, although limited, proved to be a great source of compassion and intrigue. While I did take several liberties to elevate the plot, in turn causing a few fictionalized moments (with permission from the man himself), the story you are about to witness is largely true.

When Henley approached me to write his life story thus far, I was reluctant to take on such a task. I am, myself, a fan of his work. I worried my subjectivity could bleed onto the page, and I already knew a great deal about the wild, old musician. Upon meeting him and hearing his desire to have his story be told, I nearly begged to be the editor of such a tale. It is one of sex, drugs, and rock and roll at its surface, yes, but below, there is a wandering heart that beats for art and humanity.

Much of this story was collected from a compilation of many recording sessions I conducted with Henley at his apartment in Greenwich Village. I would set up a microphone, wield my pen and paper, and allow the man to speak about his life. I asked very few questions throughout the process, instead opting to allow the space and silence needed for him to remember many of his triumphant events.

To my surprise, the details he could recall—ranging from specific dates to precise dialogue from conversations—caused much of the story to write itself. However, much of what he said was out of order, and he often found himself backtracking to retrieve an anecdote or a detail from a previous event. This is largely where my editing was required. Some large pieces of the story are directed quotes from the mouth of Henley. The selected lyrics from the discography of Beach Sirens were approved by Mr. Henley, Mrs. Cavansky, and ROT IRON Records.

I shall note the scale, Dear Reader, as I'm sure you are well aware, is quite great. The professional life of Henley has been nothing short of expansive, hence the need to divide the book into three volumes. The volumes were named by Henley, as were the chapters and the title of the work as a whole. The work is also approved by Joe Henley, and still to my giddiness, has expressed a liking to it.

So, Dear Reader, where does this story begin? For many, it begins here—or perhaps it ends here—when I sat across from the musician in his living room, on a quiet January afternoon, and hit record.

[*Transcription from my first recording session with Joseph Henley.*]

January 31, 2033

Me: Okay. Now it's recording. See?
Joe Henley: Oh, very good! I was wondering if I was going to have to get off this seat and show you myself.

Me: No need, Joe. How do you feel? Are you ready?
JH: I suppose I'm as ready as I'll ever be. Was that your first question?

Me: Call it a warm-up question. Now that was an answer.
JH: [*Chuckling*] Perhaps we should start over.

Me: That's alright. Let's get into it.
JH: Okay. Where should we start?

Me: I'd like to start by asking, how are you?
JH: Today—ah, today, I am well—thank you for asking. In three hours, the sun will fall below that bank there, on University, and then another day will come to a close. But to spend that time doing this, and here with you, this is a treat. I do enjoy your writing, by the way, fantastic work. I'm just glad to be seated here and finally sharing the truth. Do you mind if I smoke?

Me: No, not at all. Feel free to do all the things you normally do.

JH: Thanks. And you? [*He motions the pack of cigarettes to me*]

Me: I'm alright. Joe, it's my pleasure and my honor to be doing this
with you. Now, let's get into it. Where would you like to begin?
JH: I was hoping you'd be able to tell me! Well, I suppose I should
start at the beginning. What should I say? [*In a goblin-esque tone of
mocking*] Hello! My name is Joe Henley. I was born in Athens,
Georgia but I was conceived on a weekend trip to New Orleans! [*Back
to normal*] I don't know, man. This is a bit awkward, isn't it? What a
drag.

Me: Don't let the microphone scare you, it's just you and me here.
That being said, we can start wherever you'd like. It's your story. Tell it
how you'd like.
JH: [*Beat*] Right. Okay, yes. Let us start the story on a quite pivotal
day. It was the day I consider to be the catalyst for all the change in my
life. Ah! Oh, I have so much to say!

Me: I understand this feeling. All you have to do now is tell the story.
JH: [*He pauses to sip from his mug of coffee*] Fuck. Okay. My life. Well,
my life was never the same after I lived through this day I am about to
tell you about. It was February of 2023. My third studio album was
released just the week before and met with *dismal* reviews. It was on
this day, I woke in this very city, only thirty or so blocks North from
here. . .

INSTANT VANITIES

Jesse David

VOLUME ONE
DYING STAR

I

Motor Oil Breakfast

I was only in New York for the weekend, stopping in to do a performance on a Late-Night show, although I cannot remember now which one. After that, I was to be sent straight back to Los Angeles for further promotion. My slumber that Saturday was interrupted by my manager ripping the comforter back, allowing a chilled breath to rust over my body. He had apparently been bashing on my door for the last hour and finally bribed the clerk at the front desk into providing him with a key. I hadn't even heard a peep until this moment when I was dragged from my bed, completely naked and useless. He slapped my cheek, babbling to me about how I must focus up, and prepare for the day ahead.

"We're going to be late. You hear me, Joe? Big day—*big* day—we need to get going," he yapped. I heard him going on about how, in all the outrageousness from the day prior, I had been spotted walking into the hotel room at half past two that same morning. Now nearing nine, a crowd had formed outside by the valet, awaiting my presence, a groundhog meant to see my own shadow.

My manager shoved underwear around my waist and attempted to stuff a sweater over my head. I stared dimly at the bed and noticed a red stain across the pillowcase. I squinted at it curiously, unsure how or why I had bled or where it was coming from, but there was no time for questions. My manager, Ant, and my assistant, Hal, came up with ways to get me into the black SUV waiting for me beyond the lobby.

"Maybe they have a backdoor or an entrance through the kitchen?" Hal optioned. He seemed timid with his offers as if Ant might explode on him at any second.

"Suitcase," I muttered.

I received blank stares.

I coughed, pulled the sweater off my neck, wearing nothing but a loose pair of underwear. I began plucking every article of clothing from my suitcase. Jumbled Levi's, wrinkled trousers, a winter over-coat. Socks were flung out through the suite like mullets on the coast. Once the suitcase was empty, I sat inside of it and curled myself as small as possible.

"It'll do. Quickly," Ant huffed, pink in the face.

I crammed my body into the fetal position and all around me I could hear the zipper growling as Hal secured me inside. The suitcase stood up and my kneecaps pressed against my eye sockets.

"Can you breathe?" Ant questioned. I could hear him already opening the door to my hotel room. He didn't actually care, I thought; he cared only enough to get paid, and I was his paycheck.

"For what it's worth, I can," I growled. "I couldn't bother either of you for a smoke?"

The top of the zipper peeled back, and something dropped in my hair. I managed my hand onto my head and felt it was a cigarette and a lighter. The suitcase began to move, feeling the rolling vibration of the hardwood floors all around my body.

"Thank you, Hal," I continued, "Not a bump but this will do."

I was rolling down the hallway, half awake, hungover, and disori-ented. The vibrations paused and I knew I was on the elevator, the inertia of the sinking space felt queer and unusual while curled so fetal. I was thumping over the tile of the lobby, then surrounded by countless voices, all at once hit with the cool outside air. Distantly there were sounds of cars honking and a general roar of engines as I rolled and clicked on the concrete. I was lifted into the trunk, more thrown, to keep my cover. After all, I was luggage to anyone's concern. I kneed my eyes, likely to leave a bruise but the makeup department would fix that. I pushed my index finger against the zipper, birthing an opening no larger than my thumb. The SUV zipped off into the city traffic. Still stuffed in the suitcase, I lit the cigarette and held it to my lips. I tilted my head up and pushed the cigarette's tip out of the little hole.

I smoked, holding the butt on my lips the way a hamster gets water, although this was far more insulting. A song played on the radio—*Mess Around* by Cage the Elephant—I focused on the track as the car sped and halted around the city traffic. This may have been one of my most listened to songs as a freshman in college. Strange now to think that only months later I joined a band of my own, and before I knew it, I found myself in this situation. The overall fast-rock style of the song felt fitting for our endeavor. Time was slipping nastily, and we still had three miles to the studio. I huffed a little too generously on my zoot for at the same moment we went over a pothole and the damn thing left my mouth and out of the suitcase. I coughed, catching a wad of mucus in my teeth and was forced to swallow. I hadn't even considered what could go wrong with lit ash sitting on the rented SUV's carpeted interior, but instead wondered what they did with all my clothes in the hotel room.

The drive was less than two miles then and we were agreeably gaining on the studio, but two miles still took far too long in the city. The smell of smoke eventually grew stronger, I was incapable of telling anyone unless I were to become frantic. If we could just make it to the building before the SUV were to catch fire, I thought, there would be no need for a dramatic episode. The smoke surpassed the potency of smell and was then capable of taste or lining a scratched heat within one's throat.

"Motherfucker!" Ant snapped, muffled in the front passenger seat.

I knew what he'd been on about as the warmth and the smoke only grew heavier. Rightfully hot-boxed. I was fine, crinkled up in my polyester cocoon. More-so a cheap casket in hindsight. And yet, the car slowed to a halt, I heard the back hatch unlock. All at once, I was yanked and thrown out from the trunk, slapping the street, hitting my entire crunched body on the asphalt. I winced; the bag unzipped.

"You *fucking* idiot, stand up," Ant continued. I did as I was told, rising from the bag. The icy January air stung my body, standing in the middle of 53rd and Broadway, mostly naked. But more alarming was the trunk snaking with flames and on top of that, my suitcase had caught fire. I blinked rapidly at the sight as Hal tossed a petticoat on my back and grabbed my shoulders.

"Two more blocks—*Stop it*—Stop looking at it. Two blocks and we're there. Understand? Let's just get there," he ordered. I paid him to do this, I had no reason to do anything but accept and trust his demands. He pushed his hands through his sharp, black hair and wandered his eyes at the crowd of spectators who had stopped in shock at our situation.

"Best you keep your head down," he added softly.

I walked barefoot through the city, stepping over fast food bags and kicking paper cups. My feet slapped and I watched them, trying my best to navigate around the mysterious stains imprinted on the cement. The petticoat covered my entire body, I folded the collar up to conceal a bit of my facial features. I heard scattered voices, some young women, some men, yelling out my name. *I'm not him*, I thought, as if it would change anything. *I am not Joe Henley.*

Before long, I was in the building and sent up to the eighteenth floor into a green room. I asked an eye-bagged stagehand if they might perhaps have a shower but regretfully, they hadn't one. Instead, I was given wipes that I could use to scrub myself down. I was also gifted deodorant and told to be ready for a rehearsal in half an hour. I would spend the next eight hours in that building. My assistant retrieved me enough coke for a line and a cup of coffee, both of which I was sure he'd attained from within the building. This mixture was how I had to jumpstart the engine every morning.

I was nursing the cup of black coffee when the door swung, in crossed Autumn, the drummer in the band. She looked considerably better than I did, her makeup done, and her auburn hair freshly shampooed. Autumn was generally quiet, shielded, but had a real bite to her when she was upset.

"What the fuck happened to you?" she grimaced. I was still in my underwear, there were remains of white powder on my vanity and my thick, brown hair was curled and greased.

"Rude awakening," I explained briefly.

"Get dressed. God, you're skinny as shit. Go to craft service and find a bagel. You need the carbs otherwise you might blow away."

I did as I was told, putting on my outfit, a designer suit. White linen blouse and navy dress pants with a matching necktie. Next, Tommy came rummaging through the dressing room. He was lanky like a scarecrow, wiggling through the room while chomping on an apple.

"Hey, Slick," he said, his movements were languid, but he was so tall, he almost moved like a pirate. He sank into a chair beside me and crossed his legs, leaned back leisurely, scratched at his buzzed blonde head. Tommy was the most interesting person I knew. He was not nearly as sophisticated as he let on, and he wasn't as stupid as he tried to make everyone believe. Not to mention, the best guitarist I had ever seen.

"Wild night. Glad you're okay. How's your nose?"

"My nose?" I questioned. Suddenly, I was reminded of the dried blotches of red on my pillowcase back in the suite, and how they'd rusted overnight.

"Yeah, you don't remember?"

"No, do you?"

"We made it off the roof of RT60. We were about a block away from the hotel when you ate shit on the sidewalk. You tripped on the curb and landed right on your face. You looked like Wile E. Coyote, I swear." He hummed a chuckle to himself, cracked another chalk into his apple and slurped. I remember standing on the rooftop with our first round of gin and tonics before deciding it was too drab to be standing up there. We looked over the edge at the vessels of 48th before heading back into the candy-colored lounge. I remember our conversations about how film had changed in the last decade, reviewing the current art scene in New York, how it all related to an art recession. "Just tell me, Slick, you alright?"

"Yeah, I'm alright. I don't even feel it."

He was quiet, grinning like a pantomime and tickled his nostrils. "*A spoonful of sugar*, Old Soul, eh? I'll see you in the green room." With a pounce of a hand on my shoulder, he patted my cheek and exited. I wiped my face—splashed it with a sting of cold water— quickly shoveled a bagel and was pushed onto a side stage across from a giant wooden desk where the talk show would take place later that same afternoon. I stared at my keyboard and placed my fingers on the keys, for the first time all day feeling any sense of familiarity.

I pressed an F minor chord with my right hand. It rang out through a speaker system and as it faded, the sound was replaced by plucks of a guitar and soft taps on a snare. I turned my attention around the room, finding the rest of the band at their places. There was Sophia on the bass, Autumn on the drums, Tommy on the guitar. They looked back at me. We'd all aged quite a bit since we'd met, being a band for more than half the last decade with two studio albums and a third releasing in two months. Staring back at me were the people I loved most in my life, but all their faces shadowed a look of worry—slight but present—and a fear rinsed through me as I watched their mild eyes. The metronome clocked through my earpiece. I counted them in.

Our latest single sprang out in the room, reverberating off the walls. An empty audience, but we played with heart. The languid push and pull of the rhythms rocked every chord, following Autumn's kick drum on every fourth, and Sophia filling the half notes with the bass. The piano was riding the bass, but my vocals were seem- ingly on their own, following the tempo only in a pattern I created.

The song ended abruptly rather than with a fadeout, a newer trend but classic all the same. Music is less about trends than other art forms. I was herded back into the green room. I sat with the others this time. The four of us—Tommy, the lanky, spacey pothead with a buzzcut, high cheekbones, a devilish basso voice and incredibly well- read in the realms of philosophy and comics; Autumn, the silent empath who hid behind a mask of sharp insolence, round faced with ginger strands and short enough to walk under a ladder without ducking; Sophia, the brunette, the well-proportioned starlet, excitable and optimistic while also tame and collected, cheery grin and sleeves of black-ink tattoos, and on the constant pursuit of perfection in her life —which leaves me, the greaseball they allowed into their lives for whatever reason, a full head of hair and practically skin and bone; a lungful of smoke and an aimless set of eyes.

We watched a screen be mounted on the wall of our green room as it spit a picture of famous celebrities laughing and chatting to the host who I was entirely unfamiliar with. I recognized only one of the actors, having seen him at a party, I was certain of this. It was Freddy Richardson, the lead actor in *The Call*, the biographical film based on the life of the writer and journalist, Jack London. He was nominated for best actor for this film at the previous year's award show. I tilted my head, curious to see it now on regular television. Suddenly bored, I directed my attention to the band. They were in the midst of a discussion when a curious thought leaped to the front of my mind.

"If I were obsessed with cheetah print, would I still be the lead singer?"

"Sophia would," Autumn began, she was used to the nonsense I spouted day in and day out. Sophia glanced up from her phone, passed a movement of the eyes to the two of us. Autumn continued, "Plenty of bassists double as the lead singer and she would have better style than you. If you were in constant cheetah print, we'd have you seated off to the right of us." I wasn't thrilled by her response.

"Joe's the lead singer?" Tommy asked in his sarcastic, low tone. I ignored him and did my best to ignore Sophia's false grin.

"It's sort of chic, though, isn't it? If you pull something like that, and you stand up for it, maybe call it *a statement in camp*, regardless of if it is or not, in five years' time *it will be* camp."

"When did *you* become so involved in fashion?" Autumn squinted.

"I would consider myself involved but not contributing."

"Same thing."

"I disagree."

We watched the talk show in silence. I lit a cigarette as a woman with a headset opened the door. She said something and I followed the rest of the band through a hallway and back out toward the stage, this time completely dark. People in all-black outfits—assistants, interns, stagehands—some of these bodies held flashlights and walked beside us. We were to follow the dim puddle of light and stare at our shoes, but I wanted to make sure I didn't bump into Autumn directly ahead of me. I might end up with a pop to the nose if I threw her focus. Someone plucked my cigarette and killed it as I walked onto the dark stage. I found my seat back at the keyboard and thought it must be around 5:45pm at that point.

Lights hung ungodly; they grew and cast an intense warmth on us. I knew from the countless mirrors on the way up I was sweating and now the golden light would make the sweat sparkle on my face. Still, I understood the routine, the performance that could not go wrong; I counted them in, and we were off.

I found myself when the music ended, the crowd gave the same applause and freckled cheers. I was standing, the mic had moved from the keyboard to a mic stand, I was doubled over, bowing for the packed audience. The lights muted, my smile faded, and we were escorted off the stage. I never ended up meeting the host and I had dinner plans with a producer and a vague acquaintance who lived in Queens an hour from then. A man by the name of Ellis Young, whom I had only met briefly at a party or two over champagne and polite handshakes. He was a good contact, however, and we both managed to schedule a dinner. In his fronting charm, he offered to cook at his own Long Island City apartment.

The car was gone so I took the subway with Hal as my parent. He studied every sign, triple-checking that we were heading in the right direction. Once on the plastic orange seats of the N train, I noticed a dimly lit advertisement for a Broadway musical—*Jazz Canal*—I knew the musical well. I knew the songs from listening to the soundtrack in college. The stained placard was a deep red color, with the title in blocky white letters. I pointed at the sign and asked, "Could we make it to that?"

"No," Hal replied.

I dipped my head and stared at the dusted floor of the cart and my dress shoes. The makeup was still on my face, mostly to hide the black eye I had received on being flung out of the trunk of the car.

Before long we were back up on the street in Queens and going into an apartment building. I knocked on a door on the fifth floor and a moment later, there stood Ellis with his shoulder-length, ginger-red hair in a ponytail, holding a cup of tea.

"Joe, it's good to see you," he said in his distinctly English accent. His voice was charming, and devastatingly deep. He would have better suited a career in broadcasting or narration had he not been such a genius in music composition. He was from Manchester in the United Kingdom, but his voice was devastatingly rich, likely due to cigarettes and not being a singer himself.

He wrapped me in a hug and asked if the two of us were doing alright, an alternative to asking why I smelt of sweat and smoke. Upon entering his apartment, I first noticed the spectacular selection of books he had lined on a shelf taking up the entire back wall of his living room. He had a sagging leather sofa, twin armchairs, and candles placed in every dead space. Elaborate, blooming crown molding etched the ceiling, plant life lived on every window in fine pottery, and the vinyl floors chirped with weight. The apartment seemed fit for a poet from two centuries ago rather than an artist and music producer today (he always said he was an artist first, producer second and I found this to be quite honest).

"I understand you're just finishing up from a performance on Late Night, is that right?" he shouted from the kitchen. He rounded the corner not a second later with a teapot clutched in one hand, cups and saucers in the opposite.

"Yes," I replied, and wondered what else to say. Luckily, Ellis continued, "Ah, wonderful. It went well, yes? That was over in *30 Rock*, yes, I worked as an intern in that building. Coffee runs and such. Hooked up with Victoria Redding in that building. 'You know of her? She was the love interest in *Breaking Bread* and, yes, she was the lead in *Chasing Windmills*. That was back—oh—must have been 2014 or so? *Fuck*, nearly a decade already. Enjoy your beauty while you have it, Joseph. And the fame! With the sounds you've been putting out recently, you must be busy every night with a different body."

I nestled on his leather sofa and before even being offered, Ellis placed two fresh teacups on the coffee table. He sat across from Hal and I in an armchair, more of a throne, him going on and on, the sound of our new single, raving about our techniques and sound. I stared off at his bookshelf.

"You have a lot of books by Charles Dickens," I observed out loud.

"I do, I really enjoy his writing," Ellis replied. He directed his attention to my interest.

"*David Copperfield...*" I read aloud. Ellis nodded, swallowing his herbal blend, "Ah, yes. That's one of his best. A bildungsroman—it is a difficult genre to guide but Dickens is a master of his art—he always said Copperfield was his favorite child."

"Mm..."

The room fell quiet as I studied the spine of the book, my head tilted at an angle. I must have looked insane with my head askew. A bent neck and increasingly inquisitive eyes. All of which I did without saying a word.

"Joe," Ellis muttered. He was hushed so as to break the silence gently. "You don't think Charles Dickens wrote a novel about the *magician*, David Copperfield, right?"

I had.

"Of course not."

"That novel is nearly a century older than the magician, mate," Ellis explained.

"Yes, yes, but the magician is quite good."

"What are you suggesting?" Ellis squinted, I sipped the tea, too ashamed to carry on with my speculation. The apartment was quiet, but I noticed his excellent stereo system, a *Pro-Ject Debut Pro* turntable on his vinyl record display stand. He had records scattered every-where, some on the coffee table, under the coffee table, stacks on the floor, stuffed crates in the corner of the dining room. With a soft clearing of the throat, Ellis fled the previous conversation, "I wanted to talk to you about your new record."

I sighed audibly, "I thought we were having dinner."

"Your album is good," he began.

"Yeah, yeah," I blew, barely listening to anything he was saying.

"But your album is also incredibly forgettable."

I clicked the teacup back to my saucer, swallowing, and found a place for it on the coffee table. The soft meeting of wood to porcelain may have been the only audible sound aside from the outside traffic. It was devastatingly clear that Ellis had my full attention. He stood up from his throne across the living room and began pacing about.

"I listened to it all the way through twice and I began to feel as if you and your band had no sense of direction this time around."

"That's sort of what we do. Without direction, we have the freedom to go anywhere. Our band has no blueprint, we just are what we are," I argued.

"This is just my opinion but I'm afraid your songs are too outlandish. Each song picks a different genre, yes. There's no cohesive-ness to the record whatsoever. Occasionally, you would tap into some-thing really special but then you'd shy away from it a track later. I mean, if this was your intent then I applaud you, but I know what you're capable of. And in all honesty, the wandering lack of attention made me— somewhat *worried*—about you, mate."

He was right. I sat in silence.

He continued, "Did you set out to create a novel or a collection of short stories?"

I had avoided all reviews of the record and now I knew why. Ellis felt the same way I did, only I hadn't been able to face this anxiety until he said it outright. I remember at that moment I wished to either be alone or intoxicated.

"Have you got any wine?"

"I do. There's salmon in the oven as well. Again, Joseph, you're a friend so I don't mean to offend you with any of this. You understand, I'm sure. It's all only honest critique from a fan. I used to be Robert Horowitz's personal assistant, and he always told me that fans will give the best reviews because nobody cares nearly as much as they do."

I nodded. Robert Horowitz was a famed film director, now in his sixties, but had created an extravagant run of science fiction films, as well as thrillers and biography pictures. Ellis enjoyed telling many people about the many red carpets he attended as a young man and how he met nearly every celebrity through his connections with this director. Ellis had even once gotten to see an early cut of Richard Lebber's *The Billionaire Tragedy* at Horowitz's house on a summer Saturday night in 2013, a full year before it won best picture at The Academy Awards. This was, to my understanding, after he had already broken into the music industry. He worked with The Inbetweeners on their historic Sophomore album, *Dream No. 99*, and skyrocketed into fame as a young music producer. *The Prince of Dissonance*, a quote from the aged tabloids. He grew bored of the music industry after a few years (restless, as most driven young men are) and tried to pivot into filmmaking, only to fall back into music sometime later.

Ellis retrieved a rosé from a cabinet and between the three of us, the bottle was gone in half an hour. He uncorked a chardonnay; it was gone in an hour. I drank most of the chardonnay, and before long I felt a burning pleasure on my legs. The sun glazed tangerine stripes across the wood flooring as the day drew close. Ellis slumped in his armchair with his wine glass held below the bowl; he observed me for a moment as if I were some sort of art piece.

"Meandering," Ellis graveled. I said nothing, unsure what he meant.

"Your album—It's meandering," he worthlessly added, "I believe the meandering is a result of fear. You were afraid to do something wrong. As if there is a *wrong*."

I listened without giving my attention. Instead, I spun the liquid in my glass, the legs stretched and fell. I repeated the act over and over again as if studying it.

"You got so caught up in the idea of creating a masterpiece that it started to fragment itself, falling inward, losing sight of intention. *Implosion*," he rang, "In result, the work you created feels afraid. Afraid to pick an identity, afraid to be nurtured in simplicity."

He paused, perhaps awaiting a response or gathering his thoughts. He played, "The moment you second guessed what you had, deciding the sound needed more, and the lyrics needed ambiguity, that was the moment you lost simplicity. You lost a clear path, and the project grew branches. *Meandering*. I've worked with many artists, Joe, I don't want you to think I'm singling you out with this critique."

I blinked to soak in the tears sheathed on my eyes. Heat pulsed in my face, and I started gnawing tightly at the insides of my cheeks. To my surprise, Hal spoke to my left, "Well, we both know there's a lot going on in that brain of his."

The three of us chuckled, mine louder than theirs. Thank goodness for Hal then, breaking up the conversation like that. Soon we went out and smoked on the fire escape with the window open, allowing strings from a spinning record in the living room to accompany us. His record of choice was *Odelay* by Beck.

By dinner, the sky was a chromatic landscape. The salmon was the best I had ever had, both flavorful and sweet with whatever he'd marinated it in. I hugged Ellis goodbye and thanked him but inwardly felt a wicked jealousy toward him. Ellis was a respected artist. He had no need to hide his face much in public. Someone would only recognize him if they were a genuine fan of his, which meant any approach from a stranger would make for real conversations on music and art. He knew most everything on the topics of philosophy, history, random anecdotes (he chose his cleanses to include black tea as it benefits a shine to his hair, and the black tea did as such; he had a glimmer to his hair, the color of changing leaves). He knew everyone worth knowing and had accomplished more in the last decade than I had in my entire life. Ellis had once mentioned in passing that he thought he had a keen eye for Rembrandt as he could name each of his paintings if presented to him. He could too recall the year it was finished, which resulted in Ellis going as far as referring to himself as 'a Rem-brat.' This made me sour. Cross. Aside from this, he was a man of natural talent, sprinkled with a stroke of charmed luck to assimilate all things he took fancy in. Such was not the case for me, having had to teach myself for years how to do anything I admired. Aside from this, he had a lean physique. A toned, clean jaw. He was without flaw and to make matters worse, he was unwillingly kind.

I sauntered along the street with Hal at my hip. Hal was twenty-five then with black hair combed to the side, clean shaven, always in leisure suits. It had been his first time being anyone's assistant and was my first assistant. I met Hal at university as a senior, the same place I had met the rest of the band. He wrote a column on our band for the college paper, *GW Today*. He was majoring in Journalism with a minor in Marketing. Howard (Hal) Walsh always intended to write for magazines to the likes of *Billboard, Rolling Stone, Rock Sound, NME.* The piece he'd decided to write on us would mean attending our shows, interviewing and spending time with us. After he'd submitted the column, Hal continued to stay out with us on weekends and sit in on rehearsals. He'd become a close friend of mine with his gentle yet straightforward demeanor, someone I could talk to about anything I needed to. I believe his column in our school paper helped propel us into fame, and so, I'd decided he'd be my assistant if success granted it a necessity.

A blue-white moon spun above us; the rest of the buildings rocked like masts of a ship. My head bobbed; the wine sloshed in my stomach creating a pleasant warmth. I was still in my suit, riding the subway back downtown and to my hotel suite where I would stay another night before leaving early the following morning. Off the train and out into the dimly lit city, we walked a handful of blocks closely. We'd stopped at a street corner, waiting for the passing cars to shuffle by when a young lady approached with her phone already in hand. She looked younger, perhaps in her early twenties, sporting a white top and bleach-washed jeans. Her brown hair braided in two, falling on both her shoulders and gold-rimmed glasses pressed over her little round face. Her puffy black jacket made it seem as if she had her shoulders scrunched to her ears.

"Uh, hi. Are you Joe Henley?"

"Yes, that's me."

"*Wow*," she started to say as her cheeks flushed red, "I hope it won't bother you to get a picture?"

I nodded, she extended her phone toward the sky, the camera flashed, she reviewed the photo. Her eyes lit up when she saw the photo as if I were some sort of New York attraction or an animal in a zoo. She now possessed a picture she deemed valuable. Though, much less valuable if nobody knew who I was. It begs the question—Would she still have approached me for a photo if she was the only person to listen to my music? Would a photo of an artist with their only admirer be worth it to them?

"Do you like my music?"

"I love it! I listen to you when I make breakfast in the morning and sometimes on the train going to my classes," she said.

"What do you make for breakfast?" I asked. She blinked, as if perplexed by such a question.

"Well, I usually have toast and tea. Sometimes I make bowls of fruit for myself."

I huffed, "That sounds nice. Do you go to school around here?"

"NYU—I'm studying theater—I'm an actress."

"What's your name?" I tilted my head.

"Aubrey," she replied, her eyes wide and mouth gaped. The light changed; the red glow of the pedestrian sign morphed to white.

"It's lovely to meet you Aubrey, and I'm flattered you enjoy the music we make. I hope college is treating you well and please be safe out here," I grinned. Hal gave a friendly wave to Aubrey and threw his arm around me. She stood in place as Hal and I marched toward the hotel. I looked over my shoulder and she was staring at her phone, perhaps at the picture of me, evidence of having met her, or of her having met me.

Back in my room, I thought about Aubrey for longer than I'd cared to. Thinking how if I'd been just a few years younger, I would have brought her up to my room. But for me, nearly five or six years older, I had much less interest in strangers, even less a fan who thought they'd known me on any sort of personal level. I knew more about her personal life than she knew about mine. This was, of course, by my design. Nobody knows me except perhaps my band. My bandmates were the only people I loved.

I undressed alone in my room and got ready for the nightly routine. I brushed my teeth, stared at my body in the mirror, a decomposing mess. I washed my face, the tan grime from the city clung on my facial pads. I climbed into the king-sized bed, masturbated, wiped myself clean with a hotel towel, and fell asleep staring at my phone.

———

Strange how only last year, I would go out in search of any substance I could get my hands on, stay out until first light, and keep going until lunch before an unavoidable crash. I had hollowed eye sockets and pimples dotted over my face. Now my skin was clear, my hair was healthier, and I looked decently put together aside from the black eye, swollen and the color of a plum. Perhaps I'd gotten it all out of my system, perhaps I was growing introverted, perhaps I was becoming tired.

The alarm on my phone sounded at five in the morning. A blaring shimmer, a click, and alone in the dark of a neat hotel room. I remember being pushed through lines at the airport and onto a plane, back to Los Angeles. I was to attend numerous interviews for our latest album, *Music to Die to*. Our previous albums date back to four years ago, beginning with our self-titled album, *Beach Sirens*. This was followed by our most recent release at the time, *Island Walkers*, put out two years later in the summer of '21.

I had countless names for records that were rejected by my bandmates. They gave criticism to my harsher reality despite living the rock and roll lifestyle, supposedly I could conclude their input kept me grounded. For instance, on *Island Walkers*, I wanted a single titled, *Am I Gay? And Other Suicidal Thoughts*. Instead, we opted to use a line from the song, titled, *Don't Get Too Close*, but I felt my title had more consequence—a misdemeanor but an earnestness—*je ne sais quoi*.

Island Walkers was nearly named *Romance Empire*, which later became a six-track EP put out after the album. We had to release something to keep the newfound craze for our band satisfied while we toured and worked on our next album. *Island Walkers* went platinum in just over a year of its release, with 1.2 million copies sold in the United States by August the following year. We followed it with a single aptly titled, *Oceanic*, that went gold in a matter of months and became our thesis for the following EP. The success of our music was relentless, headlining festivals across the world and finding ourselves unable to turn on the radio without hearing our single from the album, *Loose Ends*.

We were on the cusp of stardom. We had already come to terms with being just another indie band. It was when we went from traveling by van to a gig in Georgia to flying private to Brazil less than a year later that we had our senses beat to death and knew we must have become celebrities. Now, three years into the lifestyle and work ethic of a rockstar, real genuine ones, I wasn't quite sure what to feel. If I felt anything at all.

Every word I said in the press junkets and interviews for *Music to Die to* rang false in my conscience. Since my dinner at Ellis' apartment, I couldn't help but wonder if my own lack of focus, of course, transpired onto the sounds of the record. If I or even my bandmates were in a state of disarray, surely our collective work of art would portray our state of mind. At this point in my life, I had turned to the stars that came before me. How did they manage their careers?

I came to the conclusion that many musicians were working in a machine, teetering between creation and exploitation in a cycle of push and pull. These artists, caught in a trap by a corporation to replicate themselves in varying fashions to suit an audience while revealing a fresh sense of growth, all embellish a state of disorientation. Some artists rise in this scenario but many fall.

I am reminded of the myth of Sisyphus, and his attempts to cheat

Death. In doing so, he is caught and punished with pushing a boulder toward the peak of a mountain. Sisyphus would eventually reach this great summit, but just as he is about to push the boulder over to the other side, it inevitably tumbles back to the base. A curse was bestowed on him to push the boulder infinitely. I always thought it to be a humorous story. That is until I found myself, the reputable character of our own post-modern mythology, to become a twisted Sisyphus.

What a drag, in all senses of the word, with my power of stardom, I have cheated Death in my own rite. Irony would have it, I am granted the punishment of my own rock, in the form of rhythm and sound, and as I attempt to conquer the summit, it rolls back to the bottom. Call it Sisyphean, my many efforts to play Death. This desire to reach the unreachable. Call it rock and roll.

II

Glass Houses And Dead Birds

Then it was Friday in Los Angeles; leaves were brushing the sidewalks, and I was on the way to a café near my apartment to meet with Sophia. My strut was leisure, knowing I'd arrive early to ensure a decent seat but with the relaxed weather, we were able to sit outside anyway. The café—Frosted was the name, if I do recall—sold all kinds of pastries and coffees. A honey-colored interior with gold and white accents. Black and white tiled floors. Spacious ceilings. Modern but tastefully classic. When I spotted her as she rounded the corner at the top of the block, I made quick effort to compose myself, brushing bits off my torso and standing up straight. As she drew closer, I pretended to then notice and start towards her. She grinned and stuffed her smartphone into her back pocket. Black denim shorts frayed at the edges. White t-shirt and cat's eye sunglasses.

"Hey." She pulled me close for a hug. "Good to see you." Her collection of metallic and gold bracelets jingled as her arms moved.

I ushered her into the café; we ordered and thankfully, we both went unnoticed by anyone inside. After standing in the line of patrons and receiving our orders, we carried our cappuccinos out to a bistro set outside the front window. My reflection stared back at me in the glass, enveloped by the golden letters stenciled and spelling out the name of the café. I turned to study Sophia's face—she was going on about a new poem she'd been writing about non-permanence. She explained how she was to use chocolate as a literary prop; for instance, when owning a delectable piece of dark chocolate, one would rather treasure it than eat it, but the latter, of course, is the inherent purpose for its creation. I was listening but tracing the outline of her natural brown hair to where it fell on her shoulders. I tilted my head to watch the sun reflect off her earrings. Sophia hadn't put on any make-up that morning and yet she was just as beautiful as she'd always looked, and at once I felt the same affection toward her from years before and surely, years to follow.

"You've been here before?" I asked, watching her closely.

"I haven't. It looks lovely," she replied.

I nodded. I pressed my fist against my head in every possible way to prop myself up. She sipped the cappuccino softly. I studied the street around us. A young lady ripped by on rollerblades. A greyhound clicked his nails on the cement; his owner, a burly man, sauntered on behind him. Across from us was a seafood restaurant, a boutique, and a hair salon. All of them looked chic, but only the hair salon was open at that hour.

"Are you nervous?" I asked, trying to sound nonchalant.

"For?"

"Ah, for the next tour, you know," I reiterated. The first show of our new tour, titled the Fatal Tour, would begin on the 18th of March in Boston, Massachusetts. The minds behind the execution of this tour were a collection of heads at the label, travel coordinators, Ant, and others, including myself. The last tour left me in a state of exhaustion and relentless misery. I feared the next tour, despite it being a culmination of our creative interests at the time. We were to wear matching black suits, tailor-fit to each of us respectively, and the stage would be outlined in a silver stand of light. We thought the idea boded well with the thesis, *Music to Die to*, and as such, making it the flashiest funeral anyone had ever been to.

"Oh. Not so much. It's on my mind, sure, but I know better what to expect this time around," she said, making eye contact. Her voice flowed sweetly like linen. Her face fell slightly, and I noticed new lines on her cheeks, either from age or the early morning.

"How have you been?" I pushed.

"Fine."

"Sophia, really. It's me, you can tell me."

She looked past me then, down the sidewalk, at nothing in particular. She was staring out at something that was not with us at present. She ran her fingers up and down her forearms, grazing over every black tattoo there. She sighed quietly to herself.

"I don't know—I have so many thoughts—I mean, there's Daniel to think about now," she said. She looked tired. I tried to push blame on the early call of our meeting, but she'd looked tired for days. Weeks. I hadn't forgotten about her boyfriend, Daniel, her partner for the last two years at that point. He found himself in her life right as our music found itself in the limelight. He was the Field Producer for many documentaries and docuseries (usually in the sports category), which granted him many unique opportunities. If he pitched a poignant enough story as a follow up, he could earn himself a paid stay anywhere in the world. It was up to him to find the right stories and center athletes as the protagonists of their own documentaries. All they had to do was answer questions in minimally-gaffed interviews and be their best, brightest version whenever a camera lens pointed in their direction.

Daniel rarely ever stayed in Los Angeles despite living there; instead, he infiltrated Montreal or Venice, Brazil or Jamaica, Athens or Portugal with his ragtag team of five or six misfit documentary crew members. How he acquired such a job, I had no idea and never felt inclined to ask. He was the type if I were to ask a direct question, he'd pretend I existed only half of the time. He was constantly lost in himself—which I always found quite irritating—but of course, who was I to judge?

"*Fuck, two years*. It doesn't feel like two years," I said, trying to sound sympathetic.

"Yeah, yeah," she muttered. She sipped more of her cappuccino without making a peep. Sophia had always been a quiet type, never one to speak about her day unless prompted, and extraordinarily polite. She was quite a bit shorter than me but stood taller with her reserved composure. She hadn't always been that way—in college, she was fairly extroverted—always excited for events and viewed them as adventures. Somewhere in the last six or so years, it had faded into this dulled presence. This never bothered me, she was always going to be Sophia. I regularly tried to make her smile because each of her smiles had the ability to rewind time, to place me back in Washington when we were only two young university students.

"Dan's a good guy, I really like him. I think he's good for you," I said, masking the distaste for the words. I didn't hate Daniel, but I hoped for more for her. He was a dry human being, that is to say, his substance was grave-natured, and his humor was monotone. He was wholly artificial. I began to conjure a daydream of her boyfriend pitching a docuseries on Artificial Sweeteners to a board of studio executives and producers, where he'd present the working title as a swinging home-run, aptly named *Daniel*. Sophia was mute, eyes bugged and glued somewhere on the bistro table; all of my conversations with her went this way in some fashion. Circles of silence. I picked up the conversation in any way I could. She adjusted, now staring down at her coffee, stirring it slowly, when suddenly she began to smile to herself.

"Yeah, he's pretty cool, isn't he?" she looked back at me, her little grin still clinging to her face. There it was, the Sophia from all those years ago. Still, a tinge of gloom sprouted in the context of her joy. It was obvious that Daniel had been kept in the dark on the topic of Sophia and I's past. He may not have known that I too knew the shape of her body when bare, the pitch of her laugh, and the rate of her breath when she slept. My brilliant Sophia. I'd thought one day certainly after all the grooves, itches and chasings, would actually pay off—once we're a little older, she'll finally give me the time of day— we'd be together in the end. No, this would not be the case. I turned to discover patrons exiting the café and stealing looks at the two of us with hooked gazes as if their attention had gotten caught in something sticky. In return I granted them the same counterfeit grin I'd given Sophia only moments before; something I was, at this point, well accustomed to.

"Remember last year when we'd do this? Just sit outside the café and talk for hours. It seemed more riveting then," I thought aloud, pulling a cigarette from my shirt. I flicked at the tin lighter half a dozen times before it caught.

She nodded, "Yes, but last year we were in France. Not only that but we did that in Strasbourg. This is your neighborhood coffeehouse."

"*Loved* Strasbourg," I thought aloud, pulling the mug to my lips.

"So did I. I loved Paris quite a lot too, or at least what we got to see of it. Something about it was so appealing to me. It had the energy of New York City but with that European charm. Has to do with history, you know. Maybe it was how the French always spoke with honesty," she gathered as if she were chipping through layers to the core of her idea the more she spoke.

"I always thought it was their bohemian lifestyle. Bohemian in the American sense, I should say, our lofty, sort of *idealistic* outlook on what a Bohemia is and should be," I said, "I mean, they must see Americans through such a modest lens."

"What we call bohemian, the French call Monday," she grinned. I saw her perfect teeth lined and white. Her teeth hadn't always been perfect like that, I remembered.

"Mm, I like that a lot," I mumbled with the cigarette stuck in my lips. I continued, "They have everything good in France. Especially their beaches—*unreal*—you remember, don't you? Oh, don't give me that face—I think we call the most special things in our life French."

"What do you mean?"

"It's all French, the good stuff. Toast—*kissing*—*inhales*—and even the most obvious staple of American culture, we call French."

"Being?" She sat with an incline, leaning forward in her seat. I blew the smoke toward the road as a chuckle grew in my chest. "Fries —Sophia, *french fries*! Those are *absolutely* not French! Well—maybe they are, I don't know."

"I think they're from Belgium," she hummed.

I continued, "I mean, Christ, even their *revolution* was more grandiose than ours. They're timeless in beauty with such little effort."

"Maybe you should move to France. Have you ever considered that?" she eyed me.

"I couldn't. Not with the band here. Plus, I'm not pretty enough for France. I don't belong there," I breathed. Sophia shook her head in disagreement, pulling a smoke from her case. Hand rolled. One of six. She took my cigarette from my mouth and used the ash to light hers.

"Lest we forget," she started, "*your* face is the result of all kinds of people who loved each other's faces. You belong anywhere you'd like to belong."

I chuckled and brought the smoke back to my lips. Once the words left her mouth, I knew at that moment that I could spend the rest of my life with her. I'd felt this way a thousand times before and I knew I was certain to feel it again. The energy when the two of us were together was unquestionable. I felt it all over my body. I couldn't resist smiling at her and she returned it knowingly. She held her cigarette out with a limp wrist. I leaned into my cappuccino, saying, "You sounded quite French just then."

We talked for over an hour that morning, sitting out in the dry winter. I'd known Sophia for years, I knew how to make her laugh, I knew what she liked and where the line was between us. I cared for her in ways I was incapable of with others. Her and the rest of the band, they were the only people I really cared about anymore.

This adventure, this ride as Beach Sirens, it would not last forever. She told me between the lines she hoped one day to lay it to rest and live on her own. Of course, these thoughts ran through my mind countless times as well, knowing we cannot count on being young, and in the limelight for the rest of our lives. We had to accept that it was our shining moment. Not three years ago. Not ten years from now. This was all we had. I felt a sting in my stomach—for her situation—her strategy. She'd set herself up to leave one family and start another. She'd be a mother. Sophia, the bassist and female vocals on several records, would shed the skin of an alternative musician in exchange for that of a caregiver. And it would happen sooner than I thought.

I went back to my apartment, only to realize the caffeine had little effect on me. The first task I set out to complete was to concoct another coffee for myself using Italian grounds. I always opted for dark roast. This and a line of coke held my body upright. I sipped my coffee at the kitchen table, sniffling every so often, and watched the stuffy Los Angeles skyline in the foreground, dusty hills beyond it. I rolled on the thoughts from my morning spent with Sophia. I tried putting myself in her position and wondered how I (in this purely hypothetical scenario) would handle being a father. Surely, I wouldn't be very good at it but there was still a pulling sensation inside of me to someday wager the possibility of having a family of my own.

I moved across the room and tried to form my thoughts into a song. There, at my Steinway grand piano, my fingers hovered over the keys. I realized then that it may be impossible to break away from music as I continuously defaulted to it in every situation. Even in an attempt to control my thoughts on a life aside from my musical career, I use melodies and rhymes to cope. I leaned back on the stool. I felt as if I'd been slapped across the face.

I spent the rest of the day in a gaunt sedation. Between preparing myself cocktails in my apartment, I would sit out on the balcony, on the third floor, suspended thirty-five feet or so above the street. The sun pressed on my face and neck, *Untitled (How Does It Feel)* by D'Angelo pulsed gently on my turntable from the living room, the sound of traffic immediately below me found itself into the mix. My apartment was on Olympic Boulevard, a luxury residence with two bedrooms, a spacious living room. Vinyl floors, beige walls, a birch bookcase and stacks of records. The only wall ornaments I'd hung up were black lacquer records that read 'Beach Sirens' and 'Island Walkers' and one RIAA platinum certification for *Island Walkers*. My apartment was hollow—I never bought anything but the occasional takeout, records, wines. It was home though, I suppose, as it did feature everything I felt I needed. Satisfaction was never located within my living space but rather derived from experiences. And, perhaps, accomplishments. Admittedly, at times even my accomplishments made me feel very little, and it was at these times that the apartment felt most like home.

———

Tommy lived in a new house in Woodland Hills, a price just over one million. The exterior had a small enough lawn that it could be balded with a pair of pliers if he wished but he insisted on hiring a landscaping company to take care of it. He had a pool in his backyard, cut out from a cement frame; a depth of six feet, enough for Tommy to stand in it and still have his eyes poke out at the surface. I spent a lot of time around his new house; he'd only just purchased it at the top of the year.

I arrived at his house in the evening after we'd finished rehearsal; I pulled my convertible against the curb of Miston Drive and the lock chirped. His house had an even tan, dark wood accents, and walls of bamboo on either side to block out the neighbors. Tommy was at the door, as he always was, fitted in some baggy denim and a marrow-hued button-down. He shuffled down the steps of his front walkway with bare feet slapping against the cement.

"Hey Slick," he muttered, yanking me close into a hug. "You smell fucking incredible. What is that?"

"I don't even know. *Chanel* or something."

This was honest. I got ready for my visit by choosing a silk, olive dress shirt half open, suede nude dress pants, birch leather loafers and a belt to match. Men's perfume. A silver chain necklace.

He held me out by the shoulders, examining my outfit as if I were an unwrapped gift and said, "And fuck, you look handsome. Like a millionaire playboy—which you are, and I wish you'd act like it—God, yeah, I'd fuck you."

He nodded approvingly at his comment and gave a definite slap on my shoulder before turning and allowing me into his new house. The floors were tiled, and he had all kinds of massive art prints hanging on his walls. His house was fairly tidy, a mounted flat screen television in the living room with a suede blue sofa. White walls throughout. The whole place was cold and felt almost clinical. *Minimal* is not a correct description, perhaps a better fit would be *organized clutter*. My apartment was minimal, with bare walls and a collection of records. My place seemed more like a staged set for a home magazine shoot. All this aside from his kitchen where it was anything but skeletal. He had more pots and pans than any man would ever need. Tommy was an excellent cook; he made several pretentious dishes when we were roommates for in D.C. White wine butter scallops. Braised lamb shanks with winter fruits. Mushroom and beef wellington. Garlic butter steak bites over a bed of pea risotto. Tommy used to tell me often if it weren't for his guitars, he'd have been a chef.

He wrapped an apron around his torso and pulled a pan from its cast-iron hook above the inlaid pale marble sink. He shouted over his shoulder, "This evening, I planned to make a smoked lemon chicken pasta. 'That alright?"

"It's alright. It's not a burger. I'm not picky though, you know that."

He glanced over his shoulder with a raised brow. "Should we stop by *In-N-Out* instead?"

I huffed a laugh, "No, man, I was joking! No, no, it sounds great. Whip me up some dinner, Chef."

I sat at a stool in his kitchen and read the paper—Tommy was adamant about getting the newspaper, even in D.C.—he never wanted to miss anything. We talked back and forth about the housing market. "Why don't you buy a house?" he asked.

"I have everything I need in that apartment," I said.

"Everything but a woman."

"Look who's talking."

The conversation delved from there into the throws of the economic crisis, new-age living styles, and the post-modern bohemian admiration toward renting rather than buying; much of our conversation was cause for boredom. After dinner, we stayed up drinking a French Pino and listening to *Richard D. James Album* by Aphex

Twin. Sweeps of electronic dribbles hopped around the living room. We discussed the mechanics of rhythm, what kinds of things we needed to try, how to empower our sound. Tommy had a myriad of philosophies for music, everything ranging from 'Saying less is saying more' to 'Folk ballads are the reason for lyricism.'

Later on, as the sky lost its color, we watched David Lynch's *Inland Empire* and sometime around the scene with the rabbits in the nightmarish family sitcom, Tommy turned to me with an excited eye. He said, "This is it: Breeding familiarity with this kind of *distortion* is what makes something uncomfortable. Fuck with the familiar and you can make an entire audience uneasy! David Lynch is a master. It's like—right—we all know this angle from stage plays or *I Love Lucy* but look—look at it now. What are they saying? Are they saying anything? It's all turned on its head. But you have to look closer than that! Or, better yet, stand further back and let this unsettling feeling take control." We talked about Lynch quite often (*Would a bathroom without a mirror over the sink be considered Lynchian?*); after all, Lynch was Tommy's favorite filmmaker. I would go as far as to call him Tommy's idol, or at least his inspiration as an artist.

We crawled off his couch and stood with our backs against the far wall, tipsy and smiling at the flickering light of the movie. The pale blue glow was the only color and shine in the whole room. We'd watched this movie and a few others plenty of times. We were in our own rite, proper cinephiles. We'd spent many nights blazed on the sofa in D.C. having spiraled talks on what makes something beautiful. Beauty is subjective, yes, but beauty is more personal than that. Born in the subconscious, beauty is something we cannot anticipate. Tommy's favorite movie changed every day, but it was always either David Lynch's *Blue Velvet* or Vincent Gallo's *Buffalo 66*—he could never properly articulate why he loved these films so much—we decided this is how we'd know if we had fallen in love with the beauty of a piece or a person. If we lost our ability to pin explanation, and if we could cherish it for what it was—regardless of precision—we'd see perfection.

———

Music to Die to was released exactly one month before I spent the evening with Tommy. Our third record was released on the 10th of February, and it was accompanied by a release party in a venue that felt a bit like The Brickroom, but it was triple the size. I opted to self-drive, arriving at the party late by nearly an hour, just as the trees splintered the sun. I knew very little of the people at this party; carved young faces, molting aged faces, elegant dresses styled by famous designers, fashion statements that were much less statements and much more the acquired attire of these events. A renovated theater in Los Angeles, stuffed with celebrities and business conglomerates to congratulate us on the record complete with a photo wall. Many told me it was one of the best records of the year, maybe even the decade. Ellis' words had seared inside me, branding themselves on the front of my brain. *Meandering.* The word was blinding. Beach Sirens' signature logo was plastered on every wall I could find. It seemed my request (a request to have a screen projecting a recent art film of mine, titled *Eleven Lipstick Licking Lads*; a film in which I sat in an all-white room with nothing but three buckets of paint and a hand of bananas, then used said bananas as paint brushes to depict a portrait of an eleven-man-orgy on the wall—a film I shot by myself in one take and that was over four hours in length) had been denied. I muffled the he-said-she-said, stirring one tonic below my nose after another, wetting every bit of my tongue before thanking someone else. I held a grin on my face with barbed wire for the first hour before retiring the act.

Events at this level were less about celebration and more a historic procedure for posterity. I caught myself staring into the eyes of guests without interpreting a single word on several occasions. Perhaps it was the overstimulation of drinks, the cameras, the exhaustion of having to shine on these people. Luckily at 10:00pm, our band was to take to the stage and play a short setlist; the first half of the set were new tracks from *Music to Die to*, our popular hits took the latter. We were told to do it in this order so people would leave reminded of why they love Beach Sirens. Our set was as follows:

1. *Clothes Off Your Back*
2. *Losing Interest*
3. *Alamosa Drive*
4. *Catholic Sex Toy*
5. *Can We Talk (About Your Wrists)*
6. *Dream (About Me Too)*
7. *I Want to Eat Your Father*
8. *Don't Get Too Close*
9. *Loose Ends*
10. *Droopy Eyelids*

I gripped my Daiquiri with such force, I thought I might shatter the glass. I threw the cocktail against my face, swallowing the rum in heaping gulps, ice knocking against my eyelids. I walked on the minimal stage, nearly meeting the audience at eye level. All the familiar faces made my hands sweat. I wiped them on my dress shirt before curling them on the neck of an electric guitar. Everyone applauded and hollered as Autumn sound-checked her cymbals, sending short crashes over the audience like waves on the ocean.

"Thank you all for being here tonight," my voice scratched through the speakers, I cleared my throat before continuing, "This event was put together to celebrate the release of our new album, *Music to Die to*. I want to make it clear, nobody is going to die tonight, not on my watch."

The crowd giggled and whistled. I continued, "While this record is music to *die* to, it's also music to make you feel *alive*. Again, we're so thankful all of you could make it. This is *Clothes Off Your Back*."

I felt my body become television static. My vision zoomed in and out while we played through the song. I'd pushed so much alcohol into myself moments before our set that I had become a lousy drunk by the end of the track. Lucky for me, by the end of the third track, I could collapse at the piano stool. I plopped down and felt my head orbiting itself. My hands played the chords merrily and without me paying any attention. I did, however, miss a few verses in the new singles; I hadn't gotten a chance to memorize them yet.

"'The fuck's going on?" I heard Tommy say behind my earpiece. I stood up from the stool for the next track, leaning on the guitar stand before taking it up and strapping it to my body. I could stand and seem presentable, but I could not walk in any cohesive or presentable manner. I swung my hand at the strings, causing a suspended E chord to ring from the speakers.

"Alright, you beautiful people—you *irresistible—fake*—people. It's time we have a talk," I chimed. I heard my voice echo around the room. A sea of empty stares faced me, a very hysterical sight. "Just know, we love you and this is a safe space. So, we need to talk about your wrists."

We crashed into a groove; the freight that was our performance proportioned with the swelling crowd. Time chomped away as if I'd been skipping forward. I don't remember much of what happened for the second half of the setlist, aside from the occasional jump from the speakers and screaming into the microphone. A roar of screams and applause rang in my ears as I drowned very suddenly in a swarming pitch of black.

"Fuck you, Joe," an aggressive tone, a real bite in the voice. I thought it was from Autumn, it would be Autumn. I tugged and my earpiece flung out and immediately, the screams became deafening. Tommy picked me up from under my armpits, my dress shoes scraping the chalked stage floor. The fluorescent fixtures in the restroom were hideous, I clenched my eyes as Tommy leaned me in front of a toilet.

"Do you need help, or do you think you got it?" Tommy asked. His tone was stern like a father. I flashed the back of my hand and leaned my face in the bowl. I stared at my slithering reflection of the toilet water. There I was, at once a vessel of life, now petrified in an expression of void—only a ghost—someone I hated. I closed my eyes and focused as hard as I could on the smells in the room before letting loose.

———

When we finished our final tour rehearsal, I decided to save a speech for when we were on the stage in Boston. I don't believe much in superstitious ideologies, but I refused to congratulate anyone until we'd at least made it that far. We left the rehearsal studio, filing out to our cars under a diffused overcast sky when I noticed Sophia crossing my direction. She jogged over in her athletic leggings and black over-sized t-shirt, spat with an anagram for *Nine Inch Nails* across the chest. She lifted her sunglasses to her forehead, squinting at me.

"Hey," she started. She was less out of breath than I was from rehearsal. I was lead vocals, but she sang nearly a third of the tracks on her own. Before I was ever involved in the band, she'd been the lead singer. This resulted in a band with two front vocals once I joined. It was unique. We never went cross about it either. Yet somewhere along the way, more and more of the lyrics were handed to me. Sophia wrote a lot of songs with me in mind to sing; she always said she loved the way my voice sounded while singing her words. Sophia was more of a poet than a songwriter and far more talented than myself. When she stood at arm's length of me in the parking lot, I could feel the magnetic forces inching me closer.

"Hey, Stranger," I said. "It's been a while."

She ducked her gaze to her feet. "Yeah, sorry. I've been really busy lately. I don't even mean to get this busy but somehow it always happens."

"It's good to stay busy. Keep yourself going, you know?"

"Yeah. How've you been? Well, since last Friday," she said with a dimpled grin. I could never hide my giddiness around her. Whenever she was within my sight, I was distracted, and all the world fell out of focus.

"I've been alright. I haven't been doing much. I've been tinkering with some new choruses if you want to hear them."

"*What*? Absolutely. Send them to me tonight, I'll listen to them."

"Okay," I replied.

"What's wrong?"

"What? Nothing. I'm alright, Soph," I said. I chuckled and made a face that said, *don't be ridiculous*. She rolled her eyes. "Listen, Joey, I know when something's wrong. I have some stuff to do tonight but call me tomorrow and we'll talk more, okay?"

I nodded and put on a makeshift smile and in my head wondered if she'd be going home to perhaps make dinner with Daniel. She capped me in a hug before turning back for her car. I watched her as she crunched through the asphalt and bent into her car. I recalled a thought from a conversation I had the week prior; I could never truly articulate the love I felt for her. I cherish it for what it is, regardless of precision, and see perfection. I drove straight home to avoid as much traffic as possible. I sat in silence for the entire hour drive as a song took form in my mind.

Winter's in the air
And you're on my mind
Coffee colored hair
Something...

I couldn't tell where it was going without my piano for support. I held onto the words, repeating them softly under my breath until I kicked into my apartment. I stomped in, tossing my keys at the kitchen counter, and laid my duffle bag in the armchair. I sat adjacent at the piano, finding the chords for the song. Again, I tried my lyrics, and fumbled on the chords:

Winter's in the air
And you're on my mind

The chord changes between *and* and *you're*. I thought about the next rhyme, instinctively changing it.

Nobody compares
With your eyes on mine
Honey, be aware
This'll be in due time

My head rocked, seemingly to assure the change in direction. Keys pressed and inversely the hammers stung. A bottle of wine rested atop the piano and without a glass to accompany, I drank straight from the rim in short swigs. Carefully placing the bottle against the paint, I clicked back into the mechanism of creativity—mumbling beneath the chords—this crescendoed into singing. My voice hung in the empty apartment.

"*In due time,*" my voice rang. Perhaps a chorus. The summit of a completed idea. I perched at my instrument, my grand machine for spinning thoughts into sounds, and for several hours I continued tinkering on the words and melodies. The wine emptied, the sun slid into the hills, and still, I sang and played until everything went dim in my apartment. The only light was artificial then, and it seeped in through the floor-to-ceiling windows, causing a monochromatic appearance in the room. I centered myself on the stool, constantly reminding myself to straighten up and push my shoulders back. I recorded the skeleton of the song, scatting my way through an intro and verses, singing the chorus with truth. Only a mere forty hours from then, I would be in a hotel room in a snow-infested Boston. I knew only one thing for certain, and it was that this song would never become anything more than a means of clearing my mind that afternoon. A rinse of frustration.

How long could this method last before it imploded on itself? Perhaps forever. Perhaps my compassions could always be funneled into chords and phrases and paraphrased and threaded—is consciousness really so limited it can fit entirely within the boundaries of language? My every emotion could be followed, examined, given tangibility and a title and a catalyst. Would anything I ever endure in this life be truly unique unto myself? I wondered. I stood up from the piano and peered out the large windows, at the grim landscape of low-rise Los Angeles. Murky orange globes and wincing yellow street-lamps cast over the city the way radiation might slowly decay a creature.

"Boston," I muttered to myself and sighed. I thought of happiness and how I longed for such a rich emotion. I itched my chest and turned toward my room to begin packing and whispering in a motherly comfort I bestowed upon myself, "In due time."

III

The Sacred Jest

"Do you consider yourself to be a good man?"

A clean-faced, bushy-nostriled journalist jammed his eyes at me, his fingers braided together and resting on his khakis. The conference room of the hotel welled with hot reporters awaiting their turn to ask me their own dim questions. Sophia and Autumn were sprawled on a sofa, Autumn twirled her auburn, wavy, shoulder-length hair while Sophia zoned out on the green and maroon carpet patterns. Tommy yawned, as we'd only gotten off the plane from Los Angeles a mere three hours before. My tongue swirled —I treated the journalist's question as if it were a very insightful ask, a question of rarity—my answer was a performance.

"Sure, I suppose," I croaked. I rested my millionth cigarette against the callus on my middle finger. "But you and I might have different meanings of the word. What if my answer is misconstrued based on the depth of your question?"

The journalist blinked at me behind horn-rimmed glasses. "Well, I suppose I mean what our society deems to be good. You know, a rule follower. Someone who might be positive and such. Someone who is caring rather than destructive."

"No, no, not *that*, man!" I interrupted. "I know what's good and it sure as hell isn't whatever the hell you just said. I meant man. Do you consider me a man? A dog could be a grown man by his nature, but he can't even say a word. Do you think a dog considers himself a man, let alone a good one? Is good and evil exclusive concepts of humanity? Let's check whether or not I am a man first."

"Ah," the journalist fumbled, and his mouth twitched. "Alright, fine. In your own definition of the word—would you consider yourself a man?" I knew he needed it. His eyebrows were turning in on themselves. I remember the journalist was twice my size but at that moment, I was the predator. I caught a brief glance by Ant; he was holding an expression that said, *play nice.* I wanted to conjure an expression in return that could embody an apology but returned to the journalist instead.

"I'm a man," I nodded. "Now, if you'd like to know whether or not I'm a *good* man, well, that all depends on who I'm sitting next to. Do you have any other hypotheticals for me?"

The questions pressed on with a circus of strange faces, each asking me increasingly personal questions. One woman with olive-toned skin, jet-black hair, and eyes as sharp as knives, asked, "When you embark on these tours, sometimes six months at a time, do you ever miss home?"

I sighed at the question. Tommy sat beside me on the sofa, our knees nearly touching. He swiveled his palm over his eyelids. Sophia had fallen asleep, her forehead smudged against Autumn's shoulder, both slumped deep in the sofa then. Autumn seemed generally uncomfortable as her chin dug into her chest, but I knew she would not budge so as not to disturb Sophia. And Sophia looked younger. An air of innocence to her with her eyelids shut and jaw relaxed. Autumn and Tommy watched as I studied them, both edging on fatigue but refusing to show it.

"I brought home with me," I said, and I realized a grin had materialized on my face.

Autumn met my stare, for the first time that year, with a look of genuine ease. Her hazel-tinted eyes analyzed me like a detective piecing together a mystery. And Tommy, striking a ripe grin, slapped me hard on the shoulder. This caused a warmth to bend on the journalist's face and for a moment, we all felt light.

"Is Tommy your brother?" the journalist pushed. The question left me so perplexed, completely unsure if she was being serious. Had she done any research on our band at all? Only one second of dumb silence went between her question and my answer.

"No," I exclaimed but at the exact same time, Tommy butted in, "Yes."

I puckered my lips to halt my voice. I became instantly enthralled wherever it was Tommy would take this. The lady journalist shot her curious eyes between us and pointed the end of her pen at either of our chests.

"He's saying no and you're saying yes," she said but in such a way it sounded like a question.

"I'm older by two years," Tommy explained. He turned to show me an honest, blank expression. Tommy and I were renowned for placing unbelievable lies in interviews, mostly to see who could make the other break character first. I did my best to contain my laughter by holding my breath, causing my chest to quiver. My face must have begun to show off my inability to control myself as the journalist sharpened her gaze.

"Is he alright?" she asked and squinted at me. Tommy chuckled, "You know how younger siblings are."

At this, I snorted so hard, I made a mess over myself from my nose. Tommy kept the cool exterior which caused more giggling to rise from my stomach. How he was able to contain himself, I had no idea. I excused myself to use the bathroom, and Tommy followed, announcing to the many faces in the room, "He can't go on his own."

As soon as he and I pushed through the double doors out into the hotel lobby, we let out a relentless guffaw, sending hoarse echoes through the sterile building. We caught furrowed brows from all around us. Employees of the hotel and guests looked on with offended bearings. We returned to the conference room only a minute later, finding our sincerest composure by way of wearing our sunglasses. We collectively survived the interviews for various articles, magazines, and columns. This meant we could all finally get the rest we valued so dearly.

———

After a brief rest, the four of us finished our work for the day and climbed up to my hotel suite where we drank and played. I didn't know they still had it in them at that point, to be such a rowdy crew to get along with. A white flash punched my eyes. As my vision faded in, I saw Tommy standing on the bed, the hoodie of his sweater up and tight around his face, holding a bottle of limoncello and a Polaroid camera. The photo screeched from the camera, dripping onto the bed where Tommy belly-flopped to catch. Sophia smoked next to an open window, staring at her reflection in a mirror and read-justing her golden hoop earrings. Autumn crunched her body on a love seat at the corner of the room with her drumsticks evenly pittering on her thighs. Chandler Press, a bony juvenile from Kentucky, and his two boys, formally known as the alternative band French Press, bobbed their heads seated in a row on a velvet futon. I discovered Chandler's music sometime in the year prior and had since been doing everything I could to get him signed to ROT IRON. The three of them—Chandler Press, Cole Gallagher, and Mason Tonga— were no older than twenty-one and absurdly talented. Not to mention, they were great company.

Our newest album streamed from Chandler's phone at full volume, sounding as if Sophia and I'd sung the whole thing into a tin can. Autumn beat her legs to the songs, and Sophia sang her verses. Tommy crawled on his hands and knees off the bed and toward his duffle bag; he shoved his hand deep inside and began to stir.

"Music to Die to? More like music *to get high to!"* he revved, yanking a crumpled bag mightily into the air. He held it in his fist as if it were a trophy. Every one of us took molly from Tommy's stash and

got the music connected to two giant box speakers. Before long, the sun sank between the windows of the buildings; the Boston skyline grew warm. We all danced to the music as streaks of gold spilled across the room. Tommy bounced about on the bed and sang along. Sophia ran the backs of her hands on the walls, her eyes closed and shaking her head side to side. She opened them, stared out the window at the sky, now approaching the hue one would associate with the color of ballet, and exclaimed, "Every sunset shows us the death of another day with the blood-stained clouds."

I crinkled my nose and almost felt angry, wondering what had brought her to say such a thing. Autumn swayed in front of me; she ran her fingers through my hair and over my neck. My attention was directed at the little ginger girl, her eyes low, her bottom lip puffing out as she unclenched her teeth. She whisked around, causing her hair to wave like a dancer.

"It's too hot in here, I need to go change!" yelled Autumn. She hooked her hand and sank her nails into my forearm. She sprang toward the door and called out, "Joe's gonna make sure I don't get lost!" I was not going to argue, having already known what she was leading me toward, but her room was only two doors down from mine on the top floor. Tommy's room was between ours. The last glimpse I caught of the party as the door drew shut was of Tommy's body flipping on my bed and attempting a handstand with his bare feet scraping the ceiling.

Autumn and I rolled to her room, hungry for each other as she struck the key card on her door and crawled inside. She'd become an animal and chosen me as her prey. She yanked at my dress shirt, attempting to pull it open with both hands. I stopped this immediately to not ruin the buttons.

"Alright, what's going on?" I asked, slight laughter simmering in my voice. She laughed too and leaned in close. I felt her gentle lips brush my ear and the sound of her whisper, "We need more music."

Even two doors down the music triumphing from my room had seeped into hers but she insisted that we also play music. We fell to the floor with opposing bass thumps vibrating our bodies as we undressed one another. This was not the first time Autumn and I had gone to such lengths. The band was actually accustomed to sexual interactions but managed to maintain team-oriented mindsets. Even in a group setting, we could always finish up and tighten our focus to work-related topics without any intertwining strings. After a certain point, we'd grown tired of strangers, fans, single serving lovers—this resulted in us turning to the people who knew us best to satisfy our intimacies.

In no time at all, every bit of clothing was stripped off our bodies. I stood over her, examining every inch of her curves as if she were a piece of art. With a dull thud, she plopped her head on the hardwood floor, glowing tangerine from the sunset. Her cream-colored skin gleamed beneath me. She smiled with her tongue pressed between her teeth; I knew it was a result of the drug. All over her face, I watched the sounds of music pleasuring her. I dropped onto her, feeling an override of animalistic nature, and pressed my lips against hers. Warmth emanated inside of me as our bodies grew closer. Finally, I pressed myself between her legs; our pelvic bones met, and I watched as her face contorted. The pleasurable touch within her devoured my senses. It was one of the few instances where my mind was able to transfer control over to my body.

After some time, I heard muffled voices from out in the hallway. Standing behind Autumn, both her hands pressed against a full-length mirror, I motioned a finger over my lips; her croons dampened. I listened closer—how curious it was—behind the many sheets of synths and beats, it sounded as if there were men distantly fighting. I released myself from her body, crossed to the door and jabbed my face at the peephole. To my surprise, Ant and two strange, properly dressed men with warped faces and heads the size of balloons, were at the teeth with each other. I flung open the door, all three men turned to face me with their lips curled. I heard Autumn call for me to just come back already.

"What's going on, Ant?" I asked sincerely. One of the men he'd been up in arms with stuck his finger at me, "Are you Joe Henley?"

"Yeah, I'm Joe Henley. What's the issue here?"

"We've received several noise complaints, including calls from *two* floors down!" he seethed, beat in the face. Ant sidestepped in front of me, a curtain of gray hair drew over the old man who I'd assumed was the manager of the hotel.

"You don't talk to him, you talk to me," Ant announced in a slick, dangerous tongue. I'd never told anyone, nor would I ever admit to it outright but in truth, I feared Ant. Anthony Mercer was a hulking Irish man and if he didn't have connections to the mafia, his family certainly did.

"Are you in charge of him?"

"No, I'm not," replied Ant, folding his arms.

"I'd like to speak to whoever is in charge of Joe Henley," the manager demanded. Ant took a single step closer to the man so his chin fell in line with the man's forehead.

"Nobody is in charge of Joe Henley. I'm his manager and you're lucky to even talk to me. Now, we had a travel coordinator get in touch with you some time ago about the band, Beach Sirens, staying at your hotel—to which you agreed. You agreed to a rock band and their crew renting out a portion of your hotel. You failed to think through the implications of your decision."

"I don't care if it's the president staying in the suite! I want the music off now!" he bellowed while the man beside him did nothing but stand there and mimic his superior's expressions. Ant maintained his cooperative yet intimidating composure.

"I'm sorry, Mr. Praud, but that will not be happening. You consciously rented these rooms to rockstars. I hope you will take this as a hard learned lesson for your future," Ant replied with his grizzly tone.

I wondered if these half-Windsor men were actually the owners of the hotel. I couldn't know for sure, but I could tell their tailored threads were expensive. I scratched at my bare crotch (I was standing completely nude in the hall with three men), and pleaded, "C'mon guys, I gotta show tomorrow night. The least you can do is let me listen to the music I made."

"Your music is vomit! I'm calling the police," the man barked. I wiped his saliva from my face. The men stampeded for the elevator. I was about to accept defeat, cut the music, and find some clothes, when Ant got straight and puffed his chest. He released a roar down the hall at the men of the hotel.

"Call them! *You fucking morons*, I'll call them myself! You don't like the way we do things, we have the power to ruin you! Fucking nearsighted *nuts*! Try me!"

Without facing me, Ant pressed a hand onto my bare chest and gently shoved me back into Autumn's suite. He slammed the door on me, engulfed once more in the dark room, a jungle of music. I turned, Autumn was standing behind me in the hall with her hands propped confidently at her waist.

"What the fuck was that about?" she shouted. She had her arms crossed over her chest. I walked to her, picked her up under her legs, and threw her body over my shoulder.

"Nothing," I laughed, reviving myself, "We're fine, everything's fine. Ant's got it handled!"

I tossed her onto the spread of white sheets and flicked on a lamp. I fell asleep beside Autumn and was never awoken to any sort of police. The hotel was quiet in the late morning, nearly silent, only the purr of Autumn sleeping beside me. She had the comforter pulled all the way to her nose, and her face appeared peaceful, not so bottled in stress and rage. I carefully removed myself from the bed, found a cigarette at the desk and slid a glass door to the side. I stepped out onto the balcony to wince at the thin air biting at my skin. The frost-covered city made it almost unbearable to stand out in the cold but my cheeks felt raw, and my head was tight from lack of nicotine. I lit the cigarette and leaned on the rail when I locked eyes with a group of teenage girls down on the street.

"Guys, *shit*! Joe Henley!" one squealed into the sky. Another flung her arms up at me, as if trying to grab me even from a thirty-yard vertical distance, "Fucking impregnate me!"

I scampered off the balcony, slamming the glass door. I shoved the lit cigarette in my teeth and sat on the edge of the bed.

"Don't smoke in here."

Autumn was awake, but when I twisted around to get a look at her, she was still face down in her pillow. I continued to smoke.

"Do you want to get breakfast?"

"I might be getting up and finding something soon," she grumbled.

I rolled my eyes, plopped backwards on the bed. She moved her face from the pillow to glare down at me with puffy, freckled cheeks and glazed eyes. "I meant *with* me—do you want to go? I figured we'd go together."

"You're not my boyfriend, Joe," she sneered. Her voice was muffled, baritone and coarse.

"Do you want a boyfriend?"

"Not in a million years. You know that."

I sighed, sucked on the cigarette and blew.

"You're getting ashes on the sheets."

I swept my palm at the sheets but only blended gray stains. I scooted myself up the bed and rolled toward her, practically nose to nose, with my right arm stretched, holding the cigarette over the edge.

"Why don't you want a boyfriend?"

She propped herself up in the bed, and lazily covered her chest with the thin sheets. She combed her shoulder length hair from her face, "The same reason you don't want a girlfriend—they get in the way of work—our art, I mean. You're my co-worker. And you're also my best friend. You can fuck me all you want but we aren't going to date. Plus, I really like my alone time."

"So, is that a no to breakfast?" She was quiet for a long time, her greenish eyes clocked between mine. The most minute muscles flexed and unflexed in her face. Careful evaluation. She looked like an actress. She sighed, "Where do you want to go?"

———

I arrived late at the MGM Music Hall at Fenway by nearly fifteen minutes. Nobody noticed, of course, which led me toward embarrassment as it had become an expectation. Despite this, the sound check went smoothly. We finished what would be our last piece of rehearsal before the show. I stood on the stage with a microphone in hand as the entire crew huddled around in a wide circle. They crawled out from booths, hallways, backstage, above and below. Once the group settled, I cleared my throat and raised the mic, feeling the cold, metallic gridded texture rub against my lips.

"I want to thank every single one of you for your dedication and focus to creating this show. I look around and I see a lot of familiar faces—I'm comforted when I see all of you. I also see a lot of new faces, which is great—I'm *excited* when I see you guys," I started. My words echoed as I spoke. Sophia, Tommy, and Autumn stood next to me each in their workout attire. Their faces still shimmered in sweat from the final rehearsal before our tour began in only a few hours.

"On the way to this venue, I was walking down the street with Hal, my good friend and assistant, I'm sure many of you know. Anyways, we passed this guy on the sidewalk who was playing his guitar and singing for everyone. He was huddled up against a brick wall with his case open and a few bucks inside—he was set up outside one of the bars around here, I didn't catch the name of the place," I said and paused, realizing I was getting off track.

"But I tell you this because he had a true veracity and strength in his performance. I stood there for a long time watching him play, and to be completely honest, I was *mesmerized*. He was out there to make a few dollars but more than that—and I could see it in his face—he was putting everything he had into playing the music to the best of his ability. Now, I know, it doesn't take much to distract me, especially when it comes to music," I carried on, and got a wave of gentle chuckles from the crew. Each in their all-black attire, some with official Beach Sirens shirts and the word *CREW* etched across their backs. This looked more like a grunge funeral, even more so once the four of us got into our show attire.

"But I bring him up because it only took one guy with his voice and guitar to get me to stop on the street and watch him play. Now, if we all take part in this idea—this simple idea that we can all contribute our specialties in a way that gets someone to stop what they're doing and watch in amazement—then imagine what we could do as a collective. All of you on this stage are here for a reason. We're here to put on the best possible show we can. We've blocked and rehearsed this set to the point that it's nearing second nature. I have no doubt that we're ready for it. But you, as an individual, have the power inside of you to make what you do stand out."

The crew was hushed, remarkably still. I scanned the stage; each set of eyes met my own. A quiet contemplation. I noticed some of them stood taller.

"I see all of you and I can't believe we're all here about to start a new tour. I couldn't have asked for a better group of people to work with these next few months. But more than that, I'm lucky to have each and every one of your performances. I'm not performing on stage with just these guys," I motioned to the band, "I'm performing on stage with all of you as well. So, let's leave the crowd mesmerized. These kids deserve a night to remember. Thanks, everyone."

The switch at the bottom of the microphone clicked, the dotted red light died out. Around the circle of the crew, I received a scattered round of chalked claps and various hollers. I made sure to meet the eyes of most everyone I could before we ventured backstage to a green room. We showered and had our hair and makeup done by our stylists, Betty and Juliet. Hal arranged for sushi to be delivered to the music hall, and we ate together in the green room while everyone else put the finishing touches on their looks. I was the frontman, the one who talked directly to the audience, asking them, *how are we feeling, Boston?* And, *are we still having fun tonight?*

I might go on to tell them how special their city is to us, and likely express our gratitude and our hope to return in the future. Yet, my appearance was rather sheepish, not having bothered to style my hair in any particular way, a five o'clock shadow coloring on my face and a dress shirt only half-buttoned from the bottom. This inadvertently became a signature caricature of Joe Henley, a sleazeball who wreaked of cigarettes and wore his sunglasses indoors. I'd press my lips on the mic when I sang. Sometimes thrusting my hips to the music as if it were life or death. Occasionally, I'd spit on the college-aged girls lining the front row, causing them to blow up in a frenzy, screaming and crying.

French Press began their set as the opening act; one hour before the Fatal Tour began. They cranked wild electric guitar and frenetic snare slaps in the auditorium, Chandler on the mic with scattered shouts. Nobody was singing along. French Press was very garage rock, it seemed they relied on the heavy thwacks of the drums to fill their set, and this drowned out Chandler Press' vocals almost entirely. Our band had opened for The Inbetweeners some four years prior, awarding us the opportunity to follow them around the country for the second leg of their North American tour (this was for their sixth studio album, *Arden*, released only months before we released our debut album). A quarter of the decade later, we could have rung up Deirdre Schellvile and had The Inbetweeners open for us. Here we were with the Kentucky-based rock band, offering them a chance at the spotlight, awaiting our turn with the crowd. It was our duty to provide what they paid and slept on the pavement for. A tremendous duty. Familiar. The final growl from a Gibson soared over the audience, fading into wails and raining hand slaps. The stage lights fell and no later the band hung up their instruments, following each other off the stage.

Stagehands sprinted past me as I snatched Chandler in a hug. He was glistening with sweat, and wide-eyed like rolling off a high. I slapped him on the shoulder, feeling quite a bit like a prideful father. He was disoriented, I could tell. I placed my hand on his cheek, his volted gaze finally found me.

"You crushed it out there, my friend. How do you feel?"

"Me? I'm fucking incredible. To play in a space that size? What a rush, man!" he bounced.

He turned and grabbed hold of his brothers, pulling them in for a relentless huddle. The image resembled my band when we were younger, fresher, with a string of goals still to achieve. Next, it would be us out on the stage. Beach Sirens—their third tour of North America—about to begin. We met with the Sound Utilities, they gave us our earpieces and checked levels under a dimly lit lamp attached to their cart. A mic pack with a silver antenna clipped to my belt. The roar of the crowd muffled only slightly; I could hear Tommy clearly as he spoke beside me.

"What are the odds you let one rip on stage?" he asked with a devious grin on his face.

"Slim to none, fuckface."

Autumn ignored us, following her cue and crossing to the stage. I watched as her body dissolved into complete darkness, the crowd turned, and a wave of reverting screams thundered throughout the music hall. Sophia flipped around, looked past Tommy, and caught my stare.

"Here we go again," she muttered. She winked and scooted out into the darkness. She looked as if she were doing everything she could to not frolic with excitement. A kick drum thoomed, the powerful, velvet kick caused a static in my chest. It spread out in the music hall causing the crowd to grow in volume. There in the darkness lay an ocean of anticipation. My heart began to pound with increasing speed. It was time. I pushed my palms across the length of my dress pants. I swatted at my nose, but I barely felt anything aside for the sharp heat from the blow caked somewhere in my sinuses.

"If you do it, I'll do whatever you want," Tommy pressed. I shook my head at him, eyes low. I wasn't having his banter at the moment. Instead, I focused on staying present and trying not to faint. We hadn't performed live in thirteen months and in a matter of seconds, I would be on stage with five thousand faces beaming back at me. Tommy growled, "See you up there, Slick. I want to hear a strong one tonight."

Tommy dissolved in the shadows. I stood alone. The kick drums dug into my ribcage, two solid vibrations from Autumn only five yards away. I took a cigarette from my breast pocket, and in three clicks I had a lighter pressed at the end, melting the paper. I dragged and held it between my fingers; I felt the roll of relief play on my mind. I heard the cue; I took one final deep breath and climbed the stairs. I followed a path of spike tape on the pitch-black floor and wandered toward the front of the stage as the thunder from the crowd shook the stage beneath my dress shoes. The backs of heads were at my feet, a line of evenly spaced security guards standing around the apron. Specks of smartphone lights dotted the room as if I were standing at the center of the cosmos. A private universe with all the stars revolving around me. I found the piano stool and sat, forcibly telling myself to let my shoulders fall. The room fell nearly silent, encompassed by bodies and hushed whispers. I pulled at the cigarette, held the burn in my lungs, and blew it out onto the stage. I watched as the smoke dissipated or blended into the ever-dark world surrounding me. They were all waiting. I brushed my fingers on the keys and found my opening chord to *Losing Interest*. The metronome chimed in my ear. This was it. I heard Sophia's words replay in my head. Here we go again. I leaned forward toward the microphone perched and bent at the top of the piano.

One. Two. Three. Four.
One. Two. Three. Four.
One. Two. Three. Four.

Final measure.

Two. Three. Four.

My fingers pressed into the keys, punting the sound around the music hall as lights blasted all four of us on the stage. The crowd burst into chaos as Autumn and Sophia joined the mix with their respective instruments. Finally, I released my breath into the microphone:

Always knew this would come someday
There's no telling what will come of this
Ain't no way for us to tell
Darling, I don't wanna leave this trust

But I gotta say my heart's been crushed
I've been staring down the barrel
It's killing me, I've been losing interest.

Sophia thumbed her bass, lining the song with a bounce. She took her verses steadily in her upright microphone with such precision to her voice. The song was meant to be a conversation between two lovers, the man losing interest in the woman. We sang the song in turns, finally completing the bridge and final chorus together. Admitting to a lost love together, we found the finality of an admiration against a gooey, synth-rock track. Tommy popped a thrashing, final, electric chord as the song ended at a clean halt. Cries flung out from the audience in a stretched wave. We weren't stopping there.

I crawled from the piano toward a guitar propped near my mic stand and strapped it to my chest. Autumn followed the next tempo into *Clothes Off Your Back*. Four distinct taps sent us into the song, a low heavenly rock ballad about sex with an ex-lover. The track fit perfectly against *Losing Interest*. Terribly difficult to let go, whether it be lovers or loved ones; sometimes those people in life feel like life itself. This was our thesis for *Music to Die to*—an album in dedication to the close relationship between love and loss—throughout our lives, we die a thousand times before we leave the world behind.

Swaying heads rocked below and above us as we played. I walked toward the apron of the stage, a vibrato wavered in the chord pressed below my fingers. The slowness of this song in particular made it sound as if the chords were spilling out from the guitar. I stared out at the young faces lining the front row, reaching for me and stretching their phone cameras as close as possible. I immediately looked away and bobbed my head at Tommy, who grinned and bobbed right back while strumming on his guitar. I moved to the mic and poured the words on the outreached hands.

If we only have tonight that will have to suffice
Promise I tried to make it right, too late to realize

Do you still think about me? Some but not all the time
I'm aware of the heat, so try the window for a breeze
I can't sleep without you, I'm so restless without you
Not trying to cause it, not too late to stop it
An animal in a trap, put me on, and take it off
Seal it tight and don't look back
Take your time, take the clothes off your back

The song ended; the chorus of applause rocked us where we stood. I looked back at Sophia to find her wrapped up in a buttery grin. We still had what it took, the four of us, and we knew it. We were back.

I squatted on the apron and dangled my feet near a security guard. I held the mic close to my face and squinted at the towering lights. I surveyed all the faces looking back at me.

"How are we doing tonight, Boston?" I slurred.

An eruption of screams followed. I cleared my throat, and a chuckled echo of my voice bounced around the music hall. It faded, and the room dozed back into a crawling quiet.

"Good, good," I continued, "We're so happy to be back in here in Boston, Massachusetts-"

A tremendous burst of screams cut me off, so I nodded and sat patiently. I observed the audience, the countless heads. I continued once the sound died down.

"We love the culture here, you know? We love the people. This city is very special to us. Special people deserve a special show. We've been working very hard to put this show together for you all, and dare I say, *I'm fucking proud of it*. I hope you all enjoy it. We're Beach Sirens, your favorite band and your dad's greatest fear."

With that, Autumn slammed the snare, and as she did, I hoisted myself from the ledge of the stage, pointed the microphone directly at my backside, and squeezed a gnarly pitch of gas. The fart released between snare hits, causing an unusual flow to the rhythm. I glared at Tommy at his guitar; he had barely been able to hold himself upright with a face changing red. I saw the burst of laughter pressed in his cheeks and astoundingly, he was able to hold his composure. Most impressive. The audience seemed startled; nobody had any time to gather what had happened before we jumped straight into, *I Want To Eat Your Father*.

The show ate through time. After the first hour, we were sporting a layer of sweat and felt increasingly comfortable with the crowd. By the end, we knew the audience like a group of friends. A party. The final song we bashed out was *Poison Oak*, our new closer for the show, a track from *Music to Die to*. Previously we would play *Red Light* as our closer but now we had two strong closing songs played back-to-back. *Poison Oak* was about my childhood, with a droning guitar and slow drums at the beginning of the song; it had a nostalgic ring to it. As the song progressed, it became increasingly heavier until I could scream into the microphone during the finale. The lights struck like lightning. Autumn ran wild on her kit, and the guitars slithered on grungy electric waves, the whole room was in an awesome frenzy. A unified high. The song faded, and I blinked sweat.

"We're Beach Sirens. Thank you so much."

The rapture slapped my ears as I unplugged the earpiece, and all four of us started our strut off the stage. Tommy stayed behind to flick his guitar picks out at the fans in the pit. He saluted before hiking off and tiptoeing down the steps. The first night of the Fatal Tour had been a massive success. I turned to find Sophia tackling my body, nearly knocking me backward into the Sound Utilities. We held each other for what felt like an eternity, yet not long enough. A moment later, Tommy and Autumn joined the embrace, and the four of us stood together with our arms wrapped around one another. My best friends.

Soon we were told to change, and we found ourselves in comfort clothes before being ordered to pile onto our tour bus waiting outside the backdoor. The four of us courted the bus, the engine patting away with a diesel smoke snake chooing from the exhaust. We tucked our noses in our coats to hide from the pinching New England cold, our noses and shoes ran as we all crossed the parking lot. We climbed up the steps to find our bunks and plugged our phones to charge. Adrenaline festered in my blood, I wanted to go to a bar, but we were to get a good night's rest in New York tonight. On Tuesday night, we would play Madison Square Garden for the second time in our careers with an audience that would quadruple the capacity of our Boston show. I spidered into my bottom bunk, below Autumn and curled into a fetal position. I used to search for videos from the show, but exhaustion took me much sooner.

———

Past three in the morning, Hal shook at my shoulder to wake me. The bus was still, and I caught shadows of bodies moseying about in the mutely lit aisle. We'd made it back into New York City. I pulled myself up from the bottom bunk and drooped a hoodie over my torso, hood up out of precaution for fans. I followed Hal into the hotel with the army. Ant tapped a button and a moment later, I stood half asleep in an elevator with Tommy, Autumn, Sophia, Ant, Hal, and there, too, was Jonah, our videographer. He had recorded segments around the stage of the Boston show for our social media presence, along with Tessa, our photographer. These were then given to our social media manager, Tiegan, to promote our band across internet platforms. Tiegan had been hired by ROT IRON, but Jonah was a friend of mine from Los Angeles whom I met at a birthday party for the award-winning actress, Vivian Wells.

Going on two years ago, Hal called one morning to ask if I would like to give my personal contact to Vivian Wells, as she'd like to invite me to an event. I agreed, and less than an hour later, my phone rang with a number I hadn't saved in my phone. I knew who Vivian Wells was, of course. She was a rising star in Hollywood. I'd seen her in films like *Breakfast After Lunch*, an independent film that buzzed around festivals and ended up with a short theatrical run. This got her into *They Do Not Grow Old*, a brooding vampire flick that I quite enjoyed, featuring a scene of a shirtless Vivian, rising from a moonlit pond. In her third feature, she took the lead role atop the Call Sheet, *Sloane's Gotta Go*, a romantic comedy about a *Wonderbread*-esque undergrad boy falling in love with the school's biggest party animal. She played

Sloane Chevalier. Doused in eyeliner and purple hair sloppily chopped at her shoulders, she amazed audiences with her range of character and likability. I'd taken a real interest in her. Not to mention, I felt we had a bit in common, we were the same age and hurtling toward fame at a monumental rate.

She personally asked me to come to her twenty-fifth birthday party over the phone; notably, she did not ask for any sort of musical performance. I agreed to attend, and a week later, I arrived a half hour late only to haunt around the open bar and the backyard pool. To my dismay, I never did meet Vivian face-to-face at her party but lingered on conversations with celebrities who would later solidify themselves into the full-blown historical entertainers of our time. And I eventually met Jonah, who had been the camera operator of *They Do Not Grow Old* (no small feat as that one was shot on 35mm film). We talked of art and lifestyle over cocktails for hours at Vivian's house, time bleeding into the midnight hour. He went to UCLA with Vivian; they knew each other well enough and became friends on the horror film set. Jonah hadn't been getting any work at the time, and after our spiraling conversation, I got his contact and put him in full creative control of our music videos from that point forward. I got him a full-time job on the Fatal Tour after shooting four music videos for our singles, which he agreed to with a face full of reluctance, as he intended to continue on his path as a cameraman in the film industry. I told him, if he gets a call, he could leave from whatever city we were playing in and continue on his journey in the film industry.

But for now, he was in New York, staring down at the waxed tile of the elevator, eyes a crackled red, a great sturdy bag hooked up on both his shoulders, doing his best to simply stay awake. I wasn't sure where Tessa was at the time, maybe had already made it up into her room for the night. Tessa was Sophia's cousin, four years younger, and went to college for a degree in Visual Media with a focus in photography. She knew everything to do with photography, whether you commissioned her for a dimly lit cage fight, or a soft wedding captured on *Kodak* film. She knew it all, and at only twenty-three years old, she was a fearless artist, willing to do almost anything to capture whatever shot she had in mind.

Ant flicked a key card my way, which I graciously accepted. I chipped into my suite and patted down the long hallway. It was the same hotel as we'd stayed at only a month ago for our performance on the talk show. It was a different room but the same setup, so I found the bathroom and quickly stripped all the clothes from my body to shower off before the water could gain a comfortable level of warmth. I wandered toward the bed. It was now past four in the morning, too far into the night for drugs or masturbation. I checked my phone for the first time in over a day. A text received eight hours ago from Ellis Young:

Lunch tomorrow? I know a great spot for us... x.

I blinked rapidly at the screen, unsure whether to reply right then. I opted to close the phone, sink into the darkness and wait until the following morning. We had no show to perform the following night. We had a Monday to ourselves in the city and I was unsure how to spend it. I ended up staring at the gray ceiling of my bedroom for nearly an hour, unsure whether I should respond or not. I wanted to rest all day, but I couldn't help but be drawn to accept the offer. I couldn't believe Ellis Young, the Prince of Dissonance, wanted to meet again. In a split second decision, I snatched my phone from the nightstand and tinkered out a reply.

Yes, although it will be more like breakfast for me...
Just going to bed now. Talk soon.

I sent the message, tossed my phone at the nightstand and shoved the comforter into my nose. The remembrance of his honest critique gnawed at my brain. *Meandering.* I wondered if the next day would be spent enduring more of his raw critique; I was sure it would infect my thoughts for nights to come. *Forgettable. Implosion.* I attempted to swat it all away, instead replacing my mind with images from the show we had just performed back in Boston, at Fenway Park. I did my very best to relish the accomplishment, then struggled to view it as an accomplishment as the images faded into nothing.

IV

IMMORTAL SPACES

A taxi dropped Hal and me on Fifth Avenue where everything felt fresh. The wind pushed flower petals through the afternoon air—pink petals of Central Park's cherry blossoms—they surfed over our heads. Just at the end of the block, Ellis Young stood on the sidewalk outside our lunch destination, a petite, bustling Euro-chic café tucked on Fifth named Bluestone Lane. He grinned beneath his round-rimmed sunglasses, which were settled on his sharply pointed nose, similar in prospect to the beak of a bird, and outstretched his arms in a wool overcoat as if to welcome us back. The widow's peak of his hairline seemingly without quarrel; his dusty copper hair brushed his shoulders, well-conditioned as a cause for a pleasant volume. This glinting man with gothic spectacles as big, licorice zeros and hair orange as a closing day, complete with a birch wool scarf, powered toward us tall and scarecrow-like. Once in arm's reach, Ellis sheathed my shoulders to his chest, providing a warm hug.

"I reserved us a few bar stools for us inside. I hope that is alright. I wasn't anticipating it being so bloody crowded this afternoon. Please follow me," he jested in his perfect low register. I gave a wondering glance to Hal, only for him to give it right back.

Once inside, we found the three open stools at tabletop seating. The café was speckled with customers, none of whom confronted me for any reason. We ordered our meals, ranging from croissant sandwiches to chicken wraps and breakfast bowls. I ordered all of us our first espresso shots.

"And if it isn't so, here we are again," Ellis smirked, "How was Boston?"

"It went very well I'd say, at least on my end. Hal?" I looked his way for an opinion. He had watched the entire concert while I performed, so I deemed his opinion just as, if not more valuable.

"First night and there were no jitters. No slip-ups from anyone. The whole show ran smoothly," Hal said, his eye contact fierce, "Yeah, these cats still got it, man."

Ellis nodded, outwardly silent but obvious thoughts carouseling in his mind. Three espresso shots arrived and slid in front of us. The brown froth swirled in blue ceramics. Ellis brought the cup to his lips, sipped without a sound and placed it back on the saucer. He reached for the packets of cane sugar.

"What about the others? How did they feel about it?" he continued to question.

"I haven't seen them much since we got off the stage, but I think we all had a good time," I gathered, staring at the swirling darkness of my espresso shot, "Yeah, it was a lot of fun." The café shot met my tongue and down it went.

"And that's all that matters," Ellis said. He grinned handsomely at Hal and me. An aura of mystery surrounded the man, it crowded between his teeth and below his fingernails. What he had been planning, I hadn't known at the time. It was a concentrated anticipation he was beginning to construct, and yet his craft could never be anticipated no matter how eagerly one could study.

We enjoyed our breakfast between spurts of kind conversation before hiking a block up to the Solomon R. Guggenheim Museum. The Guggenheim, an art museum, is an architectural behemoth. A circular building with a slanted walk spiraling up the walls, all wrapped in sleek white. Every few feet on the inclined path was an art piece displayed on the wall, spotlit with a plaque providing the artist and the title of the piece. The all-white precision of the interior made standing in the center at the ground level feel as if you were existing in a giant rib cage.

Ellis paid for Hal and me to explore the museum while he had a membership and required no pay. He knew extensive bits about the art temporarily inhabiting the space and had various takes on the meaning of each piece. A giant canvas, as wide as fifteen feet and as tall as twelve, smothered in black paint aside from one solitary yellow square, somewhere along the left of the painting. My first guess would have been Rothko. The three of us stood in front of the painting, Ellis with his wool coat draped over his forearm.

"You might be wondering what warrants an art piece as simple as this into a museum of this stature. Any guesses?" he asked, to neither one of us in particular. I looked to Hal who gave a lazy shrug of the shoulders. Hal looked very tired, understandably so.

"There," I began. My finger extended in the direction of that yellow square, so bright in contrast to the pitch paint surrounding it, it almost seemed to glow. The golden patch was no bigger than a post-card but zeroed the spectator in its direction, seemingly demanding their attention. As if the glowing canary edges were more of a ship amongst a dark ocean, a lifeline, a wandering good idea, a speck in time, a visual ping of optimism against a storm of negatives. However, to be interpreted, my eye began to linger out and away from the square, swallowed in the darkness, filling out the rest of the painting.

I answered, "That's the artist."

Ellis took one step away from the piece, Hal and I watched with twisted necks. He almost glared at it, grinned his brilliant marble teeth at us.

"I believe so. I had to be careful not to stand too close. Too close and you'll see the brush strokes," he hummed. I took one step back to hear him clearer, muffled by the whispers of patrons whirlpooling the structure. He pushed amber strands of hair from his face and said, "This piece, as most art does in my opinion, has little to do with detail but how it is displayed as a whole. It's not to be fragmented or else the illusion will fall apart. Not to mention, whatever emotion it gives you will also dissipate. Art is the closest magic we may ever find but it only works if you believe in it."

Without warning, he turned and continued up the slope, rounding the walls and glancing passively at smaller pieces hanging about. I caught up to him, intrigued to hear more, and Ellis provided, "The artist is Cameron Caswell, he's from the city. This museum almost always features an artist from the city, but the emotions of such works are universal. Wouldn't you agree?"

"Yes," I said, nodding at the floor, "I'd second that."

"Why do you think you were able to find the purpose of his piece so quickly?" he wondered. We passed groups of university students, couples, singles, aging families as we ventured relentlessly up the slope.

"I don't know, I guess I just felt a connection to it."

"No, that isn't why."

"Well, why do you think so?"

He halted on the slope, leaned down toward my face and muttered, "Because you are an artist yourself. And artists, all the honest ones anyway, are inherently lonely. You felt a connection, yes, but it was not the piece you connected with—you felt connected to the one constant, unresolving feeling that every artist both yearns for and despises," he paused, shifting his concentration between both my eyes, "*Loneliness*, that's what was displayed in that piece. You felt it too."

I didn't say a word, just kept staring up at him. He flipped around and continued forward.

"Why did you agree to spend time with me today?" he asked. I stared at the back of his head.

"You asked."

"I asked, yes, that much is true. You didn't have to say yes. There must be some sort of mutual attraction that compels you to me. Not to say it has to mean in a romantic sense—it could be a creative way— or what have you. That, or you had no plans today and knew whatever I had in mind would be more interesting than anything you could do on your own. Or you just wanted to be nice, appear like you care, keep the contact with that famed music engineer intact. Let me be clear, I don't fault you for whatever it was."

"It was honestly a blend of everything," I admitted then. He stopped at a painting, a farmer in a field sheeted in a layer of snow. The dying crops golden along the bottom, in rows, and scattered clouds above, in a chilling blue sky.

"Look," he said, "A Van Gogh."

He analyzed the canvas for a moment, before he snapped his attention to me.

"Why don't you move to the city?" he asked. He sounded so sincere in his curiosity; I blurted a chuckle. He cocked his head at my amusement, patient for an answer.

"I don't know," I said, "I like the city, I do. But I'm not cut out for it. It's a great place, it makes me feel very alive. It's just not home."

"You need to erase *home* from your vocabulary, mate. That word has no meaning for people like you," Ellis spoke. I furrowed my eyebrows. He poked at his temple and continued, "The home of an artist is the mind. The sooner you realize and live by this idea, the freer and more spirited your work will become. Let go of your notions of a masterpiece. Allow simple ideas to be simple. No need to bloat an idea with meaningless corners in a space better off round."

As he finished his phrase, he brought both arms into the air, gesturing out over the ledge of the slope, out into the museum as a whole. He laughed to himself freely and brought his arms back in, finding their way to the front pockets of his dress pants.

————

Hal split from us, optioning to continue upward and enjoy the art, while Ellis led me through a doorway, into a corridor of the museum with statues and sculptures featuring prominent contemporary African aesthetics. He bent his knees to squint over the sculptures from every angle and drifted his attention to a window looking out over Fifth, over all of Central Park in bloom. The sun skated the ponds, the flowers colored vibrance in the trees; the whole picture was more impressive than anything in the museum.

"What is art to you?" Ellis asked. His gaze relied on the image out the window.

A silence followed. I sighed, "Art to me," I said aloud, and breathed with more weight so as to prolong the time. "Perhaps art is a collection of what it means to be human."

Ellis chuckled and placed his palm against the bottom of my back, "I urge you to think on the question longer. On your own time, of course; you don't have to answer me today."

"What about you, then?" I asked.

"Sorry?"

"What is art to you?"

Ellis thought only half as long and connected his knuckles behind his back. An inquisitive figure, surely, and he met my stare.

"I believe art is a device by which people seek to defy their own mortality. There must be something comforting to an artist who can paint a portrait, and it continues to live long after their time on Earth."

He paused and seemed as if he, too, was grappling with the imagery. Ellis wet his lips and recalled his stance, "Perhaps the impact they leave behind, no matter the size, is them—and they aren't truly gone, Heavens, no—their art becomes their new form, so to speak. A form of multiplying complexity. Interpretations of their mind appear, genius or moronic, what does it matter? Truly. An artist is discussed beyond the grave! That is power. Quite a powerful force, art is, wouldn't you agree, Joseph?"

I nodded with prying eyes.

"The many filmmakers and actors I've met in my years need not worry about death anymore," Ellis was telling, "They have a catalog of their achievements forever imprinted on film celluloid—or, I suppose much of it is digital now—the message is all the same. And you have your music, eh? Long after your time has come and gone, long after this conversation, once we're both gone from our physical forms, what is left of us? Dust to dust, yes, so they say. But in my apartment, there are three vinyl records pressed with reliable mimicries of your voice and true words of your mind. This is a step toward permanence —in some respects, mate, this is true—and you, my friend, the heart-throb of today but tomorrow, who knows? You are a figure destined for a permanent mark on the culture. Like Elvis, or Cobain. That's you, and it sounds quite peculiar to say now, but I do have a keen eye for talent. I wouldn't be where I am in these industries without it. And I believe, between us, there may be a quite interesting combination within our grasp."

"Ellis," I murmured, "What are you trying to tell me?"

He didn't say anything for a moment. We stood in a fixed silence, carefully assessing each other before Ellis began to smile again. He spoke up, "It's my attempt to convince you of a collaboration."

"You want to collaborate on music?" I questioned.

"More than that. I think you and I could create art, whether it be music or whatever interests us, with a fresh lens. Not revolutionaries but spinning traditions in a new light. Or who knows, I'd wait to see what happens if you were to agree. I do also have an idea for a— program of sorts I would like to develop—it fits alongside my vision for the art I am seeking to create. I know it all sounds very cryptic now —I cannot say more at present—but I will say, it is something I do not wish to execute alone."

My silence took its turn. I looked out at the city from our window view, soaking in the sun rays pressed through the glass. I recall being quite unsure what to say.

"But I just started this tour," I muttered anxiously. It was an unconvincing response, even for myself, as I had always wanted to collaborate with Ellis Young. It had been a dream of mine even if only to meet him in passing. Yet ten years on, finally faced with the opportunity to marry our skill sets, I chose against it.

"We would have the future to look forward to. You don't have to make a decision now, but it's something to think about," he cleared. He turned to me, the sun bent on the side of his face, hazing an orange afternoon light against his cheek. He leaned down and pressed one hand against the back of my neck. His nose brushed mine before suddenly our lips touched, and he kissed me. I felt entirely disoriented. Before I had any time to process his move, he broke the kiss and stared at the floor, breathing quietly but with a real weight. He returned his attention to the city as if becoming acquainted once more with his composure.

"Right," Ellis whispered. He cleared his throat, "I'm not trying to sway your decision. But I like you, Joseph. I want to create with you. Just consider it and stop calling Los Angeles home," he said. He led me out of the corridor and up the top of the spiral, without saying much more. His intentions were undoubtedly clear. However, Ellis seemed genuinely flustered, matching my disarray. Hal stood at the top, admiring a painting of four young adults smoking and drinking at what seemed to be a diner or a lounge. The clothes and hairstyles of the group gave clues to a 1970s setting, smiling and contemplative, the group in deep conversation.

Hal caught sight of us and together we staggered down the spiraled slope, eventually landing back on the waxed ground floor. We exited the museum, out into the calm March, cultivated with bodies crossing every which way. Ellis withdrew his sunglasses and hooked them over his ears.

"Gentlemen, it was a lovely afternoon. I have business to attend to but I'm glad you both came along," he chimed, and brought Hal into a hug, telling him to keep a close eye on me. Hal smirked and agreed before Ellis next faced me. He wrapped his arms around my back and spoke into my ear, "Loneliness dies in company. There are tricks around the truth of the artist. Consider it."

He peeled away as if he hadn't said a word and excitedly huffed a sigh, looking us over.

"Take care, Ellis. I'll be seeing you around," I said.

"I'm sure of it," he replied.

He joined the swarm of life streaming the sidewalk, his fiery head of hair was lost among the heads of New York. Ellis had been nearly an inspirational figure. I'd seen photos of him in magazines, or in the background of videos while The Inbetweeners recorded *Dream No. 99*. I was still a kid at the time. Then to discuss music with Tommy, who understood producing to a much greater extent than I had, the name of Ellis Young breached the topic of conversation quite often. He was now in his late thirties, showing no signs of gray, and presented a charisma unique to himself. Acquainted and friendly was the extent of our relationship up until I visited his apartment in February. This visit on that afternoon in Queens must have been the catalyst for something within Ellis. Our relationship changed in that museum, and it was irreversible. He seemed to have arranged it to be this way, as if it were all going according to his plan and each beat was by his design. Ellis was indeed a designer—a designer of minds—he was known to withdraw specific emotions out of artists. I knew it was a setup. It was strange, and I grew weary of him; Ellis was little more than a stranger.

———

In the cab, Hal looked me over and said, "Joe. Are you okay?"

"What?" I blurted, smacked out of a deep thought. I'd nestled my internal chatter to the front of my mind, but Hal sat leaning forward on his side of the car, his gaze bouncing around my face.

"Yeah, I'm fine. Just thinking," I said. Our conversation took a decrescendo as I turned once more to face the window. A silence filled the cab aside from the hissing rumble of urban traffic. The cab dropped us back at the hotel, I got caught in the lobby by two boys at the coffee bar and they achieved a digital picture with me. I clocked into my suite and stumbled to my bed, mentally drained from the day. It was approaching six in the evening and my stomach ached.

I sent a text to Hal asking if there were any decent sandwich shops nearby and if he could arrange a delivery. He sent the menu to one he deemed most suitable for my taste. Half an hour later, he rapped at my door. The door spread, revealing Hal, holding out a black plastic bag. He was really quite good at his job—when he felt like it.

"You got yourself something, right?" I asked. He nodded, grinning, "Yeah, I did, thanks."

"Would you like to come eat here with me?"

Hal shrugged—he nodded again—and I stepped to the side to allow Hal's welcome. In the kitchenette of my suite, a small table for two awaited us. We ate our sandwiches. I folded a recycled napkin, tattooed with the round logo of the restaurant, and patted it against my lips.

"Today was very bizarre," I broke the silence. Hal stared up at me.

"Why do you say that?"

"Ellis—He was acting very strange all day. It was at the museum, and he asked if I wanted to collaborate with him," I explained.

"On a new record, yeah? Good, good."

Hal adjusted in his seat, scratching his wood-flat stomach and looking past the glossy window to the city skyline. Clouds of cement blinded the sky, pale threads stretched over the infinite line of buildings.

"No. He didn't specify. I figured it would be until he went on about—well, I'm not sure what exactly—he said any art I'm interested in creating," I went on. I began folding the copper wax paper into a perfect square and discarding it back in the takeout bag.

"I don't see anything wrong with that. You two seem to get along well enough."

Hal burped quietly, a puff of air, and uncapped his San Pellegrino water, pouring a swig.

"Hal," my voice lowered, muddying it; I leaned forward in the chair causing the wood to sigh, "I don't know any other way to say this. He kissed me."

His eyes grew and lips pushed to this side, I thought for a moment he might burst into a fit of laughter. Hal focused himself and squinted at me, "*He did?*"

I nodded, refusing to break contact. After a second of soundless weight, I continued, "I can't make any sense of it. It was as if he was trying to seduce me but not in any romantic way. It seemed manipulative to my senses, like he chose intimacy as a means of getting me to agree to his business proposal. And he wouldn't even tell me what the business was!"

"Did you like it? Maybe you're queer," Hal offered in a sincere tone.

"No, that's not it. It seemed almost genius. Sociopathic though, yeah? It worked on me at the moment, I wanted more of whatever connection I'd developed for him. But as we left the museum, thinking about what had happened, I realized it was an act of persuasion. A twisted one, too. Why would this prodigy producer want to work on music with *me*?"

"I know why," Hal said, and really gulped his sparkling water. I winced, unsure how he could handle the carbonation burning his throat but held in anticipation of his answer.

"You have something he doesn't," he said.

"What do I have?" I laughed; his comment seemed so provincial to me.

"I don't mean to make you out as some solipsistic figure, but you can hardly leave this hotel without being hounded by people desperate to even just be near you. It's *unreal* to them. You're like a god, or a fictional character come to life. Most people have studied you through videos on the internet but to see you *in person* causes them an adrenaline rush. I've seen it, you know what I mean. Something familiar but impossible, like the resurrection of Christ—maybe it is solipsistic," his thoughts wandered. He contemplated beneath a quivering lip and started, "You're famous. Maybe, and I'm not saying this for certain, but maybe he wants to latch onto that. You know, try and use you as a vessel into that unsteady wave of limelight."

"Fame fucking blows," I hushed. Hal nodded with exaggerated up-downs, his expression reading understanding, "You know that. The band knows that. I know that. Ellis doesn't know that. We all want what we don't have. Greed is a part of being human in many ways. Think about it, he wants what you have—you want what he has —and if you got what you wanted, to reverse the roles, do you *truly* believe either of you would be satisfied?"

I nodded. "So, the kiss was out of greed then," I said. I was fragmented, attempting to piece it all together. Perhaps Ellis and I were different in the same way. Or the same in a different way. Hal rose into a laughter and when I gave him a look he explained, "Well, for fuck's sake, dude! Who's to say he doesn't just actually like you?"

Raindrops tapped and bounced against the window, clinging and sinking. In a matter of seconds, the drizzle evolved into a steady rainfall. I watched the tears slip against the glass for a while, letting my mind settle around what had occurred that day. A while later, Hal left for his room to get some work done. I stayed put in my suite as the storm carried over, listening to our newest album, convincing myself it was perhaps a focused record. I pulled up the music video for *Losing Interest*. The four of us appeared on my little screen, all wearing matching blue pajamas and playing our instruments on an exaggerated bed. The bed, mostly green screen when we filmed, was made the size of a football field with white sheets stretching yards and yards away from us. We played the song as pillow feathers swam around us, giving the effect of standing in a field of snow. Beneath the bed, revealed in CGI cutaways, lurked two glowing, yellow eyes of some unspecified monster preying on us. The whole thing was admittedly well done, partly in thanks to Jonah, but some aspect came across as entirely artificial. I felt that the video had no correspondence with the song. The lack of focus between the song and the video was apparent, I began to wonder if the fans noticed it too. Ellis noticed, that much, I was sure.

My eyes stung while I watched this version of myself standing alongside this version of my band. While it was images of us, captured a year ago in a soundstage in Los Angeles, these four were no more than characters flickering on a six-inch screen. I closed my eyes, and the stinging sensation heightened but simultaneously brought a sense of relief. A painful relief as my vision collapsed into darkness. I thought back to where our band started, back to that whispering fall semester at university.

V

THE STAMFORD RECORD: A-SIDE

I grew up in the unassuming Athens, Georgia and led a fair childhood alongside my two older sisters, Beatrice and Dianne. My mother taught eighth grade Social Studies at the middle school I attended, and my father worked in a cyclical haze as a sales associate for our local Nissan dealership. This meant that at the pinned age of sixteen, each of his children received a used car that ran well enough to get us through college. When I became this titular age, I received a dingy silver Honda Civic on my birthday. The dashboard displayed six booked digits, spelling out how many miles had already been clocked on the vehicle. Sixteen was also the age I was warned to begin choosing which college I should like to attend when I finished high school, or at the very least, narrow my options down to a few good choices and begin applying. At the time, however, it felt like high school might never end. Oh, how time dragged on as a teenager. How was I expected to ponder my next four years of schooling when the current four served as their own little eternity?

As a family, the Henley's were considerably well off, in a decent sized house in a decent neighborhood. I had decent grades and decent friends. I rode my bike to convenience stores, listened to Green Day on my iPod and played *Tony Hawk's Pro Skater* on my Xbox until sunrise during weekends. I discovered pleasure and depression at the same time; the internet was briefly fun. I received brochures for colleges in the area, and a large part of my consideration went toward Georgia State University, but I didn't want to be close enough to home that my parents could visit me at a moment's notice. I had a profound yearning for independence, even from a young age. I knew I wanted to navigate the world on my own terms without parental guidance. I also knew I wanted this before I could even decide on a field to major in.

I had done choir all four years of high school and it was one of the only things I quite enjoyed. I spent most lunch periods in the choir room, either seated at the piano or talking with my choir teacher, Mr. Leonard Barett. During my senior year of high school, Mr. Barett asked where I might be attending college, and of course, I hadn't a clue. He recommended I apply to George Washington University, in the mix of the District of Columbia. It was his alma mater, where he learned much of his own teachings. He thought it might be a good fit for me, especially given my attention during his classes and my grasp of musical language. Several months later, in February of 2015, I received a letter from GWU. It was carried between thumb and forefinger by my mother; the letter tapped the old countertop one morning where I sat with a plate of scrambled eggs. I tore it open to find a letter congratulating me on my acceptance for the Fall Term of that same year to pursue a Bachelor of Arts in Music degree. Music quickly became my life from that point forward and while I was still unsure what I wanted to do as a career, I knew I wanted it to somehow involve music.

The start of my sophomore year at George Washington University was a breath of relief as the summer spent back in my childhood home dragged on for far too long. My parents helped me into my dorm room for the new year, having driven the entire way from Athens the day before. My new roommate, Christian Soenick, was an English major. He was a quiet boy with golden hair and eyes that magnified when he peered through his bulging, oval glasses. He wore the same outfit every day, a dress shirt covered with a sweater accompanied by khakis. I wore mostly shredded, old jeans bagging into the leather collar of my signature scuffed-up boots. This was accompanied by daily band t-shirts. I also kept my hair untamed and long enough to scratch my slouched shoulders. Despite our physical differences, Christian and I got along quite well on the rare occasion both of us were in our dorm room. It was just the three of us unclosed in my cinder block cutout in the middle of D.C.—my parents idly fascinated by the space—I hadn't met Christian yet, I only knew his name and major. As for myself, I kept my printed schedule in my back pocket, folded and chewed with scattered coffee stains, and only printed the day before.

My father helped me shove a few cardboard boxes beneath my bed. The entire room gave off a familiar, sterile air. Stark, bone walls. Two back-straightening, navy-blue generic wooden beams, the very wood used for our wardrobes, a kind and natural wood. The single chipped window at the end of the room gave a damp, natural light, facing a line of more dorm window cutouts on a brick wall some five yards away. My father stood up and smacked his arm around my shoulder, pulling me in close for a side hug.

"Have fun, J-Man," he muttered. I nodded, staring at my half of the room. I would learn in only one hour that Christian was out getting hangers and laundry detergent; he, too, would insist on us sharing. I wondered what he might be like. I wondered what the new year might bring. Last year I kept mostly to myself; I never attended any parties and didn't join any clubs. This year, I was determined to change that and fully indulge in the college experience.

After spending a final dinner with my parents in a Thai restaurant, they walked me back to my dorm building a few blocks through the city. I stood outside the glass doors on the sidewalk and hugged them goodbye until Christmas. After a full minute, I pulled away from my mother, studied her shoes, and glanced at the city behind her. The sky aged into a cherry tint. Streetlamps began to putter into being. My mother rubbed her hand against my cheek and smiled at me with what I knew to be a sting of melancholy. I tried not to look at her too closely as her brunette hair was beginning to turn silver, and her face was aging at a rapid pace. I didn't want to think about how old my parents were getting. My father, his gut poking below his chest and hair atop his head so short it was like moving your fingers against a suede, gray and old. I was their youngest of three, now fully grown —or so I thought at nineteen—I would turn twenty in December.

"Take care of yourself. It's a new year. You're going to have a good time, I know it," my father folded his arms and nodded, a half smile crooked on his face.

"Don't be a stranger," my mother said with a choke in her throat, "I got you that phone for a reason. I like to hear your voice every now and again."

Her words cut deep in my stomach. I chuckled to relieve the anxiety, "I will. I promise, Mom."

She gave me a second hug, gripping me tight, and letting go. They told me they loved me, and they'd see me at Christmas. It was the middle of August, and as my parents shuffled back to their minivan in the aching heat of D.C., I felt December grow further and further away. There was fall break, but it being five days long, I would stay put in my dorm. Or so I thought.

———

Luckily, classes began only two days later. I had my new Music course (Sound Technology I - Introduction to Digital Musicianship), a Poetry Lab, French, and an Economics course. Considerably a light workload by my standards, making room for my first year in the Jazz Ensemble (playing piano) and my second year as a member of the mixed choir named the University Singers. I was a Tenor with a peeping voice, which I am led to believe gave me some leverage in the audition, not to mention a quiet recommendation from one Leonard Barett. The University Singers gathered twice a week to perform and practice choral arrangements. I was studying so much Latin, I was becoming fluent in the language. It was here that I met Sophia Baker, also a sophomore, majoring in English.

Sophia Baker was born in the summer of '97 in Norfolk, Virginia. By the age of two, Sophia was in full custody of her father as her mother fell to a demise consisting of alcoholism and physical abuse. Her father cared for her in every way he could while working as a Lineman on call and living in a two-bedroom condo. He could afford this for the two of them, as Linemen made good money as they were always on-call. If he was called in at midnight, he'd gently wake Sophia to tell her he'd be back later. *Do not answer the door for anyone, Soph.* Young Sophie became well accustomed to being home alone and, of course, she had the kind, old neighbor's number on speed dial if she needed anything.

Some mornings, her alarm clock would screen, signaling time for school, and she'd get herself ready for a new day as a student in the first grade. Sophia would be sure to make it to the bus stop at the front of their subdivision, early and prepared. By age five, Sophia had decided she wanted to be a singer, like all the pop stars she saw on TV and printed on teen magazines, twirling on magazine stands at the checkout of grocery stores. It wasn't until she got to high school and deepened herself in her AP English courses, that at the age of fifteen, getting her nose pierced for a second time and sporting increasingly odd outfits, she decided she wanted to be a poet instead. She shifted gears completely, while still practicing her singing and not entirely letting go of the dream, Sophia began to research which schools had the highest success rates for literary figures. She eventually funneled into a select group of schools, and on the list was George Washington in D.C. She applied to each of them, eighteen in total, as a junior in high school. She graduated, and by August of the same year, she settled into her new dormitory, in her new room with her new roommate. Sophia had only ever lived with her father and the prospect of having a new friend, not to mention a girl her age to live with, excited her. She entered the room to discover a shy redhead fumbling with coat hangers on her side of the closet. She was a quiet Music major named Autumn Gladis.

Autumn was not always so reserved. She was a few months younger than Sophia, born in October of the same year. She grew up in a small town half an hour outside of Boston, Massachusetts with her mother and stepfather, who both proved very caring parental figures. Her adoration for music began with her stepdad, who loved music, made obvious by his extensive collection of records and CDs. Whenever Autumn agreed to a ride with him in his pickup truck, he would play all kinds of music for her, but the most common genre was rock. Autumn quickly grew attached to the sounds. Electric guitars and basses. Rampant drums. Her stepfather took note of how well little Autumn seemed to understand rhythm; she often played on upturned buckets or patted her hands against the kitchen counter in perfect time. So, on her seventh Christmas, she tore the wrapping paper on a pair of drumsticks and gave her parents an absent stare. Her first-ever drum set was tucked away in the garage, fully set up and sparkling.

She became obsessed with the drums. She focused on bettering the set throughout primary school and joined the marching band to play drums during school hours too. She knew the practice would help; any practice was worth it to her. Autumn had a short roster of batshit, awful boyfriends who either beat her head against the passenger window of a Charger or screamed at her when they got home from parties, both drunk and barely able to stand. This was the first instance where Autumn instinctually became closed off emotionally. She took solace in her drums hiding in the garage. It was all she had, her only passion, her only friend. She refused to let anyone else into her life or her heart, out of a subconscious fear that she might get hurt again. Her younger half-brother, Liam, notes that growing up she rarely even talked to him. She auditioned for GWU's Corcoran School of Art and Design, a Bachelor of the Arts in Music, like me. Autumn was accepted into the program on the same day I was and began her time at university with a chest full of anxiety. I saw her in my Comprehensive Musicianship class last year, the girl who kept her head down and talked with nobody unless necessary.

As a freshman, she made it into the Symphonic Band and focused on percussion. She roomed with Sophia Baker, a girl who, when not engulfed in a book by Plath or Austen, was kindly plucking away on an electric bass guitar in their room. Autumn quite liked Sophia, the quiet girl with wooden hair and book page skin the same as hers.

Sophia took a liking to film photography, lying in the grass and smoking weed with her friends. Autumn kept to herself and wore her ginger hair styled just over her eyes. Over time, however, Autumn opened her heart to Sophia and eventually discovered a common passion for music. Soon the two young women began writing songs together in their dorm room and in time, they would become best friends.

This leaves Thomas Murtaugh, the last of the band, a Music-majoring freshman with blonde hair halfway down his spine and the height of a basketball player. Tommy was born on the Fourth of July in '98, putting him a grade behind the rest of us. He was born into a stern Air Force family living in Charleston, South Carolina. It is also worth noting that Tommy may have been the only one of us with any sort of natural talent. He could pick up any instrument placed in front of him and play it well enough within minutes. Saxophone. Violin. Piano. Pianica. Flute. Trumpet. Double Bass. Guitar. However, Tommy was always much more focused on what could get him high. Tommy was never one for the standard education. As a child, he could be found heaving with pellets of tears hitting his homework at the kitchen table most nights. By the time he made it to the eighth grade, his group of friends had discovered the awesome abilities of marijuana. He frequently got stoned in his high school's bathrooms between classes and would practice band rehearsals completely blazed. Tommy was willing to try anything as long as he was safely away from the tyrannical forces of his parents, who seemed fixated on keeping their boy in line.

By sixteen, Tommy watched as his older brother, Oliver, set off on his own adventures in the U.S. Air Force. Tommy felt sick at the possibility of having to follow suit. He urgently decided to look into colleges. He focused on schools for music, or how he saw it, the only thing he might be good at. He decided to attend the great George Washington University within the heart of the country with the backup plan of the College of Charleston just down the road from home, in case he didn't make it into GWU. But Tommy made it into the Corcoran School without having to try very hard at all, with a simple application and an effortless audition. He felt safe as he hunkered into his dorm room and raged on his electric guitar, hooked up to his amp and with headphones on, lighting a joint and letting loose. It was at this moment when his roommate, another heavy-lidded freshman boy, poked at his shoulder and offered to buy some bud. That was the moment Tommy Murtaugh, freshly eighteen, became a drug dealer with what was considered to be the best weed around campus.

His customer base grew until one day, he was approached by two beautiful sophomores rooming together as prospective buyers. The first time Autumn and Sophia walked into his room and met the wall of musky smoke, they noticed his teal Stratocaster leaning on a stand and asked if he played. Sophia excitedly asked Tommy if he knew how to play and he cooly picked up his Stratocaster to show off a handful of riffs he'd been tinkering with. It was perfect and the girls were awestruck. A week later, Sophia returned to ask if he would like to practice with her and Autumn with the possibility of starting a band. Tommy liked the idea of being in a band, especially if it was with these two sophomore girls. That next Friday, the three of them gathered in one of the music rehearsal rooms to practice together.

Their first band rehearsal occurred over a month before I began stealing glances at Sophia Baker during our choir rehearsals. She was a beautiful soprano but never stuck out like some of the much more determined female singers. I'd seen her in my poetry class and knew of her from our previous year in University Singers. Though, she and I had never even said hello. I never worked up the courage to say anything to her, instead choosing to wait until that evening to bring her up to Christian.

"Do you know that girl, Sophia Baker?" I asked Christian from across our room, twirling in my desk chair and tossing my smartphone in the air, catching it. Empty Styrofoam boxes with spaghetti sauce and plastic forks dispersed on each of our desks. Trap music hammered softly on either side of our walls. We both had our lamps on as there was no overhead lighting in the dorms. I had just stuffed my completed homework assignments into my binder and redirected my attention to Christian sprawled on his twin bed with his magnifying spectacles facing a novel.

"Is she an English major?" he asked while splitting his attention to finish the paragraph.

He was deep in another one of his science fiction novels, something of a holographic cover and a futuristic astronaut wielding a fire sword etched into its center. He raised his head and bookmarked his place without looking. We both understood he would be unable to focus on his novel until the conversation subsided. Despite this, Christian provided his attention without any hint of frustration.

"I think so. She's in my poetry lab. She has brown hair, maybe five-five, five-six," I described.

"I think I know who you're talking about. She has a few tattoos?" he squinted, his bug eyes flattening.

"Yeah! That's her. Do you know her?" I questioned in a hopeful tone. I stopped twirling around and leaned forward in the chair, facing Christian in a pose that a father might assume, on the edge of his sofa during a big sports game.

"No. Not personally anyway," he paused and thought for a moment. "She was in a few of my classes last year—and this year we have Fiction Writing together—yeah. I've never spoken to her though."

"Have you ever seen her with any guys?"

"*Guys?*" Christian clued.

"Or girls. You know, *romantically*," I said, really exaggerating the last word. It occurred to me Christian likely wasn't paying much attention to who was hanging on the arm of who or too much of anything to do with *romance* for that matter.

"I don't think so," his voice faded out, before, "Oh! I saw her in the University Yard with a guy and a girl once. I didn't say anything to her though. I just waved and she waved back."

"A guy?! What'd he look like? Were they *close*?" I interrogated my frail roommate.

"No, no, they just seemed friendly. He had long blonde hair—ah, to be honest—he sort of fits your style," said Christian. I could tell by his careful voice that he was trying not to sound insulting. I was not offended. I stood from my desk chair, and lightly kicked it to the center of the room, leaving it twisting. I placed my hands on my hips and peered out of our single window for only a moment watching the other students across the way in their own rooms, under gloomy light, studying or chatting. I turned back to Christian, and his bug eyes blinked at me.

"University Yard, you said?"

———

The next day I sat my bag in the wind-combed grass and plopped down beside it, surrounded by peers and strangers filling out the sun-stretched University Yard. The courtyard featured brick paths poking out from between buildings in all directions; the paths lead into a statue at the center of one George Washington who stood tall and ugly. Across the yard, my eyes surveyed for Sophia by focusing on every brunette girl or blonde boy I could feasibly see. I sat for hours, eventually shifting between courtyard scans and catching a page or two of *The Wild Boys* by William Burroughs.

Eventually, I hoisted myself to my feet and packed my belongings. The sun was streaming through the buildings in cupid colors and the chocolate-covered espresso beans I'd bought at a cafe a few blocks away could only tie me over for so long. I threw my bag over my shoulder as I turned to notice three distinct bodies at the very far side of the yard; I hadn't been able to see them before with how other students had shielded my view of this particular area. One Sophia Baker sat wearing olive overalls and a mustard yellow shirt; sunglasses masked her eyes and brown hair snaked elegantly in the breeze. She was sprawled over a blanket next to a shorter girl with a sunset-colored haircut, a button down and corduroy pants. They were giggling in the direction of a young man with long blonde hair; it had to be the one Christian mentioned the night before. He sat with his knees pulled to his chest, but it was obvious just how lanky he was. All three of them were pale as vampires but still they sprawled out in the warm coatings from the dying sun.

I cut across the yard at an anxious pace. I made for their direction, and stopped at the edge of the blanket the trio lay on. All three heads turned and stared up at me expectantly; I realized then I was out of breath but denied my lungs to heaps of air. My mind dropped every opening line I had prepared as I stood less than a yard away with a quivering lip. I caught details of their appearances, everything from the ginger girl's sand textured cheeks to the boy's untamed face acne. He wore a white t-shirt with the Aphex Twin symbol. Sophia's wrists and fingers were covered in gold jewelry, her forearm had a blue-black quote written on it reading, *The Red upon the Hill*. I recognized the quote, a line from an Emily Dickinson poem referring to the sunset; it felt out of body to read it with the dotted red sun slipping in my peripheral vision. A curious quote. A coincidence, too. The images flashed in less than a second, and the trio of faces watched my flickering expression with stupid anticipation.

"Hey," I blurted with eyes on Sophia, "You're in my poetry lab, right?"

"Hi," she started, taken aback by the bluntness of my approach, "I am! I'm Sophia, this is Autumn and Tommy. And, it's Joey, right?" she asked. She knew my name but wasn't sure of it.

"Yes. It's nice to meet you all. I just wanted to say, I really liked the poem you wrote for the first critique. I think it might have even been the best in the class," I bellowed, doing my best to sound confident and cool.

"Oh, well, thank you—I liked yours too—It felt very free-form. Very *sing-song*," she added. She was not at showing any hint of awkwardness, was instead flattered and rather excited to discuss poetry. It's also possible she remembered more of my poem than I did of hers.

"Thank you. A lot of people have said my poetry sounds like songs. I don't know if that's a good thing or not," I chuckled. I didn't want to overstay my welcome. I became suddenly aware of my presence, and it struck me like a bolt of lightning. I flicked a wave at the three of them, "I have to get going, it was nice to meet you all."

"Likewise," Tommy said with a deep chalky voice, he brought his hand out for me to shake it. I rattled his hand and waved a hand to Sophia.

"See you around. And, really, thanks for the compliment," she waved back but when I waved at Autumn, she only looked at me. I exited the courtyard following one of the brick walkways with a heavy focus on my stride in case they were still watching me. I made sure to remember their names, holding their images steady in my mind and labeling each of them. *Tommy. Autumn. Sophia Baker.*

———

The next University Singers rehearsal began in the practice room. I arrived ten minutes early with a full stomach after eating an early dinner in the cafeteria with Christian. He went on about how I really should read *The Silmarillion* by J. R. R. Tolkien since I was a self-proclaimed poet, and I had enjoyed The Lord of the Rings trilogy. The whole endeavor left me a bit exhausted. I excused myself from dinner earlier than usual. I informed Christian that I wanted to be sure I would make it to rehearsal on time, which was partly true, but I wanted more to see Sophia again.

When I entered, the singers were already huddled in groups around the risers and conversing before Professor Johstono began his rehearsal. I opened my binder, flipping to a bookmarked tab for a rendition of *Kyrie* when I felt a small tapping against my shoulder. I spun around to find Sophia looking up at me with a reddish grin growing on her face, practically matching the crimson red flannel she wore.

"Uh," she thought aloud, "So you're a singer too?"

I couldn't contain a breath of embarrassed laughter. She must have felt the same, mimicking me, and as it subsided, I focused on maintaining eye contact, "I guess I am."

She held her music binder at her chest and looked at me with her big, dark eyes, "You didn't tell me that! Do you like singing? I mean, are you good at it?"

"I like to sing—I wouldn't say I'm good at it. I've just been doing this since high school. I'm a Music major. What about you, do you like singing?"

Of course she likes it, you moron, I thought to myself. We'd been in the same choir for over a year at this point and had never once made conversation until this point. It clocked that this may be the first time Sophia noticed me at all.

"I do. I've always loved singing. It's my happy place," she said dreamily.

"It suits you. I think you're really good," I said.

"Thanks—so, do you think you'll make it to the Hungary trip at the end of the year?" she asked. She was referring to the tour we were to take in the spring semester. Every two years, the University Singers went on an international tour to perform in some of the world's most impressive cathedrals and churches. This year was one of those, touring churches in Budapest. I'd never left the country before.

"I hope so," the words fell from my mouth. Professor Johstono pressed a C Major scale on the piano, the rising keys blew around the room. As if programmed to do so, every one of us, including Sophia and I stopped whatever we were doing and marched to our places on the risers to follow the notes with our voices. I followed her bright red flannel, an easy identifier, as she positioned herself on the top riser at the far right of the choir.

———

The rehearsal ran nearly two hours. I found myself thankful that I ate dinner beforehand. Far too many times, enough to be considered foolish rather than a misstep in time management, I'd gone to the evening rehearsals on an empty stomach. I was feeling chipper and surprised to find the black hands of the clock reading a quarter to eight. I walked through the hallway with the rest of the choir, all traveling back to our rooms when Sophia ran up beside me. The breeze from her pace hit my back a second later.

"Hey again," she said, smiling, "So I'm meeting my friends, you met them, Tommy and Autumn, tomorrow in one of the rehearsal rooms," her voice trailed off. I wasn't sure what she was getting at before we passed a locked door, she struck her index finger at it, "This one! That's where we practice."

"Practice for what?" I asked, genuinely unsure what she meant. Tommy and Autumn were not in University Singers; Sophia giggled at my confused expression.

"We started a band. This is where we've been practicing. It's only been a few weeks so far, but I think you should join us or at least stop by and see what you think. Oh—I forgot to ask—do you play any instruments?"

I had taken piano lessons throughout my childhood; it was another one of the constants of my decent upbringing and what helped shape me into a fairly decent person. A woman named Mrs. Duescher showed up at my house every Wednesday after school for an hour-long lesson. I'd played piano for a decade and considered myself quite good, good enough to get into the Jazz Ensemble. I fancied the piano quite a bit, and I enjoyed reading music; I often listened to classical music on a casual basis. These things never struck me as odd, more just hobbies or enjoyable ways to pass the time. I still wasn't entirely sure what I wanted to do as a career out of college but deep down, I'd wanted to be a conductor to an orchestra. Although the yearning for this career felt so unachievable, I never told anyone of this dream.

"I can play the piano but that's about it," I responded after chewing on my answer. It was a lie. I knew my way around a guitar. I could also play double bass, which meant I could play electric bass guitar. I could blow into a saxophone and a selection of other brass instruments.

"That's great! None of us can play the piano. We're more of a rock band though. Or alternative, I guess we aren't sure what we are yet. Do you like rock music?"

"I *love* rock," I said, truthfully.

"Hell yeah! You should stop by then! I was thinking about what you wrote in our poetry lab," she said as we pushed through heavy, double doors into the evening campus. The streetlamps were powered on. The city wore its nightly sound of vehicles humming and whistling, crickets creaking down in the roots by our feet as we followed the caravan of choir students down the block and toward the dorms. She continued, holding her *New Yorker* tote over her shoulder, "I thought it was really good! And it *does* kind of sound like a song. So, I was thinking, maybe we could turn your poem into one."

The melody of her final sentence bent more like a question than a statement. A proposal. I thought it over for only a second or two, listening to my leather boots chomp on the cherry-red bricks.

"That would be really cool actually," I said, "I'm so down for that. Tomorrow, you said?"

"Yeah, tomorrow at six. Is that okay?" She seemed eager so I nodded. I quietly looked at her every time we passed below the white glow of a streetlamp.

"That works for me. I'll be there," I said. My stomach started tying itself together into sharp knots when I caught her immediate satisfaction by way of a genuine smile.

"Awesome! I can't wait for you to see what we have going on. I'll see you then," she started slowing her pace. She turned in the opposite direction, and I realized her dorm was not this way at all. It may have been a block or two away for all I knew. The dorm buildings of GWU looked more like apartment buildings sitting on the edges of city blocks. Our campus was the city.

"Oh, I'm sorry," I said aloud, "I didn't realize you were that way."

"It's okay, don't apologize! Six! Tomorrow, Joey," she rang as she trotted back into the last minutes of sunset. I watched her tote bag bounce against her skinny jeans, her scarlet flannel shrank as she retraced her steps up the block. My lips curled into a grin. I stood, watching her, and thought to myself, *The Red Upon the Hill.*

———

I tried the silver door handle and to my surprise, the rehearsal space had been unlocked. I slid into the chilly darkness of the room, fingering for a light switch along the cinder block walls coated in thick, thick paint. I found it twenty steps in on the right, on a board of six switches. I flicked each down the line, illuminating the room in a gruesome, fluorescent glow. The rehearsal space was nearly empty, aside from giant black cases, mostly square in shape, though some matched the shape of a guitar. There were chairs stacked as many as fifteen high, several towers of seats arranged against the far wall. There were two practice rooms with wide windows. Music stands and chewed sheet music (likely older than I was) were spread and scattered and tossed about. At the center of the space sat an upright studio piano. Wooden, maybe ivory, a dark beautiful wood with a glossy finish.

I was alone. The room was deafening in the absence of sound, forcing my mind to develop a steady, softened wave. Whether it was the precise sound of air particles swimming against one another or entirely made up—ghost sounds—I could not tell. I checked my watch, it read 6:02pm. I was late and yet the first to arrive. I stepped through the carpeted room, hearing each press of my boots into the fabric with considerable detail. Had they forgotten? Perhaps they had rescheduled and were unable to contact me. Were they here only two minutes ago and when I decided not to show, they ditched the rehearsal entirely? Were they in some sort of danger? Was it all a prank to waste my time?

My thoughts snowballed into insanity just as metal clicked and the giant door swung to reveal Tommy with his Mötley hair ruffled over his face. Behind him, Autumn and Sophia poured into the room. Sophia picked her gaze off the floor; her face shimmered when she saw me standing dumb and slouched in the middle of the room, "Hey! You beat us here!"

Her eyes were glazed and pink as were the others'. Their smoke session had run later than expected, causing them to be late for their rehearsal. Nonetheless, they all had a quality of excitement that made the three of them bounce toward the cases in the room. Tommy paused, he turned and shook my hand.

"I'm glad you could make it. Sophie says you play piano and sing," he said. "I think that's awesome. And I read your lyrics, there's some good shit there."

"Actually," I started. I pulled a folded paper from my back pocket. I'd rewritten my poem into song lyrics, retitled the poem and given the words more of an edge. I didn't tell them, but I had stayed up until nearly two in the morning transcribing my own writing into something more equipped for music. "This is the poem, but I rewrote it to have a chorus and a bridge, all that. Verses too."

He raised his eyebrows, slouched his lips as if to say *impressive*. He read over the lyrics and nodded, "This is good."

"Thanks. I think it still needs work but at least it's a start, right?"

"Let me see," Sophia chirped. She walked up to Tommy's shoulder and did her best to peep over it. Tommy scoffed at the mousy girl and handed her the creased paper. Sophia's eyes rocked back and forth across the page. She finished it quickly and clocked a grin at me. She giggled, "*Dude*, I love this. Like, it's *really* good. Do you know how it would sound?"

I had thought about the melody of the song absentmindedly while writing the lyrics, cooped up in my dingy dorm room, cracking the top to a new Heineken once an hour. Christian didn't drink much but obliged to take one from the six-pack I'd obtained from an upperclassman. He was intrigued by my mission to turn my poem into some sort of rock song. Between chapters of his sci-fi novel, Christian would peek over my shoulder to follow my progress. I could hear the song and maybe even the instruments arranged in my head when I read them over. A phantom band performing with sounds yet to exist.

"I have an idea of how it goes—but I'm not sure how to show you," I admitted.

"Sing," Sophia said. She stretched her arm, the paper crunched against my chest.

"*Now*?" I yelped, and instantly turned pale.

Autumn paused in her efforts to quickly assemble her drum set, seemingly intrigued by the new boy forced to sing in front of three strangers. I glanced back at her and up at Tommy, arms crossed with all his weight on his right leg. I remembered the studio piano to the left of him. Without a word, I crossed the room and sat at the stool, the three of them watching me curiously. I read the first line of the chorus, thought hard about the melody, and tried the piano. I got it wrong. Wrong again. After a full minute of quiet patience on their parts, I fingered along and found the melody that I heard in my head the night before.

I moved my left hand to the chords on the far left of the piano. Dark, rich chords rode beneath the chorus. It had a mystifying, near-melancholy ring to it. I closed my eyes, boot pressed against the left sustain pedal and played it all together. I opened my lips, allowing my voice to ride the melody of the keys. I sang the entire chorus:

> *Swallowing diamond pills*
> *And I'm watching cars collide*
> *Running off this bender*
> *I'm scalping heads*
> *My hair is thinning*
> *But I'm letting go*
> *Of this countryside tonight*
> *I fight the urges*
> *Watch as the buzzards cry*
> *I've got arrows in my spine*
> *I force myself to swallow*
> *Swallow, swallow diamond pills*

I was so lost in the sound and movement I felt from the piano and my voice, I'd forgotten all about the triplet audience standing in the room. When I blinked, I glanced around and was confused by the three spectators, as if I'd just awoken from a dream. All three were still. Autumn was sitting on the floor next to her kick drum. Tommy's arms were sheepishly at his side. Sophia's mouth was slightly ajar. She frowned, "Did you come up with that just now?"

The familiar ghost sounds returned to the room as she silently awaited my response. I heard and felt the blood pumping beneath my skull.

"The chords—yeah—I mean, I could hear it in my head."

Blank expressions.

"What?" I questioned. My face started to burn. I wasn't sure what to make of their quiet. I almost felt betrayed, leaning on anger, as if they were hiding their opinions. Whether I'd done terribly or decent or even well, they wouldn't say, that is until Autumn piped in, "Where the fuck have *you* been?"

It was the first time she'd acknowledged me as a human being in her presence. It was, too, the first time I'd ever heard her deep, charcoaled voice as if she were a heavy smoker. She hadn't been, of course; this was just her voice, I came to find out. All four of us broke into laughter, unable to contain the humor of the discovery. Even I was unaware of being able to do something like this. When I'd taken piano lessons, I always practiced classical pieces. I never thought to make something of my own. Not to mention, this was the first time in two months I'd played a piano, since summer back at my parent's house in Athens. I was perplexed and slid my eyes to the piano, watching my fingers hover over the keys, trying to memorize whatever I had just performed before I could forget it.

The rest of the band got set up and, before long, we learned how each instrument rested against the other for support. They plugged their own ideas into what I had created with the chorus. They showed me the two other songs they'd been working on: *Cowboy Face Paint* and *Vertical Dreams*. Both were decent enough. I figured out how to play Tommy's guitar parts on the piano, and Sophia's bass part as well. The songs were simple, and now able to hear my improvisations with the keys, they discovered ways to amplify their parts. A perfect storm. Lightning in a bottle. We spent four hours in the practice room, only interrupted once by a janitor checking the trash bins. The janitor informed us we could stay until ten but would appreciate it greatly if they could lock up the building around that time. We stayed in the room, teaching each other how each instrument fit into a song. A field recorder sat on a music stand, recording every noise from the entire session.

———

By the time we knew we had to wrap things up, the song I'd written the night before had turned into a half-finished rock ballad, tinges of sorrow in the verses and a bleak chorus with a heavy, dripping guitar riff underlining the whole song. They even allowed my piano to remain on the track. One question we kept away from asking: who would take lead vocals for the song? Before my newly anointed position in the band, I understood Sophia to be the lead singer. She plucked her bass and practiced in front of us where the singer would take the stage. But for our newly born track, named *Diamond Pills*, I'd been the only one to sing the song other than Sophia taking a crack at the chorus every now and again. But even then, she was singing with me and never on her own.

I slipped the folded lyrics into the back pocket of my bitten jeans. Autumn clipped her cases tightly together and stood; the room looked exactly as it had when we arrived, including the mess of sheet music. Tommy stuffed the field recorder in his backpack.

"That was awesome," I blurted. My excitement was hard to contain. Tommy patted me on the back and mopped the hair from his eyes to see me.

"I think you have a talent, my friend. I'm glad you found your way into our lives. I mean, *fuck*, what if it was fate?"

"*Tommy*," Autumn groaned.

"No, seriously! This guy walks up to us out of nowhere in the Yard—like he's some kind of a *Messiah*—and now we're making music better than ever. I mean, this is what we've been *talking* about!"

We left the rehearsal room, clicking out the six switches and slamming the door. Tommy tried the handle, jiggling aggressively; the door was locked. The four of us clicked down the vacant hallway. I had to consciously keep my face muscles from forming a smile. I finally had friends at school. Real friends, not just acquaintances I tolerated, not just Christian and his band of Hobbits, no, these people thought like I did. They talked like I did and walked like I did. We wore similar clothes and followed the same bands. We shared similar interests and dialects, all from different places along the East Coast and hoped with fingers crossed to achieve something greater than ourselves.

Tommy placed his palm directly on top of Autumn's scalp; she swatted him away, instantly saying, "'The hell is wrong with you?" There was a real sting to her tone. I knew then not to cross her even if she wasn't necessarily upset.

"Couldn't help myself. I can see completely over your head," Tommy chuckled. "Hey, Joey, you wanna come back to my place and smoke a bowl?"

"Which building are you in?" I asked, admittedly interested. The thrill of creating music with all of them caused a peak of adrenaline I was still rolling off of. Not to mention, a newfound intimacy created by following a tempo with three other people. A symmetry of the minds.

"The Dakota," Tommy replied.

"Me too. Yeah, I'm down," I said. I tried, eagerly, to sound reserved, holding a lazy composure.

Sophia pushed through the double doors, back out into the familiar tones of street life in D.C. The stars were faint. Vehicles burped along the avenues with headlights flashing us. Sophia turned to look at the rest of us, a smile growing slowly across her face.

"Same time next week?" she asked all of us.

"Where *else* would I be on a Friday night?" Autumn asked with a lick of sarcasm in her tone. "Yeah, I'll be there. No plans, you know me."

"I live and breathe for this band now, Soph. You'll see me next week," Tommy answered in his basso voice. "And as for our regular

Mozart here, he will be there as well. I'll make sure of it—I'm not letting him out of my sight."

Sophia laughed. Her eyes met mine. Much like the love songs suggested, it felt as if time began to slow from its normal pace. All at once, time was frozen for the two of us and yet, the moment ended before it could even truly begin. My body was hot. Infatuated.

"Cool," she murmured. "See you next week!"

I blinked and started toward the dorm building with Tommy; Autumn and Sophia crossed in the opposite direction. I was still caught in the headrush of Sophia's stare, spiraling through increasingly imaginative scenarios. Would I have a chance with her? Would she ever be my girlfriend? But a different question rolled forward, flashing in my mind and making me feel like an idiot.

"Wait!" I shouted, twisting around, the two girls doing the same. "What's our band's name?"

"What?" Sophia cried back. Her voice was mostly lost in the skiing wind tunnels that ran the blocks.

"*What's our band's name?*" I repeated, louder, howling down the street. Her and Autumn were small at the top of the block. Sophia cupped her palms around her mouth and began to shout. "Beach Sirens!" she screamed back at me as cars blew past us. Strings of headlights. She called out once more, perhaps for good measure, and her voice blew down the silver streets. "We're called Beach Sirens!"

VI

The Stamford Record: B-Side

From that moment forward, my life was changed, although we did not, at the time, understand the gravity of our creation. We continued meeting every Friday night, skipping out on blistering parties at fraternity houses and weekend drinking binges in hopes of creating a new song or perfect an older one. By the time quarter finals were afoot, we had four tracks, all of which we continued to practice with immense focus. I had acquired a habit, absentmindedly, of pressing on the edge of my desk into a sort of imaginary keyboard during my lecture halls. University Singers and Jazz Ensemble became a gold mine, with sheets of written music placed in front of me twice a week; it became a means of studying for Beach Sirens. Admittedly, we took many ideas for our own music. With sheet music, I was able to physically see and study the progression of melodies, and how different sections fit together like puzzle pieces or an equation. Math was far from my best subject, but I found myself regretting not signing up for at least one Algebra class that semester, recognizing how the class would better my abilities as a musician.

Thanksgiving approached. We would have from Wednesday to Sunday off to celebrate the approaching holiday. It was decided one night in Tommy's room, while the four of us passed around a loaded bong in a merry circle and blew wisps of fog into a box fan plugged in beside his bed, that we would spend the break together. None of us would be going back to our families, despite how much Tommy's parents desperately wanted him home. He called to inform his father he was far too busy with studies to make it back for the holiday; he wanted to focus rather than waste time on one of the more insignificant American holidays. This was somehow enough for his father to let Tommy stay in the capitol for the Thanksgiving break.

"We could all stay at my parent's summer house," Tommy growled with smoke foaming at his mouth. He blew the rest of the smoke into his box fan in an attempt to dissipate the smell. Tommy's dorm was always a filthy wreck as he had the entire room to himself. Outside his room, there was a common space complete with a bathroom, a fridge and kitchenette. There, too, was a second door identical to Tommy's, which led into his roommate's dorm room. This door always remained locked. His roommate, Michael Shiffler, was hardly ever seen. To my understanding, the young man was a stickler for anything related to drugs, alcohol, sex, infidelity, or rock and roll. These broad terms, however, were the only hobbies and topics of interest for Tommy Murtaugh. The two respectfully kept an arm's length distance apart and rarely gave the other anything more than a greeting.

"You guys have a *summer house*?" Autumn questioned.

"Yeah, it's up in Connecticut. We actually used to live there. My dad bought it when my mom got pregnant with Oliver. But he got stationed in Charleston when I was a year old. They decided to rent the house out but now it's empty, we just use it as a vacation home for the summertime," Tommy said, so *matter of fact*, he practically brushed the anecdote off his shoulder. We all stared at him and each other with unarmed looks.

"So let me get this right," I began, "Six hours away—yes—six hours?" Tommy nodded. "*Six hours* away, there is a big empty house —and we could go practice as much as we wanted."

Tommy kept nodding as he kissed his lighter to the bong. He pressed his mouth to the glass and inhaled, bubbles burped at the base. I could almost swear that Tommy was more intellectual when he was high, he was certainly more focused and presentable. Almost as if the drug brought him to homeostasis. I looked to Sophia and Autumn for their reactions, we all shared the same face of revelation.

"I guess we should start packing," Sophia said, although it was more of a question. We all focused on Tommy. He tugged his head out of the bong and surveyed the circle, "What?"

"Can we go?" Autumn asked in her scratchy voice.

"Like, do you have a key? Is this something we could really pull off?" Sophia added.

Tommy raised a finger and clenched his throat. His eyes slammed shut, and a second later he erupted into an explosion of coughs. He focused up and knocked the hair from his eyes, "Yeah. There's a code on the door to get in. It's a pretty place too, there's a garden with statues and shit. The backyard has a trail down to a river. It's sick." The three of us exchanged growing looks of disbelief after his every detail. Our music retreat became more enticing as Tommy described the place.

"Oh, and no neighbors—not anyone nearby, at least—see, it's on, like, nine acres of land," he croaked. He looked at me, holding in laughter with sore eyes, half open. "*Dude*, when I was a kid, I used to *love* going to that house. Summer was cool as *fuck* out there, man. I used to call it the Castle because the whole house is made out of these —sort of—stone blocks."

He snorted to himself, maniacal like a hyena, but it came off strange due to having said nothing particularly funny. He was far more gone than the rest of us and not nearly as riveted by the idea of uninterrupted band practice. Maybe he wasn't as focused while high as I was led to believe. We spent the rest of the night sitting in the room, eating Oreos and drinking beers, Tommy dunking the former into the latter. I watched him perform this dunk of Oreo into beer and quietly labeled the behavior as psychopathic. We continued to plan and discuss our plans for the holiday getaway in which we could rehearse and record music to our heart's desire.

———

Tuesday after our classes let out, essays were turned in, tests were finalized, we packed up Autumn's Honda SR-V and headed toward North Stamford, Connecticut. It was past one in the morning when we pulled off the tree-squeezed back road. Stone half walls lined the edge of the property. We made a right at the mailbox—a black '240' ran vertically down the aged wooden post—*240 Farm Rd*. This was our destination. Down a winding dirt road, past various cedar trees and white oaks, the silhouette of a house spread in the gray field. We parked in a gravel driveway, the four of us slid out of the car and crunched through the rocks, sounding as if we were walking through snow. Ahead of us, at the front of the car, was an extension of the house, a long hallway, so to speak, with four large windows running along the stone architecture. To the right, this protrusion led to what appeared to be a two-story guest house complete with french doors at the base. It was only twenty feet from the car with what seemed to be a limestone path leading to the house. And to the left, a great, stone mansion sat empty, ghostly in the dark.

Another winding stone path led through the front garden. Menacing statues. Bird baths and dry fountains surrounded by flower bushes and unkempt hedges. The attractions cast long black shadows in the night and stood highlighted in pale streaks from the cold moon overhead. Tommy led us through the path, twisting around a large statue of what appeared to be a winged angel, praying with her hands parallel, her head tilted toward her shoulder. She stood over six feet tall, her stone face looked down on me with a gentle stare as we trotted around her. Arriving at the front door, Tommy punched a four-digit code into a padlock, the machine screeched, and the lock turned.

Once inside, we were met with a grand foyer; the moonlight scrubbed the marble tile from windows at the back of the house. The house was cold, and eerie; a chandelier with glass ornaments hung directly above us. To the left, a winding staircase led up to a second floor. Tommy pressed a golden button on the wall, and the chandelier lit instantly; I was bewildered. "Is *that* the light switch?"

The cover was a scratched gold plate but rather than a switch I was used to seeing in houses, there were four punchable gray buttons, maybe once also golden but worn down and bronzed with age.

"Yes, this house is very old," Tommy said, his voice echoed. "This is how switches used to be a long time ago." Tommy led us up the stairs to begin a tour of the home.

When we rounded the top of the staircase, we entered a loft space with a banister to look down over the first floor. The carpeted second floor featured a seating area with two armchairs and a coffee table. An oak bureau sat opposite, wedged between two doors with golden handles that led into two of the bedrooms. Each bedroom had its own king-sized bed, raised with four maple posts, all etched with absurd detail. The second floor had four bedrooms total, all quite identical. Still, there were three baths and a bar off in its own room. Behind the bar, off in the far right corner of the room, a second staircase led to a frog loft with seemingly another bedroom with a full bath. The loft had another set of french doors that led onto a wrap-around balcony, overlooking the garden and pitch dark trees at the front of the property.

Back on the first floor, the foyer led into the right of the house with a living room, all antique furnishings, my eye took note of the mini-grand piano displayed in the corner, or further still behind a wall was the kitchen with an island and built-in stovetop. When we cooked breakfast on the island, we could see out the floor-to-ceiling windows into the backyard, a shaven field with a path leading toward a line of trees. Beyond the trees was the river. The house had a spectacular dining room past the kitchen, a butler's quarters that led back out to the kitchen, and a door at the end of the hall that led out into the long hallway toward the guest house. The whole place overwhelmed me; it was a century old with furniture acquainted to its age, but with appliances and renovations from the last decade.

The interior of the home presented itself like a haunted mansion, but the exterior, when bringing in round after round of instrument cases, appeared more like a quaint, countryside cottage. It felt ominously like a structure out of time. Even at night, it seemed as if we'd stumbled upon something medieval or like we'd found a witch's house deep in the thick wood. We brought the cases into the guest house, knowing it might be quieter there with no sounds of the ice machine on the fridge or a laundry machine whirlpooling. We didn't even bother unpacking the cases that night. Instead, the four of us locked the doors to the guest house and drowsily fumbled together through the hallway back toward the main house.

We all decided on our bedrooms; mine had deep blue walls like the bottom of the ocean. The bed had an ornate comforter with matching throw pillows. A wide, old desk was propped between two brittle windows, both of which were drawn with heavy drapes. The desk looked to be five hundred pounds or more in weight and of intricate design. My bedroom had a lamp on either nightstand guarding the massive bed. This bedroom had no private bathroom, instead it was out in the hall. Although a simple trek, I didn't even bother brushing my teeth, instead stripping my clothes to the floor and climbing in the silky, dust-coated sheets.

I assumed my friends were all asleep in the rooms next to me, but I wondered if they were also awake and studying the flowers carved into the white crown molding of the ceiling. I twisted the knob of the lamp twice, taking out all the light in the room. I existed in a space of absence. In some ways, I felt less than absent. Almost as if I were a ghost. Back in my dorm, or even back home in Athens, my rooms always had faint light either cast from streetlights or charging devices or the general radiance of a city that clung in the clouds back in D.C. Here, out in the country of New England, in an unfamiliar place with three people I hadn't known three months prior, I felt the loneliness of my decision. The total dark befriended absolute silence to portray the illusion of nothing. I was fooled too.

I forced myself to focus instead on the music and memories we might create during our stay. The four full days we had in Stamford could be a real event, I thought. This was relaxing and necessary. These hopeful thoughts were necessary to ease the mind I knew was as black as the countryland, and off I drifted, out and away from the crowded reality.

———

We spent Wednesday morning at *the Lakeside Diner*, ordering a dozen donuts and holding our coffees under our pierced noses. Huddled around a fading square table, the four of us discussed the three songs we already had and what our plans were for the break. We decided a reasonable goal was to make two more songs and head back to college to finish the semester with a total of five well-conceived tracks. But despite our intentions, this was also a break to do whatever we pleased. We spent most of that morning running around town with our chins tucked into our scarves. The four of us wandered the Stamford Museum, boggled by the Stamford Planetarium within the Bendel Mansion. The Bendel Mansion looked similar to Tommy's summer house but was much larger in scale with more impressive architecture and mythic sculptures. We traversed the wonderful nature trails of the Bartlett Arboretum. We twirled around the center of the Herb Garden, applauded by the wistful audience of tea leaves and medicines grown in the earth. We took leisure in the many paths, enjoying the nipping sunshine that pricked our faces between tree branches. Countless beautiful gardens. We could have spent all four days befriending the elegant nature but decided we had work to do. It was nearly evening when we returned to the house off Farm Road, and we went up to the bar in the main house to mix drinks.

Tommy hopped behind the counter in one fair swoop, landing clapped on his feet and turning to us like an acrobat. "What'll we be having tonight, ladies and *gentleman*?"

"Rum and coke," Autumn rumbled, failing to hide her grin and rolling her eyes in consequence.

"Make that two!" Sophia stretched on a caramel leather couch across the bar room, making her body long like a cat. She was twirling a thread of her hair in one of her hands.

"Vodka soda," I added.

Tommy rummaged around behind the bar returning a moment later asking, "Is ginger ale alright? I don't see any club soda. I wouldn't trust it even if I did."

I nodded and Tommy tended to his bar. Three drinks later, Tommy carried flour glasses and a bottle of scotch and led us toward our makeshift studio. I swayed down the long hallway that connected the mansion to the guest house, following behind the three of them with a bubbly body. We were all buzzed as we staggered toward the studio. Tommy opened the door and flicked the lights to reveal the beautiful set up we had. Notably—there was no piano—my primary instrument. I expressed my confusion to the others.

"It's alright, man! You'll just have to sing," Tommy announced, pouring scotch about one sixth of each glass. He handed me a glass, so I sniffed it. Wild musk from the liquid. "Oh, don't look so down about it! At least you *can* sing—I mean, fuck, look at me. *No* vocals of note here. And look at Autumn—"

"Watch it."

Tommy extended a hand toward Autumn from across the room and bowed his head as if a wordless apology. Autumn continued to adjust her cymbals and snares while perched at her drum set.

"Yeah, I can do that," I chimed. I hadn't even thought about what I'd said before it was out in the open. I looked back at Sophia who must have noticed my anxiety. She grinned and said, "We'll both sing. Or we can take turns. Either way, it'll be good practice."

I shook my head and took a sip from my glass. The scotch refused to go down but with applied force, I managed the warm poison to my stomach. Sophia accepted a glass, swallowed a bit, and sat it at her feet near her guitar stand. The cable connector sank into her electric bass. She flicked the power on her amp and a low hum sizzled from the amp's speaker. We had a real setup in our makeshift studio. A microphone for Sophia and me to share, a microphone pitted in front of Autumn's drums, and two XLR cables snaking from the amps into an audio interface. We could now record our instruments in a far superior quality than a field recorder. And in the silent guest house, it was our opportune moment to record. Each of us had headphones with long wires that tangled around the floor. We heard our instruments at pristine clarity, and the metronome clicking around in our heads. It was quite the setup, all of which was Tommy's personal equipment he'd lugged up from school.

"Testing, testing, *hello*. Hello, hello, hello," Sophia spoke into the microphone. Her voice was crisp and smooth in my headphones at the highest quality, as if she were the voice of my consciousness. "Okay, we have, *Cowboy Face Paint*, *Vertical Dreams*, and *Diamond Pills* to practice and *maybe* even get some damn good recordings." She sounded like a sexy radio host. I had to stare at the rug to hide my smile.

"How're we feeling? Are we ready?" Sophia turned and Autumn sprang her thumb to answer. Without thinking, I swallowed a mouthful of scotch. My knees buckled. It was better than wobbling, I decided. Tommy hit something on his laptop, the metronome rang in my head, sounding like a never-ending sway of Newton's balls or a steady game of ping pong. Sophia brushed her lips on the metal cage of the mic; her eyes peered up at me, only inches from my lips. "Ready? *Cowboy Face Paint*—One, two, three, four."

Autumn added her drums to the next measure and riffed in that space until Tommy jumped in with his screechy guitar lick. Sophia underlined with her bass and gave me a nod so wide I briefly wondered if she'd been stretching her neck. But instantly, as if a primitive muscle flexed in my brain, I leaned into the mic and pouted out the opening lines. To my surprise, there was a strange echoing effect; my voice doubled, I could hear my real voice swallowed in my head as if I were underwater, but a second layer of my voice, suited in audio effects, overlapped through the headphones. It was sharp and dreamy. It was pop. I was so shocked to hear my own voice, but I was on autopilot; it felt similar to swimming, feeling each layer of my bandmate's contributions in my blood, and singing the song like it was always meant to fit in this space of time. I swooped into the chorus:

> *She can take her big city*
> *But it really is so passé*
> *A mouthful of anxiety*
> *But she's got nothing to say*
> *I'll stay here in my small town*
> *Working hard and making history*
> *Yeah, I'll be making history*

We recorded each track a handful of times, becoming increasingly drunk as the night went on. I felt like I was under a spell, singing with Sophia through the fluidity of time. I was deeply moved every time I got to sing each song, like a profound sense of belonging—a thread stitched to hold the others in place—the keystone to an archway. My body swayed unknowingly until I clocked Tommy snickering at the movement of my hips. By two in the morning, we were intoxicated, giddy and overwhelmed with the idea of having three recorded tracks (yet to be mixed or mastered, something Tommy would attempt later). We listened to them through the surround-sound speaker system back in the bar room, dancing and bouncing around like witches in the forests of Salem, feeling every movement of our songs. Sophia and Autumn pranced around on the leather couch—Tommy shook and craned his body with a full glass in hand, splashing copper-colored liquor on the hardwood floors—and I stood in quiet infatuation with these three people. We listened back to our demos; each of them was a genuine catch and to the ear, sounded frighteningly professional. I blinked, perplexed, with one sober question loaded in my brain, *how did we do that?*

———

Thanksgiving morning, Sophia suggested we make a special dinner for the four of us to celebrate not only the holiday but our labors in recording the new songs. Tommy agreed and offered to cook for us. The only establishment open on the holiday was a local Hispanic corner store. We were all in agreement that it would be worth it to have a Mexican feast and support the local business. Sophia stood up from her stool, hands pressed on the ledge of the island counter. Her hair was up in a messy bun, and wood-plated glasses accessorized her cheeks for she had yet to put in her contacts. Tommy scratched the happy trail up his bare stomach, sporting only gray sweatpants sagging on his waist. His eyes were puffy and glazed from hardly having woken up not thirty minutes ago; he squinted back at Sophia.

"Let's get going," Sophia announced. Tommy stretched his arms over his head, causing a series of cracks to clink from his shoulders, airy knocks hollow and sharp. He made a satisfied groan and reset. "I'll drive if that's alright. Are you two coming?"

He was referring to Autumn and I sitting across from each other at the kitchen table, the wall of trees behind us fell out of focus in the large windows. I was reading more of my Burroughs novel with recently brewed coffee in front of me in a clay mug. Autumn sat across from me, huddled in her oversized hoodie, reading some article on her phone. She scrubbed her eyelids with a finger and graveled, "Do I have to go?"

She was the last to get out of bed between the four of us and had barely adjusted to the morning light. I caught her routing a glance in my direction, but it zapped away just as quickly. I was already looking at her, and I realized I'd been doing so unknowingly. I looked back at Tommy, hoisting himself onto the counter.

"I'll stay here with her. Is that okay with you guys?" I asked.

I caught Sophia's look of surprise, but it quickly transposed to approval. "Okay! Yeah, that's fine. We got this. Don't we?"

She seemed to need Tommy's reassurance, but his delayed nod ended in a yawn. Sophia walked around the island and yanked at his arm.

"Alright, let's get going so we can get back. Don't you own a shirt?" she glared. Tommy hopped off the counter and headed upstairs for his suitcase. Sophia tightened her pair of Converse on her feet and waited for Tommy by the door, who descended a moment later. He clawed the keys to the SR-V resting on the entry table.

"We'll be back in a bit!"

Sophia's voice echoed through the hallway and into the kitchen. I swallowed the dark roast swirling around my teeth and set the mug back to the table. "See you in a bit! Be safe!"

The door slammed and suddenly I was alone in the large summer house with Autumn. She looked at me, but I could not read her emotions. Not blank—far from it. Overwhelmed seemed more fitting. Shut off, even. Somewhat menacing and all the while, an eye of curiosity. Before I could say anything, she stood up and moseyed over to the Mr. Coffee machine. She pulled a matching mug from the rung and filled it, mixing spoonsful of sugar into the mix. She creaked into her chair across from me.

"So, what kind of music do you like?" she asked. Her voice was deeper, raspier in the early morning. Her scratched, velvet sound was annoyingly attractive. But more questionable was how she'd snapped out of character, suddenly becoming someone else entirely with her question. I blinked, waiting a moment and strategizing my response.

"I really like The Doors," I replied. Again, she was unreadable. She did not respond. "And, you know, I like modern music just as much as the next guy. Beck, Muse, The Killers, uh—TOOL, Paramore, Chili Peppers—" I kept rambling everything I listened to at the time, with her hawk-like stare heating my face.

"I like the Red Hot Chili Peppers. They were my first concert, actually," she said, interrupting me.

"Nice," I said. The room fell to silence. I sipped my coffee and tried to think of something else to add. The yellow sun cast itself on the gray lawn just outside the window as the morning birds hovered above and fluttered down toward the back deck. They chipped at a birdfeeder and cocked their heads at the empty bird baths. I returned my attention to Autumn who was staring off into the gloss finish of the kitchen table.

"What about you?" I finally asked. "What sort of music do you like to listen to? Any guilty pleasures?"

"Uh—yeah," she responded. She sounded miserable at having to answer a single question.

"Well?"

She was quiet for some time. She sighed and asked rather shyly, "Do you ever listen to any musicals?"

I chuckled but reset when her face flushed. I knew she was embarrassed, so I quickly composed myself and found a response. "I actually really like musicals. I listened to them a lot throughout high school. Yeah, yeah—*West Side Story, Singin' in the Rain, Wicked*—"

"*Love Wicked*," she said. "Do you like *Phantom?*" Autumn leaned forward in her seat; the chair peeped from the change in weight. As she leaned in, I seemed to catch a glimpse of her—more than her—as if I had precisely positioned her in the sunlight to catch a hidden shine. Jarring. Exciting.

"*Phantom of the Opera*? Oh yeah, that one is great too. I take it you like musicals then?"

"It's my secret. Don't tell *anyone* I told you I like them. I mean it, Joe. But they're what I would listen to all the time as a kid. I credit musicals for introducing me to music."

"I don't know who I owe credit to. Maybe you guys," I said cheekily. Nothing in return. I asked, "What's your favorite musical?"

"I would have to say *Rent*," she murmured, looking at the table. Her septum piercing caught the morning sun from the giant windows, aimed back at me. I winced and moved my head to the side.

"What about you?" she asked.

I thought for a moment. "Have you ever heard of *Jazz Canal*?"

"Yeah! That's one of my favorites," she replied. *Jazz Canal* was a musical that had only opened around six months ago at this time and was not generally well known. It follows a group of six university graduates as they go from kids to parents, all the while attending their favorite bar. The real tragedy of the story—or perhaps the genius of it—is how as the show progresses, the group begins to unite less frequently, and soon there are less and less friends who attend at all.

"Who's your favorite character?" she asked.

"I think Bendy. Yours?"

"I'd go with Rolan. I think she's *vastly* misunderstood."

I smiled, nodding. I liked her answer. She sipped her coffee and held it close to her chest.

"Have you ever seen a show on Broadway?"

"No," she replied. "I've always wanted to go but I've never been to New York. Well, I've been to the state but not the city, you know. One day though, I would like to go. I would love to see a real show on Broadway, but I guess we'll have to wait and see."

"Maybe you'll perform on a Broadway stage someday," I said. An attempt to sound optimistic.

She tiffed, "Not Broadway."

"Well, why not?" I asked, leaning forward in my chair, shrieking with the wood on wood.

"It's not my art. I can love it from afar. But it is not where I'm meant to be."

I stared at her. I looked deep into her hazel eyes as they looked back at mine. A certain fear existed there and after only a second or less with our eyes touching, they returned to the table.

"Well, I'm going to go take a shower." She stood up and crossed the kitchen, only to pause at the archway leading back out into the hallway. "What are you going to do?"

My brain was vacant and perplexed. I was unsure as to what she was trying to say. It seemed there was a message between the lines she was trying to communicate without actually saying it. I couldn't decipher her code. She had a strange aura. Too much time was passing.

"I don't know—I'll finish my coffee—then decide what to do after that," I responded lamely.

Autumn shook her head and walked off toward the stairs, taking her coffee mug with her. I heard her go all the way up and then nothing; I was alone in the house again. I looked to my right, out the window, following the gravel walkway all the way to the heavily guarded woods. I knew there was a river somewhere beyond, but it was too dense to see from the house. I finished my coffee, washed the mug and hung it back to dry. I moved to the living room just behind the kitchen and sat at the mini grand in the corner. There was dust on the wood cover. I brushed my hand over it to reveal a gloss finish. I opened the cover and was at once greeted by the patterns of black and white. I pressed a key, and loudly it kicked out from the piano. I jolted, practically bouncing on the stool, and instantly adjusted my ear to focus on the nearly unintelligible drone of the shower going.

Besides the soft hiss from above, there was myself and silence. I felt the freedom to tinker with the piano and practice some of muscle movements. And in no time at all, I veered from classical renditions to creating my own melodies. I'd developed an altered melody and found the chords to follow it. I played it over and over and over. An hour passed and I was humming over the song when Autumn crept down the stairs. She had a navy GWU crewneck over her torso and black athletic shorts. I watched her step into the living room and slump into the couch. She pulled out her phone and scrolled, hunkering in with her head resting on the cushion.

A moment more of my humming indistinctly over the song and twirling some words in my head before I decided to try them together. The piano stopped, filling the room with silence, before I started the song over again with my voice quietly added:

I need to live a thousand lives
So maybe once I can get it right
I feel like I'm losing it
But I take it how I choose it
Leave me alone so I
Can relive it a thousand times
And I could fill a museum
With memories of you and me
Now, without you by my side
My darling, I'm just passing time

. . .

I repeated the last two lines. I riffed in that space for some time. I moved notes—up a step or down a step—up an octave or down an octave—and tried to find the best sound. I thought of Sophia while coming up with the lyrics. I stopped to sip my coffee, but it had gone cold, biting back against my tongue with a metallic taste.

"What's that one called?" Autumn asked. I glanced up to discover her green eyes peeking over the top of the couch.

"I'm not so sure yet."

"Did you come up with that just now?" she asked, almost sounding angry. She stood and walked to the opposite end of the piano, leaning her elbows into the gloss finish.

"While you were upstairs, yeah," I said.

"Play it again!" she demanded. I played my new song for her once —then again—and noticed her fingers pattering against her thigh. She kept time and created a rhythm. For the second time since I met her, I saw her smile. And once again, I caught a little glimmer of Autumn.

———

The weather turned gleeful and welcoming. A watery golden sun beat down on the shaven lawn and prickled bushes, even a cross-stitch of black and hazel fell on the forest floor that masked a crackling river. Sophia and Tommy made it back home, forearms loaded with paper bags. Tommy began preparations for the steak with a cigarette freshly lit and hanging from his teeth. Autumn and I conversed in the living room for quite some time about music and poetry, focusing on Rimbaud, Cocteau, Hart Crane, and Verlaine. Sophia frolicked into the living room, light on her feet and leaned over the piano.

"Tommy says the river is safe to swim in. Who wants to go down to the river?" she asked excitedly.

"I'll go with you," Autumn replied, and she achingly rose to her feet, her knees popping in the process. She blew an embarrassed giggle.

"Joe, are you coming?" Sophia questioned. She wore a bright smile on her face—one I thought relentless—one that might never fade, no matter her age. Her energetic desire to be open to the world could never falter.

"But I didn't bring a swimsuit," I peeped.

This prompted Sophia to push air from her lips and roll her eyes. She crossed her arms and leaned her weight onto one leg. "You men are such prudes. *I'm* going skinny dipping. And you're absolutely welcome to join if you change your mind."

Sophia turned on her heels and fled the living room with Autumn accompanying her side. I teetered into the kitchen to find Tommy on pause, hands on hips and he mumbled, "There they go."

I followed his sight out through the giant windows to find both Sophia and Autumn stripping their clothes in the backyard. They were pulling every stitch from their bodies, revealing more glaring pale skin to the sun. Sophia was first to stand stark with her bare backside facing us in the kitchen. She stretched her arms into the sky, and her body glowed as the pale light reflected off her skin. Finally, as the last of their clothes landed on the back deck, Sophia and Autumn stepped off into the grass and ran out toward the trees. The two young bodies shrank into the wood and vanished.

Tommy glanced down at me; a grin curled in his cheeks. He plucked the cigarette from his mouth and offered it to me as a bit of relief. I had never smoked a cigarette in my life before this very moment.

"Slick," he charmed. He'd never called me that until that day. "You look like you could use a puff of this." I accepted the stick with wisps of pale smoke crumpling at one end and held the opposite between my lips. I allowed the smoke to course through my lungs and fool my brain. I realized just how much I was beginning to change.

———

Once Tommy finished his preparations for dinner, we sat out at a four-chaired round table on the back deck reading books and smoking under the glory of the autumn sun. We sat across from each other, sunglasses over our eyes, a pack of Newports between us on the tabletop. Neither of us said it, but we were mutually awaiting their return. And when they finally did, the two of them made no effort to hide their bodies. Sophia and Autumn trekked casually side-by-side back up the expansive mound of dying grass. They glanced left and right and eventually stepped barefoot on the wooden deck; their hands pressed firmly into their hips. I looked to my right and got my first good look at the two of them; Autumn was completely shaven below the waist while Sophia was the opposite.

"Hello," Tommy greeted. His voice fell lower than normal, an octave or two below his usual call. Sophia giggled. She sat in one of the chairs at the table between Tommy and I, and reached for the pack of cigarettes at the center and lit one.

"Hello, boys," Sophia answered. Autumn took the last chair. The four of us sat around the table, Tommy and I with our sunglasses on, as we pretended to be reading our books. I would stare at the same page of my Burroughs novel for five whole minutes and interpret less than a single phrase.

"How was it?" Tommy asked with a disciplined casualty to his voice.

"It was really nice. It was cold at first, but we got used to it quickly," Sophia said.

"Yeah, it was good. There was a fallen tree across the river," Autumn added.

Tommy did not look up from his book. "Did you guys try to cross it?"

"No! That would be so dangerous!" Sophia giggled. She smoked and puffed into the blue wind. I wondered how the chilled air and blaring sun must have felt all over her body. I was making myself excited—visibly so—I took periodic glances at her body beside me, before ultimately forcing myself to focus on my book. I didn't have any real place on the page. I had stopped paying attention to the prose nearly two pages ago. My strained appearance must've been obvious even masked with my shaded spectacles because Sophia took a bite at me.

"Joey," she began, "Why don't you join us? It really is a lovely day for sunbathing."

"Hm?" I pretended I hadn't heard her. She grinned with her cigarette held between her fingers. Limp-wristed and held at eye level. The trail of smoke began at her temple and made a ghoulish pale string into the sky. Her wet hair had turned black and slicked back on her head, she shined like a vinyl record. Beads of water still clung to her chest. Her shoulders. Her hips. She turned to Tommy to see if he would take the bait, "What about you? Won't you join us?"

Tommy sighed. He flipped his novel over and slapped it against the table. Even through tinted lenses, I could tell he was looking right at me. A look that said, *might as well*. He stood up from his chair and pulled at the seam of his shirt. Off it went, tossed on the deck. He hooked onto the stringline of his sweatpants and in one swoop, his bare legs revealed in a flash. Tommy stood for a moment, seemingly allowing everyone a good look.

Autumn and Sophia flashed smiles with teeth at the sight, Autumn even hummed a low chuckle in her breath. All three of them directed their attention to me. I looked back at my friends, upset that I was now the only clothed one. I had become the minority, the one that stood out. I stood up and tugged my t-shirt off my back and tossed it to the side. Anxiously, I unzipped my shorts, pulled them to my feet and tossed them onto the warm deck. I fingered the edge of my underwear but paused with uncertainty. I was unsure how this was going to affect their image of me if they saw me in such a vulnerable state—this thought was short lived.

I shed the last of my garments. I quickly sat back in my chair and pulled my body close to the table. I snatched my book and continued to stare at the wordy page but my mind was spinning, the blood pumped through my head with wild thumps. I couldn't focus on anything other than the fact that I was in the nude with three spectators. True, they were also in the nude, but I felt my stomach turn at my relentless vulnerability. I could not deny though that the sun's great snuggle felt extraordinarily delightful all over my skin. A liberating bath of whispering wind that seemed to freckle all over my body. A freshly warm coat of sun made me feel relaxed and less naked.

"Hey," Sophia poked, "Put the book down and spend some time with us."

I glanced back at her. She was still smiling with her devilish gaze. She leaned back in her seat and put the cigarette back to her perfect lips. I was not certain what was going on until I felt her toes brush lightly against my testicles. I thought at first it might be an accident until she made it clear with more confidence to her force. She pressed her foot gently into me; it caused me to flinch at the forbidden pleasure. So, I set my book aside and decided to pay attention. Sophia leaned forward and handed me the cigarette from across the table. I accepted it and she snatched my sunglasses.

What occurred next, I had never anticipated happening in my life. She leaned forward on the edge of her chair, bent one arm and supported her chin while the other found its way below the table. Her hand touched me gently, then massaging until I became erect. My erection stood straight up, practically hitting my stomach, and she tightly motioned her hand up and down. Waves of undying warmth hummed in my waist. Casually, she smiled and took the cigarette back from my mouth. She asked with a jarring casualty to her tone, "So what did you guys end up doing today?"

"Joe wrote a new song. And *of course*, it's fucking good," Autumn said. I looked to her to say thank you but was too taken aback to discover Autumn leaning forward in her perch with her own left arm moving beneath the table. Tommy leaned back in his chair with his hands interlaced behind his head; he sported a grin on his face.

"*What*?" Sophia chirped. She shot a look at me, never stopping her motion on my penis and equally never mentioning it. "Why didn't you tell me you wrote a new song?"

"I just," I couldn't get the words out. I felt all sorts of pleasantries. A plethora of phantom touches that prickled out from my waist. I tightened my abs and said, "I just came up with it today."

"Well, when we get back inside, you have to show it to me," she demanded. The incredibility of her tugging little hand began to build on itself. Her velocity steadily increased. They talked for a while longer with informality and neglect of our current situation. I noticed Sophia's unemployed hand disappearing under the table to act on herself. I stopped listening to whatever it was they were discussing. They were nonsensical topics at this moment. I couldn't hold my focus on anything besides Sophia seated to my right and her working hands. It became a total takeover of my consciousness. An illusion.

Tommy leaned forward and gripped Autumn's shoulder. The conversation broke, Sophia and Autumn directing their concentrations to his gaze at the table.

Sophia's hard strokes slowed a moment as we all turned our attention to watch him in admiring anticipation. His face contorted, squinting his eyes. His neck strained. And we, his audience, were respectful and curious. He sucked air into his chest rapidly, and froze. A moment later, he exhaled, long and weighted; Tommy's body relaxed. Autumn leaned back and wiped her hand dully on her thigh then returned to the place between her legs.

Sophia picked up her pace, broadening her movements. I locked eyes with her, her brown eyes were gleaming in the sun. My attention darted rapidly between her figure and her face. Flawless. Unbelievable. Impossible. Sophia looked at me with desire and determination. She whispered, and when she did it was as if the rest of the world fell away, into a blinding white, and she spoke, "Come for me."

As the words left her mouth, all at once the pleasure tensed my whole body. I locked into an arresting heat coursing through my blood. I rocked forward in my chair as my breath increased. My head felt relaxed, as if I were slightly high. Sophia smiled happily and wiped her hand on her stomach, rubbing it into her milky skin. Tommy leaned in to assist Autumn. My hands trembled as they found their way to Sophia. After petting the skin of her legs, I allowed myself to glide the top of my fingers over her lips. I found the slick crease and it clung to my fingers as her breaths became longer drawn.

Before long, we migrated out into the grassy yard. In the acres of gray, we intertwined. A wonderful sense of animalistic behavior took control of our bodies. We were high on the human body; one would think we were starving for it. When our intoxication subsided, we glanced at one another, and burst into laughter as if it were unavoidable. We dressed and ventured inside to finish the preparations of our holiday feast. None of us mentioned what had happened outside that afternoon, letting it sit quietly in our minds and never beyond. I felt alarmingly prideful of our secret and became calmly obsessed with the images. I quickly yearned for it to happen again. As Sophia and I set the table in the dining room, the only thing I could think about was how I wanted her once more. But a larger contemplation of remorse for the situation sank deep in my stomach; more than her lust, I wanted her love.

The whole mix of opposing emotions almost made me lose my appetite and excuse myself to be alone for a while. I tried to see the light of the situation, as strange as it was. I felt lucky to be her friend, to be a part of something as intimate as a band, and to have her consent in an intimate encounter. All of it garnered my gratitude. I decided I should maintain my appreciation even if she and I were to never be committed, for I found nothing in this life to be as romantic as artists finding moments to create with one another.

———

After our dinner party, we spent the rest of the night engaged in the same activities as the first. We chipped away at two new songs and drank heavily at the bar. We fell asleep by three in the morning. Drunk, high, burnt throats and bloated stomachs. Only this time, we didn't move to any particular bedroom, the four of us passing out on the leather sofa, myself in the armchair, Tommy on the floor. And so, the rest of our Thanksgiving weekend went in a glutenous pattern. We woke up every morning hungover, cooked each other breakfast, wrote songs and read literature, and engaged in sex whenever we felt like it. By Saturday morning, we all woke in the flesh and none of us bothered to put anything on, knowing it would be more of a hassle to dress just to undress again. We were comfortable enough around each other and far enough out in the country to not have any need for clothing at our countryside cottage. We drank heaps of liquor when the sun melted into the hills and heaps more coffee by day. We were balancing a sinful nature with a dedication to work, and to us it felt wholly artistic. Despite our thirst for lust and desire to smoke and drink, we finished the weekend with a total of seven songs, written and recorded. Our seven songs, once mastered back in Tommy's dorm room after long days of classes, would change our lives forever. The seven track EP, titled, *THE STAMFORD RECORD*, would soon become our first tangible artifact bred from the minds of Beach Sirens. It was a real piece of art and we, the four of us together, served as a single creator.

———

Our last night in Stamford, the four of us lay out in the grass, staring up at the twinkling stars, clearer than I had ever seen in my life. A complex grid of dazzling light. The sky was practically blue again from how visible everything was, down to each pale prick of starlight. We were piss drunk with spinning heads; the earth tilted back and forth below us like a great sailing ship. We were spread evenly and formed a cross, or an 'X' formation. Each of our heads met at the center.

"Did you really come here every summer?" Sophia asked.

"Most summers, yeah. Sometimes we'd vacation somewhere else."

"That sounds like a dream," she replied, quietly, almost a whisper.

Then, Autumn, "So this is what money can buy. Pieces of paradise."

Tommy chuckled, "That would be an excellent song title!"

Something was on my mind. I cleared my throat and said, "Hey, Tommy."

"Mm?"

"Do you like your father?"

The wind raced against our bodies and through our hair. It combed the grass and braided the tree branches. This wind was the only sound for a moment, a comfortable hush. Tommy thought over his answer before finally, he groaned.

"I suppose I like him. He's okay," Tommy replied, "He's a little uptight about shit—Why? Do you like your dad?"

I stared at the stars, and responded quietly, "I do—though sometimes I wish he were dead—I mean, I love him with all my heart but sometimes I wish *one* of my parents would die. And I don't want it to be my mom—I think because I still need her—or worse, soon she will need me."

Silence followed.

"Why do you want your dad to die?" Autumn asked softly.

"I don't want him to die," I explained, nervously. "I just wish for it—as if it will make me more interesting—or I'll gain more experience from the pain. I really don't want him to die though—I bet I sound like a psychopath."

Sophia, "You're not a psychopath, Joe. My mom is addicted to the same thing I've been drinking all week. But it's gonna kill her someday, you know? And sometimes I wish she'd just leave already."

I chewed my cheek and felt like I was going to be sick. I felt ashamed of what I said, like maybe I should learn to keep my mouth shut. "I'm sorry," I said, but Sophia began to laugh.

"Don't be! She fucking deserves it," she said. "What about you, Tommy, which parent are you choosing?"

"Which one am I killing off?" Tommy asked.

"Yeah."

"Dad," he croaked.

"And you, Autumn?"

She was quiet, seemingly cautious of her answer like it might manifest into a terrible reality. She spoke so gently, her baritone voice nearly blended in the sound of the river, "I don't want either of them to die." And it silenced all of us. Out in the field, the stars watched down on us. We lived together beneath our sliver of sky.

Autumn continued, "I'd pick my dad though, I think—I don't know—it couldn't be my stepdad. If I really had to choose between my stepdad and my mom—I'd rather choose myself."

Tender, mindful, silence. We allowed the sounds of the earth to fill the conversation for only a moment. Her parents meant the world to her, and the realization hit like a stabbing pain to the gut. I felt ashamed of the conversation. I thought maybe she would cry but I knew she was far more shielded than to allow that to happen. Autumn would rather be silent with her agony than let any of us know it existed. We would be there for her if she were ever to open up to any of us or if she ever needed to ease the pain.

"I like that answer." I tilted my head to get a better look at her. Autumn turned to face me, and she closed her eyes; they were wet and glinting in the moonlight. She still managed a smile. It was a needed exchange.

Tommy began to cry. The tears found him quickly, and he shot up, wiping away tears and smudging his palms on his lids. I sat up too, and the girls followed. We were all alarmed by his sudden breakdown. I placed a hand on Tommy's shoulder only for it to be swiped away.

"Don't fucking touch me," he warned. Sophia leaned toward him with a hand hovered over his thigh. She glanced at Autumn and I, hesitating to attempt consolation. Instead, she asked, "Tommy, what's wrong?"

He sniffled and wiped his face with his wrist. I did everything I could to focus on my friend rather than feeling the orbit of the planet. I inched toward him.

"Tommy, man, tell us what's going on," I urged.

And after a few deep breaths, he sniffled, "It's just that—I think this is a perfect night. I don't think it's going to get any better than this, you know? I don't see how it can. So, what's the point?—This, all of *this*—It will never last."

Sophia gave me a look, uncertain but I saw she recognized what he was saying. And I did too. All of us knew what he was feeling. What was the point of going on if the best was now? We would never be as young as we were at that moment ever again. Never as free. Never as beautiful. Never quite as naïve. Never so alive.

"Let's just try to enjoy it while we're here," I mumbled. When the words left me, Tommy slowed his sniffles. He turned, and we caught eyes, his shimmered like glass. This was the first time I noticed how blue his eyes were. He looked at me with such fear and I watched as it drained, slowly, and turned to comfort. He nodded, "Okay."

On Sunday morning, the four of us sat at the kitchen table eating scrambled eggs and English muffins with strawberry jam and butter. We had yet to pack any of our belongings, instead focusing on our last breakfast together before returning to school. Back to school meant back to classes, back to clubs and jobs, all of which meant not being able to spend every waking moment together. The four of us had become so synonymous with one, so much so that I wondered what I would do by myself when I split off from our group of tightly intertwined minds. Autumn sipped her coffee, her legs crossed and set it back at the table. Tommy leaned forward in his chair and clicked fork to plate, shoveling eggs onto his English muffin. Sophia poured herself a second glass of orange juice. The sun from the wall of glass warmed us and made our bodies gold like treasure.

"So, are we going back to meeting every Friday then?" I mentioned. There was a tick of sorrow in my tone, almost sarcastic. I looked to Sophia and Autumn for any input.

"Maybe we can spend the New Year together. I know my dad wouldn't mind," Sophia said, always trying to implement her positivity to the situation. "My house isn't nearly as beautiful as that—but it would still be nice—maybe. We can make it work!"

"No, I know I won't be able to. Strong tradition in my family. I will have to be home, Tommy mumbled with a mouthful of scrambled eggs. "Especially since I'll be the only son home at the end of the year."

Sophia turned and rested her hand on mine. "We're still going to spend time together. We will always make time for the band, no matter what."

Tommy scrubbed his mouth with a napkin and offered to take our plates. He stood and cleaned the dishes at the sink. The four of us gathered our belongings and organized our bags. We each wearily picked an outfit for the drive back, all of us zipping or buttoning our overcoats and lacing our boots. It was time to return to school for a new semester, and we all seemed to understand our futures together were uncertain.

But our predictions were true. We continued to meet every Friday evening in our practice room, repeatedly getting lost in the music for four short hours just as we said we would. We spent the rest of our Friday nights together, usually in either Tommy's cramped room or back at the girl's dorm room. I began looking forward to every Friday, and it helped me work through classes each week with the addition of a clear end goal. I only saw my roommate a handful of times more during the school year.

When I went home for Christmas break some four weeks later, I was obsessed with the idea of getting back to school. I played the piano in the foyer of my house nonstop to make sure I didn't forget any of my parts in the songs. My parents could not believe how attached I had become to the piano, singing, and writing. I wrote frantically; I scribbled out lyrical prose about how much I loved my friends or where I hoped to be someday. And how I found such purpose in doing so. How I longed for the city. How I longed to never do anything else but play music with the three of them. How I longed, indeed.

In May of the same school year, we released *THE STAMFORD RECORD*, so it became available on all streaming platforms. Much to our surprise, our EP performed fairly well for a college band, and we became something of a local celebrity at our school. So, the following two years at George Washington University were spent in a band. Every party we attended, we would bring along at least one other member from our group. When one of us got a fever, each of us would check in on them to make sure they were okay. We did everything together; we became inseparable. It wasn't a conscious thing, it just was.

When I turned twenty-one the following December, Autumn and Sophia had just turned twenty, while Tommy was still nineteen. After

Christmas break, I bought us alcohol every Friday to drink in Autumn and Sophia's new apartment in Arlington. We all got jobs in our third year; Tommy and I worked as delivery drivers in the city, Sophia interned for a publishing company and Autumn worked for a great wage at an independent record shop (better wages than what any of the rest of us made). Our worlds revolved around each other; an orbit held close with music as our gravity.

We stayed in the city that summer to work and stayed in our apartments. It afforded us the opportunity to work more frequently on music and try new experiences. Every weekend we performed small gigs, drank ourselves black in bars (the other three had fakes), and spent countless nights together wagering in long conversations about the meaning of life or saying nothing at all and focusing on sexual activities together. It was the bohemian dream, that summer before our senior year. We skyrocketed in popularity all around DC as our discography grew. I once found a Beach Sirens sticker stuck on a restroom mirror in a dive bar; I glanced at the sticker, a symbol of pride, and stuck my nose on the sink to snort a line and splash my face with cold water. We all weighed less than what we had a year ago, but we each weighed immensely heavier in ego. Between tripping acid, snorting cocaine in increasingly unique situations, and sleeping with every fan that said they'd heard of us, we felt unstoppable. We became the essence of rock and roll.

We all quietly worried about what might happen once each of us graduated and went our separate ways. All four of us had bright futures to lead, and the orbit of Beach Sirens was only so strong until it wasn't. Without college, there would be no need to stay in D.C. Unless we found jobs in the city, it would be more of a hassle to stay. Our gravity would slip, and we all knew it was coming. I tried hard not to think about it, but the thoughts blackened my brain each night. I might have to go back home to Athens and become a music tutor or worse, I might try to work with my father at the dealership. Luckily, once our senior year began, our luck changed.

For the freshmen coming into our university in the fall, we arranged with GWU to play a short set in the auditorium. What we didn't know was a sharp young man named Hal Walsh would be seated in the audience. In his second semester at our school, he published his article covering Beach Sirens in the school paper, *GWU Today*, and it caught the attention of many of our peers. It caught the attention of a freshman named Teddy Mercer, who decided to attend our show at the Songbyrd Music House in the fall of our senior year. Teddy approached me after the show as I stood at the bar, both of us damp with sweat, and he explained to me that his father was a music manager for a record label named ROT IRON. His father had heard of us through his son who had taken a liking to our music. His father was Anthony (Ant) Mercer, a burly white man of Irish descent. We got in contact with Ant, who signed us to his label the moment as Sophia, Autumn and I graduated in the spring of 2019. We decided to hold on the offer for we only had eight weeks left until we completed our degrees. Tommy, however, got so excited about the offer, he dropped out of school before he could start his senior year.

After a split-second decision, our twenty tracks were owned by ROT IRON, home to other bands we enjoyed, like Crosswired and Baby Mullets. Our twenty tracks were whittled into twelve tracks and re-recorded in a professional studio in Los Angeles. The process took roughly two months in total. The label allowed us to write four new songs in that space, which was much more impressive than our practice room at GWU. Finally, on the 8th of November 2019, our debut, self-titled record, *Beach Sirens*, was released to the world. The four of us went home to our families that Christmas as college graduates and contracted musicians. In the new year, we began discussing our first tour, which would span four countries.

All was going better than we could have imagined, that is until we found ourselves unexpectedly locked in our apartments for all of 2020 thanks to a pandemic that spread around the globe. We spent lockdown in an almost constant state of drunkenness as we all felt we were being held hostage. In total solitude with a world shutdown, we replaced our grim thoughts with weed and anything else we could get our hands on. We huddled in our apartment worried and strung out (Tommy and I lived together by this point but we spent almost every night at the girls' apartment). We wondered if we'd ever get to perform our music live. Or if we'd even get to keep our record deal with all the chaos happening globally at the time. We decided unanimously that our best chance at survival would be to continue writing new music. It was our form of medicine. For the next nine months, we focused our efforts on our art and in all, we created a total of twenty-two songs.

A shimmer of hope arrived in January, nearly a year into our solitude, when *Beach Sirens* became certified Gold. The record label sent many gifts to us in D.C., and in return, we sent them a completely new LP. We wrote the entire album while quarantined and we hoped it might impress the label with our efforts; perhaps it would be good enough to keep our record deal. ROT IRON responded to the album with extraordinary praise.

Our sophomore record, *Island Walkers*, released on the 25th of June 2021. We had so much to prove and we were a band locked together in a space for several months, so the obvious outcome was a new record. The suffering from that year led us, the band, to our toolkit of creation in an effort to make sense of it. As is always the case with artists. The album became a worldwide sensation. At any hour of the day, we could tune into a pop radio station and be met with *Don't Get Too Close* or *Loose Ends* blaring back at us. We attended award shows and lavish parties in Los Angeles and met faces we had only ever seen in magazines. Everyone knew who we were because of *Island Walkers*. This time, a tour was put together and we would play shows one hundred times the capacity of our bars in the city.

Our lives had been forever changed. The alterations were so immediate and instantaneous that none of us had any time to keep up. Between uppers and downers, nodding our heads at whatever we were told to do, and being herded onto planes, buses, private cars, sprinter vans, it all became quite overwhelming. We were the talented, young pets of the label. If we took the fraction of a second it took to blink, we thought we would certainly miss something, so we all learned how not to blink. With fried eyes and steel-shattering freedoms, our band became drenched in the powerful glow of the limelight. We played across North America. We played across Europe and South America. Shows in Brazil, Mexico City, Kansas City, Toronto, Lisbon, London, Paris, Munich, and Milan. We played Madison Square Garden in February of 2022. That same month, *Island Walkers* sold its millionth copy. We saw everything we ever wanted to see and did anything we had ever wanted to do. Anything was possible for us then. Once we realized our power, we became frightened by it. We became immortal.

VII
Denim Dogs

Our colossal return to Madison Square Garden became a standout with quite a corrosive success. The show sold out. I made sure to reserve a private suite for Ellis to attend the show, but I was never made aware if he'd decided to attend. While I stood on the stage and peered out at forty thousand eyes back on me, I wondered if any of them belonged to Ellis Young. That night, I exaggerated my performance in hopes he had been watching, with a grand speech in the middle, and more dancing than I'd done in all the rehearsals combined. Why had I wanted him there so badly? I had little time to think about him as I was whisked away to different cities all across the continent. It would be several years before I ever encountered the alluring Ellis Young again.

We played in stadiums and theaters throughout North America. We were pushed onto stages in Toronto, Montreal, Pittsburgh, Philadelphia, Newark, Baltimore—finally we'd arrived at Washington D.C. It was a reunion of sorts to be back in the city where the band originated. The four of us stayed out late with fans and revisited our favorite bars and caught up with the bartenders. Ahead of us still were Cincinnati, Indianapolis, St. Louis, St. Louis, Nashville (two nights), Charlotte, Birmingham, Atlanta, and Jacksonville. We would play in Tampa on a Saturday night, then not play again until Wednesday in

New Orleans. I scrubbed the sides of my fingers against my eyelids, the painful relief crackled like sprinklers.

The tour was becoming a successful venture. To my surprise, our fans seemed to like *Music to Die to*—or, at least, they hadn't despised it as I had begun to. I wondered if it was Ellis who instilled such a distaste for the record or perhaps my lack of appreciation as a touring artist. As the tour progressed, city to city, we began to make headlines with major news outlets and across social media platforms. Many articles highlighted our calm, focused demeanors—traits never before seen from the band up to this point. I read one article from a music journalist who coined our new style as *somewhat avant-garde* but truthfully, we were approaching our late twenties and exhausted. I began to feel my knees and back after each performance. We were at the peak of our success but fatigued—the media interpreted it as a newfound maturity—and despite my adoration for the band and our music, I grew sick of the career.

After each live show, I returned to my hotel and hid until morning—or climbed onto the bus and pulled the covers over my face. There, beneath the old comforter and alone, I could reflect on the fading memory of the show only hours before. I stood center stage and stared out at thousands of faces gleaming back at me in the darkness. An otherworldly sense of euphoria. In situations like these, it becomes difficult to absorb the moment, and instead, the most rapturous shows of my life become a blur. Then without any time to decompress, I was pushed into a new hotel. Too many nights spent lying on my back, staring at the pale ceilings. I would ponder my humanity. Was this how one should spend their youth? Was this sacrifice? I questioned if I was the one in control of my life or if it was the team of people who catered to me all across the country.

I no longer had to ask for drugs. Everything I ever dreamed of trying was delivered to me or was already at my disposal. Our lunches were planned. Dinners were forced. Everything I once had to do for myself was now done by someone else. Subtly less than human. Faces often asked if I was doing alright. If I need anything at all, I need only let them know. Fake grins. Express thanks. Careful head nods to show my acknowledgment of their communications. I grew further from myself as each day passed. I would lie awake in the too-perfect bedding, struck pale with anxiety, and wonder what it was I had been trying to accomplish at this point in my career. But then I would always remember, if not this, what else is there to do?

Some musicians live to perform but my ambition aches to create rather than recite. Once the art is what I consider to be finished, I only wish to release it and let it be. However, in my line of work, I must hold the carcass of my creation with thin strings, an undead marionette decomposing more every night I show it off in the thick gloom of each venue. I arrived at work each day to play a character. I sat at the piano with my friends all those years ago to create musical compositions and now I am to perform a musical stage play—I should be in character as myself if I were only so extroverted—so one dimensional. My sense of self was strained. Cold nights. Waves of pleasure seeped through my body with whatever drug I chose. Tommy got me into the habit of crushing opioids and snorting them, something always quite regretful; I would have to quit shooting things into my nasal cavity if I wanted any chance of maintaining my health.

Blackout drunk. Brief memories like snapshots of me tripping on black city pavement. Chewing on the potent textures of psychedelic mushrooms, kicking them back and plugging my nose. Tommy and I lied on the frigid vinyl of private suites, watching as the world dripped into obliteration. While high on anything we could find, we'd pour more glasses of liquor and sit across from each other on the floor. Our heads drooped so low against the wall that our chins pressed into our chests. It was midnight in New Orleans; the two of us were bunched up in some luxury hotel. I smoked a cigarette to keep myself occupied like an infant in possession of a pacifier. Bits of ash crumbled into a tiny anthill between my pecs.

"Why are we here?" I grumbled, the cigarette bobbing as I spoke. My face congested and my breathing audible. The soft purr of my hoarse lungs gave me satisfaction for I knew I was at least alive.

"To play a show," he replied from across the room. His black body slumped into the wall created a dark silhouette. The city's plasmic glow cast through the windows to provide only a smear of definition to his face. A single dot of bright orange at the end of his chin; it pulled away, and his head grew into a black cloud and dissipated. All of it was only hints of Tommy.

"No," I said and shook my head. I searched for what I had meant to say and coughed. I blew smoke and queerly held the cigarette between my fingers. "Why are we alive? What is the purpose of us being alive?"

Careful silence. We took drags of our cigarettes. We swallowed bourbon from the clacking whiskey glasses. Our throats burned hot like dying coals. Emberred lungs and backward eyes.

"Purpose is whatever you want it to be," said Tommy. His voice was scratched. He choked to clear his throat and swallowed audibly.

"No, *no, man*. There has to be more to it than that," I graveled. My attention drifted as darts of rain began powdering the window. The shadows of the droplets burned onto Tommy's profile. Ghostly tears.

Tommy sighed. He said, "Some would say God, or whatever that means to you—He determines why we are here—He determines our purpose." He paused and chuckled, "Wouldn't that be nice? That feels like a neatly wrapped notion—maybe that's the answer we're searching for—the question is, are you gullible enough to fall for something like that?" His tone was earnest as if he meant it genuinely and not in any condescending way.

"I cannot believe it!" I piped. I shook my head. "But the option of evolution and adaptation rings sort of easy, too. I think, whatever happened here, with all this that we call life, had to have occurred entirely by accident. This formation of mass and energy is unethical but what's more, it is," I wandered the tip of my tongue, "Unsustainable."

"Glass half empty, aren't we, Slick?" Tommy laughed. His cello hum calmed my thoughts. He kept me grounded and present. "Well, my friend, maybe it is all by accident. Although most would call it a miracle." His voice faded into a whisper but with the room so still I could hear every vowel, "And if that is the case, we were granted just enough development to question it but not quite enough to answer it. What a shame that is! Our five senses have limited us from the abstractions of existence."

"Mm," I nodded. I let his words roll around my brain. "The answer is somewhere but not in our grasp," I said aloud. The rain continued its subtle window taps. Silver strings on the gloomy glass. I smoked and sipped as Tommy continued deeper.

"Not within our grasp of understanding. We live in boxes, yes? This *room* is a box. Our *minds* are boxes. We thrive in structure. Whether it be physical or—ah—in the metaphorical sense. Our species has evolved by the use of structures. But even then, our structures are inherently wrong. They are all our own designs. I can't argue though, they work just well enough for us to get up in the morning and go to work."

"What do you mean *wrong*?" I questioned. "What does that mean?"

"Think about it, Henley. Take *time* for example—one of our more useful structures—it's wrong." His words were stretching, almost as if he were falling asleep.

"Why?" I asked. For a long time, Tommy did not reply and I briefly wondered if he'd fallen asleep. "Why?" I asked again, louder.

Tommy responded by way of asking a series of questions with lengthy pauses between each of them. "When was the beginning of time? What happened at the *start* of time? And what happened before that? When is the end and what comes after it? Do you see what I mean?" he asked. He paused and I heard the ice tick in his glass.

"It's a self-induced paradox. There is no beginning and there is no end. What we call *time* invented beginnings and endings. We think too linearly to see the greater abstraction. A wristwatch is reliable. A clock on the wall is measurable. But it cannot be correct. Because we invented the measurement, true only because we say so. Time is as real as the gold in Fort fucking Knox, my friend."

"So, if not time—then what?" I asked. I crammed the end of my cigarette into the vinyl flooring.

"I don't know. I'm just a dumb animal running around a planet." He giggled lowly to himself again, and admittedly I began to do the same. We practically fell onto our sides, sliding down the wall and catching ourselves on our elbows, laughing at the puny notion of our lives.

"Pretty insignificant, aren't we?" I huffed while desperately attempting to regain my balance against the wall.

"You could say that. It doesn't matter what we do here, not really, at least. The way I see it, if we do whatever we please without harming anyone, what fucking difference does it make? Do you want a hundred years here eating plants and taking long walks? Or do you want forty years here and give in to all the pleasures?"

"I don't know what I want."

"Neither do I. And that's okay. Just don't get all hung up on it because again, we aren't even really supposed to be here at all."

"Which could also be wrong," I countered. I knocked my glass back to catch the remnants. A boulder of ice pounded my nose. I knew I was too drunk to stand and pour another glass. I was magnetized to the hardwood.

"Could be. Like I said, just an animal. I cannot perceive the wider abstractions the same way a dog cannot perceive what's beyond the neighborhood. But what I'm trying to say is—if our entire existence was *actually* accidental then there is no purpose. You know, the way ecosystems fit together like puzzle pieces could *only* be due to adaptation. So, what we call *purpose* might have no role in it, maybe it's simpler. Life could be an accident; it doesn't mean it can't maintain itself."

"You make it sound like a disease," I grimaced.

"You said it, not me."

"We're rock stars. Thousands of people every night scream for our attention. And yet, every person in the venue could very well be the greatest phenomenon to the universe," I said. I turned my attention to the slithering rain over the urban night. I thought about how quickly time was passing. Only three hours ago, I had bowed to another unwavering storm of applause. But how could time pass at all if it was false?

I closed my eyes and focused instead on the soft sounds of falling droplets.

"If you think you're famous, that's fine, but nobody outside of our atmosphere gives a flying fuck about you. Unless they heard what we created, huh?" He snarled, lips curled and laughing again.

"I suppose that's the only thing I know to be true."

Tommy swallowed; I heard the ice hit the bottom of his glass. "What's that?"

"Sound is not limited to human beings. If all life were to cease, the waves of the ocean, the wind through trees, the burning of the sun, it would all still create sound. A bow across a string is natural to the universe."

"That's good," Tommy replied. "Yeah, Slick, I think you're right. Sound and maybe color as well—although I suppose color is light—light and sound. They continue to exist without life. Mightier than time. More powerful than life."

We were quiet. Tommy continued, "And we forge them into emotions—the tools and weapons of the artist."

"Yeah," I said. Lost. Feverish and comfortable. Sick and alive. Contemplative and woeful. "Light and Sound. They're like the children of mass and energy. The truths of the universe."

And in his darkened whisper, "If this even *is* a universe. Because we invented that concept as well." Even in the sharp shadows of the hotel suite, I could make out his crooked grin from across the shadowed room.

"We sound like fucking morons," I huffed before teetering into laughter.

"I think we sound pretty cool," he snickered.

Our laughter subsided. Then, another thought crept up inside of me. "But if what we think of the universe to be true—you know, spiraling out forever in every direction—then we are not the anomaly. It cannot be by mistake."

"Supposedly, yes," Tommy responded, "But that means there are infinite mimicries of you and I sitting in the same room, having the same conversation."

"How can it go on forever though? That seems impossible too—maybe space is like time," I wagered. I felt ill-equipped for such thoughts. I groaned annoyingly.

"Nothing makes sense now," I said while holding my palm to my forehead. "It's all too lofty."

"That might be the most intelligent thing you've said all night," Tommy bickered, hoisting himself with the wall as support. He crossed to the kitchenette and held the bottle of bourbon. Tommy swayed back through the room and slid down the wall beside me. He refilled my glass. He leaned his head back on the wall and made a thud. We stared across the hollowed landscape of shadow. The constant drone of calm rain sounded like the ruffle of someone turning over in bed sheets.

"The more we seek answers, the more questions will arise," Tommy said to seemingly nobody in particular. "We know so little. Everything is likely wrong. Take love for instance—that's entirely inexplicable—although we may sooner understand love than anything to do with existence."

Everything felt buzzed and rolled in numbed vibration. I blinked only to not feel it.

"So, what should we do about it then?" I asked.

Tommy scoffed; he placed his hand on my shoulder. I looked at him and caught a twinkle on his glass held out in front of me. My glass clicked against his. I watched Tommy as he held the rim to his lips. He spoke delicately, "A wise man once said to me, let's just try to enjoy it while we're here."

The following morning, we fled to Houston, Texas before sunrise. I slept through the travel, bumping and snoring on my bottom bunk while Tommy lay across from me sound asleep. We arrived in Houston at midday. Our stage set had already been erected within the magnificent 713 Music Hall. I sat in the audience with our lighting director, Travis, when Jonah approached and asked me for a moment of his time. I obliged the videographer, and together we followed the bloody exit signs and fled through the backdoors of the venue. At once, I lit a cigarette just to have something in my lungs. Houston was pale, dusted, and smothered in an obliterating heat. There I stood outside the venue in the blazing sun and squinted at little Jonah at my side. He set his *Dixie* cup of dark coffee atop a sun-faded trash bin as I hooked a pair of shades over my ears. He lit his own cigarette and stood near me with his head facing the pavement. He had black, curly hair. A crooked beak-nose pointed into a messy beard. He looked as if he hadn't eaten in days. Translucent framed glasses that dragged to a tint. He was all skin and bone, slouched over and talked with a soft Western draw. Anytime I saw him with a moment to spare, and if not a camera in his grasp, it would be a quick break with a cheap cup of coffee.

"So," I said, in an attempt to start the conversation. He was seemingly nervous, never meeting my eyes. Squinting and hiding at his feet from the white and blaring sun.

"Yeah, man. I'll just come out and say it," he started. He sniffled and scratched his nose. "You said I could leave the tour if I was hired for a camera job on a film production. And—well—I got an offer," he said, kicking the toe of his shoes on the asphalt. He cleared his throat and said, "I've had some discussions, but I'll be the B-Cam Operator about a week or so after this North American tour wraps up."

I blinked, admittedly taken aback. I asked, "A film?"

"Yeah—it's a horror film, actually. I think it's going to be a good one too."

"Who's directing?" I asked. I blew smoke, and sniffled.

"Ah—well, it's this Italian director. He's new and very young. Fresh on the scene, you know. Apparently, he's made a big name for himself in Europe. He acted in some Italian sit-coms, or something like that and decided to take a crack at directing. So, he made a few short films—but this is his first time directing a feature—and it's a Mid-Budget horror. His name is Luca Krzyżewski."

"What's it called? The movie, what is it?" I asked.

"Right now, it's called *Mass Hysteria*. That could change."

I nodded. I wasn't sure what to say. We would have to find a new videographer quickly, unless we decided to ditch our idea of chronicling the tour. I hadn't seen any of his edits up until this point, but we'd have to hire someone to replace Jonah at once.

"That's fucking awesome," I charmed, and let out a soft laugh. "I'm happy for you. I really am! You deserve this, man." My heavy grip landed on his shoulder and caused him to sway. "You're too talented to be hanging with us all the time. I still appreciate all the time we got to spend with you."

"Thanks, Joe," he started, and pinched a little grin and met my eyes. "I really appreciate that, especially coming from you." He took a drag from his cigarette and added, "I know this guy—his name's Bradley—I went to college with him. He's back out in Silver Lake, but I think he would be a perfect fit for this kind of work. I can give you his contact if you're interested."

"Yeah, absolutely. I trust your recommendation, my friend." I nodded at Jonah and expressed more praise, "This is going to be so good for you. A horror film! How exciting." I inhaled and exhaled a wraith of smoke. Jonah nodded in return but went quiet. His attention fell to the pavement once more, and a face of concern fell over him.

"How're you holding up?" Jonah asked. I was left blank by his question. While he was someone I trusted, we were not exactly close enough to tell him the honest answer at the forefront of my mind. All the sweat-wrapped nights spent getting increasingly less sleep. Befriending the crimson numbers on the hotel alarm clocks, relishing as the glow of time ticked forward. I knew my appearance was changing—there was no hiding it—sagged eyes and gray cheekbones. Instead, I provided, "I'm alright. Honestly, all of this," I motioned to the venue behind us, "It's all a bit overwhelming sometimes."

"You play it off well, my friend," said Jonah.

I put out my cigarette, scraped the end against the blacktop, flicking it in the trash. I turned to Jonah and met his eyes, albeit behind my shaded lenses. "This film you're going to work on—you think it will be any good?"

He coughed, and recovering, he nodded, "Yes. I really do." Jonah crushed and tore the cigarette butt below his shoe. He continued, "I heard about the director, Luca, back when his short films started making some noise. He's been trying to sell this script to every major studio in Hollywood. And from what I've heard about it and what little I've read, it's wild—it's bombastic—it's demented." This was the most exuberant I ever saw Jonah, creating motions with his hands as he described his picture.

"Sounds like something I'd like to see."

"I think you're going to love it. And really, I wouldn't be leaving if I was not absolutely sure—"

But I cut him off, "No, no. None of that! We had a deal, you and I. Remember our talk at that party? The one for Vivian Wells. We are artists first and foremost. We can make money, but we must always follow the path toward our art. This is why we're here and I understand you have your own path just as I have mine."

I swallowed as a shiver trickled up my spine. Was this my path? I wondered. He glanced up over his glasses. He said, "I agree. And funny you should mention Vivian Wells. She's playing our protagonist." A grin branched across his face.

"Really?" I noticed my body slouch. I became self-conscious just at the mention of her name. I adjusted my weight to the opposite leg and attempted to appear cool. I followed, "Have you talked to her?"

"Yeah, she and I went to UCLA together, so we had a bunch of film classes together. She hasn't officially signed on, but she says she's supposed to sign a contract soon. Vivian believes in this project as much as I do. It should be an interesting shoot. Lots of makeup effects, lots of night shoots. All in good fun of filmmaking though."

"I wonder how she is," I thought aloud. My imagination wandered to thoughts of the actress. Thick, clean eyebrows and straight blonde espresso hair down her back. Sharp and pointed eyes. Her high French cheekbones angled on her face. Her name grew more recognizable with each passing day as soon she would be the new princess of Hollywood.

"Why don't you ask her? You have her number, don't you?" Jonah asked.

"I think it was a burner number to get me to go to her party. I've never actually talked to her face to face," I answered, and slouched.

"It wouldn't hurt to try."

I mustered up as much of a smile as I could bear. Jonah snatched his *Dixie* cup from the trash bin and opened the door for me. Off went the shades, back into the controlled darkness, echoed floors and a familiar sickly climate. Following a corridor back to the green room, Jonah and I talked more about his film—I kept asking increasingly detailed questions to keep my brain distracted—and I wondered if I'd ever see him again. I wondered more about this Italian director, and Vivian Wells as the star—I quickly realized I had never thought of how films are made. I knew of lights and cameras and actors, but I hadn't thought much more into it. Surely, it could not be too far off from my line of work. Between conversations with Jonah and my own wandering imaginings, I found myself becoming increasingly interested in the world of film.

———

I grew jealous of my dear friend Jonah and saw his resignation as a form of escape. As the tour prevailed, languid and rhythmic as it were, and with myself at the center of the ecosystem, I gave up control of my mind. In a vicious pattern between day and night, sleep and awakeness, aching alone in a hotel room in contrast to the roars of twenty thousand screams dealt out in desire for me. I drank bottles of liquor —straight *Crown* and *Hennessy*—anything to hide my nearsighted field of thought from the terror that struck from the sharp contrast. Alone in the dark was more alone than in light. And I thought of light and sound —few of the natural productions of energy—and thought more about the band and time. Time, in its infinite spawn of paradox, dealt still in absolutes; and a promise of end, at least to life, at most to space. Time is merciless, a train without breaks, an ever-thrusting motion forward with no known way of stopping it.

Each city was a blur, somewhere I'd been before, but now without the wonder in my gaze. Buildings without roofs. Windows illuminated with tungsten glows or are vacant and shrouded in a dreadful darkness. The hollow and foreboding faces of strangers, so many faces, with one eye stretching back on me as I walked past. My nose faced the concrete as I attempted to hide my likeness to the famous body I inhabited. Caring parents called to check on me. They expressed how they loved me so much; they would often say, call us soon and we love hearing from you. Each call brought about an aching guilt. Love was found in my band members—Sophia Baker, Thomas Murtaugh, and Autumn Gladis. With my addition, we became a singular title. We were all impermanent beings of life, and of light and sound, but we existed as creators of a title destined to outlive us. Beach Sirens was nearing permanence, but I kept questioning whether or not that mattered to me.

Soft conversations with Tommy or Autumn or Sophia. These private words shared with my best friends were bound by the vibrations we generated every night, performed in places where patient minds would pay to bear witness. We talked more and more about what our lives might be like outside of the band, and the future beyond it. I never made much contribution to this talk as I felt this band—this miracle of time we spent together as one—was my life. And having to conclude in my mind that perhaps there will be a time when I am no longer synonymous with the name Beach Sirens only made me wish to be drunk again and forget about the whole thing. I recognized the irony in this.

Yes, I would rather waste a memory lying on the floor all night, skull pounding, stomach heaving, than share a beautiful experience with those I love the most. I skipped most dinners to sulk like a child. This was the push and pull—I was left nauseated. Tommy did not understand this twisted mindset but understood the part where I would get fucked up, only for Tommy it was an account of a good time. He never hesitated to indulge in a bit of substances with me if it meant we were doing it together, like brothers embarking together on a journey away from sobriety.

During our stay in Atlanta, the two of us stumbled on the streets, and staggered through dangerous regions; only we were not present enough to comprehend our unwelcomeness. We were drunk off an unknown amount of vodka and traversing in the new clothes we'd bought in the city. Small talk, nonsense. But to me, some of the best words were exchanged between us in these endless summer nights, these awesome accounts of walking through the face of fear because we'd sloshed away our understanding. Gray, fabric skies. Mud-colored buildings cut together. We walked past a *Hertz* car rental with the stringy yellow sign glowing and snakes of light bumping around it from the drag of our minds. City lights made a spectacle. College students with headphones on and minding the ground below them. The only colors were muted shades of black, beige, grays, off-whites. This was the genetic makeup of a city. Hazy fog made streetlamps echo their illumination and draw harsh edges to their fill of light, solid blocks of sodium haze, coning onto the cement. Clothing shops with the lights out—mannequins petrified and staring back at us—our reflections on the black glass cast ghostly faces over their vacant expressions.

And back in the hotel, feet propped on a side table, eyes closed and neck bent back on an armchair, we sang a refrain for a song we'd created out of improvisation. Tommy sagged across the room, cigarette between his fingers moving along the frets of an acoustic guitar, strumming out a cool tone of string-hums in the congested room. Only a dust-clumped lamp beside the bed haloing any sort of light, over half of his face, he strummed along, head slightly bobbing while I sang the words that came to mind.

Break of dawn for the callused days,
The sun over the city sports a red haze.
I'm on the road, calling a cabbie a taxi.
He curbs the sidewalk; I fall in the backseat,
He turns up the radio and turns up the street.
I blink and I recognize the melodies.

I shout and hit the glass to say, 'Hey, that's me!'
On the radio, he squints; barks, 'Quiet down!'
I slump in the seat and begin to frown;
He turns the volume to mute my sounds
So I called out to him to just let me out.
Cabbie squeezes and puckers, begins to pout,
'But, my friend, this is Fourth and Columbian.'
He stumbles and mumbles something in Mandarin.
I whisper out curses, lining with adrenaline,
So I unbuckle and lunge myself
Out of the cab and toward pedestrians.
There, on the corner I lie on my back
Only to hear to my right that pale, dull crack!
All I could see was sky like an ugly cement
Before I close my eyes and start a descent
But screams and hollers keep me awry
For I see to the right that canary car die!
The cabbie I called a taxi wore a red spleen
And by God, I can't believe it,
From my pricked ears and vision torn,
My song blared out that crooked machine,
And I was singing to watch it burn.

The song was recorded on my phone, etched into time with a digital replication of our new sound. We decided to name the track *Denim Dogs*. I found this on my phone the following morning with no memory of when we'd decided on a name. But listening back, the lulling drone of the air conditioning, the truth in the scratch of his fingers moving between frets, and my charred throat dry as sand against skin, there was a near-nostalgic, comfort to the sound of the recording. This method of creating songs was usual in our infancy as a band but now had nearly gone extinct due to pressures of studios and formulas for radio-pops that brought smiles to listeners and executives. But this was honest—and more, I felt, existed outside of Beach Sirens—it was a creation of two friends at a moment in time, when all felt lost, and yet they found themselves together to create something out of beauty to express the emotions sparking around their brains. Two friends—two brothers, as far as I was concerned—with everything gained and everything still to lose. And what joy this realization could bring with a guitar and a rhyme.

We never spoke of it that night in Atlanta but we both knew we were leaning on one another to stay afloat. This contradiction of wishing to make music rather than tour it, and to run amok like young boys, but also to shield the gnawing reality; we don't know how to do much else. And the horror this can bring to a person, that if this one Hell I have conquered is taken away from me, the rest of the world will become worse. It became a self-induced prison sentence. But staring into his alcohol-rinsed eyes, I saw he felt the same way without ever having to say a word. His guitar was just as brilliant as his theories of the universe and oftentimes spoke for him. And the tour pushed on still, the beat of illogical time, the power it held to age us at the rate we'd chosen. In the relentless blur, that self-induced pattern of there but never there, and pushing back against knowing this time was meant to be enjoyed rather than squandered. This was all happening but none of it was happening.

My parents were in attendance at the Atlanta show. With the buzzing echo of my voice from the sound system, I dedicated a song to them near the close of the show. Cameras cut to their faces, smiling and shy in their private booth. I turned back to watch the screen. My own two parents—my father with his arm around my mother—ten feet tall and glittering on diamond LCD screens. Their faces turning in, a tear rolling across my mother's cheek as the crowd of twenty thousand voices applauded her and my father. This was the image I remember most of my parents. Two simple people living in the quaint town of Athens, Georgia—faces made out of joy itself—but I saw their hidden terror and confusion with the chant of thousands directed onto them. I thought to myself with trembling knuckles, *See? This is what it feels like*, as if it were their fault. I knew they were unsure how I'd gotten to this point in my life as the screens burned giant projections of their faces. I saw how they felt, an expression only visible to a child who grew up learning their faces; I saw the intense realization of just how mad all of this was. In turn, like a gunshot to the head, I locked into acquaintance with my own madness.

———

Jonah stayed on for the rest of the American tour. We hired his recommendation, Bradley Barton, a clean faced kid from UCLA with big ambitions but even bigger hair. Black frizzy dreadlocks and thick-rimmed glasses. It came as no surprise when I asked who his favorite artist was, he replied with Jean-Michel Basquiat. He would fit right in with our production team; a great addition when we landed in London that October. London was our first stop in Europe, playing at the O2 Arena. That was only a mere two months away at the time; it was the birth of August and I was packing my belongings in my Seattle room. Between swigs of white wine, I remembered what Jonah mentioned about Vivian Wells taking the lead role in the horror film. I searched her name on my phone and found an article posted ten days ago with the headline: *'Mass Hysteria' Finds Its Lead with Vivian Wells*. A few taps along the phone screen and I found her name and number in my contact list.

I typed out a text—backspaced—typed out a new, and read it over a handful of times. I touched my thumb to the screen. Message delivered. I rid of my phone and heard it thumping across the white bedding. My mouth fit around the wine bottle so I took a queasy gulp. Once my room was fully packed, my suitcase neatly prepared, sheets piled on the floor, buzzed and forehead tapped in sweat, I checked my phone again only to find my lonesome text awaiting a response:

At once I had thought it cheeky or even charming but reading it again, I thought it could be taken aggressively. I went pale in the face and light in the head. Hal helped me into the bus as we headed toward Boise. It would be several wretched hours later when my phone let out a cry. We were all on the bus, staring through tinted glass at tall white windmills clocking in the distance. I walked back to my bunk and unplugged my phone to discover a notification from Vivian Wells. My face shimmered as I read over the LCD words sizzled on the screen:

> Jonah!! What? We can share his talents, can't we?
> Besides, I'm just playing a part in the movie :)

I frantically crossed my fingers around the screen to form a quick reply but hesitated to send a message back with such immediacy. I instead waited to hit send until nearly half an hour later. This way of communication continued back and forth for the next couple of days while I sang on stages in the American northwest and Vivian went about rehearsing her lines. The day I texted her, she had just wrapped up her final press interview for her most recent movie, *Brand New Color*. The film was a World War II period drama surrounding the life of Josephine Baker—played by Mona Gretchfield. Baker was a black French singer and dancer during this period and, as the story goes, enamored the Nazis with her beauty so much, Baker was granted access into Germany. While she was a famed dancer in Paris, she was a spy for France. She took note of German military secrets and strategies in her sheet music. She did so by the use of invisible ink and success-fully smuggled these plans back to the Allied Powers, in turn helping defeat the Nazis. While Gretchfield portrayed the titular Baker, Vivian Wells played her adoptive daughter, Stellina Baker, who recounts the story of her mother in the opening and closing scenes of the film.

Brand New Color was set to come out that September, also when pre-production would begin on her next film, *Mass Hysteria*. This film would be her fifth feature, her second time as the protagonist, and her second horror film (following *They Do Not Grow Old* respectively). It was only after *They Do Not Grow Old* and *Sloane's Gotta Go* that Vivian began to get the attention she deserved. She was emerging as a name everyone knew, and I could not help but feel a connection with her. Did she also stay awake at night, afraid to walk down the street and buy cheap dinner? She was a genuine Hollywood Star, among the vogue of cinema at twenty-six years old, and never caught looking anything short of glamorous. Yet she liked to do horror films; I quite enjoyed the genre and suddenly my thoughts of her grew increasingly fond. And as the days and shows dragged by, I became closer and closer to her through my phone screen. We were the same age, and both of us artists fell into a world of tremendous fame. We both were still learning how to navigate and deal with such a craze. One night, while at a private dinner with the band, Autumn questioned my newfound infatuation with my mobile phone.

"You've been smiling down between your legs all night, Joe," Autumn started. "I'm well versed in what's down there and it isn't much to smile about."

We were seated in a private room at a restaurant, *Portland City Grill*, in Portland, Oregon. Hal reserved the room for us that same morning and now the lot of us were to enjoy a nice evening together but it seemed I had been spending too much time staring at the phone screen. Autumn was to my right—to my left sat Hal, and the rest of the way around the table, Ant, Tommy, Sophia.

"I'm texting Vivian Wells," I whispered, rolling my eyes. Autumn's face lit up with immense shock. I didn't have to keep a low profile, but I kept my voice low enough that perhaps only Autumn would hear.

"The actress? Like, Vivian Wells from *Sloane's Gotta Go? That* Vivian Wells? How'd you even get her number?" She asked, greatly intrigued, practically bouncing in her seat. She seemed to know I was trying to keep the ordeal quiet because she scooted her chair closer to mine, causing a series of high shrieks against the floor. I caught whiffs of her hairspray and noticed her pearl earrings for the occasion. Her chin rubbed into my shoulder as she attempted to read my messages.

"I went to her birthday party two years ago—going on two years," I explained. Autumn looked so lovely that evening; I could tell she put a lot of effort into herself. Black dress fit to her figure, the pearls, a golden bracelet of a serpent wrapped triple around her wrist.

"And you're talking to her?"

"Well, yeah," I huffed and glanced around the table. Hal and Ant were deep in conversation, as were Tommy and Sophia; the anxieties lightened. As if I were engaged in some criminal act, I hadn't wanted Sophia to know I was talking to Vivian.

"Yes, but, you're *talking*-talking," Autumn said, and she lifted her head. She smiled knowingly, only inches from my face. I debated taking hold of her hand and walking her to the restroom for a go right then. Yet I held restraint as it was a quite nice dinner. This sort of thing used to happen exclusively with Sophia, and Autumn with Tommy, but things had changed—as Sophia had been in a relationship for two years and Tommy remained a complete mystery. For the last six months, I had only had sex with Autumn Gladis. I thought Autumn would be a bit taken aback by Vivian, but she seemed more enthralled by my ability to even talk to her.

"I guess you could say that," I added in a hushed voice. "I'm not really sure where it's going to go just yet."

"Please invite her to a show, Joey! *Please*! I want to be her friend so bad," Autumn urged. Her brows turned up in a near worrisome expression.

"Alright, alright, I will," I agreed. Then I moved close, narrowly missing her cheek, and brushed my nose into her rusty hair. I whispered, "But it's a secret."

Autumn grinned and leaned back in her seat. She pinched her thumb and forefinger together over the edge of her lips, and zipped them shut, completed with a wink. I glanced across the table and noticed Sophia glancing back. She quickly diverted her attention back to Tommy as if nothing had happened. I wondered if she heard any of the conversation or if she saw my closeness with Autumn. To my surprise, Autumn kept the secret, although it wasn't long before everyone learned of my attachment to Vivian. I kept my end of the deal with Autumn and invited Vivian to visit one of our shows between her rehearsals for *Mass Hysteria*. She agreed. Vivian drove out from Los Angeles to attend our show in Glendale, Arizona where she and I would meet for the very first time.

———

I made sure to reserve her a backstage pass. The hours crept by before our show at the Desert Diamond Arena. I grew anxious and my nerves flexed below my kneecaps, under my fingernails and in my ribs. I drank two bottles of Oregon-pressed Merlot, one right after the other while waiting for Vivian to arrive. As everything began to blur and my steps declined to a shuffle, I crawled out of the green room, and sauntered down the hall and toward backstage. As soon as I came to stand behind the curtain, I caught sight of a figure marching toward me. I glanced to make out the stranger, and it was Vivian Wells, powering through the shadowy aisle of black and chromatic trunk cases. She stepped over taped cables and approached me with an extended hand.

"Hey," she said, looking up at me. An unaffected soprano ring. I accepted her hand and shook it lightly.

"Hi," I peeped. I examined her in a prompt once over. Her high-pinned smile revealed perfect teeth. Her brunette hair waved down her back. She wore a white Beach Sirens t-shirt though seemingly tailored into a crop top, paired with a black leather skirt and boots to match. Sophia glanced between her and me in the wings of the stage and I felt an ashamed pinch in my throat. Autumn smirked with her weight pressed into one leg before returning to a conversation with Ant. I found Tommy passing through, and upon registering who I was with, he raised his eyebrows at me. I motioned for Vivian to follow me somewhere more private; at least somewhere without so many of my friends' curious inspections.

She and I hung around the green room as our opener, Lola Pop, took to the stage. I was used to being drunk by this point in the tour and had a decent grasp on myself; my confidence, of course, was higher than ever before. I walked and talked with a loose swagger akin to the rockstar aesthetic. A wild and constant bass beat heavily from the stage; it caused muffled thumps to vibrate the walls of the green room. Lola Kalili was a brilliant artist, a twenty year old with a special ear for the Alternative Hyper Pop genre. I grinned at Vivian while I leaned against a vanity and we both tried to ignore the vibrations on the walls. I continued looking her over as she was quite beautiful, and she giggled on an olive suede sofa.

"What?" she asked nervously.

"Nothing," I replied.

"No, don't give me that! It can't be nothing, it's never nothing."

I chewed on a toothpick between my molars. I pushed off from the vanity and stood up straight. "Well, if I'm being honest—You're shorter than I was expecting."

"Oh," she chirped, politely taken aback, "Is that a bad thing?" She shrank into herself as a wave of self-consciousness weighed on her body. I was quick to pour a chuckle, so as to reveal my tease.

"No! Not bad. It's just a thing. You look so big up on the movie screen."

"Most actors do."

She leaned her chin onto a balled fist and slouched over her lap. She spaced out on the frosted cement walls. I pulled a chair around from in front of the vanity, a director's chair with wooden legs and arms.

"Have you been to Arizona before?" I questioned as I fell back in the chair.

"I haven't. This place is so beautiful though—I love the architecture—very unique. I thought about studying architecture when I was going to pick a major. But I decided not to go to college at the last second, and did what I'd done since I was a kid."

"You've been acting since you were young then?" I asked.

She smirked. "I've been acting since I could speak. My mom is an actress—you probably know her—Nora Spencer?"

"Yeah—yeah! I know her!" I exclaimed. I hadn't known many actors, and could rarely put a name to a face. But I had known of her mother. Nora Spencer was a darling starlet of romance films some thirty years prior. Nora Spencer was among the likenesses of Meg Ryan and Julia Roberts. I paused a fraction of a second, taken aback by the connection to the famous actress. "No shit? Wow."

"Yeah," her voice fell apart. And the room went quiet for a moment. She flashed a big grin and asked, "So, what about you? What do your parents do?"

"My mom certainly isn't an actress, not by any means. My mom is a middle school teacher."

"Really? What subject?" asked Vivian, perking up on the sofa.

"Social Studies—she's pretty incredible at it—*Mrs. Henley*."

Vivian flickered a smile, her eyes fluttered. "And your dad—what does he do?"

"He sells cars," I snickered. I rose from the director's chair and started back toward the vanity.

"So, he's a smooth talker. Could he sell me a car?"

"If you're ever in Athens, Georgia, you bet he could. Do you smoke?" I asked and picked a red and white pack from the vanity, no larger than a box of cards. I stuffed one of the paper sticks on my lips and fingered my pleated trousers for my lighter.

"Oh—No, thank you. I don't," she answered and turned in shyly.

"Right," I said. The lighter clicked shut and returned to my pocket. I tucked the cigarette into my breast pocket and asked, "But you drink, yes? White wine, perhaps." I moved toward the Merlot on the coffee table.

"Yes, occasionally," she hummed highly and flashed her brilliantly white teeth. I poured a glass for each of us.

I asked, "Are you excited for this new movie?"

She accepted the glass and slumped into the sofa with an exaggerated groan, her eyes rolled and hung at the ceiling. I blinked, unsure what had happened until she sighed audibly.

"I'm just ready to get *going* already! See, there's this awkward time between signing onto a project and when we actually start filming that fills me with such anxiety—I can hardly stand it—it's unbearable. Everyone knows I'm going to be in the movie, and they start to preconceive in their heads what I might act like! I just keep working on my character until I start to forget who I am."

"Jesus," I mumbled, then more audibly, "So, are you Vivian now?"

"Yes, I think so."

"You *think* so."

Her dimpled smile took shape on her face again. By this point in our meeting, I was really beginning to enjoy its presence. I watched her as she thought quietly; she wore much of her emotion on her face.

"I can't know for sure. Who is *anyone* really?" she sighed.

"I know the feeling," I said and took a sinking drag of bloody wine. The wine went down easy as honey but stung like thorns.

"Do you enjoy acting?" she asked.

"I've never tried it."

This caused her to break into a giggling spirit; I tried to decipher if it was earnest or not. She chuckled out, "Oh, *please*."

"What?"

She smacked her tongue to her teeth and replied, "You may not be in movies but take a look around! You have your own green room, just like I would on a movie set—except yours is much nicer—all things considered. And you perform on stages! You have cues and stage directions, lines to learn and such. And rehearsals, rehearsals, rehearsals. So don't think I don't see it, you're not the same person on that stage as the man standing in front of me."

"Is that a bad thing?" I asked, rubbing my chin.

"It's just a thing," she charmed, followed by more giggling. I noticed then just how often she liked to laugh. Her joy was contagious, and it was this moment when I felt a distinct shift in my body. This smiling girl looking back at me caused a tingling warmth in my chest. My breath tightened; my heart throbbed. I rounded the coffee table, wine glass in hand and pressed into the sofa beside her. She watched me intimately. Her sharp eyes radiated a wash of complexity, the equivalent of burnished copper.

"I like the sound of your voice," I heard myself say, "It's very nice on the ears. Has anyone ever told you that?"

I wasn't expecting her to blush. She said, "Luca tells me all the time that I have a good voice. Great for character."

"That's the director of the new movie, yeah?"

She nodded, never taking her eyes off mine. Her body shifted more toward mine. "Yes. And he's such a lovely man. A wonderful artist, too! He's such an inquisitive mind and, you know, he's only a few years older than we are. I believe he recently turned thirty-one. But I think you two would get along great. Maybe when we get started with filming you can stop by our set!"

"I would love that," I replied. I felt the muscles in my cheeks beginning to ache from the constant smiling. She adjusted away from me then and took a robotic swig from her glass. She glared at her boots.

"What?" I questioned, and a fear prickled through my body.

"It's nothing," Vivian said.

"I can't be nothing, it's never nothing."

She huffed. She turned her head, but it hung low, staring at my side. She muttered, "I don't know how you did it, but I already like you."

"Is this Vivian talking?" I asked. Her eyes met mine.

"Tonight, I am Vivian," she grinned.

I chuckled. "If it makes you feel any better, I feel the same way about you."

Before I knew what I was doing, my hand on the back of the sofa had moved away and fell beneath her chin. My fingers slid along her jawline and parted around her ear. Her eager stare refused to break for even a moment. We were silent, hearts pounding and patient. I swallowed. I started toward her; Vivian followed. The press of her lips began intense and fell into a tender movement. I followed her swaying motions until we became attuned to one another. My heart felt frothy, and my cheeks flooded with a brilliant heat.

When our lips parted, my desire for her had reached profound heights. I softly bit at her bottom lip and a shivered wave of her breath fell into my mouth. Then we broke away and quietly, we learned each other's features.

"I think I just found my Romeo," she breathed, the words blowing from her mouth. Vivian giggled; I rubbed my thumb over the dimple of her grin. The immense fear and attraction that grew together in my chest was a sensation that could only be described as falling.

VIII

ATRO CITY

Back in my apartment, I sat huddled against the side of my bed. Short breaths huffed in and out of my chest. The following night was the 19th of August or, as my schedule referred to it, our show at the Hollywood Bowl. It was the end of the tour until the international leg began, the first show performed in London's O2 Arena at the dawn of October. It was nearly fall again— so soon had the summer gone. How had I let another summer slip through my grasp? I tried to recount memories I'd made through the year but nothing of any note came to mind, instead, I winced at the recounts of drug binges and panic attacks—the only constants to my life—besides the fresh sheets on a different bed every other night. In an attempt to combat the aching sensations of my heart's downbeats, I recalled the memories I had that worked as an antidote, those loving memories from the days back in D.C.

I focused on the flickering images of Tommy and I sitting beside each other on the floor of our old apartment, twisting knobs, and messing with the creation and reconfiguration of sound. Back then, if we couldn't find the precise sound we were searching for, we'd record our voices and morph them into the monstrous noise only available in our heads. We were blasphemous, carefree, and wonderful. I would exit my bedroom in a California-Sober daze, at hazeled sunrise, to discover Tommy propped up on one elbow, asleep on the sofa with a guitar spread across his body; six or more beer bottles and a collection of bongs created a topographical cityscape in a unique, almost high-art chic. Back then, we could throw a song together in a night, slap a title on it, and forget about it. So many songs still in our inventory from those days and all quite good—*Armadillo, Backpack Race, The Cassavette Children, Blood Ranger, Peeping God, White Philanthropist, Bedtime Stories, Train Dreams*—The library of unreleased songs grew to outlandish proportions, well over two hundred tracks.

And on occasion, while visiting Autumn and Sophia's apartment, nearing on morning and still thumping around, we would all find ourselves grooving to some new tune made on the computer or we would attempt to replicate fundamental elements from other genres. I distinctly recall a party in D.C. where the entry fee was taking three shots of vodka in a single swallow. Once inside, music blared with 808 growls. The congestion of smoke created an ocean of fog, enough to cause the guests to appear as dark shapes at a distance. Drunk girls without tops or glitter-caked eyelids slurred questions about what it's like to be in a band. I'd spot my friends somewhere else in the apartment blurring their minds, and join them in a sleazy quest of self annihilation. There was one party in particular in which I awoke on a futon to find myself staring back at a baby, who himself slumped cross-legged and trilled out his own songs from across the sea of sleeping bodies. The party was thrown by Joseph Randolph or as everyone called him, Black Joe, and I was in turn referred to as White Joe to help differentiate. His girlfriend was a scrawny, round-faced girl with long blonde hair named Andie—I never bothered to learn her last name—she was from Houston, accent and all, and I was always blown away by how in love these two used to be. And still are, as I heard later they got married and now have a family in Virginia. Black Joe was a real close friend of Tommy and me as well as a remarkable acrylic painter. All of his paintings were mostly hand drawn artworks, frosted over with blotches of thick paint. His art reminded me of France in a way but of the dessert in another.

The memories were a dying flame, a brittle mask in the foreground of my veins beating to death. And as the tears sank to my jaw, I thought about giving up for the first time in my life. Not just giving up on the band but life and the overwhelming nature of consciousness. I convinced myself that my art was subpar, at best decent, and I would never truly create anything masterful or definitive, especially due to my methods of songwriting. *What is masterful?* Is a masterpiece something that lives on for ten lifetimes after your own? Does that equate to true permanence in the world of art? Nothing about my life was permanent; everything that lives at this moment is but strands of rope rubbing thinner with each passing day until one day everyone will move on. Perhaps what we consider to be masterful—whatever legendary pieces of art come to mind—was a result of an artist long ago, who only needed to pass some time or feed themself.

I did, however, notice the clear irony of the situation, as I had no greater fear than that of dying with unfinished work to do—this is a direct conflict with my notion of giving up art and life as a whole. The gnawing voice in my head urged me to get up and continue the relentless wheel of pumping music from my mind to my fingertips. Translations. The connection of my throbbing brain to the keys kicking delicate pings—another form of neurotransmission. To cast an idea from my mind unto the movement of my pen was to cast lightning from a stormed cloud unto a metal rod.

I wanted urgently to lift my head from the edge of my mattress and find myself at my piano to explore these concepts, but instead, I was frozen still. I felt glued to that spot in my bedroom, my back against the bedside, staring at the dust-coated, wood flooring and the shadowed cutout of my bathroom. I could stare at my phone—I could scroll through videos from fans captured from the tour—I could watch content about anything in the world—I could read about the next year's election or watch people having sex or watch an episode of television or dabble in internet conspiracies—I could pile up the information in my head and scroll past countless photos of friends and strangers alike.

I felt nauseous then. After two hours of persistent phone usage, everything grew out of control; my skull invented a sensation akin to implosion. It was this paradoxical trigger that propelled me off the floor and so completely spring-loaded that I hurdled forward. I caught myself with my palms slapping the wall and a dull thud echoed around my muted apartment. Now, as I was up and on my feet, my entire peripheral shifted white from the even spread of cloud-colored paint. I felt the sturdiness of the structure. The wall was coarse, but the paint created an illusion of silk. It was enough to remind me of the physical world and ground me back in reality. I stood there for a long time tracing my fingertips over the wall—the minuscule, uneven textures—soft and honest like skin. I kept reminding myself over and over that being alive was enough; I shouldn't worry about the outlying constructs or the infinite possibilities of life. *I am here*, I thought, *as is this wall, and together we are here and touching*. That is enough.

A droning hum grew and shrank from the speakers at the front of the stage; it was low, nearly a growl, and though it seemed infinite, there was a certain anticipation that stretched from the sound. A building toward resolution. I stood center with Tommy to my right and Sophia to my left. I turned to face Autumn behind us, silhouetted on the black riser, adjusting her stool. The crowd wailed a ripple of screams, thunder, and cheers. The tempo started its tick. Everything in its right place. I cracked my neck side to side and the earpiece didn't even budge. Instinct. On the downbeat I became possessed and snapped back in character—dancing, leaping about, sprinting back and forth across the stage, a crazed pendulum—the Hollywood Bowl. Fog machines yawned waves of clouds, turning our lights to beams, and struck them out over the crowd. Rows and rows of faces stood in front of their seats, moving in time with the music, and creating a tangible energy in the outdoor venue.

A few tracks into our set, the energy refused to die. My heart kicked against my ribs, I turned to Tommy and found myself unable to contain my grin. He returned the smile, and in that moment of shredded innocence, I felt childlike and comfortable. We hadn't been this happy together on stage in a very long time. It was the last night of the North American tour and I wanted to go out on a high note. Perched at my piano, my hands rested in their natural positions. Ticks of water flecked and clung to the black and white keys, as up in the sky was a coming rain, with threaded droplets racing onto the stage. And out at the crowd, the silver strings scattered over the endless ocean of bodies. But I continued to smile. For the first time, I felt like nature was present with us, attending and adding its own flare to the show. I pressed into the keys and sang into the next song just as my hair began to drip and crawl with beads of water.

Everyone attended the show at the Hollywood Bowl. Daniel Cavansky, Sophia's boyfriend, was out there, somewhere amongst the crowd. A handful of notable film actors, peers in the industry, celebrities, and friends of friends. Vivian was notably absent from this show as she was busy with rehearsals for the approaching film production. And yet, with an army of phone cameras pointed up at me, I thought perhaps she might find a clip from the show online—with her on my mind, and myself on the stage, there was a sudden shift in my composure.

I climbed on a speaker and ripped off my dress shirt, no longer white, but rather transparent and soaked, revealing my skin anyway. The crowd lost their minds, ballistic and I traced my steps back to my microphone—my spotlight faded out—Sophia became shrouded in a splintered gold. She switched her bass for an acoustic guitar. She stepped forward and sang into her microphone, far enough away from me to be on her own, close enough that I could take in all of her features. Her black lace shirt rippled in the chopping wind; her black lipstick would smear the mic if she were any closer to the microphone. Her eyebrows slanted up as she sang with closed eyes. And her words —her precious words—echoed out onto a crowd of nearly twenty thousand people. But she looked so alone there under her light as if she were telling a secret to herself. I commonly thought that perhaps Sophia should have been the full lead singer of the band, the band she started, and I should be the one pushed to the left of stage. She was the one who came up with the name Beach Sirens. Sophia had the care and the leadership for the band that I simply did not wield. And yet, here she was, capturing the attention of thousands of ears and eyes, allowing herself to be seen.

I turned to Autumn as Sophia sang her ballad, and when she caught my gaze, she smiled back at me. Her teeth flashed with genuine joy. I tried to hold this image of her in my head, as if I could focus so immensely that it would burn into memory. Even now, looking back, this image—like all memories seem to do—loses its details and begins to fade. But an overwhelming sense of gratitude sank through my body. I turned back to the crowd and saw them all swaying to Sophia's calming voice and strums. I thought of how many nights I spent in total disregard to these intimacies. I disregarded fans who loved our band, and the band as a whole. I took a real one in a billion opportunity for granted. Without all the swaying bodies, we'd still be broke and working dingy jobs, music on the sidelines of our lives. Maybe we'd have split ways by now and thought up new plans for how to get by.

The crowd at the Bowl was the best we'd ever had. Their energy was better than any drug I'd ever put in my body. Between songs, around the halfway point, I stretched and my thoughts began to pile inside of me. I didn't want to take this moment for granted. *The end of the tour*, I thought, as I focused myself. I bit my cheek until it began to bleed. This epiphany of my luck and my appreciation for all that surrounded me was cause for celebration. In a split-second decision, I leaned in, pulled the mic from the stand and stepped toward the apron.

"How is everyone? Are we still doing alright?" I asked. A thunder of screams. Vibrating thumps from Autumn's kick. The waves of sound clattered in my chest. "Right, well, good. Your energy is fucking fantastic—I hope you all know that." More screams followed; arms extended with open palms; their hands clawed the air in an attempt to grab hold of me.

"Listen, listen—I want to get real with you all for a second— We've been touring now for the last five months, give or take, and it's been an absolute pleasure. I will admit to you all though—" I paused. The mic fell to my side, gripped tight in my hand as the wind skid across my face. Dark skies and silent rain. Cold strands of black hair rippled across my vision. I thought to myself, *I am alive and this is happening*. Then I thought it over again. Such an obvious thought that can become lost in a world of privilege and great indulgence. The mic returned to my lips. Water slipped off my nose.

"I will admit this tour has not been easy for me. I've had frequent panic attacks, spending long nights awake and alone, wondering if anyone is still listening to the music we make. You know, massive success will do that. I couldn't stop asking myself, 'Is this fame? Is this really what I want?' There's a lot of pressure to create the right piece of art for your audience once you get to this point," I paused once more as the crowd broke out in verbal condolence; many voices shouted out, '*No, no!*'

"Where I am, there's more walls put up around your freedoms as an artist. And I became unhappy. *Very* unhappy. To the point I thought—I don't know, maybe life isn't worth living," I said, and my voice choked. I dragged the silence. The faces of fans stared back at me for an urgent resolution. A few scattered phone lights dotted the audience. I cleared my throat, "And, you know, I look at these three next to me on this stage and—there's no other way to say it, they're my family. I love them. They are undoubtedly my best friends in the world. I can't quit out on this because that means quitting on spending time with the people I love the most and you just don't do that.

"So, I pushed through, I wore the nice clothes and wore the nice smile, and now I've made it back home. That's what a grown up does when faced with a difficult task. But still, I keep wondering if this is all there is to it—I wonder if this is the peak—I wonder if there is anywhere else to go from here. Maybe we're scratching the ceiling. And I would look in the mirror before every show to ask myself, 'Do I look happy?' And now, I stand before all of you and ask—*Do I look happy?*"

There was a visible discomfort across the audience. A few speckled replies yelled out in answer to the question. The rain slithered down my back. Everyone began looking at each other. I had created a mass confusion. They were visibly startled.

"I don't want there to be any barrier between us," I began, and a hand fell on my shoulder. Sophia looked up at me with wet black hair and a worried expression, "Joe, c'mon, let's keep playing."

"No," I said, accidentally into the mic and glanced back at the crowd as a wire of embarrassment bent through my legs. Sophia took a step back. I cleared my throat and filled my lungs with the copper-scented air. "I want you all to know how I'm feeling because I think it's important for you all to know. It's real and I believe relationships are built on trust. There's a lot of pressure for the performer to be happy, and energetic, and give you all the performance you paid to see. I mean, some of you have been camping outside since last night," I said merrily.

The young women along the barrier front row nodded. "You!" I exclaimed, "Yeah, you guys, that's fucking *unreal* to me. Kudos to you all. People are *sleeping outside* of venues to see us perform. It's fucking surreal. As many of you know, this whole lifestyle of fame and success is still new to the four of us. It can be fucking exhausting at times—so I found myself getting lost in the travel and stress of making sure everything goes alright. Do you get what I'm saying?"

I lowered the mic a second time, this time trying to gather my thoughts. I scrubbed a hand over my mouth. I noticed in the far distance a group of bodies close and discussing in the control booth. "Alright, alright—I'm getting to the point. The point is, I'm no different from any one of you. I have a job and I stress too much about it sometimes. I get sad and overwhelmed. And, while I'm being honest, I procrastinate cleaning my apartment too! Not that I have that much to begin with but I'm *human*. We all are. And tonight, I realized—while up on this stage—we're human beings who've come together to take a break from the overbearing shit in our lives and have a good time. So, I say fuck it to the logistics of the show, and the stress of making sure this machine is well-oiled. Tonight, if you all don't mind, I want to have a bit of fun with you guys. Is that alright?"

The crowd was louder than ever, claps and whistles and throat-scratching screams of reassurance. "And, hey," I started, the crowd slowly decreasing in volume, "I want you all to know, tonight has not only been one of the best shows of my career, but one of the best nights of my life. So, thank you all for being here. We wouldn't be here without you. We're not going anywhere either. We're Beach Sirens, the best band *in the fucking world*!"

And I spread my arms out wide, my head tilted up at the sky as freckles of storm colored my face. The shouts and approving hollers washed my body like a trip of ecstasy. The exhilaration was a shot of confidence, and as I circled back to the mic stand, a guitar strapped across my bare chest and pick laced between my fingers, I kept my eyes low on the crowd, "Let's have some fun then."

"What the *fuck* was that?"

Ant slammed the door back on its hinges, a loud metallic slap as the door handle crushed against the back wall of the green room. A great jolt caused my body to flinch, eyes fluttering and body wilting. Ant stormed through the room, shoving boxes and trinkets out of his way as his massive body barreled toward me. He halted in front me at the vanity and huffed air, with a weaponized finger in my face.

"You think this is a free therapy session for you? You think you can just say anything you fucking feel like while you're up on that stage?" I stole tiny glances at the rest of the band, just as wide-eyed and filled with terror as I was. As the door ached back toward the frame, a small body squeezed through just before it shut. It was Tiegan, our social media manager. She tried to pop her head around Ant's hulking appearance, shouting minuscule peeps toward us before he finally swiveled around and looked down at her.

"Hey," she squeaked. She wore a messy acorn bun. Round rimmed glasses. Septum piercing. She continued, "Before you murder our lead singer, I thought you should know, right now, his is the highest trending name in the world. Beach Sirens is topping the trending pages too. And it's all positive."

"What? What? What are you saying?" Ant grumbled, his face was a violent red. He was still in a mode of attack; my least favorite version of the man. He turned to meet shoulder-to-shoulder with Tiegan and peered over as she scrolled through her phone. I was eternally thankful for her stepping in at the last second and possibly saving my life. I was silent and allowed his mind to be changed. He growled after a moment and turned back to me. "You're on thin fucking ice, you understand me?"

"Hey—I thought it was appropriate. No, really! You know, letting the fans in on some truth about me," I said in my defense. Far too long I'd been viewed as some sort of God. When all anyone sees of a person is through video clips online and photos from performances, an aspect of humanity is lost. I added, "I dunno, I thought it was sort of important for them to know what's going on."

"You don't get to go up on stage and tell a crowd of twenty thousand people that you're suicidal. You just don't." His gray eyes were weighted behind his round glasses like two orbed fishing sinkers.

"Twenty thousand sounds a little off. How many views does that video have, Tiegan?"

Ant took a honking step forward, close to my face with a forceful finger at my chest. He warned, "Stop it. You don't even have social media, Joe, why are you so suddenly concerned with connecting with your audience?"

"I could have social media," I said.

"Would you like one?" Tiegan piped in. I shook my head with a face that said, *now is not the time*. But I quickly returned to Ant, "Look, I'm failing to see the issue here. I haven't done anything new. Why would I not want to connect with my audience?"

"When you're on that stage, I don't want you to be Joe Henley. I want you to be Joe Henley, the lead singer from Beach Sirens. Copy? I don't want you to bring up how hard it's been for you mentally. The last thing your fans need on their plate is to know you're fucking sad —and they sure as Hell don't need to worry about whether or not their favorite artist is going to kill himself. You think *your* life is hard? Really? If your life is so awful, maybe you'd be better off institutionalized, *huh*? Look at me, Joe."

I turned away from him with my head shaking in disagreement. I wanted to breathe smoke. My fingernails clenched so deep into my palm, I could feel the skin ready to break.

"Hey," he said. And a gentle hand on my shoulder. "Joey, you know I always want what's best for you—that goes for all of you—that's what I'm here for. It's my job to be stern with you so we can continue this journey. But you got lucky with this one, kid. It could have just as easily been spun into a story of a pretentious celebrity crying on stage. Does that make sense?"

His new approach of kindness made me feel vulnerable and I understood what he was getting at. I nodded. It was a confirmation that I would have to keep playing the character; a parody of myself. There was me and there was the man on the stage. All the enchantment of the night's show was replaced with a dull heaviness resting on my throat and chest. I hung my head low, taps of water jumped from my strands to the floor. A weighted quiet floated in the room like a thick dust. Ant cleared his throat.

"I apologize to you all. Go ahead and change and I'll meet you all outside." He opened the door lightly upon his exit, and he took notice of the dent in the wall from the handle whacking into it. Ant placed his hand on Tiegan's shoulder and led her out. I felt my cheeks turn warm like an electric stove. My eyes quivered with tears damming on the lids. I slid out of my chair and sniffled. I tugged the towel from around my waist and ruffled it loosely in my hair. It was mostly a way to hide my face as I started to cry.

"What a fucking prick," Autumn cursed and crossed her arms.

"Joe," Sophia said, and she stood in front of me. She muttered, "I thought it was pretty cool what you did tonight."

I forced a grin. Autumn stepped in front of me and rested her hand on my shoulder. "Fuck him. We're never going to be mad at you for telling us how you feel."

I nodded, I leaned my forehead on the waist of Autumn's pants.

Her hand ran up and across the back of my head. Her touch was comfortable and motherly, and all at once I felt a familiar love for her. My love toward all of them—Autumn and Tommy and Sophia—was perhaps the strongest effort of care in my heart. It was equally my greatest fear, that of losing them someday to the responsibilities of life. Something shifted, my breath caught in my lungs, and my tears could no longer hold on. I cried softly into her side as she rubbed the back of my head. Sophia and Tommy scooted their chairs closer and consoled with just a hand on my knee or for Tommy, a strong hand on my shoulder. My best friends were there, as they always had been for me. When we were together, four became one.

———

September now in the great Los Angeles, leaves had yet to change but the air began to thin. At this point in the year, I was moving through stages of delirium, waking up each day and waiting patiently for the day to end. I took Vivian out to only two parties before she became very busy in pre-production of *Mass Hysteria*. One of these parties was thrown by Simon Powell, an acclaimed producer, and I prayed I wouldn't run into Ellis Young while wandering the party. I came to find out he was on the guest list but never made an appearance. I should have turned white at the existence of myself between Ellis Young and Vivian Wells; I wondered how the two of them might get along.

The other was a birthday party for a breakout artist, Elara Carpe, who had three alternative tracks in *Billboard*'s Top 10 at the time. She was turning twenty-two, and the party was held at her house in Beverly Hills. The loathing I had toward parties became monstrous, to the point I had to arrive drunk or at least a little fucked up in order to participate. But Vivian loved the party scene, and she was embraced by it, so I did whatever I could for her. She warned me immediately after the tour ended that soon she'd become unavailable due to her allegiance to *Mass Hysteria*, but I hoped her veering attention wouldn't disrupt the development of our relationship. I assured her I would be patient with her. A week later, she was moved into an Executive Producer role on the film and suddenly she was taking calls and attending virtual meetings most days. I was left by myself during sun up to occasionally tinker on the piano, scribble lyrics in my notebooks, or attend my own calls with Ant and ROT IRON.

It seemed like suddenly the band was very busy with their day to day lives. A month off from work and everyone had seemingly disappeared. Autumn would call to check in with me every so often but Sophia left every message unanswered. I fell into a tradition of leaving her a string of desperate text messages—*Hope you're doing well. Miss you. J.—Soph!! How's life?—Hey! Checking in*—met with no replies for weeks. Eventually, I eased the pressure. I felt there was no point in bothering her after a certain point. Besides, Vivian was texting me frequently every day, so the festering loneliness was often tamed. But every time I bunched up on my sofa to scurry around on my social media, a familiar weight would return across my body. Sophia's social updates were constant—her feet in the sand at sunset—her morning cup of coffee with the steam still twisting off the top—sitting across a white-clothed table from one cheeky Daniel with his neatly combed hair, olive skin, and thick eyebrows.

My immediate reaction was anger. I couldn't understand why she would grow distant especially when I hadn't done anything to prompt it. What had I done to her? I questioned myself and my previous behavior on the tour. The rage congested my brain; I could feel it physically pulsing. I resented her in some ways, and worse, any mention of remorse for the dying friendship would be met with instant regret, furthering our distance by great amounts. This caused a shift inside of me. If I caught a glimpse at one of her updates, a terrible gloom clung to my heart and sunk its teeth.

I felt sentimental about our old, loving friendship. We used to tell each other every new bit of gossip in each other's lives and ask for feedback or advice. We used to look forward to talking to one another any chance we found, and we would relish the opportunity. We would become excited to see one another. This was fading fast. Soon to be nothing. Perhaps once we landed in Europe, we would act like strangers, or at most, co-workers. We would be respectful and passive to one another but never find ourselves walking the long hallways of stadiums while chatting endlessly about a childhood memory or a recent story that the other was *simply not going to believe*. I had so much I wanted to say to her, but it felt as if I had lost her entirely. I sat on my hands in an attempt to not text her anymore—I had to let her be her own person and live her life with whom she chose—but I had still everything to say to her, and explain how much she meant to me, and how badly I wanted to be a part of her chosen life.

It was no secret that I loved her. I'd fallen in love with her back in college when we were first starting out as a band. Back when she was energetic, always hopeful, a gleam to her eye. And I loved her still, in a new way but still love, as I appreciated her careful step through life—her slowness in the everyday—her patience for the world around her. She had changed and so had I, but I never lost sight of that adoration. When she came to me two years back to disclose that she intended to date Daniel, I assured her they would have their space. Before then, we'd been inseparable, going everywhere together and spending most days attached at the hip. Anyone who knew Beach Sirens knew how close the two lead singers were. Sophia and I were always closest to each other, Tommy and Autumn were close in their own fashion. She knew how I felt without my ever having to say the three words out loud to her. I never once thought she'd stop speaking to me—it might have been the worst thought I could conjure.

Tommy was an even bigger question. Sophia would at least text Autumn, but Tommy was completely unresponsive aside from a text to Ant once a week. While bumping around my apartment, Autumn would call and ask if I had any updates on him and the answer was always no. Her stress began to transpire onto me, so I, too, began to worry about our young Tommy day in and day out. Where had my friends gone off to? Long drawn headaches. Unshakable anxieties. I started to cut back on blow in favor of Xanax. I had an amber prescription bottle on my bedside table, gleaming in the morning sun every day I woke. The prescription was made out to Howard Walsh— I should note, I never asked Hal how he'd gotten it but it wasn't difficult to piece together. I tried to sleep through every day, perhaps to fast forward to October. I became so familiar with sunset; it became the only time of day I truly realized—the first signal that another day had come and gone. It meant I was one step closer to being reunited with everyone, wherever they were, whatever they were all doing.

To my surprise and to my comfort, Autumn kept in contact with me. She was the only one who made an effort—she would call to make sure I was okay, if I'd eaten today, what my plans were. This resulted in my confiding in her, someone I trusted and needed in my life. It was around this time I began calling her nearly daily, and we set a time to visit. I told her I missed her rather than admitting to not trusting my actions if I were to remain alone. While this was the truth, it was not the whole truth.

———

I arrived at her house across town, a small village-style home with four-sided columns trunked in a line at her front porch. Tangerine light striped the vinyl siding and turned the chipped beige into gold. She had an old two-story home and lived with her roommate, Mazy Diaz, not because she was hard on cash but because they had become best friends in the last two years. Mazy was in a band named Gauze Moth, consisting of her (Lead Vocals, Keys) and her younger brother, Oliver (Drums) and another artist named Melinda Reichart (Guitar). Their band was more dream-pop rather than alternative—much to the likes of Cocteau Twins or Siouxsie and the Banshees—not entirely in the mainstream but with a strong and quiet following. It was Mazy who answered the door when I arrived.

The door swung back to reveal a young, pale-skinned girl—the top of her head came up to my chest—seemingly wearing only an oversized t-shirt with a graphic of a toad. And what a quaint toad he was! He held a mug in his grip and stood on two legs, sporting a beanie and a vest. Mazy's soil eyes found me on the upward glance. Round face. Uneven cut of hair, short and curly. Winged eyes and fake freckles. Her face grew in eager excitement to see me again, as I'd only visited once before, almost a year ago by then.

"Joe Henley! Come in! Please! Oh my *god*, how have you been? I haven't seen you since, what? Halloween it must have been! You look thin, are you on a diet?" This was the question she decided to pause on for a response.

"Ah—no—no, I'm not." I wasn't sure how to respond as she stepped aside, widening the jaw of the doorway. I crept into their living room. A large wall of white shells was stuffed with books of all kinds. Plants in various neutral-toned pottery lined the window seals and baked in the evening sunshine. I stood behind their suede sofa and used it to balance myself as I kicked my shoes off, placed neatly beside their entry mat.

"Well, no worries," she muttered, "I'm making a green bean casserole and a vegan sweet potato pie for dinner. You're welcome to eat with us!" She practically leaped off her feet, rocking back and forth between her heels and her toes. Hands tangled behind her back. Careful stare. I felt the need not to be rude, but a growing uneasiness welted inside of me. "I'm okay—thank you—of course. I'm sorry, I ate just before I left."

This was a lie, in fact, I hadn't eaten at all that day, but I wanted to move along. "Do you know where Autumn is?" Mazy struck a finger through the archway leading into their kitchen.

"Through there, she's on the back porch," she said with a half grin. Thin lips, cherry velvet lipstick. I started through their kitchen before turning in the archway, Mazy now turned to tend to her plants. "And Mazy?"

She hummed a pitchy tone, grinning again and facing me. "I'm doing well—to answer your question. How have you been?" I combed my fingers through my hair. She straightened herself, hands pressed on her hips and huffed a sigh.

"I'm alright, thanks," she answered. Mazy seemed to draw a blank, whisked away by a quiet wandering thought. "It's been an interesting year. It's hard to focus on music lately, especially being independent.

But we're finding the time." Another pause. "Getting by. That's my answer, getting by."

I nodded. I felt a diluted sense of regret for not inviting her to open for us on the tour. Why we hadn't done it, I wasn't sure. I enjoyed her music, and she was best friends with Autumn. I decided it was the stress of the tour and booking that made me forget about Gauze Moth entirely. Then, in their archway, I made a mental note to have their band set as an opener sometime in the future.

"I understand. At least you have your roommate back. Sorry for stealing her away all the time," I said, adding an artificial chuckle behind it.

"Oh, yeah. Well, she's great. We have to share her, don't we?" Her voice shrank as I edged toward the backdoor, slowly, enough time to admire the pearly backsplash of their kitchen. Three wooden stools evenly spaced at their island. A dinner table with six chairs. The smell of the casserole in the oven. A blackboard with a mint-colored chalk scribbling a list of groceries needed. Everything vegan-related.

"That's right!" I called out to her before opening the backdoor. Outside on the back porch, Autumn sat cross-legged with a glass of wine, staring at her phone. The door shut behind me, and it was loud enough for the sound to warrant her attention; she blacked her phone screen and passed a warm smile in my direction.

"Hey," I said. I collapsed into the plastic lawn chair bleached by the sun, opposite her. She reached to her right to a short side table and poured a glass of wine.

"Hey yourself," she replied and handed the glass. Her fenced back-yard was mostly bare aside for a brick fire pit with three more lawn chairs, two newly planted lemon trees, and a small boxed-in garden with a variety of herbs and vegetables. The ending sunlight sheeted the far side of her lawn, the rest blocked by the shadow of her house. We focused on that patch of copper-colored grass as if it were a piece of art, and in many ways, it was.

"How are you?" I asked.

"Fine. Relaxing and enjoying the time off."

"Me too," I said. I didn't feel like getting into the bloodshot nights in my apartment. I longed for my apartment on tour, and now that I was back, I wished hard to be back in the terrorizing cycle of traveling. In many ways, I felt ungrateful and as if I was incapable of satisfaction, but I was beginning to think something much larger may be wrong. Seated beside Autumn, my hands began to tremble, so I pressed the rim of the glass to my lips.

"Have you seen Tommy recently?" Autumn turned her attention, squinted eyes on mine. She uncrossed her legs and adjusted in her chair. I swallowed and cleared my throat.

"No, I haven't," I admitted, "I've left a few calls, but I've gotten nothing back from him. Have you heard from him yet?"

"No," replied Autumn. Her voice was muddled, and I sensed her tinge of worry. We were both silently slipping toward grim thoughts. I maneuvered the conversation in an effort to keep her happy.

I asked, "And Sophie, how is she?"

"She's good. Yeah, good. Last I heard, her and Daniel were spending the weekend in Joshua Tree. I think she's well." This was cause for me to swallow more wine—my glass empty faster than I anticipated—I motioned to the glass. Autumn blinked before reaching for the bottle and going to top me off again.

"How are you, Joey?" she asked.

"Like I said, I'm well." I became conscious of my drinking, diluting myself to sips.

"No, really," she started. She watched her wine carefully, and muttered, "Are you okay? I know the tour wasn't easy for you. I saw it almost every day, but I didn't want to bring it up. If you want to talk about it, we can."

I wasn't sure how to answer, she knew the truth but my mind betrayed honesty. It was never to be spoken of. I swallowed, blinked and gazed at the lit grass, smaller than before. I said, "Ah, I don't know." But Autumn was patient as she always was whenever she became concerned. She was never quick to talk of herself but would wait in silence to hear the feelings of someone else.

I started, "Touring is not easy—and I know we've discussed this before." Lengthy nods from Autumn. "It's like—everyone in the world is watching you, and you temporarily—sort of—lose yourself, and as soon as you walk off that stage, the illusion is broken. And you're almost slapped in the face by reality. The second you get off, nobody gives a shit. You're just a guy, nobody's chanting your name—and you're alone! And, and," I looked around for the right thing to say, "Back in that hotel room, it's just fucking you. You know? *You* know."

I placed my hand on hers resting on the arm of her lawn chair. Her expression was unaltered, and deeply focused on my words. I sighed and pondered a conclusion.

"I guess I gave into the solace of those rooms, even more so than last time. I learned it to be an outer shell of myself, like I was the nucleus and I wouldn't be fully functioning without the rooms as my cell. And, honestly—a cell could mean many things—I trapped myself in there, after all."

She nodded. Silent. She clicked her tongue and said, "You know, I was always just one room away and would have talked to you whenever you needed." Generosity swelled in her tonsils.

"I know, I know. I began to relish loneliness though—really lean into it, you know? It's hard to explain. It's as if I sought out to overindulge in this unpleasantness of the situation. Maybe it was immature."

"It wasn't immature. Please don't say that. I've just been really worried about you since the last show. You didn't tell me you were feeling those types of things. I had no idea."

"I know, but now I wish I was back there, back in the cities and on the stages. I wish I could do it all over again and actually have some good fucking fun. But it's over again. I can't remember much of anything either. Now I'm having a fucking pity party."

I stared at my boots on the wooden planks. Autumn was quiet.

"I'm sorry," I mumbled.

"No need. We were all there with you—I just like it to see you happy."

"Me too."

I focused on as little as possible, batting tears wrapped on my eyes.

I coughed and attempted to compose myself. Not here, I kept saying to myself. Not again, not now. Enjoy this moment. I nipped a cigarette from my breast pocket.

"Could I snag one?" she asked. I withdrew an additional smoke and handed it to Autumn; she thanked me. I burnt the ends and puffed. Her eyes squinted, low, and arms extended with the cigarette twisting smoke at the end. A rushing heat swelled in my legs as I watched her do it. She looked back at me a moment later and a knowing smile grew into her face.

"Something on your mind?" she asked. I shrugged my shoulders, as if to throw it off but both of us knew what I wanted. She scoffed from her front teeth and shook her head. "Why don't you just go to Tommy's? Maybe you two need some time together, just the two of you."

"I could," I replied. I wasn't sure what else to say; admittedly, I thought her idea was bad. I wanted to provide Tommy with the space he seemingly desired. I countered, "But what if he isn't home?"

"What if he is?"

I stared at her for a long time, watching her pull smoke into her body and brush it back over her top lip. Sometimes I wondered about Autumn, an undefined wonder, for she fascinated me constantly. But my more present feelings toward Sophia always took center of my mind. She kicked my shin and laughed. "Cut it out, Henley! You horn-dog," she cried, "Don't make me call up Vivian Wells and tell her you're acting out of line!"

I chuckled and backed off; I continued nursing my glass of wine. We sat next to each other enjoying the last moments of summer until the bottle was empty. We talked over a variety of subjects—what places we would venture to first when we arrived in London, how things were developing between Vivian and I, and what I had planned for the weekend—Autumn was adamant I go check on Tommy before I do anything else. I followed her inside and thanked her for having me.

"Are you sure you don't want to stay for dinner?" Mazy asked, her lids low with a facing up glance. Despite her flirtations, she was not the one I wanted that night. I grinned kindly, "No, thank you. I'm still stuffed but next time you guys feel like having me around, I'm more than happy to come back for dinner together. Really, thank you."

The two of them saw me out and I walked back to my car parked on the street. I skid off through the neighborhood with my phone in hand, Tommy's number ringing in dazed blurbs through my car. The call went straight to voicemail as it had so many times before. I recalled Autumn and how she wore her concern. I knew I had a duty to fulfill, if not for Autumn, then for the wellness of Tommy. After a U-turn I was headed in the direction of Tommy's house. I was back on Reagan and headed toward Woodland Hills where I hoped to find my best friend.

———

I pulled into Tommy's driveway and parked behind his black BMW gran coupe. I glanced up at his house; the windows glowed yellow with skidded lines from the blinds. The whole place was shrouded in darkness from the bamboo trees lined on either side of his lawn. I walked up to the front porch and pressed into the doorbell. I waited there for a long time, hitting the doorbell every so often, before I began to think up awful scenarios. Five minutes went by and I was still standing out in the night. I tried the front door, and curiously, it was unlocked. Entering his home, I passed an unkempt interior, full of records and comic books splattered across the living room floor. The television flickering on the local news channel at a low volume. His kitchen seemed cleaner than the rest of his house but with takeout boxes piled high on the island. The kitchen wore a pale flickering glow from the living room television. The trash hadn't been taken out in days, weeks maybe, and the stench was thick. He was nowhere to be seen. The creeping sensation of sterile loneliness crawled on my back and the local news wasn't helping.

I cut out the TV to become swallowed in pure darkness. Rather than silence, I heard the muffled running of water streaming from somewhere on the second floor. I followed up the staircase toward the noise, growing louder as I climbed, and turned toward the master bedroom. A wild smell hit my nose, notes of vomit and sweat but something unfamiliar to me. I guess it was metallic and fetid, but I knew it was unbearable, and I pinched my shirt over my nose. My eyes began to burn looking around at his shadowy bedroom. The bed itself appeared normal—his clothes were in a pile outside of his open closet. The fan was on, rocking from the high setting, his record player skipped at the inner most groove of a vinyl and still, behind a closed door, the shower was running in his bathroom. The light was on, causing a rectangular halo to outline the doorframe. I crept closer, inching toward the door. I leaned my knuckles into the wood. Three gentle knocks.

"Tommy?" I pressed my ear against the door, listening hard for any movement. Nothing. I tried the handle, also unlocked. Steadily, I inched the door further, and there he was. Tommy stood in the shower, head down with his chin pinned against his chest, and eyes closed. He was wearing a full suit, complete with boots, completely soaked with steam waving off his body.

"Tommy," I said again, a violent urgency in my voice. I walked across the bathroom, stepping through puddles of water from the glass shower door that had been wide open. I called his name again, louder, and still he was unmoving. Standing and breathing, yes, but unresponsive.

"Tommy, what the fuck!"

Finally, Tommy muttered something. It was so quiet. No voice left his body.

"What?" I stammered.

"Are they still out there? They're trying to get me," he mumbled louder, just barely enough for me to maybe make out his words. I grabbed hold of his shoulders, swung him to face me, and like the pop of a firecracker, he exploded. His eyes shot open, wild and red. He latched onto the front of my shirt and hurled me to the floor.

Before I had any time to catch my breath, my head slapped the tile, and my vision edged on white before returning with a haze. And the dull pain crescendoed on my skull, equally causing a ringing in the ears. High-pitched, unwavering, ringing. I knew Tommy was going ballistic on me, going on about the bats! *Bat people*! But my foreground was out of focus, instead the gnawing whiplash of my head took everything out of me. I struggled to find my breath as Tommy continued to lurch my body around on the floor, helpless and lost. I felt like a ragdoll but was only trying to stay awake.

I wasn't sure how much time had passed when Tommy had enough and got to his feet. I recall the image of him running out of the bathroom and leaving me breathless on the tiled floor, hearing the shower running from what sounded like miles away. After another span of vicious time spent catching up to the moment, I was able to gather myself enough to peel off—turned over to find the shower puddles rusted—they had all become somewhat pink—surely a mixture of something diluted in water. I patted the back of my head to find a thick red drooling down my hand. But no emotion was able to come forward, still locked into an unsteady delirium. I latched onto the wall and crawled out of the bathroom.

"Tommy," I croaked. It was meant to be a yell, but my brain couldn't figure it out. The bedroom was tilted, slightly off-axis, and I held the wall all the way out of his room and down the hallway. The hallway was tipping over—I held onto the wall like my life depended on it—and maybe it did as a trail of steady, red dots dribbled onto the floors behind me. A scary sight, I remember, but my attention shifted when piercing crashes rang from the first floor. I carefully made my way toward the sound; each step was a fight to remain conscious as the warm stream of blood soaked into the back of my shirt. When I got downstairs, I found Tommy holding a cast iron pan as if it were a sword.

"What do you want?" he questioned. He flipped the pan in a defensive manner. He screamed once more, "What do you want?" My care for the situation had fled, instead focused purely on survival. I leaned against the banister at the bottom of the staircase, head bobbing around, everything swelling and fading. I tried to focus on pulling the oxygen in and out of my lungs.

"Tell me," he screamed, "Tell me now!"

I couldn't pull any words forward—I took the final step down the stairs and that was it. My mind disconnected from my body, and all at once everything was fading out entirely. The dimly lit living room fell on its side at a rapid pace, catching an extreme white, before I heard a crack against the floor. That's when everything went black.

———

Tommy kneeled over me with stained hands and bandages. He was changed, no longer in a suit, rather a t-shirt and sweatpants. I had no idea what was going on, but I was still lying on my back in his living room, only now a wadded-up towel was beneath my head.

"Hey, man," he said. He smiled but in an embarrassed and knowing sort of way. I tilted to view out the windows and noted the sun pressed on the blinds. The pastel wash of sunlight hung on the walls, the floors, over the two of us.

"What time is it?" I asked.

"Nearly nine in the morning. Do you want to go to the hospital?"

I tried lifting my head but only learned of a humming headache.

"I don't know why I'm not already there, man. What the hell happened?" I gritted.

He scrubbed a hand down his face and took his eyes off me. He looked afraid, which wasn't common for Tommy. He retreated to a quiet laughter, a farce he wore very well. He admitted, "I don't know. I was going to ask you. The place is a fucking wreck though, I know that."

He helped me to my feet and rather than going to the hospital, he propped me up on his couch and made a bag of ice for my head wound. He'd strapped three layers of gauze around my forehead and cleaned me up pretty well—a hoodie from his closet replaced my bloodstained shirt—he took care of me, but I knew he was off-center. It was when he stood in the kitchen, now reassembled, at his espresso machine, I watched him slowly make two cappuccinos. He was frantic, and I recognized his twitches of worry and fear.

"So, you don't remember anything?" I asked. He turned his head but never fully around, he shook his head.

"No, no. I can't remember. I have a feeling I made all this mess though."

His response irritated me. How could one get so far gone and not remember a thing? A moron, I thought, an honest-to-God moron. "Yeah, you did," I said, heat caught in my voice.

Wisps of burnt wood. Rich and chocolate senses sprouted through the house as the espresso machine groaned. He made an effort to turn his body around completely. He faced me, though from across the house, in his kitchen.

"I'm sorry, man—truly, I am—I don't know what I was thinking."

He carried a mug my way with one crooked finger hooked around the handle. Before sitting next to me, he shot to the windows, peeked through the blinds as if expecting to find something foul. He locked the front door. Tommy sunk onto the sofa and sipped at the espresso with foamy slurps.

"Care to tell me what's going on?" I asked.

He crossed his legs and tried to look rather sophisticated. Dried blood dusted on our hands. He cleared his throat and began, "Well, I was reading this book a few days back—Fiction, you know—from an author I read quite a lot. And it followed this drifter—a writer—who did LSD every day for like, twelve days in a row. And I was thinking to myself, you know, that's *nothing*. I can do that. In fact, I can *double* it."

"Tommy—" I began, and my voice was shallow. His name was the only word I got out before he cut me off.

"And, of *course*, I kept seeing increasingly violent images. It was the most terrifying shit I've ever seen. These people—winged people —they have wings like bats, and they crawl across my floor. They hide in my clothes and such. They keep coming back for me and it all feels so real at the moment—less than real life but more than a dream."

"So, you stopped then?"

No answer. I leaned forward and gave him a sterile look. After a moment or two, he seemingly gathered the courage to speak up.

"I did three times the normal amount last night," he whispered, his voice trembling.

I shot back on the couch and cranked my neck up to face the ceiling. The confusion and madness left me scattered. What awesome ignorance could lead someone to such idiotic experiments? Perhaps it was arrogance, though I often thought ignorance was the spawn of arrogance.

"But it's not as bad as you think! You can't get addicted to acid," he said, as if it would convince me his behavior was reasonable.

"You can get addicted to anything under the fucking sun if you want it all the time!" I barked back. I was furious. Here I was feeling played. I had gone to check on my best friend only to find out he'd been consuming hallucinogens in a spree for false reality. It was destroying his brain. His behavior was different from what it was on tour already. He was unfocused, darting his eyes around. Alarmed. Always on. He looked like he hadn't slept in days—I hadn't had much sleep either—I noticed the irony in being so afraid of losing him.

"I can't! But, listen, I'm stopping right now. I flushed it all as soon as I came down and saw what had happened to you," he said, all very quickly. He took a deep breath and leaned in close, "Joe, I *never* meant to hurt you. You have to believe me, you're like a brother to me and I would never do that to you."

"We are brothers," I corrected him. "Just no more fucking acid, man. You're frying your brain."

His eyes diverted; they zipped around the floor before shutting. A tight nod. I sipped my cappuccino and analyzed his behavior. I was coming down from my fit of anger toward him, which translated to pure worry. He was my favorite person aside from the girls. But every boy—every man—needs another man they can put their trust in. Together, they might make a decent soul.

IX

The weather was kind on the worst day of my life. Tommy and I sat around scraping callused fingers against the frets of our guitars and toying with new distortion pedals when Vivian rang me up to say her film pushed shooting until after the new year. She would be flying back to Los Angeles the next morning, so Tommy and I still had the whole day to do as we pleased. Neither of us said it but we were spending more time together to keep the other in line, this way we wouldn't lose track of the other. Last I heard from Autumn, she was helping her roommate produce a new single, spending all her time in a studio space they'd built out in their garage and Sophia was nowhere to be heard from. The four of us were to leave for London in two weeks' time. We had a logistics meeting that morning in which managers and ROT IRON heads joined on a video call to go over all the prospects and technicalities of our travels. It was also the first time I saw Sophia in weeks; only half of her face displayed in the pixelated box of a smeared computer screen. She wore her sunglasses out in the sun of Joshua Tree where she'd been with her boyfriend for the last however many days.

I felt my knees ache; my stomach tightened. The last time I sent her a message was well over ten days before, again met with no response. Yet there she was, a formation of pixels on my screen, spending half her attention on the meeting and the other half on whatever she had going on off-screen. I couldn't stray my thoughts from her, and in turn, I lost most of the logistics discussed in the meeting.

In the evening, Hal arrived at my apartment. He'd called me only hours before, with such confidence slicked on his tongue as he spoke; he was coming to pick us up and the three of us were going to go to hit a handful of clubs. This was something we hadn't done as a group in a little over six months and I believe all of us were quietly excited. This would later become the most guilt-steeped decision I ever made, a decision drenched in nightmare, one that would take years to grasp in my head. I rose for the door at the three sharp knocks, and there stood Hal—slicked, black hair—a sage green blazer and matching dress pants—a jagged, chromatic chain around his neck, the top two buttons of his shirt undone. He ducked in the apartment and swiveled to find Tommy stretched on the sofa with an unplugged Gibson laid across his stomach; he gave his full attention to Joel Schumacher's The Lost Boys blasting on the television.

"*Hi, Michael!*" Tommy was slightly stoned and quoting every other line of dialogue in the movie, in similar inflection, only a much deeper tone. His cherry-chewed eyes sagged and he grinned at the cheesy effects of the vampire flick. Tommy wore a beater, an open button-up and a pair of drab, blue jeans.

"Hey, Tom," Hal said. Tommy lifted a hand in greeting before returning it to scratching the guitar strings. Hal navigated across the vast and mostly empty apartment, he flicked his keys in the air and caught them again in his palm. Hal scanned and said, "You guys ready to go yet?"

"Fuck, is it that time already?" Tommy groaned from the sofa. He rose with dramatic effort as if he wore an old character in a stage play. He crossed the apartment on his toes and found his shoes for an evening out.

Hal dropped his bag on the dining table. He rummaged through it while shouting back, "So, Joe, we're off to London in twelve days— twelve days left of our private *vacays*—Sophie's off doing whatever the fuck—then we're back at it. And this got me thinking, as always, you know—my boss is gonna need some drugs, right?—*right, right, right* —so, just as God intended, you come across a good opportunity, you take a good opportunity. That's what I do—for you. And me, I guess —look, what I'm trying to say is, I have a pretty fucking crazy stash for our Europe travels."

Tommy sat up and watched as Hal plopped a brick of cocaine on the table. It was a quarter after four when he revealed the brick, and I would never forget the dull thud it made against the walnut-stained dining table. I would never forget any of it; Tommy's neon orange and green bong on the coffee table reminded me of a sherbet dessert; I wore two rings on my left hand and a metal chain on my right, none of which were expensive but one of the rings Autumn had bought for me while out at a market in Texas; I had on a beige button shirt tucked into my pants, all of which I'd thrifted; the temperature outside that day was a high of eighty-three degrees Fahrenheit and a low of fifty-eight.

This and more, every detail, every sense, every word, indefinitely etched into memory like names on a gravestone. I learned over the years to stop replaying this hour in my apartment but even still I can drag it to the foreground of my mind and replay it as if living it again. I remember Hal as he turned, a gaped grin branched on his face, he clawed his hair back and sighed. Hal was proud of it, I realized, but he had no idea; none of us in the apartment had a clue; that brick of cocaine resting on the kitchen table was laced with fentanyl, and if any of us took it, we would be dead in minutes.

"What the fuck," I muttered, but Hal heard it. He visibly buffered before resetting and walked toward me with arms stretched out defensively.

"Joe, look, I was downtown last night, and I was at this club. I met this guy—a photographer—he said he's worked with Simon Powell. You remember Simon, *right*? You hung out at Simon's party a few weeks ago? Yeah, well, this kid, Damion—he's new to the industry and still trying to find his footing, bless his heart—but he *loves* coke— fucking loves it—he gets all his shit from New York. And he says he gets a discounted price in exchange for photographing sets." He was freckled in sweat, his speech running long and fast. He was obviously strung out on something, and I tried to pin which drug he'd taken while listening to his story.

"So, I'm talking with this guy, and he pulls out *this brick*—broad daylight, you know, fuckers at the other tables are looking at it, I start freaking out—" While he was explaining his story, Tommy and I exchanged a quiet glance. "—Anyway, he says he'd sell me the entire brick for twenty-five hundred bucks. He says he has five more at home, *and* he's selling it to me for *more* than he pays for it out of New York. So, I'm sitting there thinking it through, and this brick is nearly half the price we pay. I mean, if we paid for an entire fucking brick—I know it's absurd to buy all of this shit at once like we're in the god-fucking-forsaken Mexican Cartel—but it's not like this goes bad, we can just knick at it while we're on our European escapade, right?"

I nodded, feeling a little uneasy about the brick sitting on the kitchen table. I swallowed and asked, "Have you tried it?"

Hal shook his head but started to carefully strip the shrink wrap, layer by layer, until I groaned, "*C'mon*, Hal, save it. I'm still good on coke. I have a decent stash in my bedroom. Go ahead and take it with you though."

"Okay, okay—" Hal darted a focused squint at the half-peeled brick. What he was thinking over, I had no idea. The kids on the television had just stolen their grandpa's car and were speeding toward the vampire's lair. "I fucking love this movie," Hal added, "Hey—Have you guys started packing yet?"

"Hal," I said. His brain was firing in every direction. I had my palm up, as if to say, *slow down*.

"What?"

"Are you sure you haven't taken any of this?"

"Hand on my father's grave, Joe. Christ, I haven't even unwrapped it yet, you know?"

He started unwrapping it very suddenly. Tommy peeked over the top of the sofa, prompting him to spring off and sloth toward us. "Did you know," Tommy began, slurring his big velvet voice, "There are traces of cocaine on ninety percent of our US currency? That's true, you can fact-check it. Although, I'm sure it applies to paper more than coins."

"Sure, sure, sure." Hal kept tightly repeating this one word over and over under his breath while carefully unwrapping his treasure. Tommy scratched his cheek and looked at me, he was absolutely stoned, he looked like he'd been awake for days, but it'd been more like hours. He must've noticed me staring at him because he started to giggle richly. Back to Hal.

"Hal, what *did* you take?"

"Coke! You *fucking moron*, isn't it obvious?"

I was practically shouting and impulsively, I landed a sharp smack against his shoulder.

"So, then why are you undoing this giant brick of cocaine if you're already high?" I questioned in a seething tone. The high of the weed kept me from bursting into a scream; I'd reached a ceiling with how frantic my body could fathom. His forehead was bubble-wrapped in sweat—a real savage—he kept licking his palm and slicing wet ends of hair from hanging in front of his face.

"I tested it at Damion's apartment first—stop—listen to me. I tested it with the shit he had out, he had this brick wrapped up and hidden behind his fucking bookshelf. But it's the same shit. He gets it from the same guy out in New York. But he said this one was special and it belonged to someone special—*like a goddamn motherfucking rockstar.*"

I replied and spaced out each word—careful with my pronunciation—so perhaps Hal would get it through his thick skull, *"I don't know who Damion fucking is."*

I watched as Hal carefully bared the powder; it was like a mummification of cake mix. He took his personal business card—pure white with indented font reading, *Howard Walsh* and below, *Artist Assistant - Music Journalist* along with his contact information—and used this to scoop a decent mound of the cocaine and settle it directly onto the cherrywood gloss finish. The mound expanded a bit, crumbs of coke dribbled down the sides of the hill and got stuck in the scratches of the table, one might only notice it from the correct angle of light. I watched these little pieces of coke stumble down the hill. Sisyphean.

I was annoyed with Hal, biting my tongue and grimacing like a child. I never asked for a brick of cocaine worth over two bands and I never would. I wasn't nearly as strung out on the shit as he was. Over the last year, Hal had gained a talented ego, which I thought ironic as he was my assistant. Still, Hal went around checking himself out in every reflection, fixing his hair, fixing the collar of his shirt or his blazer, and talking up any girl he chose in any club he chose. He'd bought a new car with the money I paid him. He needed me, everything in his life was due to my career requiring an assistant. None of this bothered me until this very moment, when he was standing in my kitchen and slicing the pyramid of cocaine into careful streaks on my table, all the while pretending we were equals.

He held out his business card and a rolled fifty in an almost menacing fashion as if holding a weapon, "Which one of you dickwads wants to go first?"

"Stop it, Hal. Cut a piece, wrap it up and let's go," I gritted my teeth.

The room fell flat. A silence took over aside from the wincing strings blaring from the film flickering on the television behind us. Hal nodded and did as he was told. He withdrew a chromatic tin, no larger in size than a deck of cards, lined with a teal accent and in cursive lettering, read, 'Anton's Mints.'

Wintergreen—everything else on the tin was written in another language I did not recognize—I tried to decipher what the language might be and decided it was, perhaps, Russian. He clicked open the matchbox tin; Hal swiped a decent bit of the cocaine into a plastic baggy on the edge of the tabletop, zipped it and stuffed it into the curious tin. I guessed enough for more than three dozen lines once it was poured out somewhere.

"Where'd you get that?" I asked, my head cocked and focused on the Russian mints capsule. Silver and blue gleamed back at me.

"What? Oh—Yeah. When I was at Damion's apartment I asked if

he had any gum and he tossed me this whole thing of mints. He says he gets them imported from Russia and fucking loves them. They weren't bad—anyway, I realized it might be a good fit for an eight ball and—shit, hey, here we are."

———

We shuffled down to Hal's top-down convertible, Tommy leaped into the backseat and I took passenger. We ended up at a club we attended frequently; it was called The Miserable Sinner, a smaller club with a clean, backlit presence to it, nearly gothic in its black and gold accents. The bouncer, Teddy, a wide Hispanic man, knew us on arrival and allowed us in. Brick walls. Black lights. Glow stick cracked and hazing neons. Purple teeth. That night's DJ on the back wall raged out with cranks and swells, bass 808's and high hats that were similar in sound and rhythm to a jackhammer; all this while the bar splashed shots of tequila straight up for a group of dolls from the Valley. There was a back room, which was where we liked to hang out mostly as the general public was not allowed in. We shuffled through the crowd of people, sideways with one shoulder leading, and eventually made it to the back room where we were allowed in once more.

The three of us squeezed ourselves into a booth beside a rapper I recognized immediately to be an artist who went by Outlyre. He was a Thousand Oaks native with a clean face and a wild bush of an afro, two years my younger. His jawline was at a right angle and his smile was of the fashion that made one's day brighter. I had one of his records, his newest release from that same year called *Causing Problems On Purpose*. Tonight he wore overalls and had a joint bent at the corner of his mouth. He was laughing at something a scrawny young lady was saying into his ear.

"Is that Joe Henley?" he asked with a scratched, nearly gone voice. I learned he had just played a show that same night at The Fonda. I practically tripped into a clinging hug from Outlyre, who was standing now and introduced me to the young women beside him. I recognized one of them, another rapper named Pythie with dyed blonde hair and shaved eyebrows. A table made up of four glowing walls and a granite top planted at the center of the rounded booth. Two bottles of champagne sat atop, plus a bottle of Crown and five shot glasses on the table.

"You want some smoke?" asked Outlyre. I declined and plopped beside him. He waved a palm over the table, "Feel free to help yourselves to anything you want, what's mine is yours. You boys just out for a good time?"

We ended up taking shots of Crown, filling a glass of champagne and the hunger for blow began to simmer in my cavities. I chewed on my cheek. Another shot. Five shots of Crown was my total for that night, plus a glass of champagne, three cigarettes, and three bong hits. Tommy was trying to tell Outlyre about something lofty, as he was always doing.

Tommy shouted over the music, "So let's say we are alone in the universe, at least from a standard of organic complexity—which means there could be alien organisms, sure, maybe even alien plant life —we would be the highest form of intelligence in the universe. It's unlikely but it isn't impossible based on what we know," Tommy went on in his dark voice while Outlyre just kept nodding and nodding with his brows pinched.

Tommy swigged on the champagne in his glass and went on, "What does that mean for our evolution then, right? If the multicellular organism evolved again, and instead of using itself to generate a twin, what if it could do something else? I mean, who knows, teleportation? Ceasing to age? Immortality? All of it is implausible but not impossible, you understand."

Outlyre began to laugh, his head shaking, "Man, I like you. You want another shot?"

"Sure. Slick, you in?"

I nodded, to which Outlyre lined the glasses and bled the bottle. Raised hands with our shots, we tipped them back at our lips and down the fierce venom went. This was my fifth and final shot of the night. Tommy began to shake his whole body, he hissed as he clapped the shot glass on the glowing table, his teeth a neon purple under the odd light. He leaned toward Hal who was charming one of the young ladies in the booth with us.

"Hey, pal, you wouldn't happen to have any breath mints on you, would you?" Tommy yelled into his ear and followed with an open mouth guffaw. Hal grinned a wicked look and reached into his blazer to withdraw the silver box. The music inhaled and exhaled; it thumped like a drying machine. I felt the alcohol creeping up on me as my mind began to drift and my body grew disconnected. I tried to watch Tommy unpack the blow on the glowing table; the girl to his left made a Soprano noise of interest when she watched him reveal a bit of it. This led to another spurt of Tommy giggling and pushing a palm over his shaved head. He leaned forward and rolled a bill to use as a tool for the drug.

As he bent over, there was a millisecond where I caught him glancing up at me, and it occurred so quickly, I thought at first perhaps it did not happen. But it did. He shot a quick glance before looking at the table. His eyes seemed to be asking permission—before deciding he didn't care. We were spending all this time together to keep the other in line. But cocaine was something neither of us planned on quitting. We'd been doing it for the last four years. We'd done it half a million times. But in that zap of time when his eyes met mine, I felt a simultaneous true and complete understanding of his thoughts. I felt, too, a crack of fear erupt in my chest.

And before I knew it, a thick, dry sniffle skid across the table. He shot straight up and tossed his head back, flicking his nostril like a kick drum. He blew out an exasperated howl and a shriek of laughter and stabbed the blow utensil in my hand. His giggling, so natural and easy for him, drained. He shook his head sharply as if wading off a buzzing insect. He took a deep breath and squinted. The woman threw her arms around his shoulders and broke into an impressed laughter, she kept telling him he did so good; Tommy rubbed his temples.

"I'm—uh," Tommy stammered. Disorientation. Something was wrong. "I have to piss. You all keep doing what you're doing." He was rocking back and forth while sauntering toward the bathroom. He walked as if he were standing on a boat, stopped and swiveled, "And hey, Slick?"

My face was pinned in an expression of disorientation, and I was unable to change it. "Yeah?" He stuck a finger at me, deadly serious. "I want you to tell Autumn not to worry, you hear me? I walk this path alone, my friend. Whatever the fuck it is."

"What the fuck are you talking about?" I grimaced. The first words that came to mind were the last words I got out before I faced his back and he was off again. Hal was smiling and licking his lips and then shouted my name across the table.

"He's the interesting one, why isn't he the lead singer?" Hal jested.

"He's shit at singing," I graveled. Blunt but honest. Tommy was best at singing when it was through the chords of a six-string. And when he sang that way, he was better than any of us. Hal reached across the table, two bodies down and latched a hand on my shoulder with such force, I tensed sharply. He laughed a ferocious cackle. He rocked my body with his grip and I felt my body losing itself, a sickness festered inside of me. I was losing my consciousness to a violent fade. I looked to my left and Tommy was gone, and I had already forgotten about our interaction. In his place, the oaky haired young woman who'd been crushing on Tommy was now using a credit card to form her own line of blow. To my right sat a woman I had never met before with a hollow face, cat eyes, and wisping platinum hair; she was speaking to me.

"So, there's only one plane crash for every seventeen million flights. But, there are over *twenty two million* flights a year. There are bound to be at least a few mistakes being that high up in the fucking sky! Yeah, it's safe but there are still about one hundred incidents a year. It's even accounted for; can you believe it? I can tell you first-hand, I've been on some *rocky* flights since I started flight-attending, to say the least," said the strange woman.

"Who are you?" I asked.

"Fuck you," she snarled and bit her lip. I had no idea what was going on. I looked back to my left where the licorice black leather upholstery now sat completely empty. Where had that mousy brunette gone off to? How much time had passed? Where had Tommy gone off too? Maybe he was with the brunette, I thought, getting off in the bathroom stall right now. An anxious prickling sparked through my body; it was the same sensation as a limb falling asleep. I must have closed my eyes in the booth, and maybe even passed out for a moment as I jolted sharply to find myself smothered in icy champagne. The group shot me a concerned stare—Hal, Outlyre, Pythie, and three other young ladies plus a neatly dressed pale man I'd never seen before—the whole scene was jarring, and I was becoming increasingly afraid. I was aware that I needed to escape; home would be much safer for me. I wanted the music to stop, the awful thump of ostentatious music, the volume turned far too loud caused a vibrating pulse in my chest. I thought for a moment the anxiety was going to boil up inside of me and burst, a vicious loss of breath and tightened muscles, my eyes heated as my tear ducts prepared themselves. I fluttered my eyelids to stop it and tried to shoo this all away.

"What time is it?" I asked the group loudly, despite my torso being newly smothered in a heap of champagne.

"Quarter after one," one of the young ladies replied. I nodded and patted Hal on the shoulder who was now in the spot where the platinum haired woman had once sat. It felt like only a moment had passed since I watched Tommy do the line. I was blackout drunk, and I knew it. From that point forward, I oriented myself to return to my conscious abilities, which meant first going to throw up the mix of drugs in my stomach.

"I'm going to the bathroom," I barked at Hal. He and a handful of others scooted out of the booth to make room for me, I gripped the leather booth and fumbled out, swaying toward the restroom in an unstable manner.

"If you see Tommy in there, tell him to finish up and get his ass back out here!" Hal beckoned as I made an uncompromising effort to stand straight and in pursuit of the restroom. My attention left Hal completely and every prick of anger in my body folded into the worst anxiety I had ever felt. I was instantly struck with a suspicion of what might have happened to Tommy; there was no sure confirmation until I made it to the restroom. My loafers clicked against the waxed, black, marble tile the whole way, deep and responsible as I went. I was right outside of the door when I tried calling his name, but nothing came. I was shaking violently, like standing out in the bare winter and pressed my cheek into the door as if I were using it for support. Again and this time successful. "Tommy."

It was all I needed to say. It was all I ever needed to say. I'd been in this situation not so long before. I pushed into the door but stopped before swinging it fully open. This time I prayed he'd attack me and leave me bleeding out on the tile floor like we had done a fortnight ago. Cold. Reeling. But would that be the case? My heart was throbbing so intensely I thought it would overwork itself and give up. I swallowed hard in an attempt to pass the lump in my throat. Please don't let it be what I believe, I chanted in my thoughts. And suddenly, as my arm pushed the door back in on itself, I became overly aware of the physical moment playing out in front of me. Like a scene from a nineties flick but this was real. I felt the wind surf over my arm and thought about how strange it was that I am alive. I am a person with a name—my name is Joseph Henley—and this is the life I am leading. I make money with my job so I can pay for my apartment and go out with friends. I like to drink coffee, preferably warm. I enjoy wine in the evenings and also singing with my friends. And behind this door is my closest friend, closer than any other, Tommy Murtaugh. I'm about to see him and he's going to be standing upright, crossing the stalls with still wet hands and smiling as he flicks water at my face.

The door pushed back. I felt my stomach ready to relieve itself of the toxic liquid as I found myself met with a completely vacant men's room beside one stall, second to the left, closed but not locked. I clicked to the door, the black restroom twinkled reflections and dim light all around. My head was spinning. The room warped and refused to stay still.

"Tommy—Hey, buddy," I called.

My eyes were heavy, half-open, stinging. I pressed into the door of the glinting black stall. Tommy's body was tangled on its side. His head was lodged between the toilet and the back marble wall behind the toilet. I noticed the lid of the toilet was closed, implying he may have had no intention of using it at all. I took one step forward and stopped breathing to study his body. I watched his chest so carefully, so carefully I thought perhaps I could see the fuzziness of the air shaking all around me. Panic.

"Tommy!" I was screaming his name. It poured from my body over and over as I thrashed at his legs, ripping him toward me and I tried to pump his chest. His face was depleted of all color, a sheet of nothing. I begged aggressively for anyone to call an ambulance despite being completely alone. I forced myself to exert my stomach of all alcohol into the toilet, a tortured plop and trickle as my stomach gave up on itself. I flushed my vomit and inner acids and returned back to my friend, wiping my mouth rid of waste. I pumped more at his chest and eventually knew it was not going to work. I wiped the tears falling from my face into my sleeve, I rested his head on my lap and surfed my fingers over his head. There was my boy. Except he wasn't there. I could tell it was Tommy, but Tommy was no longer there. I felt my stomach slug heavily and light as a feather, I thought for sure I was going to be sick and rested my forehead against the stall.

"Wake up. Wake up, Tommy!" I screamed until my throat seared with a burning flame. My muscles were eager to be used. Every part of me continued to shake as I stared at him. I stared and stared at his face, the oldest it would ever be. I knew it but shook the thought away. No, I'll call the paramedics and when they get here, they'll know what to do and how to fix him. He was going to be fine, and I had overreacted. The adrenaline continued to course despite the fact that everything was going to be okay. Someday, when Tommy and I are old, we are going to look back on this day and laugh. I watched his face sink from white to gray. His shoulder and left knee would twitch in short spasms as all functions slowed to a stop. And I continued petting my palm over the top of his head.

Minutes before, everything had been fine. Hours before, everything had been perfect. We were watching a classic film, enjoying our Saturday afternoon, all before I'd gotten angry at Hal—that was the first moment I pieced it all together. Ten minutes of my undivided attention on Tommy, my boy, and suddenly, something snapped. This was Hal's fault. But rather than rage, all I felt was desperation. As I placed blame and realized my internal decree, I heard the door to the men's room blast open at once. I heard Hal shouting my name and Tommy's name between cups of laughter, telling us to hurry up and get back out there. And slowly he shuffled on the black mirrored floors—his shoes left skid marks from never fully picking up his feet —and he leaned into the wall of the stall. His face giddy and dazed, but falling, falling, falling into a bewildered horror.

"What did you do?" I cried, looking over my shoulder at Hal with tears sagging down my cheeks. He shook his head—worried eyes darting all over the bathroom as he pieced the images together—I kept my gaze steady, locked on his and asked again, "What did you do?"

———

The days following Tommy's death were spent in a cycle of sleepless nights and a series of faded, far off days. I spent the first day speaking with detectives, answering their questions (*you were with him only the day before, is that correct?*) then sitting alone in my apartment. The world felt less colorful—less real—further away. I sat around with an aching stomach, my boiling hands clenched hard. Shadows stretched and wrapped the room, cutouts of light projected from the windows slid up the walls. Darkness became more familiar than the day. And still, questions from police, discussions with the label (*I believe it best if we postpone the European tour leading into 2024*), silence from Sophia, long sessions in stillness—this all grew into a rhythm, one I could follow.

Last I heard from Autumn, she was in the same state of being. Unable to move. She felt like a piece of herself had died along with him. And still, I held onto the impossible chance of his return. Tomorrow, I thought, tomorrow he'll call me up and ask to watch a movie or practice together. These thoughts of tomorrow are likely what kept me alive through the first weeks of his passing. Even at his funeral—a vast service in a bolstering church stuffed with plenty of family and countless faces I had never seen in my life—I shook hands, made quiet conversation with his Aunt Carrie, who apparently had babysat him while his parents went out of town for their anniversary each year, or his cousin, Diana, a lawyer, a beautiful little thing from Denver (*If you ever need anything—anything at all—you have my number now. Even if it isn't law related, feel free to call me.*) and through it all, the reason I was able to generate a smile, summon such an air of poignancy, was all due to a disconcerted optimism that I would get to see Tommy again someday. This hopefulness and the statements in which I'd sheepishly persuaded myself to be lies, kept me upright—present—motivated to see my best friend again soon. I couldn't wait! I was so excited for him to call because I missed him, and every day without him was an agonizing challenge.

So, I stayed up late and fought with these contradicting thoughts. I detoxed off cocaine; an evil terror instilled in my skull that I might meet the same fate. If I unknowingly snorted fentanyl into my system, I would be dead by dawn and in the news by noon. Everything that was tangible felt less dimensional, somehow discounted, and in my head all of my possessions were less real just for existing in front of me. I tried convincing myself it was all a bad dream when my theory of tomorrow began to wear—*all of this is a bad dream and I'll be waking up momentarily*. Any day now. I kept my ringer on so as to hear when Tommy would be calling. I smoked cigarettes on my balcony, in my kitchen, in my bathroom seconds before stepping into a shower. The showers I'd chalk with steam, forcing myself unconscious from the absurd heat. Movies reminded me of him. My piano gave comfort but in a nostalgic, self-conscious sort of way—twisted, betraying sounds. My kitchen grew increasingly vacant. An ashtray on the crumby countertop. Boxes of Chinese takeout, stained and aged. Half-read books. Lighters. Sunglasses. Too many rings for my fingers.

One day in early October, I crawled into the shower and sat bare on the ground. That same day I was meant to be playing in London but instead, I curled into myself on flat, charcoal tiling. My head leaned back against the polished stone lined up the wall and stared into the fogged glass. I fell into a trance of distinct memories—often memories of when Tommy and I lived together—our dingy Arlington apartment. The little movies caught at the front of my mind. The most ridiculous moment, while listening to one of our songs at a blushing volume, grinning and buzzing off beers, Tommy danced in the kitchen with such elegance, as if he were trained in foreign dance and chose that moment to reveal it. I later found out that the music and the alcohol blended to create this one special instance in which he could dance, and his dancing was so brilliant, so unique, fate felt less of theory then.

The absence of cocaine in my system made for a great deal of lunacy. I nearly crashed my car a number of times driving around town with intense brain fog, forgetting where I was going and losing track of time. My head would throb for an hour with an intense headache, and the next, it would go completely limp, seemingly useless. I thought of cocaine most of the day, wanting to do a line when the thoughts of Tommy would dig themselves too sharply on my skull. I smoked nearly a pack of cigarettes a day for over a week straight, drank several cups of coffee, and slept nearly fifteen hours a day, waking up in the glazed evenings. Paces taken around the apartment. Placing the needle on a record, carefully lifting it back, dropping it again, and lifting it once more. I felt animalistic—the most insane I had ever felt up until that point—and shrouded in a shadow of anxious guilt for the death of my best friend.

Tommy and I had been doing coke frequently since I was around twenty-one years old, we were both welcomed to it at bars and eventually gifted it when we gained a status of notoriety. I never thought this snowy powder, so brittle, so associated with triumph, would be the poison to crumble the foundation of my life. Was there anything I could have done to stop it? I'd heard so much about death and thought maybe I'd be better equipped when it finally got close to me. But the way it clings is like a mold—the weight of it so thick and chalk dry. I could have never imagined how intensely my muscles would ache. The greatest trick of all was how death could so intrinsically convince one of self-blame. And in some ways, I still believe I had something to do with the death. Tommy would reasonably be here if I had convinced him to stop doing drugs altogether, but instead, I only swayed him enough to quit the drugs *I wasn't taking*. Drugs I partook in were still fair game because I hadn't wanted to knock it either. Selfish. A shame.

This coke, if I had taken it, would have fatally struck me alongside my best friend. As fate would have it, I stood still—like a stranger in traffic—I existed without a face, alone among many, with people counting on me to stay alive. I tried to forget who I was, to distract myself from all responsibilities. And the trees grew exhausted, slouching their arms, letting go of their leaves. The air lightened, from a push to a brush. The attendance of the sun lessened. The people began to change with nature in unison. Knit sweaters. Corduroy olive tones and burnt oranges accented on bodies. Fewer pairs of sunglasses forked through hair, more cuffed beanies and winter caps with stitching lined parallel to eyebrows.

I lit a cigarette and held the crisped smoke in my lungs, this way I knew I could breathe. I sank my arms into my favorite denim jacket, worn and eaten over time, and dug my fingertips along my sinuses out on my balcony. My phone had been off for several days, an unknown amount of time, I didn't care. I didn't care about anything besides my friend who was taken away from me. I hardly had any dreams around this time, but the visions of Tommy flashed like pistol cracks in my brain, the images of his body and my intuition that recognized it was Tommy, but he was not there. A hollowed shell stripped of all aspects that made it truly beautiful.

X

Chasing Sunsets

I spent the entire night giving statements to authorities on the night I lost him. Then, at around six in the morning, I chalked my knuckles on Autumn's front door. I hadn't even told her yet and I didn't want to call her as I knew she'd been sleeping. So, I drove half-awake and half-alive, and parked on the curb as I'd done only a few weeks before. This time, Mazy did not answer the door. After two attempts and several minutes, Autumn appeared in the doorframe with her raised cinnamon cheeks, her hair twisted in apricot strands, and in an oversized DOORS t-shirt. Her annoyance left her face once she saw my eyes baked like two pink suns. Tear marks crystalized on my cheeks. The moment I saw her in front of me, I was reminded of the reality of my presence—the rough, tangible texture of the night before scratched against my heart.

"What happened?" she asked, low and alert. "What's wrong?"

I followed her into her bedroom where I sat beside her at the edge of her bed; I blinked my attention between her potted plant on the shelves and her concerned expression. I sighed. I told her everything—just how quickly it happened—I told her of his last words—do not worry about him, he'd said. But why Autumn? All the while, her face fell lower and lower until it seemed like all life had left her. The complete devastation was so apparent, an absolute hopelessness. She looked like she'd been tortured.

Windows shot paper cutouts of light across her bedroom, across her canary comforter and the mahogany vanity with its precise veneer work. She was crying now, too, silently, turned away so as not to let me see. The gentle intensity of her breath was the only sound besides the wind tumbling through the branches outside. Finally, she wiped her face with her sleeve and chewed on her cheek.

"Tommy," she started. I wasn't sure where she was going to take it. I noticed her gripping her bed sheets as if it were a hand she needed to hold. Pale knuckles. I placed my hand on hers in response and it seemed to give her strength. After a moment of breathing, she said, "I'm not good at relationships. They always end in total disaster—for me, you know—it's hard for me to really trust anyone."

I waited patiently for her to finish gathering her thoughts with drawn space. She whispered these words through choked inhales, "I fell in love with him completely." Tears patted her bed and her head struck my shoulder. "I loved him, and he loved me. I believed him when he said it. And we had a plan that after we finished being a band, we'd run away and be together." She barely got the words out before breaking completely.

I thought hard; I sifted through my memory searching for any hints at their behavior. I slept with Autumn twice while on the previous tour. Had Tommy been upset about this? I furrowed my eyebrows. My thoughts began to separate, becoming further from each other and out of focus.

"What?" I heard myself say.

"Tommy was my true love, I know he was," she repeated, then, "This can't be happening—no, no, this can't be happening—it can't."

She repeated the latter phrase over to herself multiple times with increasingly higher pitch as if a distressed chant. I had never seen Autumn cry in this fashion before in my entire life. I placed a meek palm on her back and began to rub up and down. I began to cry with her, though quietly, as I wanted to be strong for her.

"What do we do now?" I whispered.

She lifted her head from my shoulder and sighed for air, "I have no idea."

I said nothing; I had nothing to give.

"I guess we'll take a break," she decided. "There's no fucking way I'm performing without him. Not now at least. I can't even begin to think about what that'd be like." She shook her head slowly. "I can't believe this."

I tried hard to find the words to make the situation lighter but as I prepared them, they all felt false on my tongue. Everything was flat. Lousy. And I decided on the darkness, the vulnerability of the pain at the forefront; maybe it's better to allow the pain to hurt than to cover it.

"Why didn't you tell me? Tommy was my best friend—if I had known about you guys—I would have never come between you two. Autumn, you have to believe me," I said, with clenched desperation. I leaned into the pain, allowed it to seethe inside my body and provided it with no bandage. It didn't need one. I could face it. For now.

"No, Joe, don't do that. We weren't together. There were no rules, you know? Not until Beach Sirens ran its course and we could give ourselves to each other forever," she said. She sounded disillusioned by the end, as if realizing their fantasy was too lofty, and although earnest, highly unlikely. It made complete sense now, how the two of them were close and walked side by side most of the time. Neither of them really had any sexual desires on this last tour, which I did find odd for someone in their mid-twenties. Perhaps this is why Autumn quietly stopped partaking in such activities with me. The pieces fit together well.

"I'm sorry," I said aloud. My voice rasped and everything ached as if I wore a sickness.

"Why?" she questioned, a twang of offense in her voice. "Listen to me. You didn't have anything to do with this. You were *helping* him. You didn't know it was going to be laced—if anything it's Hal's fucking fault—but you were his best friend. Please understand that you were his best friend he ever had. And he loved you too. You didn't do this, Joey."

My tears dotted her sheets next. She seized my chin, turning my face forcefully parallel with hers in a sweet temper.

"Promise me you won't blame yourself for this," she whispered. I took turns between both of her rich eyes. I wanted to be in her arms. She was one of the most beautiful girls I had ever met, though I had never thought about it at first; in fact, I originally feared her quick temper, always defensive and biting. But over the years, I grew to know her as well as she knew herself. I saw her hardship as if she'd worn it on her sleeve—and I saw her confusion, her internal struggle —all of this became facets I soon admired about her. I grew to find adoration in her ability to push through suffering, to sift through the world with a cleaner filter than the rest of us. She was resilient, sentimental and far more human than myself. So, I nodded to show her I understood even if it hadn't been entirely true.

And she told me everything. Every question I had, she was willing to answer me then. And the more she told, the more everything began to fall into place for the two of them. Her confessions shot me back to the apartments when in our final year of college, we moved to Arlington for cheaper rent. Tommy and I spent plenty of time at the girls' apartment, and the girls at ours; the girl's apartment became synonymous with the meaning of home to the point that I never noticed when Tommy snuck over one night to be with Autumn. He crunched through the December snow and made his way up to the fifth floor. He sent her a message rather than knocking as to not wake Sophia. Tommy raced over when Autumn confided that she needed to see someone—but not anyone—she needed him. And what happened to Autumn was an anxiety attack; that particular night in December had been a relentless one.

Autumn developed anxiety mostly when she was young, and it carried over to adulthood. Her chest tightened. She couldn't breathe. Her heart was going to burst. Was this what a heart attack felt like? Tommy pushed his fingers against her cheeks and ran them back through her auburn head of hair. But something took control over the two of them that night, and upon their intimacy, that something changed the two of them forever.

That was, as I was told, six days before my twenty-fourth birthday; three weeks before the new year; five weeks before our first studio album would be certified Gold; and thirty-four months before Autumn would confess this to me. That was all the allotted time they had together—nearly three years—in a quiet, masquerading romance. While Sophia and I would have morning discussions over cappuccinos in France, the two of them would be off at The Louvre, or kissing in the sweetened air of Versailles. I spent most of the time completely infatuated with Sophia; the two of us wore fascinated eyes as we took in as much of the world as we could. I never noticed how close Autumn and Tommy had become until now, and now it revealed itself with such immediacy.

Autumn and Tommy would sit closely on the bus but keep themselves apart in the green rooms. Calculated. I was impressed by their attention to detail. But more, I only wish they had told Sophia and I about their love for one another and had tried to make it work. There was no sense in hiding it from the rest of us. On the Fatal Tour, Tommy was always off with me getting drunk and high, tripping on some sort of psychedelic. I learned how upset this had made Autumn. Tommy's self-defiance of his mind and body was unfair; I could agree with her that in seeking to destroy himself, it would mean destroying her. This resulted in them going silent with one another in the weeks that followed the tour, back in Los Angeles and waiting for Europe. And this was the catalyst. This was why Tommy insisted on tripping so hard and often on acid and weed; his escape meant he could handle being apart from Autumn. Of course, I could never have this confirmed but I knew him well enough to know this was the most likely conclusion. It was also why Autumn was so eager for me to check on Tommy, genuinely worried about her lover.

Tommy's passing was hard on all of us, with the assumption that Sophia was handling it in her own way. Autumn kept in touch less and less with each passing day—falling into herself—implosion. I knew exactly how it felt. I found myself increasingly aware of what was keeping the band together, that being myself. I was the keystone to the crumbling arch. If it wasn't for me, the band would have surely broken up before this dreaded incident. Could I have stopped this? Was my selfishness to blame? I couldn't allow myself to focus on this, and instead thought up the opposite. I spent every day wondering when he would come back and when the four of us would get back to making music. But that would never happen again.

———

It was November in Arlington when Sophia pressed a far step through the snow, eventually making it up the street toward me and Tommy's apartment. She made it to the fourth floor and was halfway into our apartment when she knocked on the door, fully swung back and practically slapped into our coat hanger. Tommy, Autumn and I spread around the living room—Tommy cuddled with his bong, Autumn sat near the record player spinning MGMT's *Little Dark Age*, and I sat at the kitchen table with my Moleskine notebook peeled open—Sophia smiled at the three of us.

"Hey guys," she said. Tommy and I gave her a glance while Autumn kept her attention on the floor, but she was the only one to respond, "Hey, Soph."

"It's here," she sang. Sophia reached into her bag to reveal a cardboard package. The thickness chewed from the days of traveling to arrive at their home in Virginia. We all knew what this package contained inside. We'd been waiting for days—weeks—for this one package to arrive at either one of our doorsteps.

In an instant, the four of us assembled at the kitchen table, and Sophia began tearing into the package. Her waist pressed into the edge of the table and she unsleeved it from the cardboard. Her hand tugged at it, and like the work of a blacksmith, the brilliant reveal of shimmering black showed itself. It wore a menacing beauty. There it was— the plastic wrap sparkling from the tungsten haze of the room—our first real record. It was the final product, an advanced release of our album pressed into vinyl and shipped for the band. An all-black background. White, digital lines skidding and colliding across the album like surges of electricity—subtle and thin but chaotic—the lines seemed like the reflective lines one might notice on the surface of water. And in bright orange, the words, 'Beach Sirens.'

The four of us huddled over the album for a long time in a seemingly stunned silence. This was it. The dream we had worked so hard for had finally fossilized into a piece of art we could see, touch, hear whenever we wanted. It was new. It was our creation; our newborn child. And we were the parents who nurtured and crafted this little piece of art with our minds and hearts for the last two years. Now, it rested in front of us on the woodgrain tabletop, nearly yellow from the dust-caked lighting fixture casting that familiar and awful rusted glow.

"Should we open it?" I asked robotically. My voice was peeped and hushed, almost a whisper.

Sophia glanced at me before she averted to tear into the wrapping. But then, "Wait!" A sharp croak from Autumn who seemed so worried by Sophia's methods. Autumn seemed to notice herself and deliberately reset. She asked calmly, "Should we really open it now?"

"Well, what are we waiting for?" Tommy asked.

"I don't know, this feels like a really big moment. Maybe we should wash our hands first before touching it," Autumn answered.

And Tommy began to laugh—admittedly, I giggled as gently as I could—Tommy shrugged his shoulders. "It's our album, Autumn. If anyone should get their hands on it, it's us. It isn't the Mona Lisa we're holding."

"Maybe we should," Sophia thought aloud, agreeing with Autumn. I rolled my eyes and gave an audible sound to accompany it. They all ignored me.

"Give it here," Tommy said, and he snatched it from Sophia. At first, he began shredding the plastic wrap with an equal veracity to Sophia, but the further in he got, he changed to tenderness. And soon, the plastic wrap was gone, and Tommy held the record naked in his hand. He pawed open the centerfold to observe the artwork inside. Distorted digital imagery like something from *The Matrix* or something similar to a Joy Division album cover. Admittedly, they had an influence on the album. White and orange lines against a matte black abyss. A pixelated ink black sea. It looked better than I could have ever imagined. On the inside, every track listed in orange with the lyrics typed out in white. The credits of the album on the bottom right. Every producer. ROT IRON. Our four names were printed multiple times throughout.

I heard the sharp inhale as Tommy pulled the vinyl from the thin sleeve. A singular, licorice black vinyl, double-sided, fourteen total tracks. A fifty minute debut. Tommy tugged at the paper. He held the lacquer disc with such care, tilting it to find the intricate grooves spiraling around the greasy void. He made a noise, a low hum, that sounded as if his mouth had been open, it would make an, *Oh*. And his hands began to tremble while holding it; tears twinkled in his eyes and he smiled, but instantly lost it. He looked up at the three of us as if to make sure we were all still there with him.

"It's really beautiful," Tommy mumbled. He laughed. He sniffled. "Um," he made this same sound over and over again to buy himself time. I understood just as I believe the girls understood. This was all we ever wanted. This was the physical proof we needed to present to the world that we were more than just a college indie band or four druggies with distortion pedals and loud drums. This was a step into the official world of music. The record in Tommy's hands was a tangible vessel to project the sounds we created. *We created sound*, I said to myself on repeat in my mind. We rewrote the air around us. I couldn't believe it but each time it felt a little more real. Increasingly, the world felt closer and a weight lifted in my chest.

Autumn positioned herself to intercept the record from Tommy and she cautiously met the record player to switch albums. The previous vinyl fell into its sleeve and ours proportioned itself onto the turntable. Spinning. The moment Autumn swung the needle back to the record, there was no sound in the room. We all held our breath. Total quiet. Then, the minute thump of the needle on the outer ring, and the silked scratch for less than a second.

A low drone swelled into the room, the first sound of Beach Sirens. And a snare. A kick. A snare. A kick. And my voice, low and collected, layered, reverberating.

Sometimes I think it's all been said before
But when I look at you I know
We left so much unsaid.
If we leave our hearts at the door
Can we call it haunted?

Tommy's eyes met mine. No words were required to know the joy in his face. Autumn grinned, equally astonished. Sophia lurched forward on her chalked Converse and wrapped her arms around mine. She shined her teeth at me with dimpled cheeks. Every piece of our lives had seemingly fallen into place correctly for the first time ever. None of us said anything but we all knew from that moment, that maybe things would be okay for a while. But more than that, life really was beautiful. It always had been. Like the rhythm of daily routine, or the beat of the heart, or the creations we wrote into our first record, life was a series of rhymes like one massive poem. Like all poetry, we could either try to understand or enjoy it for what it is.

It's not easy to take notice of the world, and especially its beauty. Our world is subtle in its beauty, never choosing to stand out, instead, it is quiet and there when you need it. Some need it every day. A reminder to continue forward. Others need it only every so often and are happily content. But the world will always be beautiful and, in turn, full of beautiful things—some of which we as human beings have created in dedication to it—art curated for the world to keep and enjoy along with the nature surrounding us.

Our world is imperfect, with hate and evil, but necessary for beauty to exist—the same as happiness only able to be truly felt as opposed to sorrow—warmth noticed only after experiencing cold. We navigate through the world experiencing all the negatives and the positives, and without the other, each will go unnoticed. Necessary. Essential. Our lives in Arlington were anything but vogue but it was the beauty of our sounds that kept us pushing forward every day, chipping away at the goal of completing our art. All of which would someday be in dedication to the world, for anyone that may want the music, or those who may need it. We curated our sound for ourselves and everyone else willing to listen.

The four of us watched each other closely as the first track rang in the living room of the apartment. Eight eyes remained vigilant. Our minds attuned. We expressed a myriad of jumbled thoughts and wandering excitement without ever opening our mouths. Our sound was real, and we were the creators. The four of us created art—created beauty—oh, we created beauty! We danced to the waves of our beauty as if we were the children of Apollo, students of music, masters of our souls. What I remember most though, was that boyish grin on Tommy's face, one so comforted by the love surrounding him and the peace he felt then so effortlessly—his long blonde hair brushing over his face, tilting his head when he becomes aware of how hard he'd been smiling—and looking at the rest of us with an expression he wore so easily, one that seemed to say, *thank you*.

———

Every time I clicked Sophia's name on my phone, I'd receive a series of six short drones before a voice explained that my call had been forwarded to an automated voice messaging system.

"Shut up," I'd tell it and end the call before the tone. I threw my phone at my bed. I wiped my palms over my eyelids and down my cheeks. I didn't know what I was doing anymore. I felt numb, and the furthest from myself I'd ever felt. I knew I was wasting my time. Then my phone buzzed in the comforter and a cold shiver coiled through my spine; I tackled the bed. I fumbled the phone through my fingers until I steadied and read the name-calling at the top of the screen. I exhaled, admittedly disappointed but eager all the same; I slid my finger across the screen and held the phone to my ear.

"Hey," I blurted.

"Hey."

It was Autumn, her toad voice lower than usual. Her voice had grown more tired, drained of life. I began to pace around my bedroom, looking at everything I owned but not really looking. The inconsistencies of paintbrush strokes on the walls. The chipped door frames. How badly my ceiling fan needed to be dusted, how badly everything needed to be dusted.

"Did you see what Sophie posted this morning?" Autumn asked. I gripped the phone with increasing force, annoyed with Sophia and her unfaltering, prancing joy she held through the death of her friend and her band. She was still off with this guy as if the two of them were ghosts and freely wandering the earth. It was now nearing Thanksgiving—two months since his death—we were supposed to be heading toward Japan by now.

"No," I replied. I did everything I could to muddy the snarl in my tone.

"She posted on all her socials today. Look at it."

"Can't you just tell me?"

"No. You're not going to believe me if I tell you."

I did as I was told and when I found her profile, I saw her most recent post. A post of the backside of her hand, familiar and small, but a silver chromatic ring dazzling on her finger. At the center of the band was a beautiful, shimmering diamond stone cut into an oval; a miraculous silver with glittered sprints of color, green and blue and red. Posted eight hours ago. Sophia Baker was engaged.

"No fucking way." The words plopped from my mouth.

"Yes *fucking way*. I just got off the phone with her, she showed me the ring and everything." Autumn knew Sophia wasn't going to call me. The haunting curiosities returned in violent flashes. Had I done something to upset her? Was she uncomfortable around me? Did she tell Autumn and make her promise not to tell me? My brain swirled with an icy weight, as if I were lost in a snowstorm.

"Oh," I provided to buy myself time to form a better response.

"He proposed at the Grand Canyon. They'd been hiking for days apparently and once they made it to the other side, Daniel got down on one knee with the sun in his eyes."

"That's—sweet," I managed. The words caused me physical pain. I was tense, and I felt the blood pumping behind my face.

"I guess so. If you ask me, I would've been pissed to be out in the middle of Arizona, drenched in sweat, and getting proposed to. Those are three things I hope never happen to me all at once."

We both laughed. But the silence that followed was palpable. For a long time, the line held at my ear was only a coarse haze. I believe she was pondering it just as I was. Sophia was going to be married. She'd been saying constantly for the last year she was ready to start a family, and now the first real step had been taken. It was real. It felt very adult. We'd gone to plenty of our friends' weddings, even performed at some, but now one of us would voluntarily exit the group and start anew.

There was also to mention, that constant fuzz pouring into my ear felt like a rope; it was as if the rope was tied to Autumn and I was holding on. Autumn was soon all I had left. And I wondered in that silence, if she felt the same way about me. Tommy was gone. She never wanted to talk about it. She wanted to talk about anything else so that's what we did. But now Sophia, ever distant from us, seemed to be making a clear distinction of her departure. The worst part was, I knew just how easy it would be for her. In fact, it was likely the easiest decision of her life. Sophia never wanted fame or fortune, or to stay in a band longer than our college years. It all happened so quickly, and she went along with it.

"Beach Sirens is over," I said aloud. It was meant to be a statement but it came out in the tone of a question. I swallowed and held my breath. I stopped pacing and stared at my shoes.

"I think so," Autumn said, her voice choking. The line fell to the familiar hum again, and we were both stuck in consideration. Maybe Autumn and I would lose connection too. The three people I loved so much for the last nearly seven years of my life would vanish entirely. The chilled aches of loneliness returned, like spiders tickling through my veins. I missed Tommy. I thought once I got off the phone with Autumn, perhaps I would try calling him again. Or I could try calling Sophia again, and congratulate her and Daniel. Or perhaps I'd go to see Autumn and pull her out of her bed. I would force her to go get ice cream with me, dairy-free ice cream so she could eat it with me. We'd sit outside and talk about the good times the four of us shared together, we'd chuckle like two old friends. I would do none of these things though.

"Joe?"

"Yeah, still here."

Fuzzy silence. I heard Autumn breathing through the phone.

"I'm sorry. I know you loved her," she said. And her words clung inside of me like hot tar. My eyelids drooped and I thought maybe I would go completely numb, or all of my muscles would give out, or my lungs would simply stop asking for oxygen. *Loved* her. Did I no longer love her? I tried to determine what I felt for Sophia anymore and what it meant to me. I couldn't be with her anymore; I hadn't been with her for nearing three years. Last time she and I ever shared a kiss was two Christmases ago.

I grew instantly tired, I felt my body swaying but unmoving, like the phantom movement from spending hours in the ocean. I collapsed on the edge of my bed and stared at the room. Chipped door frame. Dust on my bamboo dresser like frosting on a cake. These things became lifelines to remind myself that I can still do things that matter. I still have a purpose on my own even if only to complete little chores. Autumn cleared her throat on the line, and I remembered I was still on the phone with her.

"What do we do now?" I asked again. I hoped she would have any sort of answer; anything better than what she said.

"I don't know. I still had no idea."

I nodded as if she could see it. I wanted to tell her I missed her. Or I missed Tommy. Or I missed Sophia. Or I missed feeling like myself. I created this version of myself to help pull myself onto stages, to hold myself up in front of thousands of faces—but this person I cautiously created turned its nose on me—now so far from human and utterly repulsive—I no longer recognized the person I saw in the mirror. I leaned forward and examined the new age marks this monster gave me. My hairline was pushed back every year. Joe Henley was a beast I created. I had to get it out of bed, wash its hair in the morning, brush its teeth, pick its outfit; I had to feed him, take him outside, remind him to drink water, remind him to smile when a fan approached him, remind him to make eye contact during conversation even if he didn't want to. He was all-consuming and took so much, I was left with nothing. Hollow.

My true loves existed in the seams of my brain. But they were all then so far apart, and some were missing. Where had they gone? The seams were unraveling. I felt the tears rocking and eventually slipping down my cheeks. I sniffled and wiped my nose with my forearm.

"You okay?" Autumn asked. I shrugged.

"Honestly, I don't know anymore."

And many seconds later, she finally said, "Me neither."

Autumn and I sat in our bedrooms as the sun fell, telling each other scattered thoughts, and revealing emotions in short phrases. I lay in my bed without brushing my teeth and watched the sky rub into an indigo sheet; needle-pinned stars took to their places. We both fell asleep with our phones on speaker. I woke in the morning with my phone plugged into the charger, rested on the pillow beside mine, and her quiet purring fluttered into my room.

———

Thanksgiving was spent at my parent's house in Georgia. We had an informal dinner, something small with just the five of us. My two older sisters were home for the holiday. Beatrice Henley, half a dozen years my elder, was the oldest of the three and attended school in New England to become a lawyer. She was at this point one year into her practice. Next was Dianne Henley, the middle child, the shortest of us in height but with the most hair. She was a real estate agent in the Atlanta area with her new boyfriend, Lionel Briggs, who was, of course, a real estate photographer. My sisters tried to console me to the best of their abilities, and Betty must have realized that the best option would be to give me my space.

"I love you, I'm here for you," Dianne would say to me throughout the entire weekend. She said it between meals, before we turned in for bed and when I would leave for coffee each morning. Betty was much more reserved and seemed as if she were waiting for me to come to her. Betty had always been the quieter one, the maturest of the bunch and in turn, had the least amount of energy. Yet she was charged and focused, having never seen her with a boyfriend until she was a freshman in college but it only lasted two years. Then Betty was alone and back on her path to becoming a lawyer with her attention set on New York City. I looked up to her the most. There is something very powerful when someone wields an undying dream, they have no other choice but to accomplish, it is rather palpable. Contagious. I loved Dianne too, but she was a wanderer. All three of us looked rather similar, as we all featured the distinctly Irish nose of our father, the curled brunette strands of our mother, brown eyes across the whole family. A family of dreamers.

The night before Thanksgiving, I do vividly recall as if it were a real memory, I dreamt of myself standing on a city sidewalk, the city itself was unknown to me and unnecessary. Ahead of me was Tommy, only he faced away, but I knew it was him. The blonde buzz cut, the greasy Levi's, his left pierced ear. I was not curious as to how we'd gotten there, or what the situation was, as is often the case of logic within a dream. And I took a step forward, the sole of my boot knocked the cement, and he must have heard the sound because his body language changed to attentive, like prey, and soon enough he was walking away from me down the block. I tried calling out his name first softly then in increasing volume, but he refused and only kept wandering away. I pursued Tommy, marching eagerly along, finally shouting at him. He would have been able to hear me. And I hadn't noticed but at some point, our stride had turned to a run, and more still, into a full sprint. My blood was quick below my skin and my knees clenched with heat as I chugged as fast as my body would allow, passing block after block as Tommy ran ahead of me.

Notably, although entirely unnoticed in the present of the dream, there was not a single life walking or stirring on the city streets. We ran block after block, vacant of cars, of people, of pigeons and dogs. I swerved around trash cans and leaped onto curbs at each intersection, carrying forward in some urban void. I kept gaining on him but oddly, as if it were suddenly real, I began to lose momentum. My stride broadened but my lungs tightened, flaming on themselves and I began to wheeze. Tommy carried his pace steady, and he began to shrink in my vision, off he went steady like a horse, smaller and smaller on the sidewalk. My boots began to skid into the cement, my stride fizzled out and I flung my arms, coming to a full stop and watched as Tommy became nothing but a white speck somewhere on a far-off block. I watched there, heaving air with a sandpaper throat, until Tommy became nothing.

I awoke that morning in my parent's guest bedroom with a damp mattress where I'd pouted out a coat of sweat. I threw the sheets in the washer before even going downstairs to greet the rest of my family. Thursday morning and The *Macy's* Thanksgiving Day Parade was screeching from the television set in the living room, there within the shimmering sixty-inch LED screen, gigantic balloons of *The Peanut Gallery* were hovering through the city streets in a militant formation. My father was helping my mother and sisters in the kitchen, already summoning preparations for a larger family dinner. Thanksgiving always brought forth my striking memories of the band's first Thanksgiving together in Stamford. I still hold no regret or shame for the activities we engaged in. I ate very little at my parents' house and said even less. They kept their distance from me and offered me very little for the extended weekend I spent at their house. Their new house was a big, five-bedroom house in Athens. I offered them a piece of my earnings some five years ago, and after several denials, they finally accepted it.

Aside from the television, it was the quietest Thanksgiving. My father liked to watch the news, but it wouldn't be on for more than half an hour before my mother would cross the living room to shut it off. The investigation of Tommy's death was still ongoing, and whether or not the drugs had been laced on purpose was yet to be determined. And if they had been laced on purpose, that meant someone was potentially attempting to murder *me* by selling the drug to my assistant. I'd heard by this point that Hal was innocent (although, inexplicably and irrevocably *fired*) but Damion, the photographer he'd bought it off of, was on trial for potential voluntary manslaughter—or worse, first-degree murder—intent to kill. The pressing concern that someone was attempting to murder me had lingered for some time but I was doing well at suppressing such demented theories. Further, I knew it wasn't the innocent photographer kid—even back then, I knew it was much bigger than that—none of this was by accident.

When I left for the airport the Sunday after, I embraced both of my parents in a hug; I made sure to tell them how thankful I was for the two of them, and for their allowing such a noiseless visit. I promised that when I returned for Christmas, I would be better equipped for conversation. Their old grins tempted their cheeks, and I felt a comforting warmth chisel at my muscles. Accompanied by a tugging sensation of disappointment for not telling them more often that I loved them and was appreciative of everything they'd done for me. Their undying love was real and they wore it around on their faces.

On the plane back to Los Angeles I thought of them and how I could never lose them. I pressed my forehead on the window, looked out at the miniature buildings and patches of shaded grasslands. I didn't want to know what would happen if I lost anyone else. My life up until that point had been a series of gains, and now I wondered if I would spend the rest of my life losing. I closed my eyes and tried to get some rest.

Then, later came Christmas, with no clear resolution on the fate of the band. Everything was up in the air between us and ROT IRON; we decided to not further our discussions until after the new year. Back at home, I engaged in more conversation with my family. I told my mother about some of the restaurants I visited during our latest tour while whipping eggnog in a large serving bowl. I sat with my father after supper, sipping Heinekens and talking about the future. He was doing his best effort to inform me about the coming technology he read about online, that of quantum computing. I nodded, half-listening to him, and half-listening to the choir of toads and insects singing and bouncing along the fresh lawn. I opened up a bit more to Betty one night while sitting in the backyard, just the two of us, oldest and youngest. It was black out and the porch lit made her a silhouette in her chair.

"I think my personality is too much sometimes," I admitted to her, buzzed and talkative. "I give myself away too quickly—whether it's people or music or whatever—I lose myself in it and then if it's taken away from me, I feel like I'm left with nothing."

Betty sat across from me in her own lawn chair with a beer in her hand and listened to the dancing sounds of the crickets somewhere far off in the silver sheet of grass. The gritted sky sparkled clearly over the quaint neighborhood. She thought over a response and finally gave one.

"You're young, Joey. I think I'm the same as you. Once we find something we like, we squeeze as hard as we can and never want to let go. That's who we are, I guess. But the more you go through experiences like this—and the more you realize that nothing is really going to stay with you forever—you'll learn not to squeeze so hard and just appreciate the time you get with it. Does that make sense?"

I nodded. I felt like crying. I had nearly forgotten how much I loved my sisters. As I look back on the intimate moments of curious relations that can only come from siblinghood, I realize I should have told them I loved them more often. There was no other person as close to me as my sisters in a literal sense but also in a feeling of familial affection.

It felt good to be home for a while. I slept easier and thought of Tommy a little less in my hometown. I went to the *Ingles* grocery store when my mom needed anything for that night's supper, and would occasionally run into a fan or someone I'd gone to high school with. One old friend in particular, Edward Esther, was more of a distant memory. Edward was now a computer engineer, a father of two little girls and took them to get all the supplies needed for ice cream sundaes. He still wore thin, golden spectacles; he kept his hair up like a greaser but now looked older, and had gained a nearly unnoticeable gut. His daughters were four and two, named Adelaide and Norma respectively, both with the same silky, chocolate hair as their father. I said my farewells, my happy holidays, and looked over my shoulder more than once at Edward and his girls. Jealousy was not the right description, no, it was yearning.

———

The holidays wandered by, and eventually, the new year came. I counted down backward from ten in my parent's living room, stumbling for my glass of champagne on the mantle. I turned to my parents. My father, grayed beard, hairless scalp, and rosy cheeks. If not for his strong jaw and ocean blue eyes, he may have begun to look like Santa Claus. And my mother, happier in weight, thick silver hair, and shrinking eyes that sparkled when she smiled. The two of them watched me smile back at them—I was wrapped in a blanket of buzz after having nearly five glasses of champagne—and I told them I loved them.

"We love you too," my mother said. She was so quick with her response; she wasted no time getting the words out and spoken to me. As if she had been waiting or hoping I would say this to her. Her eyes turned in, I thought she might cry. My father snagged me around my arm and pulled me in close for a side hug.

I chuckled and studied my charcoal dress shoes. I felt his lips near my ear and he mumbled, "We're always going to be here for you, Joey. We're always here for you, don't you forget that."

I felt the tears rise beneath my face and my body turned hot. I loved them so much but felt wildly embarrassed then. I know they had read every tabloid and news article that came out about Tommy's death. They knew I was there and held him when he died. They knew about the cocaine, the drug habits, they knew everything. But they never mentioned it—not until I was ready.

I was then twenty-seven years old. I used to be the lead singer of the alternative pop band, Beach Sirens. Now, I wasn't sure who I was. I wanted to focus on being Joe Henley or at least find new ways to entertain the beast. I watched old flicks with my father on their sofa, everything from *East of Eden* to *The War of the Worlds* to *The Good, The Bad, and The Ugly*. My mother made us sandwiches. I started waking up earlier to go on walks with her around their neighborhood with their dog, Lana, a massive, ash-furred sheepdog. I rummaged through boxes of my old belongings in the spare bedroom, discovering short stories I'd written in elementary school, yearbooks, baseball cards, action figures and terrible drawings. What interested me most was the finding of my old choir binders from both high school and from George Washington.

Within these bound books I found all sorts of music. One of particular interest was a booklet that featured all the music from Mozart's *Requiem*. It featured all voice parts, as well as the piano. It was a beastly book. I saw my notes along the margins, parts to watch out for, when to hold, dissecting each syllable of Latin to make sure I got it correct. I was a tenor in the piece, hidden firmly in the middle of the voices. But I remember studying the *Requiem* in my freshman year at university. Sophia was there too, and she had to study the alto part. I thought of how the last time I'd truly looked at this booklet, I hadn't known her yet. I saw the massive history between us flare below my skull.

I ran my finger along the runs. The notes stamped into the aged sheets. The massive builds in the score. I found myself listening to the music in my head. *Kyrie*—the second movement—the basso tones rang low and languid, followed by the tenors and altos performing quiet runs, and the sopranos took the lead with their runs finally, and the four parts finally came together. Exquisite. Precise. I heard every voice part and when I read over the piano, I could hear it as well.

Something occurred to me then. I flipped to my sheet music from high school, some I hadn't seen in a decade. I ran my eyes over the music, and still, I could hear the voice clearly in my head, as if someone were singing it directly into my ears. I could nearly feel the vibrations of the voices. I glared. I set the sheet music aside and grasped at the electric keyboard atop the closet. I lowered it down with ease and plugged it into the wall. I thought of the piano in *Kyrie*, the sound I had just heard in my head, and replicated it with my eyes clenched shut. Upon my comparison, I had performed just as Mozart had written.

I could hear the music. I spent the rest of the day in the guest room fiddling with the electric keyboard. I wrote out a movement of my own while hunkered in the room, a six minute piano piece I named, *Bugbear*. I wrote out the four voice parts that accompanied, and everything else I had in mind. I could hear it clearly between the sound within my skull and the physical protrusions of waves exuding from the keyboard. I created the short piece first on average line paper, then translated it into sheet music by darkening the lines into a bar staff, skipping a line and continuing on the next.

By supper time, I completed my single movement, just for the thrill of my newfound ability with reading music, and the intuition of sound I knew was so secure. I spent three hours total writing out the piece; the six minute movement composed of angelic tones from the altos and sopranos. The whole piece was sliding, aromatic, practically melting into itself. That is until the latter half of the piece when I allow the voices to find each other, and I included an addition of a harpsichord. The beauty of the piece took shape as I imagined all the sounds and melodies combining for the final few measures. I could hear it ringing in a cathedral space, shimmering off the walls. I stuffed the sheet music into my travel bag and went to help my mother set the table downstairs.

The following day, I received a text while sitting on the back patio. I turned Oscar Wilde novel, *The Picture of Dorian Gray*, upside down so the innards rubbed the glass tabletop. I read the message and who had sent it. Vivian wrote:

> Happy New Year. My heart goes out to you. If you'd like to visit our set, I would love to have you.

She was, of course, referring to the film set of *Mass Hysteria*; last I heard production began on the 10th of January. This was the first message I had gotten from her in the last two weeks. It was my fault we hadn't continued our connection; I tried to grow into her but each passing day after losing Tommy, the more difficult a relationship proved to be. We saw each other only twice after Tommy's death and she seemed to respect my space and for that, I will always be thankful. I needed solitude.

I stared out at my parents' spacious backyard—the dead grass had taken a gentle brown—the leaves pedaled down to die softly on the earth—the perfectly chilled wind feathered against my neck and arms. It was a beautiful day even in the midst of winter in Georgia. In place of snow, there was sunshine. There I sat and thought over her text and wondered if this was something I would really be doing next. North Carolina was not so far away. And for the first time in my whole life, I had nowhere to be. I nodded to myself and the decaying nature that kept me company; I smiled, and it gave me strength. I hadn't smiled in a long time. To Vivian:

> Happy New Year to you as well. I hope the production is going well. I would gladly visit.

I blackened my phone screen and sank a bookmark into the novel. After one final moment in the winter afternoon, I stretched and headed back inside to tell my mother what I had planned for myself next.

VOLUME TWO
YOUNG MASTER

I

Truths Of The Universe

The first time I set foot on a movie set I wore my chestnut scuffed boots strapped tightly around my ankles and took a brisk stride down the street toward the men carrying a speed rail and hulking lights that faced stretched sheets on metallic frames. January air speckled the skin of my neck; I tugged the collar of my leather jacket up toward my ears. The tone of the morning was so dreary; the sky was wet cement. My cheeks were sagging.

The production that morning was filming in a neighborhood in Wilmington, North Carolina. The chosen neighborhood was lined with beautiful old homes, some of standard Southern Colonial architecture and others of a Victorian Revival draw. Ghastly Queen Annes. Stout Craftsmen peppered in between but the most prominent was by far the Colonials.

The night prior, I'd rolled into town in my parents' old Honda Civic, it was nearly midnight when I checked in at my hotel downtown. Now half past eight in the morning, I parked the Civic a block away and trotted down toward the film set. My boots clucked the wide sidewalk with the beautiful homes on my left and their manicured lawns, grass long dead in the winter and looked like bread dough spread flat from their entryway to the pavement, a constellation of dew droplets still clung and webbed about across the top; on my right would be the street but the view was blocked by giant work trucks, long eighteen-wheelers with white box behinds, a red logo stenciled along the side. The trucks varied in size as I pressed on toward the house at the end of the block, the one lit up by colossal lights hoisted onto tire-wheeled stands, taller than even myself.

I approached the house and stood at the face for a moment or two, completely dumbfounded by the chaos ensuing around me in every direction. Men and women of all shapes and shades lugged their carts on tired wheels up to the front of the house where the windows were spotlit by the circular lights. The lights were magnificent, much like the stage lights I had seen many times before, but these were at least double in size. And still, persons were carrying translucent makeup bags at their hips, clothing racks with outfits labeled and sleeved, hidden from the elements; others were passing out call sheets and switching their walkie batteries like drugs; others still were frantic —dense men hopped up the chinky metal lift gates of the work trucks —they cared for all sorts of metal equipment inside; some duties I was familiar with from the music world and others I had never seen in my life.

This wasn't completely unfamiliar to me as in the world of music, a lot of the same equipment exists. C-Stands, the cameras and their lenses, the tripods (called *sticks*), the restroom trailers delivered to the set (referred to as the *Honeywagon*). Everything in the world of film had a name and I was mostly oblivious to it. When I acted in music videos for Beach Sirens—the last one nearly two years ago—I saw this chaotic scramble but on a significantly simplified scale. We shot a handful of our music videos on location, but most took place in a studio soundstage. To my understanding then, around half of this film was to be shot on location, while the other half was to be shot back at the studio lot where two soundstages hid sets built for the film. Regardless of their plan, most of their process was completely lost on me.

I stumbled back on the sidewalk, nearly bumping into a burly, elderly woman with fantastic blue eyes and rust orange skin, several chins but a genuine smile, a bag at her side with several hair products and spray bottles lodged inside (visible due to the translucent nature of her bag). She greeted me, "Good morning, sir." And I returned the greeting with a smile that could only be a fraction of the warmth of hers. I scampered toward a tree then, and all at once, a group of young voices from various spots around the house shouted in militant unison, "*Second Team!*"

My heart twisted in my chest and my breath was caught. I wiped my nose on my sleeve and huddled into myself, into the tree and did my best to blend in. White sprinter vans were dropping more and more of the crew off behind me but still no sight of Vivian. I knew how these things went, I watched as two young men with a young lady jetted the legs of a black canopy toward the sky, and black tent sides followed along the legs, creating a closed-off tent complete with a zipper acting as a doorway. This, I knew, would be where the director or the cinematographer was likely to hide for the day and slither in and out to give notes and talk to virtually none of the crew.

I looked desperately for a white tent, likely to be a makeshift green room or a changing room for Vivian. Perhaps her green room would be inside of the house they were shooting in. My blood was racy and hot, I felt increasingly like an interloper. I dashed toward a young lady with curled blonde hair waving down her back, her jeans tucked into her hiking boots and a maroon scarf made her shoulders appear hunched.

"Excuse me," I said, and she flinched. She turned vapidly and gave me a weird eye. I continued anyway, "I'm looking for Vivian. Uh, Vivian Wells. I'm her—" I thought for a slice of a second on how to name myself, "Friend. I'm her friend, and I was wondering if I could get a call sheet from you."

"Uh," her eyebrows bent in, creating an upside-down V above her eyes. She was afraid, perhaps confused, and calculating how to handle the situation best. She said, "One second, sir."

With this, she swiveled on her heels and faced away from me, now really hunched over and murmuring into her black walkie-talkie complete with an antenna. She turned back to me, "Someone is coming to talk to you in just a second."

The young lady stayed close to me but far enough away for her to feel safe. She gave a detectable glance every few seconds while we both waited for whoever was to meet me with more information. I felt insane and out of place. All I wanted was to see Vivian again or feel any sense of comfort, any familiarity. It was only a minute or two later when a chromatic-haired man with an equally silver mustache came strutting toward me with a welcoming hand. I accepted, shaking firmly as he said, "Good morning. Ford Palmer, I'm the location manager of this production. How can I help you?"

Again, I explained I was only in search of Vivian. He gave the same disturbed and suspicious gaze. I started to explain but paused halfway. I groaned and turned my attention back to the young lady who had helped me before.

"I'm sorry—Excuse me," I said, and the young blonde tensed. "Yes, you, what's your name?"

She looked at Ford with a worrisome expression then back to me. "Katie."

"Okay, Katie, what are your top five favorite bands right now?"

"My top five? Uh—I guess, The Delectables, Beach Sirens, Do You Mind—"

I raised a hand, and she pattered out.

"Beach Sirens," I said. "I'm the lead singer of Beach Sirens."

She stared at me hard for a moment or two before her face flipped on itself, her eyes stretched wide, and her jaw gave up. She exclaimed, "Holy fucking shit. Yeah, *yeah!* You're—Joe Henley?"

I nodded. She looked back at Ford—he was less than amused.

"You're a singer?" he asked. He folded his arms over his protruding beer belly tucked into his belted trousers. He brushed his fingers over his salt-haired lip.

"Yes—Sir—Mr. Palmer. I'm, uh," and I leaned in close as if I were telling him a personal anecdote, "I'm dating Vivian Wells. But it's sort of a new thing—we haven't even told our managers—and we definitely haven't told the press. So, we're trying to keep it quiet, you know."

I withdrew my phone to show him a photo of Vivian and I posed together backstage at the Arizona show, her head resting on my shoulder, me with my earpiece in and a paper-thin layer of eyeliner tracing my sockets. I pulled back to find Ford nodding slowly. What followed was this location manager conversing with someone named Olivia who was waiting for me back at basecamp. I was told to head toward the mall, less than a mile away, where basecamp was planted in the middle of the parking lot on the South end, and Vivian was in her personal trailer. I hopped back in my Civic and followed the address given to me without any argument; zipping toward the mall to find my Juliet.

———

In a flash, I rolled into a parking space close to basecamp and walked into a maze of red and white trailers chalked to the asphalt. The setup was expertly done, much like the arrangements at music festivals, with buses and trailers that created narrow alleyways with doorsteps complete with welcome mats that led up into each trailer. I searched for one that could be Vivian's when a door swung open behind me. There stood a young lady with caramel skin and cornrows, she stood tall in the doorway and gave a healthy grin. She wore thin, oval glass frames resting on her nose and her bleach-washed overalls appeared baggy on her thin body.

"Hello," I blurted.

She bounced down the four black stairs with a waving hand, "Good morning," she rang, "I'm Olivia! And you must be Joe." I nodded to show I was him, for now, and crammed a cigarette against my teeth.

"It's lovely to finally meet you, Olivia. I've only heard good things. What is your role in all of this?" I asked, motioning with my arms stretched out toward the city of trailers as a whole.

"I'm the Second AD, I make the call sheets, among other things."

I nodded again, unsure what to say, but changed my face to show I was impressed. 'AD' stood for 'Assistant Director,' and there were typically three or four of them on or around any given production;

they kept the production in line and on schedule. To fill the brief silence, I flicked at my cigarette. "Do you smoke?" I asked.

"No, no, not anymore."

I rolled my eyes. What was becoming of this world? I blew a tangled wisp of smoke and looked back at Olivia. "So—I hate to be so blunt—is Vivian around here?"

"Yes! She just stepped into HMU—" she squinted at her watch, "Roughly three minutes ago. So, she'll be in there for the next hour."

Olivia walked me to the Hair & Makeup trailer, and handed me her printed call sheet, already folded in several ways, coffee stains blotched at the corners, highlighted and annotated in red ink along the sides. She explained that the scene first up did not include Vivian, which is why she had a later call. The first scene was with another actress I hadn't heard of who was apparently my age but playing an eighty year old woman. I glared at Olivia as she attempted to explain the plot of the movie to me, but I fell into a familiar daze, nodding and saying, "Oh, wow, yeah," while I studied the way in which my boots kicked the pebbles along the brownie asphalt.

Olivia knocked before instantly swinging the door open and she motioned for me to follow her up the steps and into the liquid fluorescent atmosphere of the trailer. Ladies with perfect makeup and peculiar framed glasses cheesed stretched grins while poking a brush at the face of Vivian. When I realized it was her, this girl with honey colored hair pinned up on her head and a pale color being applied to her face, I failed to contain my relief, my full body joy. The anxiety of the morning slipped out through my feet; Vivian shot up and attached herself to me with both arms squeezed around my back. The ladies in the trailer hummed chuckles when Vivian loosened her grip. A face of white makeup created a ghostly face on my black t-shirt.

"I'm so glad you made it," Vivian purred. She bit her lip and swayed with her arms still wrapped around my body. I pushed my fingers around the back of her neck and nearly got caught in the stitch-work of pins in her hair.

"I'm just happy to see your gorgeous face again," I hummed. And

I leaned down to kiss her. I pressed into her soft lips, soft as cake, and quickly ejected before I could find myself too entranced by her.

Snickers rose from one of the ladies in either the Hair Department or the Makeup Department. I turned to find the voice, she was short and stout, in the second half of life, with thick, silver hair and even thicker spectacle frames, colored maroon. She motioned her hand, and I shook it lightly as if it were a child. "Wanda," she said with five fingers pressed on her chest. Wanda was in Makeup.

I nodded and said, "Joe. It's lovely to meet you." I hadn't thought to ask which department she was in because then the next woman, Noreen, introduced herself, in Hair. Noreen was my height, paper thin, rich dark skin and hair buzzed short and dyed bleach blonde, similar to how Tommy liked to keep his hair in his last years. There was also Sylvie, a young, black haired Ukrainian woman with milk pale skin, also in Hair. Dora was the last, in the Makeup Department —I couldn't tell her age but knew she was either thirty or fifty or anywhere in between—Hispanic, gorgeous black hair fluffed with a side part, and wore a sky-blue jumpsuit, I practically bit my tongue from attempting not to ask her where she got it.

The ladies allowed me to sit in with them while Vivian went through the 'works' as it was called. They had a deadline time to have both her hair and makeup ready to go; the ladies were so skilled in their professions, that they flew through their hour with alarming grace and carried healthy gossip throughout the process. I was awestruck watching them apply Vivian's licorice black, bob-cut wig. It was second nature for them. Soon enough, she was ready. Vivian looked noticeably different, as she was about to be in character, no longer the actress infatuated with the rockstar, but instead a junior at Dacre College, looking to get a summer job as a caretaker for an elderly community neighborhood. This plot turns on its head, as I learned through the production process and upon getting my hands on the script some weeks later.

In the film, the elderly residents of this senior neighborhood are all in on an elaborate, demented scam—the scam being young adults, ages twenty-one to thirty, have secretly murdered their grandparents and now dress in their clothes and apply makeup to be eligible to live in this community—whether it was merely a fucked up premise or some sort of social commentary, I never really knew. It was Luca's brainchild, and he never cared to go over subtext.

Vivian tiptoed across the parking lot in artificially aged black Converse, blue jean shorts hiked all the way up her legs, and a tight, purple tank top. She flashed a smile over her shoulder when she noticed I was following closely behind her; I still felt severely out of place in the walls of red and white trailers. "Are you coming with me?"

I told her I would, absolutely, and together we climbed into one of the glimmering, white sprinter vans with her team of hair, makeup, and costume representatives. One of the young costume department ladies asked me nonchalantly how I was liking Wilmington so far and at that point, I hadn't seen much. I hadn't even been in the dainty port city for twelve hours yet. I noticed then that the van was without seatbelts as we pushed off the parking lot, towards the neighborhood. We were let through wooden traffic barriers placed by local police (hired to close the street for the film production). The van tumbled to a halt outside the house and out leaped Vivian along with her team; I was the last out of the van, and caught sheepish eye contact with Katie, the first-team production assistant (*first-team* meaning the actors, meaning Vivian), who still stood at the front of the house.

"Wait here," Vivian instructed. She skipped to the side driveway of the house and into the black tent. Katie scurried after her frantically, who was trying to motion her into the house for the scene. Just before I had arrived the cast rehearsed and blocked the scene. Now, it was nearly eleven in the morning, and Vivian's time to get in there. Once the director said action, she would pretend to be her character, Madeline Price, and get through the second scene (out of four) for the day.

I was motioned into the black tent where I met the scruffy digital imaging technician and the director of photography, Donna Murray. Donna was only five feet tall, slender with a bob of black hair. A slender, pale face despite her age and a thinly pointed nose. She had facial wrinkles where they were not due; the wear and tear of the film industry seemed to reflect plenty physically on the crew (and conveniently not the cast). Donna squinted up through bulky, square-framed emerald spectacles.

"This is my friend, Joe Henley, be good to him!" Vivian was eagerly whisked from sight, so I stood alone in the tent with Donna and her technician friend.

"Hi," he said, an extended hand that I shook politely. Donna motioned for me to sit next to her in one of the fold-out director's chairs.

"Is it taken?"

"Does it look taken?" she quipped.

I sat next to her and combed my fingers together. I did my very best to remain respectful, patient, and quiet. Donna leaned on the edge of her chair; she was peering at the three giant monitors—two of which reflected what the cameras inside the house were capturing, and the third was digital information, waveforms and color wheels. She murmured for the DIT to adjust something a fraction, the image boosted its shadows so minimally only she would notice.

"You're the DP," I said, although my pitch rang more like a question. Donna grinned with her teeth, but it fell quickly. She kept her gaze on the monitors, watchful as if she were preying on a creature in the wild.

"What do you think of this?"

Suddenly, the emerald frames were pressed back at me. I blinked. I knew what her job was; she was the final-say in the overall lighting of the scene, the angling of the camera, the lens chosen for each shot —*cinematography*—it was aptly named. This was the genetic makeup of any film, television program, music video, commercial. The cinematographer, or the director of photography, was of equal importance as the director. And here she was, peering at me with her fist pushed up under her chin, legs crossed, posed in a classic posture of insight.

"Oh—it's great," I replied. I glanced at the monitors. The windows were blacked out, I'd noticed it when I got out of the van. Giant, black sheets of cloth were boxed outward with enough room to place a light on a stand within it. These blackout boxes covered the windows. This gave the illusion that perhaps this scene takes place at night and the few lights within the blacked-out boxes gave the illustration of moonlight drooling from the back windows of the house.

The dual shots displayed on the monitor were of a bedroom with a cold light ribboned through the windows, the rest of the room dark, and a warm, copper light from a bedside lamp gave distinct contrast. One angle wide, the one beside it closer. Did I love it? I wasn't sure, but I knew it was appealing to the eye.

The old woman—or, I suppose, the young lady in enough makeup to appear as an old woman—crawled into the bed and stared straight into the lens. The camera angle flung to the floorboards. Some adjustments were being made, and I caught a quick glimpse of Vivian's black Converse in the corner of the frame. I struck a grin thinly.

"Yeah, no, it is really good. I don't have any reference to the film, but this feels—cold—in a good way. It's also a bit distant—I'm not sure if that was intentional."

Donna grinned so wide her cheeks pushed to the edges of her face. She replied, "It was. This is the language I speak in."

I chuckled and asked, "What does that mean?"

"Luca is in there directing his film as if writing a novel. He says everything he means to say through dialogue, blocking and arches. What I mean to say with my work lies more in the abstractions. This language of cinema I must create is poetry. I create images that cannot speak so I must say everything I mean to say without ever saying anything at all."

I noticed her voice had a whispering chalk-like quality to it, rounded and distinctive. *German*, I decided. *Or perhaps Icelandic.* Her bangle bracelets jingled on her wrists as she readjusted in her chair. "You see, in cinema, we use light to create emotion. It is not to be taken literally. In life, we have no perfect lighting in darkness, we have no soundtrack in the air. But in cinema, we allow ourselves to believe in these things—they are visual poetry. In the light, in the dark, above and below. Poetry is like life—yes—it is all around us, we just have to look a little harder to see it and understand it."

My vision clicked to the monitors when I heard a voice shout out, "Rolling!"

"Rolling!" I heard the PAs shouting from various distances.

The monitors were still in their frames and a red dot appeared on each monitor. The cameras were then swallowing all the information of light constructed by Donna's precision—captured into digital data—the modern cinema picture. And it was beautiful to watch. Horror, yes, but human all the same.

In the scene, the old woman lay on her back with the linen sheets wrapped at her chest and her fingers braided. An icy light from a full moon blew in from the window. Over cricketing floorboards, Madeline Price filled the doorframe; the old woman remained still, eyes closed and likely deep in sleep. Madeline rocked on her heels as she stared lovingly at the old woman before giving in; she tiptoed over the swollen green rug lying in the middle of the bedroom floor and gave the woman a curtly kiss atop her forehead. Madeline reached for the lamp and just before clicking it off, whispered, "In a little while."

The tangy light that once held a comfortable gloom over their faces was lost in a snap. Only the chilled moonlight outlined the textures of their faces, Madeline's black bob cut turned violet. She held a moment in the silent night before she rose and exited the room. The cameras did not follow Madeline on her exit. Instead, one camera began a slow push-in on the old woman asleep in her bed. The angle crept forward, nearly unnoticeable as the frame began to shrink and the woman became steadily larger. The camera tilted and rolled into a bird's-eye-view above the old woman. I felt I was watching something I may have not been supposed to see, and yet I could not look away for even a second. Then, as the camera settled onto a new angle, the old woman's eyes shot wide open, looking straight through the lens.

I nearly flinched but steeled my muscles all in a fraction of a second. The red dot disappeared on the camera; the monitor image tossed around the room, revealing the ceiling, C-stands, flags, a boom mic, and shot down to show the floor once more. The production assistants roared outside the tent, almost instantaneously, "Cut!"

"So, Vivian's friend," started Donna.

I turned to find Donna peering at me with her grin crooked on her face like the Cheshire Cat. She uncrossed her legs and leaned forward in her chair, and it squealed lightly. "What do you make of this filmmaking now?"

I saw it. The poetry she spoke of before. The craft that went into conveying emotion through the movement, the sound, the lighting. It was like a dance shaped into a story. I looked at Donna and said, "It seems like a ballet."

"Are you a filmmaker?" she asked, her tone was sincere as if she'd asked, *Are you from around here?*

I chuckled, "No, no." She continued to peer, awaiting further information. I swallowed. I thought of Sophia—of Autumn—of Tommy. I saw their faces. They felt like ghosts. I remembered the reality, and in turn, the gravity of Tommy and his real absence, how I would never see him again. I had to keep going, I had to get up every day without him, I had to respond to this woman before she repeated herself. I chewed the inside of my cheek and sighed.

"I'm a musician."

———

The most curious bit about watching Vivian act in her three scenes that day was how I completely lost myself in each take. Every time the cameras rolled, and the red dot returned—a watchful, red hazing eye —I fell into a lopsided trance. I was in the world Luca and Donna were creating and Vivian was no longer Vivian, instead, there was only Madeline Price. One moment, I could see Vivian behind the makeup and the wig and costume, I saw her giggling as the crew told her anecdotes, and the next, with the militant sound of the PAs, she was gone. Vanished. There stood only a fictitious character from the mind of Luca Krzyżewski. It was incredible and admittedly jarring to watch.

I never found a chance to go into the house that day. Instead, I was ushered with Vivian back to her trailer for lunch, then back to the set where we stayed until nightfall. I never met Luca that day either, he spent the entire day within the confines of the shooting house. So,

I had no idea what the man even looked like. I did get to catch up with Jonah outside of the house; we caught each other next to the craft service table. He looked up from the coffee pot and saw me there, unlit cigarette at the ready, and practically lost his mind at the sight—a face he knew although in the incorrect setting. Finally, it registered that he was not dreaming and everything around him was real.

"No fucking shit—Joe Henley."

"I should have called you and told you I would be out here," I chuckled as he pressed his cardboard cup to the foldout table. He crossed under the white canopy and pulled me in for a hug—it was the most uncomfortable hug I had ever partaken in, as he was strapped into some sort of tactical vest; I later found out this vest was the connection for him to carry a leveled camera at his waist, called Steadicam. It did exactly as the name implied, a camera operator could keep the camera steady with a large and frankly, dangerous, arm attachment. It took an incredible amount of training before one could use one of these professionally.

"What the hell are you doing here?" Jonah asked with a big grin, he scratched at his beard and under his baseball cap.

"I've gotten closer with the lead," I said. Jonah made a noise similar to a ghost stereotype.

"*Woah, woah, woah!* Don't tell me *Joe Henley* is going to settle down," he said in a sarcastic tone as if this was entirely out of the realm of possibility. I shrugged, scuffed up a laugh as I watched him drop a dollop of Half-and-Half into his black coffee. I had never seen him drink it any other way than black. I lit my cigarette and tried to determine if Jonah was a different character in this environment. He held himself taller, a straight back, he looked stronger and more confident. This was his mojo, I decided; this was his forte. One of the production assistants asked for him to return inside, he held his coffee cup at eye level and said, "Cheers, Joe."

They wrapped filming that day at eight sixteen; the PAs made sure everyone knew. I walked down the block to my car and returned to my hotel where I sat patiently for a text from Vivian. She had still to get out of hair, makeup and costume. An hour later, I was casually making my way through the downtown blocks to her hotel where we crept up into her room for a glass of champagne. Vivian showered and returned a moment later in a robe and her hair swirled into a cloudy towel.

"What did you think of the movie business?" she asked.

I was lying on my side across her bed, my boots and bomber jacket huddled near the provided desk. I scoffed a handful of air between my teeth before taming an answer, "It was—it was unreal—I don't even know how to describe it."

"It's a dirty, chaotic circus every single day and if a day goes perfectly smoothly, no hiccups at all, that means something has inherently gone wrong in itself. But it's addicting. Like a runner's high. Somehow, it seems a burst of endorphins crack in the brain when you hear the word, 'wrap.' Or sometimes it hits you while you're working. You look around at the lights, the cameras rising on massive cranes and you think—ah, there's that movie magic I've heard so much about—that's why we endure the hardship. That's why we wake up in the middle of the night and get home at sunrise."

"I will agree, you sure do work long hours," I said, grinning and propping myself on the bed in a pose I thought might look slightly more attractive. I reached and gently wrapped my hand around hers. Mine was large and tanned in comparison to her dainty palm.

"*I* work long hours. *You* work so little; it would be easier to say you work long *minutes*." A giggle kettled from her lips. Vivian hopped on the bed, a scoop of champagne flung from her glass and slapped the bedding. She peeped as she dabbed at the white comforter with her robe. I watched her in such amazement, her shift in self. The woman in front of me was so far from the apprehensive university girl I watched on the monitor screens only hours before.

"You're fantastic." I heard the words mumble from my lips, "You're absolutely incredible. It's like you said—magic—whatever it is, you have it inside of you."

She hummed another giggled, low and buzzing like a bumblebee. "You really think so?"

I nodded. She crossed her legs and took a sip. "I'll let you in on a secret—Joe Henley—I don't know how I do it either."

We laughed together at this. I sipped the champagne, and studied the glazed vinyl floors, gray as concrete but grained like oak. I went on about how dazzling it was to watch her act. I felt my attraction for her rising inside of me. She laid on her side across the bed and I laid opposite her with my arm bent to prop my head. I stared straight at her, her cheeks flooded pink, and she looked away.

"What?" I chuckled and placed my hand on top of hers.

"You're looking at me," she mumbled and dipped her face into the bedding. She lifted her head a moment later with a stuck grin. Her honey blonde hair stitched the rim of the towel wrapped high on her head. I looked her in the eyes, her oceanic, hazel eyes, and said, "You're easy to look at."

———

It wasn't until the seventh day of principal photography that I finally met Luca Krzyżewski. I kept asking Vivian when I'd get to meet him, but he was always far too busy for introductions. That is until halfway through my third day visiting the set. We had just begun a company move from the exterior of a country club, back to the movie studio on 23rd Street, ten minutes away (*five klicks away*, I heard the PAs chirp on a walkie). I followed Donna closely as if I was her child. I ended up sitting next to Luca on the bus, although I didn't know it was him at the time; it was the first time I met who would become my long-time collaborator, and a lifelong friend. Bronze skin—a mane of black hair that fluffed around his head, and in twirls hung over his eyes—a blacked out, long sleeve shirt and scraggly dark wash jeans in their last stage of life. He had a five o'clock shadow, salt and pepper. Fingernails gnawed down fine. He gripped a red binder and a tablet with both hands on his lap. I thought nothing of him; most people on set seem to go without too much notice.

"Hi," he said, and when I looked over, he was facing me and peeling the strands of black hair from his face.

"Hi," I replied. I wasn't sure what to say. A devilish smile spread on his face, it was then that I saw how strained his eyes were, lumps sagged below. He said, "You remind me of the Mick Jagger."

His accent came out then; the strong, Italian lineage rolled in his mouth. His naming Mick Jagger as *the* Mick Jagger threw me before I couldn't help but smile back.

"You look like Edward Scissorhands," I said, flashing my teeth. "But maybe after a summer vacation."

Luca began to chuckle, "I *wish* I were the Scissorhands!" Luca readjusted himself to better face me. He squinted his eyes. "What do you do, my friend?"

I realized then that he thought I was a member of his crew rather than a visitor. I cleared my throat and thought of the best response, "I'm involved in music. That's what I do actually, I'm a singer."

"Ah?" He lifted one of his eyebrows. "You are not crew? You are a *visitor*? A visitor from where?"

"I'm from—" And suddenly the phantom words of Ellis appeared at the forefront of my thoughts, they flashed and rang; I responded, "—I don't really know anymore." Luca nodded with a quizzical eye.

"You are mysterious man. Like Jim Morrison but not so attractive," he said. His lips curled. Clay colored sunlight flickered on his face as we passed by a wall of trees.

"Like Bob Dylan but taller and with less to say," I added. Luca chuckled heartily again.

"I like you—tell me, what is your name?" His voice curled high as he asked the question like climbing a scale. I looked him over; it felt like looking in a mirror.

"Joe."

"Joe? Luca. Nice to meet you, Joe." And when he extended his hand, everything clicked into place. The director, I thought, so this is Luca. Luca Krzyżewski. We talked the rest of the way back to the studio. The van passed the front gate and dipped into the main aisle that separated the rows of soundstages. Giant, scarlet numbers painted on the side of each stage. To the right, stages one through four and to the left, stages six through nine. Stage ten sat behind all of them, the biggest soundstage the studio had.

This was the place. Black sheets of asphalt spread between each soundstage, alleys stuffed with silver trucks and forklifts, thick strands of black cables braided together in metal baskets or snaking through alleys and basecamp. The stages we were using were three and four (stage two was also in use but it was converted into a cafeteria space for the catering company, *Slashed Catering*). We stumbled out of the van, just outside of stage four—the sets built within the stage were named:

'INT. - TUNNELS'

'INT. - BASEMENT'

'INT. - HALL BATHROOM'

Luca turned, confused to see me. I stood sheepishly with my hands at my sides, unsure what to do with them. He tilted his head, "Are you not going to lunch?"

"Not hungry."

Luca chuckled. "You are very strange, Joe. But I understand. Come with me then, please. *This* you will like."

And I followed him toward the stage. He twisted the silver handle on a red door, and into the stage we went, hit with a blast of cool air and a red painted line a few feet from the wall. The door slammed and sunlight was completely forgotten; now we lived in a different world. The walls themselves were painted black some time ago and dusty now, and huge metallic beams supported the structure. The sets within the space looked odd, they appeared to be unfinished buildings from the outside, with exposed wooden beams and shells made up of plywood. But inside, there was magic.

Led up by a ramp, I entered curiously into a grungy basement with greasy concrete walls, still smelling of paint from the fake grime added to detail. There, across the room from me was Luca, the film-maker, thumping his heavy boots on the wood floors, the man who birthed the idea for this hideous place. I still tried to wrap my head around the volume—the creator of marvelous stories and their surroundings—surroundings I now physically inhabited—stood before me, like a god in his own kingdom. He was only a shape in the darkness, a black skeletal figure with a spiked head. There, completely lost in this horror landscape brought to life, Luca spoke to me low and carefully in the basement, "Joe, my new friend, this is the power of the cinema."

"This is amazing," I heard myself mutter. I stood in a basement, as all my senses recognized it to be so, and yet the stairs led up and onto a ramp where we walked back out into the vast warehouse space, complete with speed rail lining the beams on the ceiling. C-Stands were stacked on a cart, giant blue sandbags huddled together on their own, and lights were prepped in positions with barn doors opened and shooting into the only window in the set.

Luca twisted around when we stepped off the plywood ramp; he chuckled, and I realized I must have gone wide-eyed at my surroundings. I followed him out of the soundstage where we met a siren sun; I fumbled for my sunglasses.

"So, you are musician? I ask, please, why are you here then?" Luca asked. He unfolded his own shades and looked up at me with a cocked expression.

"It's a long story," I replied, trying to avoid the complexities of such a question. But Luca grinned. "Ah, Joe, we have time. I am a storyteller! I am interested in your story too. Please, we walk now. And you tell me your story, no?"

And we walked through the alleyways of the stages, passing golf carts and stake beds, lift gates half drawn with the smell of weed flowing from within. We talked of how I ended up on his movie set, and of how Luca had gotten there himself. I offered him a cigarette and we smoked in the arteries of soundstages, talking about movies and music, light and sound, and I understood him to be an admirable artist. He must have felt the same about me for we became a seemingly inseparable pair from that day forward.

———

The rest of that week, I was no longer attached to Vivian's hip (any break she had she often liked to spend alone as well, the job of an actor is far more taxing than anyone is led to believe) but instead in a director's chair labeled 'Guest' beside Luca Krzyżewski. I learned plenty about filmmaking, and what films to watch, and what films were best viewed alone, and what films were best viewed on mute. Luca knew of my recent loss and what I was experiencing in this chapter of my life, and he recommended films that might help me through such a time. *Ikiru*, *The Seventh Seal*, *Hereditary*, *Good Will Hunting*, *The Basketball Diaries*, *A Ghost Story*. I learned where my new friend came from.

Luca Demetri Krzyżewski was born in Milan, Italy in December of 1991, making him four years my elder, almost to the day. His father, Borys Krzyżewski, was a Polish painter. To my understanding, Borys hitchhiked across Europe at the age of twenty-three and eventually found himself exploring the city of Milan where he met his future wife, Lucia. She was attending the University of Milan and studying Italian Sign Language (LIS), American Sign Language (ASL), and the English language. The two fell in love but Lucia had plans to explore Europe and America herself as a translator and told Borys it simply would not work.

Borys was a persistent man—he challenged her—he continued his expedition around Europe with his acrylics and his pencils. Any chance he had, he would purchase a postcard and write a letter to her. Although, he had no idea where she was in the world after she graduated. He knew she got an opportunity directly out of university, which led her first to Rome, then a month later, to New York. It would be four years of wandering Europe on his own with a stack of postcards reaching a thickness wider than the postcards themselves. Then, at the age of twenty-seven, Borys was in Belgium in a small flat he'd rented for himself, fixing air conditioning units by day, painting vigorously by night with nothing more to do (besides a daily pint at the pub). During the day, he'd go back out on the street and set up his canvases in his favorite spot of his favorite park, Parc de Bruxelles, and charge ten euros per portrait. He was in high demand, not for his charming looks but for his skillful hand and distinct artistry.

One day, he noticed a group of young women lying in the park, three of them, with bronze skin sparkling and black hair waving over their shoulders. As the story goes, Borys gathered his belongings, wandered over to where they laid, and asked if he could paint them just as they were. But, yes, one of the women was his true love, Lucia. And that night, back at his apartment, he gave her the stack of postcards he'd been waiting four years to give her. And the night after, at her hotel, she gave Borys a stack of her own postcards from across two continents, all love letters back to her traveling painter. It was a year later when Luca Krzyżewski was born.

Luca grew up a fairly normal child in Milan, his father now a successful painter, spending most of his time at a studio, and his mother teaching at her alma mater, but little Luca loved watching television. Both his mother and his father loathed how often they'd find their son planted directly in front of their new, box television set. They told Luca to play outside with the rest of the boys. Have fun! Make memories! But watching television programs was all he wanted to do—until he was eight years old, and his father allowed little Luca to come along to the cinema to watch an American Hollywood film called *Gladiator*—everything changed forever.

Luca was reborn. He began playing the character of Maximus everywhere he went. While Borys hadn't known the film would be unsuitable for an eight-year-old, he recognized the passion his son had found and he was thrilled to learn his child was an artist too. In high school, Luca began doing theater and studying Shakespeare. He auditioned for plays outside of his high school and the first role he was given was, astonishingly, Lucius in Shakespeare's *Julius Caesar* at the Elfo Puccini Theater, just northeast of the heart of Milan. He was only seventeen when he played the stoic attendant of Brutus and with the attendance of a filmmaker named Alfredo Saccini in the audience of opening night, he was whisked off to play heartthrob roles in Italian-produced television series. This went on for nearly seven years when even Luca began to notice he was aging out of the teen heartthrob aesthetic. He was twenty-five when he quit acting and used his money to produce his own short films.

Luca had finally found what he wanted to be, what he wanted to do with the rest of his life. He loved every second of being behind the camera, being in charge of what went into each frame and how it was executed. He edited all his films himself, which meant there was no fat, there was no need to do another take or to add a line because he wrote it in the past, and he knew how it would be edited in the future. It was this incitement, and this needled control over the process of his art that made him such an expert filmmaker. Not only that, but he was naturally a kind human being and extroverted; he was a young man everyone seemed to like having around.

Luca Krzyżewski was twenty-six when he won the Short Film Palme d'Or at the Cannes Film Festival 2018—the highest achievement for a short film, except perhaps the Academy Awards but even then, it's widely received that Cannes Film Festival is of higher stature —his short film was a drama about a thirteen year old boy who finds a tunnel beneath his house, named *Landfall*; the tunnel was apparently a metaphor for anxiety.

This short film, *Landfall,* was the first to have any substantial funding and a real crew, with real catering and real location agreements and city filing. It was the first time he hired Donna Murray on any of his productions who was from Iceland, as I had guessed. Donna grew up with doctor parents and wanted to make a name for herself as a cinematographer. She first did wedding shoots, then did videography for real estate, and finally evolved to cinematography for music videos. Then, for a rate less than she was already used to, she decided to shoot Luca's short film when they set up a video call—not because she needed the money, but because she liked the boy—Luca and Donna spent all six days of the shoot practically inseparable; their minds were perfectly in tune with the desired aesthetic and overall feel of the film.

The following year, Luca began writing his first feature film. He promised to bring Donna back. He had a producer at a major Hollywood studio ready to produce nearly anything he submitted. But

Luca, being a true artist, knew he wanted to take his time. It would be three years before Luca submitted his screenplay and to no one's surprise, it was dark and metaphorical, a sort of Gothic poetry like a screen adaptation of Edgar Allen Poe—but most of all—it was brilliant. And so, pre-production began when Luca and the producers agreed upon Wilmington, North Carolina with a modest, low budget for his first horror feature that was set to premiere in theaters fourteen months after shooting wrapped.

Luca spent several weeks driving around the port city in the passenger seat of Ford Palmer's pickup, making more red and blue notes on his already tattooed script, and preparing himself, meeting after meeting, for the greatest challenge of his life. However, seven days into shooting his film, on a quiet, late Thursday morning, I met him after shooting the first scene of the day with three scenes left to film back at the studio, and he was focused—cheerful—wise. He showed no physical signs of distress or emotional disruption. He was at peace and seemed more interested in me and showing me what it was he did. I sat and listened and learned as much as I could about the filmmaking process from Luca, Donna, and Vivian.

The next day, Friday, the First Assistant Director, Tyler Verrina, called lunch (*Alright, everyone, that's six on the dot, let's make it safe—Gretchen's gonna get last man? Great—bye, go eat, please*). The crew shuffled out of the giant elephant doors into the picturesque, watercolor sunset and toward stage two where catering was set up. Vivian plopped in a chair beside where Luca, Donna, and I were seated, just outside of the set where two monitors were set up. Our monitor setup was minuscule compared to the giant set that towered over us, although it was just a craft of spruce wood on the outside. It looked like a giant treehouse was built right inside of an even bigger warehouse. Luca's assistant, Hunter, appeared with two bags of takeout from a nearby Italian restaurant that Luca adored. I thanked Hunter and he nodded politely before he shot off to hide somewhere.

Vivian groaned. I leaned over to brush the black bob wig from her forehead and kiss her when I realized then how much she looked peculiarly like Donna. They looked like two twin sisters or clones seated next to one another. Still glancing between the two of them, I blurted in a questioning tone, "Luca."

"Mm?" He said with a mouthful of spaghetti waterfalling and spooling from his pinched lips.

"You wrote this movie, right? All of this is your idea."

"Si."

I continued to stare at Vivian and Donna. Nobody seemed to mention it, but the protagonist of the film was certainly made to look like the cinematographer and longtime friend of the director. I minded their business and cracked into my plastic cupped salad. Vivian leaned her head back, Donna dug into her dinner plate from catering. Luca wiped his chin of orange.

"Joe, I think you should be filmmaker," he said.

This comment prompted a giggle from Vivian before she replied, "Sure. Let's convert him to the dark side. Who knows, maybe he'll fit right in. But then again, I do like dating a rock star."

"I'm serious! Joe has the eye, the filmmaker eye. Donna, you agree? You tell me about this boy," he said while gesturing a cupped palm toward Donna as if asking her to put something in his hand. Donna nodded without ever looking up, focused on dicing her chicken risotto with her tiny plastic cutlery, "Yes, I believe he has what it takes. He is an artist, after all."

I'd made a few films before but nothing remotely close to the Hollywood chic captured in these soundstages. I made art films, much to the likes of Andy Warhol. For one particular film I made, named *Hypnos' Playhouse*, I set up a single, static shot of myself in a giant, abandoned warehouse, and filmed myself sleeping in a sleeping bag for five and a half hours; a second camera I had on a tripod filmed my unconscious body at a closer angle, and this camera plugged into a stuttering box television to my right. This allowed for a secondary, optional, flickering angle of my sleeping face. I recorded a soundtrack for the film in a single take with an electric keyboard in my apartment during the middle of the night. This was the style of off-putting, post-modern, ironic art house films I enjoyed making. No lines to memorize, no point to it all, up to interpretation and something that could be shown on a wall in an art museum (most were upwards of five to six hours long anyway).

"Joe," Luca hiccupped, "You make career change. Please, yes."

"What?" I asked, genuinely taken aback.

"What yourself! You do not have to always be Joe Henley rockstar. You can be Joe Henley filmmaker!"

I scoffed. Luca set his plastic fork in his pasta. "Why not? You know that the average person changes their career three to seven times in their lifetime? That's real, look it up! And almost half of teachers quit teaching in their first five years. *Unreal* statistic. I know—before you say—I know, teacher is much different from film director. I am aware."

"That is an unreal statistic, Luca, yes, but—I've been working in music professionally for the last eight years of my life—I don't have any intentions of stopping either."

"Without band, what will you do?"

"Luca," Donna jabbed. She had a frightening motherly tone in her voice, sharp and meaningful. Luca caught my stare, and he looked away quickly, down at the floor. A shameful contemplation. Luca put his hands up defensively, "I am sorry if I make you upset, Joe, you know that is not what I mean to do."

And although my salad suddenly ran devoid of taste and my stomach was numbed, full of nothing but bloating, and my legs felt raw, I managed a smile. I replied, "It's alright. It's a good question. You know, right now, I just want to focus on my relationship and think about music after some more time has passed."

I said this while knowing that tomorrow morning, every website would receive word that Beach Sirens would officially be taking *an indefinite hiatus*. Anyone who has read this about a band before knows this is the translation for 'the band is breaking up while leaving the severely unlikely option open for someday returning.' It was a decision made by Autumn, Sophia and I in a group call with Ant and ROT IRON. This salad was the first thing I'd eaten in almost two days and was only just now starting to feel a little bit better.

"In meantime, I would love it if you stayed with me," Luca stated.

He was proud of himself as if he were doing me some sort of service with this proclamation. I knew he meant well, and I was really beginning to fall for the oddball European artist. He flicked the black hair back on his head and gave a boyish grin, wide on his hollowed cheeks.

"I'd love to, but I also don't want to intrude. I really do like being here, but this is your place of work—"

"No. Joe, please, please," he started. Luca shrugged with a huff of air, "Fine! You don't have to be filmmaker. But I like having you around—you are real artist—we stick together. So, please stay here and watch me make cinema."

The buttery concrete floors fell out of focus as I clocked the notion. A change of scenery. Something new to try out in this only attempt we get at life. I thought of Tommy. I was older than him and always would be; while I continued on with life, he was fossilized at twenty-five. He would have loved the soundstage and the movie sets. If I were to stay and be a part of this film, it would all be in dedication to him. I grazed at the inside of my cheek before turning my gaze toward Vivian.

The only other person I would want to make sure this was okay with was her. After all, I would assume Vivian would want some time spent apart from me, her new boyfriend, so she can focus on her craft. She caught my stare and lightly dipped her head in a single nod. She smiled, and even under all the hair, makeup and costumes; she caused a warmth of security to replace the sinking sensation that choked my body. She made me feel, for lack of a better term, whole.

Back at Luca, grinning with tomato sauce staining on either side of his lips. I raised an eyebrow at him. He was a peculiar individual, to be sure, but already someone I considered to be a friend.

"Okay, I'll stick around."

Luca nodded, and a thin smile twined into his face. For the rest of the day, I watched quietly as Luca brought his film to life. I began to understand the importance of a leader, the importance of trust and friendship. I was skeptical of this new and unfamiliar environment; it all felt quite alien to me then. The point I kept returning to, while staring at the tall, shadowed rafters overhead, was that I truly had nothing better to do.

———

"Do you know why I wanted to become a filmmaker?"

Luca was standing right in front of me with a red and neon green glow illuminated across his face; a twisted, neon lit Heineken sign hung on the chewy brick wall and cast all sorts of strange hazy colors. We stood at the bar with one forearm leaned into the chipped wood when two new Aperol spritzes slid toward us. Luca changed his attention toward the drink, sipped, closed his eyes, and to the blonde bartender, "Grazie." Then back to me, "Well, *do you?*"

"No," I replied. We'd only been in the bar for twenty minutes at most and this was already our second drink. Luca loved Aperol; I was indifferent to it. It was a peppy Saturday night in the downtown bar, hidden underground with century old stone steps leading down into the slum. To our left, a Q ball cracked at the apex of the pool rack, a college aged boy leaned back with the pool stick swinging up toward the ceiling. To the right, a group of six sat conversing at a high-top table with a round of beers. Luca and I were discussing the idea that perhaps not every question has an answer, that's when our drinks ran dry. Now, he was leading me back to our table in the Flemish brick bunker, where Vivian Wells and Donna Murray sat closely with their own cocktails.

"Neither do I! This is what I mean—not every question has an answer. Meaning of life? See—no real answer—most people are not willing to accept this, and some waste their entire lives in search of the answer that does not exist! Bah, but who cares? We all live as we please! Because on a long enough timeline, all of us in this bar—all of us in this country—all of us *living* right now *and* in the past—it will all be forgotten. So, who cares? Let everything roll off shoulder, and smile! You understand, no?"

"I do," I mumbled, loud enough to hear over the music. I kept my head down as we wandered across the bar, but everyone seemed to be preoccupied with their own fun. I slumped back next to Vivian; I didn't notice when I put my arm around her until she cuddled closer into my shoulder.

"Good!" Luca plopped on the wrap-around seating, not quite a booth as one side was open, but the same style of cushioning. A light spruce table with all four glasses muddled together with various heights and various amber hues like fossils twinkling in the dim light of the room. Luca continued, "*You* make sound. Brilliant! Powerful! Donna, my love, she make light. She paint these—these—magnificent portraits of light and color, yes? They are so *magnifico*. What I do—I combine these two. Sound—the light—and the absence of them when needed—and create the moving picture. And no, no, no, *I know what you think!* I know what you think, *Joe!* The pictures are not moving, that is magician trick. *Illusion*. But if I make you—BAH! — Jump? If I make you jump from your seat, or I make you cry, or I make you laugh, then, my friend, that is the picture moving *you*. And if I can do that with the light and the sound, and you feel it, that is real magic. Understand?"

He finished most of his ramblings with 'understand?' I suppose as a way to make sure I understood everything he was trying to say. Whether he wanted to make sure I understood his second language (he first learned Italian as he lived there the first twenty years of his life, he also knew Polish and licks of French; he was practically fluent in English at this point) or if he wanted to make sure I was following another one of his meandering ideas about the universe, I am yet to find out even now. And so, I nodded to show the European filmmaker that I understood.

Luca tossed a glance around the table and straightened when Donna was smiling knowingly. She was an incredibly intrinsic person.

"I ramble again," he said. "Joe, please, tell me how you are doing. I read about your band on *indefinite* hiatus. What does this mean?"

I sighed, the words still cut but I'd had enough time to digest them by now, "It means my band is likely done. And maybe we'll never make music again but we're still on the label just in case. It's a very technical situation but in my eyes, I'm not in a band anymore." I took a large, heaping slug of Aperol.

"What are you going to do now?" Donna asked.

"I'm going to keep living every day because it's beginning to feel like that's all I can do."

"And I hope you don't mind my asking—making music—is that something you're interested in continuing?" she questioned.

When Donna added this, all eyes fell on me. Even Vivian tilted her head to note my expression. I swallowed and stared at the table. I stared so hard I thought I might break the glasses. But I said, "On occasion, I think I'll continue music. I don't really know. Music is like my breath, you know, I can't go very long without it. If I'm being honest, being here with you guys is enough—this—this is what I need right now."

Donna and Luca found each other's eyes for a flash of a second and exchanged warm grins, as if they were my parents, proud of me and saying more with their eyes than they could ever say out loud. Then, Luca slapped a firm grasp on my shoulder and rocked my body, the same way Tommy used to.

"You believe in God, Joe?"

"Not so much."

"Good. No need. You have everything you need here. Nothing will happen to you when you die. Nothing happen to your friend. He is just no longer here. And this is okay. This is how we pass the energy from one to another, whatever it may be."

I nodded, I felt my eyelids growing heavy again and my stomach weighing me into my seat, "You're probably right." And I took another swig from my glass. Now, I just wanted outside to smoke but I just ran my palm up and down Vivian's back.

"Psh. I am right! Like the Catholics say, ashes to ashes, dust to dust. Our bodies, you and me, we are dust. Everything break down to the same thing," Luca said as he drew dangling strands of black from his face. "But it is the energy inside of us that makes us different. There is this special energy in the trees, this special energy in your pets and the tomatoes. This energy is special, because it makes life, and from birth to death, it moves—and when it moves, it makes change. Change is what life is. Start small, grow up, grow big. Then gone. That is it! So, I say, embrace change! No matter how big or small."

Luca shook his fist as he finished his speech. I grinned and looked around the bar, doing my best to memorize the moment like a snapshot in time. These strangers will remain at this age in my memory. These young people moving their bodies, clicking pool balls on the velvet tables under muddy lights, spilling the foam off their beer glasses as they narrowly duck from whizzing darts, new faces fumbling from the steps into the lair and taking in the scene just as I was. This was a moment, I realized, one to be filed away as one of the good times. Time refused, however, to keep still. All of it kept moving—moving forward—in the standard motion.

I turned and Luca had just placed his spritz back on the table. He swallowed and with scrunched eyes, he said, "Do you believe you were placed on this planet to make music?"

"I don't know. Maybe."

"Maybe. Maybe so. Or maybe you were simply put on this planet, for no reason at all, and you want to make music. Why can that not be enough?"

The whole nihilistic outlook made my knees ache. I felt the gnawing sensation lining the muscles of my mouth.

I excused myself, "I need a cigarette." I traveled up the stone steps with Luca close behind. We reached the top and stood in the gritted alleyway, at the far end where it opened back into the street, twenty-somethings crisscrossed every few seconds like the extras in his movie. I bit the end of the cigarette and drew a sharp burn of dark smoke into my lungs, filling them, fuller and full, and out.

I nodded to Luca, handed him my lighter and relit the conversation, "My friend used to say our brains are too complex, to the point that we've overcomplicated almost everything. We add steps, and like you said, we ask questions that don't have answers. It's like the curse of consciousness."

"Why do you think dog is so happy?" he asked and blew all the smoke from his mouth and cut into the January chill. I scoffed at the question, "Good point," and hunched my shoulders. A group of young ladies strutted toward us; one gave a lengthy stare at me in the darkness before she decided I wasn't Joe Henley, and descended into the bar.

"Just do whatever you want. It will not make a difference in the end," Luca said, "All your songs, all my films, they will all be lost with the human race someday. All of it will be gone. All music, all literature, all poetry, all art. It will be destroyed with the species. *So dark*, I know, so brooding! *Brooding Luca*. But truth! Acceptance. No more humans mean all of us goes away too. And that is okay."

"Which means there really is no God." I focused on my breath and watched the hot air wisp from my mouth; it became difficult to differentiate between smoke and breath in the mustard smog of streetlights in the alley. Above us, an inky, wet contraption of fire escape hunched against the brick, all the way to the silver sky. Luca chimed in again, "But lucky for us if there was God."

"Why?"

"We are artists."

"What does that have to do with anything?"

He chuckled softly, "What? You think Heaven have more artists who creating beauty, or you think they have more accountants and attorneys?" His chuckle quickly shot into a snicker. When he took a sip of his drink, the conversation had an intermission.

"This spritz," he continued, "Well-made here." I agreed. Luca cleared his throat, "Enough of the Tolstoy *Confessions* talk! It make me *nauseous* to run in circles with these thoughts all the time. Like jogging in place, never going anywhere, except I get exhausted. What shall we talk about?"

I tongued the question, and said, "What is your favorite film score?"

"Ah, bella domanda! Good question, Joe. I choose *The Shining* score. So haunting! The music is like ghost on its own. It is as if I should not be listening—a powerful score—and you?"

I hadn't thought about it before. Tommy and I loved watching movies together. All four of us would watch plenty of movies together, especially when we lived in D.C.

"*A Clockwork Orange.*"

An attentive gaze. Luca was glued on me as if I were a painting he'd felt a profound connection to. "Really?" He asked, a tinge of ecstatic desperation in his voice like a child who was just told he could spend the night at his friend's house.

I nodded.

"Do you think you could ever make something like that?"

"I don't see why not."

Luca flicked the butt with thumb and forefinger and the red light zipped toward the sidewalk. It bounced and pattered out to nothing. "Funny, though. We both chose Kubrick films."

I shrugged my shoulders. "He's a master. One of a kind."

An honest look spread across his face. His eyes held quantities of curiosity, effortlessly, the two little brown beads were comforting and warm. "Joe, I am happy you are here. And I am happy you have Vivian. You have me now too, understand?"

"Thank you," I choked. I sucked hard on the cigarette. I felt weakened by his words, but all the while overcome with an overwhelming urge to engage in a big hug with Luca.

"Vivian, you really like her?"

"Yeah. Yeah, I do."

"Maybe she is the one, no?"

I hadn't thought about this before. There was always the aspect of soulmate that I pondered occasionally, especially as a musician. Was Vivian the one I had been waiting for? She certainly made me happy and was someone I found incredibly easy to talk to, to get along with, and had plenty of reassuring qualities that could make for a great companion in this tread of life. Perhaps this was it? I was twenty-seven. If not my soulmate, at the very least, it was something I should have thought about. Was a partner what I wanted? I felt my head grow.

"Look, I am not trying to scare you," Luca chuckled. "Was not trick question! Just my curiosity. She is my muse, for lack of better term. This is how you say it here? I mean to say, she is the woman I want to act in all of the films I make. I want to make sure she is happy, but I want my new friend to be happy also!"

"Who knows," I complied. "Maybe so. I guess we'll see what happens."

"You are like Romeo. She is Juliet! Let her know how beautiful she is to you because that is what they like to hear. Well, in my experience. *Fuck*." He swirled his spritz and glanced at the stairs. He seemed ready to head back inside.

"One more question," I prompted, and he lifted his eyebrows. "How is it you don't have a girlfriend or a wife or anything like that?"

He grinned and the black hair mopped over his eyes, but he left them there. "Joe, my friend, in my experience, I am no good at relationship. Look at me! Always on movie set. I have never married because of this. So, I have found loophole." He led down the crooked steps.

"A loophole?" I questioned. He nodded and shook his index finger around, "I do not go around telling every person this, Joe! *Al cuore non si comanda*. I find loophole by hiring the woman I am in love with. That way, when I see her and work alongside her, work becomes more happy! And work becomes something I look forward to—more than I do already—it make me that much better of a filmmaker."

I stopped in the doorway of the bar as everything fell into place. I couldn't help but grin, of course, I knew.

"Donna," I said. Over his shoulder, the slyest nod and a half smile blew from Luca before he sought our table again. It all made sense, him and her, and it was so genius of him. I immediately thought of Sophia and how I had tried to do the same thing. Images of Sophia through the years fluttered through my head like the sun blinking between trees—chestnut hair, and dough eyes—I saw her rings, her dimples, her tattoos—*the Red Upon the Hill*.

I squeezed my eyes shut. When I blinked them open, I was back in the bar with the strange group of filmmakers. Luca plopped into the booth seating and the back of his head landed on Donna's shoulder;

he glanced at me with one brow bent up as if it were caught on a hook, "Carpe Diem, Joe. We are here now!"

And he laughed, a laugh so highly contagious and beautiful that the four of us laughed together; Vivian was the loudest and continued to giggle long after the rest of us subsided. We ended up ordering more drinks, discussing so many topics, another round and conversing some more. It didn't matter that it was after midnight. This was a connection—this was what artists did together—this was life.

As we stumbled back to the hotel a few blocks away, through the frozen air with our arms slung high over each other's shoulders, we sang my song, *Loose Ends*, loudly and ironically. I could not break my guffaw at the performance Luca gave, shuffling ahead of us in the tangerine-lit streets, soaked in shadows and dingy streetlight, as he tried to click his heels while poorly reciting the chorus, then tripping on the uneven sidewalk and nearly cracking his skull on the pavement. He straightened and turned to face us as we caught up to him in the pale darkness.

"I'm okay!" He threw his arms high over his head, his gray sweater shot up too, and we all saw his caramel stomach. When we caught up to him, his eyes doubled in size from something over our shoulders.

"*Molto bello,*" Luca mumbled to himself; he was stuck in a trance, his jaw soft. Then, he whipped his phone from his pocket, a sober light bled across his face as he fiddled around for the camera setting. "*Gah!* You, you, and you. Stand in line right here. This light—so perfect! Donna, angioletto mio, you will love this, promise. Stand! Smile, big smile! Joe—you must also—please, *please!*"

Luca got the photo he wanted after a few tries. We were all drunk and bonking each other's noggin as we squeezed our eyes to try and focus on the smartphone image, brighter on the screen than in real life. There was me on the left slouching in toward Vivian, who was flashing all her teeth and looked like maybe she'd had her eyes closed, and Donna on the right with a tranquil pose, a grin so peaceful she reminded me of the Mona Lisa. To Donna's left, there was a figure in the glinting reflection of the storefront window. A 'closed' sign skewed half the face, but it was obvious, even in the shadowed murkiness of the reflection, that it was Luca with his Robert Smith hairdo in utter disarray.

I begged Luca to send it to me, at which he obliged. I stared at the image as the four of us went up the elevator where I would sleep with Vivian in her suite—the other two a mystery. I felt a single tear make a wet crawl on my cheek, almost frightening me as I quickly wiped it away. The picture of all of us made me feel so eager yet so terrified—please, I thought, please don't let me lose them this time; this time I want them to be with me forever.

The idea of praying crossed my mind. The way I would sometimes overhear my mother doing in her bedroom some nights. But the image was enough, proof of what was, a symbol of hope. By this point, I hadn't even touched the key of a piano in two weeks. The longest I'd gone since I was twenty years old. What bothered me though, was how I did not quite miss it. This new world I was slowly unraveling was peculiarly of more importance to me now. Maybe Luca was right. Maybe I am here, and I simply *enjoy* music. Is that enough?

Vivian keyed us into her room and shed her clothing; I followed. In the darkness of her hotel suite, our bodies collided. Then, I lay in the center of the bed, wrapped in a thin silk of sweat with Vivian purring asleep on my chest, and for the first time in so, so long, I was happy. Different, and entirely new. The thought simmered in my cheekbones, and I thought perhaps the tears would return but I was so drunk and tired and relaxed that I drifted toward sleep instead. I am content.

II

This Is Not Happening

The box of light in Vivian's little hand projected countless short form videos of content. She swiped seemingly endlessly through the repetitive, and frankly annoying, homemade entertainment. Each individual user could upload their short, vertical videos to this app on their smartphone to potentially go viral or make money off it. While most claim they only wish to inform or simply have fun by making such videos, deep in their psyche, they too are hoping for a chance of this fame and glory when the tip of their finger meets with the pixelated glass to send a haptic message through the handheld computer to complete a task we call, 'post.'

Vivian enjoyed watching these videos on terrifying loops and even making some of them herself despite the fact that quality, lighting and overall editing of the videos were generally lacking especially compared to the craftsmanship I was witnessing seated next to Luca day in and day out for the last few weeks. A baffling sight to behold, the difference in quality and technique, and yet the value of entertainment was held on an equal pedestal. I wondered what Luca might've thought about these bewildering, short videos on the smartphone.

It was now Saturday: we had just finished the halfway point of the shoot. On Thursday, Jamie from craft service, an ogre-esque man with a jolly attitude and dull eyes, went around with a wicker basket full of sugar cookies with magenta frosting that read, '17/34.' This, of course, meant it was day 17 out of 34, and therefore, when we all arrived at call time on Friday (Crew Call: 3:00PM—the cast and crew could expect a late night), we would officially be shooting the second half of the production.

Shooting began on the 10th of January and would finish on the 26th of February had it not been for Presidents' Day on Monday, the 19th of February, in turn making the 27th of February the final day of filming. This day was a Tuesday, which reserved Wednesday through Friday as makeup days or rain cover days, in case anything was to go awry, and additional days became necessary.

Everything in film is planned to the finest details; even the grittiest precisions are peer-reviewed, triple-checked, quadruple-checked, and signed off on after meetings, emails, cross examinations, discussions and countless late nights in the production office. This all has to happen before cameras can even roll on a frame of the final film. And it takes months.

After Luca's screenplay was greenlit by the studio and officially sent into development, the film was given a budget. For this particular film, that budget was twenty million dollars, which sounds like a significant sum of money, especially in 2024, but in reality, this was considered in the business to be a 'low-budget film.' Offices opened at the movie studio in unassuming, charming Wilmington, North Carolina. A few weeks later, there are hallways with offices to house the unit production manager, the production designer, the director, the director of photography, the assistant directors, the art department, the accounting department, the locations department, the transportation department, and many more.

The minds began working vigorously to plan the most detailed calendar anyone had ever seen. This is all to make sure that, for example, on Valentine's Day of 2024 at exactly midnight, the crew would break for lunch on time which is crucial because Vivian Wells has a Changeover immediately when she's back in from lunch. This means she had to remove her wig for a less-stressed wig, redo her makeup, and change her costume, all so she was ready to shoot a scene from the beginning of the film, whereas only an hour before, she had been screaming and straining her eyes to create real tears in the titular climax of the film.

It was an intricate dance, and if everyone paid attention—if everyone gave at least a bit of a shit and their undivided attention to their individual tasks—the train would arrive on time, and the film would have no need to break into the rain cover days at the end of February. And so, as it goes, the Production Office, with the ever-looming date on their calendars scribbled in as, 'shooting begins' or 'principal photography,' they begin to hire and fill out a complete crew for the production (meanwhile, in the casting department—some people are physically in the production office while others may be elsewhere in Atlanta or even LA or New York—the cast of the film is hired on, and extras are booked from an online advert).

Time pressed forward; the start date began haunting everyone. By the first day of production, everyone was groggy and fumbling to find their footing in the pitch darkness before sunrise, cold air causing their noses to clog and their eyes wetting from the cutting frigid nature of the weather. Every first day of a new production is a jumble of jittering excitement, a real shock to the nervous system, mixed violently with a sour hollowness felt below the skin, as if forcing the body to take another step despite the begging to go back to sleep. It was a fight—more than that, it was a choice—every single person on the crew out under the black sky, in uncharted territory and sprinting, sweating, lifting Hercules' weight in gear and doing mathematical equations off the top of their heads all before the sun has even shown interest in rising, have all decided this is where they wanted to be. It is a special day. All the soldiers stormed headfirst into battle.

By the middle of the production, the crew divided into two—half decided to hold onto their undying sight of potential for the film and chose a gleeful, hard-working attitude for the rest of the film—the other half could give a fuck about the film and were already in negotiations for their next project or quitting the industry all together. This seemed to be the mix I was encountering each passing day in the production and the baby purple, frosted, sugar cookies were either met with praise and cheery appreciations or snickers, scoffs and watching as they tossed their treats to the garbage.

But now, it was Saturday. Peace. Slow down. Saturday morning and Vivian would have a rehearsal that afternoon with the Stunt Coordinator, her Stunt Double, and Luca for only an hour but still, she wanted to lie in her hotel bed that morning and do something she referred to as 'rot.'

"Let's just rot for a while," she said with her giant brown eyes fluttering and she giggled lowly across the pillow, the white sheet pulled just over her bare chest. The sun stapled vertical bars of light through the drapes; the thick double-layered curtains slithered as the exterior AC unit hummed a brisk chill up into the room. By this time, I was no longer staying in a separate hotel from her. I had a room just a few doors down and paid for by the production, yet I spent all my time playing and resting in Vivian's suite.

Vivian found her phone on the nightstand, plucked the charging cable from it and found the app that stored the endless feed of videos, videos I noticed to never have much of a meaning to them, let alone any sort of quality. After a few minutes of upward swipes with her thumb, I felt a shiver of annoyance.

"How long do you usually watch these?" I blurted the question.

"An hour or so," she answered kindly. A petite smile grew on her face before her face slouched back to the empty sort of gaze into the little glowing box. In one hour, she would turn that screen black and see her dead, expressionless face peering back at her in the darkened reflection of the little box cutout. She'd breathe in and out, already bored from the lack of stimulation, staring at the dark box, and it would never cross her mind that a dark box would be her final destination someday, lying on her back and staring up at darkness, finally one with the black box.

"Let's do something else. Let's go find some coffee, huh?"

Vivian either ignored my comment or she was too enamored with the nothingness of content.

"Viv, c'mon. Please? Does Luca know you spend your Saturday mornings watching this?"

"Who gives a shit?" She sounded offended by my comment. I swallowed and stared past her phone, making the foreground blur into a soft fuzz and watched the curtains ripple in mini waves like a small, beige fabric ocean. I watched as the sounds to my left changed from song to song every few seconds. I tried not to think of what great minds would think of my situation. Would David Wallace be understanding of it? Would Thoreau pass a look of disappointment? Finally, I heard my voice belting the lyrics to *Loose Ends* on the screen but pitched low—the song had been altered—slowed down by two hundred percent—and I felt a jolt of anxiety scamper over my veins. I sat up in bed, bolt right.

"What's wrong, baby?" Vivian asked. I'm not sure when she started calling me by a pet name, but it was recent, and it still felt unnatural to the ear. She rubbed my back, her fingers thumped over the bony mounds of my spine, each facet tightly wrapped in skin and nothing else. I needed to quit smoking, I thought, but absolutely not today.

"I'm okay," I lied. I felt as if I had stared at the interior of the Sistine Chapel for too long and had accidentally strained my eyes from focusing on every crack I found on the ceiling. I decided at that moment I had been spending far too much time, far too fast with Vivian. An overabundance of pleasure circled back into suffering. I became too familiar with her brush strokes instead of viewing her as the piece of art she was. I didn't want to hate her. I would never want to get to that point in a relationship where the companion becomes a nuisance. If the sound of their voice could evolve into a sharp chalkboard, it was no longer love; remaining there would be an unsustainable fear of being alone. I ripped the covers back and hopped out of the bed. Too much on the mind. I slipped my denim around my torso and pinched my belt around my waist.

"Do you promise you're okay?" she asked, and she looked very startled.

"Yeah, yeah," I mumbled.

"Well, you don't seem okay." She was looking away from her phone then.

"I'm fine, Viv. Just going on the balcony for a smoke." I leaned across the bed and kissed her on the forehead before retreating from the premises as quickly as I could without making it seem as if I were, in fact, not okay. I chewed on my cigarette and thought of the irony, oh, the irony! Vivian worked relentless hours to create such definitive art and yet, within the same medium, chooses to indulge in the tired, chastised interpretation. Could the videos she watched even be considered art? And why did I care so much about how someone else spent their time?

Then, leaning over the balcony and looking at the crumbling shack of a brick building and an alley where a line cook hunched over on an upside-down milk crate and smoked his own cigarette, I had a shuttering thought. I liked Vivian Wells, I liked her a lot even, more than most girls and yet now, for a brief moment, I wondered if I only liked the *idea* of liking Vivian Wells. In that brief moment, I dug further and wondered if perhaps I chose to like her because it would fit my aesthetic to be with an actress. A Golden-Age Chic. I wondered if perhaps I chose to like her because I lost all my closest friends simultaneously, one legitimately, and had nobody else to turn to until she took the call of fate to show me the comfort I was so desperately in need of. Was the subconscious really so powerful? Perhaps the subconscious exceeded consciousness, but I could never know for certain due to it being outside of my mind's waking control.

All of this shot through my brain in a flash, like an atomic wave, my neurons connected and sent the message around—perhaps I did not like her—and I replaced the thought just as quickly. *No*, I thought, *I don't want to think about this.* I decided to bury the idea as far into the crummy depths of my brain as I could, where I kept my mistakes (they often needed to be reburied every so often) alongside thoughts of the grim, thoughts of self-destruction. No telling what would happen now if I broke ways with Vivian and decided to go back to my life in Los Angeles. Then, a new thought took over, more a question: *Does that old life still exist?* It couldn't exist now, not with the band broken and my apartment a reminder of all the depressive, cold, lingering memories. I felt my stomach rising so I flicked the cigarette and watched the dart of orange-red bounce into nothing, fading into the portrait of the line cook on a smoke break.

A final thought as I stood there for a moment longer and absorbed the prickling wind skidding across my bare stomach and arms: the only thing keeping me happy is doing exactly as I have been. Learning to love and experiencing new art. So, I swallowed hard; I made sure the thoughts were well locked up and turned to the door to jump back into bed with my wonderful girlfriend. And she really was quite wonderful. We continued going on dates in the city. Mornings spent at a new cafe each morning, traversing shelves of quaint bookshops in the quiet downtown and counting ducks in the ponds of the city's parks. For a few afternoons whenever she had the opportunity, we sat out on a blanket on the beach, bundled in wool sweaters with our feet tucked into the ripples of sand.

"We should move here," she muttered with her nose turned into the center of my chest. I could hardly hear her voice, yet the words were clear enough. Of course, this could never happen—but in that instant between her purr of thought and my tiny response, I thought of how romantic it would be indeed. Much to the comforted notions of Monroe and Miller in their New England estate but more the realization that I could do as Sophia had done. Perhaps I was capable of leading a normal life. What a normal life was, I wasn't quite sure other than what I'd seen of my parents and my siblings. That, too, of some of my friends back in D.C. or Los Angeles but even those were unconventional. I turned my head to press my chin to the crown of her head and spoke, "If that's what you would like, that's what we will do."

An additional day was added to the shooting schedule. The leftover shots were to be done in stage four with a giant blue screen for visual effects. It was Sunday afternoon, the 19th of February, and I had just received a call from Luca asking me to accompany him a few blocks away, to *Purple Parakeet Billiards*, yet another underground bar with a number of pool tables, darts, and a jukebox. I met him at sundown and we both had a round of vodka sodas as I examined the limited selection of music on the jukebox. Luca tapped the thin of a silver quarter against the plastic chromatic finish.

"I have place I would like to see," said Luca with the glass against his lips, muffling his words into a shelled echo. The ice cracked and twinkled as he swallowed the remnants. He clicked the sweaty glass on the bar top behind him. Luca loved to drink, though normally he fancied wine much akin to myself; tonight was a special occasion, according to Luca, as he stated in his phone call. We ordered another round of cocktails, and I remember thinking I should have wanted cocaine but somehow, all urges for the drug had seemingly subsided, and how strangely wonderful this new sensation was. I felt lighter—like I was free from the waking devastation caused by the awesome powder—and I grinned to myself with the knowledge that I was clean of all drugs besides the likes of my cigarettes and the drink. I decided these were necessities for the creator like me, fuel to the artist, if not the best toolkit any craftsman in the trade of creation could buy.

What Luca had in store for us took place a handful of blocks away, and the two of us walked side by side into that good night, swaying into one another and using the other for support. We arrived at the intersection on Market Street where a bolstering erection of a water fountain sat in the dead center of the road. The streets of the intersection curved around this giant fountain, seemingly more of a statue without the water running, a mound of sculpted cement like a colossal birdbath lodged in the circular road that went around like that of a merry-go-round.

"Is this it?" I asked. And Luca slapped the center of my back as he doubled over in a horse's laughter.

"No, no! There!"

He pointed, I followed the index finger to a brick building, nearly black in the night, with six stories, puncturing the web of clouds stitched overhead. Bars outside the windows of each apartment gave the impression each had a little balcony but as we grew closer to the building, the rusted railings were no more than a foot from the windows and had no metal floor for anyone to walk out on. We crossed the street and surveyed the corner of Market Street and Fifth Avenue where the apartment building stood.

"What's so special about this place?" I asked, my voice hushed. Luca had turned the corner into a cutout in the building, almost as if it would lead into an alleyway of sorts but instead was only enough of an intrusion to fit a spiral square staircase leading all the way up the floors. He yelled back, in a sort of shouting whisper; he hissed, "I want to get inside!"

I cut the corner into the cubby in which lay the stairs and spotted Luca already nearing the second floor. I called for him to slow down, please wait for me, but it was no use. He stopped at the door when he found it locked and blew a string of curses in English and Italian under his drunken breath. Higher he went, in some fit of insanity and tried the door on the third floor and the fourth, fifth and sixth, all locked and I did not follow once I arrived on the landing to the third floor. Luca moiled down with his head all loose and sat on the stairs for a moment, right on the icy metal. We were wedged in those stairs where the walls of the building faced each other with windows only a few feet apart. I decided it should qualify as an alley when I looked over the edge of the molting handrail to see the garbage dumpsters the size of a postage stamp.

"This apartment building is history," he began to explain.

"What?"

"*Casso*. Sí, Joe, I know—all buildings have history—bah, bah, bah. I explain when we get inside. Come, my friend, please, we have other paths to explore."

He was slowing down the stairs, as I was, for the state of our minds was far too off-kilter for a fumbling descent. Carefully, we finally arrived at the earth again; Luca rounded the brick exterior to the front of the building but before walking all the way to the front entrance, we both stopped at a window. It was at eye level, the both of us, and it seemed we noticed at the exact same time how the window was slightly cracked. Luca turned to me with a knowing, blank stare.

"No."

I shook my head. This was all I managed to say before Luca

shoved the window higher and the opening became wide enough for our bony figures to slither inside.

"Hoist me up, I'll pull you in," said Luca.

"Luca, we don't even know if this unit is vacant, there could be someone in there right now! Asleep for all we know! And you want to break in?" My voice was a whisper but so full of attack it was similar to the shriek of a viper.

"You hoist me, I peak my head in, and if I see any furniture, we close window and go home. Deal?"

I rubbed my tongue over my teeth and looked around our environment. All the gothic houses and brick buildings beyond were all dead, aside from gas-lit lamps with tickling flames on a few front porches. No sign of any other people. I decided and sighed with a bite to my throat, "Fine."

Luca slid into the building with such little effort and for a brief moment, I was completely alone on the inked street. Not a second passed before a gray hand reached out from the black box and grabbed at me. Luca lurched me upward and I kicked my feet against the brick, climbing up the wall and into the building. In through the darkened slot, a whiff of cold breeze across my face as my head whirled, then a dulled whack as my skull went numb and fuzzy. Disoriented, my body yanked to its feet, and the silhouette of Luca and a dash of red light against the left side of his face.

"Are you alright?" Luca whispered. I looked around the space. All was completely sheeted in shadows, darker than black and colder than winter, all this aside from the clear stamps of crimson light that glowed from the few windows in the long apartment. No furniture. No other people. All that was in the apartment was on the wooden floors, decades old, laid out was a scraggly old rug, one that was large and circular in the living room space. Each step we took created distinct and present whines and screeches in the old wood, wrinkled from time, shifted by years of use.

We examined every room of the apartment. The unit was long and thin, a single hallway served as the spine with ribs of bedrooms, bathrooms and such growing out on the sides. At the very end of the apartment, where we fell into the unit and opposite the front door, this was where the living room and kitchen were. Everything was outdated and seemingly hadn't been used in years.

Cockroaches idled on the windowsills and a rat practically tripped over itself to escape when we opened the door to the bathroom. I went to use the bathroom and when I returned to the living room, I found Luca lying on his back and eyes fixed on the ceiling. A hideous sensation ran through my body, and I dashed toward him, only to cause him to jolt.

"What! What!" He yelled without a voice in his cloudy colored whisper.

"I thought something had happened to you."

"No. Just lying down for a minute. Join me, Joe, please. Lie down." He patted the blue rug next to him, at least I thought it was blue. The mix of scarlet glows and unforgiving shadows stole most every other color. I lay on my back just as I was told and stared up at the ceiling.

"This is it. This is how it really looks. How it smells. How it *feels*. Hm."

Luca was seemingly growling. I turned to look at him when the light of the room flicked away from red and into a jolly green. It was brighter than before and the windows shot the leafy hue onto the walls and floor of the vacant unit. The traffic light at the intersection had changed just outside the corner apartment. We were truly alone but the wind brushed the windows, sending a ghastly breeze to where we lay.

I was focused on the breeze and my spinning head when Luca continued, "Maybe not exact apartment, but the building where David Lynch shot *Blue Velvet*. I take you here because you mention that *Blue Velvet* was your friend's favorite movie."

I was silent for a moment. I had to process what Luca had said to me and process the truth of Luca mentioning Tommy. Flashing memories of watching Lynch's films with Tommy in Arlington. Inquisitive discussions and pressing vulnerabilities. I thought, too, of

Luca, how he had broken into the apartment not for himself, but for me.

"Really?" I asked. I couldn't think of anything else to say. I was left speechless at the kindness in Luca's heart. He was such a genuinely kind soul. Admittedly, through glazed eyes I peered at his pitch silhouetted lying beside me and wondered if he might be an angel; perhaps Luca was sent into my life to save me. Maybe I was meant to meet Luca. Maybe a light was always guiding me but now that light was a person, a friend, an equal. This was someone I looked up to and cared for, someone I gave myself over to and respected. I thought of whether I should ask him about this, the question at the tip of my tongue, and finally, after a charismatic silence, I did.

"Do you ever think things happen for a reason?"

Luca did not take long before he began in response, "I have thought about this many times. Still, I am unsure! I like to think it is no; nothing happen for reason, but then something new comes along—I feel so deeply, I cannot explain—and I think it has to be purpose. Fate, as we call it."

"How is it that my best friend adored *Blue Velvet*—then, he passes away and I feel the most alone I have ever felt—only to end up in the real apartment building where his favorite movie was shot? And with a film director no less."

"What do you think it means?" Luca asked, in a tone as if he was genuinely trying to get to the bottom of this, like a detective with all the clues but none of the solutions.

"I don't know. I know he would have loved this."

"Enjoy it in his memory then. Enjoy it for yourself."

I nodded. The light of the room changed again, this time a wicked yellow, nearly amber. I said, "Of course, I will. I still have to wonder— I wonder why we're here at all—I can't stop thinking about this monotonous life-gazing prospect every day—I get nowhere with it! I think it has something to do with beauty, I've determined. It's a theory. I think sex is intuition—but music, books, cooking, *fuck*, even *cinema* at times, that's all something to do. It's like, we're here for no other reason than to pass the time."

The squares of light scattered about that black room returned to red once more. This was the darkest glow of the three colors and now everything felt further away somehow, and my chest tightened. Luca beside me reached for his face and began rubbing his fingers into his temples.

"Oh, *shit*. I feel like I have been in this exact moment before. But I know I have not. Could not have."

"Deja vu," I optioned.

"Casso! And you say *deja vu!* You are right on time to say this! The window was this red and the wind this strong. You say, *we're here to pass the time*, then I have thought, *no, time is passing us*—and I lie on the floor on this same old rug, so familiar! This is really happening —this is real."

"Yes, and you know, some people claim that— *fuck*—what was I saying?"

My head was spinning, a whirlpool in my mind from the slush of alcohol. I felt strongly like how I used to feel with Tommy, and worse, I felt nostalgic for the nights we spent drunk and high in similarly shaded rooms. I tried hard to focus on what we'd been talking about.

I continued, "Sorry—what I was saying—some people claim that deja vu is the universe telling us we are exactly where we're supposed to be. Everything has lined up with fate."

"There is this word again. What is with you and fate? It is interesting idea. You believe this, no?"

"No."

"Ah? Fate or deja vu?"

"I don't believe the very real sensation of deja vu is an extension of fate," I said.

"You don't think the big universe could have some say in what we do on such tiny planet?"

"Tommy used to say technically we know of very little truth in the universe. Maybe nothing at all, actually."

"Yes?" This was Luca's way of asking for elaboration or to continue. It was admirable, I decided and smiled.

"Yeah. Tommy, my old friend—he would always go on these

long tangents about how life is pointless and nothing we do in life will ever *truly* matter over a long enough timeline—but he'd argue it was more beautiful this way. He was a nihilist—he always thought glass half empty was, in turn, a glass half full—very paradoxical but somehow, he always managed to make sense of it. And he'd make sense of the entire world around us, from the fabric of existence to the fallacy of time. It's funny actually—he was a pretty remarkable thinker."

"Why do you say this is funny?" asked Luca. I adjusted my head on the rug to face him, the light red then blotted back the green. He tilted his head to look back at me, the black strands of hair waving around his head in a mane on the rug. Despite the murk of the space and the quiet green, a real desperation grew on his face. He mumbled, "I only feel sad when I hear you say this."

"Well, as he used to always say to me," I explained. "The only thing we as a species concern ourselves with is the knowledge of our mortality, and that single, dreadful thought has spun out to create societies and trades—and frankly, all our economic systems rely on the fact that we are mortal—which spawns the necessity of choice. If we were immortal, no choice would *really* matter. If we lived forever, we would eventually make both choices."

Luca slipped silent a moment, I assumed to translate all the words I said in English and to interpret the idea itself. He turned his head again back to face the ceiling and muttered, "I see—but what if one choice is more painful than another? Humans love in pleasure. I say, we choose based on the happiness we gain from it, no?"

From that comforting green, back to the dull yellow.

"Sure. But like Tommy always said, we know so little of the world. And I believe him. Think about it, we assigned names to every single known thing in our universe. Every word I speak is one of many ways to say the same thought—I'm communicating a thought to you in this language so you can understand it."

The traffic light beyond the window reverts back to red and I say, "We're likely the only life in the history of time and space to ever do this."

This caused a scoff from Luca. He folded his arms despite being laid flat on his back.

"Bah! It happened once before, it could happen again! You think humanity is accident! But you also think you were placed on earth to make music. Fate or not, Joe? My friend, you speak in paradox. Like many of the great philosophers! *Contradict*, is how you say? Joe, you do not listen to me!"

"What?" I asked.

"I say to you not every question has an answer. And this is okay. Why do we need to think these big questions at all? We are here, aren't we? Let it be enough, yes?"

"But there's just so much to think about," I argued. So much to think about. So many monstrous ideologies and philosophies and questions, so heavy on the mind it causes a physical ache. I used to be in constant amazement that not everyone was thinking about these same questions. How can we all go about our days when there are these unanswered questions with cores still unexplored? Green light hit the room.

Suddenly, Luca flung his hands into the air.

"Old trick! Old, old trick, this ponder of life—be happy, *you idiot!* All that you say, it has been said before. It has been thought about hard by man before us. Books about it. Art throughout history go, hm, let us ponder the big question. No need to say it again. Like the Talking Heads, *say something once, why say it again,* no? Tolstoy driven to be sad man by thinking too hard about this," Luca rambled, his arms were bright and creating big motions.

"Joe, you try so hard to understand everything around us but what are you making? Maybe there is no self—try not to focus on you or where you came from or why you are here, my friend—these things do not matter because you are one of few who have the ability to create beautiful things. Art! We are artists, no? True, like Tommy say, we know very little about world. But the sooner you can admit to yourself that you, and all of us, should not *care* about this answer, we go to be better people and you—better artist."

The crinkle at his side caused my attention to shift as he muddled around in his pocket to fish out a cigarette, make that two, and gift one. He propped himself on one arm, lit the cigarette and the gleaming dot was a contradiction, in its bronze, to the green spill of spots around us. I lit mine with his metallic lighter and handed it back with my thanks. We puffed on our cigarettes for a while, heads flat against the wooden floor of the living room. The wind crooned wildly from the open window. Luca had another thought, and returned to his propped-up position, I thought to get a better look at me.

"I hate idea that all art must have meaning. Analysis, fine—I study cinema. But I separate it from beauty. Beauty can only exist with expiration date, otherwise it is only interesting. Rocks are interesting. Flame is beautiful but fleeting." He waved his dainty cigarette around and the orange glow grew, too hard to focus on at once, and became like a blazing worm.

"You understand? Just like *us*. Easier to say this way, no? Art is best when the artist does not fear it. You talk of this *so much!* You are not philosopher—no Socrates—no Hobbes. You are musician who is afraid of death and does not want anyone to know it. Yes, you do— stop making this face—it is okay not to think about death every single day, Joe."

I shook my head in disagreement. "That's easier said than done. And I'm really not afraid of it, promise. You think I would write music about it and discuss it so much if I were afraid of it?"

Yellow light. I propped myself on my elbow to match Luca next to me.

He said, "Yes. You're afraid of why we die. Why must you die someday? The loss of self is scary, I agree, we all agree! It is why our hands shoot away from stove when too hot. Natural to protect yourself from death, yes, but we do not need to ponder *why*. No answer. We are here. Alive and we had no choice in this. We have a choice to *live* though."

"So, we keep living," I said. Red light. A maniacal grin sprouted on Luca's face and in the shrouded dark of the apartment, it was a haunting image to perceive.

"That is what Tolstoy say. That was his confession! We're alive now for some reason. And we must live on. We are both capsules of energy and—eh—we are what is it—*mass*, no?—baked into little living pastries with so many ideas—and you know what else?"

"What's that?" I questioned, and just as soon, I received a healthy blow on the shoulder. Luca threw up his long, thin arms once more. His silhouette was a terrifying sight and now the two of us had naturally moved to a sitting position with one palm planted behind our backs to support the weight.

"You do not listen to anything! Deaf musician, *bah*."

Luca paused to smoke his cigarette and sprinkled the ash on the rug. "Say it with me—*artists*—we make things that outlive us. We do it for different reasons, maybe in your case, it is fear of dying without legacy. Yes, that would fit you very well. Or me, I really enjoy the process of art. Films are too fun to make! Like *high* they are."

The process is what I love about music. And while I enjoy listening to it when it's done, the sensation is nowhere near the joy of creating music. It is how a mathematician must feel in the midst of an equation, a scientist in the depths of an experiment. Something for the mind to feed on.

"I feel most like myself when I'm creating the music," I heard myself say. I blinked in the bloody light of the unit.

"Ah, you are like me then—I was hoping so—*real* artist. You create because creating for you is like water. You cannot go long without it. No escape from creation but also, you are so thankful to have occupation."

"I think creation comes from a need and a desire. The desire is—"

"The desire is a feeling of control. I know," he said. Luca nodded.

"Joe, you are so easy to read. Like children's book, you are! You talk of all this philosophy and big idea but *my god!* You just feel so helpless and afraid of impending dread we all march to—like soldiers on the beach—we walk together toward death. Boohoo!"

A quick smooch at his cigarette before finishing his thought. He began fumbling over his words, drunk and trying desperately to stay in English. He continued, "Everyone from the noble to the sinner, we all go to be alone in death and the energy go somewhere else. You accept this and think less about it—or else you will waste your life—you miss all this miraculous life right here."

He turned to look into my eyes, he even held my wrist. Green light.

"Joe, right now—you are in club—secret society in universe. This what we call being human. Be more grateful because you will not always be a member. Expiration date, you have! You will age out and go back to energy in the stars."

I hung on to these final words, relaxed them in my brain and thought of how correct my new friend was. At first, I'd perceived Luca to be not as smart as Tommy was, but it was this night that I decided he was actually far more intelligent. I felt cross at my private monologue but knew Luca was another special person in this vast world. I felt lucky to have met him in this intersection of life, where our two manifestations of souls got the opportunity to interact.

I blew smoke from my mouth and Luca did the same, we both watched as the clouds of curling white floated into the other, becoming one, and snaked into that emerald light. An enchanting green. This beautiful color will leave, I knew, and just as soon, it was replaced by gold. The color green, the smoke, they had both dissipated. They became a piece of the unit we'd broken into; we were trespassing on the property, trespassing on Earth.

Luca spoke once more, "What else?—fuck you. Fuck you for making me think about all this. Why can we not just be normal? Two drunk men alone in dark apartment should be talking of something else."

"It isn't exactly fun to think about this sort of thing day in and day out. It's like you said, time-consuming," I explained, and the light fell quickly into that awful scarlet again, like spilt wine.

"It remind me of when you notice breathing, no? And you are conscious of pulling air in through your nose, into your lungs, and *out, out, out.* All becomes muscle effort when you think about breathing, and you have to wait before your brain return to it with no thought. Understand, Joe?"

I understood and felt the air growing and dying in my lungs at my command. Through my clogged nose, my muscles expanded and worked together at my chest, and back out through the nose. I groaned audibly; I crammed the black end of my cigarette on the frigid wood just off the edge of the rug.

"Christ," I twisted, "Now I'm thinking about my breathing. Fuck you."

"Fuck *you!*"

Luca shoved my shoulder and we both rose into joyful laughter. I shoved him back and he cursed in Italian. He swung the strands of black hair from his face and took a final puff of his cigarette before putting his out as well.

"Joe," said Luca, his voice low.

"Yeah?"

"You are good person—I am glad to live at the same time as you—and be your friend."

"Me too," I said.

"I mean it. Serious! See? *Serious.* I know men do not tell each other this often but I say it to you now with truth in my heart. Not so easy to find true connection in this world. You get me and I think I get you. We must stick together for the rest of our time as human."

"Okay," I laughed, "As long as you and I are in the club, we will be friends."

"Allies," Luca growled.

"Who are we against?"

"I am not so sure—taxes, maybe."

We both laughed at this and when it subsided, we sat in the silence of the room with only the wind as our witness. I thought of how profoundly lucky I was to even know him at all. When you meet someone you care about so deeply, or understand them on a level far deeper than the surface, you hope it will last forever. Through the toils of life and the strides taken to achieve greatness in our short chapter as people, sometimes we are Sisyphus regardless of skill or talent. It is our friends who help us, and they show us we can always try again. To know someone for a very long time, that may be the most beautiful thing of all.

"I'm glad to be your friend too," I mumbled, only loud enough to hear over the breeze cutting against the aching windows. Green light.

"No more ponder questions without answer. From now on, we are creators with no fear. We make art that is simple, unaware, and honest."

"Why those three things?" I asked.

"This is what the best art is composed of. No bullshit. No urge to be great. It is great without comparison. It only is. You agree?"

He stared at me, his eyes black but familiar. The moment, long intimate, was one of complete vulnerability. I thought I might begin to cry when I swallowed, and nodded to show him, yes, I do agree.

"We are creators without fear," I agreed, and he smiled.

"Creators without fear. Friends in club of humanity. Allies against taxes."

I laughed again, not because what he said was humorous, but because his willingness to communicate in English was admirable but jarring. I was seemingly seated next to Frankenstein in the gloom.

"We watch *Blue Velvet* tomorrow, no?" Luca hummed.

"Okay." This was the last thing either of us said before we were both too mentally drained to continue our demented ramblings that would go on forever given the opportunity. Our minds were capacious. Untrustworthy. We didn't stay in the unit much longer after this, as Luca and I both knew how the plot of the film shot in that building played out, as the protagonist breaks into the apartment but is caught by the owner. This unit was surely vacant but as we began to sober, we knew it was in our best interest to get out of the building as quickly as possible.

The light was red when we collapsed onto the sidewalk once more and I stared back at the three traffic lights in a line, watching me like the heads of Cerberus. We hurried on through the downtown streets and split for our hotel under that ink-bled sky, arriving at the entrance and ignoring the clerk at the front desk. It was after two in the morning when we'd parted ways for our own rooms without saying goodnight or anything in parting. Only a nod of the head with both our doors parted, and we turned in, both knowing of our crime and our connective minds with the invisible string that twined us together. What else we knew undoubtedly, we were, in fact, creators without fear.

———

I spent much of my time learning about film, seated directly next to Luca, absorbing the process, reveling in the curious nature of the industry. Luca explained the details of every shot, even why Vivian wore a red sweater in one scene and blue in the next, saying it has to do with emotion, and how there will be subconscious impacts on the audience in a theater—blue being sad and cold, red as raging and hot. All of it was in order to portray emotion on that moving, flickering screen through the means of storytelling. Through this formula, I felt inspired by the many moving pictures I saw every day. Some time ago while out downtown in the port city, I bought a little black notebook, the traditional size. It was with this notebook that I began measuring out five horizontal lines, with the treble clef to the far left, and would write out music that I heard in my head while watching the scenes.

I carried this practice back to my hotel room where I stayed up early into the next morning writing out in the notebook what I thought to be music that elevated the scenes I witnessed being shot. The ideas were to be played on piano, and in my hotel room I had my old electric keyboard from the closet of my parents' house. I absorbed myself in the music between cigarettes and cups of tea or cardboard cartons of cranberry juice, and it felt so fulfilling, so nostalgic, the equivalent to reuniting with an old friend. I felt whole again while tinkering through my methods from which I would discover the perfect sounds to my ear, the precise and solely correct steps in each melody. I had a field recorder, of course, that caught much of my samplings from the set of the film, although muffled as I was usually not in the same room as Vivian or whatever actor was performing their scene that day. But it was enough to take me back to the moment, to be present in the space, and find myself with physicality in each scene. And again, while under the golden flush of my bedroom's many lamplights, I could close my eyes and hear the music that ran within each scene. I knew it, as if it were always there.

Somewhere along the way, while shooting in one of the many gray soundstages on the studio lot, Luca took notice of the particular inscriptions in my notebook. We'd been filming a scene near the end of the film; the house we'd been filming at when I arrived on my first day of the production, was now built on the soundstage. The entire interior duplicated down to the most intricate details. A knick on the trim. A scratch on the window where the branch outside had dug into it, and the branch there too. Similar floors. The railing of the stairs was so similar, I could not tell the difference. At times, while standing in this set, I forgot I was in a set at all, and thought I was back in the house in the quiet, strolling neighborhood. It was a beautiful, intrinsic, sickening facade of reality.

And the scene we were filming involved the house being set ablaze, which called for a fleet of SPFX (special effects) crew to come in and work. They had controlled flames in the windows and scattered flames on the floor or walls, all of which were coming from burners and valves that regulated the flow of fire; a meticulous grid of gas lines were constructed into the frame of the set from the days of pre-production (everything planned down to these details). Outside were giant tanks of gas and the number of fire extinguishers became nearly tripping hazards with the amount placed on standby.

To watch the fire swarm the set with the naked eye was admittedly underwhelming. Then when watching playback on the monitor and seeing what had been captured in camera, it gave the very real effect that, yes, this house is burning to the ground.

The house was on fire, Luca and I were sitting outside of it in the concrete shadows of the stage, I had my notebook tilted toward the orange light from the monitor screens so as to see what I was writing. I felt a flick at my shoulder, I looked to Luca and pulled an earphone off from the side of my head.

"What is this?" he whispered.

"Music."

"Music for what?"

I shrugged. Luca mocked me with an exaggerated shrug.

"Tell me," he said.

"Music for the scene."

Luca glanced at the monitor, at the notebook, and then back at me again. He tossed the black hair from his face and, while there, gave a good scratch on the head. He shot his eyes at the monitor but was still facing me, and leaned in. Slowly, his face was approaching mine but his focus on the monitor. Closer, closer in the darkness. Then, "Cut!"

Off somewhere inside the burning set, another voice I recognized to be Tyler Verrina, "Cut there! Kill the flame, kill the flame, let's make it safe." Which ignited a chorus of frantic but speckled voices yelping sharply, "Cut! *Cut, cut!*"

I heard a frantic movement to my right and found Luca ripping his headphones from his skull and placing them on the little stand in front of him. A Production Assistant stood over us with his walkie cupped in his palm, James was his name, he said, "Luca."

This single word was to get the director's attention. Luca nodded back at him; James pulled the walkie to his lips and held down the button on the side, "Good with Luca." The two of them had gotten into such a rhythm with the process that very few words were needed between the two of them to keep the production moving forward.

"Alright, moving on to our next set up," the quiet tenor of Tyler in the set. The PA choir mirrored his words once more, echoed in the walls of the giant stage. There was an entire two-story house built in the stage and still held room for maybe twice more of the same next to it.

"You write music for my film?" Luca asked. His voice was low, despite the only other person near us being James. I watched the chaos ensue around us as Vivian was given a robe and Katie took her out of the soundstage, her black bob of hair bouncing as she made way with a brisk step. Donna crossed into my sight then, nearly a twin to Vivian, and she trekked straight into the set as the SPFX department cut all the flames out of the house. Luca nudged me, a gentle jab at the shoulder, he was chuckling, "Joe! *Scatterbrain!* You hear me?"

"Yes—sorry."

"You write music for my film?" he asked, repeating his question.

"Well, sort of."

"What you mean, *sort of?*"

"I was just writing it. Not for any reason in particular. It was all just coming to me, so I decided to write it out."

"Can I see?"

I obliged by showing him the notebook, jammed with staffs of music in treble and bass, jotted ideas on the edges and notes written in words. I had scribbles above a staff that read 'piano here' or 'violin.' And on occasion, I had music written for voice parts, inspired by the symphonies which at the time I was becoming infatuated with. Pale was Luca's face as he curved his wrist, the pages fell on one another like leaves in the fall. It was quiet besides the chatter within the set just before us and the minute scuffle of shoes on the concrete floors around us.

"*Così bella*," Luca whispered. I picked up enough to know he was finding infatuation by the work. He turned to look at me.

"Why did you not tell me you write music like this?" Luca asked. He spoke so quickly, like he was in real pain, with his face twisted in distraught.

"I don't usually—well, I wrote a piece during Christmas at my parent's house—I say it's a movement, as I intend on writing more, but I've been here doing this. And I don't know," I fumbled for an explanation and resulted in telling him plainly, "I could just hear the music."

"Were you ever going to show this to me?"

"I hadn't thought that far ahead but—yeah—I guess I was going to eventually."

He leafed the tattered, coffee-stained edges of paper once more in a quiet concentration. I rubbed up and down my bicep awkwardly while waiting for the conversation to continue. I thought of getting a third cup of coffee at craft service on the far end of the stage. I glanced at the crafty setup, a blotch of sour light loomed over the table of snacks. It was, of course, after two in the morning but there was a city of life within the structure.

"Joe," Luca caught my attention once more, "Please, will you show me what this sounds like after we finish today?" He was excited, like a child given a gift. I nodded, and smiled unconsciously at the sight of his joy, how he tossed his arms up and shouted.

"*Meraviglioso.*"

He was right, it was wonderful. We were all a piece of a larger art, and it felt wonderful. I let him continue to scan the pages when I got up to find a cup of coffee. The coffee was fine, but I was not expecting us to finish the day only an hour later, half past three on a Thursday morning. I was wide awake driving back to the hotel.

When Luca and I returned downtown, he followed me to my room. It was in complete disarray, travel bottles of vodka drained and in a small pile, a wincing sight at the aging fruit I had on the television stand and so many piled towels swirled up in a hill outside of the bathroom door. The makings of a suit splayed on the hotel room floor. My dress shirt stretched on the ironing board. Smears of ash in the sheets. A faint smell of cologne, enough to sting the throat. We stepped over my clothes and suit pieces and wine bottles and books to the electric piano on the study desk at the far end of the room. I motioned for him to follow me, and he plopped into the giant armchair in the corner of the room.

"Okay, hold on, hold on," I muttered.

I powered on the keyboard and within seconds the interface lit and glowed a pale patch of color against the muddied copper tones of my room. Luca cleared his throat, presumably from the cologne stench; he was scrubbing his face with both hands. His greased locks rocked in front of his face—he made no effort to push them back— no, not at this hour.

Without warning, I pressed into the chords for a track I hadn't known at the time would later be named, *Madeline's Theme*. And it would become an iconic movement of music in the world of film against all odds and entirely unbeknownst to me and my hopes. It was only scribbles in the notebook that night, but Luca shot up from the armchair when he heard it. Resurrected. Reborn. He was in awe of the sounds I had written and then played for him; I even showed him how some of the tracks written for voices would sound. I sang to him and played for him for over an hour. He began to eat the sugared, battered fruit on the television stand.

He paced the room, "This is it, this is what will make the film. This is how we elevate the emotion of my picture!" Stopped at the edge of the room, and turned on his heel, he paced with his back to me still rambling, "The light—and the *sound!* There it is—this is what you say, Joe! The truths of the universe! It is the marriage of life and we still use them to imitate it."

He stopped, scampered across the room—narrowly hopping over the mounds of clothes and trinkets—a halt at the edge of the desk and knelt to my level.

"My friend, please, will you score my film?" he asked.

His brown eyes hovered on mine, they paced their focus from each of my own, and a silence took shape over the digital keys from the piano that previously furnished the air. I thought hard about what I might say next. I thought of how this decision might involve the very perception of my name in aspects of history, and how it might repurpose the trajectories of life.

Finally, and rather easily, I gave a nimble nod of the head, solidifying my position. This curt nod transformed me not only into an official member of the film crew, but a creative partner with Luca Krzyżewski. I tried to think elsewhere of words like 'composer' or 'soundtrack,' or anything that might cause me to lose my sense of identity. I did not want any words to define me other than 'artist.'

Creators without fear, I thought, and focused on the words. Luca tinkered the air conditioning unit down to a comfortable temperature, and a groaning fan kicked on. We held cigarettes between our fingers, as we always did, and lit them. We sat across from each other with crossed legs and exhausted complexions.

"If they don't want us to smoke in the hotel room, they should let us open the windows at least!" Luca charmed. He peeled a drape back on itself and rang his knuckles on the hulking glass. The wretched night was stiff on the opposite side.

"Joe Henley, I know what I say before when we were drunk, but I reconsider now," Luca continued with his appearance still hooked through the window. A curling smoke rolled from his hand, which was rested on his knee. Both my hands played on the keys but stopped to pull the zoot from my mouth and ask, "What's that?"

"I think it was fate that brought us together."

I said nothing in response and instead studied his words. Perhaps he was right. I couldn't help but wonder about all the tragedies I had to endure to arrive at this very moment of my life. All the many highs and all the dreadful lows that felt so desperate for forfeit. And here I was, seated with an artist I admired, a friend I had the opportunity to collaborate with. Surely, the tragedies were unfinished with many more in the future, but the courage to continue forward, and know another moment of joy is possible, this could serve as a vessel of truth.

What Luca said next, I will never forget. He sat with his profile shadowed. The halo of the hotel lamp wrapped around his mane of hair. Facing the window, at the waning night, slipping between our fingers like the ash of our cigarettes.

Luca spoke, "Fate is as real as the wind—it is something we may never see. Yes—maybe it pushes us along—and with its help, we arrive where we are meant to be. And blown over the sea, here we are."

III

FALLING LEAVES

Vivian scrunched her body as she rolled from the bed, prepared for the floor, and with a thud, she was on her feet. She turned back to face me. A wild grin. Honey hair tangled and pointed in every direction. My bones ached with knocks and cracks when I rose second, like the stretch of an accordion. Still, I watched her and her stance, as if she were placed on a field for a sport. We'd only just awoken, and she was ready for playtime, but I was far too exhausted from the shortened slumber we'd been getting each passing night.

It was just past noon on Saturday. Only seven days left of shooting on *Mass Hysteria*. The previous week, I'd gone to a music store and purchased a used, battered violin to stray my songs on, despite never having played violin before. Back in my hotel room, just a few doors down from Vivian's, the violin sat out of its case with its bow beside it on the armchair; the electric piano sprawled on the study desk, and my computer opened with software to record and play music.

"How are you always so exhausted?" Vivian said with a synth of laughter. I shook my head with the round of my palm pressed into my eyelid. Without warning, Vivian stripped the shirt she was wearing. She stood completely nude in front of me as I took in every detail of her figure. She danced off to the bathroom and I followed her into the shower. We cleaned ourselves while carrying easy conversation.

"Sing for me," Vivian hummed, and her voice bounced around the tiled walls.

I sang. My voice hung low and old. She listened with her chin pushed into the pit of my chest. Vivian grinned so hard and often, I began to wonder if she ever grew tired of it. I sang Elvis Presley's *Love Me Tender* to her. We swayed our bodies, locked together, my arms tight around her back under the spiraling drool of the shower head. My voice echoed and when the last words of the song rang out in the mucky, thick of the bathroom; she peered up at me with an affection so earnest, I became rightfully startled. The last thing I needed was for this young lady to fall in love with me.

"Joe," she said with a questioning tone, "Where are you right now?"

"Here," I lied. "I'm here with you."

She shook her head in disagreement. We hadn't known each other for only a few weeks but she knew me well enough to understand I was not with her at that moment. My brain was elsewhere, admittedly entirely focused on the original score I was creating for the film. Every second I was not working on the score was spent thinking about the score. An obsession with the idea of it grew in my brain like a tumor. I decided to tell her the truth, and how I would be writing the score for *Mass Hysteria*. To my surprise, she gleefully accepted my honesty. We talked at great lengths about my work on the soundtrack.

Out of the shower, we toweled off and hopped back onto the bed. Vivian unwrapped her towel. It slid from her body to leave her utterly exposed. She spread her legs and made a noise, a low and precocious hum of laughter. She was a little, angelic body—without flaw.

"What?" She asked with a perched, knowing brow and again wore a wicked grin. I couldn't help myself then. I found myself crawling from the edge of the bed to my face just between her thighs; I stared down at the mound resting so sweetly between.

"What a shame," she whispered. I stopped my movement. My

chin hovered just over the start of her stomach. My palms surfed the bare edges of her waist like a breeze over sand.

"What?"

"You're writing a soundtrack to our movie—but it's that beautiful voice I find so attractive—it is unlike anything I've ever heard before. I wish to hear it every single day for the rest of my life."

I chuckled, "If I keep up the cigarettes, it won't be very beautiful much longer. I need composition as a backup plan."

"Or you could stop smoking. Don't make that face, Joe!" She clicked her tongue and blew a heavy sigh. I watched her bare chest rise and fall. "I never want it to go away—I wish we could both just stay this way forever—perfect in every way."

She glanced down to where our eyes met. A brief silence took hold as we dashed our gazes over one another. We both seemed to agreeably think to ourselves, *yes, we are both quite perfect right now*. Finally, as if she no longer wished to focus on this epiphany, Vivian gently drew her eyes shut and leaned her head back; she pushed my chin into the start of her stomach, the Adam's apple within my throat rested directly on her vagina.

"Won't you sing for me?"

As I opened my mouth and began to sing *Love Me Tender*, the vibrations of my throat hummed below her waist. Vivian's entire body began to contort beneath me. My voice dug into her—the perfect target of pleasure—and she thrust her hips into my neck. I continued to sing, her legs trembled, and she fell into a fit of pleasure. After the encounter, she curled back on her bed with her smartphone to traverse her daily intake of media content. I lay beside her and studied the eggshell ceiling for as long as I could possibly bear. Only twenty or so minutes passed before I was up on my feet; I threw a sweater over my shoulders and went out the door back to my room, and back into the rhythms of writing the film score.

———

I wrote the entirety of the soundtrack in that hotel room of mine over the course of three weeks. The soundtrack was created with my laptop and a semi-modular analog synthesizer. My toolkit for the score consisted of my second-hand violin, my 88-key electric keyboard, a slick bass guitar, and an array of my and Vivian's vocals. When I had a full rough draft of the soundtrack, four days after the production of *Mass Hysteria* wrapped, I had a score that sounded a bit more like an ambient record. It was, of course, an electronic hybrid score that gave more of a pleasantry to the sound. The film's audience seemed to agree. The effects of my keyboard and synthesizer, doubled with the dirty, handmade quality to the whole soundtrack, made for a gritty digital sound. The bass and its accompaniments were dark and pulsed with the symphonic qualities I tied in with the acoustic and classical elements. It was as if I created a remix of Stravinsky or a retraced, post-modern cannibalism of Copeland.

On the final day of shooting—the 27th of February, in stage four—we were shooting scattered pickup shots of characters against a blue screen. It was a massive rectangular sheet of perfect blue, nearly stretched to the ceiling of the soundstage and just as wide, precisely lit to eliminate shadows. Luca sat at the monitor with little focus on the monitor, instead his attention lay on cracking his pistachios. I wandered into the stage with my notebook, a binder, and my laptop all tucked under my arm and upon spotting the director with the long black hair, I trailed a new path in his direction. Luca turned at the soft sound of my approach and his face crescendoed to a certain giddiness.

"Joe! My friend, please sit!"

I plopped into the chair beside him and asked him how he felt on the final day of the shoot. His eyes wandered the interior of the metallic classical soundstage. It was a sight to behold; just as one might imagine for a film shot a century before. Luca nodded wisely and as if speaking to anyone who would listen, he said, "This stage is where Brandon Lee was shot dead while they were making *The Crow*. Special effects crew, they think they have every bullet checked, sent in from Hollywood, ready to go! *No.* Son of Bruce Lee. *A star.* Dead on the floor with a piece of metal in his stomach. He drop his prop, his bags of groceries—and he yell 'cut,' himself. The special effects and the crew—they carry him out of this stage—and he is dead."

I looked about the stage, the bleakness of the shadows and the tangles of light seeped through the windows into the house, but those shadows; I thought if I stared into that eclipsed darkness for just long enough, I could catch a glimpse into what comes after. Luca must have seen my flushed complexion, a ghostly pale quality that drained my face of heat and he continued, "*The Crow* was about man who returns from the dead to avenge his love. Beautiful, grunge, gothic film. Thirty years ago, this film was released. When I was just freshman in high school, I saw the film for the first time in little cinema over the summer. I was in Crema with friends, and they do the ten-year celebrating screening, one night only. After the movie is over, I decide this Crow, I want to be like him. He will fight—even in death! Powerful. *Potente*. It is Shakespeare, and he is Banquo, no? This is why I grow out my hair. The film has massive impact on my life. I tell you this to say, I think it is all purpose. I was meant to be here, in this soundstage, with the phantom of the Crow watching over me, and creating gothic film like one I saw as a boy."

I nodded. The shadows between the window cutouts stared back at me. They felt alive.

"Maybe you're right," I said. He patted my shoulder.

"Unspeakable! Fate and wind! I just wanted to tell you this. You have seen *Crow?*"

I had. It was a favorite of mine as well. The haunting makeup of that ghastly face, and the pitched lines that stood straight over his eyes. All the features of the man who would perish as the character, elevated, and closer to death than he had ever thought. The man of beauty and talent—on the shoulders of giants—masquerades as a character of death only to face the demise of which only death can supply. Tragedy. Travesty. Irony. He was far too young to be lost. A year older than myself when he perished as I stood on that very stage. And yet his image, especially in his legendary black and white, will live longer than any other and it is that of a dead man in a fictional tale. If a man dies while acting as a ghost, does the fiction follow his soul? It is the closest instance of life imitating art, and it happens to be at a moment of exit.

Throughout the day, whenever there were free moments, between taking photos with the crew and cast, lunch and the production office handing out black sweatshirts with 'Mass Hysteria: Cast and Crew 2024' dripping in a bloody purple font across the chest, I injected many moments of presenting pieces of the score to Luca. I had seen him only equally thrilled a handful of other times in our week of knowing one another but this time it felt entirely intimate, and a closeness developed as I watched him listen. Luca was now a dear friend and someone I'd hoped to collaborate with for a very long time.

The final setup on the final day was an extreme close-up shot of Vivian—a single tear was to fall from her eye, the camera would dolly down, tracking the tear as it fell, and stop at her lips—ending in a grin. That was the final shot to be filmed in the entire production and it would be done within the main house on the soundstage. Vivian requested she be alone with her music and her headphones, I obliged her requirements and sat with Luca and Donna and James, the PA. Jonah was chatting with us by the monitors as the final shot was lit.

"Ready for First Team, let's step Vivian in, please."

The words chirped from James' open walkie (his earpiece was not plugged into the radio; his walkie sounded out in the open, generally frowned upon I learned but it was the last day, and things were becoming increasingly lenient as the film had wrapped principal photography all but this one, particular shot). The voice on the walkie came from Tyler, undoubtedly, and his voice doubled from where he stood within the set, in front of us; Tyler's head poked out of an open window.

"Where is she? Do we have eyes?" he asked, impatiently, only a head. It was his duty to wrap this film on schedule and have everyone home for dinner that night. He would walk away a hero and a respected leader in the eyes of the crew.

"She's stepping over now. She had her headphones on," Katie replied with her voice high on the open walkie.

"Great. We can wrap Second Team with their thanks, they're

welcome to stay to the end. Monica, you have done so amazing," from Tyler. A dimmed cheer within the set. A moment later, Monica, Vivian's stand-in tiptoed down the front steps of the mimicked house.

Vivian strut across the stage, headphones in hand, with Katie at her side. She never dared to look anywhere but at her shoes. She was wearing blue slippers provided by the costumes department as most of her costume did not need to be worn for the shot.

She entered the set and seconds later, her eyes, two beguiling worlds of brown, filled the frame on the monitor. The red dot appeared in the corner of the screen and numbers lined the white grid outlining the frame. The door into the set was open, and we sat close enough around the corner for Luca to bellow in his smoke-congested, nasally scratch, "Action, Viv."

After a second or less of staring seemingly down the barrel of the lens but actually, millimeters to the edge to trap us all in the illusion of the film, a single tear formed and boiled on the rim of Vivian's right eye. It trembled, growing, and let go; it fell across the sculpted valley of her face. There the image followed that single string of sorrow, slipping further and further until it found the crease of her lips. The tear escaped to the seam of her mouth and the camera held in a weighted pause—I held my breath; I felt my abs flex—and a subtle, vivacious grin turned upward, both ends going U-shaped just enough for elegance—a declaration of powerful release.

"Cut," Luca whispered, but I was the only one to hear him say it. The rest of the crew remained silent, caught in their automatic load of equipment, and watching—we were all focused on her performance —so rich and pinned with perfection. Something nearly impossible. "Cut," Luca repeated.

"Cut," James said straight into the brick of his walkie.

"Cut," said Tyler from within the set, and so, "Cut! Cut, cut," the rest of the PAs chimed in agreement. A bell shrieked twice and the red twirling bottle lights on the soundproofed walls died and froze. At the monitor, the lens went wide and soft, then back into a crispness of secret comfort; Vivian was still on her mark, wiping her single tear from her jaw and giggling at something Jonah was saying beyond the camera. The aged hands of the Hair and Makeup teams dusted and poked at Vivian's face. James, our trusted PA, asked the director if he'd like to go again.

Luca nodded kindly as he watched Vivian, his muse, on that screen. "Once more for safety. But we got it," he announced.

I felt a leap in my chest, a felt movement of shock—excitement and pride, but despair—everything must come to an end. If this project were to be realized, to be seen as a film, it would have to end. The camera reset and Vivian reincarnated her performance; another tear fell into a grin. The camera cut once more, and Vivian returned. Her character, Madeline Price, was no more, alive only on the silver screen. James pressed the side of his walkie and gave a look toward me as if to say, *are we absolutely sure?* And I nudged Luca, he jabbed me back instinctively but caught sight of James over his shoulder. He provided a second, more militant nod, "Wrap on the picture, James."

That was it. Tyler Verrina jested over his walkie (which he always treated more like a handgun, twirling it old-West style and shoving it on his belt only to unclip it again quickly and repeat the motion), "That is a wrap on Vivian Wells—Ladies and gentlemen, that is a picture wrap on *Mass Hysteria*—That is a wrap on *me!* Thank you."

James' walkie cut out and I flinched, surprised; I thought maybe that was all Tyler was going to say. I leaned in at James' side where he clenched the black box. A static of radio air puffed out, coarse like beach sand, and Tyler rang out, "Thank you to everyone on my team and on the entire production for your hard work and dedication on this production—I know it means a lot to me, Luca, Donna, Vivian, Olivia back at base—You guys have been possibly one of the best crews I've worked with. Lots of love to everyone here—thank you."

The sandy sound cut out again only to be replaced with an exasperated howl from the masses, high and wailing like a police siren that stirred out a whining screech of giddy intentions. All around me in every direction of the dim stage, the lights shot up, a squealing brightness overtook my sight; the crew members crawled out from their nooks and shadows to celebrate, if only for a moment, and everything became alive and frenetic in a matter of mere seconds.

"Christ," I blurted. Luca hooked the acute angle of his elbow on my neck and kissed me hard on the cheek. He tossed me away so he could hold both of Donna's cheeks in his and present her with a softened kiss on her lips. Luca then turned and sauntered up the steps of the stage for a speech; everyone was rapturous, and champagne seemingly appeared from thin air.

They all celebrated and drank, and what's more, there was an apparent 'Wrap Party' taking place at a bar the following night with the whole destination bought out for the night. There was an open tab to drink as much as one could handle. Were all film productions commemorated in such lavish extremities? With Luca and Jonah locked in a prideful embrace to my right. Vivian skipped across the stage. Her wig was gone to reveal her hair still pinned into a sort of cap—she sported her robe I had come to expect between takes and latched onto my body with a leap. All I could think about with such sureness was how this place, this strange industry with its curious operation and bands of freaks, was where I wanted to be.

Vivian pressed her lips to mine and held them there for some time —all the noise of the jittering space fell out and it was only the two of us and our careful touch, the gentility of our breath and the sensation of brushing each other's faces—before we let go and the exterior world swallowed back into life, like a conscious crack beneath water. Still, our gaze did not falter.

"You were right," I muttered. She rubbed the palm of her teeny hands up west of my jawbone and up through the backside of my hair.

"What's that, baby?"

"It is a circus. This whole place—all of it—it's one, big, fantastic circus."

She danced her vision around in a sidestep, checking in on both my eyes and almost seeming fearful. I chuckled in reassurance, "No! In a good way! I love it—all of it!"

And she sprouted a giggle, revived and certain once more. I thought she might tell me she loved me then, but it never came.

Instead, we embraced in a kiss once more, where we both knew we were sufficiently comfortable.

———

The official soundtrack to *Mass Hysteria* was mixed and finalized months later when I was back in Los Angeles and staying with Vivian at her house (I use the term staying to avoid the term living). It was then I adjusted all the measures, rounded the edges, and generally shaped each track of my score in accordance with each scene as the final edit was locked. Luca and I went back and forth through phone calls and emails to finalize what would be the score for his Mass Hysteria. It was a big step for both of us and he needed the score to be completed before he would enter the process of ADR (Automated Dialogue Replacement). They would then do a final mix of the film with my score smacked over top of his picture. Luca lived in California; he stayed in a voguish rental in Carlsbad. I recall he had plans to move closer to the city.

I spent many nights walking the sidewalks of Beverly Hills with my headphones on and listening to the soundtrack; usually, I would jot down two or three notes to fix when I arrived back at the house. At a certain point, it turned into a routine, and without any distinct date or time, the notes subsided, and I would go outside while listening to pieces of the score without making any changes. One morning while walking the lavish avenues, I paused to glance at my shoes; I realized the score was complete.

Vivian and I spent that summer traveling Europe; we had the means to do so. We presented to each other our favorite destinations in such cities as Budapest and Prague, even Warsaw, Berlin, and Brussels. While in Cannes, Vivian and I spread out on a beach and allowed the sun to wrap our bodies like bedsheets. We laid out for an hour or two, flipping every so often and reading our novels we'd brought from home. Vivian lay flat on her stomach, pale as a portrait and reading her Margaret Atwood novel through shaded frames and eating candied walnuts. I asked her how she liked the story so far.

"It's really good," she said, "How's yours?"

I was reading a novel by Haruki Murakami. I had been an admirer of his work since I was in high school. I had always adored his worlds, and how he chose to present them, drenched in dreamlike qualities.

"It's good, real good—I'd say it's even mesmerizing," I paused, and nudged her, "Much like you."

She giggled—that humming of closed laughter—I grew to adore this sound more than any instrument could create. I brushed my palm down her back, and we grinned at each other. We returned to our fiction while next to one another in delightful comfort. I understood the tranquility that came with companionship. Whether I was truly falling in love or not, I may still not know, but I did believe I was. I have come to understand that love, among other emotions, will present itself if you go searching for it.

We wandered countless cinemas, opera houses, bookshops, and cafés. Vivian would strut ahead in large strides with her jeans high on her waist, over her belly, a crop top loose and flowing in the summer drag. She taught me more about cinema (added to my repertoire already stocked by Tommy and Luca before her). Her favorite films were, in no particular order, were as follows:

Thelma and Louise. Regular Lovers. Frances Ha. Raw (2016). *Persona. Halloween* (1978). *Clue* (1985). *The House of the Devil. Moulin Rouge. Amadeus. Matilda. In The Mood for Love. Vertigo. You've Got Mail. The Virgin Suicides. Stanley Kubrick's Lolita. Pan's Labyrinth. Juno. The Dreamers.*

All of which I enjoyed—*Amadeus* and *The Dreamers* most of all —I felt as if they were pieces of art that shared a secret with me. I have always found it to be such an important thing when one discovers a piece of art that speaks to them. Occasionally, an artwork is created, and it will whisper back as if to say, *I see you and I understand; you and I belong together.* Not to mention the riveting sensation found in a piece of art, the sensation similar in stature to falling in love.

I watched the many fantastic pictures my dearest Vivian deemed worthy of my viewing. I, in turn, presented Vivian with a list of records to listen to, while we were on the train between cities. I believe we were somewhere between Frankfurt and Paris. Thumping in our cart, my hand resting on her thigh and an earbud pressing to each of our ears, I played her a variety of albums and, best of all, she sat and listened. She really listened and she often smiled.

"I liked that one a lot," said Vivian, her eyes turned up at me; the flicks of sun through the window cast a halo around her hair. We had just finished listening to Bob Dylan's 1969 *Nashville Skyline*.

When we returned, Vivian had one month before production began on her next film, *Gravitas*, from an American film director named Bernadette Claude. Claude was a pudding-blonde woman of high intellect and a trace of bitterness toward many of the grotesque men who clung to the film industry like mold on a wall. *Gravitas* was to be her third feature and was based on her early twenties when she got her first job in the industry as a film loader, and all the turmoil and tribulations she had to face to even get even one her scripts read. Part comedy, part drama, part exposé. The film's distribution was to be handled by a well-received independent studio with a certain *je ne sais quoi* in the arthouse realm (in this era of cinema, the company was a highly regarded studio among avid fans of cinema).

While Vivian was prepping for her next role, between rehearsals and calls with Bernadette, I was tapped to compose the score for another horror film from the director Theodore Sellers. The film followed Montana ranchers in the late 1980s who stumbled upon abandoned nuclear bunkers on their newly purchased land. Only within these bunkers do they discover a horrific, humanoid species of creature inhabiting them (The picture starred Frederick Richardson, an actor who I was growing fonder of as his career began to take a real shape). It was called *All Along the Wrath Lands* and had wrapped production that summer while I was on vacation. Teddy had apparently been a mentor figure for Luca, and when Luca sent him a few scenes of his debut feature, Teddy's first question was, *who in the hell composed that score?*

I signed onto the project. So, while I was being sent clips and references to use as inspiration for my first accompaniment to a midwestern gothic tale, Vivian was zeroed on molding a performance fit for the creator of her own kaleidoscopic autobiography. On top of our new endeavors, we decided to purchase a house for the two of us to live in together. While I did spend many days in a row at her house in Beverly Hills, I still had the lease to my apartment. So, I purchased a house for the two of us to live in, somewhere we could call home together and within the comfortable walls, we could catch glimpses of a shared future.

We were exhausted by the hustle and congestion of Los Angeles and decided to embark on a new chapter of our lives in Santa Barbara with a newly remodeled Spanish bungalow complete with a brick courtyard and cliff view patio. We were close to West Beach. The house had more space than we needed, I knew, but felt compelled to the aesthetic of the house when it was shown to us. It was not lost on me how far I had succeeded since finishing primary school, barely less than a decade before then. It was only Vivian and me. The word, *family,* was on the tip of everyone's tongue.

By the time everything was settled with the house and the two of us had moved in—Viv had her home gym properly set up; my studio was set up in its own building, a sort-of guesthouse, across the hedge-walled gravel walkway—it was time for her to leave for New York. And what a pity it was for her to have to go back to work. The two of us had spent so much of our last few months confessing to each other the stories of our pasts, tossing around in colorless sheets—changing them just as often—challenging the other to cook increasingly complex meals for dinner and teaching the other phrases we knew of different languages.

"Tout est bien qui finit bien!" Vivian might have said.

"Ich verstehe nur Bahnhof."

"*Bella!* Il mattino ha l'oro in bocca."

"Eh—*prego?*"

"I better *not* be!"

But the fun was over. The house grew much larger. Now it was the 1st of September. Each morning, I rose with the sun and fell back with it. Vivian had managed to get me back into shape over the duration of the summer—training exercises with her and her trainer,

Loren—home workouts, sunrise meditation, yoga, reading, meal-prep, higher rates of protein consumption, daily vitamins, drinking water more often but not too often and, most of all, cutting out the fucking drugs. I vouched to maintain the concoction I would surely keep until the end of life, that of coffee and cigarettes, or as I call it, my reason for getting out of bed. I now had a thin layer of facial hair, a pepper that some mornings just looked more like dirt smeared on my face. I hadn't liked the scruff very much, but I knew Vivian preferred it.

"Why do you never grow out your facial hair? You'd look good with a little stubble," she often expressed.

Every few weeks, Luca and I made an effort to meet with each other and catch up on our lives and have a meal. I can say with truth on my tongue, I was comfortable. Between colossal venues, absurd studios, clubs, jets and vans, wretched hotels, and short breaks at my old apartment, I spent the last few years of my life in a jammed cycle of wicked pace. I could finally breathe, and the air was kind. I would never forget about Beach Sirens—I would never hope to forget about it—but I had turned a corner in my aging, and I was thinking about the band much less frequently. I was nearly twenty-eight and was in the midst of severing ties with the rockstar within me. Sophia and Autumn and Tommy, the trio I cared for with every ounce of my body, sat respectfully in the back of my mind and allowed me to slow down. This is not to say I never thought of my bandmates, those of whom I consider closer family than my literal immediate. Vivian and I fancied bike rides through the beach town every now and again. It was a relaxing afternoon activity for us.

One breezy morning, Vivian and I stopped in at a coffee shop we frequented. Most of the surfing crowd and locals knew after a certain point not to bother us but every now and again, a tourist or beach-goer would gather the courage to confront Vivian or me and ask for a photo. Some wanted photos with Vivian, others didn't know who she was and wanted a photo with me, but most wanted both of us in the photo. I no longer despised the photo opportunities if it meant getting to be in the picture with Vivian. Truthfully, it felt good to find a picture posted of Vivian and I posing with a fan, as if we were a couple that could inspire a generation with our class and balanced lifestyles.

One young lady with brunette hair cut off at the shoulders and a star-crossed gaze, decidedly still in high school, carried a sun bleached copy of *Little Women* below her arm. She tapped Vivian's shoulder while we waited at the pickup counter, my arm pressed into the faded black countertops.

"Excuse me, Vivian Wells," she started, and she took a deep breath. "Can I have a picture with you and Joe Henley?" she asked, with all the sweetness to her tone she could muster. It was very common for people to call us by our full names. They did not know us personally, so in a weird way, it made sense they would not say only our first name.

"Of course, dear," Vivian rang. She leaned toward the phone extended in front of the girl. A digital impression of my and Vivian's faces moved onto the screen and she snapped the photo, enveloping an abstract postcard where the three of us had been in that moment of time.

"Thank you! And I love your movies, Vivian Wells! I really love *Sloane's Gotta Go,* all my friends and I quote it like, *all the time!* 'You can't just make up words, Sloane!' 'All words are made up, you fucking squid!'"

We all laughed at her impression of the film and the young lady turned to me. She tilted her head, "And—I wanted to ask—do you think Beach Sirens are ever getting back together?"

Vivian's face flushed and she went tall, like the sunshine had washed from her body. I felt speechless. What was I to tell her? I didn't want to disappoint her. I fumbled with my tongue against my lips and thought of how to best navigate a response, a response that I wished to know as well. The young girl must have noticed because she puttered, "It's okay, I'm sorry—you don't have to answer that—I love your music, I'm sorry."

"No, no—thank you—that means a lot. The truth is, I don't

know what will happen with Beach Sirens. I suppose there can always be hope."

"Even though Autumn is making her own band?" she asked.

I squinted at her, my brows pinched.

"Don't you know about that? Don't you know about her new record label?" the girl asked.

"No," I replied, blinking and confused. "My Autumn? Autumn Gladis?"

The girl nodded. I chuckled due to the perplexity of the news.

"This is the first I've heard about it," I answered truthfully.

"Oh, wow. Well, it's called Acid Ick—and I read she's starting a band," said the girl. She dipped her eyes to the black and white checkered floors. "I read it in *Rolling Stone* magazine last week. Yeah, I guess she's doing pretty well."

All three of us went silent only until the young lady's name was called from behind the counter, *Carleigh!* She swiped her iced coffee from the counter and thanked the barista, then turned to us, "It was really nice to meet both of you," she said, now less anxious than before.

Vivian offered to sign the inside of her book and Carleigh accepted the invitation. I cocked my head as Vivian scribbled her own name on the inside, across the page from where it read, *Louisa May Alcott*. How strange, Vivian's name was of more value to the young girl than the common scripture that followed it. It wouldn't be long —not long at all—before one of Vivian's films or my records could be reduced to a canvas for a new personality to scribble their signature on. I tried not to think too much about this. On the bike ride home, I decided the only thing I wanted to worry about was the feeling of the breeze melting around my face and the trees stirring over my head.

For the first time in my life, I began noticing the intricacies of nature. I sat in my courtyard patio, on the tomato-colored brick foundation, under a layer of shaded branches and watched the bumblebees as they sauntered from flower to flower, center to center, and gathered their pollen. Bumblebees rely on pollen and the flowers rely on the bees. A unity of reliance and trust. I sat on my patio with my coffee each morning and tried to whittle that very phrase into only a word. What is it that was all around me? The fabric of which the entire web, seen and unseen, held itself together by the contribution of each bit of life. It only took a week before I decided the summary of my phrase, *a unity of reliance and trust,* was very simply, *love*—and it was all around me.

It bloomed in each flower, it was stuck to the fur of the bees, and it was in the honey. Love was blowing in the wind, it ruffled my hair, and it ran in my veins. It was not so easily seen, and more difficult to see when one pushes through life in a cyclical, demanding manner, but something I have come to learn through life—love can be seen and it is best seen through the eyes—not only the eyes of a lover or a dog but for every living thing, from a lamb to the grass it lies in; everything has its own eyes. Look into these eyes, and this love I speak of shall reveal itself.

I was a baby again. I became curious about how color presented itself to me. Curious how right angles always fit and why the world functioned with these angles. One blinking Sunday morning while Vivian was off in New York, I was in my airy studio writing a new piece to a piano concerto I started back at Christmas. *Bugbear* was the name of the movement I wrote at my parents' house, then I was working on the third and final movement. This piece had nothing to do with the score for *All Along the Wrath Lands*. I reserved weekends for my own projects, as I found it quite important to reserve time for my own projects. After an hour or two, I decided to stretch my legs and walk out to the mailbox. Inside was various mail for Viv, plus a single letter inscribed to me and whose name should be imprinted on the top left corner of the teeth-toned envelope but Sophia Baker's. The address line:

2687 Stratford Dr. Austin, Texas 78746.

I couldn't believe what I held between my fingers. I'd spent several nights staring at the lavender ceiling, sweat sponging on my skin—Viv, dead to the world on my right—and there in the warm darkness I would wonder if Sophia, my first love, ever thought of me. Yes, I had thought about her much less frequently, particularly since I had such a wonderful young woman in my presence most every day, but at night, the back crept forward and urged my thoughts. I shredded the letter and found a smaller card inside with a hyper-realistic photo with an absurd cleanliness glowing back at me, a photo of an archway and a grapefruit sky outlined by braided clouds, the foreground of which was Sophia in a white gown, Daniel in a navy tuxedo. Their eyes scrunched and they wore buttery awkward grins, forehead to forehead.

YOU ARE CORDIALLY INVITED TO THE UNIFICATION OF
SOPHIA AND DANIEL CAVANSKY.

What's more, a golden press of numbers kernelled apart from each other, spelling out in a yellow chromatic gleam:

5 - 10 - 25

I moved my lips without words, *May tenth of two thousand and twenty-five.* Every cell in my body began a process I thought could only be described as surrender, and all at once my stomach tensed and chalked like water added to a bucket of cement. A violent flash of memories stamped through my mind. They brightened and faded out slowly, like flicking out the lights in a room and watching as the bulb slowly died. The card requested I 'RSVP' if I decided to attend the event; there was a space at the bottom for if I chose to bring a guest. I thought of Vivian. She'd met Sophia the same night I met her for the first time. I tried hard to think back to that night but most of it was fuzzed out, I had been too drunk and too zooted by blow to create any memories with proper structure.

I sent the slip requesting my reservation back with both my name and Vivian's name written on it. I thought to try calling her instead of sending back a physical declaration, but I caught the grievance of last year when I had spent all that time trying to call her. She could have her space, and I could have mine. I decided maybe it was better this way, and someday, perhaps, I'd think of her for the last time. *Health.* This was a big word for Viv. She insisted we be as healthy as we could be, and that meant the mind as well as the body. I was unsure if Vivian would even be able to attend the wedding given her always changing schedule but knew she would like to keep the option open.

By the time the wedding came around, Vivian was caught up with work—she had a mandatory set of stunt rehearsals for yet another new film that would shoot that summer, a dystopian, climate-fiction film about the climate crisis named *Niño*—and I very nearly could not make it myself, but I knew I would make any excuse necessary to attend her wedding. I was invited to see Sophia again, and on what should be the best night of her life. It was an important event, but I kept my thoughts on the subject close to my chest, a secret for only myself. Nearly eight months later, wiser and older, I did attend the wedding, and I attended alone; this would later become one of the best decisions I ever made in my life.

IV

The Wild Idiot

I arrived at the venue around early afternoon; I paid and tipped my driver before the car crawled out and away from the celebration taking form atop the hill. The wedding was held at a peculiar place best suited for upper-class, modernist, golf-centric households named Tepler Clubhouse—a white stoned clubhouse with an outdoor patio and terrace—the terrace was dotted with tables; tablecloths drooped over the round edges, a bony white shade like melting candle wax. There was a photo wall of a rustic aesthetic (it was simply wooden planks stained and nailed together into a wall and pinned with a string of bulb lights and assorted flowers). A dance floor lay vast in the foreground of a suited band who were pressing out the final refrain of *Somewhere Only We Know* by Keane. The band paused only a moment before twinkling into *Paper Rings* by Taylor Swift.

A marble bar top and a pale glass wall of alcohol beyond; the bar featured mostly wines, not that I'm one to complain, also beer but nothing good—vodka, bourbon, rum, Aperol, tequila. The bartender sank the cork and—*pop*—it zipped upward and curved, then falling, it landed in her palm. I was astonished; curiously and instantly attracted to her. Brown, frizzy hair pinned in a bun. Freckles sanded over her face. Black button-down slim to the waist.

No. Stop it, I told myself. I had to conjure images of Vivian, both provocative and innocent, to keep myself level-headed, focused on drowning my ego.

"Well, well," a voice from behind said. A familiar tone, a deep and feminine ring I knew of only one woman. As I twisted myself around, I could hear her approaching as her flats crunched through the gravel, and then there she was. Autumn Gladis. She stood ten paces away with all her weight on one leg. She folded her arms and grinned.

"Hey," I blurted.

"Hey yourself. Nice beard."

"Oh–" I started and subconsciously bent my elbow to rub a palm over my cheek, finding the rug-like texture brushing through my fingers, coarse and prickly like fresh cut grass. "Ah, thanks. I don't think I'm going to keep it."

"No, Joe, I wasn't saying anything. I really do like it. It suits you," said Autumn. She chuckled lightly and uncrossed her arms. She wore a black dress that stopped at her knees, it was rather form fitting with a slit up her left leg, up to her thigh. Black sandals. A silver necklace with a charm I recognized to be a butterfly. She sported her fluff of red hair shorter than usual, and a lighter shade like marigolds in bloom. She was a pleasurable sight. I saw the signs of recent aging on her face, around her eyes; her green eyes bobbed over my appearance, and I recognized I'd been doing the same.

"You look really beautiful," I said. And she grinned at the pebble floor beneath her feet.

"Thank you," she said. The smile faded, replaced with a melancholy—no—it was as if the melancholy was always there, and she'd only masked it with a smile. More than melancholy, it was fatigue. I hadn't seen it right away but with her half-present concentration, her lids magnetized toward the ground, it was clear she only made an appearance out of obligation. I made the ten paces and put my arm around her waist in an effort to lightly persuade her into the venue.

"How have you been?" I asked. "I heard about the label you started. Acid Ick. I like the name."

"You can pronounce it like *acidic*, but you have the right idea. I'm glad you like it. It's something I've been working on getting up and going for a little while now."

"What is your plan with the label?"

"I'm—" She stopped herself from continuing. She seemed perfectly normal, nothing extraordinary, but caught on her words.

"What's wrong?" I asked.

"It's just that—I'm sorry, Joey—I was afraid to tell you. You remember Mazy, don't you? My roommate from LA?" she questioned, in a tone of distress.

I nodded and she nodded too; a supposed assurance came to light from mirroring one another. Autumn continued, "Mazy Diaz, yes, her—she was doing her own thing with Gauze Moth, and of course, I was doing my thing with Beach Sirens—" Her voice choked on the name of our band. She sniffled and managed, "Basically, she and I had an idea to start our *own* band. And I know—she was doing pretty well with Gauze Moth, but she wanted to go bigger. So, I invested some of my money into starting my own independent record label. Anyway, I basically signed myself onto the label but was really making Mazy my first client."

"So, you're still drumming?" I questioned. We'd stepped into the venue at this point and absently found seats for the wedding ceremony. We were in the fifth row on Sophia's side. I'd received countless stares from the many guests; I never removed my gaze from Autumn the whole way as to avoid them.

"Yes, are you joking? I'm never going to stop that. I made *Acid Ick*, and then Mazy and I officially formed our band. It's called Dead Girls Club. Mazy is on vocals and guitar and keys, I'm on drums, and a girl named Freya Morris on bass. We've made about— five—yes, about five songs so far. And once we have a few more, we're going to play a few shows around Brooklyn before we release an EP."

I straightened in my seat as if I'd been bitten by a pest. "Sorry–did you say Brooklyn?"

"Yes—that's where I live—in Brooklyn. Mazy and I have lived there for about a year now. You'd know that if you ever reached out," said Autumn with that same, chummy bite to her tone. She looked at me with her scouring gaze, squinted and was ready for attack.

"*Easy,*" I teased, completely unafraid of her antics. It was a family style bond we shared. Or perhaps it felt that way due to the ingrained familiarity. To see Autumn that night felt wildly nostalgic; I stressed on the presenting lines of age that took shape on her face. I wondered how long until we both had gray hair. Would we ever see each other again after tonight? Were we destined to conjure the same cyclical small talk at events such as these for the rest of our lives? A horror struck my bones when I realized I would see Sophia in a matter of minutes. She would be in a white gown and walking down an aisle toward another man while Autumn and I watched in discomfort. And Tommy was elsewhere, forever lost to us, yet we were expected to smile.

"Are you okay?" Autumn asked. A pinching wave of heat had shot through my body like a syringe full of flame. I suggested a confused look, "I'm fine, why do you ask?"

"You look pale. Are you still on drugs?"

"Do I look like I'm on drugs?" I scowled angrily. Autumn gave a real scan over my face and shrugged.

"Actually, you look clean—and muscular—*damn*. What is Vivian Wells putting in your water bowl? How is she by the way?"

"We're doing well," I nodded, "We just celebrated our one-year anniversary with a trip to Sicily. It was surprisingly hard to plan because of everything she always had going on. But it went well—yeah — very well."

Autumn nodded back. It was always one of us nodding for whatever reason. I felt admittedly nervous. Autumn crossed her left leg over her right and grinned a devilish grin, "And you're a composer now."

I flashed my teeth and looked to the ceiling; Autumn pushed against my shoulder.

"What? Are you not allowed to talk about it? *Baby's first film score*. Oh, Joe, I know all about *Mass Hysteria*. You don't need to keep anything contractually safe with me."

"How did you hear about that?" I blubbered, and frankly, I was taken aback by her comments. I hadn't told anyone outside of the people who worked on the project, not even my own parents or sisters.

"I have my sources. But I really am happy for you. Do you think the movie is going to be any good?"

I glared a single eye over my nose. Of course, it would be good. It had to be because it was created with precision and care. It was crafted by one of my favorite people and he believed in me to help execute his distinct vision.

Your score, yes! Your score, magnifico, this excellent score will be the glue that holds my entire picture together, my friend.

I remembered that I hadn't seen Luca in over two months by the time I was seated for the ceremony. I had little time to float on the thought before the ceremony commenced. First, the band strung a rendition of the *Bridal Chorus* from Wagner's Lohengrin (often simply referred to as *Here Comes the Bride*), a tune so infamous, it was attuned to folklore, synonymous with the few other movements and jingles we seem to know from birth. How can a tune become so universally known? Why can I not remember learning or hearing such a tune for the first time? It seems more natural, as if the sound were always with us, and as common as the birds.

These thoughts were crammed to the side for the growing concern over setting my gaze upon Sophia. Perhaps she'd not meant to send me an invitation and I was there by mistake, maybe it was only for Vivian. Perhaps Sophia had not known that she and I were in a relationship. My palms were sweating ferociously; I dug my palms into the thigh of my dress pants to wipe them dry. Pairs and pairs of groomsmen and bridesmaids walked with arms interlaced, they moved through the center aisle toward where Daniel stood in his tightly fitted navy blue tuxedo.

Daniel's blonde hair was flopped to one side to cover the balding spots. He was a tall fella with a long face and thin, dark lips. His eyes never seemed to be fully open but now he was grinning cheek to cheek until something changed, and he began to cry. I knew who was behind me then as everyone in the crowd contorted in their chairs to peer behind them. I stopped breathing; I closed my eyes and tried to focus on the tempo of the music.

One, two, three, four.

One, two, three, four.

One—

A hand braided into mine at my thigh, one with an alert sensibility and awesome grip. It was Autumn's hand; she stared back at me with an expression of concern. I took a heaving breath. I stared into her hazel stare for a moment longer before she grinned. Together, we turned our bodies to face the back of the room. There was a woman with brown hair done up with such brilliance, it shimmered like silk. She stepped forward, slowly, at a ticking pace. She wore a simple white gown that flowed around her ankles. This woman held tears in her eyes but refused to let any fall and I recall she was smiling with ease. She walked side by side with a man I knew, her father I'd known for years, the man who raised her by himself. All this as she stepped closer with each beat of the song. As she was only a few steps away, she looked at Autumn. She looked at me.

In that single, prick of time—the measure it would take to blink; nearly unnoticeable—I caught her eyes on mine. There was Sophia. She and I stared at each other in that briefness, only a flash, but everything puttered to a surreptitious slowness. A surge of adrenaline shot at a lightning pace, like a drug, and my eyes grew. Her eyes on mine, I felt the most vulnerable I'd ever felt in my entire life as if I were a wild animal. To everyone else, she seemed to be wearing a mask. A character playing the bride with exaggerated sadness and thankful expressions; *I am so lucky: it's my wedding day.* And yet, she caught me and registered that it was me, her old best friend, whom she was looking at for a needle of time, so short in measurement that nobody else would have any time to notice. Her expression moved toward comfort. All at once, I saw beneath all the many layers of fancy; the young girl I'd fallen in love with walked past me. And she seemed to have seen me, too. Sophia looked gentle and relieved to see her old friend.

More of an old hat now, I thought to myself. The moment had

gone by so quickly. It took less than a second—a rather dense portion of a second—and I would think on that single knick in time for an enormous difference, much longer than our meeting of the eye. She'd already made it to the altar and the ceremony was beginning. The officiant, pink in the face, began as anticipated. We are gathered here today. He charmed the couple and told of their love that began when they met five years ago.

I noticed Autumn's hand rubbing up and down my thigh so as to soothe me. There were two people in the room who could read my thoughts before I even knew of them. And one was next to me, able enough to comfort me. While holding my hand, Autumn had reached across her torso to run her hand on the length of my thigh, and it was doing as she intended. My breathing returned at a normal rate. I was so thrilled to have her next to me for the length of the ceremony. I felt better than I had in months as if I had rediscovered a piece of myself that I had thought lost. I decided I would remain at her side for the rest of the pale night.

———

Dinner was a choice of chicken or chopped steak. I chose the chopped steak (Autumn chose the chicken) though I only picked around at my plate. I grew weary of dinner and instead returned to the attractive bartender for round after round of champagne. I graciously accepted a slender slice of vanilla cake as dessert. I'd had a full bottle of white wine by the time Autumn held my hand and walked me out to the dance floor. Sophia and Daniel performed their first dance together to *Landslide* by Fleetwood Mac; it was a cover but the female vocalist in the live band did such an exquisite job, I thought it could have been Stevie Nicks in the flesh, if not better. The song ended and they counted into a new song and the guests were invited to join on the dance floor.

"Fuck," I groaned. Autumn continued toward the floor but began to sway. This was her introduction to groove, and soon she would discover the music.

"What?" yelped Autumn, over the volume of the band.

"They're playing a rendition of *Annie's Song*," I explained.

"That's John Denver, right?"

"Yeah," I chirped.

"Why is that a problem? It's a romantic song!"

"He wrote this song because he was fighting with his wife," I said. "Apparently, they had this big blow up and he left to go skiing in Aspen or something. He said it came to him on the ski lift. Isn't it strange that this became such a classic wedding song? Something that spawned from the tribulations of marriage?"

"What? Joe, that makes the song *even more* romantic! What did John Denver write at a low point in his marriage? He wrote a fucking *love song* to his wife. Love will always have tribulations, but you always overcome them and find each other again. That's what love is. It's finding each other at every turn. It's wanting to spend your life with one person despite all the boring, cyclical, shitty, aspects that come with it. You love someone when you'd rather have them there at the end of every sick and stupid day because they make it a little less sick and stupid."

I blinked and she bit her lip while watching me, she was searching for what I'd thought about her speech. I heard myself chuckle; I wrapped my hand around her waist and stepped her out onto the dance floor. She leaned her head onto my chest and without ever saying a word, we danced together to *Annie's Song*.

The evening pursued in the classic fashion of a wedding celebration, and Autumn mingled in the crowd as the sky draped into black. I cradled my glass of wine to the edge of the dance floor then swayed inconspicuously to a table on the terrace. Rolling blue hills. Little balls of light flicked throughout with tiny quivering glows surrounding them. I leaned on one of the white-clothed tables and sipped at my glass. I thought it really quite amazing how even out there, life inhabited those magnificent ink hills. People are everywhere and everywhere there is nature. You haven't got to go very far to find something familiar.

"Joey!" called another. A voice with such shining familiarity. I became startled at the call of my name and a shock bolted through my body as if I had been struck in a storm. A splash of white wine flung from my glass and pelted on the cement floor. I twisted around to find the newly wedded bride. She slapped a hand over her lips to keep from bursting into laughter.

"Hey," I started, "You didn't see that did you?"

"No, of course not," she jested and added a roll to her eyes. She stepped forward and extended her arms; she plopped her body onto mine in a bearish hug. "It's so good to see you! You're so muscular now! And maybe it's the beard or the suit, but you look sharp."

She spoke with a new inflection. I hadn't seen her the longest out of anyone and she then felt, unfortunately, like a stranger. "Yeah, yeah, thank you. You look absolutely gorgeous—and what a beautiful ceremony—congratulations, Soph, really," I said with a conscious grin on my face. Every few seconds I adjusted my facial muscles to ensure that I was still holding it high.

"Thank you. I hear you're a composer now. Is that right?"

"Ah—Yes—I'm scoring films at the moment. I'm about to begin work on my third one."

"Well, that is very exciting! Congratulations! That's something I don't know if I could ever do but it's so fitting for you. You always did love sitting at your piano or with a guitar and coming up with melodies. Writing entire orchestrations, though—that sounds like a daunting task. Seriously, I love that you're doing this. I'm going to have to get your autograph before this is over," she said, and her voice fluttered into a laugh. I couldn't quite tell if she was joking about the last bit.

"What about you? What have you been doing lately?" I asked.

"Writing poetry."

I stretched my face to show my amusement; Sophia grinned and chuckled, "I know. Fitting, isn't it? I'm trying to get a poetry collection together; the only problem is, I want it to be quite good."

"Fuck, you could say that again."

"I knew you would understand! It's so difficult being a perfectionist because you're just not satisfied until—until—"

"Until it's perfect, Soph."

"Yes!" Sophia leaned forward: her elbows pushed acutely onto the table; she pointed at my glass. "Do you mind if I have a sip?" I shrugged my shoulders and offered a sky-faced palm. She yanked it by the stem and took her sip—more fitting to call it a gulp, two heavy gulps, most of the glass—and returned it to the cloth floor of which it perched.

"Are you alright?"

She shot her gaze from the inky hillside onto me again. She seemed somehow taken aback by my concern. "Me? Yeah, I'm okay. I promised I wasn't going to drink tonight and then—well, wouldn't you know—you show up."

She must have noted my hurt expression as she recharged, "I mean, I'm happy you came! But fuck, if there isn't a history here! I was terrified of seeing you again. I was afraid the second I saw you, I'd pick up a cigarette."

"Just any cigarette?"

"I don't know! Out of your pocket, off the floor, who knows! Do you still smoke?"

I nodded. She nodded too.

"Right, figured as much—okay, let me ask you this—if you haven't changed completely, I'd assume you still have an obsessive personality. Hey—no—just hear me out. My question is, does Vivian ever get upset with you when you're working on music?"

I attempted to reflect on my last year to determine if this was a common trend. If I recall correctly, she had been standoffish to my decision to spend so much time in the studio space as time went on. At the time of the wedding, it had only just begun and that night, I hadn't known it would continue to get much worse. Little trends like these sprout in relationships without a glancing eye. Problems between people can often start out as invisible to both. Yet they grow into problems so large, they shroud out the love and care felt from the beginning. Dangerous. I nodded at Sophia. I made gentle notes of her physicality. Her brunette hair pinned and done up precisely. Golden earrings swayed around, on her lobes. A simple golden necklace clasped high on her neck. The black drawings etched down her arms lay in their correct placement. I read over the one I knew, the one I cherished, the one that might never leave me, *The Red Upon the Hill*. And a golden ring, elegant and new, wrapped around her finger.

She picked up the glass again and swirled what was left of my wine. I nodded in answer to her question. She took the invitation to down the remanence before she said, "Daniel gets upset if I choose writing over hiking or going to a game. Usually, it is a basketball game but sometimes other sports too. He'd really be perfectly content if I blew him every morning and played tennis with him every evening."

"So, then why'd you marry him?" I blurted and felt the instant horror of realizing I'd said it out loud. But to my surprise, Sophia began to laugh. She had a hand pressed on her flat stomach as she chuckled. It seemed we were both beginning to feel the wine.

"Daniel really is a good guy but God, he loves to think about himself. Consider him so introspective, he turns in on himself, and he ends up with his head up his ass."

I chuckled at this, but Sophia did not. We sat in silence for a moment. The band was still jingling out covers from behind us, but the night was the loudest element from where we stood. The gentle breath of the wind and the creaking voices of the crickets were our score that wonderful night. I stole another glance at Sophia from across the standing table and she was looking back at me. I quickly looked back to the hills.

"Joe," she said, "It really is good to see you again. I'm sorry I never returned your calls or messaged you back—I was so scared and felt like I was losing myself at that time—I just needed to take a step back. I needed my space to find myself again."

I swallowed. A blister of thoughts coursed through my brain like fresh water. She needed her space, but, really, she needed to be alone with Daniel. I knew she wanted a family. The reality was, she needed to block me out of her peripheral vision if she were to move on and commit to Daniel. It was the only way. I knew it, this violent realization, like being rightfully imprisoned. I laid my head in the guillotine with gentility and grace; this is where I existed and I was patient.

"It's okay," I finally replied. "And I forgive you."

"Thank you."

"For calling me an obsessive personality, that is."

"You are! I'm not saying it's a bad thing because I am also obsessive. We're obsessive artists, the truest and most insane kind."

Out of nowhere, Sophia was thrust into the sky with two hands cupped under her armpits. She yelped and kicked her bare feet. Down she went gently back to firm ground and Daniel wrapped his arms around her waist; he planted a big kiss on her cheek. I used to do that some four years ago and now this was her husband, her devoted person to care for her for the rest of her life. He locked on me and gave a firm half-grin, the kind a man gives to another man in passing, accompanied by the most minute of nods.

"Hey, congratulations," I charmed, arching my brows and stretching a hand.

"Thanks."

Daniel's palm clapped into mine, creating a hollowed slap. Blonde hair combed to one side, his long features and an arched nose bent at the tip to the likes of a bird beak. Squinted blue eyes and a porcelain row of teeth fenced into his visible gums. Daniel Cravansky was so familiar, perhaps I knew him from somewhere. He was a tall, lanky man, and although an assuming type, I could practically smell the danger he felt with me talking to his bride.

"Are you coming back to the dance floor, babe?" Daniel asked with his hand petting down her back.

"Yes, I'll be back in just a minute," Sophia hummed and pecked him on the cheek. As he turned to walk back toward the dance floor, in the blinding background of pearled lights I caught a row of groomsmen casting wicked stares my way. Aside from the freaks, I noticed Daniel's final squint at my body before he turned off as if I wasn't meant to have caught the look.

"I guess I should be getting back," said Sophia with her eyes at her feet, "It was really good to see you again, Joey. And you're next."

"What? Getting married?" I laughed, practically guffawed at the very idea of it.

"Would that be so bad? Besides, it would be lovely to be at Vivian Wells' wedding. That sounds like a wonderful time!"

"Why can't Autumn be next?"

"Autumn is never getting married, she says so all the time! Now, she says she'll never even date again. We'll see about that."

"I guess never say never—that goes for all of us. Send me a copy of your poetry collection. I want your autograph too."

She grinned and gave me a parting hug. Her hair smelt the same. Sophia would forever carry my heart, even if hers wandered elsewhere. I accepted it at that very moment; to accept such a grievance was worse than swallowing a large stone. She pulled away from my chest and said, "Isn't it crazy where all of us have ended up? It's like if I had to guess where we would be now—you, me and Autumn—I think this would be one of my top guesses."

I wished her a lovely night and told her how it was great to see her again. She was a beautiful bride. She was exactly as I had often imagined her to look in a wedding dress. I wanted it to be me at the end of that aisle with my entire chest, and played back the memory from Daniel's point of view several times. The result was an overwhelming heartache, a twisted sensation of collapse and weight. I leaned on my table out on that dreary, dim terrace and stared at the empty wine glass. While I felt lost, I could lose myself still more. I thought of indulging in a great drink.

I returned to the open bar; the pretty bartender filled my glass to the rim as best she could.

"Do you bartend a lot of weddings?" I asked. She looked at me with her brown eyes, then focused back on the pour.

"Yeah, I have a wedding to work almost every weekend. It's good fun and I get to see a lot of lifelong memories get made. It's worth it." She sounded younger than I expected but now I was the closest I'd been to her all night. She seemed maybe only around her early twenties in age. She handed me the glass with a quivering rim and I spilled a splash on the white of my cuff.

"Thank you—and—may I ask," I started, "Do you know who I am?"

She tilted her head at an angle and scanned my face over and over before she said, "No, I'm sorry. I don't know who you are."

I sighed, admittedly disappointed despite my year in solitude, and threw a large tip into her little jar. I scratched my beard; I took a wide, heaping slug of wine down my throat and said, "Neither do I."

———

I wandered around the venue only to find Autumn seated inside the clubhouse on a random chair in a pale sea of vacant seats. She stared at the altar with a tilted gaze, as if hypnotized—perhaps magnetized—intrigued by the perspective. She had a glass in her hand when I sat beside her. She greeted me as I sat but very little was exchanged out loud for a worthy stretch of time.

"Are you drunk?" she finally asked, and I nodded my head without a word.

"Yeah, I think I am too."

I said nothing in response. I was focused on breathing and simply happy to be seated. That is all until she asked, "Do you ever think about the past? You know—how things used to be—or have you moved on already?"

"Sometimes. But I try not to."

"Why?" she pushed.

I was focused on her, but a distracting stimulation ran terribly in the legs, a dull warmth as I thought about Autumn. I thought of all the memories and images I had of her in my head, all the provocative poses. I cleared my throat and sighed, "I'd rather think about what's happening now."

Autumn grinned up at me; she was so close to me and as my brain rocked back and forth with a skull utterly still, something took control of my conscious behavior. She leaned her head on my shoulder and the simple touch of her hair against my neck sent a hot stroke through my body. I very carefully placed my hand on Autumn's knee and down—down—onto her inner thigh. I watched as my body worked against my mind and noted as Autumn accepted my physical gesture.

"Let's just focus on now then," she barely said under her breath.

Autumn provided her signature cutting look and I knew what would happen next. We took a car back to the hotel where I followed her into her room. The hotel had all the stamps. The air conditioning unit below the window screeched a tin sound. Thick drapes, triple layered. A desk with a lamp, a television mounted to the wall. A mysterious carpet with mosaic designs, darkly colored, like a stone path that led me to her bed. On the bed, still completely made with four pillows, two on either side, and atop the sheets, Autumn sat and hooked her finger below the straps of her dress. She stood up on the edge and allowed the dress to puddle into a mess at her feet. She dropped her underwear and bra. She turned, and I saw her completely naked in the darkness. She stepped out of her flats and crossed to the lamp in the corner, she flicked the switch and a somber, tungsten oval glowed on the ceiling.

As I undressed myself, slowly and awkwardly, as my cufflinks and double-buttoned pants caused trouble in my drunken state, Autumn boarded her bed and spread out on her back. She watched as I fumbled to relieve myself of every article of clothing.

"Do you need help?"

"I think I got it."

Finally, I removed my clothing and climbed on my hands and knees over the bed and onto Autumn. I felt her breath spread across my face. Her face was just as beautiful as it was two years ago, the last time we'd done this, in the Boston suite. Her face blurred and doubled, and I blinked several times to keep myself focused.

Our eyes found each other and locked together. Then, a sunken despair sucked through my body, quickly, as I became suddenly very aware of my awful, frigid situation. Autumn was naked and drunk below me, half of her body illuminated in the dim light, the other masked in shadow. All was familiar. Everything was comfortable and lustful. And before I could turn back, before I could put my clothes on again and drift into an alcoholic sleep on the terrible carpet of her room, we began the terrible act.

I remember little of the occurrence, either from intoxication or regret, and soon enough, it was over. I recall her green eyes were gray in the lowness of the room. Her bare chest huffed up and down, filling before it deflated just to fill again. The twinkling butterfly charm of her necklace creased between her and the start of her breasts went in and out of my vision. And we looked at each other, examining the other's features, now aged and new; we touched each other's faces and felt each other's skin more intimately. We brushed each other's hair with our fingers like paintbrushes melting on a canvas. Finally, Autumn grinned again, and she closed her eyes. Everything vignetted into a collapsing, curtained fade; the room faded, and Autumn faded, as the trill of her breath lolled me out.

V

Brides Head

If I existed, I thought, *I would hate myself.* A pale bluish streak of light painted a skinny post on the white, topographical surface of the wall. It was the only shape in my field of vision. I blinked to make sure I was alive and I, in fact, was but felt the fury of the toxins in my blood; all this to say, I did not feel alive.

The weighty intrusions of my infidelity pressed my head, a squeeze so tight I thought my skull might crack under the sizable pressure. Autumn lay beside me. I felt the skin of her body pressed against mine. I rolled around to find her there, her body still and unconscious. She was again filled with a presence of vulnerability, and a chilled purity. The mirroring image of her two years ago in a Boston hotel suite caused my memory to cross.

The air in the room was sick. I released my body from the sheets and shuffled out into the central cavity of the room. I sucked at the inner lining of my cheeks; it'd been maybe twelve hours since my last cigarette and now the biting ache in my mouth had returned. I found a cigarette and went into the bathroom, flicked the switch and the overhead light flickered on with a yawning fan. I sat on the toilet seat and smoked by myself with the door shut.

What had I done? The crushing sensation of raw, mortifying guilt refused to vacate my head, and the attempt of a second cigarette back-to-back only made me long for a glass of water. No more of this shameful lingering in my past. I would make a soft escape before Autumn awoke and go home where I was known as an honest man. I put out the cigarette and before leaving the bathroom, I realized if I had truly wanted to be this idealist honest man, it would entail a confession to Vivian of what I had done. *Adultery*. A new iteration of a scarlet letter and one engraved on my heart like a scolding brand.

I twisted and bent over the toilet bowl, the water still hovering upward after I'd flushed my cigarette butts only a second before, and engaged in the horrendous endeavor of vomiting. Violent splashes of filth, their scents and stings were of an acidic sludge. Poisoned breakfast. I wiped myself clean, or somewhat, and returned to the room to rummage the floor and find my clothing. I did myself decent and took one last look at Autumn. Her bare backside was only half-covered by the white sheet at a vertical shield, as if she were dual toned. I could still hear the dainty hiss of her nose breathing in and out, a different breath than that of awake, one reserved for only the depths of sleep.

What I felt for this woman had always been what I refer to as an unresolved conflict. I never felt certain of her and I working in the sense of a relationship, but I did find Autumn very attractive, and I did feel very comfortable spending time with her and confiding in her. These were the checkboxes for the necessities of a partner. She knew how to make me laugh. She knew what upset me and how to keep me away from it. We could sense each other's emotions and their outcomes—a trait that could not be translated into words, instead communicating through a primal understanding—seemingly intuitive, but no—this is the reward of a long and well-exercised love. We would spin out a beautiful child, a quite desirable family.

She was the love I would never face. She was a soul I'd looked past due to an infatuation with her best friend, who ironically was no longer a part of either of our lives. Sophia, my dearest, was now entirely unavailable. Curious too, the moment Autumn and I reunited, the result was a night of infatuated love (regardless of the tribulations). I leaned across the bed and kissed her as lightly as I could on the forehead, a soft comfort in my body, but it would never last. The curl of a heartache burrowed itself in my ribs at the very moment my lips left her skin. *Goodbye, Autumn*, I thought, *I do love you, and someday, I will get to see you again.*

———

I returned to my home in Santa Barbara that same day; Vivian would not return home for another nearly one dozen days and when she did, she showed up sideways, a bobbing head and clean face, caramelized crust around the eyes and fatigued expression. She went straight to bed. I had planned to tell her immediately of my betrayal of our love, but it was her demand for slumber that constituted a thought on my head; *this could wait.* I waited until she awoke and then waited until after dinner, and waited until bedtime, and waited until the weekend. I waited for her to finish her final two weeks of filming, and for myself to finish the final touches on the score of *All Along the Wrath Lands.* I had one week remaining to bow up the score, with the hectic commute into Culver City to record at the Barbra Streisand Scoring Stage with Theodore Sellers. This all happened just before I received yet another inquiry, this time from a highly regarded film director by the name of Conrad March. I have seen all of his films! I should be a tremendous fan of his work in film as well as the collection of poems he wrote. A master of his craft, both in poetry and his visual story-telling, which was still poetry in its own right!

Conrad March directed many films, among them, my favorites: *Clement Dr.* (1988), *Method No. Nine* (1992), *Drifting on Zero* (2004), *Fetid Petrichor* (2011), *Blood Thinner* (2018). Now, at the age of seventy-four, he was beginning to make his next film, titled, *Only in Dream.* A call was set up for the two of us to discuss the potential collaboration. I was rightfully nervous on the phone with him as I felt the screen shiver from my discomforted hand against my cheek.

I stood in my studio with broken sunlight dead on the wood floors and spaced with my phone in my palm, reading the number etched on the screen and knew it was him. Upon my greeting, I heard the shortness of his sentences, which, I would come to realize, was just how he was. He spoke in a low tone, a throat charred by years of tobacco pipes and rolled cigarettes alike, and he spoke with slowness, something I interpreted to be a lungful of fatigue.

"Joe, I can hear you," he started, and so slowly, I could hear his distant, wisping breath on the line before he continued, "I saw *Mass Hysteria*—the Luca Krzyżewski picture—I enjoyed the music you made. It was a haunting masterpiece. You are a very worthy composer of our time. I should be—some kind of moron—to not work with you in my lifetime. I'm making a picture. I will have my assistant, Nellie, deliver it to you. Let me know what you think."

Nellie delivered the picture by hand in a manila envelope the following Monday morning and I read it all in one sitting in my studio; it was a masterful work of fiction. All his films blended this profound sense of viewing a real moment occurring on screen, only to then shift to a dream-like voyeurism, a feeling as if interloping on the emotions of a character, personified and made literal. Theatric. Poignant. Substance at every inch of the silver screen was the operation of Conrad March. *Only in Dream* seemed to be a final step in his expedition of cinematic simile.

The film was about a boy, Malick, who finds a film canister in the woods. He takes the roll home and loads it into the projector to find an old man with a head of gray, flickering on his bedroom wall and instructing him on where he could be found. The film takes place over the course of the boy's lifetime, depicts his trials and hardships of life and becoming a man, and by the end of the film, the boy has grown old. Malick is aged, nearing midnight, and has lost sight of what he was in search of. He sets up an old camera and pleads for his younger self to find him. A metaphor, of sorts, a painful wink to an audience, that yes, March was aware of his mortality and limitations of time. It was an exquisite piece to read and the dialogue throughout was poetic, melancholic, and cerebral.

I agreed to the project and began work on the score straight away at Conrad's request, months before production would even begin. The first thing I knew I wanted to get into was *Malick's Theme*, which I would comprise mostly from a subtle nod to crime noir with a dreamy, reverbed saxophone, hitting all the lowest notes possible. The arpeggiated low-note sax ran as the backbone for the theme; I wanted the sound to reflect a calling from his older self. Malick, as a child, however, was very bright and energized, so I played the same melody of theme only transcribed onto the clarinet, used in a breathy, airy high tone.

Everything in the score, I knew, I wanted to have that dreamy sound to it, which called for plug-ins, echoes, and reverbs. But further, I wanted everything to have a demanding presence, as if it were guiding the viewer at a subconscious level. This would likely only be a detail of incitement to accompany the story. I sent *Malick's Theme*, as its first draft, over to Conrad and the next day he called me once more to tell me it was perfect.

"Do not change a measure of your composition. My boy, I will edit around it," he said over the phone. It was then, with my heart fluttering and a chest of giddiness, I felt like perhaps I was inching curiously toward my rendition of purpose.

———

It was while working vigorously and often on this project that everything in regard to my personal life came crashing down all at once. It began in the late afternoon with a sun ache over the studio; my inspiration muddled toward empty. I kept having distracting thoughts the entire day—if I am to be honest, it was the entire week or longer. I was stuck replaying the memory of Autumn and I, the brief scenes I could remember, and my imagination filled the gaps. Our lustful performance in the heated pursuit of each other's bodies was animalistic and hot. I could see her pale breasts tinted yellow in the light of the room, them bobbing, inflating, and deflating as I continuously took more and more of her breath away.

Without ever making a conscious effort to do so and alone in my quiet studio, I had unbuckled my belt and undone my dress pants. I masturbated to the memory and felt no wrong; I was able to momentarily dissipate the clouding guilt. Vivian's name would cross my mind and only her name, but it felt like a joke, like something that never really much mattered at all. My forearm grew tired and burned as the pleasure challenged in my body. As I caught the image of Autumn achieving climax in my skull, like catching the reflection of light against glass, I was able to do the same.

My mind slowed to a crawl, and I knew I would be making no more progress today. The silence of the space realigned, as if it had been off balanced by the quiet beating. I felt alone but in a distorted way, a way I can only describe as stupid. The sun had gone from gold to pink anyway, and I buckled my pants once more. I saved my work for the day. I made my usual path from the studio, across the brick path, the patio, and through the backdoor. This landed me in the kitchen, where I took the liberty of preparing dinner. Vivian would be home soon, warned by a text message prior to my self-absorption. I prepared a light, grilled chicken with sweet peppers, herb goat cheese and garlic honey mustard. Once I began cooking, I was able to shoo off all the distasteful images I had conjured in my mind, as if it hadn't occurred at all.

Vivian clicked the front lock and walked briskly toward our bedroom; I could hear every squint of her tennis shoes against the hardwood floors as she shouted, "Hey baby!"

"Hello," I returned, and I really was trying to sound enthusiastic. I flipped the hissing chicken breasts and checked the sweet peppers on the silver pan. I heard her enter the kitchen a minute later, the stick to the floor hinted at her being barefoot and I remember thinking this was curious until she forcefully flipped me around. There stood Vivian, and to my great horror, she was nude. She took a few steps back to allow a superior view of her figure. Her completely hairless and artificially tanned skin.

"What's this?" I asked. I was alarmed. I was retracting infinitely within my mentality. She could not know this, however, as it would destroy her. I hoped aggressively in the breath between my questioning and her response that she'd explain she only wanted me to examine a sunspot or check something on her body.

She instead, of course, giggled. And she stepped forward, while she spoke sweetly and daringly, "I wanted to surprise you. I've been thinking about this all day." She snatched my wrist and positioned my fingers between her legs, already made slick and warm. The whole image happened far too quickly to even keep up with what was happening. She pushed my wrist upward and my fingers followed; they effortlessly sank into her. She moaned softly at first until she stood on her toes then flattened herself back to her feet, she repeated this movement many times; her moans evolved to piercing neck-bent yelps.

"I want you right here," she growled. Her eyes were wild, and cheeks flushed raw. She removed herself from my hand and made herself comfortable on her knees. Terror prickled through my body as she undid my belt and yanked eagerly at my dress pants. I'd lost my breath but decided to help her by undoing the button, and down they went along with my underwear. My penis was not even half erect but still she held it upright between her fingers, limp and dead as it was. A pitiful sight and I felt the heat instead in my face, simmered into a devastating embarrassment. Vivian did as she intended and shoved all of it into her mouth; I stared down at her in a state of delirium. I nearly fainted. I watched her, her honey hair up in a ponytail, swaying with the bob of her head. Her naked body on the white tile floor, seeing the heart shape of her back and her toes peaked out behind it. *I should be aroused*, I thought; these were all the ingredients for a perfect surprise.

Of course, this sort of surprise usually only happened in the shower and occasionally in the car, on a long enough drive. Once on a hiking trail and twice in the pool. Never in the kitchen and let alone while I was cooking dinner. The stress of cooking, my recent ejaculation, and the damning weight of guilt within me made the whole situation nearly intolerable. The prominent memories of Autumn held at center stage, sweltering, more and more of Autumn. It grew and grew like a tick in the skin, leeched and alive. An anxiety that could not be killed by any technique of breath. My penis had yet to grow. It was still completely flaccid, and minutes had passed, Vivian was still continuing with the tired motion of her mouth. She hadn't even noticed me checking the chicken behind my back. The anxiety built inside of me until I reached a tipping point, and I'd had enough.

"Viv," I winced, I'd tried to keep my voice as neutral as possible. Her face unearthed from my penis, and she looked up at me. I didn't know what else to say to her, I was brimming with frustration. "I can't do this right now—I'm sorry—maybe after dinner or something. But not now, and not right here, alright?"

She looked dumbfounded by what I was saying to her like I'd just told her a secret. It dissolved—crossfaded into betrayal—a look of distrust. Dissatisfaction. She stepped up off her knees and brushed them off, she placed her hands on her hips and tears welled in her eyes.

"Are you sure?"

"Yes, Viv—I'm just stressed out right now. Maybe later if you're still feeling up to it."

"Okay," she said, and I took note of how her voice rose in pain, the second syllable of her response high and broken. She took one final glance at me, and I recall it was a face that left me in a state of devastation. She held a fresh hatred within her. Now was not the time and I could not simply flick off the stove and give in to her antics, especially after the prelude I'd fancied myself to with my fantasy of Autumn. It was pure hatred. She turned and I watched her storm off, and how strange it was to watch a woman, nude as birth, storm away in a fit of rage. I heard the shower-head honk in our bathroom followed by the crashing shrill of water. There was nothing I could do then—the damage had been dealt.

———

After we ate dinner, cleared plates and glasses, she wandered to the bedroom and began getting ready for bed. She barely said a word during dinner. She sat directly across from me and stared only at her plate. Every question was met with a single word response. It wasn't until we were doing the motor function of removing the throw pillows from the vast bed that she spoke up with a question.

"Did you cheat on me?"

I blinked and looked up from the pillow I had loaded in my fist, I met her eyes and did everything I possibly could to hold them there. I felt my cheeks brighten but still crossed my brows.

"What?" I practically shuddered. Did she know? How could she possibly know? I tried instinctually to appear disoriented by her question, a face of innocence on my trial. She placed her hands on her hips again and grimaced.

"Fine. What changed then? Because the Joe I know would have jumped at the opportunity. Do you still love me?"

"Of course I do. What kind of question is that?"

"You don't act like it, Joe." Fiery whips in her intonation. Tears reddened on the rims of her eyelids. I wasn't sure what to say or if I should just outright admit my secret to her. How might she react? What was I to say to this woman, whom I was sure I loved, as she unraveled?

She put her face in her hands and rocked forward and back. She recovered and stood up straight, sniffling and sighing. Her eyes shot to the ceiling and in doing so, tears beginning to flick down her cheeks. I watched her, awaiting an explosion, but was instead met with the opposition. Implosion.

"I cheated on you," she whispered.

I had no response. For my half of silence in the following moments, an overwhelming relief curiously arrived, only to fade. Once it was totally gone, I was sucked from control; a fleet best described as nothing would crash land—yet it wouldn't. It was the lack of presence, devoid of positive and negative, I existed in an emotion of profound emptiness. Shameful, disoriented betrayal. She and I were an adored couple. We did so much together, and I knew right in that instant, it was over. The end came without warning. I would find myself alone again. Truthfully, this notion hurt much more than anything she had done to me. The fear of loneliness overtook my body, and I flushed pale. But I knew I had to respond, and I blinked, remembering that I should speak.

"Can I ask—who?" I asked. My voice was rough like the teeth of a saw.

"Freddy. Freddy Richardson." She sounded annoyed that I made her say it out loud, annoyed with perhaps herself that she slept with an actor I'd verbally praised, one of my current favorite actors working in Hollywood. He had been nominated for Best Actor for his performance as Jack London. He was one of the leading stars of his generation. What's far worse, however, was how he was the lead actor of *All Along the Wrath Lands*, the film I scored the year prior. And finally, a sheet of pain rocked over my body, swaying in calm, hurtful waves. I felt my brain deteriorating.

"It was my last night in New York while we were shooting *Gravitas*, that's why I didn't answer your call. Do you remember? He'd been doing ADR for some movie, and we met on the street. He invited me up to his apartment, and we had sex. I was there for less than two hours before I left. It was a one-time thing, and I even went back to my hotel that same night."

I was decidedly hushed, much like a predator about to attack its prey. "Freddy," I started, and the rest of my sentence crescendoed into a violent outburst of malevolent screaming, "was doing ADR for the same fucking movie I was working on at home, Viv!"

She paused, shocked, and swallowed hard. I continued, quickly, "What the *fuck* were you thinking?"

"*I don't know!* Don't give me that shit. Why won't you fuck me?"

"Because I—" and I paused, squinted at her and pointed a finger. She nearly grinned, I could see it, but she held back. She had me right where she wanted me, in a mutual checkmate. I sighed, "Fuck! Fine! I slept with Autumn—at the wedding—*after* the wedding. Christ." I felt insane. I was made of flame.

She clawed a pillow from her side of the bed and launched it at me, it jetted past my face, a near miss. She wasn't sure what to do and leaned in to bellow a snarled scream, "That ugly bitch? That's why you won't fuck me? At least cheat on me with someone pretty. That way I don't feel like chopped fucking liver."

I took this personally and the hatred I felt toward her was edging on my skin, so hot I thought the heat could bleed from my pores in an outcry of evil sweat. I wetted my tongue before I sprang in brilliant retaliation, "I was shitfaced! I mean, we were *both* drunk! I barely remember it, and the lights were off, for fuck's sake! That was only two months ago but you waited, what? A full year later? Were you sober with Freddy?"

"Yes, I was sober. What kind of stupid question is that?"

I started laughing, a full-chested guffaw with all ten of my fingers sinking through my hair and into the flesh of my skull. "That's so much worse. That's so much fucking worse," I mumbled this softly on repeat, pacing up and down the length of the bed.

"Stop—stop it, Joe! Your story doesn't even make sense. You won't fuck me because of something you can't remember? I wanted you *tonight* so maybe I could move past this miserable mistake I made. We could continue to be together! What? *What?* Talk to me."

I shook my head, again laughing, unable to fathom the ridiculous words leaving her mouth. I pinched the bridge of my nose, "That's not how it works. You can't just forget about these kinds of things." I wiped my nose on my sleeve and inhaled—I held it and chewed on every realization as if everything she admitted had just finished processing—a Polaroid with the ink finally developed. I spoke softer than before as the energy fled my veins, "I won't fuck you because I felt guilty for what I'd done. And you felt guilty too, which is why you wanted to. It makes sense, I get it, but Viv—look at us—we both cheated on each other."

Vivian glared at me; I could see from the corner of my eye. We shot the same grimace back at each other. She turned around and sat on the edge of the bed. There was no sound for a measure, a long heaping off, only the subtleties of our congested noses. Total forfeit.

"Maybe we aren't supposed to be together," she mumbled, and the latter half of her phrase dove into a whimper. And her shoulders shuddered, her head bounced lower and lower. The quiet sniffles and exhales of her crying began. I stood behind her for a prolonged period in a complete state of shock. I walked around the bed and sat beside Vivian, my sweet, giggly Vivian, now pouting and her forehead dipped onto the round of my shoulder.

"Maybe we're not," I agreed. A low, calming tone; it reminded me of my father's voice. "That doesn't mean we have to hate each other. We both like each other, yes, and we both enjoy spending time together. That much I believe we can agree on. But the second we got away from each other—and away from this house—we both took the opportunity with a different person."

She only continued pouting, her tears moved warm and wet on my skin. I let her cry and thought perhaps it was helping. My palm surfed up and down her spine at a comforting pace. She breathed and eventually, the crying began to subside. The storm had passed. A wild wreckage had been left behind.

"I'll move out. I'll move back to LA," she said quietly.

"Are you sure?" I asked, as the pain in my chest and arteries filled in again. I hadn't wanted her to leave. I wanted her to stay with me where all was kind and comforting. The loneliness was practically tickling me, ready to fully consume me once more. True, she and I were never meant to be together. And yet, the disturbing chill at the idea of being alone, without her nearby or any knowing of when she'd return, left my body weakened.

"I'm sure. You don't have to go anywhere," she answered. She lifted her head from my shoulder and crossed her wrists over her cheeks, tugging tears as they moved. The deed was done. I looked at the woman, formally my partner, now on the set path toward becoming a stranger once again. My body ached as I was sure hers did as well. A year and a half of memories, gone in a flash, broken with all the grace of snipping rope. We were untethered, decidedly temporary lovers. Perhaps we were always fated toward demise and assured distance. If she or I were to find a magazine or an article or a post featuring the other, we'd discover a dull tense and interpret the face as familiar but gone. A hollow distance would grow between the photo of us and the other viewing it. It might become nearly awkward to see her on a billboard or moving on a screen, less of a connection than those who hadn't known her at all.

———

Vivian did move out, quickly too, the following week. It was a Wednesday when our relationship collapsed; our truths overcame our facade of love, and she was gone by Monday. She took the final trip with her remnants back to Los Angeles with the help of her assistant, Pasha, and returned one final time for a hug goodbye. She opened the front door without knocking and there I was, still seated on the bar stool of the kitchen island, and staring at the natural polygraph etches in the marble countertops.

"There's a package out here for you," she said, waving a thin, cardboard box.

"I heard them come," I returned shortly. I still couldn't believe how quickly everything had fallen apart. I was still thinking it over, like a VHS tape caught on a frame and becoming increasingly distorted. She set the box on the counter and sat down beside me.

"I'm sorry, Joe."

I nodded, my blinking every so often serving as little signs of being alive. She rested her head against my shoulder again and I felt a million micro-deaths cut through me. I wanted to lash out. I wanted to scream, to express myself completely, to toss my body about and make my pain known to her. I could show her what she had done, and what I thought of it, but no. That required too much energy. I was exhausted. Drained. Too old now for any such misbehavior; I'd become too wise for any such drama.

Instead, I rose from the stool and embraced her. The top of her head pushed into my lips the same way it had a thousand times before. This time, however, things would play differently, and I would not plant a kiss upon her head. Regretfully, a whiff of her scent got caught on my nose; this would be the last time I'd know this smell and I wilted at the assurance. Vivian moved away after a long moment. She waved with growing tears and whispered, "Bye."

"Goodbye."

She drifted to the front door. It opened, Vivian walked into the blinding white, and it closed. A hushed suction of a sound. All noise went out the door besides the occasional breath from the air conditioning or the stirring of the refrigerator. Besides these minute indifferences, I was alone. I stood in the face of my greatest, oldest, and most reliable enemy. I wondered how long I would be able to bear it before I fell to its power once again.

I did not move from where I stood in my kitchen. How much time had passed? Ten minutes? Half an hour? Longer? I remembered the package Vivian brought in for me. The package was motivation enough to cross to where it lay on the counter. I held it upright in one hand and pet my fingers over the soft cardboard knowing Vivian had recently held it. Truthfully, I felt insane at this pitiful notion. I ripped the top back, flipped it upside down, and a green velvet hardcover book dunked onto my open palm.

How to be Alive Today by Sophia Baker. Advanced copy.

Each letter was imprinted deep into the woven hardback and stenciled in a golden foil. It was a thin book, less than two hundred pages, surely. It was beautiful. I opened it to a random page, a poem named *Boston*. I flipped to another page. A poem named *What You'll Find When Searching for Love*. Every page featured a different poem, though some took up two pages. It was a magnificent work, but I was too mentally drained for any poetry for the moment. I closed the book and sat back at my bar stool, where my chin found its place on my folded arms. I watched as the sun grew into midday. I hadn't budged. It had been hours without movement.

I had to face the awful truth—I was a player in the destruction of the relationship—an entire team. There was no winning from the moment I brought my fingers to the inside of Autumn's thigh two months prior. A very small fraction of myself knew it was over then too, despite the weight of the spirits in my stomach, I knew that leaping sensation of violation. I wondered, perhaps, if Autumn knew it too. A rush of wrongful excitement, a mutual understanding as if to communicate to each other without a word spoken, *we absolutely should not be doing this and that makes me want you even more*. This crawling gnawed at my cranium grew until it translated into a more refined conclusion. Maybe, all this time, it was Autumn I'd longed to be with.

I nearly sprang to my feet to call her and see if she'd want to come over until I remembered she was across the entire continent. I could go to her in Brooklyn. I nearly thought it could be a nice surprise until I realized just how freakish I was becoming! I had to do something I thought impossible—learn to enjoy the unenjoyable—know what it is to befriend myself and learn to be alone. This would take several painful weeks. It was a similar sorrow and full body dread like getting clean from a drug. I became depressed and spiraled alone in my room, every memory of Vivian dancing in front of me like her ghost wandering through the house.

———

At first, I made little progress on the score for *Only in Dream*. I spent almost all that July entirely alone in my house. A handful of weeks passed me. I only left for groceries or to replenish my cigarette stash or to drive and clear my head at night. That is until one early afternoon, I crossed through the blaze of my patio and stepped through the glass door into my studio. The heat batted through floor-to-ceiling windows; a glow filled the room. I sat at the stool in front of my piano, my faithful friend, and played *Malick's Theme* from the sheet of music I wrote in my work binder. From then on, I had returned to work and found again, that unrelenting pace of creation. I worked with my head down. I had to concentrate on tempo, rhythm, and the progression of the music. The centrality of the score was complete, that being the themes, and all that remained was to experiment and morph these themes into complimentary pieces to fill out the score.

Near the beginning of August, I noticed I had fallen into a circadian cycle. I rose around eight in the morning to coffee and a single egg, then to the studio where I would work and work and pressed myself forward without eating or doing anything besides writing music until after two in the afternoon. I refilled my coffee. I ate canned chicken or shredded tuna around this time. I returned to the studio to engulf my presence entirely in the muscles of musical arrangement. By the end of August, the score was nearly complete, meaning I had a first draft of music that was over five hours. An array of options that could be whittled down to fit the length of the picture. I had all the dailies and early edits of the film sent to me to better adjust the score.

December came quickly, and I noticed how much free time I truly had. The score was my only obligation, and I had worked on it for twelve hours a day, seven days a week, for months. And all of fall had gone by, now crumbling into winter. How could it already be winter again? Years began ticking by at an increasing, and frankly frightening speed. The days were truly shorter by December and night took hold. I was still in my routine of experiments with sound in my studio, only now it was no longer for work; my work for *Only in Dream* was on pause until the film was edited. I experimented and created a new sound out of survival. It was the only way I could keep my mind occupied. I would sit in my studio inventing new instruments out of metal pipes or strings, even rubber bands and ruffling leaves while a microphone perched overhead. I hadn't known what I was seeking to create, it was only a way to pass the time.

That's all we can do anyway, isn't it? Pass the time. We're alive so we might as well do as we please. The more I experimented, the more I remained curious and filled my days with discovery. I realized this and began going on daily walks. Walks up and down the beach, a twenty-minute commute. Then, one day, from seemingly nowhere, it turned into running. In the rancid ice of winter, my body took control and began to jog, then the pace through the sand picked up, and I was running. I was alone on the beach, my nose wet, and my ears raw. I ran and ran, listening to the flooding roar of wind brush my face, the crackle of my shoes shoving into the dense bed of sand. I was running. I wanted to feel the chill in my lungs, the way it would soon hurt like they'd been squeezed. I wanted my lungs to feel as if they were bleeding, to feel the cuts on my eyes, my heartbeat in my skull. I tried to run to a steady tempo, counting each pressured step in the sand.

One, two, three, four.

One, two, three, four.

Sometimes I felt all I had was counting. These measurements of time kept me present: it kept me conscious and acted as a security feature to prove I was alive. It could be used anywhere, as if it were a trick I could pull out of the back pocket of my brain and use secretly to keep myself from spiraling.

One, two, three, four.

One, two, three, four.

Now, I was picking up pace but attempting to keep my breath under control. I had to transpose the time signature in my head. I tried to keep my breath steady, in through the nose—hold there, only a step or two—and out through the mouth. I ran first only a mile and paused to catch my breath. I walked leisurely with the ocean to my right, the sun to my left, peaking through the beach houses, huffing and holding my side. That is until the hunger returned, and I ran a second mile. A third mile. Four miles in one day.

I ran every single day. I was lean in no time. I couldn't get enough of it. Between the sounds I was inventing in my studio and the running along the wilted beach, I was always counting. I was able to focus my mind on my ability to count, and soon I was forgetting about Vivian. Autumn. Sophia. Even Tommy. I was counting toward something, it seemed, only it was a mystery to me then. I was counting toward a better time—a better tomorrow—a new movement that might feature less sorrow. I held a throb of deep heartache, and while I sought to mend it, I would carry it with great remorse and try another step.

VI

Can't All Stay Forever

I should have liked to die. My brain was a pendulum that rocked from optimism to pessimism in awesome sways, which resulted in some of the lowest emotions I have ever had to endure. If I ever felt too joyous for too long, I knew soon misery would return, and it would cast itself on my consciousness like a blemish. I thought of the poets and the philosophers, how I understood the words they'd strung together to mediate their intentions with suicide; it was less about death and more about escape. Less about the pursuit of a painful Falling Action and more about the yearning to have never been born at all. My methods to distract myself, whether it be music or running, could only ever be temporary to the leviathan-sized emotion inside my mind. A common misconception—*suicidal* is often referred to as a state of mind—it is an emotion, not a conscious endeavor.

True, in the moment and looking back on it now, I see the great whining I submitted myself to. *I should have liked to die?* A man with such monumental achievements, a man who had evolved into a modern-age composer; is he the man who should like to kill himself? The answer is not the man, but the mind; a mind struck with a diseased depression is a rampant one. Curable, yes, but only temporarily and it would always return again, likely when it was least wanted—least expected—possibly when you'd just barely forgotten you'd ever had it at all—the canker sore of the brain—a weight you lose but that comes back no matter the amount of caution and exercise.

This sinking, icy dread I had toward being alone was enough to spawn the depression once more, a black cancer to manipulate me, and to have faced this haunted suffering alone, I should have liked to die. Everyone has thought about it—once at least, twice or thrice—every person who lives has thought of how they could create their own ending. A pain so relentless and clogged in the stomach, seeded in the intestines and sprouting gothic roots and thorny branches to eventually fill the entire body with such terrible hurt. How to ease the pain? How to get rid of it? One reliable answer, quick and sharp, that of a rope knotted into a noose or as I had planned, a concoction of Xanax, marijuana, a glass or two of bourbon while listening to *Death-consciousness* by Have a Nice Life and lay in bed until kingdom come.

Instead of joining my brother, Tommy (he should be so livid in the beyond, watching down on me as I cut my own life short when he had no other choice; not to mention his dissatisfaction at discovering he was wrong and there was, in fact, a great Beyond), and instead of returning to dust while the dust is ripe, I brought myself out of bed every morning to run until I felt as though my lungs were bleeding. Not terribly difficult for a man like myself, who smoked upwards of half a dozen cigarettes a day (this was my cutback fund as well; while I was in Beach Sirens, it was a baker's dozen). Humbling, of course, to have such putrid thoughts of suicide while key muscles in my thighs and calves ached bitterly in the Christmas chill, knowing I had to push myself further. In this heated disagreement, this reliable, comfortable pain I'd granted myself to distract from the greater evil, I became entirely aware that I am no God.

Yes, of course, I am human—but many fans slip into a nonsensical state and seemingly forget the man in the music videos, the glamorous articles, the award show broadcasts, the talk shows, the fashion shoots, the short films, the radio shows—*he* is human. I am no angel sent from the clouds to create music, no, I am a man who was in the right place at the right time, met the right people, and was proficient enough at playing guitar and piano to take the shape of a star so a group of suits could meet their annual quotas. I am no revelation. I am a man with a hobby and like-minded, successful acquaintances.

———

It was moments before sunrise on the Santa Barbara beaches and there, I stood, dressed in tiny shorts and shoes strapped hard to my feet. The salt wrapped the air like shrink wrap and I stood in the middle of it, stretching my calves and wiping the crumbs from my eye sockets. My eyes stung. No people on the beach besides myself; no figures as far as the eye could see and the first light began to glow like a dying wick, a tattered pink aura on the horizon of an excellent blue night sky. Those stars stitched above mirrored on the water in a glittering choreography, one full of pirouettes. I hit play on the music and my earphones prickled out the opening piano chords to *All My Friends* by LCD Soundsystem.

I was off. A steady jaunt down the spine of the shore and counting in time with the music, with my pace, with my breath, with the mathematical sealant hidden in thin air. I ran a total of five miles that morning at my leisure but the nibbling remembrance of my reality, I quickly realized, was still seeping through the cracks. And it all became clear, there on the beach, now populated with scattered distant figures through the salt fog, there would be no outrunning these terrible thoughts. All the running reminded me of the dream I had, the one in the city, chasing Tommy and never reaching him. The dream had become recurring recently, so I was having the dream nearly once a week or more. Here, on the beach, I could imagine him running in the sand ahead of me, and it would cause such a stir in my focus, I had to look elsewhere. Head down, earphones still plugged and raging on LCD, I ran up to my car parked in the public roundabout, panting, and dragging my shoes on the faded asphalt. I went home, showered off, and made my single fried egg and cup of black Napolean coffee. This was how I started my twenty-ninth birthday.

I sat at the kitchen counter at the same stool where I'd said my final goodbyes to Viv, now muted in the bewitched stoney tones from the end of year mundanity. The fretted consistency with this downer of emotion was how it prevented any sort of stamina in my day-to-day routine. I woke up earlier to run because I knew if I did not keep this stern formula, I would default to staying in my bed every day. I had nowhere to be. I had nothing to do besides possibly make music but even then, I had yet to be called for any new projects. So, I got up only to run and cook my petite breakfast, and watch videos on my smartphone of humorous people and informative people and naked people. This was how I could numb myself.

Around noon, I had yet to really do much of anything else for my birthday. I sat at my cast-iron bistro set in the courtyard and reviewed a new piece of music I'd started. Black ink scribbles. Skinny blue ink revisions. No title for it just yet. *Bugbear*, my piano concerto grown from a single jotted idea, had become fully realized. I'd written it in the last year and though I had yet to publish or sell it, I thought it might be best suitable to spend my time with my teeth pressed into a new project. *Bugbear* helped me through a raging mess of grief and complications; when it was finally at a place I felt I could no longer improve, the meanderings of my mind returned instantly. Something to chew on would help. I crossed my legs in my wool, pleated dress pants and rested the sheet music on the bistro table. I reached into my inner coat pocket to ruffle around until I found my paper cigarette and steel Zippo lighter.

The flame clicked, and the paper curled with red neon, crackling and hissing behind the shielded hand. *Ah*, that stuffy charr soothed me like a hand pacing the back of my neck. That burning oak chalked my lungs in a fabulous twist I cannot describe so easily as I can feel. Only a few puffs before my phone began to spit a sound; I leeched it from my pants and swiped to answer a call from Luca.

"Joe?" He asked, his voice was long, he started at a low tone and swung up.

"Hey."

"*Ciao.* Happy, happy birthday, yes!"

"Thanks, man," I said and blew smoke. I watched as the ghostly grays expanded and faded in the invisible crisp. Then more of Luca's voice through the phone, "You do anything special for the big day?"

"Just relax, I suppose."

The line fell silent and static, and I thought the call might have dropped so I pulled it from my ear to check, only to hear the Italian man's voice pushing through again. "I need to come visit you. Apologies, I am bad friend. I am! *So busy!* I am still writing next picture, but once it is done, we mount the saddle again! We ride at dawn."

I chuckled on the line. "What's this one about?"

"It is about love! It is about loss. *Friends, lovers, family, yes*—all the connection we make with people—You remember I tell you *The Crow* is Shakespeare, but also gothic pulp cinema, no? This make me think, *why do I not try to do this?* We love people—and when they are gone—they are like ghost."

I nodded, thinking, before I remembered he could not see me. "That's already been done before in some aspects, hasn't it? *Hereditary* comments on loss. Even Conrad March's *Dreaded Harvest* is adequate with this idea."

"*Bah, bah, bah, Joe!* Think too much, you do! These Hollywood men—they ask me, 'what movie is your next film going to be like?'—I say, 'It is like *Hereditary* meets *Sleepless in Seattle.*' Then I watch their heads turn. Now I have their attention! A lot of pitches start this way—even if it is vague—but my movie will be much different! Very personal to me. And unique, no? Do not want to get into it right now."

This was Luca's way of telling me not to ask any more questions. I sighed and looked out ahead of me; just down the brick path, lined with skeletal shrubbery and grass, was my little studio. The structure was all beams with windows filling in the spaces—a wooden back wall with several, shining instruments hung up—a brilliant, stained front deck. It was barely larger than a typical shed, possibly smaller than my own bedroom, but it housed my entire soul within its walls. Luca and

I both dealt in artistries that require the participation of the senses. And we'd both gotten to a point in our careers where the art could not truly begin without first writing it out on paper.

"I would like to see you again, Joe. I hope you have been doing well last few months. I know it has not been easy." His voice fell apart, and that terrible hiss returned in my ear. I winced as images of Vivian flashed inside me like a Rolodex stuttering on each frame. Her laugh, that innocent giggle, I could hear it as it clung to my eardrum. I could see the back of her head as she rode her bike ahead of me, and honey-colored hair swimming out in the wind. I could see her careful glance at me from across the room. I could feel her head pushed into my chest, her hair pushed into my lips.

"It's alright. I'm okay. Just taking it day-by-day," I finally said.

"That's all you can do, my friend."

Strokes of wind, naked branches ticking against each other. I slapped my hand over my loose sheet music to prevent it from curling up and into the sky.

"Well, I let you go," he said, and the embarrassment obvious in his voice made me feel it equally. "I know you have work to do. But you will score my next picture when the time comes, no?"

"I will. Thanks for calling, buddy."

"Do not mention. I love you, friend. Ciao."

"Love you, Luca. Thank you."

I ended the call and slid the phone back into my pocket. Why did I have to miss Vivian? Was it heartache or guilt? I could not decide which was more tragic. How am I to know the difference with certainty? I refused to tilt into resentment toward Autumn for inadvertently causing the end of my relationship. It was my fault, not hers. My feelings and thoughts were at odds with one another any time I put effort into investigating them—had I loved Vivian or had I loved the companionship and niceties she brought to my life? The larger, hulking question I tried to ignore—*did I love Autumn?*

I hadn't been able to tell. This was a period of my life, at the age of twenty-nine, when I began to feel the immense terror of possibly never finding a life partner. While not a necessity, I knew it a comforting notion to have someone around to talk to at the end of every day, or someone to drive me to the ER if I were to break a bone, or someone to show all of my favorite films, or someone to look at me when they think I am unaware, in turn, making me feel quite special. Had I loved Autumn or had I gravitated toward her for providing me a genuinely intimate moment? I should be dreadfully in love with Sophia if the tables had been flipped—and yet, I still cried most nights over my loss of Vivian. Or was that over my loss of companionship? Was it only my yearning to distract from my default introverted nature? Had I even loved the woman I would frequently discuss marriage with? Would I even be questioning it if it was true love? Nothing made any sense and the pressure was building up, and my chest was filling with sand—an incredible weight—and I would strip the sheets from my vast, freezing bed, and I would remove my clothes as I began to sweat, realizing it would be another night without any real sleep, many sections of sleep divided into quarter hours every hour; nothing made any sense until I arrived at the notion to fling my body from the bed and storm down the hall—feet clapping and echoing on the dead vinyl—and finding myself on the stool in front of my piano. With a bellowing breath I would first play a scale of G major. Then, I played a sound, a set of chords I associated with balance—and slowly, with every pressing enchantment—nothing needed to make sense.

———

Music is not something I can consciously create, instead it comes from thin air. It is a derivative of an uncontrollable churning within the conscious, and all I can do is obey it. It was January. I had done a few Spotting Sessions with Conrad March for his latest film. *Only in Dream* was picture-locked, meaning there would be no more changes to the edit of the film—and Spotting Sessions, simply put, were when I sat down with the director and a room of heads to discuss the score for his picture—yes, we'd already decided on a few basic themes, which made the process significantly easier—and by the end, after learning Conrad's emotional objective for each scene, I not only had a decent idea on how to transpose my themes, but I could hear the music flowing inside of me. Motifs I'd written, simple hooks, had been cast into a spiraling collection of music, bound together with returning familiarities for each character's sound, and if I may, connecting the audience to the characters on a deeper level.

It was thanks to these Spotting Sessions that I began to bounce back from my depressive slump and suddenly I found myself very eager to create again. That last year, I'd been trying new and unique ways to invent sound, many of which found their way into the score for Conrad March's *Only in Dream*, including the use of a Reverse Violin. This creature of an instrument I crafted was an abomination and did not work well at all. I removed the strings from my violin—I removed the horsehair from my bow—I strung the horsehair from the pegbox, down the fingerboard, and to the bridge. No easy task to twist it just enough that it will fit, but not so much that it disrupts the sound. And I put my violin strings into the bow, which took me days to figure out how to do correctly. Finally, I had it, and while it sounded awfully distorted and faded. Occasionally, in music, a terrible sound can be exactly what is needed.

We, as creatures, are incredibly accepting of the dream world. Dreams—founded on their impossibilities and dis-attached qualities from our rules of reality—suddenly *become* reality. The entropy of dreams and what we allow ourselves to believe when there are no boundaries to nature, I find to be extraordinary. We are welcoming of the oddities as the creators of our own illusion. Conrad March carefully captured a decadent vista of this notion through his landscape of cinema. It was not difficult for me to cling to his art, to decorate it with a sound that would ultimately magnetize itself onto the photography.

His portrait of a dream was also what it meant to be alive. I had a traditional orchestra brought in to play the pieces I associated with scenes of everyday life—the aspects of growing up, plus what it felt like to change as a young person and all the learning involved—so the orchestra grew from only a single flute (the representation of a young

Malick at the introduction of the film) and evolved into a full orchestra by the time he was fully grown.

But it was in these celestial qualities of the film that I really got to explore sound. I have had certain people ask me how I achieved such magnificent tones. Others have asked how I made the percussion sound as if it were wind chimes clanking around in a metal bowl. I didn't have the bravery then to tell them that is exactly what I did. It was a world of experimentation, and the many dream sequences in the film blurred the idea of life and death, and blurred the idea of time, constantly changing time signatures, sometimes two different signatures at the same time. This was nothing new, but it also is not easy to make into a singular sound.

I wrote countless iterations for each theme, providing them all as options to Conrad, electric and acoustic styles, but all were derivatives of jazz. I found myself indulging in the sounds of Billie Holiday, Duke Ellington, Django Reinhardt. I listened plentifully to the works of Leonard Bernstein; he served as a leading inspiration for whom I should arrange an orchestra. I went mad with the possibilities of channeling and controlling these inflections of sound waves all around us. I even recorded the sound of a cigarette crackle and used it in the final mix. I had the final edit of the film sent to me, and with the overwhelming amount of strange and jazzed music I had written for the film, all I had to do was work it down to fit over the edit within the comfortable solitude of my studio. I wrote twenty-six hours of music for the film; only two would be heard in it. The picture was engraved onto my brain, and soon enough I had it memorized. I had the finished composition, two hours of an original score, saved to a file on my computer.

It was March when I completed the score, and my ProTools file was then sent over to the picture's Orchestrator, whom I had yet to ever meet. My mockup for the score was entirely in his hands (I kept several backups but still, I was weary of sending it to a stranger). The score was then recorded in five days, from the 13th of April to the 17th of April, with the helpful hand of many people in the studio in Culver City. I had to make the painful decision not to conduct the orchestra for this particular score, as I wanted to spend as much of my time as I possibly could in the booth with Conrad March. The gray man gave very intricate notes to conform to and at first, it had annoyed me to have these notes but later became such a blessing to have worked with him at all.

Conrad March passed away at the end of the year, on December 9th, only three months after his film premiered at the Venice Film Festival back in early September of 2026; not only did it premiere there, but it won the *Golden Lion*, the highest prize of the entire festival. I attended the festival, of course, and ended up staying behind to watch many films in that year's lineup. I found myself slouched in the velvet cushioned seats at screening after screening of everything from lurid, avant-garde dramas to foreign art-house short films. During this time, Luca had been filming *When the Bleeding Stops* in Toronto, Canada. My dearest Luca invited me to come visit the set but through all the bustle and lavish indulgences I became involved with in Venice, I simply did not get around to it.

I agreed to score the film, however, and kept in close contact with Luca during the entirety of his shoot in Canada. His sophomore film was shot as smoothly as his first, with more experience and a higher budget this time around. The film was another horror flick, although it leaned more into the genres of romance, drama and thriller. He compared it to films directed by Ari Aster and Nora Ephron during our phone call, but I found it to be wholly original. The first half of the film revolved around Matthew Myron and Alana Emilio, a young couple in their mid-twenties, who are maneuvering the difficulties of adulthood and sprouting a charming romance. The film opens with Matthew and Alana meeting each other for the first time at Alana's older sister's wedding. Their love begins to blossom. Forty minutes into the picture, Matt proposes to Alana, to which she says yes—this leads to a montage of the typical wedding circus, and ends with the couple purchasing a giant, century-old, Victorian to be their home and project to work on. All this only for Alana to pass on quite suddenly from a heart attack. Suddenly, Matt is alone and adrift; for the next hour, Luca explores the emotional weight of loss and depression, even betrayal and madness as our protagonist, Matt, attempts to continue living but is haunted at every turn.

What I love about his film is how the protagonist does not wish to flee from the ghost within his home because he knows the wandering spirit better than he knows himself. When we see this terrifying image of a pale woman whose feet hover ever so slightly off the linoleum, we are struck with a twisted pang of yearning. It is profound and heartbreaking—and truthfully, it was exactly the film I needed to see at that time—Vivian did not star in the film. Instead, his new lead was a beautiful young lady named Sasha Dean Parker, who had graduated from the NYU Tisch School of the Arts only a year prior.

The last half hour of the film spirals into a full horror film; the horror does not spawn from the haunting but from the madness the protagonist is driven to, and the film ends with a profound message, said but never spoken; *no feeling is final*. A breath of Rilke was within the picture, and the haunted melodrama balanced its two definitions; there are beauty and terror, and one cannot exist without the other. Luca had once again created a modern-day horror masterpiece and it was with this film that he would later be compared to the likes of Wes Craven, Mike Flanagan, Alfred Hitchcock, and most personal to Luca, Dario Argento.

I was happy to be working with Luca again and while I regretted my absence on the set for his latest feature, I also understood my role in the historic binding of *Only in Dream*, Conrad March's final bow in art, and the twilight years of his life. I recall during one of the final days of the Scoring Sessions in Culver City, Conrad pulled me aside as the musicians were gathering their belongings and heading home for the day.

"Joseph," he said, "I wanted to thank you for agreeing to score my picture. I think you have elevated it in ways I could only—well, only dream of," said the elder with a chuckle. I smiled, thanked him, and we hugged for a brief moment. He was a giant fellow, with a full beard and still with a head of hair, all frosted white as the page. When he pulled away from the hug and looked down at me with the soft eyes of a gentle giant, I noticed he wasn't just looking at me—he seemed to be studying me. Somehow, I knew he was not to dissect my physical attributes but rather, he was trying to analyze what lies beneath. I was quiet for a long while until March finally cleared his throat. I asked if he was alright.

"I'm sorry, my boy. It's just," March said and paused. "I do believe I am in the presence of a young master."

VII

THE APARTMENT COMPLEX

I had moments of insecurity. I worried perhaps Autumn wanted nothing to do with me as I walked the arteries of New York City. December had officially begun, meaning soon I would be turning thirty years old and somehow another year had passed by in a winking fashion, yet the larger, more strenuous issue at hand was that it was the 2nd of December—the second out of five days to record the score for Luca's feature, *When the Bleeding Stops*, with a full orchestra—and I smoked my last cigarette that morning while walking to the subway stop in West Harlem. I was staying with my older sister, Betty, who had a job at a firm and made enough money to support herself, but only enough for herself; she was able to afford a decent two-bedroom apartment in Hamilton Heights.

I stayed in her spare bedroom and in the morning, conjured a Nespresso with ghostly steam rising from the mug. I drank it and sat by the window half-open with my last cigarette fading between my fingers, and waited for my turn at the bathroom. The sensation of waiting on her felt briefly similar to childhood, and a needle of nostalgia heightened my senses—only now, this felt more deliberate as we were both now grown with jobs and lives—it was cause for a generalized ease of conscious, no need for any arguing anymore, no fighting over hot water—now, it was what it was.

Betty had an entire floor to herself; the place was less of an apartment and more a condo. She had the second floor at 55 St. Nicholas Place. Built in 1920, the four-story house was sandwiched tight between its neighbors, a gray brick tower with iron bars over the first-floor windows. The deadbolt cracked and the key unsheathed from the lock, I was leaving behind Betty by an hour. Then, I scuffled down the street, passing the corner laundromat and scattered boulders of garbage netted together in black bags. My boots knocked on the asphalt like the clucks of horse hooves as I crossed over to St. Nicholas Avenue and stopped at Texas Star Snack Joint; they served excellent breakfast sandwiches. With a breakfast bagel in a foil wrap, I tipped the jar before ducking into the subway directly to the left. The air changed, suddenly warmer. I bought a metro card that allowed for unlimited rides on the subway for the entire week I was there; I would be making several trips up and down, and I wanted to save as much hassle as possible.

I stood at the edge of the platform, just before the yellow blistering bumps plated on the ground as warning tiles and hounded my sandwich. On the last bite, I balled the foil and shot it into the trash bin. I got on the C train and took it all the way down to the 50th Street stop where I hopped out and up the stairs onto the corner of West 49th and 8th Avenue. Bodies gushed from the exit and into the blending jungle of Manhattan, swarms of people with placid expressions as if they were all a bunch of mannequins who had seemingly gone sentient. I passed the West End Bar and Grill to pop into the questionable smoke shop beside Times Square Diner & Grill. Just for a moment, the general roar of the city lowered as I crossed up to the counter.

"Hey," I greeted. I pointed a finger at the teal and white box stacked up on the plastic shelf behind the clerk.

"Newports, that's it." I gave the clerk a ten and told him to keep the change. I was running late as it was. *How does anyone do this commute to work every single day? Does Betty really do this five days a week?*

She worked in Greenwich Village and had been doing it for over six months by this point, I suppose after six months she'd finally gotten it down to a science. I was disoriented, blinking and shuffling and always trying to find my bearings. The last time I'd been in the city was to perform at Madison Square Garden and I had an assistant then. I was now on my own.

Nobody seemed to recognize me as I openly walked the streets. I had a fairly put-together beard at this point in my life, curled and dark brown. I might have looked like a shoegaze version of George Lucas while he was a young man in the 1970s. Hard to believe it was nearly three years already since I was last in New York, performing for crowds of thousands—tens of thousands—and it had now been over two years since Tommy passed. The anniversary was back in September. Now, I didn't have time to ponder these thoughts too long, as I knew over eighty musicians were at that moment tuning their instruments and rosining their bows, awaiting their composer but more importantly, their conductor.

Luca would have liked for me to be in the booth with him where he could pass notes on the music of his film. He and I were a team, of course, although generally, he had fewer critiques and in place, a giddy boyish excitement. I shared this excitement now, for I had convinced him to let me conduct. And Luca would be waiting for me there. Luca was now too hooked on the notion that New York City might be the greatest place to live in all the world.

"It has energy to it, Joe, you cannot deny. You know what I think it is? It is a collective nature in humans. We come together, work together, build and feed this utopia. You feel it, no? It is electric!" said Luca only the day before while we sat across the street at Kyuramen. He slurped his curry ramen from his bowl, bit into a pork belly bun; we were tucked in a wooden booth with a curtain, and we were hungry after a long scoring session. Luca asked me to move out to the city with him and while I generally wanted to, the idea of my last friend in California moving away shot a terror in my bloodstream. I simply did not have the energy or the drive to get myself to New York.

It was stressful enough as it was and with my career change—a pivot that seemed to happen without much drive, I noticed—and with my lack of funds, there was putting the house on the market and finding an apartment in New York that I liked enough to want to wake up in it almost every morning. A hassle it was, indeed, much like the city. Luca refused to give up on it though, he was likely the most passionate soul I ever met. And Autumn was here too. I'd tried making plans with her the night before, but I saw a message from her after rehearsal saying she'd like to reschedule.

I tucked my box of cigarettes into my overcoat and kept my chin at my chest. I was only about two blocks away from the scoring stage and blowing hot air into my palms, scrubbing them against one another and returning them to my pockets. I zigzagged down the street and finally made it into Gortyn Temple Sound Studio, a recording and mixing studio on 46th. Once inside, I was hit with a blast of heat rather alarmingly to the face and quickly unbuttoned my coat and crossed for the coat rack. In the space, there were roughly one hundred bodies, casually dressed, of all colors and shapes, a beautiful fluidity, and we were all connected—there was always an undertone of quiet exhilaration as if we were trying to always look calm about how enthralling our situation was—together, whether playing the instrument, working in the control booth or casting the gliding movement of the baton, we formed a work of music.

Luca practically tripped over himself as he maneuvered the intricate cabling and microphones woven around the space. He was walking down the few steps from the control booth, where inside sat the team. The team consisted of little brunette Lena Briggs, our Lead Engineer, only twenty-five years old and had started as an intern, who operated the soundboards and controlled the faders on every microphone. Lena was seated next to our Score Mixer, Bernard Potsey, a lanky man with a ponytail and kind smile, who used a computer to edit the music. Bernie also granted me and my orchestra the ability to hear a click track when we wore our earphones. Lena made sure we could all hear each other, and Bernie made sure we were all on the same track. Christopher Pyreck was our Music Editor, so he chose the best takes from our sessions to compile the score and generally help create the master of the definitive version of the score that would end up in Luca's film. Finally, was Percy Thorpe, a gray-haired man, tan skin and normal build—I guessed then double my age—who was the orchestrator. He took my file of the score I made on my computer (referred to as a mock-up) and turned it into a written score and further, feathered each instrument into their own part, providing sheet music for each musician based accordingly on their part.

"Good morning," Luca said and embraced me. We'd seen each other less than twelve hours ago and yet he had the energy charged and pointed at me. "Let us continue today, yes? Lots of work to do. We are harnessing beauty!"

Percy was behind him, coming down the stairs. I'd met Percy before this project and knew him well as he had helped me publish Bugbear, my first concerto. It was performed by a symphony in St. Louis that same year; it had been a remarkable night. I hadn't been able to contain my festering emotions and the moment I got back to my hotel room that night, I wept quietly to myself, enthralled by the childhood achievement. I used to do this occasionally after a Beach Sirens show, but this performance, and from where I sat in the crowd and got to witness it myself, nearly achieved the impossibility of making music tangible to me. I felt like I was touching my sound, embracing it, even physically comforted by it. It was my child. And it was one of the best moments of my life. I owed a lot to Percy and was always wondering how I could ever begin to repay the man. I started by making sure our orchestra contractor hired him for this score.

"Harnessing beauty?" Percy croaked, repeating Luca. He had one of those old, crystalized voices that scraped on itself from years of smoking. "Is that what they call it these days?" he asked. Percy seemed more like a cowboy than an orchestrator. He reminded me of a late Burt Reynolds and walked with a similar swagger. He had a classic Italian gravitas to him with an always raised brow, his hair still full and pushed back, and squinting every time he donned a smile.

"I thought we agreed to call it the structure of air molecules," I snarked. Percy gave out his A-list grin. He was chewing gum, I supposed Nicorette, and he too hugged me and gave a firm pat on each shoulder.

"*Wavy air.* Groovier that way," he graveled.

"Did you have coffee yet?" Luca asked. I nodded and said something like *yeah, yeah, yeah.* Luca took me up to the booth where I greeted the others and he gave me some notes. The difficulty of a film score is the math involved, less of a tempo and more of a puzzle. There is a precision to hit with timed marks, much like an actor might have to hit their physical cues within a space. We had the film edited and displayed on a screen across from my podium. I faced the screen to see the film, but the musicians faced back at me, and all their focus pinned to my hand as I struck each swaying beat.

I was listening to Luca's critiques, mostly about wanting extra measures added or subtracted before a scene ended. It was quite a sinister score I'd written. I had begun the score back in September. Luca had already wrapped shooting *When the Bleeding Stops* by then. For this work of music, I decided on the piano as the centerpiece of the score. It gave a lullaby sort of quality, and a familiarity in the melodies. Yet, when the romance began to contort, the score followed and arpeggiated downward into minor keys and darker tones.

"This piece too," Luca said, and he pulled out a sheet of music he had dogeared. He sat cross-legged in a cushioned chair at the back of the booth, that way he was certain he wouldn't accidentally bump or destroy anything with the very expensive soundboards. I squinted at the sheet music he had now splayed face up on his lap. He uncapped a pen and struck through the title.

"New title."

"Why?" I asked. Not offended, but I was confused about why the title mattered so much to him. I named most of the pieces based on what was happening in the scene, a sort of chapter title for myself to keep track of, or in certain cases using a piece of dialogue. This piece was from the protagonist of the film creaking around the house at night. He is seemingly alone. But the wraith may lurk. I named it *Dead of Night*, fitting, or at least I'd thought it was.

"*Dead of Night*—I understand the expression, yes—but it makes no sense."

I glanced at the rest of the room. Everyone seemed to be quiet, and awaited an explanation as to what Luca was heading toward. Luca shrugged, "My friend, *dead of night* would be morning."

I blinked. "So, what do you want it to be called?"

"Let us call it—*Chasing Sunset*—I don't know, that sounds lame, no?"

"No, it's good," I said between my teeth as I was biting at the fingernail on my thumb and staring through the window at the orchestra ready to begin. "Let's go with that."

I thanked everyone in the room and headed out toward the stage. A vast wax-linoleum room with spaced rows of seating, music stands facing back at them, bars and sticks of microphones both hanging and sticking up from the ground jetted out from all over the place like a construction site. Sky blue rectangular slabs of mesh soundproofing decorated the cabin-esque, wood-paneled walls; a raised station with an in-ground podium for the composer, elevated three feet; the podium oversaw the entire room of musicians seated at the edges of their seats and beyond them still. The silver screen that would project the film and six brake-light-red zeros below it. There were folded-up risers for a choir later in the week. The heat turned off as we got ready to record and all the quiet hum of the room washed out, and only our combined breath and the subtleties of our movements were left alive. I took to the podium, up the two short, wooden steps and sternly forced myself to suppress my stressed thoughts of Autumn and whether I might get to see her that evening.

The hundreds of eyes watched me and caused my worries to become more potent with intimidation. I was not afraid of the orchestra, as I had stood on stages at music festivals and arenas alike with audiences of an imperceivable size, but it was my general lack of experience and how I was nearly making everything up as I went along. On my first feature with Luca, I had not done any scoring sessions, as I recorded all the music myself with the handful of instruments I had, plus the artificial electronic sounds I could use at ease. This was far more intimidating despite their polite faces so undisturbed in any fashion; patient too, much of them far older than I was at the time.

"Good morning, everyone. I'm so glad to be seeing all your beautiful faces on this fine Tuesday," I boomed. This comment was met with scattered chuckles or loose exhales. I brushed my fingers through my beard with the charm of a philosopher and realized it was a nervous tick. My hand shot to the edge of the podium. "I just want to reiterate what I said yesterday; there is no place I'd rather be in the world than in this room with all of you. I can't thank you all enough for being here and helping make this score come to life and—in turn —making Luca's picture come to life."

The heads were nodding, some became distracted and were either checking their instruments, adjusting their postures, wiping their noses on their sleeves, or fluffing through their pages of music.

"Let's begin then, shall we?" I said and their attention fell on me. The room was mine. I picked up my earphones and pressed them over my head while I asked, "I'd like to begin with strings, beautiful strings, please! We're going to start with *Dead*—well, *Dead of Night*—now it's called *Chasing Sunset*. I know—I'm trying my best to keep up, same as you. Okay then," I projected as my voice trailed out.

They shuffled their sheet music and scratched out the song title, each of them wrote the new title in pencil and reset themselves. Each of them began pressing their instruments close to their bodies, scooting to the edge of their seats. The eyes of each performer peered at the page before moving to watch me for a downbeat. I placed one hand at my hip and the other carved the air with my trusted baton at the ready.

"Ready? One, two, three, four."

As my baton shot down, and into the first beat, the bows quivered over the strings. Hair against stranded metal, they created a hypnotizing effect on my body and soul. And I stood before them; I led them through the waves.

———

When the scoring session ended for the day, we were ahead of schedule. The files were digitally recorded at 48Khz sample rate, 24-

bit word depth, Broadcast Wave files and saved onto plenty of backups—backups of backups—as was industry standard. Christopher, the music editor, took three backups with him to continue his work at home that evening. I took a backup; the studio was sent a backup, and Luca had a backup as well. Something Luca had negotiated that was considered uncommon and therefore remarkable was convincing the studio to let him be the lead editor of the film. Luca went to extreme lengths to access such creativity within his projects. Taking the role of lead editor was just one of them; and have it be noted, he did have other editors on the project.

Luca was an inspiration but doubled as what I deemed to be my equal. I recall that week spent in New York, and how I waited for a call from Autumn. I was desperate for her ever since Viv and I had split. I was checking my phone maniacally but also slumping into the booths of matchbox diners and suave Manhattan restaurants to discuss life and art and how the two complimented each other. Luca had become a close friend of mine and without my noticing, he became my best friend. I knew it when I looked at him, at his tanned complexion, his pitch-black hair always splayed out in jagged directions. Luca was the kindest spirit I'd ever met; he was forgiving and altruistic in ways I can only really describe as angelic. He was a star guiding me from the darkness I'd been slouching toward in the year prior, especially due to the direction of his newest picture. I saw myself in Luca, like tiles in a mosaic; I often wondered if he saw pieces of himself in me.

Luca followed me back to my sister's apartment in West Harlem where we paced up the stairs and into the spare room. It was already a quarter after ten, but that night was the earliest I'd come home, and my sister was still awake. The three of us lounged around in the living room for two hours while we shared a Pinot Noir. Luca and Betty got to know each other. I have always found it to be an interesting circumstance when two sanctions of people who are both dearly close to you meet the other. I noticed the jarring image, then, as my best friend chatted calmly with my eldest sister, her head thrown back in laughter as the gloomy, droll filmmaker charmed with his Italian accent.

"I should be going. No idea how long it will take to get back," Luca announced, stumbling and holding his empty wine glass by the bowl. He was headed for the kitchen around the back wall of the living room. It was half past midnight then.

I looked at Betty who had already been looking at me. Without verbalizing a single syllable to one another, we communicated our agreement on the situation.

"Luca. Why don't you stay here?" I asked.

It was quiet for only a moment. The glass clinked the countertop. Luca's head poked back around the wall, neck stretched and sticking out. "Serious?"

"Yeah," Betty said, looking at me. "You can stay. I have blankets and stuff—"

"You can have the bed, I'll take the floor," I offered.

Luca shot squints between the two of us sitting on the sofa. A sort of situational analysis as if searching for hints of faltering or a disingenuous nature. A short smile peaked on the edges of his lips before he burst into laughter. The rest of his body was revealed from the kitchen as Luca took a model's stride back into the scene. He swayed over the vinyl flooring and to his spot on the couch where his lofty torso folded and fell back; puff went the cushions as his body molded into it. "You Henley's—So kind! I love you both—*both of you! Ti amo.*"

We sat out on the fire escape and smoked cigarettes; I thought Betty was going to bruise a lung with her obnoxious coughing fit. She turned in only a moment later; she had to get some rest for work the following morning. Only Luca and me. We sat out on the fire escape for another hour, well into the night now but not *the dead of night.*

It was two when we wandered in and found ourselves in the spare bedroom, neither of us bothered to turn on the lights. A varnish glow streaked the floor and the bed from the half-drawn curtains. Quietly, Luca began to undress. First, his shirt was tugged at from his shoulder blades and tossed to the floor; he kicked off his boots and began to undo the buckle of his belt. I became admittedly timid at the situation —I felt strange seeing this much of Luca exposed—a muted clank of metal as he fiddled around in the dark, only a silhouette as he stood in front of the window.

My shirt unbuttoned just as fast so as to not let a single moment fall awkward; I tried to catch up to him. In the quiet of the room, Luca stood in his underwear, and swiped a pillow from the side of the bed. He took a throw blanket from atop the armchair at the far side of the room and tossed them both at the center of the rug.

"What are you doing?"

"*Sleep*," he said. He pulled the corner of the blanket to create a makeshift bed.

"I'll take the floor."

"No—Joe, no—I am guest. I sleep here."

"Then why don't you sleep up here with me?"

He stopped. We stared at each other for a moment, sizing the other up. Was he thinking the same as I was? My heart was thumping rapidly in my chest—I could feel the blood kicking with a drumming anthem—I could feel it beating around my skull and arms.

"You are sure?"

"Yeah. Don't be stupid, come on."

"*Hey*," he groaned in a warning tone, then under his breath, "*Bah, bah, bah.*"

We pulled back the covers, I slid my legs under the sheets. A few seconds later, Luca lay beside me. The covers rolled up to our necks and we stared at the ceiling. A silence fell on the room. I thought perhaps the violent throbs and adrenaline coursing around my body could be heard, which only made me more anxious. I kept a zeroed focus on staring at the dim ceiling, listening to the muffled skiing of vehicles outside. Luca faced me with a turned head on his pillow.

"Joe. Are you okay?"

I turned to face him. I tried to find his eyes through the myriad of darkness.

"I'm okay," I chirped and tried to sound kind, but I overcompensated for a too cheery ring. Luca chuckled, he shifted his entire body to face me, "You know what this remind me of? This remind me of sleepovers as a boy."

"Yeah?" I shifted to match him. Our chests were so close I could pick up my arm and it would wrap around his back. He only chuckled and I couldn't see but knew he was staring back at me.

"Yeah," he returned, with a rich depth to his voice. Something within me shifted, and my motivations transitioned toward a certain hunger. I inched my body close to his until the tips of our noses were practically touching. The air between us became thicker. A strange warmth kicked up in my chest, and I lost hold of my patience. I leaned in, pressed my lips to his, and rested my palm on the back of his head. I pressed hard but I was only trying to be purposeful. I exhaled long through my nose, relaxing my body. His breath changed, as it became short and intense, and evolved into an anxious huffing. Before I could withdraw myself, I realized he was disturbed by my action.

Luca quickly snatched my wrists and with intense aggression, shoved me away. His hand trembled, his fingernails sank into the skin of my wrist. Luca held me far across the bed and it seemed as if he were analyzing to ensure this was a safe distance. He was out of breath, puffing for air, and he seemed to realize this; his grip loosened.

"So sorry," he muttered. "So, so sorry, Joe."

I swallowed, nearly afraid of him. He turned his body to face the ceiling and for a long time, we were quiet. I felt a raw aching sensation of embarrassment shroud my body. Finally, Luca spoke, in a half-whisper, his voice scratched, "I love our friendship. I want to create art with you for the rest of my life. Cannot do these things with you, okay? Understand?"

My lungs were tight. I thought the anxiety in my body might cause my heart to implode. I felt tears rock on my eyelids. I said nothing in return, too petrified to create so much as a breath. Luca reset his throat again and whispered, "Goodnight, my friend."

I whispered back, broken and only in silky consonants, "Goodnight."

The next morning, Luca woke as if nothing had happened, and he pretended to be interested in the window. We found our clothes; I showered quickly and we drank coffee at the four-seated dining table. He told me stories from the production of *When The Bleeding Stops* and he seemed so unphased, as if nothing had happened at all. The entire time he spoke, the travel to the scoring stage, and the whole day recording, the night before was all I could think about. Though I felt unbalanced, I understood why he decided to disengage from the act. I felt dull. Why did I always do this? Every person I cared for, I mistook what I felt for attraction and ruined a piece of my life by reveling in the decadence of pleasure. I never had love without lust and never lust without love.

After work that Wednesday, Luca said he had plans and went back to his hotel without getting dinner with me. I went back to my sister's apartment and sat at the kitchen table in complete silence as a shell of a man. My phone vibrated in my khakis. I absently drew it out and expanded the notification. A message from Autumn—she'd been very busy this week but wanted to get together over the weekend if I was available—the short message was concise and not at all assuming, but it was enough to make me feel revived after my stint with Luca. And I felt a half-hearted optimism that Autumn could help make me feel content with life again.

———

"Here it is," said Autumn with her arms outstretched and a pace ahead of me on the brick. I'd only ever seen Central Park from a distance until this day, the 6th of December, just over two weeks before I turned thirty years old. We met at the corner of 86th and Central Park West; we finished recording the score for *When The Bleeding Stops* only the night before. Now, it was morning, and I had the whole day dedicated to Autumn. I felt free, much to the likes of a bird, and we were drifting through the sky together. She looked older still—a face toned into a grown woman's shape—but with a complexion of peacefulness I had never seen before. I got the idea that she had finally arrived where she wanted to be both in terms of location and career.

She made a face, "What?" I realized I'd been smiling at her and only shook my head.

We ventured further into the park. There was a serene quality to the place, I found it in direct contrast to the lurid city visible between the trees. Autumn told me about her band, how they recorded their first full record and how it would be released next year. We walked side by side, clicking our black boots on the crusted stone, maple leaves swept themselves, dogs on leashes trotted along, joggers tiptoed quietly past us. A ghastly freeze of wind blew past and left invisible cuts on our skin.

"Our album is called *An Impossible Shade of Black*. We're still finalizing the mix, but it will come out later in the year, I think we're set for August."

"So, what is the impossible shade?"

"It's impossible. Don't think so hard about it."

Our silences were filled by the intermediate scuffing of our shoes and the rustle of leaves like thousands of flipping pages. Looking down at Autumn, I noticed her staring up at the trees. My gaze followed up to her interest, up into the cherry-chocolate leaves clinging to the branches.

"They are pretty, aren't they?"

"What?" she asked.

"The leaves," I answered, "All the winter leaves."

Autumn hummed a closed laugh, and I looked at her again. When she glanced and caught my confusion, she rolled her eyes wide and finally said, "It's not winter yet. It's still autumn."

I nodded and tried to think of what else to say but I was too distracted by the idea of Autumn. Though she walked beside me, she was also hidden in the weather and the earth, a force which held the two together. I studied the trees harder, and the patches of grass turned a brittle brown. We sat at a bench and watched a school group of children chuckle by with their infant legs pounding against the stone. Their puffy jackets made them plump; their cheeks were rosy and cheerful.

Autumn blinked slowly with a cool grin on her face as she watched the line of children go by. She was calm at that moment, and she tilted her head to an acute angle. She squinted at the trees overhead and spoke in a low voice, "Do you ever notice how the leaves look a bit like music notes? And the branches are the music staff. It's like a composition that conducts itself. When the wind pushes the branches, the leaves make music."

I thought of the wind, a gentle push of fate, and how it flipped the strands of orange across her face. I returned to the trees and tried to find that poetic connection between this girl and the season, how the two seemed to share a beating heart.

A maple leaf plucked and sputtered from its place on the branch, a fallen note, it was music, and it was falling—falling wasn't right though as the word seemed to conjure an image of accidental descent but this was intentional—no, the leaves were leaping. Leaping down in a drastic slump, and in music, a drop to possibly create dissonance. A dissonance where some will find beauty in the strangeness, much like autumn as a whole, or Autumn beside me with her fingers folded beneath her thighs to keep warm. The leaf tapped the earth and skated onto the path where we sat, and it paused for only a moment before it was off again into the flurry of nature.

———

If I had known this day would later be deemed one of my more important days, I might have tried to make a better note of the time. The day was dragged from beneath our feet. She took me back to East Village where we wandered the endless shelves and floors of Strand Books. The cozy red accents of the interior carried us about—we shared steam-curled mochas served at the cafe hunched into the wall —customers hid in the arteries of shelves, necks bent to their palms and lost on pages facing the ceiling. We explored the floors above and below until our cardboard cups were empty and left to walk with tensed muscles through the steely air of Broadway.

She took me back to her apartment in Brooklyn, a two bedroom with vocal flooring and floral rugs galore. Inside was Mazy Diaz, her round-faced brunette housemate from Los Angeles, now her band-mate and colleague, along with Mazy's recent girlfriend who had made the move with them out to New York. Mazy's girlfriend was named Pala, a Syrian-American with a natural glint in her eyes. She had thick, brown hair and used very strict consonants in her English.

"Nice to meet you," she said with an emphasis on 'meet' and shook my hand softly. I smiled behind the oaky beard on my face when a white blur slithered between my legs. It was their cat named Rimbaud, just a quiet puff of snow that sauntered gracefully through their apartment. The ladies treated me to afternoon tea; we sipped London Fogs, and we talked about music and how well the new band was coming along.

"And you—you just scored a horror movie? That's fucking insane!" Mazy slapped her temples and shot her hands in the air. "It's the same guy that made *Mass Hysteria*, right?"

"Yes," I chuckled.

"I loved that movie. Have you seen it, babe?" Mazy peaked at her armpit where Pala was cuddled against her breast on the sofa. Pala puckered her stare up at Mazy, "No." A polite squeak.

"We have to add that to our list! You scored that one too, right?"

"That was me," I said and curled my lips.

"Unbelievable. That's the coolest thing ever. You and Autumn are the best musicians I've ever heard in my *life*."

And I looked at Autumn, arms crossed, and weight pressed into the edge of the wall, watching the scene play out, and our eyes locked on to one another's. I thought for a moment I was looking at perhaps my mother or one of my sisters with the profound and overwhelming blanket of comfort that shuddered through my body. It was the pleasure of a drug but without the shame. I saw her, I knew her; I knew this woman so well and finally understood her. We were nineteen years old when we met and now in the sunset of our twenties, we continued quietly examining each other like pieces of art. In that moment, as her roommates faded into a piece of our peripherals, I felt sure I could spend my life with her.

———

"One last thing. Close your eyes," she said.

I did as I was told, complete blackout with purple blobs bursting on my eyelids. I felt a sheet of thick paper move into my fingers. I gripped it, and Autumn said, "Now, open."

I glanced at what was a ticket for a Broadway show. *Jazz Canal.*

"I thought this would be something we might both enjoy."

I rubbed my thumb over the glossy finish of the paper and glanced at Autumn. I could not contain the smile on my face and neither could she. The date on the ticket was for that afternoon. We fled from the corner outside of her apartment and started back toward Manhattan.

We sat beside each other, third row, and watched the performances playing out ahead of us. Singers and dancers twisted and belted on the stage, and we sat close enough to perceive a break in illusion, that of the sweat and makeup layered on the face of each actor. Curiously, I had a very difficult time maintaining focus on the immersion of the musical. More than the typical acknowledgment of everything on the stage being false, urging the viewer to believe they are in a fictional bar named the Jazz Canal, but due to the distracting nature of forcing myself to have a good time. I was locked in a conversation with myself, studying the artistry and reveling in the experience, because in two hours it will have passed. The show will only be a memory and soon later it will fade and distort, for better or worse, and someday, possibly thought of for the last time.

A terrible conversation. This caused a storm, as did the girl beside me who was becoming more and more a menace to the space between my temples. I felt as though I allowed it to happen. Looking back on this exact pain of my life, I do realize the exhaustive yearning to replace the companionship left so empty in my heart, even over a year after splitting with Vivian. A profound grief had settled within me, and I did not know a cure. I was confused—many nights I would lay awake and predict where our relationship may have gone had we just made love that night—how much longer would it all have lasted? Decades? Years? Months? Maybe only a matter of days or even hours. Perhaps we would have been together forever though, had I not slipped, had she not slipped, and we would have found ourselves married and I would be wearing a golden band while conducting, and she would be pregnant with a girl, a creation I could truly treasure. I'd reached the conclusion that Vivian, the heiress of Hollywood and soon to be the queen, was never meant to be my soulmate. And the crushing realization made me want more than ever to find the one.

This show was both Autumn's and my first time seeing a Broadway production. She'd lived in the city for over a year, nearly two by this point, and was only just now getting around to seeing a show. How strange for someone who credits her career and art to this city's greatest craft. Part of me wondered if she was waiting for me to accompany her, on the off chance we had the opportunity. Perhaps she'd made a promise to herself all those years ago that someday she would take me to see a show on Broadway.

Then there was the question of Tommy. As I glanced at her hand resting on the armrest in the darkness of the theater, I wondered if she still felt devoted to him—my best friend—or if perhaps, she could open her heart to me. Though Tommy was no longer with us, he still occupied the space between our hands. Was it wrong to want her? Tommy and Autumn and Sophia had always been my closest friends. Surely, Tommy would like to see the two of us happy and together given the circumstances. Besides being acquainted with Autumn in the physically intimate way, I knew Autumn in the closeness of her emotions too. I knew what she had been through, and the physical trauma she endured from early relationships. I knew of her distrust of the world that began with her father.

Over the years, Autumn slowly opened herself to me and I felt lucky; I felt a yearning to learn everything about her over the course of the rest of my life. When the lights came up on the show, a fanfare played—members of the cast came jogging from the wings and bowing center stage—the sea of bodies in seats and Autumn took to a standing ovation and I followed, not without wondering what it was I had just watched but not paid attention to.

"What'd you think?" Autumn asked. She had her large wool coat wrapped around her body. We walked through a metallic tunnel of scaffolding on the sidewalk. It was nearly midnight. We'd stopped in Junior's Restaurant for a slice of their original cheesecake at the bar before then heading toward the subway stairs. I insisted on walking her home and we both knew I was hoping to stay the night but neither of us said it.

"I knew it was going to be good, but it blew my expectations out of the water," I lied, I even picked a subtle tone to seem as if I were more excited but wanted to play it off cool. Not an easy thing to do, but living with an actor will teach you more than Stanislavsky or Meisner ever could have. I scratched my nose and quickly returned my hand to the warmth of my coat pocket.

"What are you going to do next?"

We walked side by side, our shoes in line and clicked on the bright asphalt lit by the whites and refractions of Manhattan. Times Square was only a block away; we could hear the thunder and see the colossal glow brimming between avenues.

"I don't know."

"I don't mean tonight—I mean as far as music goes—as far as life goes."

"I don't know," I said softer and quicker than the time before. Life then was an endless series of planning and pivoting when things failed to play accordingly. We made it back to her apartment and Rimbaud chirped at me with dilated eyes, two black zeros, and pressed his jaw into my calf. The cat leaped to the dark kitchen counter and Autumn went on ahead toward her bedroom. The apartment was silent, as silent as a Brooklyn apartment could be, with the surrounding worlds still dressed and in performance.

"Are your roommates home?" I asked.

"No, they're still out." She was yanking her arms from the sleeves of her coat.

I asked Autumn which bathroom was hers and when she pointed it out, I locked myself inside for a moment. I urinated at the side of the bowl to minimize any sound of trickling and flushed. I moved to wash my hands but noticed her bamboo wood toothbrush with black bristles, a whitening toothpaste still full, a peculiar pink residue around the sink. I looked closer still and noticed this residue wasn't just pink, but brown like rust. To the left, on the vanity, a crusted clump of black. It took only a fraction of a second to witness the perplexity of the thing before I registered that it was blood. There was a dried yellow substance surrounding it and I tried hard to ignore the mystery. I washed my hands eagerly and felt my chest contorting. I focused on myself in the mirror to change the topic in my mind. I ran my fingers through the new silver streaks. I hadn't hated aging the way everyone else seemed to. Perhaps I aged like wine? Why was there dried blood all over the sink?

I opened the door and smiled at Autumn who was still unlacing her shoes on the corner of her queen-sized mattress. Her room had the same airy, greenhouse aesthetic that her bedroom in Los Angeles had perfected. She threw her old Converse at her closet, hardly a closet; she had a clothing rack with baskets beneath it, and she got up and walked across the room. She landed right in front of me and put her palms against the fabric of my sweater, then pushed into my chest.

"Joe, I want to be very honest with you." When she finished her opening line, all the sound of the room fell out and there was only the hustle of engines cheering outside. She cleared her throat, "I don't know if I can be in any sort of relationship right now but—"

"That's fine. I don't want a relationship right now either," I blurted.

"*Fucking Christ!* Let me finish! I was *going* to say, of course, I'm going to let you stay over tonight. Yes, we can mess around. But I want you to look at me, Joe," she said, and she sounded hurt. I did as I was told. Those hazel eyes I knew so well felt like returning home, a nostalgic kaleidoscope that transported me back to being a kid. Autumn spoke slowly with an emphasis on every syllable as if she were reading from a book, "Do not fall in love with me."

We were close enough that she had to transfer her eyes from the left and right sides of my face. She was waiting for an answer though I did not know what to say. What would happen if I fell in love with her? Out of a place of annoyance, I felt compelled to ask. But I knew it would only patronize her and perhaps disrupt the moment when we had already gotten so far. Whether I had decided within myself to obey her request or not, I bowed my head and said, "Okay. I won't."

To this day, I'm not sure if I believed it, but it worked well enough at the time. I battled quietly with whether I should ask Autumn about the blood and the other strange fluids around her bathroom sink but I didn't want to embarrass her. It could've been anything.

Instead, we stared at each other while we stripped, and once we were both completely nude, we examined each other's bodies. We'd gained some weight, not much but noticeable around the waist and arms. My muscles from last year had diminished a bit. I was covered in hair, no longer to the likes of a marble statue, now I'd gone and become realistic. Autumn equally had more hair I hadn't seen before. While many would find our sight to be off-putting or possibly unattractive, I was overcome with a wave of the opposite, and I stepped forward to embrace her. We hugged in silence in the center of her bedroom where outside a honey tinsel splayed on the street and against the dead trees. While standing on our bare feet over a thin rug and listening to the shielded motors stirring in the night, we rubbed each other's backs and looked at each other's faces. We prolonged this step, taking in the features of the other before slowly leading each other toward the bed. The routine played like it had a thousand times before but how curious it was—performing this act of love never got old—but somewhere along the way, we had.

VIII

Always Drawing Sixes

Betty and I went down together to our parents' house on a cheap flight booked two weeks before. We arrived and stayed up until midnight so the family could all wish me a happy birthday, and while I felt quite lucky, something sinister settled on my nerves. The chilly twist of a blade had muddied deep in my stomach, an endless pit of blackened void. Thirty years old. No longer a boy; I already knew—I had years to ponder the eluded revelation—I had time to experience the heartache of my slipping youth without full anguish. I knew this day would come, no longer the young master and sooner only the master. Now was that time. Tommy may have debunked time as a concept, but age was still rampant on my body and as I stood in the same bathroom I knew of when I was twenty years old, one decade ago, now with a full beard, a wider build and increasingly apparent bristles of silver hair streaked over my ears. Where had the time gone? Perhaps Tommy was right, and the time had never been there at all.

In the New Year, I dragged my feet back to my Spanish bungalow in Santa Barbara. With a glare in my eye, I put the house on the market and set my sights on New York City again. That way I could be closer to Autumn, and to Luca, who was still toying with the idea of moving to the city.

"I know a guy who will get us apartment in Manhattan, good price, just have to wait until June!"

"I can't wait that long, Luca," I groaned with my fingers dented on the bridge of my nose. I could not stay with Betty until June without guilt, and I refused to stay in Santa Barbara.

Luca sat with his fist under his chin across from me in a coffee-house out in San Diego. He shook his head, visibly deep in thought, and wondered how the two of us might end up in the city. He never made even the slightest mention about what happened between us that night, leaving me further jaded by the absence of intimacy. I had fallen to incredible lows, for a string of weeks I would stare at the picture of Donna, Vivian, and myself (and Luca's dark reflection) from our night out in Wilmington. I would often cry while studying the photo. I zoomed in on each blurred grin and recalled the joy I once felt. These sessions of weeping would either evolve into messy sobs, or worse, fade into a nothing-haze of numbing.

Moreover, I would sit in front of my computer monitor with Vivian's vampire film, *They Do Not Grow Old*, pulled up and paused on the frame in which Viv rises from a moonlit lake with her bare chest exposed. I would pleasure myself to this particular frame from this particular film, and when it came time to finish, I would close my eyes and picture the night in the hotel room with Autumn. This was the only way I could pleasure myself. A remarkable and bizarre ritual of embarrassing actions. If I ever thought about the night with Luca, even for a second, all hope of successful masturbation would cease and instead, I could expect to find myself anchored to the couch with cooked eyes.

It was early in the New Year and the first time I had seen Luca since I finished his film's score. We lipped on hot macchiatos over a discussion of how we would get back to the city as quickly as possible, and as cheaply as possible. While I was a famous musician, I also hadn't toured in two years and was no longer on the rockstar salary, which was never as much as one might be led to believe in the modern age. Across from Luca, I was building walls within my mind to block any thoughts of him from that night. Instead, I thought back to the

interior of my house that had already been diluted down to a formation of cardboard boxes, a paper-brown pixelated image. I couldn't
focus on anything besides getting back to the city. Back to Autumn.
Back to the music.

That night, my last in New York and in Autumn's apartment, still
covered in sweat and wearing only the blue from the night sky
through the window, she played the debut Dead Girls Club album
she'd recorded with Mazy Diaz and Freya Morris. Most of the tracks
gave a sound I can only describe as psychedelic alternative-rock
ballads. Alternative rock was the obvious genre, most of the music
held a very rageful presence about the state of the world and how
women are treated even decades into the twenty-first century. My
favorite of their tracks is titled, *Central Concern*. A drooling, rock-
heavy ballad about a missing young woman last seen in Central Park.
A three-minute jabbing track with wailing guitars and describing her
final whereabouts in the city, it's followed by a minor-key minute-long
piano solo as sounds of Central Park at night play over it. There's even
a reverbed police siren cooing somewhere in the mix. It's haunting—
it's jarring—it's frankly extraordinary. They were achieving lyricism
that mattered, each song was more than just pretty lyrics, they had a
bite to them that demanded attention. *An Impossible Shade of Black*
would go on to become a classic album, one that would become
synonymous with the culture of the time—and suddenly, Dead Girls
Club and Autumn Gladis were mainstream rockstars.

Autumn was the puppeteer behind the charade. Her record label
had offices and a studio space in Williamsburg. Autumn was not only
more famous than she had been with Beach Sirens but now she was in
charge of everything. Looking back now, I believe this is why her
success played out the way it did because Autumn had a very specific
image and brand she was hoping to achieve this time around. Beach
Sirens may have always been her stepping stone toward her dream
project. Autumn had a new fire in her soul I had never seen before,
and it balanced her out. Suddenly, Autumn was no longer resentful
toward the world, less critical and defensive, more open and patient.
One aspect I noticed that never faltered in Autumn was her palpable

focus on her dreams. This is how it goes for a true artist. I did not want to diminish this flame lit within her, instead, I should have liked to watch it burn.

Any further time spent in California was deemed a waste. I wanted to be wherever Autumn was, wherever the art was being made. I was only back in Santa Barbara for two weeks of the new year before I turned around and made it right back out into the city. I took little more than what I could fit in a few suitcases, some clothes, some instruments and some books. The rest was all stuffed into storage or sold off. The bungalow had yet to be sold, but I had to promise Betty I would only stay with her for one more week. I had less than a clue as to what I would do, that is until something by the push of the wind led me to where I was meant to go—a curious email in my inbox on a Tuesday at St. Nicholas Place.

———

"You're not going to believe this," I said and hopped onto Betty's bed beside her. It was ten at night; she'd gotten home from a day spent at the firm and taken a shower so hot her skin was raw. She was now lying on her comforter in bedtime shorts and a large-sized Radiohead graphic tee, and every few seconds she fingered a green grape from a ceramic bowl beside her; it landed on her tongue, scooped back and popped in her molars. A mug of chamomile tea twisted its heated breath on her nightstand. She might have looked like a disappointing, post-modern Cleopatra as she half-sat, half-lied on her bed with the towel swirled on her head and watched some reality dating show with a class of early-twenties statues. I rolled over onto my back with my laptop bent at the angle of a boomerang and scooted up to where she was propped up with two pillows.

"What, Joey?"

"Just read," I groaned. The laptop patted onto her thighs. She clicked a button on the remote and the television paused on a frame of a shirtless man arguing with a woman in a bikini, only the shot was distorted by a fuzzed-out, green frame, and I realized the cameraman had been hiding in the bushes. If the camera captured a truly candid moment, and the two on screen thought they were having a private discussion, then they would be open with each other to sort out the disagreement. Human, yes, only now it was being broadcast for millions to watch and destroying their privacy. The alternative was that the reality show was not so realistic, possibly scripted or near scripted; a field producer or someone of equal stature might have been around to nudge the story in a predetermined direction, at which the altercation between the two on-screen was mostly fake and maybe even rehearsed. I folded my arm behind my head, squinted at the television and tried hard to decide which of these outcomes was worse. Then, to my right, "Holy fuck."

What I had Betty read was a message I'd received earlier the same day from a New York-based program by the name of the New York Artist's Haven. It was related with the American Composers Forum —an organization I had heard mention of in the last month—but I was unfamiliar with NYAH; I came to find out it was a new organization that had yet to begin its processes. It was set to take effect in New York in the coming months. Their intention was to provide promising artists with the residencies they would need to work on their artform full-time rather than having to juggle their art and their jobs.

The message said, *Here, at NYAH, we firmly believe artists need plenty of time to ponder their work. We plan to provide the time and funds in order for their art to flourish in ways it may never have before.*

From the brief message in the email, they wished for me and a group of select other artists in other various professions to create new works to showcase New York Artist's Haven and gain sponsorship with the recognition of young blossoming artists creating for the institute. The organization wished to commission a symphony.

I'd paced around the Harlem apartment all day as if I were in a century-old Noir, a scruffy detective with my eyes on my socks, a cigarette beneath my nose and two fingers pinching at my beard. Why would an institute choose me? Perhaps many musicians were all going to be writing symphonies, and they would choose whoever wrote the most pleasing one to present. Or did it have to do with my status? I was still a household name for much of the youth. Many would be drawn to NYAH as an organization if Joe Henley of Beach Sirens had written a symphony commissioned by them. Or perhaps it had to do with my nomination at the Academy Awards—Best Original Score, *Only in Dream*, Joseph Henley—this had to have played some sort of role in all of this.

I hadn't done so many podcasts and online interviews with various news outlets in years, and suddenly the press junket for *Only in Dream* came around and it was like dusting off an old instrument and recalling the placements of each note. A symphony was surely very different than a film score. A film score had beats to hit, measures to meet, and each scene worked as a visual description I could translate to sound; the photography and direction captured in movement led me to the music. I was left to my own spiraling mind and ended in a tangled mess by the time my sister had returned home only to wait a while longer for her to find herself comfortable so we could discuss.

"This is actually really great," she said, then quiet as she was reading it over a second time, "Yeah, wow. Congratulations, buddy." She smacked the laptop back to my wool trousers and fluffed her fingers through my hair.

"That's it?"

"I don't know," she shrugged. Betty popped a grape in her mouth and reached for the remote, but I became animated, leaping from the bed with my laptop in one hand and the other wiggling around in the air. "What am I supposed to do? I've never written a symphony! Who are these people anyway? How did they get my email? Do I even take commissions? I don't know what I'm supposed to do!"

"Did you see how much they're offering you?"

"Of course I did! I've been reading this over and over all day!"

The offer she was referring to was a clean, tax-free payment of one million dollars. The laptop clapped down on itself and bounced on her comforter before it settled and sank; I put my hands on my hips and shook my head. "When might I catch a break?"

"When you're dead," said Betty with lazy eyelids stuck to the television screen. Was the program candid or not and why did I care? There was the larger issue at hand. I tried to maintain her attention, but it was no use. I wandered before the television to the window on the opposing bedside. I thought to call Luca, but I knew he would tell me to take the opportunity, and say something proverb-esque like, *my friend, right now—you are caterpillar—you must spread wings! Fly from cocoon, be the butterfly! Yes! You name Symphony Number One, The Birth of a Butterfly! You can have the title. I do not need credit.*

I thought to call Autumn, but I knew it was Tuesday, and she would be preoccupied with her ever-present duties in the offices of Acid Ick! Records in Brooklyn. I thought of taking the subway there, but it was an hour commute, and I didn't feel like going outside. Betty was my only hope, and she could only congratulate me.

"What should I do?" I asked very seriously. My arms fell to my sides, patting my waist. Betty groaned and paused the television again, she shot her head at me and spoke through the mutilated grape sloshing in her cheek, "Are you seriously considering not taking this opportunity?"

I nodded. She scoffed, "Joey, you said you've never written anything like this before but that's a big, fat lie because I saw a video of that orchestra in St. Louis playing that piece you wrote. *Bugbear!* Yes, that one, and dude, it was *really fucking good.*" I couldn't help but smile at the playful, cat-like eyes she gave me when she said that last part, but then she reset. "Please don't sell yourself short or convince yourself you aren't good enough because I'm telling you right now, as a fan and your sister, that you are."

I hadn't thought about *Bugbear* since its debut. It was my first concerto and the first piece of music I began working on following the tragedy of Tommy's death. I felt I had no control over my life, and everything had fallen into turbulence, but the intimacy of writing each note on the page bred a type of control I absolutely needed at the time. I was patient with each delicately chosen tone; as I shaded each quarter note and finished with a stem, I felt a sliver of dominance on the world. I could declare the sound as mine, and when it was played, it was my power.

As I recalled all these emotions, I tried to imagine the volume of work and dedication an entire symphony would take. Mozart was only eight years old when he composed his first symphony, although it was his father who put the ink into the page. Beethoven was twenty-nine when he wrote his first symphony. And yet, I was older still when I received this commission. Perhaps my fire had already shined its brightest flame, or perhaps I had yet to really shine at all. I lay in bed that night and again stared up at the ceiling, the amber cutouts against the void, and tried to crack a decision. Nothing would permanently sway to a definitive answer for another two weeks—two weeks of wandering the city with my head down—two weeks of sleepless nights.

I should have been excited by this opportunity. It was a near-blank check to create whatever I wanted, however I chose to do it. There were the gnawing thoughts of Autumn. She said she would never be with me, and I wondered at this, if it might actually be true. Despite our many fallouts, I knew I felt happiest when I was with her. Whether we tucked ourselves into a random diner at midnight or took the other to a rooftop party in Brooklyn or the Bronx. It felt like a relationship even if it wasn't and I was more than thrilled to be playing the part. Though she was often busy, far busier than I was, and yes, the work would do me good. I was happy, and which mattered more to me? My familiar dark side was approaching me again, I could sense it, and I knew I had to do something to make a decision.

Many days were spent in the apartment. A routine developed as I stood over the turntable, the soundtrack record to *Only in Dream* orbited, and I sank a needle into the crackling vinyl ravines. I would stand in my sister's living room, staring at the opened window with a cigarette between my lips and unsheathing my baton to follow along. Occasionally, I would cross to the volume controls and crank it to a level I deemed reasonable before edging on a neighborly disturbance. Then, I flicked my baton about in a diamond formation, counting the rhythms to my original score. I nearly danced as I imagined myself back at the scoring stage with the full orchestra watching me as their guiding force.

My baton, as similar in physicality as it felt in the hand, seemed more of a wand to a wizard who was able to conjure symphonies. Perhaps I was fit for the commission and I let my own wilting ego mask my intrigue. Could this be my purpose I was so keen on discovering?

This baton was crafted from matted birch wood, with a copper, black and tungsten handle, of a weight that allowed it to rest at the side of my index finger, the shaft projected out and balanced ahead. It felt comfortable in the hand as it had for many years. This tool of the conductor was gifted to me by my parents when I graduated high school, as I was still intent on conducting orchestras, or at the very least, taking part in one.

This gift meant more to me when I received it on the evening of my graduation party. There, with my calmed nerves caressing the wood, nearly pointed, and feeling the rounded end of the handle. It was one of the gifts that leaves one speechless rather than the fabricated versions of immediate cheerfulness after pulling back on the wrapping. I thanked my parents, my two wonderful, ever caring, parents.

"You're welcome, sweetie," my mother said, and a hand snaked through my hair. I remember this moment when I received the baton, in its blue gift box complete with a bow, with such care as to preserve the memory in the best condition. I never want to forget that moment —when I realized my parents took note of my passion and provided a tool—a tool that implied an achieved future. And best of all, as I stared down at the thing in Betty's apartment and rubbed my thumb up the stick, as I had when I was eighteen, I felt like I could see the time that had passed.

I felt the weight of the dozen years between me and my former version; I was completely in awe that that boy was the mind and body I once inhabited. We were, somehow, impossibly, the same person. One with the dream of conducting, and the other having conducted an eighty-person orchestra some weeks ago. I stared at the stick with the same compassion I felt as a boy, only with a far wiser and mature compassion, a learned calm from years of battle.

I closed my eyes and focused on the music of the orchestra and my melodies pressed in vinyl. I couldn't explain why but it was nearly more profound than the records I made with Beach Sirens. This score was the result of a culmination of musical ideas and revelations written throughout years of practice and pain. Here it was, a symbol of my growth; all my efforts pressed into the grooves of a vinyl. It was as if the raging storm within my brain—the storm within every artist —was at last channeled, and this vinyl record was the metal rod that finally tamed my electric force. *Some things will never change*, I thought, and it is true. I am that boy with the twinkling gaze at the mysterious future; he resides in me through memory and the chambers of my heart, and I felt his little celebration in my brain.

I opened my eyes. Alone in the apartment still with a gray breeze rolling in. I put out my cigarette. The little paper stick teetered down the levels of the metal-grated fire escape. I made sure to tidy up by the time my sister would arrive home from work. She had a routine of her own, and it involved her changing into a matching set of sweats before making a very small dinner, and watching her favorite television shows. I did my best to keep out of her way. Betty occasionally asked if I had found a place to live yet, or if my house in Santa Barbara had sold—this made me desperate, tormented by her worthy questions— she laid off quickly when she saw how visibly ill they made me.

I had to make a decision soon and every day I felt further conflicted. I was at war with myself—unable to take hold of my life and make a firm choice—that is until those two dreadful weeks passed. I would dawn my petticoat and scarf to wander the streets and try for a final decision, as I had for the last few days. A splitting Wednesday of early February was the day I relearned a face from my past, and brought forth a range of emotions I left behind years ago in this very city.

———

I sat at some punched out diner on the Lower East Side with my nose hovering over a ceramic mug of coffee, full to the brim; the place was called Golden Diner, it was in a black-box frame outside of a surrounding facade of mars-red brick—jagged fire escapes, curbs of snow rounded on the edges of the roads—the Manhattan Bridge suspended above jetted into Brooklyn. I sat at a table for two, only the bench across from me was vacant and granted me access to view out the lacy drape-drawn window at the bus stop and the graffiti sprayed in sharp angles over a mailbox, and a fire hydrant across the street. A man leaned against the bus stop pole with one leg hiked and bent in a flamingo pose and stared down at his smartphone, scrolling and listening to music through bulky headphones. Inside, the white walls were efficient, and chromatic stools lined the bar with pine green patchwork over the cushions; men in white shirts and fresh aprons kept their heads down. Their hands worked vigorously behind the glass, some with their backs turned and zeroed on the stovetops, preparing everything from an egg and cheese, tuna melts, butter pancakes.

I had the email open on my phone screen. I'd read it over that morning in the apartment, waiting for the subway, and now in the diner. I still hadn't been able to decide whether I wanted to accept the commission, although it would make finding an apartment in Manhattan much easier. I still couldn't lease a place at the El Dorado but that seemed overindulgent anyway. I'd seemingly lost my fame, or it had become diluted with the death of my rockstar persona, and only a handful of people a day approached me now—some in the subway, some in the diner—most queried for a quick photo and returned to their business.

I adored this lifestyle. I used to crave privacy when Beach Sirens hit its peak and was sure to never lose sight of my gratitude for this new introverted life I now got to lead. I still had the opportunity to make the invention of music a viable career. I felt completely reborn in a sculpt of my design. I was still writing and creating music full-time, but I now afforded the ability to be myself, free of the weight of the press. I did consider myself lucky and did everything to not lose sight of the notion—after all, if asked to hammer a nail to a wall, I would likely fail to properly execute—if asked to write a piece of music that may provoke a specific emotion, it comes naturally.

I exchanged the email for a screen of apartment listings on my phone; I didn't want to think about the symphony commission anymore. I wondered if I should try calling Luca again as he had gone silent with me in the last few weeks. This only lasted a minute before I sighed and darkened the screen. That's when a light rap drummed on the window over my head, and my attention shot up; standing there in the gray wind with an orange wave of hair surfing to the right, in a long black petticoat and sporting a grin, was none other than Ellis Young. He crossed out of frame, headed for the front door, and as if I were a marionette on invisible strings, I lunged to my feet when Ellis entered the diner. A bell sounded, and he pushed his sunglasses onto his head.

"Well, well," he said in his familiar low tone, and he reached for my hand, and tugged me in close. His arms wrapped around my body; flecks of snow clung to his cheeks and hair. I paid no mind to the guests stealing their glances as Ellis pulled away to examine my appearance. He placed his frigid palms against my bearded cheeks and nodded.

"It's a good look—I mean it—but I know this face anywhere. How are you, Joseph?" he asked.

I told him I was fine and motioned for him to join me, he hunched onto the bench without ever removing his coat. He grinned again, and it looked as if he hadn't aged a day since I last saw him seasons ago. Cleanly shaven face. A sculpted jawline. His ginger hair was long and well maintained. He was somehow just as youthful and vibrant as before and while I wanted to be irritated by this, I could only feel delighted to see the old friend.

"What are you up to these days?" he said. I blinked, at the table I stirred a silver spoon through my coffee and tried to decide what to tell him and what information to withhold.

"Still writing music actually—only I'm scoring films now." I nodded as if to assure myself of this too. He brightened, "Ah! Yes, I knew about that. I read the interview you did in *The New Yorker*. And if I am correct, you're nominated for an Oscar! Congratulations, Joseph. You're going to love the awards show, it really is a treat to attend."

I brought myself to achieve a smile.

"Have you eaten already?" he asked. The truth was I hadn't, but I no longer felt like sitting in the cutout diner. I'd sat there for an hour already and I refused to drink the coffee in front of me; I knew it had gone cold.

"Where are you off to?" I asked, in an effort to dodge his question.

"I was off on business in the area and now heading back to my studio in Greenwich."

"You have a studio?"

"Joseph," he groaned, as if disappointed. "Of course, I have a studio! A bloody good one, at that. Cost me more than my flat in Queens. You're welcome to come along and see it. I'm working with an artist right now named Yvette Adair, have you heard of her?"

"No, I can't say I have," I said, and again looked at my muddy coffee, stirring it and clinking the mug.

"She's a painter from Agde, a little town in France. She's really quite remarkable. I'm helping curate her first art show in New York."

"Not a musician?"

"No, indeed, not. I work with artists of all natures, Joseph. Come on and I'll show you."

I paid the check and followed Ellis back into Greenwich Village where we climbed out of the West 4th Street Station, now on Waverly Place with the Waverly Diner to our left. Brilliant greens and reds spelled out the name of the diner and stretched a neon haze in the February flurries. We walked up a block; Ellis led with one shoulder poked forward, becoming thin as a knife and slicing through crowds of people. We hung right across the intersection; his studio lay hidden in a peanut butter chocolate building.

Ellis turned toward the entrance—a tar-tinted glass door— he punched a series into a keypad. The door was completely blank aside from a bright yellow decal reading, 'VELVET PIE STUDIOS.' The font reminded me of a detective noir comic book, perhaps because the color reminded me of Dick Tracy's trench coat. I stamped my cigarette on the sidewalk and followed him; we climbed a flight of shrieking stairs to the second floor where written on a bronze plaque was again the name of the studio. Velvet Pie.

Ellis fingered a code on a number pad, it lit green and finally, we were inside. The space was not at all what I was expecting. Ellis wandered ahead of me and peeled his coat and placed it on an empty coat rack, below he wore a vanilla knit sweater, visible above the neck-band was a white shirt and black tie. He was properly dressed like a gentleman, like a man before our period, just as I enjoyed presenting myself. I circled the wide space to behold the brilliance of the studio.

There was a vast open space facing back out onto 8th with several windows that bled light into the room. The adjacent wall was covered head to toe in mirrors and a bar for ballet. On the opposite side of the room were three wooden desks piled high with paper and typewriters and fountain pens, plus easels and canvases in the corners and at the center of the room. The canvases, blank and others with speckled art half-turned to life, were gathered in a semi-circle as if they had just recently painted a model, but upon further inspection, they were painting two ballerinas practicing across the room. The ballerinas were all silhouetted. I rubbed a finger over the strokes of black and noticed the shade melting on my finger. The paint had yet to dry. This had been done that same morning.

Paintings lined the walls as well as papers with poems, prose, haikus and sonnets pinned up for anyone to read. A 16mm film camera lay in a perfect Styrofoam cutout within a hardshell case; said case sat open as if one had forgotten to seal the camera inside but the film magazine was missing, implying the entire roll had been shot. What was going on here? There in the back, down a short hallway with no dead space on the walls and instead insistently packed with decadently framed mirrors, was a series of restrooms, a kitchenette, closet space and, to my surprise, a second staircase.

On the second floor, behind another locked door, was the music studio. A black mini grand piano rested in the furthest corner under the same dead light beating in from the windows. Music stands. Sprawling sheets of music across the floors. Microphones, a drum kit housed by soundproofing, a recording booth, amps, books, modulators, pedals, brass instruments in cases. Beside the mini grand, lined on the front wall that faced out at 8th featured twin lounge chairs—a Victorian suede sofa, cherry red with wooden accents—a coffee table with a golden bottle of Xanax, a pack of American Spirits and empty coffee glasses left with only a muddy ring stained at the bottom—a wine rack between two of the windows and a mini fridge. More still was the back wall, on the opposite end of the room, full of soundproofing and amps stacked in a row. Each wall had guitars propped wherever they fit. Boards, mixers, interfaces and consoles alike splayed across a line of desks. The only artificial light within the room derived from a few lamps near the lounge chairs and coffee table, plus a gothic chandelier curling in on itself in a brilliant gold, with more than four dozen bulbs and treasures hanging from the piece. Ellis flicked a light switch and the whole chandelier brought the room from an icy cave into a bohemian paradise.

"Holy shit," I murmured, the words cascaded from my mouth in barely more than a whisper. "You have everything in here, it must have cost you a fortune."

Ellis snickered lowly as he crossed to the back wall where he cranked a little space heater, and a hellish red blaze glimmered on its cage.

"Accumulated over time. Oh, wait until you see this!" he chirped.

He cantered to the main desk, a triple monitor display with a minimalist keyboard and mouse, but he bent and reached into a side drawer. He fished around a moment before revealing a pistol. I have never known much about guns, but this one was silver with a wood finish. A menacing metallic weapon. The moment he revealed it, he might as well have withdrawn a venomous snake. A cold cancer fit to his palm.

"Is that loaded?" I asked. I tried to sound calm and cool about it but even I noticed the shake in my voice. He chuckled, "Yeah. Mental this one. This is a Kimber 1911. Safety's on, Joseph, don't fret. It takes a real heavy pull to fire it. Anyway, this is my security system while the doors are unlocked." He twisted it around in his hand and extended it, gesturing for me to hold it. I shook my head, "That's alright."

He shrugged and hid it below the clutter in the desk drawer. Ellis scanned the room to show other details I might find interesting. Instead, he turned and plopped into the maroon lounge chair across from the space heater and clawed the tiny yellow box on the table, tapped the head of it on his palm and withdrew a cigarette. He motioned for me to take one. I did. He reached in his coat for his monochrome Zippo and lit both.

"So," he started and blew the first air of smoke. "Welcome to my studio."

"I see!" I still had my coat on, back turned to him and holding my cigarette between my fingers, the other hand deep in my dress pocket. "I mean it, Ellis, this is a wonderful place you've made. I should have recorded a record here."

"It's never too late." Ellis smoked and leaned back in the chair until it was only on its back two feet. He plucked a bottle of red wine; I'm not sure what kind. "*1927*, this label reads. Exactly a century old —shall we?"

I raised my hand as if to shake it away; I said, "It isn't even noon."

"All the more reason to drink it now, don't you think? What's the point in waiting when we're ensured now and not later? We're old friends, after all, are we not?"

"We are," I said and realized I'd been stepping closer to the lounge chair opposite Ellis.

"Great. Sit. Drink. Smoke. Enjoy everything while we have it."

I did as he said and sank tenderly into the chair. He found two empty wine glasses on the coffee table, glared hard at them in the light of the chandelier, and decided to pour. He handed me a glass and he must have worn my resistance because he spoke, "No need for the long face! Come on, it was an artist before you that drank from this same glass! It could have been Elara Carpe or Yvette Adair, Freddy Richardson or fucking Mick Jagger!"

I sat up in the seat and accepted the glass but gave an inquisitive scan, "Freddy Richardson hasn't been here, has he?"

"I don't know," he said and sounded far off like he was genuinely trying to recall if he'd seen the actor. "It was an example. Why do you ask?"

"My ex-girlfriend cheated on me with Freddy Richardson," I choked gently on the words and swallowed a swig of red. I wiped my lips with the back of my hand and when the conversation had gone quiet for too long, I looked up from the coffee table.

"What?" I asked. Ellis was smiling behind his balled-up fingers over his lips, his index finger stuck out, pointed up at his right eye.

"Nothing. Just curious."

"Curious?" I asked.

"About what happened with that girl. *Vivian Wells.*" He said her name in a nineteenth century British accent, long and drawn out. I rolled my eyes, "To tell you the truth, we both ended up cheating on each other. That's why we never ended up getting married." And Ellis snorted abruptly.

"What is it now?" I questioned, becoming annoyed.

"You were going to *get married? Really?* Joseph, that is not the life of a true artist. Settling down means—settling down! It's right there in the name! Plus, I don't see why you'd want to date Vivian Wells anyway."

"Why do you say that?"

"Her mother is Nora *fucking* Spencer, mate," he drooled on the name, and it was quite the legendary name. He scoffed, then, "She's never had to work for anything in her life with a mother like that! You were dating someone who has never experienced even a *taste* of suffering, and you wanted to *marry her.*"

"Yes, that's what I wanted. I loved her." I was offended and had my brows pinned together yet still I sat relaxed in the chair and smoked. Ellis shook his head, "No true artist wants to be held down like that—no true artist *can* be held down like that. That's how you know she wasn't a true artist; she just saw how easy it would be to follow in her mother's footsteps and did it—not to say I blame her—wouldn't you?"

"You're wrong," I growled. Ellis shut his eyes and raised a hand as if to say, *be calm.*

"I don't mean to pester you. But you are a real artist—I know it. I've known it for years and I've been waiting patiently for *this very day* when we'd get reunited and look! Fate has brought us back together. Isn't that just wonderful?"

"I don't believe in fate."

"Oh, don't you though? You can't possibly believe none of this is happening without purpose, or without motivation! Life imitates art —art imitates life—we are actors on a stage, only the world out there," he pointed his half-ashed cigarette toward the pale windows, "*Out there,* the world is both our stage and our audience. So, like any director, I ask, 'What's your motivation for the scene?'"

I rolled my eyes. "Let's talk about something else. How long have you had the studio? I could've used this for *Music to Die to.*"

He blinked and brushed red hair from his face, he held his cigarette and wine glass in the same hand to uncross and recross his legs. "It's been—oh—must be seven years now. Yes, seven years, that's right. I leased it just before lockdown—and here we are."

"Well, it's a lovely space. And 'Velvet Pie Studios,' that's a great name." I was trying to act cordial but the whole situation was festering a myriad of anxieties below my surface. I was humming with an intense dread from discussing my past. Ellis rubbed his eyes, noting none of my tremblings; I knew I had contained myself well.

"Yes, I agree, great name. The whole place is in the midst of an override at the moment. So, it won't be 'Velvet Pie' for much longer. We're not changing much inside, what you see is mostly what will stay. I'm working on changing things on the business end."

"Is that right?" I pulled a large heaping wave of smoke into my mouth, filling my lungs as much as I could contain before I stamped my cigarette on the ashtray. "So, if it isn't 'Velvet Pie,' what will it be called?"

Ellis lifted himself from the lounge chair and planted himself in front of the window. He stared down at the world, his stage, crossing and moving along down below. "You wrote *Bugbear*, yes? The piano concerto with your name on it, that was all you?"

"Correct. I started it Christmas of '24, finished it Christmas of '25. It was performed by a symphony orchestra in—"

"In St. Louis. I was there." He turned his face ever so slightly from the window, only a fraction but enough for his eyes to refocus on me. I felt a freezing paleness shudder through my veins. How had he been there? I was at the event and yet I could not recall him at all. Surely, I would have noticed but perhaps not with the volume of attendance. That night had an audience of more than five hundred bodies. A thousand ears directed their attention to my handwritten notes—two of which belonged to Ellis—I felt ripped inside out, and nearly afraid of him.

Ellis blinked and suddenly his eyes were on the wood floors, thinking, and then said, "Joe—I wish you'd listen to me. *None of this* is happening by chance." He took a step, his loafer pressed into the floor causing a merciful yelp, and he took one step closer around the back of the lounge chair. "You know by now I'm a fan of your work. I've been following you closely since we last saw each other. Forgive me if I overstepped when last we met—I knew I wanted to see you again."

"What?" I whispered. My heart pressed against my ribcage. It became increasingly difficult to breathe. Ellis clicked his tongue and took another step closer to me. "I wanted you here. So, I devised a plan, and do forgive me if it sounds at all psychopathic. I sort of gave up when you started dating Vivian Wells, I figured I'd lost you completely, but then I heard she was dating that other movie star and you—well, you're here. You finally made it."

He took another step, placing his glass on the table, then another step until he was only an arm's reach away from me. His lids were low and staring down at me in the chair.

"For the last year, I have been working on creating an organization with several benefactors and partnerships. I've never been much of a businessman so it's going a little slower than anticipated," he explained. He glanced beyond me, at nowhere in particular, and a smirk grew on his face.

"It's called New York Artist's Haven. It's an institute I'm starting for artists of any gender, race, physique, what have you, to be under an umbrella that gets their work properly reviewed and shown—"

"No," I whimpered. I couldn't believe what I was hearing and now my chest was physically rising and falling, my sweater inflated and deflated. "You're the one that—"

"I'm the one who commissioned you for a symphony and brought you back to the city. Speaking of which, I haven't gotten any word that you accepted the request. What's the issue?"

I was speechless and whirling, I darted from his blue eyes to the room. Ellis walked a handful of paces back to his lounge chair and sat. He reached for his glass and took a swig. I swallowed. Despite my admirance toward Ellis, a shield began to build inside of me, under-standing he held many secrets.

"I know it's a big decision. You're the only musician I've queried. I want one artist of each form to dedicate a piece to Artist's Haven. Currently—well, if you decide to join—there will be five artists total on the payroll. I have big ideas for this program, yes, I do believe it will be *my* masterpiece. I want to create a world with a familiar image. 'Artist-in-residence' was a term from the Renaissance, much to the likes of Michelangelo and Da Vinci. *Apanages.* The brightest age of art that we still look back on and gawk at their creations. I will be using my resources and power to resurrect the idea with a refined group—one mind for each art form."

"I'm music," I said, but in a questioning tone. Ellis nodded. "You're music. Yvette is painting. Others will take other forms, and so on and so forth—It is my vision to replay our past because I see what is happening! Art is falling to such inscrutable lows. In a world where content and creation have become falsely synonymous, is it fair to say we are enjoying the art of this generation or merrily consuming it?

Consuming leads to consumption, consumption leads to gluttony, and gluttony becomes addiction—we become addicted to these outlets of pleasure. And we all know the slippery slope of numbness. We will soon no longer discover the delicacies of art, in all its pleasures, lying in patience and quiet—things becoming so unfamiliar now. We are in a second Renaissance, Joseph, but they have seen nothing yet.

"And this is why I wish for you to join me. I will not so much be creating history, as I will be *curating* it. At this moment, I pay for three out of the four artists to all live here in the city. I pay for their apartments, their utilities, everything—all on top of their commission to create art. However, Sumitra Patani—she's our poet—refuses to let me pay for anything. All she accepts is the money. See, artists need alone time, time to do absolutely nothing, so desperately. I can provide these struggling artists, these *geniuses of our time*, with the opportunity to create their masterpieces. And I want you to be a part of it."

I still didn't have a proper answer for him. I continued my dead stare as I hardly believed a single word of what I was hearing and how I ended up here. Wronged was not the right word, I was amazed. I wondered at how he had orchestrated such an event and how he ad managed to catch me in his web so effortlessly. I cleared my throat, swallowed; I never took my eyes off his.

With a sigh, I asked, "Why me?"

"Because I sincerely think you are the most talented musician I have ever met in my life. I see it in you, how you're present but always listening to something else. You're listening to the music that is constantly formulating within your head, and that is something not many can do. You are special. Different. And I want to give you the opportunity and space to unravel the triumph within you."

I gulped. All of this was happening so suddenly and whether it was the half glass of red, or his powerful presence and his woeful pitch, but I knew my answer before I even pretended to contemplate. I considered my alternatives. I hadn't heard from Luca in the last week. I had no idea when my next film might call. And then it dawned on me that this opportunity in my lap was perhaps once in a lifetime. Perhaps this group will all be ensured successes—it could be studied in a history class someday. I had my spot firmly planted within modern culture, a household name still, and yet, what would it take to become a name in history? How does one make such a transition? I tried to consider if I was even capable of such genius, as I had yet to know what I was even doing. I'd only been writing scores for two years and felt like an extreme novice to the form. My curiosity to explore this possibility, however, interested me and was infinitely more appealing than any amount of money. I wanted to find out how far I could push myself.

"Okay—" I started, and a shiver wrapped my body. "Yeah, yeah, I'll do it."

And he grinned handsomely. "I'm thrilled by your decision. I'll have someone reach out to you with further details. Shall we grab lunch?" Ellis downed the rest of his red glass until it was translucent and pink. He wandered to the desktop and glanced at a notepad but purposefully led himself toward the exit.

"I'm busy," I said. Ellis made a pouting face. I continued, "Some other time—but Ellis." He raised his brows, cocked his head and stood patiently at the door. "It wasn't you that brought me out here."

Ellis looked truly perplexed by the comment. "Is that so?"

I nodded and he stood quietly, waiting for further information. "I planned on moving here to begin with. I'm still looking for somewhere to stay. But let me ask you—was our encounter at the diner also planned?"

Ellis slipped his hand from the knob and into his pocket. He crossed back through the studio, carefully stepping over cables and empty glasses. He was once again just in front of where I sat in the maroon lounge. "No," he admitted, "But to me, that shines a stronger argument for fate, wouldn't you agree?"

I was silent. I leaned forward to place the wine glass, still half-full on the coffee table when Ellis' outstretched hand breached my peripheral, an invitation to help me to my feet. I looked past it, at his face.

"Well?"

"Well, what?" I asked.

"You can stay with me in my flat. You've already been there once before, don't you remember? I have a separate room and more than enough space for two. You can attest if your memory serves you. Something temporary. And don't give me the annoying modesty, I just want a clean answer on whether you'll take it."

My lips moved but no sound left me. I gently clapped the glass on the table and reset. I cleared my throat and thought hard about how I should answer. If I were to move in with him, it would be as if I were living with my employer. Although, he was less an employer and more a friend who wanted to see what I was truly capable of. In all honesty, I wanted to know as well. There was plentiful risk involved, so the option became terrifying. Not to mention, I did not take Ellis Young to be an honest man. Yet my options were slim, dwindling with each passing day I spent in my sister's spare bedroom. I needed a job, and I needed a place to live.

There, in the studio overlooking 8th, I made the decision that changed every trajectory of my life. All other outcomes ceased. Ellis stood over me, his palm stood out and faced the ceiling. His eyes stayed on mine. He was patient in the midst of silence before I finally spoke.

"I'll take it."

"Good," Ellis grinned. "Then take my hand."

VOLUME THREE
FERVENT SOUL

I

DESIRE AMONG DECAY

I returned to Los Angeles only once more and then never again for the rest of my life. I ran out to sign a deed that officially transferred my Santa Barbara property over to a new owner whom I never actually met. I earned a healthy sum of money from the house, which I stashed away in a savings account for emergency purposes. I was to stay in the City of Angels for another excruciating four days as I awaited the Academy Awards. I had a tuxedo suit designed and tailored for the event, all to the credit of the ingenious fashion stylist, Alfie Baxter, a Los Angeles native but with the creative flair of a European. They styled my attire for other award shows and events in the last odd years. The tuxedo featured midnight blue trousers and a matching jacket; in a dim enough setting, as it would be in the Dolby Theatre, the silked threads would appear black. Alfie optioned the idea of a tailcoat and a chain, but I decided I didn't want to make too much of a statement, opting to attend in an unremarkable fashion. I was new to this kingdom of the modern Pythians, these decadent royalties of the motion picture arts. My plan was to smile at the lenses, cross gracefully to my seat, be quiet, and leave. I had a glass of champagne with my sister, Betty, and together we found our assigned seats as quickly as possible, and I waited for the whole event to be over. I first invited Autumn as my plus one but over the phone in early

February, she hesitantly declined the offer. I was beginning to wish I had never even been nominated as I was altogether nauseated.

The whole fiasco of the awards show was a fright. It all moved incredibly fast; camera operators walked alongside every person in a mostly quiet room, and sweeping camera cranes shot over the audience. It felt as if I were on a movie set again and it was all so surreal, recognizing most every face surrounding me. They all instinctively knew to sit and act as an aristocratic version of themselves. Elegant grins. Suave applause. I might have been in the fifth row from the front, off to the furthest left seating in the auditorium, and to my left was only a half wall and a fire exit. The camera operators stepped around my left side all night with their giant cameras hooked to their bodies, sweating a storm, wearing earpieces to know who to focus on. I must have focused on these operators more than the show itself.

"And the Oscar goes to," said an actor in a dazzling crimson gown, her black hair done up in a high braid. I focused on the charming elder man to her left, an actor I recognized from a few films I'd seen growing up, now approaching his sixties and reading from the shimmering envelope in her hands.

"Joseph Henley, *Only in Dream.*"

I was too focused on the camera woman two rows ahead of me and racking focus on me—the lens seared into my face like a frightful beam—then too stunned to register my name had been called from the stage. I furrowed with an angled stare as the actor on the stage turned in a grin and seemingly scanned the auditorium for me. I fell into a perplexed glare as faces in rows around me turned their bodies to applaud, grinning and nodding their handsome complexions, flashing their ceramic teeth and it finally clicked that I had won the award. Betty rubbed her hand against mine as I gripped sweaty into the armrest. I had gone pale, I knew, as I saw myself projected on the screen. I rose feebly from my chair and limped to the stage. I fumbled as I accepted the statue, much heavier than I had anticipated. It had a real mighty feel to it, icy cold and I noticed my fingers smothered their sweaty oils over the gold finish.

"Wow," I muttered, and I heard as my voice projected across the auditorium of goliaths. I blinked. I was a sheet of white standing handsome but fearful. I swallowed. My speech came out in a frenzy— I thanked Conrad March in a heartfelt farewell as the sea of performers sat in an unmoving silence, allowing me the space to explain how much I truly enjoyed my time with the creative collaborator.

"He was a truly kind soul and someone I quite looked up to," I said, and I paused to reflect on the words, but I wasted time. I surfed for the correct way to describe the man, but the truth of the matter was I hadn't known him that well at all. He was one of the most important filmmakers from all of history, comparable to Stanley Kubrick, Alfred Hitchcock, David Lynch, and yet, I only ever saw him in a work setting.

I thanked my parents and my sisters, and I wasn't sure who else to thank on the stage. My brain drew a blank and I realized how few people I had around me. In the front row, glinting eyes watched me like porcelain dolls, patient and sterile. I should have become entirely enthralled and yet completely terrified by the sight. I began to step away from the microphone with my eyes falling to the impossibly reflective floor, mirroring a darkly warped image of my face, the one I most seemed to agree with when I turned back to it in a jutting motion and spoke, "And to all the musicians in Los Angeles who helped bring this score to life! Without all of you, there would be only symbols on a page. Thank you, thank you, thank you."

I felt good about it although I forgot to thank the Academy, and I decided it did not matter. I was ushered backstage, someone offered me a glass of champagne and a series of portraits were shot of me with the little statue. It did not have my name on it at first; I was told that there would be an engraving later at the after-party. Then, I was ushered into a new space and submitted round after round of answers to journalists in a press room. I stood at a microphone with an Academy Awards backdrop splayed behind me; the journalists, the cameras, the lights, the microphones all pressed in on me and I felt my fingernails digging into my cuticles.

"What does it mean to you as a musician to move away from the world of rock and roll and into the world of composing for feature films?"

"What was your favorite aspect of working with Conrad March and how has his loss impacted you?"

"Will you continue creating scores for films or do you foresee yourself returning to Beach Sirens or performing in a band again someday?"

Admittedly, all were great questions, and I was baffled by how exhausting it was to articulate the very abstract answers I had in my head. My returns existed as barely attached fragments of thought—how was I to weave them into a response through the use of my tongue? Some thoughts are too withdrawn and inhabit the mind as nonrepresentational to any language. I did my best despite this assurance, and it made for many bland answers. This was followed by the option to either return to my seat or go to the greenroom or to an after-party.

I returned to the show and watched as *Only in Dream* won the award for Best Motion Picture of the Year. Then it was off to the Governor's Ball. I watched as my name, the one provided from birth, was slowly etched into a golden plaque under a little white lamp. I could not take my eyes away from the sight, afraid to blink, terrified I might miss any moment of the event. How was it that I had found myself here in life?

I pride myself on not caring about the awards or the rapture as a creative, but I could not hide the sheer thrill of being recognized for the stupendous work I had put into the music. I drank champagne and introduced myself to the faces and voices I had known my entire life, all under the lavish chandelier lighting. I was invited to one of the after-parties, the one hosted by Alexandria Graben, an actor from several films and a background on Broadway. It was one of the best nights of my life and I returned to my hotel room at two in the morning (Betty turned in around midnight and shared a ride back to the hotel with Deborah McLelland, who had been nominated for Best Original Screenplay), and I felt as if I had just witnessed what it meant to achieve the highest status. Was it the extravagance of the night that made me swelter with giddiness or had it been the award itself? I knew the answer, yet I felt so similar to the little freezing statue staring back at me on the hotel desk. Golden. Tommy would have gotten a great kick out of this. I wished he could have been present for the moment. I wished to spend my night in celebration with both Tommy and Luca, but neither were anywhere close. Luca had gone from distant to entirely unreachable. My mind remained clouded—I wondered more about what I might do with the statue when I got back to my rented bedroom in Queens—I wondered if I was capable of repeating myself. I wondered where to go from there.

———

Back in New York, it was finally time to begin work on my anticipated symphony. I had giant notebooks at the ready for any scribbling of an idea I may come across, including the pages I toyed with during my old life in Santa Barbara. I signed a contract with Ellis that bound me to the creation of a masterful composition with no real end date, only necessitating that I provide him with an eventual finished work. I was officially commissioned. In regard to the deal made with Ellis, he would pay me however I chose for my work, whether that be all at once at the beginning, when the composition was finished, or in a series of payments throughout the process. I opted for the finish, as I wished to not find myself overzealous with the funds, and besides, I hadn't much need of it as I now had a sufficient amount of money from the Santa Barbara property. Not to mention, Ellis was allowing me to stay with him for free.

Ellis' apartment had not much changed since I had last seen it at the age of twenty-six. The Queens apartment had a wave of natural light from large windows facing west. His record player was seemingly always on and spiraling a vinyl record, more still, he had freshly brewed Colombian coffee every morning in the pour-over. He kept the apartment spotless; his shelf of books was properly dusted, and I found myself examining it in awe of his collection. Most of the books were rare, and because of such, the house had to be kept at a specific temperature to not ruin the binding and pages. I didn't notice much about the temperature.

Every morning, I would rise and find what was left of the pour-over and find Ellis either watering his plants or reading a novel in his armchair. One morning I found Ellis resting in his royal blue armchair with his red hair caught in a bun, wearing his reading spectacles, legs crossed and sporting a knitted sweater.

"Good morning," I chirped. I had on a pair of comfort shorts and my crew sweater earned from *Mass Hysteria*.

"Morning," he returned with a glimpsing look, only to return to the novel. Moby's *Innocents* record spun out precious noise from the speakers. I slapped my feet across the living room and into the kitchen, over the pearly tiled floor, and found a mug in the cupboard, a large, handcrafted ceramic. I obtained my black coffee and smelt the tangy aroma, like a thick chocolate, or a bonfire.

"What are you reading?" I arched backward into the leather, all the skin of the sofa croaking against itself until I found a comfortable position. I gulped a bit of coffee down my throat; the hot liquid found its way at the bottom of my stomach.

"Rereading Milton's *Paradise Lost*."

"Do you ever read anything enjoyable?" I jested. I earned a hearty scoff from Ellis before he returned, "Life is too short to be reading bullshit, Joseph. I urge you to pick one of these books and start finding new ways of thought."

"Where should I even begin?"

Ellis thought for a moment, he pierced a tea bag in the nook of his novel (he always preferred using tea bags as bookmarks as they gave his books flowery scents). He made hums of intrigue to himself as he skated around the shelf. "Ah!"

He scooted a binding, clothbound, and walked it around the coffee table and I accepted the stretched novel. Mary Wollstonecraft Shelley's *Frankenstein; or, The Modern Prometheus*.

"Have you read this one?"

I shook my head, staring at the minimally bound edition. "Give it a go, we'll read together."

I did, and I read the first bits about Victor in the frozen lands of Antarctica, his birth in Naples, his experiments in Ingolstadt. Reading was a sensation I did not approach often but I always felt great admiration for those who enjoyed it. It was not so different from reading music as it required a great deal of work within the brain to find an immersion that existed just past imagination. Ellis loved reading and I sought to please him with my efforts but found myself fully earthed by the stories written with such diligence.

In the short time I lived with Ellis, I learned very little about his personal life—he was very particular about sharing anything regarding his past—until one night in the safety of his apartment and after a splashing good time at a restaurant called Vetro, he provided me with a version of his history. We were both drunk off two bottles of white wine, pouring the bottles' remnants between our two glasses. Ellis began to tell me about what happened to him as a child, entirely out of nowhere like filling the shadowy silence with an anecdote that might keep me intrigued. Then, the most curious thing happened, it was as if I were in control of my drunken consciousness, like I was having a lucid dream. Very suddenly, I knew it would benefit me to force myself sober and pay attention (or, the best attention a drunk man *playing* a version of sober could offer). I memorized only a handful of details from that night.

Ellis was born in the Spring of 1984, making him a full decade older than myself, in Blackburn, an industrial town in Lancashire, England. To my understanding, he was very quiet but an excellent scholar. He loved reading since he was old enough to understand it; his mother would take him to the library. He hid within the pages of these conjured worlds and whenever he wasn't involved in the intimacy of reading, he was playing the violin or anything else he could get his hands on. Ellis began playing the violin at a very young age when his parents discovered he had a talent for the instrument during a music lesson. Ellis grew up relatively poor, he lived in terraced housing with his mother and father but with just enough money to get by. His parents rummaged up the money they needed to purchase

Ellis a secondhand violin for his tenth birthday and from then on, his instrument became his only true friend.

His childhood was fairly kind until the age of fourteen. His parents, Terrence and Helena Young, loved each other completely, the kind of love some spend their entire lives searching (or waiting) for. Terrence worked at a steel manufacturing company (I hadn't found out what his mother did). His father, at the age of forty-six, died in an accident at work—while assisting on a project, a fragment of steel no larger than an arrowhead shot up and cracked his forehead, to the same effect of gunfire. Ellis, as I understand, generally liked his father and hid in his room the entire summer holiday.

Helena did the same, barely able to provide Ellis dinner anymore, and the two of them began to diminish in their bedrooms in an aching silence. They felt the abundant absence of Terrence, their provider, their entertainer, their light of hope, and now all was lost. His mother passed away seven months later from what was believed to be a broken heart. Rather than receiving funds at the cost of his parents' lives, Ellis found himself at a further loss as he knew his parents were in a great deal of debt with the bank. Ellis was a methodical child (methodical still), and he knew to pack his belongings and run away from home before he could be placed in the foster system.

Ellis told me all of this—from his parent's death, one right after the other, to his adventures with scavengers in Blackburn as a boy—in a matter-of-fact tone, as if he were teaching me a piece of history he had no affiliation with. I returned with the backstory of my family and what it was like growing up in Athens with my two sisters. It felt shallow compared to the tragedy he had to endure. I could not imagine the suffering one would experience at such a young age; Ellis was fifteen years old and living in alleyway dumpsters, playing his violin on street corners for change, begging for food around Blackburn. It wasn't until he was sixteen years old that he had gathered enough funds to take the train into Manchester. From there, he explained, his life was flipped around, when an executive for a major label caught word of a 'street prodigy.'

Apparently, a video of him playing the violin had gone viral on the internet. When Ellis explained this bit, I hadn't believed him and dared for it to be shown to me. Of course, the footage was real—a video of sixteen-year-old Ellis, with a shorter cut of red hair, only skin and bones, wailing on the violin in languid quivers, etching into the strings like a fiddle, all to his heart's merriment. The video was certainly dated and taken on an aged digital camera with smearing fragments of light and a stuttering framerate, even the date was stamped on the corner of the video: May of 2001.

"Wow," I whispered as the recording moved from teenage Ellis to the sidewalk and then black. "And look how far you've come." I patted him on the back, and he exited out of the video on his phone.

"Yeah—it was, what some may call—*humble beginnings*. I didn't make it over to America until I was twenty-one when I started working closely with The Inbetweeners. The rest is history, as we know it thus far." He scuffed a somber laugh and rubbed his eyelids. It was the middle of the night in the dying winter of Queens.

As I understood it, Ellis did not allow himself to get drunk often and I felt especially lucky to share the experience with him. This brief and limited insight into his past was all I knew of Ellis Young—he much liked to maintain this air of mystery about him—I knew he'd always been a gifted musician from the time he was a child, that went without question. Though rather than learning to play music, it was as if he was picking it up again from a previous life. I related to Ellis as we both knew that in certain instances, music meant survival. For someone I deem one of the most important people in my entire life, I knew at this time so little about who he was. It wouldn't be until much later that I would begin to uncover greater secrets.

———

The weather was beginning to turn on Brighton Beach. By midday, the seaside was sprinkled with tanning beachgoers, but the early morning still called for extra layers, so Autumn was wearing a straw tweed sweater and jeans a few steps ahead of me with Mazy's new dog, Vincent, stuck on a leash and propelling her forward. She leaned back and bobbed as the chocolate Labrador urged in the opposite direction, looked over her shoulder at me with her cat-rimmed sunglasses. The widest grin held on her face. I walked slowly behind them, grinning back and not saying a word. No words were really needed, and I tried to capture every detail of the moment to better serve my memory. I noted the harsh wind thrashing through my hair and how the salt stuck to my skin. Autumn wore a black Dead Girls Club trucker cap, and it suited her well.

We lazily made our way down the beach corridor and discussed her band's debut album that would be coming out in the fall, as well as my lack of inspiration for the grueling symphony. Eventually, we were side by side and I felt comfortable tossing my arm around her shoulder, rubbing my palm on her arm to keep her warm, which doubled as a sign of affection.

"I have a question," I said. I wondered if what I was about to say was a good idea or not.

"Okay," Autumn said, talking loud enough to be heard over the wind.

"Why didn't you come to the awards with me?"

She paused, staring straight ahead at the length of the beach that seemed to unravel outward in a long, tan stripe. The world to our left was occupied by the boardwalk, buildings and a lifeguard stand wrapped in a fabric of morning fog and to our right: the blue glass infinity, with glints from the newborn sun skidding the surface, and ahead of us: Vinny, the chocolate lab dabbing his paws in the sand, leaving tiny marks and trotting along, endlessly joyful. "Well—it's not that I didn't want to go."

"Then what?" I realized I sounded too firm. Notably urgent. I quickly added, "If you don't mind me asking."

"I didn't want any presumptions to be made about us," she said. I could hear the tone in her deep voice, a rising poison and her rage was returning. I hadn't meant to provoke anything.

"It's okay, I was just curious," I replied and tried to lay the conversation to rest. I swallowed. But what had she meant by *presumptions?*

Vinny had his nose tickling the ground and a little crab sucked into the wet sand.

"Presumptions," I heard myself say aloud, repeating her use of the word.

Autumn sighed aggressively. "Look, if it was just you and I on some red carpet, you would have absolutely put your hand on my waist. And then every magazine cover from here to Los Angeles would have some headline about us possibly being together."

I was perplexed by her answer, and in turn, fumbled for words. "What? Those tabloids spread all kinds of lies! That's what they do," I argued. My arm slid off from around her shoulder.

Autumn continued, "And then my parents would be asking about it, you know, and Sophia would see—"

"Sophia?" I cut her off, betrayed by the mention of her name. "Sophia—what does Sophia have to do with any of this?"

"She's the only other person *involved* in whatever this is."

"Like hell she's involved! She's married and writing her fucking poetry books now. We'll probably never see her again!"

"Let's not forget that if it wasn't for her, you and I would have never met—and let's not forget that given the opportunity, you'd still be swooning over her instead of me."

I frowned; my lips quivered. "What are you talking about?"

"You heard me." She had her bottom lipped puckered the way she always did when she got in a fit of anger. She reminded me often of a honeybee, a kind creature you might like to hold if only it would not sting. I knew I was over Sophia because the iteration of her I'd fallen for in college was no longer real. There only existed the new Sophia who wrote her poems and lived in Texas. She led the kindest life out of the three of us, all that remained. I had no intent of continuing on the topic—the virgining fight was not how I anticipated the morning going. I backed off and the conversation subsided for a span of time. I walked beside her with my hands in my pockets as I watched my boots leave moon prints on the beach.

Once we had reached the end of the beach, in an area with no bodies in sight, we let Vincent off his leash and the retriever frolicked and sprinted the beach freely. Autumn brought out a neon tennis ball to fling into the clearing fog as day broke on the water. Now, in the late morning, we played fetch with the dog until he was tired and panting. We sat side-by-side and watched the specks of runners come into view in the distance. I thought about how not so long ago I had been on the other side of this perspective, breaking the ocean's wind with my stride, tears coating my eyes and keeping my breath in time. I turned to look at Autumn, and she stared out at the silver waves slapping over themselves, her hand supporting her chin with her knees pulled in and the dog panting beside her.

"I could live here," I said.

"Is that right?" she returned, unamused. She never looked away from the sea. A gap returned to our language, so I wet my lips and spoke concisely while we both looked into the horizon, "I'm sorry."

She hesitated before she replied, "It's okay."

"No, I don't think it is. I may not be the smartest person in the world, but I do understand how much you value your privacy. And the least I can do is respect it," I said, and I was watching her. She looked at me, her sunglasses over her eyes but her eyebrows tilted at an angle, upwards into sadness. Her lips shivered and I couldn't tell if it was due to the breeze off the ocean or from the emotions transpiring on her face.

"Joe," she said and stopped. She positioned her lips to say something else and even placed her hand on mine. I waited patiently, tossing my focus all over her face as I still waited for her to speak up until something inside of her recalibrated. Her face fell and she sniffled, her peachy cheeks and their freckles matched the sand floor. I wanted to kiss her but refrained as I thought it could be deemed contradictory. She raised her head again and formed a smile on her face, a smile that seemed difficult to generate. I let it be, mimicked her expression, and stood to dust my trousers. Vinny went mental when I stood up, prancing around and tangling himself on his leash. I reached out my hand to my oldest friend and helped her to her feet again. There is no feeling quite like entangling one soul with another but how painful it is when it comes time to detach them. In the bindings of life or beyond, there is an inevitable farewell. Souls, I have learned, do not like to let go easily; they require a great and terrible force to leave each other forever.

———

The first artist I met who had also become involved with New York Artist's Haven was Yvette Adair, the French painter. When I walked into the studio, there she was on the floor with one leg pulled to her shoulder and the other stretched flat. She was scribbling something on the page of a blank notebook, her back turned to us, a frizzed mane of pale lilac colored hair, dyed some time ago, now fading toward her usual blonde. Her head bobbed about with headphones smushed over her ears. Ellis looked at me with a small grin, as he stripped his overcoat, and he motioned for mine as well. He led me closer to the young artist, at a sure enough distance to not startle her when our shadows would inevitably cross her notebook. She was surrounded by easels, all done up with fantastic paintings.

Her art was somewhere between Figurative and Baroque, yet a chiaroscuro to the works. I could not believe what I was looking at— it neared caricature in ways I cannot so easily describe—they were mostly portraits of people with broken faces, swirling in on themselves or fading freely as if they were puddles. The defining feature seemed to be the thick acrylics dabbed directly onto the canvas. So dense were the dollops that the paintings might as well have been three-dimensional. They were vaguely portraits, instead, it was a *feeling* of a person in each painting. There was the idea of a face staring back at me but then there was the private skirmish below their eyes, lining their faces, on their lips. And admittedly, even after all the praise, Yvette was still a better artist than I had anticipated.

As we approached her sprawled on the floor, she was sketching out four different faces in four different styles, each separated into a quadrant of the page. Ellis' shadow flooded the page, white to gray, and she cocked her head before she glanced up and grinned. She peeled away her headphones and stood up to embrace him.

"Hello, Ellis," she mumbled with her face in his chest. She looked at me with a squinted gaze, an analysis with a playful air. "Do not tell me," she said, and I quickly caught the thickness of her French accent. She peered with a sharp scan as if she might have known me. "Are you Joe Henley? From Beach Sirens?"

"Among other things," I returned in a lively tone. Her hand sprang out and I accepted it. She shook with a great deal of force and blurted, "I adore your music! I listen to it all the time, even still! It got me through college! You and your band, I love very much."

I chuckled and motioned toward the splay of canvases scattered around her. "Thanks, but I have to say, you're quite the artist yourself. You're really good."

"Not *good*," Ellis broke in, "She's the next great artist of history." His arm wrapped around her, and she hummed sweetly as he stared down at the top of her lilac hair and said, "She's one in a billion. One in *ten* billion. The world will know her genius. That's why her art exhibit is at the end of the month."

"You must be very excited," I charmed with a curt nod.

She nodded. "I am quite excited. And for this symphony, Ellis tells me about!" she exclaimed.

"What?" I heard myself say. The two of them looked at me. Ellis looked alarmed but he reset instantly, as if he, too, understood that he needed to maintain his composure.

"Had I told you about that?" Ellis squinted down at Yvette, then to me. "I apologize, Joseph, it must've slipped my tongue. Not to worry, Yvette can keep a secret, can't you?" asked Ellis. He eyed the young lady as she nodded, and her cheeks blushed a pinkish hue.

I wasn't as much worried as I was surprised. Something wafted over me, I recall, and I suddenly felt very cold at the idea of following through with the inquiry. I played through the many scenarios of me confronting Ellis to tell him perhaps I should not commit to this after all. I should continue scoring films with Luca, that was the path I belonged to. Yet at the time, I did live with Ellis, and I wondered if his sincerity only went so far.

It is true that I was his main protégé for his program. Not to mention, Ellis and I had been living together for over a month—now the beginning of Spring—and how quickly the seasons change. I would have to put a decent melody to paper at some point.

I remained quiet the rest of the day and when we got back to his apartment, he tried asking me about what might be wrong with me.

"I'm fine. Promise, I'm alright," Joe replied, a version of myself I was portraying that night. One of my many masks in circulation.

"Are you sure? Because you've barely said a word all day. You look like you're on bloody autopilot."

I wondered if this was my life veering in the wrong direction. I felt that up until this point I knew what I was doing and perhaps things did happen for a reason. I remember the careless confidence I'd adopted when I drove up to North Carolina without a second thought. Where had that gone? I suppose that was for a girl, not only that but a girl I still find flashing around inside of me. I saw her in my dreams; she and Tommy agreed to exist there.

Now, I was leaving everything I knew. Luca was to be moving out to the city in June and Autumn and I spent nearly every weekend together at that point. We'd managed a schedule of Friday nights being our night together, often going out to see a movie or get dinner or see an art gallery.

It's not a date, Joe, she'd always say, and she'd glare whenever I reached to hold her hand. I would lie and say it was to keep her warm. She would do all of this and yet, every Saturday morning, I would wake up beside her in her bed. I knew her then better than I'd known her previously, and I was beginning to know her better than myself. I knew which spots on her body were the most vulnerable and what remarks would make her laugh and which ones to keep to myself. What's more is I really loved it this way—my body felt hollowed out —had I fallen in love? When I was with her, I felt as if for the first time in my life I was finally attuned to my more comfortable self. By mistake, I was too far into my thoughts and forgot to respond to Ellis. He snorted.

"Fuck, look at you! There you go again! We can talk about *anything,* mate, *anything,*" he said. "Whatever is on your mind, I'd be more than happy to sit and listen. Should we have a drink then? I wouldn't mind that."

Ellis slouched into his big armchair and was unsheathing a mint from its packaging he'd received from the French restaurant he treated Yvette and me to earlier in the evening. Claudette, on the corner of 9th and 5th Avenue. Yvette thought it was a cute gesture, I could tell by the eyes she gave silently across the table, but that's all she thought. Ellis loved dining, he practically lived for it, he loved it almost as much as he loved breath mints. I watched as his cheeks caved inward, nursing on the little peppermint.

"That's alright—thanks Ellis—I'm just tired," I decided. He nodded, and I saw he hadn't believed a word of it. Still, he looked me over.

"Go get some rest, Joseph," Ellis said calmly. I told him goodnight and hid in my bedroom where I tried calling Autumn again. Tomorrow was Friday and I wanted to try and get a plan arranged for the weekend. It wasn't until the following evening that she got back to me.

I stepped out of Velvet Pie and withdrew my humming cellphone. At first, I thought it might be Luca finally responding after several months of quiet but once I read the name of the caller, I swiped with veracity; I held the phone to my ear and wiped my nose. I watched as a motorized scooter with takeout strapped to the back skid past an idled UPS truck with its hazards blinking; a gush of pale wind bristled over my body, and I suddenly wished I had brought my coat outside even though it was approaching the middle of spring.

"Hey," I said, doing my best not to sound nervous. I knew who was on the line, and Autumn's voice said back, "Hey." She was quiet. Hesitant. She sounded exhausted and weakened.

"What's wrong?"

I was tucking my body together as people passed me by and I squeezed myself toward the door of the studio, looking back at my reflection and examining my beard. But as the silence prolonged on the line, I began to feel the chilled anxiety clogging my body. I waited and tried to stop fidgeting as I lost feeling in my hands. Autumn spoke again, abruptly and quickly, and I had the idea of what she might say before she said it, "I think we should stop seeing each other."

Everything softened. Zeroed out. A radical deafening I'd not learned until this moment. My desensitization hadn't had enough time to kick in and mentally I was left bare to the wound. My heart began to pierce, and my knees began to throb. I wanted to escape this pain, this all too familiar pain and just be away from it for a while and yet here it was again, taking hold of me once more.

"Oh. Okay," I said.

"I don't think it's healthy for either of us. I want you to go live your own life and I don't think I'll ever really want a boyfriend—not anymore—I want to do what's best for us now." Her voice was somehow deeper and scraped as if she had been bedridden and now fully ill. I thought maybe she had the flu and simply didn't want to be seen that weekend.

"That's okay—I know the rules. You said not to fall in love with you," I said back with an air of optimism.

"I know but this way we can't even be tempted. It's not fair to lead you on when I have no intentions of settling," she groaned and paused to sigh. "I know I can't let you in completely."

"Right." I swallowed. A group of tourists held hands and clicked pictures of the buildings and of their children, the oldest daughter gave me a prolonged stare. I smiled back at her though my eyes were swollen and glossy, blinking and fluttering to keep from the tears rolling over me.

"I'm so sorry, Joe," she was saying on the line, muffled, deep and lost. "Let's move on and maybe someday you and I can be friends again. We always worked best as friends, anyway."

"I thought you and Tommy were good friends too," I said gravely.

The silence that followed was tense and ridiculed. I felt the heaviness of my attitude before I realized what I'd said and immediately knew to back off, so I stayed quiet and awaited Autumn.

"I'm trying really hard to just be the bigger fucking person and settle this, okay? Can you just go with it so we can be adults about this? Please?"

"Yeah, fine. I'm sorry," I muttered. I wasn't even sure if it was loud enough for her to hear as the wind blanketed on the phone.

"Okay," she chirped, resolutely. She gathered herself but it seemed like the burst of energy had been tiresome for her, like somehow just speaking had worn her down. "Well, look, this isn't goodbye. I just wanted to call and get this off my chest. I hope you have fun writing your symphony. And I can't wait to hear whatever it is you make next."

"I'll try—thanks for calling—and hopefully I'll see you around then."

"Bye, Joey."

"Autumn," I blurted out in an effort to stop her. In a split decision, as I wondered if the call would soon end, maybe it would be years before I talked to her again or got to hear her voice, I urgently attacked at the muffled static.

"I love you," I muttered. It was curt. Unanticipated. Something I had to say or else it would consume me like a virus. At first, there was nothing and it felt like a large gap of time, but really it had only been a second or so. I jerked my vision all over the sidewalk below my feet, wondering what she'd say in response to my manic attempts to maintain something unfeasible.

"Bye."

Three distinct bleeps crooned in my ear, and I took the phone away to see that the call had ended. The tears that transpired from my eyes were now elsewhere; they lined my jaw and tapped on my collarbone. I stood there for only a moment in the chaos of Eighth, debating a cigarette or greater self-destruction. *I've lost another one,* I thought. Somehow, I kept losing all the people that mattered to me. Was I a bad person?

My fit was apparent as I sniffled and whimpered stupidly on the sidewalk. Docile and complacent. All the wandering bodies pretended not to notice me. These strangers' purposeful subtleties in staring up at the April clouds or examining the flourishing cornices on the exterior of buildings across the street were oddly comforting. If I was a rock star, they couldn't look away. If I was unhappy, nobody would even pretend I existed. I went back into the studio feeling subdued, hollowed out by the one less person in my life and I felt as though the earth was a sharply bitter place to live. New defenses began padding over my resentful heart as I climbed the stairs toward the second floor, wiping my tears on my sleeve and pulling a cigarette from my breast pocket. If this was the response I got for caring, I would only care for myself.

———

Yvette had her art show presented in a stuffy warehouse in East Williamsburg toward the decay of April, the birth of May, and though I had invited Autumn previous to our divorce, there remained a foolish piece of me that believed she would attend. I held onto this fraying hope as I continued fading from everything that made me who I was; I myself began to fray. The warehouse used to be a steel factory but was renovated sometime in the last decade and now served as an event space. Walls of cement blocks stood firm and coated in layers of white paint. Gloss finished concrete flooring. Makeshift walls were added to make the space more of a maze rather than an open interior. Out the backdoor, a quaint patio space with a bar. On arrival, there were two men at the front serving as event security, as well as accepting donations for NYAH and handling admission sales. But I was with Ellis, the creator of NYAH, so the two of us were let in without much resistance.

Yvette was on the first floor, not far off from the entrance and Ellis and I were going to congratulate her. The turnout was better than anticipated, Ellis informed, as crowds of young and old dragged around the art space. Yvette had her back to us; she wore a distressed sweater and what appeared to be pajama pants with blue and white stripes falling vertically down her leg. Her lavender hair fell to her shoulders; she wore earrings dangling from her lobes as golden ornaments and I was trying to make out what they were. Ellis tapped her on the shoulder, and she turned quickly, beaming, and hugged him. I was kind, I knew how much all of this meant to her.

"This is really wonderful. Congratulations," I likely told her. She thanked me and gave me a brief hug but was careful not to spill her gin and tonic. It wasn't until Ellis got roped into a conversation with another guest that I became inversely alone with Yvette, and so I panicked at the realization I had to actually participate in a substantial dialogue. We both watched as Ellis drifted off into the wall of people scattered throughout the space, some idle in conversation with a glass in hand, others with cocked necks and peering at one of her paintings spotlit on the white wall and taking a step every few seconds toward the next. I looked back at Yvette and grinned.

"He's really remarkable," I said. I blinked and wondered why I'd said that. Yvette grinned back and nodded and when her earrings jostled, I knew the pendants swaying from her lobes were tiny gold plated daggers.

"Yeah. He helps a lot," Yvette said and tucked her hair behind her ears before moving her hands to her hips. "I'm glad you could make it. Still so awestruck by you! *The* Joe Henley at my gallery."

Yvette mimed what might be fainting with the back of her hand on her forehead, her eyes rolling back. She giggled. I couldn't think up a response to the point the air neared stale before Yvette continued, "You are writing a symphony. Ellis told me this. How is that?"

"Yes, that's right," I said. It was difficult to manage even this as I had technically been commissioned to write a symphony four months prior, yet I hadn't a single note of the composition completed. I grinned, "It's going really well."

"I cannot wait to hear what a symphony by Joe Henley would sound like—it will be amazing," she said, and I could see the genuine excitement on her face. So, I did my best to maintain a charmed expression. She introduced me to a round of people, some that I knew, some I didn't. Influencers, writers, actors. Somehow, Ellis had managed to apply his skill set as a producer toward his efforts on this art show. NYAH was going to be something special. I looked at him across the room, laughing with a woman who I quickly realized was Teigen Delacre, one of the most famous folk singers alive. Ellis caught my glance for only a moment, but it was time enough for his grin to grow a fraction, a minute fraction reserved for my attention to detail. His expression was a way of showing off the two little worlds that were his eyes, welcoming those who looked. And yet, I could not see beyond. There was this charm he wore, this face worthy of study for the sake of aesthetics, but no further did the eyes allow. As if more of an objectively beautiful portrait but without the soul.

I worried about the symphony. Ellis was on the verge of becoming an important person in history—it was an innate feeling, something felt but without explanation—he'd be known as a curator for this artistic period we were living through. Moreover, he had an air to him that demanded intrigue. I recognized his cusp of glory; soon his name and face may be the work of chisel to stone. My inability to even scratch the surface of a composition made me go dull as if I were doing him a great disservice.

I went into the back where there were fires in steel cylinders, a bar, and a web of string lights overhead, crossed and pinned along the pergola. I crossed a stone path to the bar where I found a familiar face standing under the web of stars. The platinum blonde starlet that came into view was none other than Elara Carpe. I called her name, and she snapped to attention, darting toward my voice and withdrew the stirring straw from her lips. "Joe Henley!"

She embraced me and made a squealing sound. I had only met her a handful of times before. Elara experienced fame earlier than myself —she was only sixteen years old when she topped the charts. Before she could vote in the country, she had met the president. By the age of eighteen, she was the bestselling artist of the year and the voice of her new generation. I attended her twenty-first birthday.

"How've you been? I saw you at the Oscars!"

"You did?" I asked, genuinely taken aback. Until I realized she was featured on a Best Original Song nomination. She had also been in attendance that night, but I had been just too spaced to notice anyone during the ceremony and we'd likely attended different after-parties. "Oh, yes, you did!" I corrected my tone and laughed distantly.

"Yeah, congratulations, dude," she rang with a bright generosity. She was still such a bubbly spirit, she went against the grain of all the other jaded musicians and industry ghouls still lurking around the world of music—and I stared at her, hoping the industry would never taint this shining soul, a diamond who remained under much pressure. Elara tilted her head, "Who are you here with?"

"Oh—Ah, Ellis Young. The producer," I replied. A grimace instantly appeared on her face, which shocked me as it was the first time I'd seen a note of negativity come over her. I blinked, confused.

"What?" I asked.

"*That* guy," she scoffed. She reset and looked me over until she realized I hadn't known about whatever it was she was talking about. "Joe, he's a fucking creep. I would never be seen talking to that guy in public."

"Why? What did he do?"

"He's always weird around girls in the studio. He's on my list of producers I will never work with. I mean, it's all rumors but I don't want to take any chances."

"Rumors," I repeated. "I haven't heard any of these rumors."

"You're a man. You've had no *reason* to be warned about him. But he can be—very—" she paused. Then, "He can be manipulative. I know you're a good guy so I think you should know about it. Just don't get too close."

I said nothing. I stared at the pale blue gravel until it blurred, not blinking. I couldn't believe what I was hearing. I tried to think back to all the instances where Ellis attempted to sway me toward his desires—the instance at the museum—the wine and hospitality—the housing and the commission. Now, I was at an art show in Brooklyn and frankly, at this point in time, he was my only friend. I had nobody else in the city to rely on and I wondered if the rumors were true, would I have the strength to let him go? I thought if I could ask Betty to let me back with her. I tried to imagine her look of complete dissatisfaction. Elara's laughter ended my fixation, and I returned to the present, away from the contemplations and the theoreticals.

"Sorry," I blurted.

"It's okay," she was giggling, and Elara said, "I'm sure I'll see you again sometime. *Be safe.*" She emphasized her last phrase as she wandered back into a crowd of young actors I'd recognized from a popular streaming show all in their early twenties, sporting threads by Balenciaga, Versace, Gucci. Once I noticed photographers approaching them, I quickly ordered a vodka soda and wandered back into the warehouse with a new shyness I'd acquired following the brief run-in with Elara. I hadn't seen this dark side of Ellis that she spoke of, but I believed Elara. I filed her words within the confines of my mind and kept them close and at the ready.

———

Ellis and I left the event together. I wasn't incredibly vocal on the way home, going completely mute in the cab, thanking the driver quietly and then going up to our apartment with overcoats hooked over our arms; it was time to retire them until next season. It was eleven at night and Ellis went straight for his wine rack to continue the celebration. He withdrew a dashing Cabernet Sauvignon.

"Shall we?"

I wanted to sleep but I found I wasn't tired. Truthfully, I only wanted to sleep so I would stop thinking. Then, with this notation, the idea of wine became all the more appetizing. Ellis poured two glasses and sat beside me on the sofa. We scooped off our weighty boots and rested our socked heels on the coffee table.

"What's on your mind?" he asked. I knew I wouldn't bring up the conversation with Elara, as the information would absolutely be denied. But time was growing, and I hadn't responded so I threw out, "I saw Elara Carpe at the bar. I was just thinking about her."

Ellis swallowed his wine, "Is that right? She's always annoyed me."

"Why?" I asked. His remark was not helping his case, and I felt like a detective filing all my evidence. He shrugged, "Her parents are voice coaches in East Hollywood."

"So?"

"So, she never had to *work* to get where she is. And her music is quite shit, i'n' it? She doesn't even write her own music. She's just another industry plant—and it would be a different conversation if she had an ounce of talent in that tight body." He was already slurring his words, and we were less than half a glass in; I knew he was truthful about not drinking often.

I resorted back to my state of fatigued quiet and as I finished the rest of the bottle, three glasses full, I was drawn out from my silent treatment and into conversation once more. In no time at all, I was lying on my back against the icy hard wood floor, Ellis lying on his bed with his head dipped over the edge, all his red hair cascading down the side and brushing the floor. He had his arms stretched toward the ceiling and in the dark of his room, I watched as his hands twisted around. Contoured configurations. Black talons, rotating and curling. We were discussing the art show and whether parties were worth it or whether creating art was the only true pleasure in life. The conversation shifted, teetered onto yet another white man's meandering lack of awareness, foregrounded by a false philosophical gaze that would cause even Thomas Hobbes to witness what should be the Leviathan of migraines—that of what makes a scene in our lives worthy of pleasure.

"If the experience will not result in pleasure, then why go toward it?" Ellis asked. He had his hand raised in a questioning way. "I believe the only reason to really live—you know, is to find pleasure. That is at the core of the human being. Once we mastered survival and made it fixed, we should focus on the aspects of what makes utopia. Our lives are like archways, and we continue going up until we find pleasure which serves as our keystone, and everything is perfect there. And then, it's all down from that point."

Ellis was staring at his hands, shifting them in the darkness, a silhouette ribbon flipping in the wind. "I think we should all begin to really act on our nature. You're at our keystone now. You must take hold of it before it's too late. Your features will diminish and soon —dust."

I swallowed. I curved my neck, and he watched the veins flex.

"On either end of the arch is suffering and it is all that we must endure," I added.

"Why must we endure suffering?"

"Balance," I argued. "Nature operates wholly on balance. Neither good nor evil, for every pleasure there is suffering. If one could manage to balance the two, pleasure and suffering, I believe it would make for a perfect life."

Ellis scoffed. "Do you hear yourself?"

"I do hear myself and I like the way I sound. It's reminiscent of what Rilke believed," I said, and when I heard myself speaking such formal language, my drunken mind fooled me into believing I was quite wise. Ellis glanced a high brow at me from the top of his bed before we both burst into a fit of laughter and after a minute, it subsided. There was only the chilled room again and Ellis continued his stance, "Pleasure can be as simple as the sun on your face, Joseph, don't you agree?"

"But too much sun will burn your face."

The pause in the conversation let me know he was deep in thought, so I cast my attention to the soundscape of motors and wind on glass. His room had a dead orange light blowing in through his windows from the sodium streetlamps; this pressed on the pine-colored walls, making a hideous combination. The wine had provided a light soothing on my skull though I remained present.

"I guess pleasure must come in short supply then," he said at last. This is what he decided on after a dense effort; I was taken aback by the span he traded for it.

"Right, a balanced supply, you could say. Too much of anything will kill you," I croaked from the floor. I swallowed and became embarrassingly afraid of my own words. Giant thoughts like these became far too overpowering for the consciousness. I watched as Ellis' arms bent and his hands landed at his sides on the bed, making a dud sound.

"And what if someone has only led a life of pleasure?" he asked. The question crawled over my body. I tried to find the answer, but the question was just vague enough to not make complete sense. Someone born into royalty might have only known pleasure. If that were so, I was led to believe the mind would create suffering for itself to endure. The smallest of sufferings were still sufferings. I blinked. "What do you mean?"

"People like you and me. The last decade of our lives has gone without hardship."

I squinted at nobody and replied flatly, "I've experienced hardship."

Ellis twisted around on the mattress, bouncing and landing to look down at me. His face was masked in puddles of shadow, hardly a face and instead light reflected off his eyes. A dark face with two yellow eyes. Long hair curtaining out from the entire horrifying portrait.

"Have you?" Ellis asked. "The rock star who moped through his continental tour and made millions of dollars? The rock star on the cover of every magazine? Who has his face on sweatshirts?"

"You don't know how terrible fame can be. Don't pretend like you know," I graveled.

"You think fame is hardship?" he hissed. I slammed my palms on the wood, raised myself so my face neared his in the inked bedroom.

"Trauma can be found anywhere," I growled.

He scoffed sarcastically and barked back, "*Grow up!* You will never know hardship. *You* will likely never experience true suffering. And for someone to look back on their manicured life with such a bitter taste is *repulsive* to me." He stopped but his darkened figure was stuttering as if he'd meant to say more, and I realized he was holding himself back. He contorted on the bed to lie on his back once more and this allowed him to stare up at the ceiling, which he seemed more interested in. Ellis continued, "You are one of the only people in the world who got to make their art and have it met with high admiration. There are *millions*, maybe even *billions*, who wish to be in that position. And what's more is that once you lost out on that opportunity, you were almost immediately given a new one. From star to maestro, you never slow down. Restless, nobody can deny but fucking ungrateful."

"I don't know how to do anything else!" I yelped out like a child. These were the escaped words before my throat caught. The room felt obliterated, and I noticed my body was trembling, my breath was out of order.

"I know—*believe me*, Joseph, I know—that much is clear to me," Ellis calmed. He continued to speak as he made his way off the bed and dribbled onto the freezing floor beside me. "You are like an angel sent down to give us music. Symphonies. I have always seen what you truly are. One day, you'll have to be sent back but you're here with us now to serve us with sounds that result in *pleasure*." He held onto the final word with a playful tone. He lay next to me, both of us on our backs and stared at each other the best we could through the shadows. By then it was past midnight and the first day of May.

I muttered into the darkness, "You try to paint me as a titan." He shook his head, rocking on the hardwood.

"Perhaps but it will not last, mate," he muttered deeply. "To me, now, in this speck of time, you have met your keystone of beauty and pleasure—" he paused and swallowed. I could hear his tongue moving in his mouth. Then he inhaled and spoke again, "—you are like a god."

———

I was in Velvet Pie the following morning before the sun could wipe the sidewalks, and I kept my chin on my throat, sweeping my heavy boots to the door. I knew the keycode, I allowed myself in and went up to the second floor where I began my day's work on the symphony. I stared out the giant windows for some time, watching as the city was reimagined. Soon, it awakened, and easily the block became increasingly populated. My brain was vacant. I paced the studio for nearly an hour, and ended up recording each violin string as a reference, then put the violin sounds onto an electric keyboard, added effects pedals before I came to the realization that I was forming music in my traditional ways rather than in what would be fit for an orchestra.

I sat at the desktop computer, swirling in the desk chair, and pulled up the score for *Mass Hysteria*. I realized the flow of the music had to follow the movement of the picture. The two were sewn into one another. Yes, each piece did work well enough on its own, but the marriage of picture and score, of light and sound, translated into something special. An emotion conveyed through sensory stimulation. I was able to recall scenes from the film in my mind as I listened to the score.

I looked back at the instruments, the countless crafts that sat around the room, quietly patient, and I was suddenly afraid. I felt more alone with the army of musical tools oddly—the blank canvas—infinite possibilities. What would I create? How could I create?

I was pondering for some time longer when I heard the bottom door chomp; someone was carrying up the stairs toward the second story of the studio. A moment later, Ellis entered the studio still in his signature tan trench coat (despite it now being early June), open and showing his faded Sublime t-shirt tucked into his bleached Levi's, shades on his eyes and hair in a tight bun. He held two coffees from a local shop at the end of the block and handed one of them to me with a greeting.

"How is everything this morning?" he asked.

"Going well—Yeah, really well," I replied, lying to him but more to myself. He sat in another rolling chair and examined the program I had opened with only a recorded arpeggio from the sampled violin. He made no expression, as if he didn't recognize what I'd done. "Can I hear it?"

"I don't have enough yet for it to be heard," I said and felt small. He nodded, removed his sunglasses, and folded them onto his white tee. He sipped his coffee and made a breathy sound as if he'd been refreshed by the flavor. He leaned back in the seat and started, "I wanted to talk to you about something."

I removed my hand from the mouse and looked at him, a searing anxiety began to clench my chest at the thought of confrontation.

Had he found out about what Elara Carpe and I had discussed? Did he know for the last third of the year I had written nothing? It would be impossible yet in the heat of a real anxious panic, anything feels dreadfully possible.

"The first week of July, or just after, I was hoping to gather everyone and spend a week upstate," he said finally, and my chest relaxed.

"Everyone?" I questioned.

"All the members of Artist's Haven, mate. Might be nice to get out of the city for a while. You know, have a week off with some peace and quiet," he said and reached for the pack of cigarettes behind one of the computer monitors.

"Yeah—yeah, that would be nice. Where upstate?"

He lit the cigarette. Puffed. He drew it away and held it queerly with his elbow on the armrest. "Just outside of Hudson, New York. *Bladen* is its name, built in 1830, sixty-four acres of land. There's a country house on the hillside, very gothic indeed, made of that classic red brick. *Surely* haunted. Anyway, I bought the house just last year and haven't been back in nearly six months. It could be a good place to go and meet the other artists, make some memories, live out some of our Bohemian fantasies, aye?"

I shuffled the new information in my head, sorting it until all of it made sense. I furrowed, "You bought a country house?"

"I bought it. In full, no less. It was not cheap, let me tell you. It really made a dent in me, but all will be recovered. A country house getaway sounded like a lovely idea to me. It's a five-bedroom house, so someone would have to double up—likely two of the girls but I don't mind taking the couch either—it comes in just over a thousand square meters."

"How big is that?" I asked shyly.

"For your overcooked American brain, that's roughly eleven thousand square feet. This studio is thirteen hundred square feet. Anyway, would you be interested in the idea? A retreat with the other artists in the program? You know Yvette already well enough but there is still

Sumitra, Katya—and Bardo. I'd have to check all their schedules to get this arranged. What do you think?"

I nodded, looking out at the floor. I thought of how I would like to meet the other artists. Perhaps the country would give me some form of inspiration as well for the symphony. As of that moment, I had nothing but an artificial violin. I wondered, too, if these new artists would become new friends and whether I would allow myself to befriend them.

All my friends throughout life had proven temporary and I developed a sharp distrust for anyone I deemed kind. They might be helpful, however. I sighed and sipped my coffee before I agreed. Ellis nodded, pleased by my decision, and I was wholly unaware of my agreement to stay in what I would soon regard a makeshift Hell.

II

The Absinthe Rinse

The Brooklyn art show was a massive success for the young artist; Yvette was only twenty-two years of age and had sufficiently crafted an established name for herself as an artist on the rise. She was mentioned in the following week's edition of *The New Yorker*. She bought a single copy and opted to do the crossword puzzle in the back rather than read her cover piece. "No need to read. I know who I am," she'd said to me as an explanation. I came to appreciate this petite French woman from a town of only thirty thousand, how she'd become a viral sensation on the internet and brought herself over to America to push herself and see how far she could take her regime as an independent artist. She had the stamina and drive to pursue these things, all while maintaining her composure as a mature young woman, free-spirited and playful. She reminded me mostly of Sophia when our band was just beginning to sculpt itself into something larger than any of us.

Someone over Ellis' shoulder read *The New Yorker* edition featuring the piece on Yvette Adair. We were in a steaming diner on Broadway called Cozy Soup & Burger, and we both powered through Reuben sandwiches, then leaned back in our seats with our interlaced fingers laid on our chests. I had a peanut butter milkshake, but was quietly crossed on the taste and ordered a glass of water. Ellis sucked at his strawberry milkshake, and I watched the pink lower in the tall glass. It was the middle of May, and we were killing time until we would return to the studio and then head to a party in the Upper East Side later in the night—the party would be held in the apartment of two lovers both named Kevin, who were coincidentally both photographers.

"Excuse me."

I looked to my left to see a woman I guessed to be in her mid-twenties, with rosy cheeks and her phone gripped tightly in her hands. She stood on her toes and rocked back on her heels. The woman spoke with certainty, "Joe Henley." And she giggled in a nervous high pitch. I was perplexed and wiped my face with a napkin, agreeing with her, "Yeah—yes, that's me. Hi."

"Would you mind if I got a picture?" she asked. She turned in her brows as if she were in distress somehow. I shrugged my shoulders, and my chair honked out behind me. I leaned over her shoulder and extended my hand as if waving at our digital reflections on her tiny glowing device. Four photos snapped onto her camera roll in a matter of maybe a second. I blinked, perplexed by how fast it had happened. I turned and looked down at the woman with her curled blonde hair tucked behind a black sweatband.

"I'm a really big fan. I've been listening to your music since I was in high school." More giggling before, "Alright, well, I don't want to disturb you too much. Enjoy your food, it was great to meet you."

I told her likewise and scooted my chair back into the table where I sighed and sipped more of the peanut butter milkshake, then shifted back toward my glass of water. Ellis cocked his head, "It's been a while since I've seen that happen."

The wording of his phrase made me startled before I recalled that, yes, I had been living with him for several months by this point—I looked out the window at Broadway.

"Fame eats you alive," Ellis said. I turned and he looked at me in a way that seemed intrinsic. He was lost on me, trying to discover something I wasn't saying aloud. "Does it bother you that you might go the rest of your life as the face of a few old songs?"

"I wouldn't necessarily look at it that way," I said, offended, and drank my water.

"No, mate, don't be cross! I just mean, you have a *real* legacy, you know? Maybe you didn't intend for it to go this way but look at that, it's real. You're now somewhat infamous, yeah? It's going to go on without you too, hope you know that."

I swallowed and allowed my glass to click the counter where the ice whirlpooled and twinkled on the glass walls. I sniffled and looked out at the myriads of faces in the diner, and quickly spotted the young woman who was still eyeing me but was now seated with a man her age. I looked back at Ellis, "What do you mean?"

"Every time you listen to *Fly Me to the Moon*, you're listening to Sinatra speak from the past. A dead man sings to us while we all dance. A man lost to time but a piece of himself lingers on. He cheated death in the most beautiful way possible. By leaving something behind for all of us to enjoy, and we all care for that piece of him," he said and picked at the leftover fries on his plate. He called them chips and offered one to me since my plate was completely cleaned and topped with a crumpled napkin.

"That's a romantic notion I suppose," I mustered as my response.

Ellis, while chewing and a balled fist over his mouth, "But I understand your notion as well, mate. The whole *everyone knows you, but nobody knows you*—it must be *haunting*—fame is a disease. Sure. But you caught it, my friend. It may lessen but it will never go away for good. This is who you are and always will be. You have a presence in our society and frankly, that comes with expectations to uphold! You have the swagger but *fuck,* man, when are you going to shave that awful beard?"

I leaned back in my seat. "You seem to think you have some sort of say in my life," I said. I stared at him, and he stopped chewing.

"I didn't mean—" His voice broke off and went pale.

"It's okay," I replied, saving him, and continued, "People so often forget that I am a real person with real thoughts—you know, *ideas,* a daily schedule, sleep medicine, *anxiety,* desires, all that. Anyone on the street will say what they think I should do next, but nobody considers the fact that I have to take a shit in the morning like anyone else."

Ellis broke into a deep laughter, his low voice chuckling, and it became quickly infectious. Ellis recovered and said, "Pity though—to grow old and change physically with all eyes on you—now *that* is haunting. Something so beautiful should wither in solitude."

I was in no mood for a philosophical talk at the moment. Sometimes we chose to speak like poets or figureheads of the Enlightenment but other times we talked like teenage boys. I tried to steer the conversation toward the party and whether Ellis planned on staying out all night. Ellis steered back, saying, *"Joseph, I'm serious!* Beauty begins with our senses. And light travels faster than sound. My eyes see something beautiful before I hear the sounds you create. How I see you is how the rest of the entire world sees you. But it will all change with time. Luckily, you've unknowingly cast a line with your music, and suddenly your beauty has a chance at an everlasting existence."

"Yeah, my physical condition is completely and entirely impermanent. Thanks for reminding me. Now, let's talk about something else, please."

Ellis grinned, patient and again, studying. "Fine. Do as you'd like. It was just a thought." He plucked at his plate of chips again but stopped a moment later and folded his arms. I watched him as he spaced out on the edge of the table.

"It seems my fame is more important to you than it is to me."

"*Oh,* don't blame me! I will *never* have what you have," he said, nearly laughing, as if what I'd said was so absurd.

I tossed air in return, thrown off by the comment. I replied, "And I can't have what *you* have! Privacy and fortune are two things I have either forgotten or never truly had. I used to get bombarded by photographers every morning while only being able to afford a single bedroom apartment for myself."

Ellis lifted my napkin and placed his plate on mine, pre-bussing the table and sighed thinly; he caught the paper check at the corner of the table. He examined it and stood, rounding the table, reaching into his trousers for his wallet but leaned toward my ear, and said, "Then I suppose the only thing we both have in common is that we worked our asses off to get where we are and are still unsatisfied. Aye?"

He tilted his head, awaiting a response, but I was too perplexed. He gave up and went to the register to pay. I hadn't understood why he was pushing his sentiment so furiously on me, to the point it felt nearly scripted. The walk back to Velvet Pie was relaxed but I still felt a soft tension between us. It would go ignored, resulting in an unresolved note. I would rewind his words in my dome like a recorder played back and wonder what he meant with his accusations and blames. I caught what I thought to be jealousy by his tone and phrasing. A fuse was lit.

————

The 16th of July was when all the artists were expected to arrive upstate. I was eager to leave by this point as I could relate every city block back to Autumn in some fashion; it brought too much heartache to revive those intimate moments. Not to mention my wandering consciousness. At this time, I was able to focus on anything but music. I had been packed for a full week before we were to leave, and my suitcase perched upright on its four wheels at the edge of my bed. I had nothing better to do with my time.

Yvette opted for the train while Ellis offered to drive me to cut the time and possibly arrive before the rest of the guests. "I need to know soon, mate. I'm not to be late to my own event. I don't wish to appear as a bad host."

Of course, I went with Ellis, and we were outside of his apartment in Queens with our suitcases in the morning mist. He had his vehicle brought from the parking garage where it mostly stayed; he had a dainty silver sports car, a Porsche 550 Spyder from 1955. There were only ninety of this particular model, manufactured by Porsche between 1953 to 1956—Ellis had one with an aluminum body (not the original aluminum, his had been restored by hand), cream leather seats and very little room for our luggage. I asked him about what we'd do with our luggage, to which he replied, "We'll just get there! Better for us to be there and worry about that later."

I suppose he could tell this explanation wasn't good enough for me as he slouched with both palms pressed into the perfectly gleaming exterior; the car's key ticking on the hood between his thumb and forefinger and twirls of ginger hair falling in front of his squinted eyes. He licked his lips and decided, "Look, I'll have one of the grounds people come out and grab them. 'Sound alright, mate? I'll give them a key and have them deliver our luggage out to Bladen before nightfall. How does that sound?"

I nodded and together we took our suitcases back up to his apartment without a word. How had he not thought of this sooner? Ellis was the kind of man who had everything planned out and knew the several variable outcomes of any given situation. He was methodical and this was unlike him. We climbed in the car and Ellis withdrew and masked a pair of round sunglasses of a retro punk aesthetic. He grinned at me horrifically with the rounded ink-black voids over his sockets. We cruised out of the city and once we crossed the Whitestone Bridge, Ellis launched the car as fast as it could go, paying no mind to traffic regulations.

"It's a racing car, Joseph! This is what it was made for!" I recall his tantalizing guffaw as his foot pressed the gas pedal to the floor and the four-cylinder boxer engine thrashed, he skidded between the cars on the freeway, our hair flickered and trembled in the manufactured wind. I tried to keep my face below the windshield, which ended just over the steering wheel, as the rest of the car was completely open. I tried slouching down my leather seat in an attempt to stop my eyes from watering in the slicing breeze. I glanced at Ellis and to my complete lack of surprise found that he was thoroughly enjoying himself and I was in awe that we never got pulled over the entire two hours it took to drive out to the country.

Finally, after two eager hours of relentless speed, we arrived before noon at a towering cast iron fence, taller than either of us. The wheels slowed to an inching crawl up to a gate and the wheels crackled on the dusty gravel. Ellis hummed, then threw the car in park, hopped out of the driver's door and pushed open each of the black bar doors, and once they were spread enough, he shuffled back to the car and trailed us inside without closing the gates behind us. To my surprise, there was no house in sight—it was all nature as far as the eye could see in the unraveling dawn of summer—fuzzy fields that swayed their green blades to and fro as flowers trekked seeds in the wind and bumblebees hovered over them and sang their baritone solos. We pushed up the hill in the tiny roadster like a hunk of steel being tugged up an emerald slope.

As we approached the top of the hillside, the gravel road seemed to flatten a bit as anticipation for the house began trembling inside me. To my left, I heard, "You know, this is the same exact car James Dean died in." It took a full moment to piece each of these words together and discover the meaning. Once I had a grasp on what Ellis was saying, I was baffled. I shot my gaze from the world and onto Ellis, off the wonder and toward hideous shock.

"What?" I yelped.

"I said James Dean died in this car! Not this exact car but this model. A compelling feature for collectors of antique vehicles, surely. Do you like cars?" he asked, and his dark reflective spectacles were facing me, so I looked away, back at the world and a feeling inside of me suggested we were close to the mansion.

"Not really," I said, frustrated by him. He'd again caused annoyance to stir inside me, but I hadn't had much time to dwell before around a bend, the gravel path ended and became a brick laid driveway with three foot hedges running on either side of the car; as we rolled up the center drive toward the house, a streaming green aisle led us toward what lay in our futures. And there up ahead was the formidable estate—Bladen, the hulking Gothic Revival country house —an imposing structure three stories high. As the Porsche Spyder grew closer still, the presentation of this staggering front facade provided more details as my fascination continued to dilate. I noticed the house was made of brilliant clay brick and featured steep pitched roofing over countless gables, coming in at inverted V's and connected with cross gables and chimneys. Had the pointed mansion been eclipsed in a shallow darkness, I might have thought I was seeing violent mountain peaks huddled together in a brooding orientation.

We came upon the circular driveway and the sports car chugged about the brick path, around an expertly attended flower bed at the iris of this masonry drive. I noticed the deviating paths that led down the hillside and toward a greenhouse while another went around back to the courtyard, and yet ahead of us was the house. Bladen in all its indomitable power. I climbed out of the vehicle, standing high, higher than before and squeezed my eyes at the edifice that would shock Hercules; I could not see any of the black shingles that slanted down the gabled roofs from where I stood at that moment, far too tall—far too menacing—everything was stretched into the blushing clouds.

"Come on, mate," Ellis was saying, and my neck navigated back to a normal line of sight, away from the highly cocked angle I'd shot up in a weary attempt to analyze the structure. "You'll have plenty of time to gawk at the exterior," he paused. He kicked up the stoned front steps, his wind-slicked hair jostling as he went, and his beige trench rumpled in his self-made wind. Ellis stopped at the front door and pressed his weight into the curling door handle, "But you really must see the interior first."

I followed him into an open space, and I learned this to be the foyer. Orbed ceilings with an ornamental finish. Velvet drapes. Custom crown molding. Two separate staircases dressed in a floral red carpeting laced together at a landing and led up together into the second floor. There were lamps at the base of the stairs, just gleaming orbs of a yolk light, and above was a terrific, golden chandelier. It hung low on its chain and was frightfully large, I feared it was larger than the car I traveled in. There were three archways, I noted, one to the right leading into a muddled room of green, one ahead into what appeared to be a sort of living room, generally a large opening with natural light, and one to the left, leading down a hallway into the kitchen. There were suitcases upright on their tiny wheels and to our right in the green room, through the arch, sat two strangers, peering over their shoulders. Ellis led me down the three short steps into what was called the gathering room, and I was introduced to two of the artists who were also part of the New York Artist's Haven. The wonder of how they'd gotten in without a key split momentarily but had to be replaced with a cordial air as it was then time to introduce myself.

"Well, well, look who we have here!" Ellis slammed into an embrace with the man who'd been seated in a sand-colored armchair. A tinge of anger at their companionship winced beneath my skin. Ellis buckled around to face me standing stupid in the room with my arms limp at my sides as he charmed with a hand over his hair. "Joseph! Introductions are in place. Firstly, I'd like you to meet the wonderful woman of architecture, the lovely Katya Baronova," he held on the final syllable over her name as she stood from the opposing chair. Katya was a young lady with long blonde hair down her back, notably sharp eyes with an icy hue, and her head so slightly tilted back. Sharp cheekbones against a round face—it was generally safe to assume she weighed less than a hundred pounds. She had frightfully pale skin, so pale it neared gray. Still, she smiled as I approached her with her open palm; we shook hands, and I noted her skeletal grip.

"Pleasure to meet you," she said. She was Russian, a fact immediately given away by the thick accent she sported, and the way in which she said *pleasure*. "Joseph is your name?" She'd added zest to my name, especially near the end, a sound I quite liked and I nodded.

"Yes, it's lovely to meet you, Katya," I said and did my best to return the strict tongue on the consonants of her name. She grinned harder, either impressed or embarrassed. "You're from Russia?"

"Yes. Not far from Moscow," said Katya. "And you are from here? American?"

"Yes," I answered and again told her how lovely it was to meet her. I watched her move as she made her way back to her seat; the man gripping Ellis shed himself and was powering toward me.

"Oh—yes, here he comes," Ellis was saying. The man was much taller than me with titillating shoulders, broad like a moose, and a stance that would be more in line with a boxer. He was a massive superhuman, one fit for Hollywood or professional wrestling, but instead, he was here. Moreover, he had a buzz cut. A thick black beard, precisely shaped, Roman. He had olive toned skin, dark and smooth. He flashed a wild smile at me, had a deeply webbed scar etched from his right ear, across his cheek that stopped at his right nostril.

"This is a dear friend of mine, Bardo," said Ellis.

And Bardo captured me in his lumbering arms, tight to the point I might have squeaked and tried to play it off as something else. He let up so I could breathe again, and slapped his hands on my shoulders. I looked up at him, "Bardo—*Bardo?*"

"Let's just say Bardo. Bardo the Sculptor," he replied.

I blinked. "Okay. Where are you from, Bardo the Sculptor?"

He grinned and I saw his brilliant white teeth. And it registered that they were fake. Veneers and expensive at that. "Belgium! Have you been?" asked Bardo.

"Yes. I've played shows there before—Oh, what is that place called? The Forest National," I recalled. Bardo's face lit with hectic joy, practically bouncing. He stuck a fat finger at my face and practically tapped my nose. "I like you, Joseph."

Bardo gave a fatherly pat against my cheek and returned to where he and Katya had been seated. I joined them at their arrangement and Ellis asked if we'd care for tea. I took him up on his offer as we awaited the remaining two artists, Yvette and Sumitra.

———

After an hour or so of waiting and getting to know one another, Yvette and Sumitra summited the hilltop in a bright yellow cab—a dot in the distance like a bumblebee crawling along the field. The driver parked the cab just beyond the Porsche Spyder and proceeded to help the young ladies with their luggage as they entered the foyer.

"And there they are!" Ellis chirped. He placed his teacup back on its saucer on the table and stood to properly greet the two young women entering the gathering room. Both were dashing their sights around the beastly interior until Ellis brought Yvette in for a brisk hug. "Everyone, this is Yvette Adair. She's a remarkable painter; the best I've had the pleasure of meeting. I cannot wait for you all to see her work."

Yvette met the other artists and upon noticing me, provided a knowing nod, "It's nice to see you again." We shook hands. Then, Ellis introduced the final artist, a pleasant young lady with carved features. Thick jet hair and matching eyebrows and the most curious amber shine to her eyes. I tried not to stare at them too closely as she placed her hand on mine.

"Sumitra. It's nice to meet you," she said. She had an accent I did not at first recognize until Ellis provided, "And this is Sumitra Patani, a Hindu poet and she's absolutely astounding at literature both in Hindi and English." She grinned at me and two dimples pierced her cheeks.

"I also speak Urdu. And Latin, which helps when I'm in France and Germany," she said. I tilted my head and asked, "Where are you from then?" Sumitra giggled and reset herself. She was the tallest of the ladies and I was desperate not to get lost in the raven quality of her eyes.

"I'm from Dehradun, a city in India. But I have been living in Paris for the last six years. I moved to Lower Manhattan just after the new year," Sumitra explained. I nodded and looked her over. She was such a sight to behold. Again, I expressed how lovely it was to meet her, and she went on to formally introduce herself to the others. Finally, all the artists were acquainted with one another. In the gathering room sat the Architect, the Sculptor, the Composer, the Painter, the Poet. And Ellis served as the Curator. Once all of us had learned each other's names and faces to match, it was time to observe the secrets of the building.

"Let's take a tour, then, shall we?" Ellis hummed to us and shed his overcoat. He tossed it on the back of his chair and tucked his sleeves up to his elbows. We followed Ellis back into the foyer so the gathering room with a jade theme was behind us. Through the center archway and between the two staircases, one could find themselves in the Commons—a devastatingly vast space, likely the size of Ellis' entire apartment back in Queens. It was a space with plenty of ornate seating arrangements, a Bechstein grand piano, a fireplace and canary silk embedded into the wall paneling to match the lemony drapes of the space. Ornamented ceilings and silver candlesticks. Ellis led us out through a side entry and into a short and cramped hallway that led into the dining hall. This dining hall featured a stretched cedar table capable of seating twenty guests and a fantastic golden chandelier overhead. Beyond this hall was the kitchen with all new wooden countertops, eggshell cabinets and a charming royal blue accent on the back wall. There was a reading nook cutout with natural light splayed out on the space, a gorgeous golden sink, a breakfast table, and black and white checkered floors. We followed Ellis out and into the cramped hallway. Through said hallway, we passed a bath, a dumb-waiter, a washing and drying room.

We made our way up the stairs onto the second floor with a western corridor and an eastern corridor. Through the eastern corridor—first, on the left, was the library. The library was a dim space with short aisles of books; shelves wrapped around each of the five walls, reaching up into the ceiling with editions. Everything from fiction to religion to manuals to biographies were accessible on these built-in cases, complete with the rolling ladder. There was no over-head lighting. Instead, the ceiling was hand painted, a fresco with a dreamy depiction of cherub baby angels flitting through a patch of clouds. There, too, was a fireplace, tables set with chess, all lit by lamps that lined the walls or the silver light that came in from the windows with the curtains drawn back.

Still in the eastern corridor were two bedrooms, one that faced the front of the house and one that faced the back of the house, over-seeing the courtyard. The bedrooms were generally colorless, instead opting for the tan stoney walls up to the vaulted ceiling where wooden beams stretched across in parallel formations. Cedar book-cases mounted on the walls, plus brilliant desks and various seating arrangements from sofas to desk chairs to ottomans. A magnificent bed at the center of the room. Four wooden columns at each of the corners raised the bed high off the ground. Three doors connected to the bedroom, leading to a private bath with dark marble finishing, a linen closet, and a rounded balcony. The bedrooms were identical—Sumitra claimed the one facing the front and I took the bedroom facing the back and the courtyard—cluttered with marble statues and walkways—and a large pool, which from the second story window seemed more like a rectangle shard of glass lying on a stone slab.

The western corridor had three other bedrooms, one belonging entirely to Bardo the Sculptor, another to be shared by Katya and Yvette, and the final bedroom was left to Ellis.

Up on the third and final floor, the attic level was a space where the ceiling peaked. Two windows showed the front of the house and there existed two more windows at the back. The space was more akin to a hallway with a bent ceiling—there were no walls—wooden floors and wooden beams alike, all covered in tapestries and rugs and hanging lamps. Exposed brick from the chimney carrying heat out of the house. Space heaters and box fans huddled in the back for anyone's use. It felt as if I were standing in a 14th century structure. There were easels and desks. A double bass rested against the slanted ceiling before it reached the floor. There was a table with magazines, a bottle of Xanax, and a bottle with a fifth left of Jim Beam. "I call this space *the Dram-Attic,*" Ellis snickered to us. My face slouched.

The excitement was enough to make traveling back down to the first floor a real chore, as I wanted to run about in this beautiful palace, my home for the following ten days. Everything from the light fixtures to the rugs, to the floral tapestries and oil paintings lining the walls, all of it was of another time—of another life—one I now wanted to live. A gothic erection in what would be better referred to as a castle than a house. I ran my fingers along the old wood paneling, where the tips never once caught on a dent or a bite. It was preposterous how each intricate detail had either been cared for or replenished as soon as something chipped or aged. After reviewing the courtyard, the pool, the greenhouse, and the fairy garden, I followed them back to the gathering room where we all shared a glass of champagne from behind the bar in celebration of our arrival, and the artists of NYAH were officially together. We'd explored the house inside and out and time had passed us so quickly—it was approaching evening already—the tour was so exciting the day diminished like how sand drains a palm.

"Right, well, I'm off to freshen up. Joseph, your luggage has made it to your quarters. If anyone needs anything, we have phone lines in each room. Dial for any service needs—or if you want to call each other, by all means—this space belongs to you now," Ellis said all of this as he stood up and placed his empty glass on the bar cart. Ellis crossed to the double doors and heaved them open; they croaked a tired sound and he tilted his head, seemingly he was dissatisfied by the imperfection. He turned to face the five of us, "Again, I can't express how thrilled I am for you all to be here. This has been a dream of mine for quite some time. So—thank you for coming—and I'll see you all at supper." He bowed and exited, his branching figure disappeared into the dim hall and then faded out into nothing.

I turned and faced the other four artists; we were now either glaring amongst ourselves or staring longingly into our empty glasses. I, too, had fallen speechless with the pseudo-strangers and wished for Ellis to return immediately until Bardo spoke up. "I understand you score films?" I looked to my left to see Bardo with his legs crossed and eyeing me with a hooked brow.

"Yes, that's right."

"Do you enjoy doing this?"

"It beats the alternative."

Bardo leaned forward in his seat. "And what would that be?"

I scoffed, "I suppose suicide." I smudged my expression and compared mine with the others, but I discovered a room of blank dissatisfaction. I thought my remark humorous, but the room was entirely quiet. I could have explained the remark was all in good fun, a joke with a haunting truth. But the rooted voice inside of me, like a tick in the nihilistic skin, thought: *no, I should have liked to be alive and to be happy.* I sighed and downed the rest of my champagne after allowing the rippling regret to devour my shape.

"The house turns one hundred and fifty this year," Yvette chimed.

"How do you know this?" Katya asked with squinted interest. Yvette shrugged, "When Sumitra and I were walking up, one of the bricks had 1877 carved into it. I can only assume it was when the house was built." I raised a brow, briefly judging her by this too quick of a conclusion before I gave up on their conversation about the house and its history, and all of it spilled from my ears as I drifted into boredom. I began to learn how each floorboard clicked into the other. What would you call these curling shapes on the rug? I grew so sick with my state of mind that I eventually excused myself and went up to bed.

In the eastern corridor, I went through the door after the library, where I found my bedroom with my luggage neatly assembled near the foot of the bed. I untied my boots, one after the other, stepped out of them and crawled like a child onto the raised bed. I pressed my face into the pillow and allowed myself to cry. The tears dropped into the fabric where they grew into a dark blotch, and I whimpered as quietly as I could despite being secluded in the corridor. I thought of Vivian and Luca, my dearest souls and how I missed them so completely. What was I doing here? I should have been with them, wherever they were. And why had they left me?

I missed writing compositions for Conrad March. I missed writing for Luca, who when I'd tried to call him only the day before, had not picked up the phone. This wretched feeling in my gut, a sunken ache—as if I were hungry with no desire to eat—and I lied still, pouting softly into the pillow, nearly unable to move. My face was permanently fixed on an expression of anguish as all I could see were the memories: Vivian in our house or Luca in the studio. And Autumn, how I felt so wrong for abusing our friendship because I was lonely. Worse than alone, for alone I could bear. It was the loneliness I battled, resulting in useless victors.

I wanted to call Autumn and apologize to her so we could move on and truly become the friends we were so good at being. I didn't want to impose. Everything felt out of place, and I was homesick, a feeling I knew well from my short-lived career as a rockstar—and more, I missed the people who had once cared about me. Where had that care gone? The ones who used to hug me, kiss me, embrace me for who I was, now I could no longer speak to them.

They were the most familiar strangers. I felt weakened by these memories—how could they possibly be true?—and yet all the more battered. Callused. I was not to let anyone get that close to me again. All I wanted was to be back in the city, and to get an evening drink with Autumn in Brooklyn, or to attend a game night at my sister's apartment in Harlem, or to discover a new diner with Luca and discuss cinema, or even to mess around on a synthesizer with Ellis in Velvet Pie. I would do whatever it took to get back home. I felt sick.

———

It was a full day after we'd settled into our newly opulent environment when Ellis sat at the head of the dining table; where once lay sliced duck breast in a heaping slather of blackberry pan sauce, mashed potatoes and green beans, now only vacant dishes. We were all full, bolstering our bloated stomachs, tipping the back legs of our chairs and holding the rounded edge of the long table, of which only six chairs were taken out of the twenty. The walls of the room were lined with more elaborate paintings, each with their custom frames, glinting by way of the exploding chandelier, which looked like a hundred golden arms each with their own tinsel. I tried not to make my gaze too noticeable, as I wanted to fit in and enjoy the moment; to be the example young artist; the bohemian with negative cares but it was all too fantastic to pass.

"Everyone," Ellis boomed, his tone was calm, but his voice projected about the space, surely hitting each original painting pinned about the walls and bouncing back in a loop. He smiled at us, myself and Sumitra to my right; across from me was Bardo, then Katya, then Yvette.

"I thought it might be beneficial if we took a chance to better get to know one another. Perhaps we could have a game night, or just drink and chat in the gathering room?" Ellis tried to gauge all our expressions, compiling an answer for himself before any of us even went verbal. He explained further, "I don't know, it might be nice.

We've all become acquainted well enough, so why not have a drink and become friends?"

Ellis surveyed the room, and eventually received approvals to his idea. Everything about Ellis seemed precise, and with such a coordinated nature, he became a brilliant host. He was still the closest thing I had to a friend at that time. Everyone was quite kind, and admittedly brilliant minds. I wanted desperately to become friends with each of them, though I refused to let anyone close enough to garner trust. I remained quiet for the duration of our dinner and chose observance and passivity. There between the lines I existed, and I remained.

After dessert, we all decided on a time to reconvene, and so, as my clock perched at the corner of my desk struck 8, I leapt from my chair and rushed down the hall toward the gathering room. I worried I might get lost on the way, but I felt certain it was just to the left of the foyer. I knew certainly to the right was the tearoom and to the left—I rounded the corner—through the archway were the other artists resting in armchairs, or sofas, feet pointed out on intricately patterned rugs.

The gathering room featured more chandeliers, although these were updated, having pointed round bulbs stretched in an Art Deco fashion. It reminded me of a club although this was far more lavish. I could see the primary color for this room was green—emerald drapes pinned around the walls and pine-colored ceiling tiles—everywhere there were golden accents.

"Well, we thought you might not show," Bardo chirped. I glanced at the room's clock on the mantle. Only two minutes had passed, and I tried not to grimace. Ellis stood behind the bar, his hair up in a bun and a cocktail shaker thrown up near his shoulder; he tossed it about for a moment before he poured the contents into a martini glass.

"Joseph!" Ellis barked. He laughed and waved a hand at Bardo, "No, no, you're right on time. Why don't you take this one?" Ellis asked with the martini held out. "What is it?"

"*Corpse Reviver,* that's what it's called, yes?" He squinted at the artists and Sumitra and Yvette were doubled over with their cocktails held pompous, nodding, and laughing. Ellis looked back at me. "Yes, well, this drink is everywhere throughout art history, or should I say the *ingredients* are everywhere. Come! Have a sip, won't you?"

I stared at the glass. The murky green-yellow fog watered down. As soon as it met my tongue, I learned a new taste of wet citrus, and of a strange black licorice. It coated my mouth the way tea would when mixed with cream, and down it went, medicine-like. It was herbal, but a great alcohol sting bit my throat. I shuddered.

"What is that?" I asked.

"Yes, well it's a shot of gin, shot of vermouth, shot of lemon juice and it's supposed to be an absinthe rinse, but I get to be a bit forgiving with the proportions. It's normally a more yellowish tinge but here it looks—what would you call this? Yvette, what would you say? Chartreuse?"

"Suppose so," I mumbled and channeled my tongue around in a motion between my cheeks, embracing each flavor, pulling them out as if they were instruments in an orchestration.

"*Absinthe,*" I muttered, repeatedly. I swirled the glass and saw the legs of green lining the sides. I knew of absinthe, the highly alcoholic drink, too high to drink on its own. A brilliant, glinting green. The drink of choice for poets and painters.

"From Van Gogh to Rimbaud, from Manet to Verlaine—absinthe was their drink. Next round, I'll show you the absinthe spoon, a remarkable technology," Ellis said with a half shot of the elixir sloshing at the bottom of a glass, a melted gem. He tipped the shot back and took it clean down his throat and rattled his head around, then growled with his head down. He stood up straight and sucked air, then spoke, "Tonight, I'll drink until the green fairy shows herself!"

I chuckled at his attitude. I couldn't believe it. This was a wholly different version of Ellis than I'd ever seen before. I'd only seen him drink wine up until this point—aside from our rare nights out at Vetro—he seemed to have disarmed his reservations in exchange for a more extroverted demeanor. I thought it impossible until this moment when he made everyone in the gathering room double with laughter at his expressive, pantomime features.

I, too, noticed that I was enjoying the cocktail, and Ellis brought out the absinthe spoon from a drawer, a floral metal utensil with prominent slits in the palm of it. The whole spoon rested across the diameter of the glass, already green with a shot of absinthe, and he placed a sugar cube on the spoon. He began to pour water over the little utensil, and the sugar cube melted away through the slits.

"That's it. It's ready to drink," Ellis grinned.

I blinked as I swallowed and hid a cringe, but the claws of the drink were unavoidable and terrible. The taste was much stronger, very bitter, even more tea-like, curiously. The drink nearly glowed, like a potion of yellow moonlight, and its breath killed my own. The devil's tea. A film coated my teeth and gums. I drank the glass and downed the final fourth of it and was met with applause from my audience, the clergy of artists.

Ellis prepared another, spilling water and alcohol across the custom espresso bar top. We laughed, and I was slipping off the leather stool. Between the absinthe's sting, its sterile poison with muddy flavor, and my drift from a melancholy mind, I found myself quickly becoming untethered—obliterated in the world of crazed Bohemia—soon enough, I would not remember anything but snap-shots like faded film.

The room went hot and lopsided. I recall my head heaving and crashing in glorious motion, drunk and detached; I watched the furni-ture float in my peripheral. Something happened but I was far too adrift. Unconscious while awake. I stared at the ceiling and saw flashes of hair, and felt my body become cold. I recall the darkened lighting and the fury of a lightning storm within the room and finding the many shades of flesh across my face.

I remember the flesh and the voices and the tastes through a speckled recollection. The harrowing tempo of some thumping, some muted bass kick, and I wasn't sure if it was from the space or all in my head. Between the heads and bodies and pleasures and sufferings, I sat in the eye of the hurricane for only a moment. I neared a feeling that existed outside of the human body, existed outside of our shells of flesh and mind. I may have drifted too far out; I may have located a realm beyond my soul in my demolition. My brain lifted in a graceful flow, riding the auroras down their glowing roads toward the heavens. Perhaps I was reborn.

———

When I awoke in the morning, I noticed first how wet I was. I was smothered in sweat; there was a pressure in my nasal cavity, a splitting headache, and a rotten taste in my mouth. Then, I blinked into vision the hardening window frame, a block of ocean foam, and to my left across the sofa, Ellis curled into an armchair while reading a brittle paperback of *Lolita*. A sea of sleeping bodies lay between us. There, too, was a monkey cooing and chirping. Its head lodged in a tennis shoe, then withdrew and sprang onto the end table, nearly tipping the vase of daffodils to the floor. It teetered and resolved itself—no smithereens.

"You're awake," he whispered. Ellis wore his signature charmed grin. I tried to mirror his face as realistically as I could manage, my left cheek pushed into a throw pillow. He sprang from where he was in the chair. He left the room and I listened as his feet tapped on the floors. I wondered at the monkey who was still curiously picking through the gathering room's many trinkets and furnishings, likely an aristocratic and eclectic reincarnation of a jungle for the young, black furred capuchin. His white head and shoulders stuffed into a sculpture of what appeared to be a copper-plated interpretation of female genitalia; I couldn't know for certain until Bardo woke, who was asleep on the wood floor. His head rested on Sumitra's chest, rising and falling.

The image of my fellow artists entangled on the floor invoked the look of nymph-like creatures, except these sleeping animals were too comparable to that of gods. I watched them with pure infatuation and carefully I sketched them into a deeply inked memory, but closer still I could see that they were slightly moving, modestly carrying out the need for breath—it seemed they were, somehow not a painting from Titian or Botticelli, but instead organic forms. Ellis returned only a few moments later with a full mug, complete with fabric steam whistling over its surface.

"Here you go, mate," Ellis said, still in his whispered tone, "Two sugars, just how you like it."

I thanked him and sat up, feeling the full gravity of my drinking endeavors the night before. My head was attacked at all angles with a sort of pressure that felt as if my skull might crack. I winced, breathing in fast, nearly a hiss.

"'You okay?"

"Fine. Might find some Advil," I answered, matching his whisper.

"Quite a night, wa'n't it?" He asked. And he chuckled; it was the first sound of his voice that morning, it crackled in a register dropped by the lack of use in the early hours. I took a shot back of the coffee, swallowed and mumbled, "Where'd the monkey come from?"

Ellis looked up from his novel, as he'd just hunkered back into his comfortable position with his legs pulled in and toes tucked into the armchair and its cushion. He scrunched his expression, seemingly startled by the sight of the monkey cocking its head and cricketing its scratched noises, whistling high pitches and leaping onto a hand-crafted mahogany console where sat a bronze statue of a heron, no taller than a bottle of wine. It patted its humanoid paw at the greenish worn beak and ticked its head robotically. Ellis seemed in a state of awe, as if the entire time he'd been seated in the gathering room with the little creature he hadn't noticed it, and now was the first time he took note of its existence. Ellis thought for a moment, studying the creature as it studied the room, then nodded assuredly, "Panama, if I do recall."

I blinked and digested his answer. I decided none of it truly mattered and sipped the coffee and waited for anyone else to awaken. Sometime later a grandfather clock gonged out a bellowing chime from behind me, I twisted my back to view the brilliant piece, the glass-casing revealed a rocking golden pendulum ornament like Odysseus' shield, with the power to tick away at the ever slipping seconds of time, and the clock face stuck at a right angle, the long arrow on XII, the short on III. I scoffed and rubbed my eyes. The oils on my face mixed as if it were a palette.

"What is it?" Ellis questioned, the bodies below were now beginning to stir, reviving from their slumber, each second becoming less of an amusement, less of a vulnerable and tender sight, more of an ooze. I waved a hand at the back wall, dressed in emerald drapes. "Your clock is broken."

"What makes you say that?" asked Ellis. "Is it the time you're on about? If it is the time, you'll be pressed to know it is honestly three o'clock now."

"In the *afternoon?*" I blurted, my voice in full, and the bodies began to stretch out between us. I recoiled, flashing my teeth as the group began to wake. What happened last night was achingly apparent. A crazed hurricane of sex and indulgence. Our edition of Venus and Aphrodite, a grand gesture to the goddesses before us. The details are fleeting but remnants scattered my thoughts at present. A night masked in hot chiaroscuro, our skin clothed in shadow, and in the face of our requited debauchery, we achieved the closest we'd ever become to gods and goddesses. The closest we may ever come to cheating death.

———

Summer paraded itself in the countryside where we lay out in the afternoon sun and drank our tea in the courtyards, played tennis together or swam laps in the pool. All was rewarded to the artists for working so diligently on masterful pieces that would soon be the face of modern art, reiterated on t-shirts and prints and find a resurgence in a sure future revival of synth-wave aesthetic (a stinging pessimism but true in the face of our misconstrued commerce). All earned, except for me. I was the only artist among them yet to even solidify a single detail toward their art. I hadn't so much as put a single note of black ink into the manuscript paper. My computer software and hard drives remained blank. My studio was much like my brain, fretfully vacant.

"Jesus *Fuck*."

Ellis was crunched in the reading nook, one leg bent up toward his chest and the other flat against the cutout of the wall. It was then the fifth day of our stay. He wore round sunglasses on his eyes, hair up in a justled bun, a bathrobe tied but loose. He had the morning paper folded back on itself and held at such an angle that the window lit an even spread on the page. The ash of his cigarette stuck to his bottom lip began to anthill on the scarlet silk of his robe.

"What is it?" I provoked as I wandered through the shrouded doorway into the overcast kitchen. Yvette stood with one hand on her hip, slouched over the stove and cooking french toast and sausage links. The aroma of the breakfast thickened the air, mixed with the oaky scent of coffee. A pot of dark roast sat on the kitchen counter; three fourths full. And Ellis, huddled in the reading nook on the farthest reach of the kitchen scooted forward and held the paper extended, cleared his throat, and held his cigarette in a feminine manner.

"*Dead Girls Club*—Could the breakout, alternative sensation, Dead Girls Club, be using witchcraft to attract listeners? Recent rumors seem to confirm this notion. The alternative band formed in Brooklyn, New York in 2024, incorporates distinct imagery of satanic and occult iconography. Upon further inspection, the picturing is said to be *real imagery* used throughout history rather than artwork created for the band. This has led to concerns of copyright infringement but given the nature of the images, that is the least of the issues at hand. The lead singer of the band, Mazy Diaz, has been seen in public holding a copy of *The Satanic Bible*—Mazy Diaz, have I met her?"

"No."

"Hm—It starts going into detail about the pentameter they use for their music—how it follows the structure of the witches' dialogue in *Macbeth*."

"It's fake," I groaned from the counter as I stirred half and half into a mug of coffee. "What tabloid is this from? It's fucking absurd."

"It's fucking brilliant, you mean!" Ellis shot up from the nook and slapped the newspaper on the back of my head. "Why haven't we thought of something like this? It's so well thought out. *Conceptual* even. What do you think? Want to become warlocks?"

When I looked up at him, he was grinning with all his spruce tinted teeth exposed. He dipped his sunglasses on the bridge of his nose. "You don't have any gum on you, do you?" I shook my head, prompting him to purr a large sigh and cross the kitchen, around the island, picking at the grapes placed in a wooden bowl. "Joseph, sooner or later, you'll start carrying gum like it's a lighter. It's just as important for your well-being."

Ellis flicked the cigarette in the sink. Yvette slapped two more slices of french toast onto a plate. "Are you staying for breakfast, Ellis?"

"Yes, dearest, I'll stay around for you," he responded, circling around to peck her on the neck. Ellis focused his attention back on me. "Really? No gum then?"

"No."

"Awful. Anyway, I was wondering what your thoughts were on your friend's *little band*. They seem to have shot higher than Apollo himself." And he hummed a high laugh with a closed mouth, a pleasant and content little giggle. Whatever he was on about, he seemed very proud of it.

"What? You mean Autumn?"

"Yes! Autumn. Beautiful name. *Beautiful woman.* I always wondered what the deal was between you and her. Seems like there's quite a bit of history more than just co-workers. I'm getting sidetracked again. What do you think of Autumn and her new band?"

Why he kept talking about her and Dead Girls Club in this manner was beyond me. He was toying with me and, frankly, I was not in the mood. "Autumn is my lifelong friend. I'm happy for her—and Mazy and Freya—and Autumn is the best drummer I've ever seen."

"I bet you feel lucky to have had her in your band then," Ellis said but as though he hadn't meant to say it out loud. He held his head cocked at an angle and despite the tinted glasses over his eyes, his eyebrows were still locked and furrowed.

"What do you want, Ellis?"

My tone was icy, but Ellis was tickled by this. He stepped closer toward me, poked a grape into his mouth, and popped it between his molars. The squashed grape rolled around in his mouth like clothes in a drying machine, and he smiled, looking down at me, "Let's invite them over."

"*Here?*" I laughed out loud. He couldn't be serious! This was no such destination fit for Autumn—sweet, viperous Autumn. She'd find it amusing but in the way a man watches his child play about in a sandbox.

"Well, why not? They're growing in stature and fast. *Bloody fast,* Joseph. Remember when Beach Sirens began accelerating at this rate? What do you expect will happen when they surpass Beach Sirens?"

Surpass Beach Sirens. The words clung to my heart in my chest, a dull pain rubbing against the organ, making it go raw. Though, it was entirely possible. She could very well become a worldwide sensation with her new band, she might, too, look back on Beach Sirens as *humble beginnings.* What of me, then? I wanted nothing more than to see her.

"I'll ask," I blurted, so shotty I surprised even myself. "I'll ask but that's all I can do." I knew it was a lie, but I just wanted to say anything that would make him quiet. If only a moment as my nerves continued to tense and I didn't want to take anything out on him.

"Great. Let me know what she decides. We'll have much cleaning to do if we have Dead Girls Club in Bladen, won't we?" He spoke loud enough so both Yvette and me would hear him clearly. The flickering grease on the pan dozed off. Ellis and I directed our attentions to Yvette—she'd been proportioning the meals on the plates.

"Breakfast is ready," hummed Yvette.

"Did you hear me?" he asked with a quizzical look at Yvette. "We'll have some cleaning to do."

Yvette glanced at me. I didn't know what to do, I was as shocked as she was at the passivity of his remark. And then, she looked back at Ellis who was deathly serious.

"Okay," she mumbled. I thanked her for breakfast. Ellis and I carried our plates into the dining room where we sat and ate in near complete silence, Ellis scooping the french toast into his mouth in square chunks while reading the paper.

"Christ, she is bloody beautiful," he finally said to nobody in particular, though I was the only other person in the room.

"Who's that?" I asked but I knew who. He swallowed and reached for a napkin, "Autumn. I hope she'll stop by. She has a perfect body, wouldn't you agree? It's mental—the proportions of her figure are angelic—nearly familiar, even—like one on a fresco."

I agonized over his comments with throbbing memories resurfacing, nights spent with her the last decade of my life. He continued, "The face though—never mind the face, mate—perhaps she'd be used best from behind, aye?"

Ellis began chuckling but I slammed my fist into the table. The force of which caused the plates to clatter and a jarring thud to resolve his humor.

"Stop it," I sneered. The words came snapping from my tongue so quickly that the phrase morphed into a single word, one word with an instant power. A bite. Ellis stared at me, perplexed by my changed demeanor, that being toward an air of hatred. His stunned look subsided, crumbling, and replaced with cautious laughter.

"What did you say?" he asked, and a single brow arched over the rim of his voided shades.

"Don't talk about her like that," I warned. Ellis' gaze searched me, a sort of full figure scan to analyze my level of disproportion. He clicked his tongue and raised his eyebrows, "Fine. Apologies. But have a look yourself, mate." He slid the paper across the table.

In full color, there was a provocative photo of the three girls standing tall and confident, all dressed in a sort of medieval lingerie, their chests and waists barely covered in netted lace fabric, and countless black strings and ribbons buckled over their legs and connected the underwear. Long black boots on all three of them. They stood confidently against a bleeding red backdrop, holding their instruments. Autumn stood between her two bandmates with her drumsticks crossed (rather than crossed in an 'X,' the sticks were held in a near-religious cross formation—only the formation was inverted—she made an upside-down cross) and held over her head. Headline: *Good Girls Gone Bad!* Sub-header: *Could the breakout, alternative sensation, Dead Girls Club, be using witchcraft to attract listeners?*

"You see what I mean, now, don't you?" Ellis questioned. I pushed the paper back across the table. "You sure nothing ever happened between you two?"

I glanced at him, and he was still wearing his sunglasses, and he bit into his sausage link causing grease to spritz from its innards.

"Yes," I replied.

"Shame—I would have loved to hear about that—and to hear about what kind of shit she's into. If I'm being quite honest, if it wasn't for you, I would have liked to be with her. One way or another, I would have," he said. Ellis' low voice tapered into a chuckle near the end. If he'd meant to upset me, it worked, and his unfathomable remarks about the woman I felt closest to had at last breached my senses. I shot the chair back from the table. I stood and exited the dining room quickly, leaving my plate hardly touched.

———

I entered the gathering room, where Bardo was on a yoga mat at the center, wearing only his white boxer briefs and socks, stretching his body. King Crimson's *In the Court of the Crimson King* twinged from the record player. He shot a glance at me, "Joey boy, good morning. Hope you all had a good breakfast."

"Good morning," I said with little charm, but I mustered up what I could. He hadn't wronged me in any sort of way, and I felt it wasn't fair to take it out on him. "Do you mind if I sit here for a bit?"

"Be my guest," he said. He rocked onto his back and continued his stretches. I thumped onto a sofa, breathing heavily, and Ellis barged into the room a moment later; I'd faintly heard his bare feet thumping against the linoleum and there he was in front of me, casting his scrunched gaze at me where I expanded myself on the sofa.

"What?" I asked.

"You're angry."

I rolled my eyes, "Very observant of you. Of course, I'm fucking angry. You were sitting there talking about having your way with one of my best friends! You think I'm going to just sit there and listen to that?" Ellis flicked the shades from his face and revealed his fierce eyes, which were sifting my expression in utter confusion as if I'd betrayed him in some way.

"What the hell are you talking about? I never say anything like that!"

"*You just did* a moment ago! You fucking lunatic! You said you wanted to take advantage of her right in front of me. What the hell is the matter with you anyway?" I growled. I wanted to whack my fist clean across his face, watch his body crumble to the wood floor, and wait to see his mouth fill with blood. I tried to leave the room again, this time passing him, slamming shoulders and rocking him off balance, but he took a step back. I powered forward, briskly out into the hall and rounded the stairs.

"Wait."

I was halfway up the stairs by the time his low, English voice was barking back at me in a tone of annoyance, as if he was upset with how I reacted. I stopped and latched onto the banister, peering over at him on the first floor. He stared back at me and after a tense beat, he continued, "I'm sorry. What I said was cruel to not just you, but to her."

"I know," I snarled back and stormed off, up the stairs and into my bedroom. I wanted to leave Bladen at the soonest opportunity. I no longer wanted to work with Ellis and write the symphony I was now bound to. I was stuck. I stood up again and thrust my fist into the bookcase—a clean smack—and several books plopped onto the floor, causing a bright rumbling sound to echo through the house. I suddenly felt everything around me was antagonist, all that belonged to Ellis, all that represented him. I recalled what Elara had told me and what word she had said specifically—*creep*. Maybe all of this was a mistake.

I sat at the edge of my bed when I decided to let go, and the tears fell from me. I was gone from myself, so far from who I knew to be Joe Henley, and this feeling of loss was revolting. I felt like an animal lodged in a trap and I had to discover a strength within me to remain patient. Numbingly patient. I lay on the bed, convulsing and finding air again. I had no other choice. I swallowed, and remained hopeful I could leave the cage soon.

———

The day was drawing to a close and I had yet to leave my room. I was hungry, falling in and out of sleep when I finally gave in and went down the stairs, running my palm on the glossed banister and staring at the psychedelic stained-glass windows on the wall. I made it to the first floor and traveled down the hall to the kitchen where Ellis was rummaging around in a drawer. I said nothing to him as he stopped whatever he was doing to watch me without saying a word.

I went to the refrigerator and slapped a carton of eggs on the center island. Inside it, I found a half dozen orbs looking back at me. I caught an image of Bardo, Yvette, and Katya outside the window, all splashing about in the pool. Bardo took a running start and leapt, diving in perfectly and rising to the surface, wiping the wet from his face. These three were the youngest out of the five of us. Yvette was only twenty-two. Bardo was twenty-three. Katya was twenty-five. Sumitra was only a few years younger than me, twenty-seven and noticeably missing from the summer image.

"Where's Sumitra?" I asked and the voice added to the silent room seemed deafening in contrast. Ellis had kept rummaging around the drawers and he cleared his throat. "She's up in her bedroom, I would imagine. She isn't much of a socialite if you haven't noticed."

I'd taken note of Sumitra. She never spoke to Ellis directly and instead spoke only to the other artists. She stayed in her bedroom often, and I occasionally peered through the entry of the library to find her reading by the fireplace. I'd spoken to her only a handful of times in the last five days, mostly to ask what she'd been up to.

The kitchen pans were hanging from the ceiling on hooks over the island. I pulled a cast iron down and turned for the stovetop, directly next to Ellis. I could feel his presence and I felt the urge to hurt him again.

"How's the music coming along?" he asked, his head down in the drawer cocking and examining as if he were a bird.

"What are you looking for?" I returned and turned the grill on.

"Gum, Joseph. *Gum!* Have you not been listening at all? Don't make eggs now, I'm about to prepare supper." I was deciding what remark I would say in return when suddenly Ellis cooed excitedly and shot his arm to the back of the drawer.

"This'll do," he said. His arm returned with a tin of mints, a monochromatic tin with a blue lining. The tin read: *Anton's Breath Mints—Wintergreen*. I immediately categorized the tin as familiar, but I could not place where I knew it. I stared at it with zeroed intent as he flicked the latch and popped a blue circle on his tongue and offered the tin toward me.

"Truce, mate? *Please?*" he held out the tin in such a way that memory caught on it like a spark against wool and the flames began.

"No," I heard myself reply. Ellis clasped the tin, and I saw the Russian language engraved the exterior. I was met with a blaze of images, bright echoes from a fretful night—the Miserable Sinner night club with Hal and Tommy all those years ago. The same tin held out in Hal's palm when he gave it to Tommy in the booth. The tin filled with laced drugs. The tin I associated with death and great fear. I took a step back from the stove and fell into the island, the marble corner dug into my lower back, and I groaned, seething my teeth.

"Are you alright?" Ellis asked, his arms out in case he needed to catch me. I balanced myself quickly and pushed him away from me with a heaving force. Ellis slammed into the refrigerator and his eyes whirled around the room.

"Stay the hell away from me," I said as Ellis tried to recenter himself. I wiped my nose and turned the stove off. I left the carton on the counter and fled for my room again, quickly as if I were being chased. The stairs screamed as I climbed, and I made it into the bedroom where I lay on the floor with my lips kissing wood. The few seconds it had taken me to land there felt like an eternity. I couldn't move as I recalled the night that featured that same tin of mints. What was it doing here? How could it possibly have been here in the back of the kitchen drawer?

My mind and body untethered, I allowed them to come unglued and gave into a full panic attack, heaving choked breaths on the floor, whimpering and whining like a great swine in terrible agony. I lay there for some time, unable to move and violently trembling until I heard the door open from behind me, it sounded miles away and faint. Light footsteps thudded on the wood toward me and stopped.

I felt a hand rest on my bicep. It rubbed up and down in a smooth glide, and lips approached my ear, shushing me. A second hand ran through my hair, and a soft whisper called to me, "It's okay. You're okay. Everything is fine and you're okay. Breathe. Focus on my voice."

I did as the voice said and soon my breath returned to a normal rate and my heart's erratic beating subsided. Her guiding whisper—her loving hands—all observed motherly and comforting qualities; soon my shaking became subdued, and I gained control of my body again. My mind unlocked and Joe Henley became realigned. I rolled over to find Sumitra, worry-eyed, on her bent knees, staring down at me.

"Are you okay?" she asked, and I noticed the fear she wore mirrored my own. I shook my head and sat up; I wiped tears from my cheeks. The vivid recreations of Tommy's death were still displayed in the foreground, but I blinked and returned to find Sumitra in front of me. I stared into her eyes—a thunderous brown color. I ordered myself to remain focused on her eyes so I would be present. After a moment of us quietly looking at each other, I finally whispered back to her, "I think coming here might've been a mistake."

Sumitra contemplated this, surveyed my twitching behavior and a single tear skid down her cheek. She wiped it away quickly with her sleeve. She closed her eyes, her head fell, and she replied, "Me too."

III

Ode To Madness

In the July heat, under a series of textile clouds and a baby sky, Sumitra spread out over the grass on a knitted blanket and sunned herself, reading a mass-produced paperback of *Watership Down*. I hadn't wished to disturb her as she portrayed tranquility, a creature in the veld, only a speck amongst the fresh green expanse from where I watched her at the attic window. After some time, I noticed her robing her figure and crossing from the open hillside and into the courtyard to the right from where I perched, barely visible at an angle. I had my cheek pressed on the glass, feeling the late morning warmth blanket my skin. I donned a loose pair of jockey shorts and scampered through the levels of Bladen and out the door, ignoring everyone else. I didn't even notice Ellis leaning back on the piano stool in the gathering room with a cigarette jutting from his jaw, squinting as I hurried out the door.

"Hello!" I shouted, intruding on the hedges, curving the stone yard without shoes on my feet. She sat at the bistro set behind the grand statue at the center. Bronze legs crossed and wagging with her robe tight on her waist, the novel splayed with her thumb pinching it open and holding it there, her elbow pressing into the table.

"Mind if I join you?" I asked. She grinned from behind her shades.

"Be my guest," Sumitra replied, and I squatted into the opposing seat. I withdrew a cigarette from my breast pocket along with a Zippo. "Do you mind?"

She shook her head and returned her attention to the story but back again, "Could I have one as well?" I lit the end and held the smoke in my lungs as I fingered the box, unsheathed one at random, and gifted it to her with the lighter. She thanked me, lit the paper, and we sat together and smoked. For a long while, she read her book. I was patient. I noticed that her arms, her legs, and neck were all lightly speckled in sweat, practically a layer that made her skin glint. It was quite the sight to study behind the ease of my shaded lenses. After some time, she finally snapped the corner of the book back on itself, dogearing it.

"Was there anything you wanted to talk about or were you genuinely only out here to enjoy my company?" she asked.

I scoffed back at her and replied, "Who's to say I didn't see you from my bedroom window, and that was enough to come down?"

"Fine. If there's nothing on your mind, I'll continue reading."

"Alright, alright," I blew out, and she won. Sumitra placed the paperback on the table and stared at the backside of the statue, awaiting me to speak up.

"I wanted to thank you for helping me yesterday," I said at last. She was quiet until she muttered back, "Of course. That's what friends are for, right?"

I nodded. And I tried to stumble on the correct phrasing of what I'd meant to say to her. "I also wanted to ask why you felt coming here was a mistake," I said, and I quickly added, "And why you're so reserved around him." I hadn't even needed to speak his name for her to comprehend. She clicked her tongue—it appeared I'd managed to toss her with this question.

"Why?" she asked.

"He's been acting—increasingly strange—and I got the feeling you might know something about it," I admitted. Sumitra stared at me from across the table, straight-faced, shades on her eyes, completely unreadable. And yet she was running an analysis of me, determining whether or not I would be someone she deemed trust-worthy. She finally licked her lips, smiled faintly, and spoke, "I liked him at first. But the first night we arrived, after dinner, I went into my bedroom. You should know that I do not trust anyone until they've proven themselves to me. I spent hours in that bedroom—searching every corner and eventually—I found something."

"What exactly did you find?" I pushed. And she studied me further, again challenging her internal negotiation to determine her trust. I breathed a giant lung of air and blew it out, I stamped the cigarette and stared back at her. She inhaled on her cig one last time, mirrored my movements and said, "Follow me."

In her bedroom, Sumitra used a great deal of exertion in an attempt to shove her dresser to the side. And with my help, the dresser heaved; slowly groaning the wood against the linoleum, we pushed the dresser until she gave up. I stopped too and watched as she bent onto her hands and knees. She looked back over her shoulder. "Get down here," she said in practically a whisper. I did as I was told and joined her.

At first, I hadn't understood what she was pointing at, squinting stupidly at the shadowed white trim lining the bottom of the wall. She rolled her eyes and yanked the shoulder of my shirt closer. My body moved weakly like a doll until I was face-to-face with the flooring. And carved into the wood, I read a short phrase, crooked and uneven. A child's penmanship and etched with something dull—all at angles and straight lines—no curves in the writing. It was aged and the date that followed the phrase confirmed these suspicions. It read:

Jasper Ellis Bartlett. Summer 95.

"Who," I muttered, only this one single word left me as the pieces fell into place. She leaned back on her knees, nodding, and her thick eyebrows were raised. She was afraid. "I don't know what's happening here," she was whispering, "but he is a *liar.*"

I pushed back on the wood, blinking as if to make sure all of this was real. It was not a dream, for I felt my fingernails digging into my shorts. I cleared my throat and made an attempt to appear calm; I questioned her, "How do we know this was this Ellis?"

She flattened, deflating on all fours, leaned back and sat down on the floor across from me. She asked, "It absolutely was him. How many other people have you met with that name?"

I made a face. Fair. She continued to explain, "Look—it says, 'Summer 95'—that would make him eleven years old at the time— and this is absolutely something an eleven-year-old boy would do."

"Okay—so maybe his mother remarried, and he chose to go by his mother's new maiden name. His father did die when he was young so that would make sense. And who's to say he doesn't prefer his middle name to his first name? That's typical," I sorted. I felt confident, in complete denial, despite my inspection of the mysterious engraving.

"Joe," Sumitra said, low and soft. She waited for my eyes to meet hers, her grim eyes looked back on me. She recalled, darkly, "Ellis tells everyone the first time he came to America was when he was twenty-one. A decade *after* this was carved into the floor." I looked away and back at the floor, unable to hold eye contact for any longer, suddenly terrified of the entire situation. I felt a cold rinse inside of me and thought I was shaking. I held my hands in front of me to confirm.

"I think he's lying about his parents. This is his family's house. Ellis Young isn't his real name," Sumitra kept whispering fast as if she wanted to get all the information out in a single breath or before anyone could interrupt her. I wanted to stop her or get out of the situation but knew I had to sit still—I had put myself here.

"It's our secret, okay?" She studied my face so I nodded to show her that yes, it would be our secret. I meddled and received information, but now I had to suffer the consequence of knowledge. Still, this name in the wood confirmed very little for me but again I filed it at the front of my thoughts. My skull now pounded, and knew I had to write the symphony to escape whatever was really happening here and whoever Ellis really was.

———

I tried all I could to concern myself with the symphony but even when seated at the Mini Grand in the gathering room, alone and playing to my own content, I felt my conceptions melting back to Ellis Young. A man who likely did not exist. There was an awful dread inside me, weighing greatly on my stomach, and I could not focus. It was possible that Sumitra was not to be trusted—perhaps she wrote that into the wood herself and used it to gain my trust and cause a stir. Yet this theory did not seem to hold up well, especially with the frightful sight of the Russian-produced *Anton's Breath Mints* tin tucked away in one of the kitchen drawers. What did any of this mean? Surely, if Ellis had been here as a child, when he was still *Jasper Ellis,* he would not have brought all of us out to such a destination where one could falsify his identity. That is unless, we'd outsmarted him but that too seemed entirely unlikely. His name may not have been what he said but I'd learned the personality and mannerisms of the man and I knew he was undoubtedly a very critical thinker.

I sat staring at the seventy-five keys stacked above my fingertips in their formation of light and dark, and huffed a terrible sigh, the only external warning to my bright suffering. When my fingers dipped into the keys, gliding and shifting my weight over each tone, it felt as fluid as water brushing over the sea. I was not a pianist, but a surfer and I was riding the sound. After a certain point, one stops commanding the piano and the piano leads the hands where it would like them to go. It's up to the player to follow the tune into the depths of the brilliant subconscious, the land of dreams—the impossible scene—the storm is tamed. It is liquid how easy and freeing all of it feels as the hands disconnect from the mind and soon, one is no longer playing the piano, instead one is listening as they play it.

I'd played into the brooding melancholy that lies in the intonation of Beethoven's *Moonlight Sonata: I. Adagio sostenuto.* An entire week at Bladen and I had yet to create a melody or harmony or chord of my own that I knew for certain would be presented in my composition. This dilemma with my brain was truly one of vile obstruction. Perhaps I had a creative soul before, but somehow, I had lost it.

One begins to wonder if they ever had creativity at all—dangerous self-doubt—the challenges were perhaps always there yet now I was not strong enough to face them. The storm of the artist had subsided, and I was perched within the eye of the storm; so there in the vexing whirlpool, I was sent further into nothing, further in madness. And the greatest conflict of all was the matter: did I actually care? Without passion, without an instinctual drive, can one still be considered an artist? I thought it was wholly a possibility that without a passionate exhibition of my project, I could only really be a musician. I wondered if I could ever encounter that irradiant artist who once inhabited the walls of my skull ever again.

Three nights remained at Bladen, our fortress of solitude, and the artists were up to their Bohemian Antics in the gathering room. Devoid of pale light, and dancing shadows, bodies and silhouettes swayed and rippled as the opening track of Pink Floyd's *The Wall: In the Flesh?*, filtered through the speakers with an awesome pounding bass and the guitars scorched out a blistering sound. As the drums went wild, around and around, speeding out of existence with aircraft effects, Yvette rapidly thumped her bare feet on the rug until the noise broke and a baby was born.

I entered the room then through the archway and down the familiar three steps and the record continued into *The Thin Ice*. I stepped one foot in front of the other, carrying myself with a suaveness. A night of *Rocky Horror* aestheticism. The green lounge with a musky orange light bent on the lamps. There were four black figures twisting and rearranging in the room. All were present except, of course, Sumitra, who I knew was still up in her room, hiding from the presumptuous artists free of shame and devoid of modesty. I danced with the group all the way through *Mother,* and by then it was time to flip B-Side.

In the wrinkled fabric sounds from the speakers, during that intimate hush, I turned in the room to find one of the four figures missing. I rounded each of them in my head, counting around the room—Yvette on her feet and dancing in a white nightgown—Bardo up on his feet, his bare chest glinting with sweat—Katya, in her long shirt, sitting modest on the arm of a chair with her drink in hand.

"Ellis?" I questioned aloud and rotated another round of the gathering room only for something to catch my eye. Bardo was flipping the record, placing the needle again and the call of morning birds and a child, an acoustic from the speakers. This wasn't it. I looked up into the bookcases, and up atop the bookcases, a form was sitting with waving knees hunched with a bent neck and watching us below. The body wore a kabuki mask, a brilliant scarlet color and glinting in the orange glow, the face of the devil with its sharp teeth splayed. It appeared to be grinning—I had to stare sharply in the dimness of the room, almost entirely wearing shadow—hollow sockets where eyes should be and I knew, with the ginger hair growing out around the mask, Ellis was gaping back at me. The ladder was off to his left and his feet kept wagging quietly from up there, knuckles white with grip on the rounded finish at the top of the case, head tilted down at me.

"Why don't you come down from there and join us?" I asked. I puffed my chest so as not to show fear at the nightmarish figure sitting above us. Yvette turned around and caught sight of him up above and shrieked; upon registering the form, she calmed and broke toward laughter. The lyrics of the song rang out in a lurid echo, *Did, did, did, did you see the frightened ones?* The devilish thing tilted its head in the opposite direction, never looking away from me and then pushed off the bookcase. He shot down the bookcase, a flight of eight feet, and landed mighty on the rubber of his boots. He stood up straight and walked over to me, tilting his head as if fascinated by me.

"What are you wearing?" he croaked, and it came out buffered behind the crimson mask. His cheeks were unnaturally pointed in sharp angles. The absence of eyes made me unsure as to where I should focus. I noted my outfit, in my beige trousers and a white t-shirt; I stood sheepishly and confused.

I asked, "What's with the mask?"

"What mask?"

His hair was crossed in every direction and his black tie was loose around his neck, the top button of his shirt undone. He took another step closer to me, staring straight down at me and I felt the eyes of the room on us. I had a goal in mind, and I refused to let him best me.

"I was wondering if tomorrow we could take a trip into town," I said with a charmed confidence. I added onto it, "I think it would be nice to see Hudson before we all go back anyway."

"We can't," he replied, almost instantly. When I pushed him further, he only said, "The Spyder cannot seat all of us and there's no signal to call a cab." The response from the room was deaf as distortion continued from the record player. Bardo recommended we keep dancing and went as far as to plead for Yvette to continue. However, I was not finished with my appliance of pressure.

"My phone works alright. How about all of yours? No issues out here? Only a few days ago you asked me to call Autumn, did you not?" I stared at the empty sockets of the mask, knowing his eyes were looking back at me.

He motioned toward Yvette and ordered, "More dancing." He shot a finger toward her, and I grabbed his wrist, hurling it away from her.

"Focus on me," I growled with more anger than I had intended. It was clear to everyone then that there was something going on deeper than exploring the town in the morning.

"How about we go into town, just the two of us? We'll go in and shop around some of the local businesses. It might be an ideal opportunity to meet the community," I continued. He ripped the mask from his face and his sharp features were then exaggerated in the stark shadows. He dully watched me as I continued, in a whisper, behind the growing tension of the vinyl record, "Or do you already know the community?" His brows turned in as he tried to appear puzzled.

"Maybe you've known them for years—or decades," I continued, "You've known this place since you were a child, haven't you?"

He stared at me, his face contorting, his cheeks flushed, jaw clenched. I thought he would burst, thrash a great deal of explosive rage on me, but he only stiffened. Petrified. I wanted to push the intensity until he popped like a needle into the skin of a balloon. His eyelids drooped and he looked at me, swallowed, and his breathing seemed to stop entirely.

"What the fuck are you on about?" he questioned in a whisper, so low I was reading his lips behind the shrill of the record. The artists watched intently, unable to hear us at all. His eyes began watering, and I had all the information I needed. I nodded, shifting between his two glinting eyes before they tightly closed. I turned and exited the room. He would never admit to his lies, I knew, but I had altered his disguise. It was only a thin crack, but it was all I needed to see through.

———

That same night I went back to my room where I dreamt about Tommy. It was a familiar dream that followed me around from time to time. One of the only constants in my life since his passing. We stood in a materialized cityscape. His back was a few feet in front of me, his head looking left and right only enough to seem as if he were enjoying the breeze. And again, when I stepped forward, Tommy did the same. He was off, at first a walk, and as I followed, coming closer and closer, it turned into a run.

We ran through city blocks, splashing in puddles, kicking litter off the curb, and moving through crosswalks. There was never anyone else in the dream but the two of us. And I would grow tired still, calling out to him, pleading and on the verge of tears. I would grow so physically exhausted, I would nearly collapse on the filthy sidewalk, gripping the side of my stomach in pain, and trying to keep up with Tommy. His backside would shrink. The back of his blonde shaved head, his kicking legs shrinking smaller and smaller. I would lose again, and again I would wake up out of breath and sweating. Alone in the gothic bedroom. Minutes to sunrise and I decided to start the day.

Ellis kept his distance the entire next day, after my harsh calling out by placidly concerning himself only with the duties of a host. It was to be one of our last days at Bladen, and I became eager to leave the mansion. I wanted to get back to the city and possibly sort out issues with Ellis, but I hadn't expected a sudden shift in my life to deviate everything from its intended path. Sometimes these days will pass in life where at once, things felt reasonably together, but soon a distinctive shift will cause a complete collapse. The empire of the cerebrum will fall. Today, the 26th of July, was my final day at Bladen for a jolting devastation would once again drag me by my heels back to the city. It was not even noon when the news reached me.

I was in the attic studio space, tinkering with sounds and desperately trying to force revelations from my crowded skull when I heard rampant thumps growing in volume. The door whacked the wall and Sumitra entered, phone in hand, the white screen gleaming on a morning news article. A real crazed look struck me; her brows slouched up at a peak. She shot toward me at the far end where I had been standing and whistling with pinched lips into a flute.

"Joe! Joe—Joe, hey," she stammered. Her words were scattered, and her voice was shaken. Trembling, she managed to say, "Autumn Gladis."

"What? What about her?" I immediately asked. I nearly chuckled at the absurdity of the name. It was a moment of cross-contamination, my worlds colliding in ways I hadn't anticipated. For a shock, I thought perhaps I was dreaming, and Sumitra mentioned my old friend in impossible circumstances.

"She passed away this morning," she said, sounding frantic and her body wavering.

"Sumitra—calm, calm—what are you talking about?" I asked.

All my premonitions were calm, stuck in a dense heat capable of being controlled until Sumitra informed me of the situation. An article that detailed the event had been posted only twenty minutes before. It was the first news outlet to publish the story, and Sumitra had been reading on her phone, only to stumble on it.

Autumn was out walking Vincent, the chocolate lab, in her neighborhood in Brooklyn. I knew this route as I'd walked it on Sunday mornings by her side. At approximately nine in the morning, Autumn was standing at the corner of Rodney Street and Marcy Avenue, her back to Williamsburg's branch of the Brooklyn Public Library, when she collapsed on the concrete. Vinny, rather than sprinting off into traffic, down the aisles of streets and alleys in Williamsburg, instead stayed beside Autumn and barked for help. Vinny was a trained service dog—*Autumn's service dog*—information she chose to keep from me in our friendship earlier that year. I stopped her when I heard the words, 'heart failure.'

I obtained all this information from Sumitra, who obtained it from a rapid, straight article, vague on details and sources. I didn't believe it, going as far as asking Sumitra if it were a joke. She shook her head with a bothered look, perhaps she expected me to explode in a frenzy of unholy panic. Then, I was able to visualize the information and thought, *Autumn is in trouble*. Finally, the flute fell to my side; it was suddenly heavy as my veins filled with lead, a feverish wash, and I swallowed.

"What are you going to do?"

"I'm not sure," I replied. My chest was beginning to deny me oxygen. I closed my eyes and felt my heart beating in pace, I could hear it in my ears. The panic was a rising tide. I squinted and stared at the dusty floor, disobeying the desire to cry, passing Sumitra in a choked voice, "Thank you. Excuse me."

I powered down the stairs and into the kitchen where Ellis was placing his final touches on lunch. I swallowed, in a daze, the floor began to spin. Everything was becoming increasingly off balance. Ellis stared at me, and I heard Sumitra following down the stairs from a great distance, an ocean away.

"What is it?" he asked. I couldn't focus on him, instead in a vignetting trap, an anxious illness, and I said in a gentle tone, "I'd like to borrow the car, please. It's an emergency."

Ellis scoffed and threw a towel on his shoulder. "Joseph, it's our only vehicle. I told you yesterday we would not be going into town—"

"It's an emergency. If you don't mind, my friend is not well and I need to visit her," I mumbled. I thought I might faint with the weight of which the words took to drag up my throat. I may never see her again. A bitter truth, I could not even muster a lie.

"Who? *Autumn?* You know what? You've been a cruel sight lately and *no*—I don't think I will let you borrow the car—I commissioned a symphony back in February and you have yet to show me as much as a chord progression. Christ, have you even *started?* You signed a contract, mate. You have a real obligation, and I don't think you need the distraction of that whore getting in the way."

There was a feeble knot tied between the mindful self and the primitive self I struggled to maintain over the last five years, and it was at this moment, in my fury of rising tension, the knot simply unraveled. With no premonition, I was at once a trembling man who stood in front of Ellis Young and next, I was a beast with grilled teeth and poisonous eyes, less than human. I slapped the platter of vegetables and sandwiches, causing a spray of color to explode on the kitchen wall. I hammered my white fists on the kitchen counter and repeated myself, in a hellish, wild scream, "Give me the fucking keys! I told you it's an emergency and you just stand there, wasting my time! I'm not asking for your permission!"

My bellowing voice was bearish—a violent, sickening roar—I felt the scratches on my throat from overextending my chords. My echo zipped through the house; I no longer heard Sumitra walking toward our conversation. She was stopped somewhere outside of the kitchen, I figured, but I was focused by my opponent. Ellis was still, pale in the cheeks and after a moment he replied, "I'm afraid I simply cannot allow it."

Autumn was dying if she wasn't already dead—my brain fought on either side of the battlefield to determine a singular belief—and I was dueling with a dictator. I navigated the kitchen island to a butcher's block, unsheathed a thin knife, and sneered an aggressive warning to Ellis.

Then, in the western corridor—I barged into his bedroom and ripped into his bedside table—there rested the key to the Porsche Spyder on a silver ring. My fist tightened around it. I left all my belongings, only the keys in one hand and a knife in the other. I passed Sumitra at the foot of the stairs, and I paused at my escape. She stood in the hallway, an ominous presence, and I stared at her long-ingly—I wondered if I should take her with me. Would she be safe?

I swallowed and darted on varying outcomes before she weakly grinned, accompanied by a single nod. I returned the nod, temporarily disabled by her, this wonderful woman, and I wondered if her or even Yvette would be safe in this house now. Would I ever see her again? I decided Bardo would protect them. I blinked back into my mission, still high on nerves, and rounded the foyer. I dashed with the objective of the roadster, which was still idle at the roundabout driveway, and when I kicked out the front door, Ellis stood with crossed arms in front of it.

"Let's talk about this," he started and winced when my pace went unphased. In my defense, I had already warned him with the blinding adrenaline stuffed in my body, and I threw him to the ground. He toppled with a briskness even I hadn't expected but the rage in my bones was then so mighty, his body weighed a twig. His jaw skidded on the stone shredding against the texture. I knew this because of the wincing sound he made, like meat being carved.

I slammed into the driver's seat and revved the Spyder, glaring back at Ellis and noticed a similar knife had fallen on the stone beside him although not the one I'd drawn moments before. His wicked expression, hassled by my wits—blended with an inky crimson lining, his marbled chin ripped open—these were the last details I glimpsed before I flipped into drive, and skid out of that circled driveway.

His curdling screams called back to me; this tantrum of cries became so loud I could hear it over the snotting engine as I zipped down the hill toward the tattered iron gates. Back onto the gravel road and chucking dust, I looked into the rearview mirror for a final time. The brick house shrank on the mirror, minuscule but malevolent, and somewhere in the image was a man—*The Red Upon the Hill.*

IV

Twin Nights

I crossed back over the Whitestone Bridge, challenging Brooklyn before I had the sudden realization that I had no idea where I was going. All my premonitions told me my quickest way to an answer would be to drive straight to her apartment. I was under the impression that she would be about, and she would even answer the door when I arrived. But hiking the six stone steps and rapping at her door, I waited. And waited. Five minutes passed and I stuck my fist to the door again. The three girls lived on the first floor, and I peeked through the windows around the house, narrowly catching frames of an empty kitchen, unmade beds and Rimbaud stretched out on a window seal. I waited on the front steps, frothing over with bursting anxiety, my stomach felt destroyed by the awful sensations, and I lay my head on the metal railing. Chipped paint fell into my hair or skidded onto the steps.

My body trembled with ferocity. I wondered if I should check a hospital or an emergency room or go to the scene at the Williamsburg Library but the city was too big. There was no telling where my friend was at that moment or if she was okay. Of course, I had yet to believe this singular article that Sumitra had shown me. We'd faced several false claims in the news throughout our careers. I decided I was going to demand that we have the article removed when I saw Autumn.

So, there I sat, and there I died a thousand times at the branching possibilities. And it wasn't until nightfall that the scale shifted, suddenly my false weight toward a misunderstanding started going dull. I, again, thought to check the hospitals but I didn't want to leave in case any of the three girls were to come home. Anguish. I thought to call the many emergency rooms and ask if she was in but they could not release that sort of patient information, not especially when it was the drummer of one of the nation's biggest bands of the year. I hadn't eaten the entire day, and my cranium pulsed with aching throbs. I stood and lurched to the sidewalk to ensure I was on the correct doorstep, and I saw Rimbaud watching me with his tail flapping about.

Defeat ran over my consciousness. I was too worn to even cry. Perhaps the girls were all out together somewhere, perhaps Autumn knew about the article and shrugged it off. *These things happened*, I knew. In the Age of Information, information is rarely true. I watched the sky blend pink, into a lavender wash, then be dyed a blue-black color like the ink of an old tattoo. The stars awoke for another night. Cars socked by with their headlights creating circular glows that wavered on the asphalt; couples passed with linked arms and pretended not to see me as they wandered by. A family of tourists clicked photos of the quaint Williamsburg neighborhood and a college-aged boy with frizzy hair and colossal headphones zipped by on inline skates and a black and brown Sheltie dog jogged on her leash by his side. The bodies became less and less as the night grew and the sky turned grayer. I sat until eleven at night when I heard shoes scuffing the sidewalk—a sound I'd heard all day—but now I heard this particular person call out my name.

"Joe?" she asked, unsure of who was on her front doorstep. My body shot up, a new sense of hope was brought about by the voice, and I saw Mazy Diaz with her brown hair back in a ponytail and her round face pinkish and shiny. I was paralyzed with happiness to see her.

"Are you alright?" I returned and nearly tripped as I rose hoarsely to my feet. She sniffled, resetting her face with the shoulder of her sleeve wiping it dry.

"I guess you heard about what happened then," she finally murmured. Her words caused my voice to be completely ripped from my throat. I was unable to respond as the finality struck—a terrible, freezing defeat bled into my body. It was a shot of despair. All over I was limp, speechless and dull. Wind rippled our clothes, creating the sound of flapping fabric, and the hiss of green leaves prickled on branches overhead. I swallowed, facing the new reality. I lived in a world where Autumn did not. The wind was light, but I thought perhaps it was strong enough to knock my feeble body onto the concrete where it could peacefully rot. I felt somehow guilty and strung out.

I continued imploding. I grew heavier as time became thick. I shook my head and realized a full minute had gone by—Mazy stared at the fossilized sidewalk and tears were stringing on my face—the world had gone quiet, so I hadn't noticed the deep blubbering noises that whimpered from my mouth.

"Come inside," Mazy said, and sniffled; she, too, was pouting then. She passed me and unlocked the door. She fed Rimbaud in his bowl, gave him more water, and prepared tea for the two of us. We sat quietly at the kitchen table, lit by the dingy mustard haze from their kitchen's overhead bulb. I sipped the tea and felt the heat land at the lowest pit of my stomach, completely empty. I needed the tea, I even needed food, but I wondered if I could handle such a task as eating.

"She had a pulmonary embolism," Mazy scratched out and cleared her throat. She spoke with a skittish voice, "Basically, she had a blood clot in one of her lung's arteries. She's had it all year and it had been resolving itself—or so we thought—but Joe—I'm sorry," she paused.

The room was patient. Mazy swallowed, "She asked that you never find out, you know, she was so sure she was going to get better. The doctor seemed confident that she would recover but I guess something was overlooked and—*Shit.*"

Mazy's face crunched on itself, and tears darted the wood finish of their kitchen table. She was silent before a jittering, vocal inhale broke her, and she wept. I placed my hand on hers and waited patiently for more information. Rimbaud had just finished his food and was now lapping tiny slurps of water from his bowl. Mazy wiped her cheeks on her sleeve again.

"She was always such a private person. She kept so much in her chest and never wanted *anyone* to know *anything* beneath her surface. Why did she do that?" she asked. I just grimaced, ignoring the question, and allowed the tears to soak my face, too exhausted to even lift my fingers and wipe them away.

"I guess she took Vinny out for her normal walk this morning, like how she did every morning, you know—but—she didn't come back. Fuck, we were going to go on *tour,* you know?" She paused, shaking her head and staring into space. I knew exactly how she felt. "It's so crazy. I went to the Brooklyn Hospital Center as soon as I heard what happened. They got into her phone and called me, so I've been at the emergency care all fucking day."

"When did it happen?" I asked. My vision was failing, I couldn't think of anything besides Autumn. Her smile. That smile was the only vulnerability she really showed me. Her skin. I knew the hue, smell, and softness of it so well that I could write pages of description. Her freckles and how they matched the shade of her hair. I tried to swallow more tea with the mug teetering in my grasp.

"On her walk. She went into cardiac arrest. Some guy on his morning run saw her and called 911—they took her to the hospital to see if anything could be done but she was pronounced dead at eleven thirty."

"Oh," I let out, but it was more of a mighty exhale and a piece of my soul left too. I was inching further from myself, spinning into a grim oblivion. Autumn had been at the forefront of every decision I made for the last six months and now if I called her phone, it would ring indefinitely. I would never see her again. Mazy explained I could go back and see her, but I told her no—I would rather not see my friend, my beautiful Autumn, in that way. I recalled the horrid images of Tommy's body on the restroom floor. I felt myself crumbling rapidly. I thanked Mazy for the tea, and we held each other in a hug for an extended amount of time, allowing me to catch the soft scents of her hair. I told her I would be around but needed time to think everything over.

A brick of loud pain had been added onto my chest when I looked back at Mazy shutting the front door, her back to me, and I registered that I'd left her alone. Mazy was hurting just as badly as I was and not to mention, she was the closest link I had to Autumn. I walked on the sidewalk as the gusted wind built on itself, and thought, *Autumn had four people closest to her.* At once, it was Sophia and Tommy but in the latter years, it had shifted to be Mazy and myself. I felt a great duty then, to have been one of her only trusted companions throughout her shortened life. Thirty years old. I blinked at the sidewalk, wondering if a curse had been brought onto Beach Sirens. Perhaps I would be next; worse, I was beginning to hope so.

———

I wasn't sure where I was going, only that I wanted to keep shoveling another boot in front of the other, knocking on the cement path and getting further and further from the truth. I fingered a cigarette from the thigh pocket of my trousers and stuck it in my teeth. I lit the end of the stick behind a curved palm and the smoke became my breath. I smoked endlessly. When one reached a butt, I was already lighting the next. And when turning onto new blocks, I was thinking about the state of my life. I was undoubtedly alone. Every person I turned to for care in this life had gone in another direction. Nobody could be trusted or taken seriously; I knew I would soon adopt the persona Autumn had so carefully developed, allowing no entry beyond the exterior. The interior was private, and while it would charcoal there, alone, at least nobody could destroy it. Bitter and unresolved. Loneliness was the enemy I would befriend, like the cloak of death hidden in my shadow, and I would allow it to accompany me in a paradoxical march toward a life led alone.

I came back to the car after one in the morning and it had

remained untouched for the two hours I left it unguarded. I did not care so much either way, the Porsche could have been stolen or deconstructed for all that mattered to me that night. I drove the car out of Brooklyn and into Greenwich Village. The Queens apartment required a key, and all the keys were currently upstate in a mansion. I had no other choice but to go to Velvet Pie Studios and slump onto the sofa on the second floor.

I parked the car on the street and hopped over the driver's side door. The form of a body cursed under his breath. I turned and watched as a strange man cantered by with an extended eye on the vehicle. I still didn't care as my resentment for Ellis took over, and I dotted the passcode into the keypad. The glass door made a sinking metal click and a green light appeared on the box. I entered the studio and carried my useless body up the second floor where I debated the Xanax on the coffee table; I debated the bong and the bottle of weed and the bottles of wine boxed in their compartments. All would have sufficed for the moment, but I was too exhausted to infect my mind. Instead, the instant I curled onto the sofa, I found myself weaving into sleep.

———

The following day was spent in a faded concoction of suffering and numbness. I woke and saw the dawn spread on the quiet studio, the furniture and instruments sat calmly in their perfect positions. The hunger I felt that morning was putrid, so I surfed the bottom floor and the cramped kitchenette. Outdated cabinets, the room was hardly larger than a bathroom. A refrigerator groaned at the front of the room and cupboards and a counter space followed it to the back wall. There was little available in the space, mostly plastic bowls, Styrofoam cups for the coffee machine and packs of sugar. There was a box of protein bars on top of the fridge. Peanut butter chocolate. I ate two of them and brewed coffee in a daze; I carried the dark roast, black and steaming in a Styrofoam cup, back up to the second floor.

I held the cup close and engaged the space heater, directing its grated facade toward my shins. I could hear the world breathing outside the windows. I twisted around to find the car was still in its spot and seemingly untouched. But scraps and paper raced around the block as a gushing wind kicked up, the sky was dark and only getting darker. A storm was coming, just as Ellis mentioned. Florida was taking the bulk of it, some of the Carolinas too, I knew. The North would only see a thunderstorm sometime in the night. I watched as people who cut against the wind lost their hats, tables and chairs were brought into restaurants and the residents across the way began plucking their plants from the window seal. I yawned, sipped my black elixir, and tried to focus on what was directly in front of me.

Again, I eyed the drugs on the coffee table, but a tremendous fear was too brought about by them. Tommy and his addictions—but suddenly a new, freshly cut fear—I had no idea what was in any of the bottles, not for certain anyway. I sniffled; the back of my hand brushed against my nostrils. Had I missed the clues about Autumn? I recalled the coughing, the low energy that I had possibly mistaken for tranquility, the blood always on her sink and the pills on her night-stand. How had I not pieced it together sooner? My friend, widely my oldest and truest friend, had been fatally ill and I hadn't even noticed. Instead, all I could do was meet with her on weekends to vent about my problems, listen to hers in return, and end the weekend in our cyclical routine of sleeping together in her bed. Guilt became over-ridden by an enormous mass of shame. I went downstairs for another protein bar around three in the afternoon but once I had made my way back up the stairs, I was too drained and depressed to take a single bite.

Then, an instant awareness stirred in my mind, leaving me incred-ibly aligned as I became concerned that Ellis might show up. The studio would surely be one of the first places he would search for me. He would be enraged by my behavior and rightfully so. He had recently ranked highest on my list of enemies. In the release of the negativity I had experienced alone in that studio, my plan was to expose him to all his lies. He had lied about being a teenager in Manchester, and I was certain he was lying about working as Robert

Horowitz's assistant. He was even lying about his name, or with-holding information about his name. My brain was spinning, wondering what else he might be lying to me about. The possibilities and the detections only grew.

I decided on a plan for if, and when, Ellis arrived. I would use the audio equipment around me to record our conversation as I pressed him on the topic of his past. I began thinking through the various paths the conversation could deviate, and I became anxious about the confrontation and how he could react.

Then, while shivering in a fit of anxiety, something miraculous happened, and I recalled a weapon, a tool for my defense, within the studio. I shuffled through the main desk's drawer. There, below a cluster of disorganized papers, was the pistol, a stubby, silver pistol. Ice cold in my palm. I found the release and the magazine slipped out, revealing a full clip of seven brass bullets pointed forward like missiles ready to be fired. I reconnected the clip and made sure the safety latched and unlatched correctly, paying much cautious attention to the handgun. I let it fall to my side and thought to hide it in the sofa cushions. *No*, I thought, *the gun is no better in the cushions than it is in the drawer.* It ended up below my belt, pressed between my trousers and my skin leading to the groin. I was not pleased with the decision, but it was all I could think of. I was not sure how much time I would have before he might arrive.

The storm was beginning to take shape. It was still dry out but the wind became terribly dark and aggressive. I watched from the window every taxi that passed the studio. I checked the gun at least a dozen times more as my mind panicked at the thought. *If the occasion arose*, I wondered, *would I even be able to pull the trigger?* I had only shot a rifle before, but it was over a decade ago and in Georgia, during hunting season. A duck out in the wild was vastly different from a man standing across the room. My senses were used up and dizziness owned me. I was sick of my recent misfortune, so I toyed with the idea of calling off the confrontation, perhaps apologizing to Ellis as soon as he arrived. It was also not too late to go back and find Mazy or Betty, who I knew would both let me hide in their apartments.

No. I had to face him or else it might never end. No matter how long I hid from him or how far I went, I was to face him sometime in the future. By nine, I decided I could slump into the sofa. Perhaps he wouldn't be home that night. I was just about to allow myself to sleep with the comforting sounds of a rising storm in the background when I heard the glass door close on the bottom floor. I shot up and swiveled at the window to see a cab's light flicker on and ease off its brake lights, then back out into the slick street.

———

A series of beating thumps went up the stairs. Rested on the desk, blended between computer monitors and synthesizers, I pressed the red button of a handheld field recorder and quietly, the device began to capture every sound within the space. This is how I was able to articulate every nuance and phrase spoken in the room that night. The night of crass finality. I shouted out to the stranger, "Ellis?" He entered the room and closed the door behind him. Bloodshot eyes, gauze mesh pressed onto the edge of his chin, wet hair darkly thickened.

I paced behind the desk with crossed arms and peered out the triplet windows onto the grit of 8th becoming highlighted by an evolving drizzle. I heard him edging closer, the floors dipped and sank. Still, I looked out the window and thought of how to confront him. My nerves were tightened. I thought this moment of clash would be easier, but all my planned tactics dissipated at the moment. All was blank.

"Joe," he said. I looked back over my shoulder. There he stood in his loose fit trousers and black button up, his brown leather boots. He looked as exhausted as I felt. "I just want to make sure you're alright. If I've done something to offend you, I'd rather we talk it out and move past it so we can continue our relationship—"

"What relationship?" I butted in with a sharpness that caught Ellis off guard. He looked as if he'd been scolded. Betrayed. I shifted my body around to face him and ran my fingers over my hair, sweaty and slick. "I don't know what you think this is—and look, I'm sorry to come off so strongly. I should have talked to you about all of this sooner. And don't worry, I'm still going to write the symphony—"

"You have to. You signed the contract."

"Right. I know. It will be done, but after it's over—after all of this is over—I want *this,*" I paused and motioned to everything around us. He raised a brow. "I want this—whatever this is—to end. I'm turning in and going home after that."

Ellis scoffed. "What home?" he snarled. I realized he was returning the inflection I threw at him. His boots pounded into the wood floors as he stepped forward. He walked all the way around the desk, and up to where I stood, he stopped just in front of me. "This place, mate, it's all you have. I don't mean this studio. I mean this city. *With me.* Face it, everyone else is gone. Don't you understand that? And I'm sorry about your friends, I am, but everyone continuously turns their back on us. We're the fucking misfits." He scoffed as if he impressed himself. I cringed.

"Answer me one question, Ellis."

"Anything, anything," Ellis said, nodding.

"Did you buy that house? *Bladen?*" I asked. I looked over his stuttering expression.

"Yes," he returned and scoffed. He winced and reset, again forming a chuckle at the question.

"Did you really? Did you not spend your holidays there? Did you go there every summer as a boy? Was it your parents' house? Are they really dead?" I asked.

His face fell into a darkened, hollow void. All emotion ceased in his body, instead he was a man of shadow. Grim. Vacant. It was the first time I felt I was seeing the real Ellis. I regretted asking as soon as the words left my mouth, and there stood only a shape. My breath grew erratic, and I leaned back only slightly enough to feel the pistol's metal glide on my skin.

"This is not something you want to get into. Let's concern ourselves with the issue at hand."

"Not until you tell me everything," I graveled. I shot a nasty glare as if to show him how unintimidated I was. It was false, but I refused to let it slip. I kept my eyes on him. "Tell me the truth about what the fuck is really going on here. Who is Ellis Young? And who is *Jasper Ellis Bartlett?*"

His vision lazily fell to the floor. I thought he might topple over, and the fury in my skin charged me. I shoved my palms against his chest and screamed, "Answer me! Who the fuck are you?"

He took a single step back and his boot chomped on the floor like a kick drum. He ran his hands through his hair, scratching deep into the red, and his body trembled. He was a nervous and wretched sight to behold. Giant and unstable. He placed his palms over his face and as if he were a trained actor, snapped back into himself, removing his hands and grinning at me. He walked delicately around the room as if his lash of violence had never occurred, and examined all the trinkets of the studio. He went around me, back to the maroon lounge chairs and leaned his gaze over the coffee table.

"I used to love going to Bladen as a boy," he finally said. He picked an ashtray, small and silver, from the table. "Curious how things change. Or was it I that changed and the world stayed still?" He replaced the ashtray and fingered at the little cigarette box. He picked one and showed it off. "Everything changes. I often find change to be a haunting premonition despite its insistence to exist in the present. This instant is fleeting as the next will be—that's not to say it's *meaningless* though—no, not if we make good use of it."

I wanted him to cut out the fat and simply get to the point. All his suffering nihilism, his tired philosophies, exhausted me to no end. I looked back out the window at the furious gusts spiraling down the block. The Spyder sat smothered in a whirling spray. I heard a lighter clicking, then paper burning. Hot tobacco burned fresh in the air.

"Let me ask *you* a question—if I may," Ellis said and slouched in the lounge chair, tossing his legs up on the coffee table. I shrugged my shoulder. He held the cigarette between two fingers and pointed it out at me in a way that looked vaguely political. "Do you feel as though you have left a legacy? Or a lasting impact on the world, something like that?" I said nothing. I gathered up enormous patience as he continued toying with me.

"See, I've been thinking about this for years now. *Have I left a legacy?* And I think I have finally arrived at my answer. Yes—I believe I have—I honestly feel as though I have, strangely enough," he paused and gave in to a grin, "You are my legacy."

The moment it took to register what he said was all I had before a shudder rippled in my body. He returned his cigarette to his lips and sucked, then blew a puff of careful smoke.

"Do you know the first time I saw you? It was a while back, going on a decade ago now. I was working with the Inbetweeners as one of their producers. When they went on tour for their new record, I went to their show in Philadelphia. What was the arena out there? Oh, doesn't matter now—but who should take the stage as their opener but Beach Sirens? It was the first time I saw *you*—Joseph Henley, the shining star. Something I have never quite seen in anyone else. You had a spark to you—something really quite special—a flare amongst the darkness."

I stood in the foreground of the pale windows, now crawling with rain droplets, and bent my palms over the corner of the desk. I went to flick a speck off my dress shirt and glanced at the recorder—I saw the growing number on the audio file—I was capturing the truth. All was going to be revealed, how Ellis Young, the self-made producer, and renowned artist, was in truth, a hack. A liar. He was smoking when I looked back at him, he squinted across the room at the crested wall paneling, or perhaps it was an eclectic finish on the double bass nestled in the corner.

"It was at this moment that I decided, at whatever cost, I would find ways closer to you," Ellis said, deep in his memory. "Frankly, I wanted to *be* you. Suppose the next best thing would be to become your closest mate, right? So, it started with the dinner plans, then the Guggenheim—but I had plans for you so much larger. *Legendary* might be a word to describe it."

"Legendary," I said and hadn't realized I said it out loud until he nodded at me, as if to say, *that's exactly right*. I tried to carry the conversation and pushed him along, "So, what was this legendary plan then?" I walked around the desk to the table where Ellis lurched for the cigarette box and held it out to me.

"Have a zoot with me, mate, please." I took his lighter and lit the cigarette. I tossed it back at him and trotted back to the desk, the only place I felt safe. He watched me for a moment as if analyzing my movements in our little game. He scrunched his eyes and leaned forward, "Have you heard of the Twenty-Seven Club?"

He waited for an answer, briefly, and continued, "It's a remarkable and fascinating discovery that goes completely unexplained. A list, of sorts, of artists who all died at the age of twenty-seven. Jimi Hendrix. Jim Morrison. Kurt Cobain. Amy Winehouse. Jean-Michel Basquiat. This phenomenon has been extensively researched but, really, it goes without reason. Seemingly so, at least. What do you think of it?"

He paused, and the endless snare of rain pelting the windows filled the space. The storm was piling over Greenwich now. I blinked with my cigarette away from my mouth. At first, I thought he was joking, then nodded and said, "You're being absurd."

We both took a beat to drag on our cigarettes. Ellis popped from his chair, screwed his body around, and made way toward the wine rack. He found a bottle of red and used a tool above the rack to withdraw the cork with an electric knock. He began a pace around the studio; his steps softened on the highly decorative rug only to batter the wood floors in an off-kilter pattern. He held the cigarette in one hand, his bottle of wine in the other.

"What you call absurd, I call extraordinary. Think about all those names! Those names now sit comfortably among the stars above our heads—if you look out at the sky, they're written in ink. There's more too, not at the age of twenty-seven but etched in time for their youthful sacrifice. See, these *beautiful* bodies have exceeded the human form. They've become legends. Or, one might say, *legendary*, aye?" Ellis spaced out on the thought, then nodded without moving his wide stare lost on the wood floor, "*Gone too soon*, they say—but do you really believe that?"

"Of course, I believe that," I said. I attempted not to burst into laughter at his growing madness. He sounded broken, as if a needle skipping on a record, cause for insanity. He reset, stopped dead in his tracks, and leaned over the Chesterfield sofa to nest the dying butt in the tray. He stood up again, swigged from the bottle quickly, and wiped his sleeve.

"Let's try this then—What is your biggest fear?" He cocked his head with those wicked eyes, lit with frenzy. What had gotten into him? Was he drunk? He felt unhinged even from across the room and he returned to his pale grin.

"Joseph! Is it not *death?* All fears stem from some desire to exist without pain, you know, to continue living without discomfort, no disruption. And pain is often associated with death. So, why is that? The thought of ceasing to exist is so infinite! It's beyond our understanding," he said with a hum to himself. The noise subsided as if he were suddenly mute. He stared out at nothing in the room, half his face lost in shadow, the other lit in the bleeding glow of the lamp. He was trembling. "We cannot process the idea of death with our limited consciousness and so we fear it. Tragic deaths are usually synonymous with pain, but such is not always the case."

Ellis began pacing around the room, bottle of red in hand, and continued, "When Sylvia Plath first attempted suicide, it was 1953, and she'd taken a fatal dosage of her mother's sleeping pills. Only seemingly fatal, as she lived, but the effects of the pills were apparently so potent, that she'd *thought* she had died! Sylvia later wrote in a letter, and I quote, 'I swallowed quantities and blissfully succumbed to the whirling blackness that I honestly believed was eternal oblivion.' *Eternal oblivion* were the words that strike me most. It sounds grandiose, wouldn't you say? Death can be grand if we allow it to be."

"What does this have to do with anything?" I yelped.

Ellis stood still and grinned. "I'm getting to the point, mate, promise."

I found myself retreating from him involuntarily, my hands no longer glued to the desk, and I was taking short backpedals. I only realized it when the floors started whining beneath me. Ellis shot a look as if he were a wild animal. He stepped forward quickly into the light of the lamp on the end table, lit from below like a creature with exaggerated features. The warm haze lining his face matched the tinged hue of his hair.

"I don't wish to scare you, Joseph!" He stood up straight again and peered around the studio space. He crossed to the golden bar cart and withdrew a glass. The wine in his bottle fell into it, filling it to the top and the bottle was empty. He tapped the bottle onto the glass top of the bar cart. He continued, "I believe there is a great dilemma to life. Do we lose our youth to age, or do we die young enough to maintain it? And my greater question is—*which is the greater tragedy?*"

I felt a yelping snap between my fingers and realized the paper had burnt into the butt. I made a cursed noise and dropped it onto the rug. I stamped it out and examined my fingers. It would blister.

"I don't want to die," I said honestly, still lightly pushing on my brand-new burn.

"Obvious. Look at you, you're at the peak of your career. You are handsome, and healthy for your age. I don't want to die either, but it must happen eventually. So many of these promising souls throughout art history died young and therefore their image of youth and beauty is embalmed in our culture. Their cut-short library of art, their messages as artists, that's what's left. *Beacons of expression.* Perishing at a young enough age as a famous person will result in dreaded tragedy, true, but it means something much sweeter than any fame could ever offer. What I speak of is immortality."

I felt a cold, icy sensation sweltering in my body. But it was a mild pain. I was lightheaded. I was beginning to piece together what Ellis was telling me and what his intentions were. My knees wavered like wooden beams in a storm. I wanted to cry but clenched my muscles, everything I could. I wondered if he would kill me right here in this room. I would join Tommy and Autumn in the constellations, and I would lose everything I loved. Gone was making pictures with Luca. Gone was the music I was so carefully crafting, only existing in the air —*sound*—the recording of sound, and its preservation, the closest we can truly get to evidence for ghosts.

"Oh," I managed. I tried to say more but even the single noise from my throat proved difficult to produce. I knew he wouldn't carry on without a response, he wanted me to react. He was proud of his artifice. I was too stunned to turn my back on him as much as I no longer wished to look at him. Ellis tilted his head at me in an animalistic mechanism, then shifted his glass to the opposite hand and held his palm out.

"Immortality in the most *ironic* way possible! I do hear myself, Joseph. I know how bloody insane I must sound but place yourself in their perspective. These instant vanities. Notice how their image is etched into eternity! They're fossilized in permanent beauty. An alignment that guarantees nobody will ever forget the artist with such wonderful promise—*a voice of the generation*—and in this promise, more generations to follow will remember them as well. Fallen idols are given the largest headstones."

A cracked blue as bright as a camera's flash lit the room with awesome, oceanic exposure. Everything went pale and cold from the windows. The noiseless flickering subsided, retinas sizzled, and the room fell back to puddled darkness. The room was all black and orange like the ponds of Hell. The rainfall swelled into a radical storm as blaring thunder followed. This thunder chomped over the studio, rattling the furniture and walls before the air was filled again. The sounds of barreling wind and rain brushed over the chewed-up glass.

"Like I said," Ellis chuckled and motioned at the horrific weather. "Marilyn is no longer Marilyn—no, she is an entity of culture. The symbol of beauty. A stamp of American iconography. A figurehead of femininity. *Marilyn will never die.* All this despite dying so tragically young," he licked his lips, looked at the ceiling, and continued, "But do you know what Debbie Reynolds looks like? Jane Russell or Doris Day? They all died in the last decade or so. They lived out full, normal, decadent lives. They relished their youth and sacrificed their beauty for a full life. No, they would not become a modern Cleopatra, that spot was reserved for Marilyn. You know how I know?"

"How?" I pushed.

"I need only mention her first name and you can picture her vividly."

Another wincing white over the room, and I wondered if the power would hold through the rest of the night. A terror split in my mind at the idea of being in this room alone with Ellis, this human malevolence, tall and creeping in complete pitch darkness. Still, as he unraveled in front of me in the light of the storm, and two end table lamps, he teetered on his false swagger and his cracked sanity. Now, he was his suave self again, held up straight and calm, his voice low and neutral.

"All sorts of artistry reside in you, Joseph. There's a great dread to life in the limelight. There is, too, that grueling hunger to leave a legacy. More than anything, you want to make being on this planet worth it. These are at odds within you, and they inflict a little war in your mind. I tried to include you in my plans at the art museum and it failed. I was too inconsiderate then. I tried to intervene following the end of your tour, at what I thought would be the very highest peak of your career. Only, it seems the aim of my arrow was off."

I found my feet planted beneath me as his words began to formulate in my head.

"What do you mean by intervene?" I asked without making eye contact with him. I only kept his tall, oaky shape in the corner of my vision.

"I was the puppeteer of an event, in an effort to cause your permanence in the world," he explained with such articulation and as if he were some form of royalty, it even followed with a hummed chuckle and a sip from his glass. I whacked my palm on the desk and watched him practically spill the wine over himself. I mimicked the raging thunder.

"Stop it! What the fuck did you do?" I questioned and remembered the pistol tucked haphazardly into my belt. I could use it at any moment, until I recalled the presence of the recorder and how I needed to keep myself innocent. That is unless he were to try and act on creating a legend out of me. I was sweating, I noticed, but also the coldest I've ever been. Shivering. I felt insane at the level of my opponent and quivering with a natural urge to flee.

"I'll say this," he began, "I know how much you loved cocaine.

And a lovely drug it is too! I met this photographer in the city, we were in some loft, and he was shooting some album cover, and I got to talking to him and he said he'd partied with Beach Sirens. A boast, to be sure, but I pressed him on it and he revealed the truth—he'd never actually met you but he'd seen you at a party once. He also mentioned that he frequented a club with a man—*Hal* was his name—and Hal was Joe Henley's assistant."

I nodded to show I understood. I wanted to leap over the desk and strangle him, to force him to the point of the conversation instead of this maddening dance. All dancing.

"So, I thought, perfect! And over the next six months, I had bricks of cocaine sent to the photographer's apartment in Los Angeles, *anonymously*, of course. I have a string of people hired to create a clear separation from me. This bloke adored blow more than anyone I had ever seen. And when your tour was finished and I caught word of you starting to go out partying again, I gave the signal to sell a laced brick to the photographer at a highly discounted rate and told the contact to keep the money. Nobody knows that it came from me or who I was in the operation. And nobody except me and a man in the Bronx know that it's laced. And then, I crossed my fingers and hoped for the best."

I struggled to interpret his explanation, backtracking on the words and piecing them together. "So—you—," I tried. He was somehow the dealer behind the brick of cocaine that Hal had sliced up in my old apartment and, somehow, he knew it would end up there. It was impossible. Then, as if he'd read my mind, Ellis spoke up again, "I'm almost there. None of this is impossible, it only seems that way. When the brick was sold to the photographer, a message was sent along. A verbal message from the contact to Damion and it ensured that the brick made its way to you."

"What?" I choked the single word out of my throat. My eyes sponged with moisture; tears built their blockades around the rims. Ellis chuckled, now feeling more powerful than ever, and placed a hand in his pocket, still pacing about and casually stirred his wine glass, "To my surprise, the brick found its way to poor Thomas. You wouldn't believe how sorry I was. I didn't sleep for days—it was dreadful—knowing I'd missed my shot."

Everything fell into place. The tension snapped. I became blinded by an untamed fit of rage. I whisked around the desk and pummeled toward Ellis. I could feel the metallic barrel of the gun pinched against the skin, and I reminded myself not to topple too far to the point of withdrawing it. His head knocked on the bookshelf. Pinned against the leather hardbacks, my knuckles curled into his dress shirt. Ellis raised his glass so as not to spill it; he took none of it seriously.

"That's not possible!" I screamed at him. Our faces were a breath apart.

"It only isn't plausible! I was going to make you an icon! Don't you get it? A known figure for the rest of history! A sacrifice any reasonable mind would make in a heartbeat! You have something so few in this world are capable of. I would kill for it! I escaped the wealth of my family and tried to rise to the top on my own, without any help but it would not work without the inexplicable missing ingredient. The *talent*. Something you have within you. And instead, my legend was wasted—"

My arm snapped into an angle and my elbow pounded against his throat. Ellis was trapped against the wall of books, now wavering and plopping from their places on the shelves. He was pinched between the shelf and the jagged bone of my joint.

"You killed Tommy," I snarled. Everything on my tongue felt viperous and pointed. I wanted to breathe his blood; I wanted to see it. I felt the hatred inside of me snapping like firecrackers, something unruly and fully consuming my mind and body. "Say it. The mints—the fucking tin of mints—I've seen it only once before; I knew it as soon as I saw it. I saw it the night Tommy died. Hal said he got it from that photographer."

I knew Ellis was lying or at least leaving out details on how Tommy's death was truthfully carried out. But it didn't truly matter to me much anymore; Ellis' intentions were crystal. Tommy's death was an accident. He was collateral in the broader scheme, that of his crazed fascination with murdering me to make me live forever. I pressed my elbow tighter and watched his body squirm, his face bending darker, from rose to purple. Another flash of lightning allowed me to see how haggard I'd made him. The breath could not escape his lungs, only sounds of puny choking and the colossal rainfall played. I could not kill him though. I let go only enough for him to catch air and once he had enough blood circulating again, he looked at me with strained eyes.

"I didn't kill anyone. I had a vision—to catch you in time—like a dead star still sending light through the cosmos. I was reckless though. I slipped."

"You *did* kill him! I want to hear you say it." I leaned my elbow tighter. I wondered dreadfully if the recorder would be able to catch his confession against his dying breath and the unfaltering roar of the storm.

"No!" he groaned. And tighter, I thought his eyes might pop from the sockets, rolling up toward the heavens and asking for grace. His mouth tried to move, and I let up. His strained neck had an imprint from my shirt, and he wheezed, "Yes! I killed Tommy! But none of this—was ever—meant for him."

I decided his words were likely of a decent volume and set him free of the lock, stepping back at a razor speed, hitting one of the end tables. I thought he might attack me at the first chance he got but instead, he held his throat with such loving care.

I watched him fall to his knees and crush into the puddle of wine and glass fragments. He looked so vulnerable in this position, so tenderly he held himself. He was genuinely hurt. His ginger hair mapped over his face as he tried so desperately to breathe, and I thought of how I'd hurt him, and the tears boiled over the edges and streaked my cheeks.

I felt a withering despair; I needed him and this full betrayal I played on him hurt so much. To know I was the one who had hurt him made me feel ill despite the truth being splayed open like a wound. I broke into a full sob and fell to my knees, equal with Ellis. I crawled along the wood floors toward him, stammering in the wicked pitch studio where he now sat in the puddle of red, nearly ink in the failing illuminance. He breathed and I placed my hand on his back, I felt his spine bend and sink with every heave. He looked at me, and despite only the sliver of muddied radiance, I could see the sadness surrounding his expression.

"Most artists create their masterpieces around their middle age. That's when they are at the perfect catalyst in their life to learn the *truth* of pleasure and suffering. As I have gotten older, I reexamined the idea. Look at you—you don't need to create a masterpiece—you are enough on your own."

I swallowed, out of breath, the two of us breathing heavily, gasping, against the background of tapping and thudding and splashing rain. "So, you brought me all the way out to the country to kill me—what about the rest of the artists? Are you going to kill them too?" I asked.

"They're all good—they're fine—but they aren't you. It hadn't mattered to me when I was developing the idea of the Artist's Haven. Before I even knew of you. It did not matter whether you or the rest of them were the best at their art form—it only mattered if one had the *potential* to create something historical—yes, the *promise* of a masterful career. *What could have been*—that short phrase, that is what I sought out. I left my family and the family business. I sacrificed everything to become a creator. I wanted to create history with the artists around me. The benefits of my theories are parallel to valor."

Ellis was a truly lost soul. A stained heart. We were covered in wine; I could smell the potent liquid wetting us over. I sniffled. He refused to break into a full fit but neared it. He pouted, "But I knew it from the first time I saw you. I knew you were so much more than sudden fame. You are destined for more! You would have been the kindest entry to inscribe in the textbooks. I wouldn't have to fake it like I would for others, no, you are *real*. That would be my gift to you. I *wanted* to give that to you."

The more he spoke and the rate at which he recovered from my attack led me further from him again. He stared down at the glass and the shaded wine, wheezing gently as if he were purring, and I steadily found my balance with my palms on the floor and kicked myself back slowly. He began muttering to himself, a soft stuttering phrase, "I can give that to you."

I was on my hands and knees turning away from him when I sensed a flailing from behind me. Like rabbits, we thumped quickly. I skidded off the floor and shot away as fast as I could. I felt a claw wrap on my leg, and I halted in a law of motion; I lurched backward into Ellis' grasp. Suddenly my head thudded, a whack on the wood floor, bouncing on my cheekbone. Completely disoriented, and unaware due to the momentary confusion, I was whipped around onto my back.

Before I could think of a defense, a blinding injection flamed at the side of my stomach. I looked down. A glass shard was cutting into Ellis' fingers while prying deep into my gut, watching as my skin tore in ways I could never have imagined. I felt sirens blaring in my head to move away from the intrusion, but everything was out of function; I was helpless and baffled. My vocal cords were retching out noises I'd never heard from myself, high and trying; I felt the glass piece exit my stomach, and the skin let it free. A gush of black ooze expanded from where the glass had dug. I watched it swell with a bulging interest and felt the coolness of air touching my blood.

The shard was then replanted. Higher and in the ribs, briskly in and out. Ellis became a new animal. He picked up his pace with increasing force and I watched as my thick blood ripped in and out on the glass like terrible maroon strings, attached and thinning out and snapping. I thought I might faint. I was trying to find air as everything tightened. I was helpless. I thought I should thrash for freedom, but I only lay still and accepted every injection, limp and dull.

Finally, Ellis had enough, or seemingly decided I was dead. Everything was quiet as the water continued its trickle on the windows like the flow of a river far off. Ellis heaved a great, whining breath. His eyes flared and pupils narrowed. I wondered what death would feel like. What might it be like to experience the final sensation? Tommy and Autumn knew of it. I was next. The realization was hard to grasp as the ideology had a profound weight to it. These were my final moments, and I stared at the regal drop ceiling tiles, golden and proper like squares of chocolate and wondered if this was the final image. The last sight to behold on the short life. It would be forgotten as the curtain closed. A cycle of cruelty.

I thought of my parents, I hoped they were well, and I imagined them young and laughing, my favorite way to imagine them. I thought of my two sisters. I thought of Sophia, Tommy and Autumn, my truest loves and those which I cared for the most from my time alive. Luca. His lovely Donna. Vivian. The countless others I'd encountered, I wanted to leave nothing out, but time was slipping, and I became fearful. I hadn't wanted to die; I had no intention of meeting death so soon, so suddenly, alarmingly. I was young and I felt ashamed of the mishaps and my mistakes, and I wanted to right every wrong and generally appreciate everything in front of me more closely and intimately. I could no longer breathe, and I knew if I continued to lie in this position, I would choke on my own blood before I would bleed to death.

I imagined death to resemble sleep before a sudden intrusion caused a birth of light. Splits of shining white like streetlamps on a dull night with outstretched needles expanding from their sources— thorny branches of the sun—these needled arms reached out toward each other in a woven neurotransmission. This constellation of pale glints braced to expand into one another like the growth of a rising dough. Finally, all is replaced by an encompassing white. A waking shimmer.

All at once, weightlessness would relieve the veins and arteries. The tethered knot of the body would release, only to float toward the sky—like a Fellini dream—yet the mind would sink with the sensation of knocking the wind out of the lungs, a sweeping kick, that same feeling as an elevator's lurch. Low, low, low, and gone, comfortably gone, collapsed and relaxing. Memories would present everything in a carousel, each memory misfiring at the front of the mind on its march toward devastation, too far drifted out to wonder where it's gone. Beyond the memories, the glowing constellation would converge into a star.

I clocked the phases of internal rapture, how I was sure to never achieve immortality even in the eyes of the culture and prepared myself for the surrender of my brain. Ellis' face came into view over the ceiling tiles, tilted and peering at me as if his greatest work of art had finally been completed. I was his masterpiece. He pushed his red hair back, slicked and darker than usual, and found the cigarettes on the table once again. My head was a foot to the left of the sofa, I reached my arm up and touched the suede fabric of it. I heard the metal of his lighter rotate then watched the sofa deflate as he lodged himself into it. I managed to push myself onto my side, moaning out a whispered sound. Ellis didn't budge, he just smoked in complete silence.

Amongst this festering pain, raw and sizzling, I felt the pistol grip refuse to let my stomach bend. And I remembered the recorder still compiling every sound on the desk. At once, I felt a wave of strength surge through me, a desire to carry on. I had to manage at least one more inhale. Then another. I created a new pattern of breath in my passion for life. I flexed myself up onto the rug. Bright stinging. It took all my effort against the pain as the rug soaked up the warm liquid from my body. Ellis scoffed at the sight of me rounding the corner of the Chesterfield sofa. He crossed his legs.

"You know what? I take back what I said. Not all art has hidden meaning."

He smoked and rocked his folded legs as if he had done nothing wrong. He had reverted to his docile charm; he blatantly ignored my scratched cries in pure agony until he finally acknowledged me with a warm grin. He explained, "The analysis of art is fine, but it's the artist I'm interested in. That's where real beauty lies. And at last . . . Here lies beauty."

He pressed the toe of his boot into my forehead, first lightly as if to barely feel the coolness of the black rubber sole, then with increasing force. He intended on pressing all his weight and I felt the pressure building as he slowly propped himself up and away from the sofa. He was about to press his full weight on my forehead. The rubber stretched my skin near the point of tearing when I found the gun.

I screamed and closed my eyes as my thumb pushed the safety off. *Only seconds longer of suffering,* I thought, and the gun was shaking in my weak hands. My arms wanted badly to instinctively thrash at his foot, but I zeroed on the pistol. Up it went and I cocked the hammer. I felt his boot begin to ease as I opened my eyes and found Ellis standing over me, staring perplexed at the gun barrel. His eyebrows started up in horror.

I pulled the trigger and there was a bright clap. My shoulders hauled back into the floor at the force. Before me stood Ellis, his eyes crossed on the barrel but following that wincing crack, a violent stamp in time of light and sound, there was Ellis but changed. As a swallow of silence temporarily sucked the damp room, I watched as a childlike wonder, nearly dumbfounded, took over his face. I thought it a soulful gleam to the eye, before they both dipped upward onto the ceiling tiles. And just as soon as it did, the world gushed toward proper speed again, perhaps even faster than ever before.

Ellis was white in the face, then red only in the neck. It grew, a black-red, like blackberry jam. His face went empty, his character broke and for the first time, I saw who I knew to be Jasper. He looked so innocent without emotion or thought, less than an animal, a curious object. Blood poured out quicker and quicker, a ringing rose in the ear, and his body went entirely limp, jutting bloody blotches and falling like a doll. It was no longer of any pronoun, no longer of any proper condition as it was devoid of what I'd known to be the body of Ellis Young.

With this thought, a jarring and terrifying revelation occurred—his body was still falling but his soul was surely above, held in place, somewhere in the room with me. It was looking down on its capsule as it rapidly shut down all its systems, the heart-thumping but sputtering and would soon slow, go frigid, and never pulse again. Ellis was dead. The action of which felt less climactic than I was led to believe. Cinema and theater and everything in our culture led murder to be some triumphant moment of release and farewell—achievement and denouement—no, it was brisk. Instantaneous. It began all in one blaring, swollen second of time and was finished in the next as *Now* morphed to *When*. Once there was a man named Jasper Ellis Bartlett who stood before me, going by a pseudonym, with a twisted goal in mind, and at their very next breath, there was a meaningless corpse plunging toward me.

I had no time to prepare as the body landed on top of me. The weight of this dumb mass smacking against me and then staying there was little to the pain I felt elsewhere. His open eyes stared at me like the eyes of a fish, never blinking, no longer moving; they were pointed at me but not staring. I used my final strengths to heave the body away from me. I pressed my palm into the biggest hole in my stomach to try and possibly preserve myself and crawled back toward the desk.

I slapped the surface until I found the field recorder, and brought it down to my level, my back propped against the desk drawers. My fingers slipped on the device, but I managed to stop the recording, smearing the device with my fluids in the process. I hadn't known if I was going to die that night, but I knew I would have proof of my innocence. I had the confession of the killer, the bent mind misconstrued by a world that held fame at a higher degree than life itself.

And I was alone again. The rain had died to spiderwebs of wet. I shifted my body, pressing my weight into one hand and the other on my stomach to look at the body on the floor. That contorted body stuck in a single position, arms twisted back, and head smashed limp on the floor in a puddle of black. His cigarette smoldered in the blood. A silent slither of smoke rose near the shape. I once thought that perhaps he was an angel sent to me in a time of need. I recall my grim opposition at that moment. A demon.

I heard my aching voice as I lunged my humiliating body onto two feet. I managed to pass the mutilated body, and mine too edged on death. Both bodies drained of the scarlet within us. I crawled fearfully down the studio steps and onto the first floor.

The door handle turned. As the door split and allowed a wedge of amber light, I saw the cascade of showering storms slanted at an angle, slicing 8th Street, and damned lightning flickering in and out on the buildings. I thought of how I wished to escape the terror that plagued the studio and stepped out onto the wet asphalt, away from the horrific scene.

What was once the epicenter of my creations, my space of safety and passion, was now tainted by an evil corruption. Haunted. I paced, one foot leading the other, into the storm, trailing red from my torso. A string of pink puddles followed at my feet. I wandered aimlessly, making it only a single block before my vision began to fade. It felt so light, so lacking in gravity, it was the woeful comfort equivalent of drifting into sleep. I could no longer feel my legs. I could no longer feel much of anything at all. I thought of Victor Frankenstein and the moment in the scripture when the creature comes to life—Victor fled his laboratory and wandered the streets of Ingolstadt in the dead of night—similar and yet wholly opposite of my scenario. Where the mad scientist created life, I destroyed it. Both are the total abominations of nature and yet, entirely natural.

V

CONCERNING THE CULTURE

I recall blinking rapidly as I came to consciousness. I took immediate note of the terrible paleness of my surroundings. Awful white light. I sat up on the paper-like sheets to scrub my fingers over my eyelids; it became hazily apparent that I'd somehow been delivered to emergency care. Cheap cabinets and a wall complete with an abstract painting. I squinted at it as if this might sprout an answer. Perhaps its purpose was always intended to be on the wall of a hospital room. Little purposes are still purposes. The room smelt like latex and rubbing alcohol and everything in my vision was blurred.

"Joe?" I knew the voice, the scratching rise of tone. There was a dark figure sitting against the hazel glow through the blinds. Their hair jutted in every direction; black claws sprouted from their head. I squinted at the figure as if it were abstract. They leaned forward, and there in my evolving clarity was Luca Krzyżewski, and he ran his knuckles on my forearm.

"Well, well, look at the sleeping beauty. Buongiorno," he said and chuckled heartily.

"Hey," I managed. My eyelids fluttered, and I was unable to maintain focus. I was in a weighted daze, somewhere between asleep and awake. I croaked, "How did I get here?"

"I do not know. I just see on the news. Joe Henley in *hospital?* I put on my shoes, I call taxi, then I wait here all night. Now you are awake! You live!"

I tried laughing but a sharp pain split all over my stomach. I lifted the bed sheet to examine what was wrong and found my stomach wisped in hair and several purple seams sewn on my skin. I later found out I received eighty-four stitches to wind up every wound inflicted on my body; nothing about my situation was fatal as the blade never punctured the breastplate or broke any ribs. Instead, the doctor informed me that I was in a rather safe state when I arrived unconscious—I'd lost a liter of blood somewhere between the second floor of the studio and the sidewalk—my body went into shock, which allowed my systems to begin to shut down. Still, I was cautioned that it was nothing detrimental to my survival in any real way.

The door clocked and Betty entered the room, her hair a mess and arming a paper grocery bag. She became dumbstruck to find me squinting back at her, blinking every so often and slightly grinning. She yelped, sort of giggling in joy, "You're awake! You're okay!"

She had purchased sandwiches and snacks from a bodega not so far away. She needed the nutrition as much as I did since Betty and I shared the same blood type. A blood transfusion was called for and Betty was there for me—always there for me.

I was only in the hospital for four more hours before I was allowed free again. They informed me of several precautions to take. I was brought back to Betty's apartment in West Harlem, where I lay in the bed I knew so well and was ordered to rest for the remainder of the day into the next. But I woke as the orange sun began to slide on the linoleum. I blinked and noted that Luca was still sitting in the room. When our eyes met, he perked and stiffened into a look of giddiness.

"Ciao, my friend, hi, how are you feeling?" he asked carefully. I shot into the air, finding him infinitely amusing, and reassured my friend I was okay. My ally against taxes. *Creators without fear.* He asked if I wanted to watch a movie. I said no, I would like to lie in silence for a while so that is what we did. Together, we studied the floor and the waning light reflecting on its surface, and I cherished the ceiling of the room I knew so comfortably. I was set to stun, my body plump with pain, and aside from my immediate circumstances, I could only think of Autumn.

I still hadn't gotten a full grasp on the situation, and I held projections of her in my mind. Countless memories made together—from our time spent in Tommy's dorm back at GWU to our close apartments and to our rapidly changing lives in Arlington, to touring and recording and touring more, to not so long ago, walking the city at her side. I didn't want to forget these memories; I wanted to keep them in focus forever. I arrived at an optimistic outlook by deciding I was unbearably thrilled to have gotten to spend time with these pleasant souls while they graced this planet and what a strange planet it is. A rock so cluttered with life—*life:* a vacation from the cosmos, dust and energy uniting to act in a play, assigned the role of a peculiar creature with a mind of its own—*a mind:* the cosmos reflected.

I shifted away from Luca in my bed and winced at my stitched torso. Gently, I allowed tears to fall due to a mix of grievance for my friends and an intense gratitude to have had the opportunity to stand by their sides, in song and in laughter. If Tommy is correct, and humanity exists only by complete accident, then a group of these impossibilities coming together for such a companionship is the greatest feat to ever happen in all the universe.

My cheeks quivered as a smile found its way on my face and my tears bled on the pillowcase; without much notice, I drifted back into sleep. There, I found myself back in the cityscape, on that familiar street and Tommy standing ahead of me. I called his name, but again it was no use; it wasn't until I started running that he ran too, like a predator on its prey. This time it was different. I started catching up to him in my dream. And as my heels grew closer to his, I stretched my hand in hopes of reaching his shoulder but something inexplicable happened—Tommy became Autumn—in the sort of logic only found in dreams where our minds are the creators and reasoning becomes subjective. It was almost as if I'd forgotten it was ever Tommy—*yes, of course, it was Autumn.*

My fingers feathered on her shoulder, and she stopped running.

The chase was over. She turned, surprised to see me, as if she hadn't known I was behind her. She looked so thrilled to see me. Autumn embraced me and for a brief eternity, we held each other. My chin dug into her fluttering ginger hair and even there, in the realm between plausibility and imagination, I could smell the signature scent that belonged to her alone.

She broke away and patted the tears from her eyes. Her hand skated onto my cheek and held there only a moment before it was off, and she grinned. I looked up and saw the street of a never-ending trail had ended, exchanged now for the typical angle of a street corner. I thought of telling her but I still decided not to, I suppose due to the subjective laws. She laughed quietly and said, "What do you look so sad for? Cheer up, Joey. You'll be alright." She playfully tapped my cheek and let go. When Autumn rounded the corner, she was gone and perhaps I could have gone around to see for myself, but my knees buckled; I was seemingly petrified. I heard Luca's Italian voice stirring in the distance and so, I turned around.

The dream fell out when Betty said, "Quiet! You're going to wake him." So, I came to reality with a slam, the dream world softening before dissolving into an envelope of darkness as if it were the end of a film in the cinema. Before the credits could begin, my vision peaked into the spare bedroom of the Harlem apartment, now the chipper morning with a freshness to the air.

I started up, swallowing gasps as I folded and felt the bandages' disagreement. I heard something that required further inspection. Not the sound of my family in the kitchen but a tone, a progression of sound, rising and crashing, in the effects of an ocean wave but with all the might of an orchestra. I heard the soft orchestra as if it were tinged by a muffled echo and it was because of this I thought the sound might be far off. I tried to listen closer, remaining awfully still. Despite its thinning distance, it was a brilliant sound to my ear. I needed to know more of it, as if it were my favorite tune, and I hoped to hear it at a volume to make it stand out. I exited the bedroom, and in the kitchen, it briefly faded, instead a sizzling filled in as I saw Luca and Betty were cooking bacon and eggs. It was a quarter to seven, the 29th of July, and it was the day I heard the music.

I felt my eyes bulge upon the epiphany, this miraculous sprout of an idea, for the quiet orchestra did not exist in my exterior world, but in my mind! It was calling to me and I needed to get back into the bedroom as quickly as possible, but I could only move so quickly—Luca glanced at me curiously before he questioned, "Do you need to be back to bed? You do not look so well." Betty went pale at the sight of me, nearly a hunchback with my insect stare at the floor. My sister and my friend escorted me back to my bed, where I lay on the sheets. Luca's head became the only subject in my line of vision, all his hair falling over his face as he peered down at me.

"Anything I can get you, please. You tell me. I will get it for you, please," he said and petted my hair.

"Paper," I muttered. I stared past him, at the ceiling, where the notes were etching themselves into the thick textured ceiling. Sprouting like leaves and fading out when I moved my vision. My brain was pounding, and I swallowed, overcome with a wave of tangible inspiration. Luca moved closer, obstructing the view of these phantom notes falling onto a staff that did not exist.

"What is it you say?"

"Please—paper—if you can find any."

A moment later, the two of them returned with paper and pens and set them on the nightstand table. I thanked them sharply and ordered them to return to their cooking so I could write in solitude. And I sharpened my many senses to listen deeper to that magnificent sound. A bellowing ensemble performed within my skull. I propped myself up in bed, and with the ringing movements of the distant orchestra, one to only exist inside of me, I inked the rising notes of my symphony. A mighty sound. With each note sloppily scribbled into the paper, the orchestra became clearer and more punctual with their harmonies and rhymes, until it was like I was standing in the hall and listening to it as a member of an audience. Crashing cymbals blended behind the barreling tread of the strings, and horns and the wood-winds found their way as if synonymous with nature's wind. To my surprise, there too was a sitar and a rumba, exotic sounds as the symphony revealed itself to me. I translated every bit the best I could with my lightning rod in hand, casting the charged storm through my body, and out to the universe through a blistering black ink.

Several days went by as I wrote in a frantic state, shifting between water and coffee and Luca watched all of it in awe. I ate only oatmeal and ignored the world. My new world became that special room where my music seeped out of my brain. From the 29th of July till the 17th of August, the first draft of my original composition was completed. The composition—if played at the typical tempos of a sonata, adagio, minuet, and allegro—ran over seventy minutes in length. I compiled my work; I was proud of the achievement. The time spent creating the project or the time spent inscribing the chords from mind to music was not all spent writing, as there were plenty of visits and time provided for police and detectives to recall what occurred the night Ellis Young was murdered.

The only interruption in the creation of my symphony was the proving of my innocence, and I found it quite nauseating. I told the detectives to immediately locate the field recorder on the second floor's desk, where ahead of the triple-headed monitor display, there would be a handheld recorder with all the proof needed to result in such a violent act. I was deemed innocent in the case of Ellis Young the night of July 27th. The judge's verdict was Justifiable Homicide—Self Defense. The entire night's events were kept private to preserve the image of the late producer.

Ellis Young was a lie. After vigorous investigation, it was discovered that Jasper Ellis Bartlett had, in fact, been raised in the small village of Lancashire, England and later in the city of Manchester but his parents did not die until he was twenty years old. Terrence and Helena Young, his presumed parents, were entirely fictional. The real parents of the producer were Kingston and Hilly Bartlett—Kingston Bartlett being the founder and owner of Bartlett Winery—as well as the Bartlett Estate in Manchester, England. His father opened six resorts, ranging from Amsterdam to Oslo. Jasper grew up as the heir to several successful businesses, and at a certain point, he realized this would soon be his kingdom. That is what led to their fatal demise, at a turning within the skull of young Jasper Ellis, realizing he could have it all if he so chose.

Kingston and Hilly Bartlett died in their mansion in Manchester because of a gas leak; it caused a powerful explosion that destroyed their entire estate—their servants—and of course, the King and Queen. Notably, Jasper was nowhere to be found at the time of the explosion. He arrived days later when it came time to take over the family business, eager to carry on the legacy of the Bartlett business. Several accounts from faculty and associates state they never once saw Jasper show any sign of distress over the loss of his parents. A fallen angel of enormous stature.

Less than a year later, Jasper turned twenty-one and sold all the companies (minus the Bartlett Winery, which he owned all the way until his death). Jasper decided to pull off a portion of his new, hand-some funds (I later discovered he had over 66 million dollars, and that was only his inheritance, which excluded the gains from piloting his many businesses) and he headed toward New York City to begin a new life as an artist. He vacationed in New York with his family nearly every summer during his childhood—they stayed in their only Amer-ican residence, the mansion known as Bladen—and this house became his new residence for a few short months as he paid for several services that would erase anything he had to do with Jasper Ellis Bartlett. By the fall of 2005, Jasper Bartlett was 'dead' and Ellis Young was his new identity. Ellis was in the city then, in his Queens apartment, and working in the music industry. He never had any innate talent or skill for music but he knew he wanted to be a part of the world of super-stardom in some fashion, to be regarded as a highly praised individual and not just for owning a wine company.

With a lot of money, one could get about anywhere they chose. So, Ellis paid out of pocket to cover the many expenses required in creating The Inbetweeners' sophomore album. In return, he asked to sit in on sessions and learn how it was all done. He was only twenty-one and I do believe the band enjoyed his charisma; how could they not? So, Ellis quickly grew to power as a leading producer, working with nearly anyone he chose as the Prince of Dissonance (his biggest draw was his ability to create beautiful dissonances and his ability to work in several different genres of music). Ellis only knew the violin as he went to a private school in Manchester and played the violin there for eight years. He kept the skill, or he must have, as I heard him practicing often in his bedroom back in Queens—the romantic tinge of strings rang out from his half of the apartment nearly every afternoon. It was the only instrument I ever saw him play.

Several musicians and now producers for several music labels have since stepped forward to disgrace Ellis—stating on multiple accounts he was a sexually and mentally abusive individual. The lead singer of Hellplex, Imogen O'Neal, made the biggest splash by coming forward and stating she had been taken advantage of at another well-known musician's party by Ellis Young. He followed her down the hallway and into the bathroom. In *The New York Times*, she specifically stated the bleak hollowness in his eyes—I felt my gut clench horribly while reading it—the same empty voids I had seen the night he tried to kill me. The night he attempted to make art out of me.

I came to realize Ellis was less than human. He was the one who killed his parents with eyes set over their bodies, focused on the fortunate hill he could then climb faster. He never played on street corners for cash. He was never homeless. He went to America to play in the sandbox of fame, which was far more enticing than any fortune could ever provide him; fortune would not follow to the afterlife, but fame had the possibility of shielding death's reign. His father was slain so he could become king but he must have steadily learned he could not become a god.

One morning in Soho, months after his death, I ran into Robert Horowitz in a café. I took to the bar top near him, explained who I was to the filmmaker, and we drank our morning cappuccinos while discussing cinema. At a certain point, I finally asked if he had ever had an assistant named Ellis Young—he hadn't. Ellis never started as an intern at the Rockefeller Center, he hadn't worked as an assistant to the filmmaker, and he hadn't met several of the celebrities who he claimed he had.

Why he felt the need to create such detailed lies was so far beyond my understanding, I nearly found it fascinating. He had accomplished much in his life, despite his demented ways of going about it, and I couldn't understand why he would continue lying. Ellis Young may have been slain and announced as a terrible influence, but something inexplicable was born out of it. The first time I saw him again was on 5th Avenue, trotting on the sidewalk, passing the Met, and there was his face sketched onto the front of a shirt. I stopped at the stand and stared at his face for quite some time—a white shirt and his face spray-painted on using a stencil of some sort, black ink dried and frayed. His finely cut face, the one I'd torn open on the stone driveway. His lips, only black lines on the shirt left me sick. His neck, free of a bullet hole, a rendition of the man before being punctured. The man running the stand barked if I wanted to see sizes and I shook my head.

I later saw the same stencil of Ellis used on social media; a jarring number of posts were created in dedication to the producer. His face was inked on every magazine cover. *Rest in Peace—Ellis Young (April 15, 1984 - July 27, 2027).* He was in Time Square, he was on the news, on the radio, everywhere I turned I saw him and saw the praise and the condolences. Despite my many attempts to deface him, and the short ripples from Imogen's statements, he was still placed on a pedestal that could not be dismantled. He was held in the hands of the people, lifted higher over their heads, toward the sky. Alive and fresh was the king. He had achieved his goal in the end: to become known as a spec in human history, given value only by what we deem it. A twisted ending, surely, yet fit for the prince. He had fallen but was now taller than ever before.

For many months following the incident in Velvet Pie Studios, I became haunted by the attack. Nightmares caused me to wake up shrieking alone in my bedroom in fits of stuttering cold. Sweat suffocated my body and wetted the sheets. I would rub my fingers over the new skin from my wounds, so soft and intriguing. It felt like I was touching someone else. It would take up to an hour to recenter my breathing and allow myself to fall back into a slumber. I began going to a psychologist to help me better understand those terrorizing dreams and to find a resolution in the event as a whole. I had lost a great deal of those I deemed worthy of care, and the psychologist aided me in finding reason. He wanted to help me someday find the ability to trust someone again.

As for the artists I worked alongside as a part of NYAH, they, too, sought closure to the event. Many of them often checked on me. Yvette ended up moving to Paris and continued her career as an artist there. The only artist who stayed in the city after everything that happened, after getting paid out by the organization, was Sumitra. This was someone I allowed myself to trust. She became a well-respected poet and a language tutor for young scholars, going between high schools and colleges, even tutoring those who went to New York University. I became increasingly fond of Sumitra, and in due time, we would spend many days together. Beginning first with her birthday party, then morning coffees, then drinks and dinners, picnics, cooking at hers, cooking at mine, and listening to any problem the other had. Neither of us gave a name to the situation; we allowed it to be.

New York Artist's Haven lived on as the organization was bought by a duo of young filmmaker brothers born and raised in Lower Manhattan, named Caden and Ernest Voigt. Caden Voigt, the younger brother, was attending Juilliard and the other, Ernest Voigt, had a massive presence online. To my surprise, upon completing *Symphony No. 1*, I was awarded the one million dollars in a series of deposits made by New York Artist's Haven. I went back to my new apartment in the city, on 11th, between University Place and Broadway as a free man—free of conviction, free of Ellis, free of the weight of toxicity and mission. I had money in my pocket equivalent to my days as a star, and scars softly recovering on my body. I had an electric mind fluttering with constant and unwavering ideas. I had myself and for that, I was complete.

———

Symphony No. 1 was presented in the Perelman Performing Arts Center on February 8th, 2028. The orchestra was a brilliant sea of fifty four black suits and stained wood, golden brass and twinkling strings; I stood at the center and ordered the music with my conductor's baton, my lightning rod. I cast my storm throughout the theater. I created thunder. I beckoned for energy and the musicians serviced it. And if it all went correctly, the audience received a satisfying range of emotions. The nature of light and sound. A combination of life working in unison to create one relentless truth. While words exist solely for the human, music could exist for all.

Still at the Perelman, following the performance and accepting several gifts and more flower bouquets than I had ever seen, I was greeted by Luca, Donna, and Sumitra, all wrapped in dazzling attire. And later, exiting the theater with the three of them, holding our breaths to brace for the night's chill, I neared the bottom of the front steps when a voice called to me once more.

"Joey!"

I turned and found my favorite sight—Sophia—in a picturesque red dress, one may call it classic, with a glittering clutch at her side —*The Red Upon the Hill*. What is more, I forfeited all that surrounded me, and shuffled through the dotted bodies, up the hill once more; the hill I would climb and climb but never summit. Upon the peak of my climb, Sophia took two steps down and leaped into my arms. I held her for our little forever, breathing in our warmth and exhaling our foggy breaths into the black sky, speckled with flurried snow. I set her down on the stairs and her heels ticked on the concrete.

"You did so wonderfully," she said, her voice already trembling from the cold, and wrapped her coat tighter around her shoulders. "I mean, of course, you were—but really, Joe—I thought you were extraordinary. It was one of the best nights of my life. I'm so glad I got to see it after all! Such a special moment."

"Thank you so much for coming," I replied, unable to remove my eyes from hers and grinning. It was like we were nineteen again, unsure what to say and staring at each other. "I'm so glad you could make it." My voice trailed out as Daniel clicked down the steps with an unconscious one-year-old girl tucked in his arm, her face squished into his shoulder.

I continued, "You and the family." I stared at the girl, her curly hair a light brunette color, and how she slept so peacefully in her father's grasp. Her name was Presley Cavansky, and she would be turning two at the end of March. Sophia chuckled, "I know. We tried to get a sitter for tonight, but it didn't work out. She really enjoyed it."

"She slept through most of it?" I asked. Sophia nodded and we both laughed. Daniel gave a stern, short nod in my direction and said, "Congratulations." I thanked him and I could sense his irritation at Sophia and I bumping into one another out on the front steps rather than in the heated lobby. I told them to catch a cab and let their daughter sleep in a bed rather than out in the cold before she got sick.

"I'll see you later," Sophia said. She rubbed the forearm of my coat. "Let's get coffee soon. Tomorrow, we're taking her on the ferry. We'll be here until Friday."

"Okay," I replied. "I would like that." She had a meeting with her publisher in regard to her second poetry collection titled, *Scissors for Heart Strings*. The meeting would have been on a call like every other, but when she received my invitation to the symphony, she decided it was a good opportunity to meet in-person and double it as a family trip. I invited Vivian Wells to the performance for reasons I could not clearly articulate—call it curiosity or weak hope—but she did not show. I dedicated the performance to Autumn, her name in every pamphlet—she was the catalyst for the symphony—and I often wondered if she placed the sound in my skull. I wondered, too, how different the composition would have turned out had she still been around, and I began to understand the importance of suffering.

There is no proper way to describe the plunging sensation of my soul as I watched my friend sink into the ground. What is worse, the casket was only faintly distinguishable from Tommy's. There she was, in her private bed in the soil; how strange and surreal and sickening. I thought, *there, that is all that remains of Autumn*. The girl I'd shared so many memories with, who I still felt all around me, was now reduced to an ornate box. That box, a symbol of her so lacking in her true greatness, represented what she used to be, her soul's old capsule, that version of her that lives now only in my brain. She was so much more than a box, so much more than a woman, she was one of the best things to ever happen to me. Autumn and I may not have been in love, but we were reliable in providing love to one another. Twin souls of the artist—honest and wandering—we were able to love with ferocity but never able to give ourselves away to the other. I had never seen anyone more dedicated to music than Autumn. And true, I looked up to her in countless ways. And so, I began to understand myself. If one sits alone long enough, that tends to be the outcome. I know what is best for me because I am the one I know best. I am my own greatest companion now.

———

Wounds matured into scars, just as they do, physical traumas served as reminders of betrayal. The body changes as does the mind. Every cell is replaced in only a handful of years and soon, you are an entirely new human being, with faded recollections of the person you were before. On Wednesday I went to get coffee with Sophia while Daniel took their daughter out to Ellis Island (likely it was more for Daniel than for infant Presley). At a little tea bar near my apartment named Whistle & Fizz, we sat outside and across from one another, like we had so many times before, and enjoyed our cappuccinos. We talked as we always had. She was one of the only people I had ever met in my life who I could speak with easily, and I couldn't help but share as much as I could with her. Something between us just clicked, but the little doses of in-person conversation were likely for the best, our greatest formula, and made our visits that much richer.

"Is a book tour anything like our tours?"

Sophia scoffed, she had her legs crossed and no longer held her head up with her elbow on the table. She leaned into her seat with a straight back. Her phone was face down on the table beside her ceramic saucer.

"In what context?" she asked.

"I don't know—any context. I know it's just you so it must be different," I said.

"It's much fewer moving parts if that's what you're wondering. Much, much fewer. It is just me and a few others involved, sometimes Daniel will visit nearby cities so I can see Presley. But the whole thing is only about a month long anyway. Nowhere near the chaos of Beach Sirens' six-month to year-long odysseys between the Americas and Europe. I go to bed at a reasonable hour, I read to groups in different bookshops, I do signings and pictures and then I usually go to dinner. It's actually quite nice."

"That does sound very nice," I said.

"Do you know what you're going to do next?"

"Me?" I asked lamely, only really to give myself more time to think. "I suppose I'll work on whatever Luca decides to do next—and, well, in the meantime—I'll continue to create for myself."

"That's great to hear. You and Luca—you two are going to that film festival in a few months, you said?"

"Yes, we'll be going out to Cannes. It's quite nice over there," I said in a dreamy sort of tone.

"Maybe someday I'll get to see it," she muttered and paused, "How are you feeling? You know, since—" her voice stopped. *Since the attack,* I filled in. I grinned at her.

"Soph, when I say this, I mean it earnestly—I think I am the best I've felt in a very long time," I said and couldn't help but smile. I felt my eyes become glassy across from her. She mirrored the grin and studied me in a motherly expression she should someday master. And I was content with this.

I sipped my cappuccino and thought of what else to say. Sometimes, I worried I would bore her. But why worry? After a decade of spending so much time together, maybe it would be a nice change of pace to bore her for once. Silence followed. Pigeons pecked at crumbs near our feet. Tommy used to like to call them trash doves. The two of us ended up walking the city for a bit, losing track of blocks, and talking. I recall the profound nature of a thought I had while walking beside her in the late morning glow, how she and I were now forever to be the only two members of Beach Sirens. There was no going back, the number will only decrease. I wondered if there would ever be a day, sometime in the future, when our music is listened to for the last time in history. Surely, that day will come. Across a long enough timeline, all history will cease to exist. History was entirely made by humanity, and it will leave with us as well. Every record of our existence will someday be destroyed and there will be nothing to ever prove humanity ever was the Great Impossibility that built cities, music, philosophies, and technologies beyond our imaginations. Does that make it any less extraordinary?

A month later, I received an advanced copy of *Scissors for Heart Strings* at my doorstep. Rather than a green hardcover, this one was ocean blue but maintained its predecessor's velvet texture. The dedication page inside read, *To my best friends - Tommy, Autumn, Joey*. She had signed it on the inside with a note: *To my first love, Joe Henley. May we cross paths again.*

It was that café visit in Manhattan where we discussed the idea of putting out unreleased tracks from Beach Sirens, including the song Tommy and I wrote in my hotel room, *Denim Dogs*. I hadn't listened to the song in years, not since our last tour. For that time, I knew I experienced loathing, but the memory has since morphed into a bittersweet nostalgia, a precious pearl of the last time the four of us were all together. This idea would not come to fruition for some time, not until I messaged our old manager, Ant Mercer, and discussions began between us and the label. At first, I hadn't known what to say to him as, when the band fell apart, all interaction with him fizzled out. I hadn't heard from him in years by the time I reached out, and to my surprise, he was thrilled to hear from me.

Joe, I am so glad to hear from you. It has been far
too long. . .

After messaging back and forth for several weeks, we crawled toward a definitive plan. A new EP titled, *The Call of the Culture*, was set to release on the 12th of May, 2028, eleven years to the day after the release of our very first EP, *THE STAMFORD RECORD*, created by our college-aged counterparts. The track list:

1. *The Cassavette Children*
2. *Between You and Me*
3. *Trying This Again*
4. *Callused Tendencies*
5. *Just Thumps*
6. *Denim Dogs*
7. *First Words*
8. *Twenty*

The last two Sophia and I wrote and recorded over the course of a single weekend when she returned to the city for another meeting with her publishing house—the other five were old recordings with the instruments of Tommy and Autumn still layered in (*Just Thumps* was a ten minute track I stumbled upon featuring Autumn messing around with her drum set)—the two newer tracks were piano ballads, mostly sang by Sophia at my insistence. It was her band from the beginning, she was to be the lead singer, and I thought it best for her to close out her own band. I recorded some vocals, although my voice had changed so much in the last handful of years given that I had no vocal training and my daily smokes, and it is blatantly obvious in the recordings. The EP would be released as a final goodbye to the fans and to the band.

I was not around for the release or to see where it charted (*The Call of the Culture* charted No. 3 in records for three consecutive weeks and *Loose Ends* reentered the charts at No. 10 in May for Alternative Rock all on its own). I did not pay much attention to the charts, or the magazines, the articles and tabloids scratching for any movement on the band. Beach Sirens was officially laid to rest and the four of us were free. I had several projects falling into place, and this was where I kept my focus. My life would be dedicated to music, to art, to the pursuit of creation and the work of the mind.

———

I was on the train with my finger pressed between the pages of a novel, and taking a break to turn my attention to the clay-roofed houses in the Italian countryside as they swam by between flapping trees. Across the cart was Luca with legs folded, his hair cut shorter and a more prominent beard now. I saw the age in his face, lining and causing a plump thesis that would become an old man. He had sunglasses over his eyes. We had been silent in our cart for over an hour, him scribbling in his notebook and looking over information on his devices, while I sat across from him and read Charles Bukowski quietly. We were heading toward Rome. The trip was less of a vacation and more of a location scout for our new film. Luca had written a new screenplay; this picture centered around witchcraft in Italy. His working title: *Nights of Daze.*

The train carried us away from Florence, which had been purely for recreational purposes. *Firenze.* It was a lovely city, where we visited many restaurants and cafés. The Odeon Cinema. The Statue of David. What struck me most about Michelangelo's formidable sculpture was how it lay hidden through a maze of art. Everyone admired the many pieces in the gallery while quietly anticipating a view of the marble man. When I finally rounded the corner, and there stood David at the far end of a great hall, under his mighty pale dome, I felt my heart grow heavy. Adrenaline pierced my blood. He was somehow greater with my eyes resting against his crystalline skin. I swallowed and shed a tear at the sight of such beauty. Closer, circling him like a prey, I came to note how much it looked like Tommy.

I was uncertain of this. I was beginning to forget what Tommy looked like. I often thought of him and his young face. I often added a smile even if it wasn't actually true. Every time I went to recall his image in my brain, it would take longer and longer—like a Polaroid developing its film but with an increasing amount of time—I wondered if someday recalling my old friend may become too difficult. He, and Autumn, may someday vanish entirely.

"Luca," I chimed.

His attention shifted to me from his notes. The train shuffled on quietly and Luca stared at me through his double black lenses. I cleared my throat, a soft chug to wipe it out and swallowed. "You remember—back after we finished the score—the score for *When the Bleeding Stops*, and we were both in New York trying to find our footing?" I said and paused; he might have looked analytical. I blew air.

"Well, I suppose I wanted to ask—why did you stop talking to me? And there doesn't have to be an answer, but it would be best to let you know how much it hurt me. I thought I might never see you again."

He stared at me fixedly. For some time, we sat in an empty space, filled in by the colorful creaking of the train and the whispering sputters of the rails. Then Luca said, "I'm sorry, I should not have done this to you, my friend. Please forgive. It was a situation I did not know how to manage. I sense our relationship was going in wrong direction. I needed time to think. But we are okay. Look at us! Like brothers. We are allies, no?"

I nodded. I wished I could tell him how it had affected me, how awful I felt at the supposed loss of another friend but instead, I let his words soar inside of me. How vile a feeling it is to lose the ones you love, like a rotten death withering inside the heart. And how strange, love is likely the closest we will ever get to feeling immortal. I suppose the two go hand in hand in this fashion. I was only happy to have my best friend across from me, happily staring out at the wiping farmlands, a reflected warmth spread on our faces from the window of the train.

"Okay," I said, to reassure him but more for myself. I wanted to tell him how happy I was to be with him, how much I loved him, how I trusted him. But he tilted his glasses down so I could see his eyes below the shades, and he grinned curiously. With his bird-like gaze, humorously, he patted me on the shoulder, and I couldn't help but laugh. I decided there was no need to express these honesties to him aloud for—somehow—he knew what I wanted to express. He was seemingly saying without a word spoken, *relax, everything is okay.* And everything was okay. The anxieties might never properly leave me be, but instead, I could focus on the passage of time, true now I could see it. How I could lie back and let it continue forward, in a nearly beautiful march, like the train softly chittering up the tracks.

Time carries on in the cycle of life and death, pushing on and on and on, never ceasing. Perhaps to spite the sensations of greed, vanity and lust. I can ponder forever and never settle on a definite answer. The best I can do for myself is do as I did then: I inhaled and exhaled and with every breath, I sank into the comfort of my seat and listened as my best friend told me his ideas for the next story he would tell— and how he wanted me to be a part of it. I looked back at the window, at the stucco houses, yellow and white, under the clever blue wash, and felt a blanket of appreciation for all that was around me. I sat and felt the swift tug of the train, pushing on, carrying me forward—I allowed myself to do nothing—and to enjoy the rest.

When we arrived in Rome, we snatched our belongings and scurried away from the train. I scuttled through crowds of Italians, gripping our luggage hard and crossed through the dim and wet underground station. We wandered up the steps, through a doorway, and into a brand-new world. We were in the heat of Rome with a golden sun, brick-laid roads and chipping structures. I followed Luca's back of the head, a cleaner black cut, and we zigzagged quickly through alleyways. Everyone wore heavy jackets despite it being the center of May. I pegged many to be tourists as they stood in small huddles and looked alarmed. I wore a black button-down and was already beginning to sweat.

Through the mug, we found our hotel and checked into our room. Luca charmed the woman at the front desk and as I looked over my shoulder, she still had her grinning expression pressed on our backs. I followed my friend up the steps, pounding my suitcase against the wall and trying to maintain a balance before we found our warm, tiled room. More beige stucco walls. We dropped our belongings on each of our beds and Luca stood, excited, and said, "Let us go get a drink!"

———

We went down to a bar near the Victor Emmanuel Monument and ordered Aperol. We shot back cafés in singular hot swallows; the rich espresso featured a fervent taste. We leaned back in our seats in satisfaction. My mind felt a new sense of pleasure from our blend of elixirs. Finally, we walked side-by-side down one of the many brick avenues and found a bench within Savello Park. We sat and watched the city move around us; the twisted trees stood tall with mounds of green at their tops. Squirrels over our heads snickered and hustled from tree to tree, causing a hiss on the branches. Bodies surfed in each direction, crunching through the gravel, and admiring the skyline of the city in the distance. Tomorrow, we would meet with a location scout named Diego and embark on an adventure to grow closer with Luca's next film. But at that moment, at the bench, I thought again to ask Luca what the meaning of any of this was.

I had arrived in Rome, and I was still myself. Somehow, I had thought perhaps along the way, I might achieve a version of myself impressive to my past. It was not a disappointment, however. I sat beside my best friend, my ally, and watched the day reach its finality. The sun went scarlet, and the sky went orange; the roofs of the city glittered. I watched the sun—*The Red Upon the Hill*—our sacred, dying star. Someday, that blistering, red dot will swallow us whole. This account of my many efforts will be gone, as will every written word, every whistled tune, every portrait and every memory. So, again, I tilted my head at it, and wondered, *why?*

Luca nudged me. "My friend, look."

I turned and followed his gaze, it was directed onto a man and woman. They were young, likely at the dawn of their early twenties. I watched the young man skid away from the woman, etching a path through the gravel pathway. He leapt and latched onto a streetlamp and became illuminated in a hazel gleam. He swiveled around on the pole, and sang an Italian version of the musical, *Singing in the Rain*.

"*Cantando* sotto la piogga! *Cantando* sotto la piogga!" The young man danced, and the woman pressed her wrist against her mouth to mask her rising laughter. He extended his hand, and she accepted. We watched the two dance with their palms intertwined. They became silhouettes against the ruby-colored sky, and even when reduced to dancing shapes, their contentment with each other's faces was unmistakable. I admired their ability to forget the world surrounding them. And all that existed at that moment were these two lovers in the park. That is all that mattered.

As if he had read my mind, Luca shifted his lips to find my ear. He grinned and muttered, "I think that—right there—might be the meaning to all of this."

———

I never forgot what Luca said to me that day. I have been deep in thought ever since. All that we do in life is eternity. We are what I have named, Singular Impermanence, but in patterns, we are infinite. The Great Impossibility. Think not of what we leave behind as crumbs. I've heard this many times, this outlook of reduction, and it is not so. Not crumbs, but seeds that will grow into a flower. A flower to serve as a representation of, *yes, in fact, you were here, too, and it was beautiful*. This owned flower will have seeds for others to use so they may plant their own. This is life, a shared garden, where we come and go, giving and taking.

We may never know if life was by accident or by design, but we may know to carry on. It is with these seeds in our pockets—the ideas in our minds—we can create. The flowers we plant are alive when we are not, they exist and blossom due to our hand. We are the catalyst of life in our own rite. And this creation is everywhere—constant, shifting, present—it may never seize and the contribution of each seed, each idea, may become a single flower against billions. Do not fear volume for without yours, there is less. You can always focus on a single star if you choose.

I am but a few pages in the story of one man, placed beside the stories of others, a catalog of what it means to be alive and a question of what it means to exist. We spend time with these people, and perhaps learn something, or best, question something. Because we choose to and do so unapologetically. We get one century, often less, sometimes more, to do whatever we choose and when we're gone, that's it.

Life flows like water, it waves around us and through us, and we are only floating by. In many ways, our impermanence is beautiful, a speckle of time, shining and singing for only an instant then never seen again. This is our limited performance. So, create because an audience may be watching somewhere yet lived, experiencing you through your flower. What you leave behind is crucial for them. Rest well with the notion that they may take your creation and use it as reference for their own. That is the greatest goal of artistry. Our feet on the shoulders of our greatest contributors will make us, in total, taller and mightier. Art is not tangible—the oil paints, the ink, the minerals and chemicals, the tightly wound strings—these are tangible —these are real. But they are not art. Art is belief. And believe what you will. Life will carry on with or without it, so allow everything to happen, all that may. Give and take from the ever-growing garden of creation. We are this instant.

INDEX

ALL ALONG THE WRATH LANDS (*Film*): The eighth feature film from director Theodore Sellers. Starring Freddy Richardson, Michaela Rice, Paul Moriarty and Woody Ranker. Photography by Nathaniel Withers. Original score by Joseph Henley. Produced by Twin Munich Films in association with God Noir Entertainment. Filmed in Livingston, Montana with a budget of 45 million. The film grossed a total of 127 million.

ANTHONY MERCER (*ROT IRON Manager*): Born May 22, 1969, in Culver City, California. He began his career in the music industry at the age of 18, working first as an intern and then as an audio technician for Bracklemore Sound. He decided to quit after five years and went to college at the University of Phoenix for business and finance. Upon finishing his degree, he returned home and began working for several artist management companies while looking to manage bands and spot gigs for them around Southern California. It wasn't until 2006 that he, finally, landed on a garage band in Sacramento, at which he mapped and sponsored an entire tour for them. The band was Crosswired. It was with this band, he grew in close connection with ROT IRON Music Group. He later managed Beach

Sirens from 2019 until 2023. He now manages Winkie Rock and Anomano, both under the label of ROT IRON.

AUTUMN GLADIS (*Drummer/Music Producer*): Born October 19, 1997 in Salisbury, Massachusetts to Amelia Gladis and Patrick Black. She was an only child before Liam Black (August 11, 2008), was born as her half-brother to Catherine and Patrick Black. Her mother, Amelia, married Isaac Krinsky when she was two years old. She did the Marching Band through high school and attended George Washington University (August 2015 - May 2019) with a major in Music and made it into Symphonic Band with a focus on percussion. She was the drummer for Beach Sirens (2016 - 2023) before she became the drummer for her own band, Dead Girls Club (2024 - 2027). She produced briefly for Gauze Moth in 2024, before she founded her own record label, Acid Ick!, the same year.

BARDO (*Sculptor*): Born July 15, 2004. A Belgian-born Italian who studied sculpting from a man named Timeo Montebello. At the age of 21, he sculpted the popular marble statue titled: *The Christ Is Me, in Me Is He* (2025). In 2026, he moved to New York City to join New York Artist's Haven as an artist in residence. Only a year later, he moved to Greece. He has since traveled the world and studied sailing.

BEACH SIRENS (*Band*): Formed on August 16, 2016 by Sophia Baker, Autumn Gladis and Thomas Murtaugh. On September 18, 2016, Joseph Henley was added as the fourth and final member of the band. Signed to ROT IRON Music Group on June 1, 2019.

[*Discography*: THE STAMFORD RECORD EP (Released May 12, 2017. Independent)—*Beach Sirens* (Released November 8, 2019. ROT IRON)—*Island Walkers* (Released June 25, 2021. ROT IRON)—*Romance Empire* EP (Released May 16, 2022)—*Music to Die to* (Released February 10, 2023. ROT IRON)—*The Call of the Culture* (Released May 12, 2028. ROT IRON).]

BUGBEAR (*Composition*): Piano concerto written in 4/4 by Joseph Henley. It took him approximately one year to complete given several other projects in rotation. It was finished in 2025 and performed by the St. Louis Symphony Orchestra on January 16, 2026. It is just over half an hour long.

CONRAD MARCH (*Filmmaker*): Born March 3, 1951 in Richmond, Virginia. He began as a photographer for the local paper and attended the University of Southern California with a major in English. It was there in California that he spawned an adoration for cinema and began to develop his own scripts. He was the director of several films: *Clement Drive* (1988), *Method No. Nine* (1992), *Pyrotechnique!* (1993), *Dreaded Harvest* (1997), *Sketches of a King* (2001), *Drifting on Zero* (2004), *Burning of the Black Wick* (2007), *Olive Story* (2009), *Fetid Petrichor* (2011), *Riverbed* (2014), *Blood Thinner* (2018), *Four Foolish Nights* (2021), *Only in Dream* (2027).

He passed away in his sleep on December 9, 2026. He was 72.

CROSSWIRED (*Band*): Formed April 11, 2007 by Seth Whitaker, Brian Maul, Terrence Mandera. Signed to ROT IRON Music Group on February 25, 2011. *The band dismembered on January 29, 2025.*

[*Discography*: *Audible Punk* (Released July 17, 2012. ROT IRON)—*Rusty Dust Bunny* (Released March 17, 2015. ROT IRON)—*Mutilated Minds* (Released July 26, 2018. ROT IRON)—*The Overflow* (Released November 19, 2022. ROT IRON).

DANIEL CAVANSKY (*Field Producer*): Born June 11, 1993 in Hudson, New York to Marie and Brent Cavansky, the ladder worked as a field producer in and around New York. Daniel followed in his father's footsteps and produced documentaries such as *Inner Lane* (2017), *Max Pace* (2019), *Forty* (2020) and docuseries such as *Nature of the Beast* (2021), *Eye on the Prize: Formula 1* (2022), *Faster than Ever* (2023), *Courtside Stories* (2024), *Trainer* (2025) *Behind the Stunt: Stunts of Hollywood* (2025 - 2027), *Making a Dent: History of*

Sports Shoes (2028). In 2025, he married bassist, and singer of Beach Sirens, Sophia Baker.

DEAD GIRLS CLUB (*Band*): Formed on April 25, 2024 by Autumn Gladis, Mazy Diaz and Freya Morris. The band was officially signed to Acid Ick! Records on May 4, 2024 (founded and owned by Autumn Gladis). They released only one album as a band, *An Impossible Shade of Black* (Released October 21, 2026. Acid Ick!).

DONNA MURRAY (*Cinematographer*): Born January 23, 1990 in Keflavík, Iceland. She moved to Redlands, California at the age of 7, and attended the University of Southern California with a major in Film and Television Production. She became the Director of Photography on the Luca Krzyżewski short film, *Forever Ago* (2017), then *Landfall* (2018). She went on to be the Director of Photography for several feature films including *Mass Hysteria* (2025), *Off Kilter* (2027), *When the Bleeding Stops* (2028), *Nights of Daze* (2030). She lives in Los Angeles, California.

ELARA CARPE (*Musician*): Born November 18, 2005 in Los Angeles, California to Brittany and Samuel Carpe and is the oldest of two children before Daniel Carpe (September 4, 2003). Her parents are both voice coaches from East Hollywood. She signed with Veneer Records in 2019 and released her first single, *Proud of It* (2020), at only 15, and was number one on the Billboard Charts for ten weeks.
   [*Discography*: *What A Drag* (Released May 26, 2020. Veneer)—*Queendom* (Released January 1, 2022. Veneer)—*Mother/Martyr* (Released February 2, 2025. Veneer)—*Norma Jeans* (Released September 25, 2027. Veneer)—*Modern Fairytale* (Released April 20, 2029. Veneer).]

ELLIS YOUNG (*Artist/Music Producer*): Born April 15, 1984 in Lancashire, England to Helena and Terrence Young. At the age of 14, his father passed away and his mother passed away when he was 15. In 2000, Ellis was 16 and playing violin on the streets for money and homeless in Manchester. He caught the attention of Harrison Clive, a Senior Executive at Monarch Sons Records. From there, Clive took Ellis in to work at Monarch Sons and at the age of 21, Ellis moved to New York City to work with The Inbetweeners and created a career as a music producer. He had the nickname, The Prince of Dissonance during his career and founded New York Artist's Haven, a program that sponsored young and promising artists, in 2026.

FREDERICK RICHARDSON (*Actor*): Born April 20, 1995 in San Francisco, California to Samantha and Xavier Richardson (the founder and CEO of Manendrake Pictures). Freddy got his first acting role at the age of 8 in the film, *Rover's Ruff Day* (2004). He was nominated for Best Actor at the 2019 Academy Awards for his role as Jack London in the film, *The Call* (2018), directed by Howard Malecki. Other credits include: *Aunt Jordan* (2005), *The Vivacious Five* (2006), *The Last Star Fleet* (2009), *Mason Hurry* (2011), *Teeny* (2012), *Grooveland* (2016), *You're a Bad Boy* (2017), *Intuition of Self* (2018), *Grooveland 2* (2019), *Papermakers* (2021), *Vanilla GunPowder* (2022), *Death of an Aleman* (2023), *The Grand Moon Leap* (2024), *Grooveland 3* (2026), *How to Throw A Punch* (2028), *Group Therapy* (2029), *Ynez and Connie* (2030). He made his directorial debut with the film, *Ynez and Connie*, which premiered at the Sundance Film Festival in 2030. He lives in Los Angeles, California with his wife, Vivian Wells.

FRENCH PRESS (*Band*): Formed on August 1, 2019 by Chandler Press, Cole Gallagher, and Mason Tonga. The band opened for Beach Sirens during the Fatal Tour before being signed to ROT IRON on October 20, 2024.

[*Discography*: *Metropolitan Laundry Day* (Released March 5, 2021. Independent)—*MoRS. Museum of Religion and Sex* (Released May 15, 2023. Independent)—*Caught on Film* (Released February 27, 2025. ROT IRON)—*Cemetery Playground* (Released August 25, 2028. ROT IRON).

GAUZE MOTH (*Band*): Formed on October 29, 2019 by Mazy Diaz, Oliver Diaz and Melinda Reichart. *The band dismembered on January 15, 2024.*

    [*Discography*: *Toil Toil Toil!* (Released February 14, 2020. Independent)—*Gauzetropolis* (Released March 1, 2021. Independent)—*Peanut Butter Dog Vol. 1* (Released May 21, 2022. Independent)—*Peanut Butter Dog Vol. 2* (Released October 28, 2022)—*Nicotine and Guillotines* (Released November 3, 2023. Independent).

HOWARD (HAL) WALSH (*Music Assistant/Journalist*): Born September 21, 1998 in Annandale, Virginia. He attended George Washington University (August 2016 - May 2020) with a major in Communications. He worked for the school's paper, *GW Today* and published an article on an independent band named Beach Sirens which shot them into stardom.

THE INBETWEENERS (*Band*): Originally named Finding Fervor. Formed on November 3, 1999 by Deirdre Schellvile, Monica Pincer, Leonard Pile, Vincent Gideon. Signed to Nobody Noise Music Group on June 8, 2001.

    [*Discography*: *Week in London* (Released April 24, 2003. Nobody Noise)—*Dream No. 99* (Released October 5, 2006. Nobody Noise, Produced by Ellis Young)—*Mercy of Impression* (Released July 7, 2008. Nobody Noise)—*Mona, Listen* (Released September 12, 2010. Nobody Noise)—*It's A Lovely Mourning* (Released August 10, 2014. Nobody Noise)—*Arden* (Released June 11, 2018. Nobody Noise)—*Watch Your Tone* (Released April 4, 2023. Nobody Noise).]

IMOGEN O'NEAL (*Musician*): Born April 11th, 1989 in Plymouth, Massachusetts. At the age of twenty-three, she took over as the lead singer of the band, Hellplex. The band went on to become one of the highest selling metal bands in music history, with their single, *Bloody Cardigan* (Released August 14th, 2015), going quadruple platinum.

JAZZ CANAL (*Stage Musical*): Lyrics and book written by George Plack. It was first performed in a workshop at the Cherry Lane Theatre, the off-Broadway theater, in February 2014. The musical eventually moved to the Lunt-Fontanne Theatre in May of 2015. It won a Tony Award for Best Original Score. It ran on Broadway for over fifteen years, ending its run in January of 2031. A film adaptation has been rumored with a screenplay written by Xavier Morrison.

JOSEPH HENLEY (*Musician/Composer*): Born December 21, 1996 in Athens, Georgia to Kent and Catrina Henley. He is the third of three children, after Beatrice Henley (March 30, 1990) and Dianne Henley (August 12, 1993). After graduating in the summer of 2014, he attended George Washington University (August 2015 - May 2019) with a major in Music. He was a member of the University Singers choir group. He was the lead singer, pianist, guitarist and songwriter of Beach Sirens (2016 - 2023). He has written the score for many films: *Mass Hysteria* (2025), *All Along the Wrath Lands* (2025), *Only in Dream* (2027), *When the Bleeding Stops* (2028), *Tooth Fish* (2029), *Not Even The Best Part* (2029), *Nights of Daze* (2030). He composed the piano concerto, *Bugbear* (2025) and *Symphony No. 1* (2028). He lives in Manhattan, New York.

KATYA BARANOVA (*Architect*): Born January 7, 2002 in Suzdal, Russia. She knew she wanted to be an architect since she was 8 years old. She attended Moscow Architectural Institute and shortly after, created the design for a mansion estate outside of the city of Moscow, named *Roza* (2025). The home featured a spiral staircase at the center that increasingly widened in diameter, much like a rose. The home caught the attention of the public and architects alike, especially for her being 23 years old. She moved to New York City as the house neared completion, in 2026, and joined New York Artist's Haven. A year later, she moved again, this time to Bratislava where she still resides and designs, though now mostly designing for mansions land hotels, she occasionally does restaurants and churches.

LUCA KRZYŻEWSKI (*Filmmaker*): Born December 11, 1991 in Milan, Italy to Italian professor, Lucia, and Polish painter, Borys Krzyżewski. Luca acted in the Elfo Puccini Theater's production of Shakespeare's *Julius Caesar* as the role of Brutus when he was only 17. He went on to act in the Italian television show, *Tentar Non Nuoce (No Harm in Trying)*, for six seasons as the heartthrob, Diego Piacchio. He then went on to direct a series of short films, *Vento Lungo* (2016), *Mio Caro* (2016), *Denti Finti* (2017), and then directed in the United States, *Forever Ago* (2017), and *Landfall* (2018), which won the Short Film Palme d'Or at the Cannes Film Festival 2018. He went on to direct feature films including *Mass Hysteria* (2025), *When the Bleeding Stops* (2028), *Nights of Daze* (2030).

MASS HYSTERIA (*Film*): Psychological horror film written and directed by Luca Krzyżewski. Starring Vivian Wells, Catherine Yeichen, Fabian Lee, Michael Pike, and Rodney Wallace. Original score written and performed by Joseph Henley. Photography by Donna Murray. Produced in association with Luca Krzyżewski's Rogue Fool Films. Produced by Olde Ornate Entertainment and Carnel Pictures. Filmed on location in Wilmington, North Carolina with a budget of 20 million. The film grossed a total of 290 million.

MAZY DIAZ (*Musician*): Born March 15, 1999 in St. Louis, Missouri. She attended the University of California with an undergrad major in Music Composition. She graduated in 2017 and received an internship at Carnel Music Group that same year. In 2019, she started the dream-pop band, Gauze Moth. In 2024, she joined the baroque rock band, Dead Girls Club. She now owns and runs Acid Ick! Records and lives in Brooklyn, New York.

NEW YORK ARTIST'S HAVEN (*Program*): A program founded in 2026 by artist and infamous music producer, Ellis Young. The program was founded with the intention of sponsoring artists and commissioning them to create their art, depending on their desired form and interpretation. The program would provide funds for food and housing and promised commission pay after the creation of their new artwork. The program is designed to 'usher the second Renaissance' and provide security to rising artists with the goal of creating and establishing new minds in the texts of human history.

ONLY IN DREAM (*Film*): Surrealist drama film written and directed by Conrad March. The film stars Joyce Ferro, Emery Higgins and Vander Allenby. Original score by Joseph Henley. Photography by Raphael Lete. Produced by Casa Roca Entertainment and Star Meadow Entertainment. Filmed in North Bend, Washington with a budget of 55 million. The film grossed a total of 180 million. The film premiered at the Venice Film Festival on September 10, 2026 and was awarded the Golden Lion, the highest prize. The film received a wider release on June 18, 2027. The film received 11 Oscar nominations and won Best Picture, Best Original Score, Best Original Screenplay and Best Sound Design at the 2028 Academy Awards.

OUTLYRE (*Musician*): Martin Terry was born October 22, 1998 in Thousand Oaks, California. He dropped out of high school at the age of 16 with the goal of becoming a rapper. For one year, he studied in private with his English teacher from his junior year to get his GED and worked nights at a diner. He got his GED a year later in 2013, and in 2016, he gained a substantial following due to the rise of music streaming. In 2019, he was signed to Triplecake Records.

[*Discography*: *Acting Up and Out* (Released March 29, 2021. Triplecake),—*Causing Problems on Purpose* (Released June 16, 2023. Triplecake) *Metropolips* (Released November 28, 2025. Triplecake) —*TUNNEL* (Released October 22, 2027. Triplecake).

SOPHIA BAKER (*Musician/Poet*): Born June 28, 1997 in Norfolk, Virginia to Amanda Whitfield and Charles Baker. She was the only child and in full custody of her father, Charlie. She applied to George Washington University in 2014 as a Junior in high school and attended the school in Washington D.C. (August 2015 - May 2019) with a major in English. She was a member of the University Singers

Choir group for the university. She was a singer, songwriter and bass guitarist for Beach Sirens (2016 - 2023) before becoming a bestselling poet. Her poetry collections include *How to Be Alive Today* (2025) and *Scissors for Heart Strings* (2028). She lives in Austin, Texas with her daughter, Presley.

SUMITRA PATANI (*Poet*): Born August 22, 1999. From Dehradun, India. She studied several languages at university and can speak fluently in Hindi, Urdu, and English, as well as understand German, Latin, and some French, Italian and Spanish. Her secret obsession had always been poetry; she often wrote poems in her own secret language as a young girl. Her secret language was called 'Sap,' and she credits the name to have a myriad of hidden meanings. She moved to the United States in 2024 at the age of 25, and settled in Brooklyn, New York. In 2026, she agreed to partake in the New York Artist's Haven program with limitations to her contract. She moved to Manhattan near the end of 2027, where she still resides, and in late October of 2028, she published a poetry collection titled, *Stuttering London*. She continues to write poetry and lives with her cat, Ham.

SYMPHONY NO. 1 (*Composition*): The first symphony composed by Joseph Henley, written in 4/4 time signature. The symphony was written freehand on staff paper. The commission for a symphony was to the credit of New York Artist's Haven (founded by Ellis Young). Henley was commissioned on January 27, 2026. He completed the first draft over the course of twenty days, from July 29 to August 17, 2026. It was performed on February 8, 2028 at the Perelman Performing Arts Center (performed by the Brooklyn Symphony Orchestra and conducted by Joseph Henley). It is over seventy minutes long.

THOMAS MURTAUGH (*Guitarist/Music Producer*): Born July 4, 1998 in Charleston, South Carolina to Peter and Elissa Murtaugh. He is the second child after Oliver Murtaugh (January 14, 1996). He graduated from West Ashley High School in 2015 and attended

George Washington University (August 2016 - May 2019) with a major in Music. He was the guitarist for the band, Beach Sirens (2016 - 2023).

VIVIAN WELLS (*Actress*): Born October 29, 1996 in Los Angeles, California to Nora Spencer and Rick Wells. Nora Spencer was an American film actress and Rick Wells was an Irish filmmaker. She has acted in many films: *Breakfast After Lunch* (2018), *They Do Not Grow Old* (2019), *Sloane's Gotta Go* (2021), *Brand New Color* (2023), *Mass Hysteria* (2025), *Gravitas* (2026), *Niño* (2026), *Saint Lawrence* (2027), *Calico* (2028), *Anyone's Guest* (2028), *Bodies in the City* (2029), *Field Goals* (2030), *Lock Jaw* (2030). She lives in Los Angeles, California with her husband, Frederick Richardson.

WHEN THE BLEEDING STOPS (*Film*): The second psychological horror film written and directed by Luca Krzyżewski. Starring Jeremiah Knight and Sasha Dean Parker. Photography by Donna Murry. Original score by Joseph Henley. Produced by Olde Ornate Entertainment, Carnel Pictures, in association with ROT IRON Entertainment Group. Filmed in Toronto, Canada with a budget of 100 million. The film grossed a total of 475 million.

YVETTE ADAIR (*Painter*): Born February 27, 2005. She was born and raised in Agde, France. She began painting at the age of 4 and is entirely self-taught. In 2025, she moved to the United States to continue her career as a painter. In 2026, she became the first member of New York Artist's Haven. In 2027, she was featured in the May 24 edition of *The New Yorker*, as an artist on the rise. She returned to France that Fall, where she still paints and resides in Paris.

ACKNOWLEDGMENTS

I want to begin by thanking my best friend, Logan, to whom this novel is dedicated to. Whether he knows it or not, he gave me the first initial seed of an idea that grew into *Instant Vanities*. Logan, we have been through everything together. From preschool to now, 20 years of friendship, I can confidently call you my brother. Your family raised me just as much as my own, every one of you are amazing.

I am grateful to my parents for reading my work regardless of the subject matter. It may not be for everyone, and yet they are always there with open minds. Thank you, Mom and Dad. And to Sariah, who I know will read this months after release. And to my other sister, Emma, who may get around to reading this years after release. Dad, you gave me notes on the original draft of this book that helped me significantly. I am so grateful for your unwavering support in every effort I make in the arts.

Caitlin, my best friend, my wonderful supporter, and the center of my universe, I am so thankful to have you. You read this book during your downtime while working on set of an unspecified television production. You too, gave me notes (You're right, Tommy wouldn't say, 'grubby mitts', he'd probably just say, 'hands'), and you were ready to read this as soon as I was able to print it. I am so thankful to have found you in this life. Your heart and soul are so important to me. I love you.

Thank you to my many teachers throughout my childhood. Everyone from preschool until I finished high school. Some of you: Mrs. Johstono, Mrs. Johnson (my two English Teachers of 11th and 12th Grade, both icons, and both showed me literature I came to admire), Mr. William Bennett, the Director of Choirs (If you end up reading this, sir, know I have a profound appreciation for your teachings on music, but also your teachings on manhood, responsibility, philosophy, and leadership), and to Mr. Eddie Hall, who even after graduating high school, would continue to check on me. He would ask about what I was writing, and offer his advice. August of 2023, his last text to me read, "Let me know when you're in town . . . Lots to catch up on." He was a mentor to me in many ways, and there for me through many hardships. I want to thank him for supporting me, practically raising me in my teenage years, and may he Rest In Peace. You taught me the dramatics, Hall, and you were someone I always respected.

I want to express my appreciation for all my Wilmington Film Crew. Every crew member in our town works their asses off on each production. I had to spotlight our production hub in the book. I wrote it to be Atlanta at first, as that made sense for the story, but I changed the setting to Wilmington. Write what you know! Wilmington is the home of many horror classics! And Wilmington, in general, simply rules.

Grandma and Grandpa, you two may be the only ones who have made it this far, and I thank you for reading every word I have to say. You treat me with a preciousness that makes me feel forever loved, and I will love you two forever. You are both wonderful, caring souls, and a beautiful gift to the world.

Alejandro, this one is for you too, buddy. You stuck with me through thick and thin. You're an absolute triumph in every art form. You're still one of my best friends, and I appreciate the friendship and memories we have created. Continue to do great things with your life, as I know you are, and keep up your art. For art's sake.

- Jesse David

About the Author

Jesse David lives in Wilmington, North Carolina, working on local film productions. He has dropped out of four colleges, written five screenplays, two novels, and directed two of his own independent feature films.

He began writing *Instant Vanities* in May of 2023, officially completing the work in April of 2025. He wrote his first story at the age of two.

www.ingramcontent.com/pod-product-compliance
Lightning Source LLC
Chambersburg PA
CBHW030328010826
48973CB00004B/922